THE REDWI

BOOK F

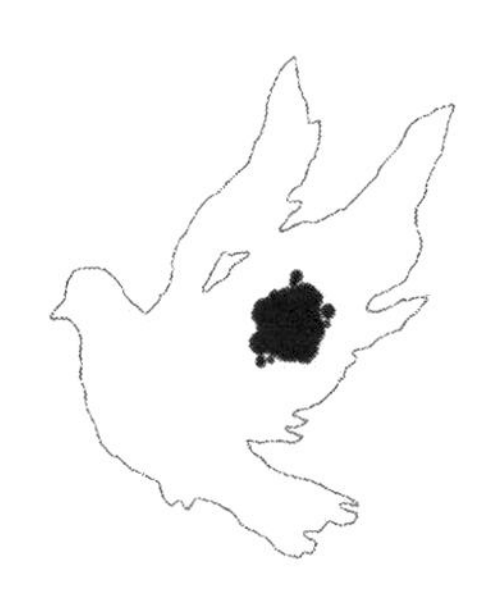

REALMS OF FIRE

SHARON K. GILBERT

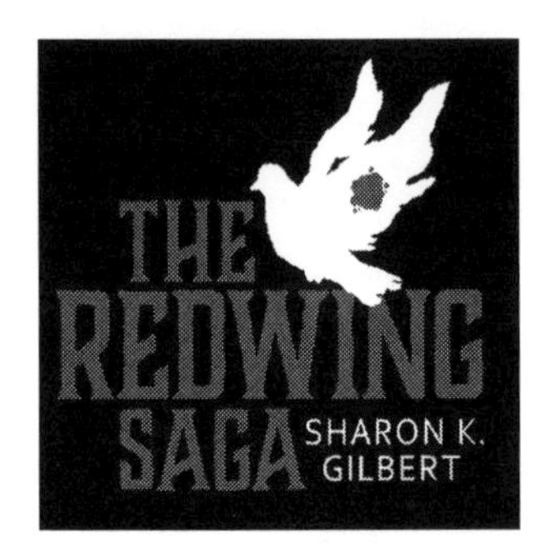

REALMS OF FIRE

BOOK FIVE OF THE REDWING SAGA

BY SHARON K. GILBERT

WWW.THEREDWINGSAGA.COM

First Print Edition March, 2019
Kindle Edition March, 2019

ISBN-13: 978-0-9980967-5-9

Published by Rose Avenue Fiction, LLC
514 Rose Avenue, Crane, MO 65633

TABLE OF CONTENTS

FROM THE AUTHOR

This book has been a labour of love. Though long in coming, it's been a journey worth taking for me. My original hope for this book was to publish it last September (2018), but travel and illness made that ambitious schedule impossible. I appreciate all who've patiently waited and encouraged me upon this long and winding road. The slow pace has allowed me to include plot twists and breadcrumbs to lay the groundwork for the next trio of books; all with names derived from chess. We're leading Charles Sinclair and his family towards the inevitable changes to occur with the turn of the 20th century, when he emerges as an influencer of men.

Most of the 'action' of this book occurs during Christmastide, which allows me to draw back the veil and consider how the 'other side' might view Christ's incarnation. In fact, I've spent so much time putting myself in the minds of the fallen realm, that Derek and I are now writing a non-fiction book called *Profiling the Dead*, which should be available in the fall of this year.

Remember, that spelling in all *Redwing Saga* books is based on British usage in the 19th century, and the language can be a bit challenging, particularly the dialects. I applaud all who breeze through these paragraphs; and some of you have told me at conferences that the Bow Bells dialect is 'dead-on'. In response, I tip my bowler hat to you.

In Christ,
Sharon K. Gilbert
24th February, 2019

To all the many patient readers who've supported me with prayers
and little notes as I've finished this book, I say:
Thank you.

Your desire to continue the journey along with
Charles, Elizabeth, and Paul makes every keystroke worthwhile.

May the Lord be with each and every one of you
this day and always.

In that day the LORD with his sore and great and strong sword shall punish leviathan the piercing serpent, even Leviathan that crooked serpent; and he shall slay the Dragon that is in the sea.

- Isaiah 27:1

And there appeared another wonder in heaven; and behold a great red dragon, having seven heads and ten horns, and seven crowns upon his heads.

- Revelation 12:3

...yonder in that wastefull wilderness
Huge monsters haunt, and many dangers dwell;
Dragons, and Minotaurs, and fiends of Hell,
And many wild woodmen, which rob and rend
All travellers; therefore advise ye well,
Before ye enterprise that way to wend:
One may his journey bring too soon to evil end.

- The Faerie Queen, Book III, Edmund Spenser

PROLOGUE

10th June, 1860 – Rose House

The boy's azure eyes popped open, wide as saucers. Something had awoken him—something scratchy and tempting. Something ethereal with a raspy voice that spoke in whispers.

His bedchamber was shrouded in velvety darkness, the only sound the somnolent ticking of a gold and black marble clock that sat upon the mantelpiece opposite the curtained bed. The curious clock featured a magnificent figure of King Arthur astride a pure white steed. The figure's position altered with the hands; the delicate changes provided by interlocking brass wheels and fine-toothed gears. On the quarter hour, the heroic king's mighty horse would advance along a concealed track towards a terrifying, fire-breathing dragon. As the rider moved ever closer, the armoured arm would slowly lift the sword higher; until, at the chiming of the hour, it pointed straight into the serpent's mouth, slaying the worm and ending his fiery reign.

The clock should have inspired a sense of history and pride in the child, but the bellicose ballet of cold marble and crimson fire ground into the sensitive boy's bones with a terrifying sense of dread. He'd hidden the clock numerous times, but the nursemaid always discovered its hiding place and returned it to the mantel. The child had learnt to shut out the persistent ticking—which often took on a grating, growling sound. Born of rare privilege and high position, the boy nearly always felt completely alone.

Charles Robert Arthur Sinclair III, known in peerage circles by the courtesy title Lord Loudain, stood tall and straight as he emerged from the warm feather bed that morning. He had measured four-foot-one-inch precisely the previous day, when his ageing nanny Mrs. Millicent Caswell, had placed her charge against the door frame of the nursery's play area.

"You'll be tall as a cedar one day, young lord!" she'd declared happily. "You might even outgrow your good father, and all the young ladies o' the county'll think you a grand catch."

The bashful boy had smiled patiently, as he generally did when trying to understand the strange amusements of adults. Most found humour in the oddest of moments, and very few appreciated the beautiful complications of the remarkable world all around them; for they seemed caught up in life's trivialities—or worse, in matters so deep and troublesome that no amount of study could unravel them.

Take his parents' recent arguments, for instance.

Ordinarily, Robby and Angela Sinclair had nothing but gentle endearments for one another, but beginning in late April of that year—following a masked ball at Haimsbury House—everything changed. Charles had gone with them to London, but he'd come down with a fever, leaving him with very little memory of that strange week. Once he recovered, the family abruptly left London and returned to their Cumbria estate, and his gentle parents commenced a distressing series of shouting matches—all of them centred on a foreigner named Prince Aleksandr Koshmar and a mysterious black mirror.

As Charles secured the buttons on his shoes, the determined five-year-old decided to search out this troublesome looking glass and discover just why his father hated it so very much.

Mrs. Caswell slept in a small bedchamber just beyond the main play area, but the fifty-two-year-old nanny snored like a bear, making it a simple matter to slip past her room without causing the woman to stir. Once through the apartment's exterior door, the youth hastened to the nearest staircase. The main wall of the broad landing held an arched window seat that overlooked the eastern park. Charles tiptoed to the cushioned seat and climbed up, peering through the leaded panes. Dawn's first rays were just beginning to paint the green hills of Eden Valley in a shimmering, watercolour pink; a stark contrast to the sapphire blue shadows cast by the statues and trees within the estate's formal gardens. The landscape looked foreboding and eerily foreign to the child's eyes that morning; as though he'd awakened to an entirely different realm.

Leaving the window, he passed by the east-wing servants' staircase. Charles could hear the rattle of copper pans and kettles rising up through the open stairwell, accompanied by the aroma of baking rye bread, cinnamon buns, and French butter sponge cakes. The hall's head baker, Mrs. Celia Carson, and her two assistants rose at four each morning to prepare large wooden bowls of dough and kindle the oven fires. Usually, Charles would visit Carson for a cup of tea and a plate of warm biscuits, but not this morning. His destination stood high above, inside the centuries-old home. Upward, all the way to the attics.

Built four-hundred years ago, the original limestone castle overlooked the western bank of Eden River. The main drive followed an old Roman road, leading modern visitors towards the west elevation of the expanded home. Consequently, the fortified castle at its heart remained concealed behind the magnificently amended wings and Palladian façade of the 18th century additions. Despite its antiquity, Charles found the original castle fascinating, and often came here to play; picturing himself as the son of a warrior marquess, learning to wield a sword whilst on horseback, or fire arrows from the defensive towers. He would wander through the armoury and run his small hands along a great blade that some claimed was nearly a thousand years old. It was called *Lann Lasair*, the 'fire sword', and it rested upon a bed of claret velvet, securely locked within a protective glass case. Despite its age, the ancient sword gleamed as though newly forged, and Charles sometimes imagined that it spoke to him, whispering of blood and destiny.

That morning, however, the sword and the towers held no charm for the boy. He walked briskly past the armoury and pulled open a thick oak door that led to the south tower. A black rat scuttled past his feet as the iron-banded portal creaked open. A blast of stale air swept across the boy's smooth face like wispy fingers of some ghostly knight.

The boy froze, wondering if he shouldn't return to bed and await his nanny's call to breakfast.

No, he told himself. *This is important. I have to see that mirror for myself.*

With fierce determination for so young a heart, the lad forged ahead, slowly climbing the narrow stone steps. The well-worn, winding stairs led to a crenulated turret where archers and musketeers once took shelter as they fought invaders from other lands and other kingdoms. Charles held his lamp high as he ascended the hand-hewn risers. His sensitive nose discerned the musty odour of centuries-old mildew as he proceeded up the anti-clockwise curve. Along the case, arrow slits provided modest hints of dawn's maturing light. At three feet high and one foot wide, the windows had seen many battles, their casement stones marked by blood stains; the last bits of life from long-forgotten men.

Charles gazed upon the shadowed ground below, picturing the hills covered in the warm blood of horses and warriors and kings; the river's clear water choked with the bloated bodies of the dead and dying. The vision sent a cold sense of dread through his bones, but the valiant child pressed onward, up the claustrophobic staircase, until he arrived at the final door. It required all his strength to push the heavy structure, but once through, he emerged into a dark chamber used now as storage. The flickering yellow flame of his lantern struggled to cut through the deep shadow. Rather than provide comfort, the dancing tongue of fire made the forest of books, sea cans, and wooden crates appear to undulate like angry trees in fields of endless night. The tall boy whispered a prayer and advanced into the unwelcoming landscape.

A series of persistent scratching sounds caught his ear, soon turning into whispers in a thousand languages all at once; seductive words without translation that simultaneously terrified and tantalised the intelligent child. In one corner, stood a suit of armour; the helmet's empty eye holes greedily watching his passage. Along the north wall, a row of sturdy bookcases guarded family histories and ledgers. Elsewhere, painted cupboards, wooden toys, musical instruments, bird cages, and scrolled iron bedsteads, patiently waited to be summoned; forlorn and abandoned, as if they'd come here to die.

The child's remarkable blue eyes accommodated to the low light as he continued through the haunted maze. Though bathed in shadow, the attics felt familiar, for Charles had wandered through these aisles of Haimsbury's *disjecta membra* many times. What imaginative five-year-old wouldn't find such a collection fascinating?

But where is the mirror? he wondered.

With only the candle's light as guide, he threaded a path through the crowded field of debris and dust. Charles passed through a series of connecting doorways, moving from the original castle to the newer sections, where modern reliquaries guarded the unused treasures of the grandest home in all Cumbria.

This newer loft included a series of round windows that ran parallel to the eaves, allowing dawn's light to enter. The scratching sound seemed to grow louder here, and he noticed several slender tree branches tapping against the leaded panes. An adult would assume this to be the source of the scratching, but Charles doubted the delicate willow limbs could have awoken him this far from his bedroom. No, the persistent sounds *must* have another cause.

He felt certain the mirror was to blame.

As he passed through the tightly packed goods, the boy puzzled through the events of the previous night. The eve of his birthday had commenced with the arrival of his father's good friend, Martin Kepelheim, just after breakfast. Then, shortly after luncheon, Prince Aleksandr Koshmar had unexpectedly appeared on their doorstep, offering armloads of gifts for Charles and far too many kisses for his mother.

Usually a generous host, Robby Sinclair showed little warmth for the intruding foreigner, and the two men had nearly come to blows following a seemingly innocent chess match after supper. By half past nine, his mother retired, blaming a sudden headache, and Koshmar followed soon after. Charles's father had whispered something to the departing prince, who'd clicked his heels and bowed before climbing to the upper storey. Robby Sinclair then ordered a decanter of his strongest whisky and drew Martin Kepelheim into the Pendragon room for a hushed discussion. Suspecting something amiss, Charles stood at the door, eavesdropping on the troubling discourse.

His father and Kepelheim argued over the mirror, mentioning a curse upon the Haimsbury family that reached far into the past—something to do with the Sinclair blood. Charles had overheard talk like this before, when he'd hidden in his father's library and listened to the inner circle members as they debated the possible identity of a future child; apparently desired by some villainous group called Redwing. Since that day, the boy had tried to discover anything he could regarding this mysterious Redwing group, but thus far, he'd found very little. His father seemed to connect Redwing to the black mirror—and to the Russian prince, Aleksandr Koshmar. Who was he? And why did his mother so enjoy the interfering man's company? Moreover, how did it connect to the mirror?

Though young, Charles had a uniquely designed logic to his mind, with the ability to perceive patterns amongst a tangle of disparate threads. Was the Russian more than he appeared? Might Koshmar be *evil?* And why did these persistent scratching noises bring forth images of gloomy places and stones of fire? He gazed out the windows, wondering if the noise was meant to lure him into the attics. If so, then he'd meet the challenge head-on; just as his father would.

As Charles progressed deeper into the dusty attic, his lantern fell upon a series of surfaces: wood, metal, cloth, even the odd jewel. Then, to his surprise, the buttery beam produced what looked like a companion beacon. A second, brighter light that shimmered seductively from the northeast corner.

It's a reflection! the boy realised.

A velvet drape covered most of the tall mirror, but a tiny hole, the size of a penny, allowed the light to shine forth like a radiant eye. A deep chill ran along his long arms, and Charles paused, suddenly overwhelmed with dread.

There's something in there.

Swallowing his fear, the child reached for the velvet cloth that shrouded the mirror. His fingers went numb, and a seductive voice whispered into this thoughts.

Hello, boy. The answers to all your questions lie within. Unveil me and behold the Face of Destiny!

Charles paused, praying the voice was his imagination.

Come find me, boy.

Warning bells clanged inside his mind, and Charles longed for the safety of his father's arms. He started to leave, but as he turned to go, the thick velvet draping slid away, as though a ghostly hand removed it. The cloth pooled on the wooden planks near his feet.

The mirror was unlike any the boy had ever seen. Rather than silver, the black surface was formed of polished obsidian, and its beveled edges etched with shapes that had the regularity of language. Charles reached out to touch the forbidding glass, intending to trace the unfamiliar words, but to his utter shock, his hand passed into it, as through an open window—or doorway.

The glass rippled, and the boy's reflection disappeared, replaced by crimson eyes set into a dazzling face.

"*Hello, boy,*" an enormous Dragon whispered out of swirling grey mists. "*Let's play.*"

CHAPTER ONE

Twenty-seven years, eleven months and seventeen days after five-year-old Charles Sinclair faced an ageless beast in a dusty attic, the mirror Dragon took its first step towards emerging into the world of men.

It began on the twenty-seventh day of May in the year of our Lord 1888, when a mysterious group called the Blackstone Exploration Society despatched a London solicitor to Goussainville, a sleepy village on the outskirts of Paris. The lawyer's name was Albus Lucius Flint, and his purpose was to speak with the Duchess of Branham at Château Rothesay, where she resided with her maiden aunt, Victoria Stuart. When he arrived at the picturesque village, Flint hired a coach for the five-mile journey, but discovered the duchess wasn't home. Leaving his calling card, the confident solicitor assumed the peeress would contact him that very same day, but two days passed before a letter finally arrived. In it, the duchess requested further information regarding the nature of Flint's business. Six additional notes passed twixt the château and *La Maison Val-d'Oise*'s room number 3 before the determined lawyer finally obtained an audience with the elusive peeress.

It was on the first of June when she received him. On that bright spring morning, the graceful young woman wore a dress of embroidered yellow taffeta overlaid in dotted silk, which rustled as she walked. Ringlets of raven hair followed the curve of her small back. She'd tucked the waist-length curls behind each ear to reveal drop earrings made of silver and pearl, which swung from her perfect lobes like a pair of delicate pendulums. She had large, almond-shaped eyes with deep chocolate irises flecked with hints of gold near the pupil rim; each watchful eye framed in thick black lashes. The heart-shaped face had the rosy glow of health, as though she'd only just returned from a brisk morning's ride. Though only twenty, the lady had the poise and self-confidence of any queen. Her perfect figure would inspire Michelangelo, and the classic beauty cause any ordinary man to fall in love.

But Albus Flint was *hardly* an ordinary man.

A tall footman, dressed in black tails and a gold waistcoat, left a chased silver tray, laden with tea, coffee, cups, and all the needed inclusions. The china pattern featured elements the perceptive lawyer recognised at once: a red border overpainted by a trio of golden lions alternating with three *fleur-de-lis*; heraldry from an old Plantagenet crest. In the centre of the plates and on the sides of each cup, he noticed the Scottish thistle surmounted by two crowns. Without speaking a word, Elizabeth Stuart proclaimed her royal bloodlines.

The footman stepped backward to blend in with the surroundings. Several minutes passed in silence. Protocol demanded the duchess speak first, and Flint wisely waited for this most royal of ladies to begin the conversation.

The duchess read through their correspondence, turning through the pages slowly, taking her time as if measuring his manners. "I pray you'll appreciate my caution, Mr. Flint," she said at last. "Will you have tea or coffee?"

"Whatever you're having, my lady."

"Darjeeling," she replied. "I'll pour, Walker. You may go, but remind Lady Victoria that we must leave for Paris no later than eleven o'clock."

"Very good, Your Grace," replied the footman, closing the drawing room doors.

The duchess poured two cups of tea. "Sugar?"

"No, thank you. And I prefer it black."

She handed him the cup, adding two cubes of sugar and a splash of milk to her own. "I'm rather perplexed as to why you would wish to speak to me, Mr. Flint, despite our correspondence. Lawyers seldom bring good news, and they generally call on my solicitor, not me."

The pale stranger managed an understanding smile. "I bring no news at all, my lady, but only a simple request. I represent a group of scientifically minded gentlemen; an internationally funded collective called the Blackstone Exploration Society. You may have heard of it?"

"No," she told him. "Is it a men's club of some sort?"

"Not solely, no. Indeed, some of our most prominent members are women. We place no restrictions on how far a talented man or woman might climb within our society. Knowledge serves as the rungs on that egalitarian ladder, but philanthropy and good works are the rails."

"I applaud philanthropy, Mr. Flint. But what have I to do with your society? I've no desire to join. Do you seek donations?"

He grinned, ever so slightly, as though mildly embarrassed. "No, my lady. Not at all. My clients seek only your permission to explore several ruined buildings on your Kent estate's grounds. In particular, Lion Hall. We understand you plan to raze it next year. Is that so?"

"Lion Hall is in decline, Mr. Flint. Long past repair or any use," she told him firmly. "Cake?"

He declined the offer, stirring an odd-smelling packet of powder into his teacup. "My constitution doesn't do well with sweets, Your Grace. An old man's digestion, you know. I hope you don't mind if I add medicine to my tea? Hot liquid helps to unlock the leaf's potency."

"Not at all," she answered. "Are you unwell? There's a fine doctor in Goussainville. I could send for him."

"No, no, dear lady. Thank you, though. As to my business, we wish to survey the ruins, for that castle helped secure the estuary during King Richard and John's reigns. Lion Hall represents England, Your Grace."

"I'm aware of that, Mr. Flint. King Richard ordered the building of the castle, but it was the Marquess of Anjou who underwrote the cost, and he who held it during many great battles. It may bear the king's French appellation, *Leon*, but that castle is Anjou; and therefore, it is *my* heritage, not England's. Those precarious ruins pose a danger to our farmers and shepherds, and I intend to pull it down and reuse the stones for fencing."

"That would be a terrible mistake," the lawyer said boldly. His fierce black eyes blinked as he rhythmically stirred the tea. Flint was cadaverously lean and spidery in form, with a lined face of alabaster paleness. Despite the peculiar appearance, the lawyer had a way about him that mesmerised anyone in his presence, and he now set all his powers of enthrallment upon the soft-eyed duchess.

"Though the castle is Anjou," he continued, "it is still part of English history. I doubt you'd wish to deprive future generations of so great a monument, my lady. The symbols upon these cups and plates reveal the powerful sinews of your family. Would you hide them by tearing down other symbols of your family's rights? You *must* allow us to dig inside the hall, Duchess. You *will* allow us. Is that not so? I'm sure *you agree* with me. *Don't you?*"

Each measured word emerged from his thin lips as if floating on clouds of sweetly scented mist. He moved forward onto the edge of the chair, so the altered tea's fragrance could enter her delicate nostrils. He watched eagerly for the telling dilation of her pupils; the slackening of facial muscles, slight drop of the lower lip. The overall willingness to listen and obey.

But he saw none of these things.

Despite all efforts, Flint's hypnotic mannerisms, salvia-laced tea, and smooth, modulated voice failed utterly to persuade his prey of anything. Instead, the performance evoked the opposite effect in the determined duchess, who responded in anger.

"Do not dare to tell me what I may or may not do with my own property, Mr. Flint!" she told him plainly, her voice as commanding as any sovereign's. "If you think me a soft target, then you've misjudged me, sir. I say again, England does not own that castle. I do!"

His skeletal hand paused on the silver teaspoon. Flint cleared his long throat. He hadn't expected a twenty-year-old woman to be so formidable an opponent. He'd need to employ a different tack with the lady.

"Forgive me, Your Grace. Though I've never had the honour to meet you until now, your reputation as a woman of high intelligence and business acumen is without equal. The Blackstone Society would never try to coerce you into improper partnerships or deprive you of your familial rights. As you say, Lion Hall is your property, and you may dispose of it as you wish. My clients wish only the opportunity to assess this historic building prior to any planned destruction. The Blackstone Society is a scientific institution that pursues knowledge; be it chemistry, physics, history, or architecture. We sincerely desire to learn more of twelfth-century construction and the activities of one of England's greatest kings. And, if possible, we should like to preserve that knowledge for future generations."

Her face softened, but only a very little. "Mr. Flint, you proceed from a misunderstanding. If your goal is to discover and preserve artifacts relative to King Richard's reign, then you'd best look for them in France. Despite being England's king, my ancestor seldom visited there, and he never resided at Lion Hall."

Flint's mouth slowly crept into a crooked little smile. Perhaps, his tea had worked after all. "*Ancestor*, my lady? You refer to the king as your ancestor? You are a Plantagenet, then?"

Beth felt a chill run along her scalp. What a foolish slip! As a descendent of Henry V's twin sons, she could indeed call Richard her ancestor, but only members of the inner circle were permitted to share the secret. One might use elements from Plantagenet heraldry here and there, but to declare it, *verbally*, was simply unthinkable!

"Yes, he was my ancestor," she answered boldly, deciding to approach the mistake from a position of strength. "As you know, one of my many titles is Marchioness of Anjou. Guillaume Capet, the first marquess, was Richard's cousin and dearest friend."

"Ah, yes, I'd quite forgotten, my lady. Your ancestry is rich with the blood of French and English princes, is it not? The paintings in this marvellous drawing room speak of that long, important history; as does Lion Hall, I'm sure. That rich bloodline must be preserved, my lady. Historically, speaking, of course. I wonder, are you aware that the Plantagenets and their influential cousins, the House of Anjou, are rumoured to descend from a suspicious liaison?"

"Why would you call it suspicious, Mr. Flint? The phrase hints at impropriety," she answered, refusing to be intimidated.

"I mean no insult, my lady. Forgive me for even mentioning it. I'd assumed you knew of the water faery Melusine—the so-called 'Lady of the Lake'. Some claim she could transform into all manner of shapes: mermaid, sprite, serpent, even dragon!" he added with a peculiar little laugh. "There are those who speak of a union twixt her and one of your Angevin ancestors. Why, King Richard himself told such tales. He believed he descended from Melusine through the Angevin blood. As Marchioness of Anjou, you would also descend from this supernatural creature, would you not?" He grinned triumphantly, stirring the disgusting mixture in his cup.

"I thought only children believed in fables, Mr. Flint," she dared say.

His smile vanished. "As a member of the Blackstone Society, I seek scientific explanations—not mythical ones. Still, it is quite an interesting tale, don't you think?"

Beth's iron will began to wane. She felt weary suddenly, and longed to take a walk or ride through the woods to escape the spidery solicitor and his odd stories of faeries. In truth, the duchess had for many weeks been somewhat distracted by a troubling relationship with a Romanian prince named Rasarit Grigor. The handsome suitor had promised to meet her in Paris that afternoon, and the thought both terrified and excited her. She wished her Cousin Paul were in town to go with her, but the earl was presently on assignment elsewhere.

"It seems as though your society knows more about the Angevin side of my ancestry than I, Mr. Flint. However, I must take time to consider your request before giving an answer. Walker will see you out."

Having failed in his first attempt, Flint bowed graciously and returned to England, rebuffed but content that he had managed to unsettle the duchess and 'set the hook' in her soul.

A flurry of written pleas followed that initial visit, containing page after page of persuasive prose; phrases couched in labyrinthine legalese that allowed enough loopholes to accommodate any future need for adjustment. For many weeks, reams of monogrammed stationery sailed across the channel twixt England and France; until at last, on the fourteenth of July, the duchess relented. Flint learnt the reason for this sudden change of mind through a Parisian colleague. Despite the London solicitor's fervent pleas and entreaties, it was a young man named Seth Holloway who'd persuaded Elizabeth to sign the contract.

The duchess had written to her longtime friend, asking Dr. Holloway's professional opinion on the Blackstone solicitation. With degrees in archaeology and ancient languages, plus a lifetime's experience in the field, Elizabeth valued Seth's advice. Rather than replying in a letter, Holloway immediately left Cambridge for Paris, spending a fortnight at Victoria's château, where he conferred with the duchess and her cousin Lord Aubrey (who'd come to look into the 'Prince Rasha' business). Both men agreed that a survey would be beneficial.

Ever the wise businesswoman, Elizabeth hired a team of expert solicitors to negotiate the contract. The final, very specific language stipulated the team restrict their activities to Lion Hall only, with surveys and mapping permitted, but absolutely no digging. The agreement also made it clear that all Blackstone activities must end after six weeks. If the Society discovered items of importance in the castle ruins, then all must remain *in situ* until the duchess approved further action.

Comprising the survey team were six paid interns, drawn from the Oxbridge elite: three from Oxford, three from Cambridge. These were overseen by a no-nonsense, retired army officer, one Colonel Sir Alfred Collinwood, a leading member of the Society and renowned antiquarian in his own right. The student contingency included a somewhat self-possessed third-year Cambridge student named Lionel Archibald Wentworth, whose anaemic attempt at scholarship maintained an inverse relationship to his pursuit of nightly entertainments. That is, the higher Wentworth's consumption of ale, the lower his marks at college. By year's end, however, young Wentworth would learn a lesson that would alter him forever: The wages of a libertine lifestyle are worse than death. Far worse than man's mind could fathom.

CHAPTER TWO

The road to Lionel Wentworth's eternal enlightenment commenced when his flustered father threatened to remove his idle son from Trinity's halls in favour of apprenticeship as an underpaid lawyer's clerk. Fearfully, young Wentworth prayed for a solution to this sticky, self-made dilemma. Not that Wentworth prayed to a capital 'g' God as any Christian might. Instead, the desperate rake offered petitions to whatever small-g 'god' might listen. Bacchus would do, he reasoned, as he spent so much time in the wine god's raucous company. The Green Man or Herne would also serve well, or even Merlin, assuming such a magician ever existed. It mattered not a whit to Wentworth, so long as the deity's answer proved favourable to his petition.

The reply to this imprecisely directed appeal arrived one Saturday evening in September, when his friend, Kip Wilson, noticed a curious flyer pasted next to the door of The Eagle Public House:

> WANTED –
>
> The Blackstone Society seeks men of good health and sound mind, willing to participate in a six-week, scientific survey. Archaeological experience welcome, but not necessary. Successful applicants will receive three hundred pounds compensation and housing allowance. Locations include, but are not limited to: England, France, Ireland, Spain, and Scotland.
>
> – Apply at Greene and Settle, Grantchester.

The enticing handbill bore a curious border of standing crows, whose crimson eyes seemed brushed with blobs of actual blood. Despite the peculiar decoration, the message of the solicitation struck Lionel as an answer to prayer, providing a firm sense of financial rescue. In exchange for six weeks of modest labour, he'd get three hundred pounds. The Society further sweetened the deal with the mention of sunny Spain and alluring France, where a man might lose himself in ribald debauchery.

Surely, Bacchus himself had answered the prayer! he reasoned.

After hastily writing to his father and receiving permission to apply, Wentworth called at the law firm listed on the handbill and spoke with a very odd solicitor named Aloysius Vermis. The man was round as a dumpling and wore a tight wool suit that caused his pale flesh to puff over the starched collar and cuffs as though trying to escape. Vermis provided the student the necessary paperwork and instructions along with an indiscernible warning that "life's turns can lead to joyful discovery or woeful regret; one never knows which it might be." In typical fashion, the frivolous student jokingly replied that Blackstone Society's new venture was certainly the former; indeed, an answer to prayer, to which the dough-faced Vermis replied in a very odd way: "Do be careful what favours you ask of a god, Mr. Wentworth. You might actually get them."

The formal interview took place on the eleventh of September inside the cheerful snug of Grantchester's Green Man Public House, a stone's throw from the idyllic banks of the River Cam. Albus Flint drank an odd-smelling herbal tea, whilst Lionel sipped warm ale before the pleasant fire, confident of his prospects. Flint opened by cautioning the eager applicant that one place, and *one place only*, remained on the roster of six interns and that two other applicants were due to arrive within the hour.

"You are how old, Mr. Wentworth?"

"Twenty-one, come the third of December."

"I see. Well, despite your youth, you have excellent qualifications, Mr. Wentworth. Classes in maths and chemistry, as well as two in geology. But are you sure this endeavour is a good fit for you? It will require physical exertion, long hours, and a sober mind," the solicitor explained from his oak chair. "There must be no doubt regarding your desire to join us. Our Society demands *sacrifices* of all its members; even our interns."

"Absolutely no doubt, sir," Wentworth insisted, completely ignoring the caution.

"You *willingly* choose to participate? It is a decision made from free will?"

Lionel bristled at the man's annoying persistence. "Yes, of course I want to join! I'd never have come if I didn't want to be a part of this project, Mr. Flint. Do you think me flippant?"

The solicitor gazed at his prey thoughtfully. "I mean no disrespect, Mr. Wentworth, but legal requirements must be met, you know. Now, the following is a standard question, so please take no offence. Is money your only reason for applying to the Society?"

Despite the innocent context, Lionel sensed a trap, and he decided to avoid it by offering the lawyer full truth.

"I shan't lie to you, Mr. Flint. It's certainly *part* of my reason. As you can tell from my resumé, my father's quite well off—a retired QC, you know—but my allowance at college sometimes makes the odd pleasure somewhat difficult to obtain. Three hundred pounds would go a long way towards remedying that deficit."

"When you say 'odd pleasure', I take it you mean drink, Mr. Wentworth?"

"A glass now and then never hurt anyone," the lanky student argued.

"True, but what of women? Are they, also, amongst your 'odd pleasures', Mr. Wentworth? Might you enjoy the soft seductions of ladies, sir? Or are there other, more unusual temptations in your repertoire?"

Lionel paused before answering. The obvious trap regarding money was a ruse to lead him into another. He felt an unsettling sensation; as though invisible hands ran along his face and shoulders, examining him. Suddenly, the brash young man felt quite naked before the solicitor's piercing gaze.

With a false laugh, he answered in a strained voice. "I find ladies pleasantly distracting, Mr. Flint. What red-blooded man doesn't?"

"Ah, yes red blood," Flint repeated, licking his thin lips. "Blood makes men do very peculiar things, does it not, Mr. Wentworth? However, I'm not here to judge. I seek only to confirm your loyalty to the Society and our mission. You are, after all, a healthy young man, are you not, Mr. Wentworth? We wouldn't want your energies siphoned off, if you understand my meaning. Blood and its associated tissues must remain pure. Besides, conducting these surveys requires long hours of taxing work. Not all of it physical. Most is mental, a strain of concentration and introspection, if you will. I shouldn't want you to be distracted by trivialities of the flesh."

"I assure you, sir: trivialities will play no part in my activities," he replied, intentionally omitting 'of the flesh'.

The inquisitor actually smiled, the crooked Jack-o-Lantern curve sending an icy shiver down Wentworth's spine. "I'm very glad to hear it," said Flint. "There is, of course, one other concern. Gambling is rife in your generation, I fear, Mr. Wentworth. Might that vice also be numbered amongst your off-campus pleasures?"

In truth, Lionel loved to gamble, and he owed Kip Wilson fifty pounds, but he had no intention of revealing what might be perceived as a character flaw to such a disquietingly nosy little man.

"No, sir," Lionel answered proudly. "No gambling problems at all. Such dark pursuits would break my poor mother's heart, Mr. Flint."

"An obedient son who loves his mother. How very *English* of you," Flint replied with another twisted smirk, as though he saw past the student's false reply and into the innermost parts of his crooked soul. "I'm sure your mother is exceedingly proud of you, Mr. Wentworth."

In truth, Lionel's ever-forgiving mother had suffered a nervous breakdown that spring; due, in large part, to worry over her son's life choices. Only recently, after spending time in a Fulham asylum, had she returned to her former self.

Flint's black eyes blinked mechanically as he sipped the dreadful-smelling tea. It seemed to Lionel that the lugubrious solicitor bore an uncanny resemblance to a carrion crow, and he recalled the peculiar border on the Blackstone solicitation poster.

"Tell me, Mr. Wentworth," the corvine examiner continued languidly, "have you completed and signed all the forms you were given by Mr. Vermis?"

"Yes, yes, of course. I say, has it grown hot of a sudden?" asked the student, wiping beads of sweat from his upper lip.

"It's quite comfortable," Flint replied icily. "The forms?"

Lionel found his thoughts growing clouded, but managed to hand the lawyer three pages of information. These included a lengthy family history, an exhaustive if not intrusive health questionnaire, a list of all courses taken at Trinity College, and the name of his 'next of kin'; an odd question, Wentworth thought, but then who was he to judge?

The eccentric Albus Flint perused the pages quickly and then added them to a large leather valise, snapping it shut with a satisfied grin. "All appears to be in order," the man declared.

"Am I accepted, then?" asked Wentworth anxiously, thinking only of the money.

"Not yet. First, you must answer three more questions."

"Only three?" Lionel sang back with feigned confidence. "Fire away, sir."

Albus Lucius Flint squared his thin shoulders, and the knobby fingers of his left hand twitched and stretched into a series of impossible shapes. He cleared his scrawny throat, making an odd croaking sound, as though swallowing a live toad.

"Very well, then. To begin, Mr. Wentworth, are you a particularly *religious* man?"

This took the smug student by surprise. Why would a scientific society care a smidge whether or not he worshipped God, or gods, or even himself for that matter?

"I'm not sure what you mean by religious, Mr. Flint. I'm not much of church-goer. Never saw the need for all that hocus pocus."

"No, no, that isn't quite what I asked. I do not enquire regarding any formal practices, but as regards your personal beliefs, Mr. Wentworth. For instance, do you ascribe to the notion of salvation through faith? Have you been, as they say, *washed in the blood?*"

Lionel laughed a bit too loudly, and he slapped the oak table. "Washed in the blood! Salvation? Do tell me I haven't misjudged you, Mr. Flint. I hope you're not with one of those Bible-thumping tract societies or a doomsayer from the foolish Pentecostals or Adventists! If so, we may conclude our business now, and I'll return to Cambridge a poorer but wiser man."

"Oh, I am hardly that," the interlocutor replied quietly as he stirred a sachet of something black and odorous into a freshly poured cup of tea. "My associations are far older than Adventists or tract societies, Mr. Wentworth. Far older than you can imagine. One might even call them *primordial*."

"Then, perhaps I should tell you the truth, Mr. Flint, and if it loses me the job, so be it," Wentworth bluffed. "To say I disdain the Church of England is understatement, but I attend their paltry services whenever I'm in London, just to please my parents. It isn't that I prefer other branches of the faith. Roman rituals hold no magical enticements, nor do the Lutherans. In truth, I consider all formal religious institutions a vanity of chains, forged from man-derived, superstitious claptrap. These comforting chains serve no other purpose than to weigh man down and prevent him from achieving his rightful, evolutionary goals. As with our ancestors the apes, we seek to rise higher, but the golden millstones of popes and priests would grind us into dust beneath their well-shod feet."

"Exceedingly well put," Flint replied, clearly pleased. "I'd thought you might be a man of clear thinking, Mr. Wentworth. You'll go far with such a progressive attitude." Flint then made a bold checkmark in the 'plus' category on Wentworth's score card.

Next, the stone-faced solicitor posed a somewhat mundane, if not entirely unexpected query. "Why do you wish to join our team, Mr. Wentworth? If not entirely for the money, as you've implied, then what else motivates you?"

Lionel finished the ale and smiled, his lean face alight with smug confidence. He'd practised this speech, having felt certain the question would arise, and therefore spun a buoyant, even prosaic thread of lengthy (though not entirely honest) claims, regarding his desire to explore ancient civilisations and expand the knowledge-base of England's ever-widening circle of callus-handed, antiquarian diggers. He waxed eloquent on the virtues of rigorous, scientific endeavour and ended with a strong hint about a keen interest in the fertile, and *very stimulating*, villages surrounding Paris; wondering aloud if the Society might have an opening in such educational venues. He even claimed to speak French with the flowery fluency of a Voltaire or Diderot—a broad stretch of the truth at best.

The saturnine interviewer's pale lips twisted into that crooked smile once more. "Ah, such a talent would be most convenient, Mr. Wentworth! There is a site near a sleepy little village called Goussainville that might suit your skills and aspirations. It sits half an hour's drive northeast of Paris, and is but a ten-minute ride from Château Rothesay, where our hostess, the Duchess of Branham, currently resides. Should you join our company, I shall add your name to a very short waiting list, compiled in the event that a French volunteer becomes ill or incapacitated for some, uh, *unforeseen* reason."

Flint's throat made a birdlike cackling sound as he pronounced the word 'unforeseen', and his black eyes blinked thrice in the same mechanical fashion as before. Despite the very odd display, Lionel nodded politely, muttering something to the effect of 'Ah, yes, I see,' and 'Quite sensible'; not wishing to appear too eager for the bawdy pleasures of Parisian nightlife.

His measured restraint earned him a second, bold checkmark.

Finally, the cadaverous gentleman in the funereal suit, leaned forward; waxwork hands steepled in a pyramid of white flesh, black eyes fixed upon his prey as he whispered in a voice so deathly cold that it chilled the student to the very marrow of his greedy bones.

"Mr. Wentworth, are you easily *frightened?*"

This final word actually echoed, as though provided with some theatrical effect; and it seemed to Wentworth that the solicitor's slack face performed a series of jerking tremors, trying to maintain corporeality. As if he were not quite a part of this world. The strange man's pupils dilated into monstrous pools of eddying black as he spoke, and he pronounced 'frightened' with a rolled 'r', rhythmically drawn out as though the word itself had magical power to instill abject terror.

Which it did.

Never before, had Wentworth felt so cold a sensation course through his body. It took every ounce of courage to maintain an impassive affect to his facial muscles, but maintain it he did, as he declared in a voice a bit too loud for the modest enclosure of the pub's snug.

"Sir, I am frightened by nothing and no one! As I've already told you, superstition has no place in the mind of a modern thinker. If I meet something unknown to me, then I rejoice in it, Mr. Flint. I do not shrink!"

Flint's thin lips spread apart into a square, and he laughed in that peculiar, avian manner at the student's bravura. A third checkmark was entered on the interview form.

He then presented Lionel with a three-page, handwritten document, that looked as though it were made from very old, very fine vellum; presumably from lamb or calfskin, though the texture seemed unusual.

"I'm very pleased to offer you the last position on our Branham team, Mr. Wentworth. Here is the contract. It contains standard language with a few, minor amendments. I'll allow you a few moments to read it before you sign. I shouldn't want you to be surprised by anything we might ask of you, come November."

The solicitor handed the student a black pen with an even blacker nib. As he took the instrument, Lionel felt a sharp prick upon his index finger, and he noticed a thin stream of bright crimson emerging from the nib's razor point.

"That's strange," Lionel muttered dreamily as he glanced at the injured finger. "I seem to have cut myself somehow."

"Strange indeed, but it will heal, I should think—eventually."

The lawyer blotted the red signature with a roller and returned the signed contract, roller, and writing instrument to the cavernous black valise.

Wentworth wrapped the wound with a white handkerchief and managed a perplexed smile. "Then, I'm a member?"

"You are a member," Flint answered with that disconcerting blinking in full force.

"Well, then," Wentworth muttered, "I'll see you in November, Mr. Flint. Forgive the impudence, but you're an odd sort of fellow. However, the Master at Trinity vouches for you—or rather his secretary, Mr. Corvis, does—and that's good enough for me."

"Corvis is a very old friend of the Society, Mr. Wentworth. You might say we've gone *through the wars* together. And now, as they say, you've signed away your life, my young friend." He grinned, the black button eyes glittering as though polished. "From this moment forward, your life will change dramatically."

To Wentworth's utter surprise and delight, the solicitor's prophetic words proved true. Over the course of the following weeks, the student's life took a sharp turn for the better. His dons began to brag on his academic progress; his horses always won at the turf clubs; his father increased his weekly allowance; and his wealthy friend, Kip Wilson, suddenly remembered that it was *he* who owed Lionel fifty pounds, not the other way round. Wilson even invited Wentworth to join the Silver Spoons Club, a secret society, usually open only to legacy students.

"Admitting a man with no family ties to the Club is simply unheard of," Wilson told his friend on initiation night. "I think some beneficent god must be smiling on you, Worthy."

Perhaps, one did, thought Wentworth.

By December, however, Lionel would regret every dreadful moment of that encounter with Albus Flint, for he would come face to face with the cruel god who'd answered his hasty prayer.

By then, it would be much too late.

CHAPTER THREE

18th December, 1888 - Charles Sinclair's Journal

I commence this personal record with trepidation. Yesterday, my beautiful wife Elizabeth gave me this splendid journal—"In honour of our one-month wedding anniversary," she told me, "and to mark the moment when you became a duke."

A duke! Who could have thought a monosyllabic word could hold so many implications within its four letters? Truly, my brain cannot fathom so strange a title when applied to myself. The staff—and even our good Mr. Baxter—now call me 'Your Grace', and each time I hear it, I look round for Elizabeth, thinking she must stand nearby, for surely it is my wife whom they address and not myself.

Ah, my wife. Now, that is a topic upon which I could write lengthy prose and fill many, many books. How I love that woman! She would be the centremost jewel of any man's crown; the greatest gift to any man's life, yet I am blessed to call her wife. Tis a wonder indeed! One month ago, we wed, and in that very brief time, we've already faced numerous challenges, a few fleeting heartaches, and enough sweet victories to fill a hundred books. My Beth—my precious 'little one'—would have no trouble penning such a history, for it is she who possesses all the creativity in our family. I am but a dull mathematician who investigates crime.

Still, Beth insists that I make a habit of jotting down my thoughts; that the discipline of writing will prove useful during the coming months. She, therefore, expects me to fill each page of this thick volume, promising to give me a new one the very moment this one is complete. Needless to say, it may take me years to accomplish my assignment.

I must say, though, it is certainly a finely crafted journal; bound in rich red leather and embossed in gold with my name, Charles Robert Arthur Sinclair III, 1st Duke of Haimsbury, on the cover. It is a constant reminder of that strange sounding title.

It's early morning, not yet six, and Elizabeth sleeps ten feet from me. Therefore, I sit quietly beside our bedchamber's cosy fire, dressed in a finely tailored dressing gown. (It's a wedding gift from Martin Kepelheim—oh, what a friend that delightful man has become!) Beyond the room's shuttered windows, a nightingale's sweet song floats upon the still night air, the perfect accompaniment to the soft snoring of Bella and Briar. Samson, Victoria's terrier, is awake and staring at me as though I should be scratching his ears rather than scratching words onto a page. These three, brave animals serve as companions and faithful watchdogs, allowing Beth and myself to rest peacefully each night. God designed dogs for such important tasks, I think. Noble creatures they are, and I'm considering adding another to our family. Perhaps, a puppy for Adele? I've already purchased a Welsh pony for her to ride at Branham, but a spaniel or retriever might be useful.

Now, to this book. I wonder just what I should say about my life? To be frank, it feels like an exercise in futility, but Elizabeth explained to me that, through diligence and careful habit; by writing my innermost thoughts, feelings, and even dreams, I may soon discern hidden patterns to seemingly random events. And that these patterns might unveil the lost years of my childhood.

As a policeman, I appreciate the importance of careful documentation and recording of evidentiary fact, but the chronicling of feelings? How will subjective self-analysis help? If I wish to unburden my heart, I may speak to Beth and my inner circle friends: Paul, Henry, Baxter, James, Reid, to name but a few. Must I, also, record my thoughts and fears on paper?

Despite my doubts, I love my wife and would never contend with her over something she clearly believes important. Thus, I find myself writing on a chilly December morn.

Where to begin? A good policeman's report begins with a summation of the facts: Though I've celebrated thirty-three birthdays, my true life began in early October, when I received a letter from Elizabeth, asking if I would call on her at Queen Anne House. To say this was a surprise is understatement. I'd not heard from her in four years, but never once in that time, had my thoughts strayed from her. I have loved Elizabeth since our serendipitous meeting at Paul Stuart's home in June of '84. That October letter is the key to my present happy state, and I thank God every day that he inspired her to send it. One day, I shall write a history of the miraculous weeks that led to my marriage, but for now, let me review the crimes and mysteries currently facing the inner circle.

Strange, I had no knowledge (that I could remember) of this august group of warriors prior to October, but now I serve as their leader. The mission of the inner circle is simple: Protect a secret royal bloodline whilst battling the plans of Redwing. That dark assembly's crimes litter mankind's history like fields of rotting corpses. Of late, I believe them responsible for the so-called Jack the Ripper murders, as well as the 1879 Cricket Ground Killings, the recent Victoria Park deaths, the Embankment Murders, and many others; including a string of assaults on women and children in the East, where a ghost-like figure attempts to lure them to suicide in the Thames.

Two known members of Redwing have been slain, and today we bury a man whom I suspect of having connexions to that horrid group. I pray I'm wrong about Lord Wychwright. His daughter, Cordelia, is fragile enough without hearing her late father participated in occult rituals. The newly formed Intelligence Branch (which I am honoured to oversee as Commissioner) has been tasked to unmask the killer or killers behind these Redwing deaths. Of course, the Home Office have no idea Lord Hemsfield and Lord Peter Andrews were members of this subversive collection of miscreants, but the prime minister knows it. It's a blessing that I report directly to Salisbury, not Matthews.

I cannot yet say if it is connected to Redwing, but our circle made a shocking discovery within two areas of my home. The ballroom, which appears to be inhabited by demonic forces; and the library, which leads to a secret passage and thence to a hidden chamber. Both the ballroom and library remain locked, with only Baxter and myself possessing keys. Martin Kepelheim is working with Dr. Edward MacPherson to clean the house of evil spirits, particularly the ballroom and hidden chamber (which Martin calls 'the puzzle room'). Thankfully, Elizabeth shows no interest in investigating these closed rooms, nor does she press me for information. I endeavour to keep dark matters from my sensitive wife by steering our talks towards Christmas celebrations. Thus far, it's working. Elizabeth's health is uppermost in my mind, and I hope to support and protect her as she carries our children to delivery next June.

Now, let me move to the true purpose of this journal: My own worries, thoughts, and dreams. As to my dreams, the content returns again and again to my parents and childhood days. Most are brief snatches of imperfect images, but a few have lucidity and even purpose to them; as though my sleeping brain tries to teach me some great lesson.

I'm not sure why, but many of these dreams include dragons, though the precise features and physiognomy of these creatures remain obscured. It's as though they speak to me from an intangible demi-monde; beyond the glittering veil of a darkling glass, casting their creeping shadows into my sleeping mind.

In last night's dream, I was here, in Haimsbury House. How often did I stay here as a boy? Though I've no memory of those visits, Martin says my family resided here every summer, which means I made hundreds of memories here—yet all remain obscured behind a thick veil. Kepelheim (whom I used to call Uncle Marty) once told me of a masked ball that my father hosted in April of 1860, and of that dance's nightmarish ending. Apparently, I appeared in the doorway at the stroke of midnight, accompanied by some hideous creature with wings.

Might that connect to these dragon dreams of mine?

Since reopening the house in late October, I've walked through nearly every inch of this remarkable mansion, including the ballroom, and there is indeed something very dark within its mirrored walls; that I do know. Our good friend Henry MacAlpin sensed it, and it terrified even his strong heart. What does that mean?

(MEMO: I must continue to keep the ballroom locked until Mac and Martin can evict these dark spirits through prayers and anointing oil. I will not risk our future children or Adele entering that hellish domain until it is safe!)

Need I explain that my precious wife is with child? Or rather, 'with children'? I've tasked our carpenters with redecorating the nursery in preparation for the twins' arrival next summer (10th of June, according to Georgianna – I look forward to holding that delightful child in my arms!). When I first toured the nursery apartment, it felt oddly familiar, but I've no conscious memory of ever having slept there. Yet, I'm told that I laughed, played, and also dreamt in this house as a small boy. At present, the apartment contains three rooms and a play area. According to Martin and Victoria, my nanny slept in the smallest chamber, I slept in the largest, and the third is a delightful library of history books, atlases, and biographies, which Adele has already claimed as her own. Only yesterday, I caught her devouring one of my grandfather's military campaign journals. I'd no idea our Della is interested in military history, but I shall try to find other memorabilia she might appreciate. I like to think she looks a little like me, as my paternal affections continue to grow. Tory mentioned how Della's eye colour is taking on a turquoise shade, similar to my own. Since Paul's father was my uncle, perhaps it is a heritable factor within the Stuart line. It touches my heart, when she hugs me and mentions being 'part Sinclair'. I reply that our shared traits are merely Stuart ones and offer hugs in return. Adele Marie! I couldn't love that child more if she were my own.

I've diverted my thoughts again, but perhaps that is part of the exercise. To return to the topic, whilst walking through the nursery's main bedchamber, I had an odd sense of *déjà vu* when touching the canopied bed. Though every window was shut, the blue silk curtains billowed without hint of breeze or human touch. There is a clock on the mantel which caused me an odd moment of dizziness. It may be that my head injury still plagues me, perhaps some lingering sensitivity caused by my coma. (The fact that I still cannot shave because of healing facial cuts is a constant reminder of that night's explosion. Beth likes the beard and the longer hair. I may keep both.) The dizziness that day nearly caused me to fall, and it was a good thing Martin and Adele stood nearby. Our darling Della is indeed a bright little thing! After Martin helped me to a chair, she continued to worry about me for the following hour, dogging my every step and periodically checking my pulse or feeling my forehead for fever. If Paul will not claim her as daughter soon, I may ask for legal guardianship.

But this clock haunts me. I cannot explain it, but the figural piece seemed to call to me; to whisper in a snarling sort of voice, speaking my name! Might I have played with the clock as a boy? It bears no maker's mark, but a genius must have built the mechanised figures. Each is exquisitely crafted, and they're designed to perform a meaningful scene each quarter hour. The players in this performance are King Arthur, mounted on a white horse, who challenges a terrifyingly realistic, fire-breathing dragon. The display is remarkable, and Martin tells me the clock was a gift from a foreign prince. Apparently, this Koshmar person gave me two of them on my christening day as well as mirror. One clock for here; the other for Rose House.

(MEMO: Be sure to investigate inner circle records of a 'Prince Aleksandr Koshmar', presumably from Russia.)

The clock is broken, so I've sent it to Paul's jeweller for repair. Martin believes this clock, when working, will jog my stubborn memories.

Now, back to last night's dream. It was exceedingly odd; as though I looked through a picture book of my forgotten past. In it, my father led me through a series of themed gardens. Father referred to them as 'our own little Camelot'.

(MEMO: I should ask Mr. Frame if Haimsbury House ever had such displays.)

Afterwards, Father took me inside, and we surveyed the house's many apartments. We toured dusty wine cellars and lofty attics. He pointed to specific areas in each of these, but I cannot recall just what he said. In the east wing attic, he showed me a tall black cabinet decorated with an undulating river. Beside this ribbon of blue, crouched a golden dragon, surrounded by seven hooded figures; each facing a tall man in armour carrying a great sword.

"It's called *Lann Lasair*," Father told me. "The *fire sword*, and it was stolen on the day I died by the same man that killed me. This man serves the Dragon. Both are exceedingly powerful and will lay claim to your blood. Solve a riddle of the clocks to unseal the chamber. Time works against you, Charles. Do not let it run backwards."

I opened my mouth to ask for clarification of these vague commands, but we moved suddenly, without warning. As soon as he mentioned time—quick as a blink—I found myself standing inside the main library. It is the very one which I now keep locked for fear that Adele or Elizabeth might wander into the hidden chamber within its inner walls. When Paul discovered it, he found one of those horrid mirrors inside, and it's my greatest fear that someone I love may unknowingly pass through that infernal black glass. I will not allow that to happen. I would sooner burn down the house first!

As Father and I looked, the library's concealed panel opened of its own accord, and we entered the passage. Using a small lantern, Father guided me through the twisting corridors and into the puzzle chamber. Once inside, Father pointed to the large marble pillar which stands at the centre of the room.

He turned to me, his dark eyes serious. "When you decipher the clock riddle, Charles, this pillar will open."

"What then, sir?" I asked.

"You'll know, son. Trust me. You will know."

Just then, a series of whispers filled the room, and Father drew me close. "Keep away!" he shouted into the glittering mirror, opposite the pillar. "He is not yours!"

I confess that, in the dream, my foolish curiosity overwhelmed all good sense, and I pulled away from my father's embrace to confront the mirror. Within its fluid brightness, I saw a pair of fiery eyes, staring at me.

Hello, boy, the voice whispered. *Remember me?*

That booming voice passed through me like slithering smoke, and I fell to the floor. The last I recall is Father rushing towards me, but nothing more.

I awoke in our bedchamber, confused and drenched in beads of sweat. The room felt cold as death, and my heart beat wildly from the dream's effect. As I slowly realised I'd awoken to reality, I sensed a reassuring warmth beside me: Elizabeth sleeping soundly, her breathing sweetly soft, and her warm body conformed to mine. Her slender arm lay across my chest, and I kissed her hand, thanking God for His many blessings.

It is the greatest joy of my life to awaken beside this remarkable woman each morning. Truly, all my happiness begins and ends in her eyes. Though I search for my past and sometimes worry about the future, I find an unimaginable, healing peace in my 'little one's' sweet smile.

As I conclude the opening Chapter of this journal, the mantel clock strikes six, and the dogs stir to go outdoors. I wouldn't want them to waken Elizabeth; and besides, I must ready myself for the busy day ahead. Baron Wychwright is to be buried in St. Marylebone cemetery at eleven, and afterwards, meetings, meetings, meetings! If I leave early enough, I may find a quiet moment to spend at Albert's grave.

Tomorrow, Beth and I leave for Branham, which means today's agenda is filled with extremes: the funeral and wake, a hundred police matters, and then an early Christmas celebration with friends and family before we leave London.

It is a strange path my life has taken. Most whose only knowledge of me comes from reading the reports and opinions in London's press probably think me the luckiest of men because of the material aspects to my life. I am, after all, a high-ranking peer (a duke, no less!) with a position of authority within government; a wealthy man, married to a high-ranking and very wealthy woman. I am friend and colleague to the prime minister and on a first-name basis with the queen. But titles, power, and wealth are but vain ornaments. I choose to define myself by the love of friends, a happy household, and most especially the love of my dear wife.

It is for Beth and our children that I seek to unveil my hidden past, not myself; and to them that I dedicate all within these pages. If this book serves no other purpose, may it grant my children and grandchildren access to my heart. May they know that I rejoice in who I presently am, for my life is filled with God's mercies and the love of family.

However, because I hope to provide a FULL history to my beloved children and grandchildren, I must continue to search for who I once was; for the boy's secrets within the man's heart. If anything there threatens my family, then it's imperative that I unearth it; no matter the danger to me. I pray this journal will aid in this, not merely amplify my deepest, unspoken fears.

It is that line from Tennyson, which so haunts my thoughts. The one my father used to quote, and that was sent to me via messenger last month: *I am but king amongst the dead.*

Whatever does it mean?

No more writing! I must shut the book, for I hear Beth moving in the bed nearby, and the lark's voice joins the nightingale in brief and joyous chorus. I must shake off the burden of self-doubt and face the land of the living.

It was, after all, only a dream.

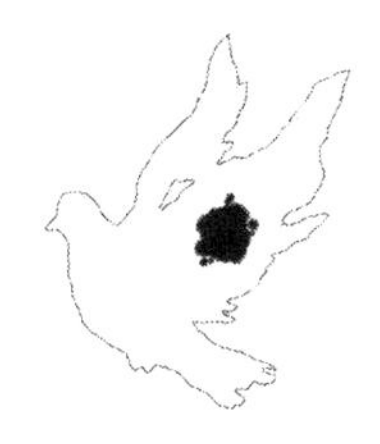

CHAPTER FOUR

Hammersmith Police Station

As Charles Sinclair locked away the journal and began to dress for the day's appointments, approximately five miles to the west of Haimsbury House, a man known only as Bleeding Jack Nobody was being booked into the police cells at T-Division, Hammersmith. The lunatic wore nary a stitch on his scrawny frame, and long tracks of red followed the veins of both arms and legs. Desk Sergeant Bill Black did his best to elicit information from the wailing madman, but the task proved nearly impossible.

"Shall we send for Dr. MacAlpin, sir?" Black asked Detective Inspector Richard Ryan. "We done all we could to keep the fella here last time, Inspector, but he broke out o' the maria takin' him to Bedlam last night."

"The Dragon's comin'!" Bleeding Jack screamed, his face upturned towards the ceiling. "He's comin'! Risin' up outa the ground like a whirlwind o' fire! Time's gonna stop, and the world's gonna fall ta darkness. Ain't none o' you coppers gonna make a tinker's difference, when them claws starts ta rakin' flesh. Cause he's a-comin'! Wif blood and fire, and he'll unlock it all!"

Black had seen madmen rave before and calmly ignored the frenzied gibbering. "Like I said, sir, he don't make sense. Reckon he's syphilitic, poor old sot."

"Have we a name for the sot?" asked Ryan.

"No, sir; nor has anyone reported a man of this fellow's peculiar description or behaviour missin'. He's unique in his appearance, as you can see. Shall I put him down as a vagrant, presumed mad, Inspector? Consign him back to Bedlam—assumin' he's inclined ta go there, sir."

Ryan sighed. Hammersmith was generally a quiet section of West London, but lately, that pleasant peace was constantly broken by a growing sense of lawlessness: Thieving, housebreaks, assaults on innocent ladies and children; rumours of a ghostly figure that lured young girls into coaches and assaulted them (some said drinking their blood); tales of masked fiends claiming to be Ripper and threatening public house patrons; even rumours of wolf-like men roaming the streets at night and stealing infants from their cots. It was as though mass hysteria had overwhelmed the entire region. But no matter the true cause behind the crime spree, Ryan and his men were run off their feet. The inspector had no time to coddle a demented syphilitic.

"Bedlam won't do, Sergeant," he declared, motioning towards a pair of constables. "This man would simply escape again. Place him in irons for now, and then send a runner to Dr. MacAlpin's sanitorium. Let the viscount deal with our Mr. Nobody. It's his cup of tea, I suppose; unravelling the scrambled minds of the mad."

Sergeant Black recorded the prisoner's information as before: Name Unknown, booked as 'Bleeding Jack Nobody'. Crime: Vagrancy, presumed mad due to syphilis. Remand to Dr. Henry MacAlpin.

Jack's wild eyes darted back and forth as a fresh-faced constable named Davey Gresham tried to place a warm blanket round his blood-streaked shoulders. The vagrant wanted no comfort. His gnarled fingers itched to hold a blade or razor; even a sharp rock would do. Anything sufficient to open a vein and release the fire demons that crawled inside him like hungry, stinging worms. They whispered of ancient kings and long-dead warriors. They sang of death and power and primordial seas. They crawled along his sagging skin and tunnelled through his feverish brain, hissing threats and derision and terrifying prophecies.

They wanted something.

No. They wanted *someone*. A human with special blood. A prince to lead the dead back to glory. A great and noble king.

And this king would be given authority over the world of men.

The authority of a mighty Dragon.

And then, all light would vanish, and the world would fall to eternal Darkness.

When the king of the dead arose.

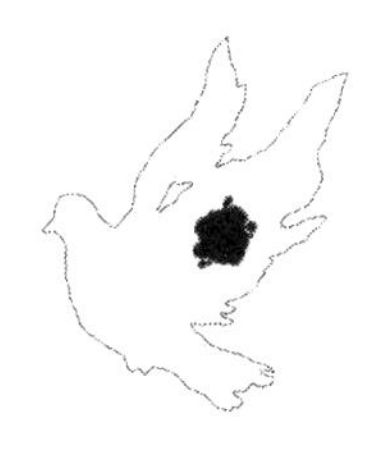

CHAPTER FIVE

Early morning, St. Marylebone Parish

Since 1835, the four hundred and ten acres of Regent's Park in London served as a restful haven for London's weary of heart, mind, and body. The grand expanse of manicured lawns and cheerful lanes was dotted with cricket pitches, bandstands, and graceful white pavilions. In an effort to blend entertainment with educational opportunities, the royal park also hosted a zoological exhibit featuring Indian elephants, African lions, slithering pythons, and fierce Bengal tigers. At the south end, the Royal Botany Society's magnificent gardens offered colour and scent, and visitors could wander the spectacular beds or enjoy a boat ride upon the sapphire waters of the park's majestic lake. During posted hours, those wishing to discover how 'the other half' lived could explore the elegant state rooms of nine private villas, including Grove House, St. Dunstan's, and Holford House. And during the summer, refreshment stands offered fresh lemonade, sweet tea, fruited scones, and jam-filled sponge cakes to slake the thirst and fill the bellies of each and every delighted park visitor, regardless of age.

Interspersed amongst this bustle of food and frivolity, a circuit of riding paths allowed upper class equestrians a chance to exercise horses whilst chatting about politics, the theatre, and personal lives. Bordering the lake, ran mile upon mile of gaily flowered walkways, lined with wide wooden benches that offered respite to the foot-weary and a viewing point for artists.

Even in winter, the park seldom stood empty. School children, governesses, lonely widows, courting couples, and secret lovers meeting for a tryst: all found the park a place of wonder and consolation. No matter the weather, no matter the time, Regent's Park was there.

That crisp December morning in 1888, as sunrise painted the elm trees of the high street with a rosy radiance, two men from widely disparate social classes arrived at St. Marylebone Church. The tower's clockwork bells had just sounded quarter to eight, when the first man, a proud Welshman named Ifan Davies, passed beneath the lychgate's peaked roof to prepare the grounds for burial of an important parishioner.

The second man arrived in a five-window coach drawn by a pair of high-stepping, dappled greys. A liveried coachman parked the crested conveyance on the east side of the street, beneath the bare branches of a regal chestnut. Overhead, within the broad canopy, a quartet of crows squatted on leafless limbs, their black eyes glistening with greedy curiosity as they watched the well-dressed passenger emerge from the coach. The birds whispered to one another in a secret language.

Is it he? they asked the largest of the group. *Whom does he serve? Shall we protect him or kill him?*

Davies took his job seriously and maintained the church and the attached cemetery park in beautiful condition. The conscientious sexton paid no attention to the elaborate carriage or to the chattering birds. Instead, Davies kept his sharp eyes on the leaf-strewn ground, diligently searching for bits of stray newspaper or other refuse which would mar the orderly forest of the dead. The lonely statuary and weathered crypts had an otherworldly look in the grey morning mist. The wrought-iron fencing and stately benches offered a comforting impression of human control, but the stern faces of marble angels, granite cherubs, and even the odd gargoyle hinted of an unquiet, pagan threat lurking amongst the Christian symbols; warning signs of unrepentant dead, of primordial chaos and retribution; an army of restless warrior spirits who waited beside a complacent land of lemonade, tea, and jam-filled sponge cakes.

The sexton shuddered. An inexplicable chill ran up his spine, as though a bony hand had reached into his soul to measure its weight. Something brushed against his fleshy cheek, and Davies swiped at it; certain a phantom's cold lips had kissed him there.

His path that morning led past a marble statue of St. Michael fighting the Dragon. The iconic tableau anchored a plot of ground owned by the Earls of Heeverswick; a line that ended in 1733 when the last earl fell ill and died mysteriously—some said of fright—

leaving no heir to assume the family name. Davies always found the face of the fierce archangel disquieting, but this morning, the chiseled features seemed positively malevolent.

The iconic pose was supposed to depict the prophecy in St. John's Book of Revelation, when St. Michael would bind the Dragon in adamantine chains for a thousand years. Conventionally, the archangel's long sword pointed downwards, piercing the scales of mankind's greatest foe. However, the artist that created this version had defiantly pointed the sword upwards, towards the throne of heaven, as though Michael had joined forces with Satan in rebellion against the Almighty.

"Good morning," a deep voice called through the thick mist.

The sexton let out a small cry, startled at the unforeseen intrusion. "Sir, you like ta scared me half ta death! If you're here for the Wychwright services, you're early, sir. They don' start 'til eleven. Seatin' begins at half ten."

The visitor stood well over six feet tall and wore gleaming black boots, a grey Chesterfield coat, and carried a silk top hat in a kid-gloved right hand. "I'm aware of that," he answered kindly. "I've come to pay my respects to someone else, if that's all right."

Davies removed his soft-brimmed brown hat respectfully. "Might that be a friend or a relative, sir? If you've need o' directions, I know every marker in this here park. I'd be pleased ta point the way fer ya."

"That's very generous of you, but I know exactly where the grave lies," the gentleman answered. "It's Mr. Davies, isn't it?"

"That's right, sir," the sexton answered in surprise. Then a smile slowly lifted his plump cheeks, for Davies recognised the visitor at last. "Well, bless me sideways, if it isn't Superintendent St. Clair!" he declared happily. "Come ta see your boy, I reckon?"

"That's right. I'm afraid I missed visiting on the actual anniversary," Sinclair explained as he shook the sexton's hand. "It's been ten years since Albert left us, Mr. Davies, though that hardly seems possible. And my surname's changed a little since we spoke last December; as has my title."

"I should o' 'membered that, my lord," Davies replied politely with a slight bow. "My wife and me was talkin' 'bout it only this mornin', in fact; over a cup o' tea. We seen that photograph o' you an' the queen in the newspaper, where she give you that new title.

Who'd o' thought you'd be a duke one day, sir? Reckon I oughta be callin' you Yer Grace, or summat, eh?"

Sinclair laughed, and his azure eyes crinkled at the corners. "Well, it all sounds very strange to my ears, Mr. Davies. I'd only just grown accustomed to being a marquess, but I prefer to keep it simple. Just call me Commissioner."

"Commissioner? I thought Mr. Monro replaced that other fella—Warren, were it?"

"Yes, that's correct. Sir Charles Warren retired for personal reasons, and James Monro has taken over as Metropolitan Police Commissioner. Actually, I'm heading up a related department called the Intelligence Branch."

"Never 'eard of it, my lord, but I reckon you'll make a fine commissioner fer it, sure enough. You always was a first-rate copper."

"Thank you, Mr. Davies. It's kind of you to say so. I wonder, have the Winstones called this year?" he asked as they walked together.

"I seen 'em a few times, sir. This summer, when they visited their daughter's grave, o' course. An' they come ta call at little Albert's restin' place—on the day, ya know."

"The sixth, yes. I'd not forgotten," Sinclair explained. "I doubt I shall ever forget that fateful day. However, other matters made it impossible for me to visit on the sixth. But as I had to be in Marylebone for the Wychwright funeral, I thought to spend a little time with him, though it is somewhat late."

"I'm sure it'll mean just as much, sir, no matter the day. And I keep it nice, just like you asked me. Oh, and there's two new rose bushes been added as well. A lady sent a man to plant them last week."

Charles walked alongside the stout fellow, his sea-blue eyes fixed upon a peaceful location near the northern edge of the burial ground, where a small, cross-shaped headstone sat beneath a graceful willow tree. Flanking the marker, he noticed a pair of rose bushes, each about a foot in height.

"White roses," the duke observed.

"So they are, sir," the sexton replied, still holding his hat. "I hope it were all right that I allowed it."

"You say the benefactor provided the flowers as well as someone to plant them?" Sinclair asked, bending to examine the fading petals of the vigorous, young bushes. "I recognise these, Mr. Davies. They're Queen Anne Whites. They're double-petaled, and the creamy colour takes on a pink tinge, just at the centre."

"That's right, sir. You know your roses, I reckon. The lady's gardener said she removed the plants from her very own garden just to plant them here beside your little Albert. I reckon you must know the lady, sir. Else why would she do such a thing?"

"Why else, indeed?" Charles replied, smiling as he sat upon a ragstone bench near the grave. "I don't recall this being here last year, Mr. Davies. Did the church install it?"

"No, sir. It were that same lady, the one what sent the rose bushes. She had the bench delivered as well. There's a Bible verse on the back, if you'd care to look."

Sinclair stood to examine an attached brass plaque. "*But I trust I shall shortly see thee, and we shall speak face to face.* Second John, Chapter one, verse twelve," he said, his eyes glistening with bright tears. "I can guess who sent these gifts, Mr. Davies. My very thoughtful wife, the Duchess of Branham."

The sexton nodded. "Aye, sir. That be the lady's name, all right. I'd forgot you remarried. Did the duchess come with you this morning, Commissioner?"

"No, but she'll attend the funeral later. Perhaps, you'll have a chance to meet her then. You say the Winstones visited on the sixth?"

"Aye, sir, they did. Left a wreath here and also at your late wife's grave across the way. Both them wreaths got soaked in the rains two days ago, and I had to remove 'em ta the compost heap."

"I'm sure they'll understand. Might I have a few moments alone?" Sinclair asked the sexton.

"Oh, 'course, sir. If you need anything, just ring the bell. You know where it is."

The sexton departed with another bow, and Charles sat once more to gaze upon Albert's small headstone. Davies and his team kept the burial ground beautifully ordered, and the simple marker looked as though it had recently been brushed, allowing the chiseled engraving to stand out:

ALBERT EDWARD ST. CLAIR
10 DECEMBER, 1877 - 6 DECEMBER, 1878
"And I will dwell in the house of the Lord forever."

"Sorry I missed visiting you on the sixth, Albert, but it's been quite hectic lately," he whispered. "That's no excuse, of course, but you're always in my heart, son. That ache never leaves me." He wiped a tear and continued, his eyes on the roses. "You probably don't feel the passing of time, but for me it's been ten years. Ten long, difficult years; most of them quite lonely, to be honest. So often, have I recalled Shakespeare's plaintive lines, for no other words convey my emotions better. For I have grieved for you, Albert, so much that once I clung to that grief as if it were my only friend.

"Grief fills the room up of my absent child," he quoted from Act III of *King John*. "*It lies in his bed, walks up and down with me, puts on his pretty looks, repeats his words, reminds me of all his gracious parts, stuffs out his vacant garments with his form. Then have I reason to be fond of grief.*"

After wiping another tear, the duke whispered a silent prayer before speaking again to his dead son. "Yet, life has at last taken a happy turn, my dear son. Grief no longer consumes my heart. Rather, joy fills it. Do you remember that I used to tell you about a young woman named Elizabeth Stuart, a duchess whom I assumed could never be more than a friend to me? Believe it or not, she and I wed a month ago, and though she's never met you, Elizabeth loves you as if you were her own."

The tower bells chimed eight o'clock, interrupting his thoughts, and the merchants of St. Marylebone hastened to prepare for Tuesday's trade. Already, Charles could hear the familiar sounds of horse hooves and carriage wheels upon the high street's well-worn, limestone setts. Amongst this clattering chorus, he noticed soft thunder in the distance. Darkening clouds rolled overhead from the east, obscuring the newborn sun, and the air grew thick and heavy as though charged with electricity.

He glanced up into a tangle of willow branches, and an eerie chill coursed along his spine. The birds had moved from the chestnut to flock above his head. Their black bodies shifted upon the limbs, causing the slender branches to wave as though the tree moved of its own accord.

Ghosts keep watch, Charles thought as he listened to the ravens whisper. *Unwelcome phantoms walk within these stone forests, waiting to snatch away life. The ancient Dragon that lurks beneath a glittering surface—black mirror of eternal doom.*

A deep voice grated inside his head, as though sharp claws dug through his memories.

"I'm waiting for you, boy."

The duke visibly shuddered to shake off the reverie. *A dream. Only a dream*, he told himself. He had police work to do and must focus on the present, not the veiled past. The skein of criminal threads before him must be unravelled; each twisted line plucked from its brother and examined thoroughly.

To begin the day's investigations, Charles had arranged to meet with his old friend, Superintendent George Draper of D-Division, to discuss a recent spate of arson fires, including one which destroyed two floors of a school just four blocks from where he now sat. Afterward, he planned to join Henry MacAlpin for a late breakfast, and then both men would attend the Wychwright service at eleven; followed by the wake and two more meetings: one at Whitehall, the other in Whitechapel.

Standing, Sinclair placed a hand on the tombstone, tears tracing his bearded cheek as he recalled the softness of his dead son's hair. "Goodbye, Albert. If there's time after the service today, I'll bring Beth over, but if not, we'll come again soon. I know you're not really here, beneath the sod, but this place provides me solace. Elizabeth and I both love you very, very much."

Reluctantly, he left the graveside and passed through neatly ordered rows of the dead, ducking his tall head now and again to avoid the overhanging limbs of shaggy yews and berry-laden juniper trees. As he neared the disquieting marble statue of the archangel Michael, an accented voice called his name.

"Good morning, Charles. Perhaps, you should have brought an umbrella."

The voice was all too familiar, and Sinclair's initial reactions were irritation, annoyance, and mild anger; but he managed to sound casual as he replied. "I'd wondered when you'd finally show your face. Have you intentionally avoided me, or has another of your kind held you prisoner?"

Anatole Romanov seemed at home in the green and stone-grey palace of the dead. The elegantly attired entity sat upon an iron-trimmed bench on the south side of the marble statue, his long fingers wrapped round the silver handle of a carved walking stick that bore hundreds of symbols along its length.

"I appear when I am needed, Charles. Join me, won't you?"

"You think I need you?" the duke responded.

"I know you do. Sit."

Sinclair remained on his feet, asking in bemused frustration, "And why do I need you?"

"It is an interesting portrayal of Michael, no?" asked Romanov, ignoring the human's question. "I needn't tell you that he is not pleased with the association."

"And I needn't say that you're changing the subject, Anatole. Why do I need you?"

"I change it for a reason, Charles. Do pay attention."

"Very well, I'll play your game," sighed the duke. Charles approached the Heeverswick plot's central anchor, touching the scaled back of the marble dragon. "It reminds me of something I saw only recently."

"The clock, perhaps?" enquired Romanov without hesitation.

Shocked, Sinclair stared at the elohim. "You know about the clock?"

"Two clocks. One for Rose House, the other for Haimsbury. However, they are not identical. Each was designed by an engineering genius named Franz Meijer. His grandson has a shop on Hatton Garden, next door to Sir Hiram Maxim's factory. You should pay him a call."

"He can tell me about the clocks?"

"He can read his father's notes. They are quite interesting. One is called 'Arthur's Victory'; the other 'Arthur's Defeat'."

"And the one here in London? Which is that?"

Romanov's head tilted to one side as though considering his reply; or perhaps, listening to a voice imperceptible to the human. "I am not permitted to answer that—not yet."

"Typical," muttered the duke. "Very well, then. Let's ignore the clocks for the moment. Tell me about Prince Aleksandr Koshmar, the man who gave them to me."

The elohim smiled. "Koshmar? One of his many names. He's not used Koshmar since his release from prison, but I imagine he'll trot it out soon."

"Is this a human or angelic prison?"

"A very insightful question, Charles. The latter type, requiring more than a physical key to open."

The duke considered this for a moment. "Do you refer to Raziel Grigor? That's impossible. You told me Raziel was bound in the Mt. Hermon stone until 1871. How could he give me a pair of clocks in 1855?"

"He could not. I refer to another of my brothers. One who is far more dangerous."

"Who might that be?"

"You've already met him."

"I meet men every day!" Sinclair exclaimed. "Can you offer no more clues than that?"

"He leaves marks upon your city, but you will uncover his tracks very soon. A friend will help."

"Stop speaking in riddles!"

Anatole ignored the reprimand. "Tell me, Charles, what you think of this statue?"

The duke sighed in exasperation. "I think it's an odd way to slay one's enemy. Is Michael supposed to be raising the sword in preparation for battle or declaring victory?"

"Neither," Anatole answered. "The artist's name was Vincenzo di Sforza. He claimed to be the direct descendent of Cesare and Lucrezia Borgia."

"Weren't they brother and sister?" asked Sinclair.

"Yes, but history is somewhat murky regarding their private relationship. Let us assume, though, that di Sforza's claim was true. If he was their descendent, that bloodline gained him position and power within Milanese society."

"Isn't Contessa di Specchio Milanese?"

The prince's eyes crinkled at the corners as he smiled. "Very good, Charles. Now you begin to see. Serena's past is also murky. Depending on her audience, Serena tells a variety of tales regarding herself, but she is also a di Sforza. Ask her about it sometime. Mention this statue and see how she jumps!"

"I will," promised the duke, "if I ever see her again. The countess is somewhat elusive. Despite our best efforts, the circle can find no record of her in London."

"She uses aliases and disguises. I shall arrange a meeting."

"You know where she is?"

"Of course, but the timing of your meeting must be right. Wait until after Christmas. You'll receive a message from me, when

I've made the arrangements. Now, to this statue. Gaze upon it, Charles. Note the intricate detail; the finely chiseled lines within the two figures."

"Why go to all this effort for a cemetery?"

"Precisely," concurred the elohim. "When the last Earl of Heeverswick commissioned this tableau for himself, he intended to place it inside a magnificent mausoleum in his honour; but the very moment the first chip of marble fell away from the block, Heeverswick fell ill. As the statue took shape, the earl's condition worsened; as though his life's blood and energy were feeding the emerging figures. At only forty-three years old, he died. But at the same precise second, the artist also died. Both men breathed their last on the same night, thirteen miles apart. The earl choked on his own blood, and the artist snapped his neck in a fall. You can make out a slight blemish; just there, at the tip of the sword," he explained, pointing with the cane. "That is where di Sforza struck his final mark. When the hammer sounded for that last time, the base of the ladder upon which he stood collapsed, and Vincenzo di Sforza fell to his death. It is a cautionary tale, you might say."

"Anatole, why are you here?" asked Charles in frustration. "And why at this statue? Nothing you do is ever without meaning."

"As I said, you need my help."

"I've needed your help before, and yet you remained hidden. What's changed? And how do I know I'm speaking to the real you?" asked the duke. "Raziel's made great sport of taking your form in the past."

The elohim laughed softly as he watched a pair of butterflies flit upon the rising winds. "As always, my dear Charles, you see beyond the obvious to ask a perceptive question. After all, Raziel and many others have taken my form often these many centuries."

"Others? Are you saying there are other creatures like Raziel roaming the earth—besides the one Trent released last month? Other Watchers?"

One of the butterflies, a yellow and black swallowtail landed on Romanov's forearm. The prince gently took it into his gloved hands.

"You and your sister should be sleeping, my little friend," he told the insect. He glanced up at Charles. "Remarkable creatures, aren't they? The delicate design on their wings has always reminded me of the stained-glass windows that decorate churches." He gave a soft whistle and then a series of quick chirps. The second butterfly turned about and made its way to the prince's arm as though responding to a call. "Here now," he told them both as he used the cane to lift the insects into a deep hollow within the nearest yew tree. "Go to sleep until spring returns to warm the night air. It grows too cold for you now, my friends. Sleep."

As if they understood, both crawled into the warm hollow and burrowed into a waiting nest of soft, dry grasses. Anatole sang softly to the tree, and a collection of tender branches turned round to form a protective lattice of deep green across the hibernating insects' hideaway.

"Do you speak to all God's creation?" a surprised Sinclair asked him.

"Of course, but as with humans, not all will listen. Now," he said, resuming his seat, "to answer your question, there are many of us walking the earth. It is why the Apostle Paul admonished believers to show hospitality to strangers; for in so doing, they may also entertain angels."

"And are all these disguised angels loyal?"

"Some, but not all," Romanov replied. "As you know, last month, Redwing unleashed my brother Saraqael. He is a particularly devious sort of fellow. Sara was once fiercely loyal and battled alongside me in the great wars, but a darkness took root in him many aeons ago and began to twist his mind. Only recently, did I witness the fruit of that fateful twisting. He's become vengeful and determined to overturn the current order of things."

"Vengeful against whom? God?"

"Yes, but also against his loyal brethren; particularly against me. It was my hand that turned the key on his prison. Sara was one of my failures. I should have seen what he'd become before he... Well, before he did any harm."

"You imprisoned him? When?"

"Nearly three decades ago, according to human reckoning."

"Three decades? Has this anything to do with me?" Charles asked.

"You're not ready for that conversation, my friend. Not yet," Romanov replied gently. "One day, you and I shall speak more of it, but know this: Saraqael is far more dangerous than Raziel. Raziel Grigor was once immensely powerful, for he understood the sacred words. He recorded them in a great book known as *Sefer Raziel*: every word that he heard spoken by the One. It is a dangerous book, containing sounds to reorder Creation. When I imprisoned Raziel, I seized the book and cast it to the winds."

"You didn't destroy it?"

"God's word cannot be destroyed, only hidden. The One has a plan to use these words, but those plans are not yet revealed to anyone but the Son. Even now, Redwing and other, similar organisations of evil men seek the remnants of Raziel's book. I have orders to allow them to hunt. The One is setting a trap, Charles, but Raziel refuses to see it. His eyes are blinded by greed and lust. This makes him vulnerable. Though he believes himself wise, Raziel is merely a tool in the hands of something far older, and much more cunning. One of the Seven."

"Can you explain that?"

"The One has Seven Spirits round his throne. The Evil One also has Seven Spirits round his infernal throne. These take many forms, but usually a dragon, for they were born from Chaos, an ancient primordial sea monster. You might know it as Leviathan."

Charles stared up at the marble figures. The dream preyed upon his mind. "Someone killed my father, Anatole, and I do not think it coincidence that you imprisoned Saraqael right after it happened."

As if to distract the human from the troubling memory, Anatole used the cane to point to the carved, angelic being. "There is more to the di Sforza tale. Though you would assume the statue portrays Michael and the Dragon; it does not. Di Sforza knew his *true* subject, for he'd struck a deal with an archdemon named Asmodeus. I know this, for I've read the sculptor's diaries."

"You mean you knew him personally," Charles corrected.

Anatole smiled. "Yes, perhaps I did. The artist had an insatiable desire for greater talent and struck the bargain to achieve it. The demon vowed to make him the greatest sculptor of his generation, if di Sforza would follow his instructions. This deceptive statue is the twisted result of the demon's dark inspiration. It is a prophecy in stone, Charles, and it depicts an ancient, fallen-realm belief that a *human* who would one day arise to become a god and rule the entire earth; a human who will side with the Evil One. This is what Redwing's rituals are all about: the quest for this deified man."

Sinclair stared at the marble statue, tracing the curve of the Dragon's tail with his right hand. He could almost hear taunting whispers coming from the Dragon's mouth; memories of long ago, of the ticking clock in his bedchamber and of a black mirror within a darkened corner; blood-red eyes surrounded by glittering shadow set within flames.

But there was more to the memory: Confusion and shouting. His mother weeping, and a tall man standing over a body; a smoking pistol in his hand. Charles could smell blood, feel wind upon his face, almost see the scene through a misty veil...

Hello, boy. Let's play.

Then someone touched him.

Charles shuddered back to reality. He'd been drawn so deeply into the cold, dark reverie that it took a moment to realise Anatole had left the bench and now stood beside him, a comforting hand placed on the young duke's shoulder.

"Do not fear the Dragon's voice, Charles. He has permission to sift you; not to slay you. But you *never* stand alone."

"Then why do I feel so alone?" he asked plaintively. "I try to keep strong, Anatole, but more and more these memories press down upon me, and I can tell no one about them. Beth has to see me as her protector, not a terrified child!"

"I understand, my friend. I do. The Dragon wants you to feel like that cowering child. It's why he calls you 'boy', but that child is far stronger than you might imagine. And you can always talk to me, if you wish."

Sinclair pulled away, suddenly distrustful of the mysterious entity. "How do I know I can believe anything you tell me? You do nothing but obfuscate and mislead!"

Romanov took no offence, answering softly, "I understand why you might think that, for my behaviour does not always conform to a human's perception of trustworthiness, or even obedience. My missions often require me to employ the art of subterfuge. The elohim of all the realms are at war, Charles. Our battles cover aeons and vast expanses of space. They make your human wars seem like child's play."

"You're a soldier?"

"Of a type," Romanov explained. "My role is difficult to categorise, but it is similar to your own; a law enforcement officer of sorts, which sometimes requires concealment within the Council of Rebels. To act as a spy, you might say."

"If you can hide within the rebel ranks, then surely they can conceal themselves as well. I ask you again, how do I know I'm not speaking with Saraqael or Raziel right now; or even some other rebel Watcher?" Sinclair asked angrily.

The prince smiled patiently. "Darkness will always reveal itself in the presence of light. Raziel and Sara may be cunning when it comes to masquerade, but a pleasing carapace cannot disguise a rebel heart."

"I try to understand, Anatole, but it's difficult. I feel completely inadequate to this task."

The elohim's pale eyes grew thoughtful. "Charles, I sense something else troubling your thoughts. You have doubts about my motives. You wonder why I allowed the castle to be breached."

"Yes, I do!" he admitted, still standing by the statue. "To be honest, it's but one of a hundred concerns about you and your kind. After the castle fire, you simply vanished! You claim that you're on my side, but how was that helpful?"

"I did not vanish, but merely altered my appearance. You and the duchess were never out of my sight. Also, I called on Lorena at Queen Anne House, if you'll recall. She told you of our conversation and my warnings regarding Redwing, did she not?"

"Yes, but now she's disappeared as well, and neither I nor Paul can find any trace of her. Have you hidden her away somewhere? Anatole, Lorena was close to accepting Christ, which makes her a target as a traitor. We must find her before Redwing kills her!"

"I have not hidden her away," Romanov told him. "However, I do know where she has gone."

"Where?" Sinclair demanded.

"Lorena is safe, Charles. That must suffice for now. Other matters take precedence for her path, and she needs to walk it alone for the present. However, she is protected. You will hear from her again, when the time is right."

Charles struck the statue with his right palm, anger colouring his face. "You speak in riddles! Why am I supposed to believe any of this? Anatole, there are times I wish I'd never met you!"

Ever calm, the elohim spoke softly. "I understand, Charles. Were I in your shoes, I would feel much the same, but if you find you cannot trust me, then trust in the One. He will never forsake you. He designed you for this task. From the foundation of the world, He knew your path and prepared you for it."

Sinclair grew quiet, his azure eyes fixed on the murder of crows now gathering in the trees overhead. Their numbers had increased markedly, filling every limb and twig with ripples of sinister black. On the highest branch of the tree, perched an enormous raven, much larger than his fellow birds. The raven stared back at the human, its yellow eyes blinking rhythmically. For a moment, Sinclair's thoughts returned to the Stone Realms and the hideous gatekeeper who'd tried to entrap him there.

You've never left us, stupid human! he heard it screech. *That is the reason behind the despair in your heart. You remain in prison. The Stone King and his Great Dragon are your masters now!*

Perceiving the human's dilemma, Romanov whistled loudly, and then called out a series of unintelligible words. The raven flew high into the air, soaring up over the church steeple and then downwards at tremendous speed, aiming for Sinclair's head. Charles stared at the oncoming threat, frozen as though mesmerised.

Without a word, Romanov raised his cane as if it were a sword and aimed it at the attacking bird. Two of the carved symbols brightened as though lit from the inside, and the raven suddenly pulled up, breaking off the attack. Charles could hear the hideous bird screaming brackish sounding words—no doubt, threats of some kind—before it vanished into the rain clouds.

"Uriens grows stronger," the elohim said. "But his threats have no substance, Charles. Pay him no heed. That is what he wants—to lure you into a false belief; a terrible choice."

"Uriens?" asked the human, snapping out of his trance. "Is that the creature's name?"

"One of them. As with all spirit creatures, he possesses many names, each describing an aspect of his history. Uriens serves a horrid and very powerful king, but the king's authority comes from the Dragon he rides."

"Is that supposed to comfort me?" Sinclair whispered as he leaned against the statue to hide his anxiety.

"Be strong and of good courage, Charles Robert Arthur," Romanov said. "Even though you walk through fire and feel the heat, the flames will never burn you, for you rest within the One's mighty palm. It is a place of complete safety."

"I want to believe that," Charles muttered darkly.

Anatole whispered to himself; the language completely unknown to the human, and then he placed a hand on Charles's shoulder, sending a warm sensation of strength coursing throughout his body. The elohim closed his eyes, whispering in that same, unknown tongue. When the eyes opened again, he spoke in English.

"I have been given permission to answer any question you wish to ask of me, Charles. Speak, my friend. What would you know?"

"Given permission? By whom?"

"By the One, of course. I follow only His commands. Ask what is in your heart, dear friend."

Charles voiced the first thought that came into his mind. "Who attacked the castle and why?"

"Raziel and his battalion," replied Romanov without hesitation. "His intent was to abduct the duchess, but the One had foreseen that plan and prepared for it."

"Yet, you left her alone!" Sinclair volleyed back in frustration. "Why would you do that, if you knew Raziel planned to attack?"

Romanov's voice remained remarkably gentle. "I left because I was ordered to stand aside and permit the assault. I understand your anger, Charles, but let me remind you that in certain battles, the best stratagem is a feint. A wise general—and the One is the wisest of all—will lay a trap to lure his enemy into making a foolish move. It is why I told Lord Salperton I would be away until the following morning. I knew Henry would use my absence to escape that night and find you."

"Which left Beth alone, without a protector."

Anatole leaned forward, his eyes misting with compassion. "Charles, my very dear friend, that sweet lady's safety was never in doubt. Do you think I would intentionally harm her?"

"I don't know. It's clear you love her, but I find little comfort in that, Anatole."

The elohim returned to the bench, taking a deep breath as though contemplating his reply. His tapering fingers danced along the ebony cane's silver handle, and his eyes took on a faraway look. Charles noticed that he touched several of the carved names as though remembering his past.

"What you say is true," he said after many minutes. "I have come to care deeply for Elizabeth since first meeting her, but I would never act on that affection as a human might. Never. Charles, I have seen what the so-called *love* of my kind does to the daughters of Eve. It is cruel, selfish, destructive—and sinful. Unlike my unrepentant brethren, I do not see Elizabeth as flesh to be conquered, but as a soul to be protected. And I will continue to do all within my power to help her. But I must *never* cross the line into sin. Raziel tried to tempt me into doing so, when he drew the two of you into the Stone Realms."

"*He* drew us in? Raziel?"

Romanov nodded. "My fallen brother believed I would yield to sin and rush after her myself—against the One's specific command. But our most wonderful Creator foresaw this tactic and provided rescue, according to His perfect plans. He used Henry MacAlpin, and even your own children, to do what I could not, Charles. The Name above all names works all things together for good, according to His purpose. To accomplish your rescue, He ordered me to assemble the castle's company, beginning before Elizabeth was even born. Each has played a role in her rescue, and all will continue to serve her and you—but also, your children."

"Children. Plural. You've used that word twice now. Are you saying that Beth is definitely carrying twins, or are these future children, not yet conceived?"

The Russian smiled, his light eyes twinkling. "She is carrying twins. During the coming decades, you and your family will take centre stage in world events, my friend. I cannot reveal why this is true, for doing so could impact your future, free will choices. Recall your admonition to Georgianna against revealing too much of your own future."

Sinclair smiled at last. "So I did. Or rather, the future version of myself will."

"Then you understand," Romanov said. "The princes and powers of the fallen realms are divided on how to combat your family's growing influence. Some advocate annihilation, whilst others believe you and your sons may yet prove useful to their schemes."

"Sons? We'll have more than just Robby?"

Anatole began to laugh, the cold breeze blowing through his long hair, making him seem as young as springtime. "I have revealed too much. You've always had a way of eliciting far more from me than I intend to tell, Charles Robert."

"You talk as though we share a long history, Anatole."

"And so we do. When you were a boy, the two of us enjoyed many long conversations together, and very soon you'll recall them, as well as all your lost childhood. However, I fear those recovered memories will bring you great pain and anguish for a season, my friend. But like the butterfly after a winter's darkness, you will emerge stronger when the light breaks at last. When you remember that darkness, you and I shall speak again."

Sinclair grew quiet, his mind crowded with warring thoughts. "I've already begun to dream about my childhood, Anatole. Of family secrets and kings—and dragons. Is that what you mean?"

"The dragon dreams are the first sign, yes. Soon, you will experience waking dreams, but do not resist them. Let them come."

"Anatole, I don't want my children to suffer because of me. How do I keep them safe from Redwing and these rebel princes?"

"Would that I could remove all the obstacles that lie ahead, my dear friend, but take consolation in this: The One will never abandon you. Not for one moment—not one second! He is ever and always nearby, and He has charged my brethren and me to keep watch upon you for as long as you live. Though you may not see us, we stand and fight beside you. Always."

Charles wiped tears from his face. "I've no fear for myself, but for my wife and children. I've already lost one child. I cannot bear to lose another!"

The mysterious angel placed a comforting hand on the human's shoulder. "I know this journey is difficult, for our presence is not always obvious to human eyes. Look to Henry MacAlpin for keen vision to see beyond the enemy's lies and masks. He loves Elizabeth and will make sure no harm ever befalls her. And you will shortly meet another who'll join her circle of protectors. Though danger stalks her steps, warriors will never leave her side."

"I'm aware of Henry's affections, and now you tell me of another man? Forgive me, if I find little comfort in such promises."

Romanov laughed heartily. "Do I hear a note of jealousy in your voice, Charles Robert? You've nothing to fear where Lord Salperton is concerned. Henry's life has been interwoven with Elizabeth's since before the dawning of the world. Just as with you, Henry was always meant to connect with her, but only as a close and constant friend. The same is true of the gentleman soon to come. Though you will suspect and like him little at first, you and he will become great friends. I have foreseen it."

Charles opened his mouth to ask for clarification, but raised voices interrupted: angry, raucous sounds of men fighting.

"Duty calls, Commissioner," Anatole told the detective.

"So it does," Sinclair sighed, heading towards the altercation.

Nearing the church, he noticed the sexton arguing with a bulky man in an ill-fitting suit of black worsted wool. Charles approached to call for calm, but before he could speak, four scarred knuckles connected with his chin and knocked the surprised duke onto the hard-packed ground.

"Go on! Get up, an' I'll show you more o' that!" the man shouted, his dark eyes wild as a pit dog's.

The shocked sexton pushed at the assailant's arm in panic. "You gone daft, Eddy?" Then to the fallen peer, he said apologetically, "Gimme yer hand, sir. I don't see no blood, but I'll go into the vestry and fetch a cold cloth anyway."

Once on his feet, Charles warily rubbed his reddening chin and then brushed dirt and wet leaves from his clothing. "That's quite all right, Mr. Davies. No harm done, though my friend Mr. Baxter's likely to complain about the stains to these trousers. I confess, it's the first time in seven years someone's caught me off-guard with a punch," he told the man called Eddy. "You should box for the Met."

Hamish Granger had been keeping a sharp lookout near the Haimsbury coach, and he ran over, ready to offer the pugilist a lesson in Scottish boxing. His employer intervened before the coachman's meaty fist connected with the assailant's face.

"No need for that, Mr. Granger. I'm sure this gentleman has an explanation."

"If you say so, Commissioner," six-foot-four Granger grumbled.

The newcomer's face turned six shades of white beneath a spotty, red beard. "Blimey, yer a commissioner? I's in a right mess now, ain't I? Look, I's real sorry, sir," he blustered. "Honest. I didn' mean nuffin' by it. It's just me brain's all afire, cause o' what 'appened. I ain't to blame, but the guv'll say I am. There's no way to explain it, sir. None at all!"

"This here's Ed Jarvis, Yer Grace," the sexton explained.

"*YER GRACE?* Lord above, tell me 'e ain' a duke!" moaned the distraught man, his face turning from white to red.

"I'm afraid I am a duke, Mr. Jarvis," Charles informed the apoplectic fellow, "but it's my Commissioner title that concerns you at the moment."

Jarvis's eyes rounded in fear. "I ain't under arrest, is I, sir?"

"Not yet, but Granger here keeps manacles in his pocket. In addition to running my mews, he is also a Detective Inspector."

Hamish withdrew the irons and showed them to the pale man.

Ed Jarvis swallowed hard. "Please, forgive me Yer Grace. I ain't in my right mind, I ain't. Mr. Quincy's gonna have me six ways ta Sunday, when 'e finds out."

Anatole Romanov had strolled to their spot. At six-foot-eight, he stood a head taller than the thick-set man in the stained suit. "I take it something has happened to upset your day, Mr. Jarvis. Might I ask what?"

"You a duke as well?" the sweating man asked nervously, running a chubby finger round his starched collar.

"He's a prince, actually," Sinclair explained, not bothering to add that Romanov's status as human was hardly implied within that statement.

"A prince!" Jarvis wailed, looking as though he might faint any second. "Don' tell me a prince seen me clock a duke on the chin! This day's gettin' worse n' worse. M'lords, I were never a part o' this. I swears it. An' I never agreed to it."

"Stop and take a breath, Mr. Jarvis," Haimsbury admonished gently. "To begin, why were you and Mr. Davies arguing?"

"Cause o' the body, sir."

"Body? What body?"

"Exactly."

"I'm afraid I'm not following," Charles admitted. "Do you refer to Baron Wychwright's body? His funeral isn't for three more hours."

"Aye, sir. That's true, but that ain't why I were askin' Davies fer 'elp. I seen it, when I 'ad ta shoo away that bird."

"Bird?" Romanov asked, his dark head tilting to one side curiously. It occurred to Charles that the Russian probably knew exactly what had happened and was feigning ignorance out of courtesy;

or more likely, to conceal his supernatural powers from the sexton and Jarvis.

"One o' them big blackbirds, sir," Ed Jarvis gasped, his breathing growing laboured, the plump cheeks reddening into bright beets. "Some'ow, it got inside the coach, so's I pulled the team ta one side an' opened the doors to let it out, didn' I? That's when I seen the lid."

Charles massaged his temples, for he could feel a headache coming on. "The lid?" he asked, his left brow arching impatiently.

"Aye, sir. The coffin lid. We don' screw 'em down 'til the family's 'ad a las' look. I tolds Mr. Quincy that no widow'd wanna see a body what 'ad suffered so much woundin', bu' 'e insisted. That's why it come up, sir. The lid, I mean."

"It opened on its own?" asked the prince.

"Like it were on springs, sir. That's when I seen it."

"When you saw *what*, Mr. Jarvis?" Charles pressed, wishing the man would simply get to the point.

"Nobody, sir."

"Nobody? What the devil do you mean?" the duke complained, the persistent headache throbbing behind his eyes now.

Jarvis's melon head bobbed up and down like a pump handle on a midsummer day. "That's the word, sir! A right devil, or a demon, or summat! Which is why there weren't nobody inside!"

"You saw nobody? I fail to see what you mean, Jarvis," the detective muttered, all good humour vanished.

"No, you sees it, my lord, you do! Nobody at all."

Romanov's smooth face twitched as he stifled an amused grin. "Not nobody, Charles. *No body*. The coffin was empty. Am I right, Mr. Jarvis?"

The driver's pale face slackened in stark dismay. "That box were empty as air, m'lords, and the body gone like it weren't never there. Like one o' them music hall conjurers done it in a magic show!"

Charles took a deep breath. "I suppose that explains your behaviour, Mr. Jarvis, and why you look ready to faint. Go inside the church and sit for a few minutes whilst Mr. Davies fetches you a glass of water. Once you've recovered, you will tell me everything that has happened this morning. From the very beginning."

CHAPTER SIX

St. Arilda's Abbey – Kent County

At the very moment that Charles Sinclair stood listening to Ed Jarvis explain about a missing body, Lionel Wentworth and his Cambridge companions were commencing the final day of their lives—or rather life as they understood it. It began with a shift in the weather, from dank chill to unseasonably mild. All clouds disappeared, blown away by a strong, northeasterly breeze, giving way to a dead calm, as though a great sea storm were taking a long breath in the Thames estuary, preparing to unleash its fury later in the day. Following a six o'clock breakfast of boiled eggs, bacon, beans and toast, the trio received word that their project leader, Colonel Sir Alfred Collinwood, had decided to spend the day at Castle Anjou with the Oxford team. In his absence, he ordered Holloway, Wentworth, and Patterson to survey a newly discovered crypt at Lion Hall.

Relieved to have a day without the stern eye of the retired army officer constantly upon them, the three men entered Lion Hall's eastern corridor at eight o'clock precisely, carrying with them boxes of food provided by The Abbot's Ghost: Farmer's cheese and salted pork in tinfoil, crusty bread spread with chokecherry jam, boiled eggs, lardy cake slices, and crisp apples. Danny Stephens had even included sealed jars of milky tea, which he'd laced with cider.

At eleven, the men paused for a break and sat upon the hall's limestone steps, enjoying the spiked tea, bread, and jam; whilst taking in the beauty of the surrounding woods. Wentworth lit a brown cigarette and smoked it thoughtfully, occasionally fanning away a persistent, greenbottle fly. The strange weather that morning was akin to early spring, and several types of flies buzzed round their faces, eager to steal a bit of jam or a crust of bread. Waving them away, Wentworth stubbed out the remains of the cigarette, for he'd observed several men approaching from the southwest on horseback.

"Who might that be?" he asked Holloway, who was screwing the lid back onto his tea jar. "Do you recognise them, Holl?"

"The lead man looks familiar," replied the professor. "He works for the duchess, I think."

The horsemen drew close, and the tallest dismounted and walked up to their spot, leading a dappled mare by the reins. He stood about six feet in height with straight brown hair that peeked from beneath a dusty brown bowler.

He also carried a rifle.

"Good morning, sirs. You're with that science team, I take it?" he began in a friendly tone.

Seth Holloway brushed bread crumbs from his palms, then shook the rider's gloved hand warmly. "We are indeed. It's Mr. Clark, isn't it? Not sure if you remember me. Lord Salter's son. Seth Holloway."

"The Viscount Paynton! Of course, I remember you, sir," declared Clark happily. "We've not seen you since last May's fête, I reckon, my lord. The duchess never mentioned you were part of this project. Is she aware of it, sir?"

Seth had a boyishly handsome, freckled face, and his sapphire blue eyes twinkled as he shielded them from the bright sun. "She is, and I hope to see her again soon." He turned to his companions. "Gentlemen, allow me to introduce Edwin Clark, the finest horseman in all of Kent. I've seen Clark ride backwards in the saddle like an American Indian, chaps. And once, he even rode bareback whilst standing, if you can believe it. Clark helped me to improve my riding skills, though he never taught me that little trick. Mr. Clark, these are Peter Patterson, usually called Pitt, and Lionel Wentworth, whom we jokingly call Worthy. I'm afraid Colonel Collinwood is elsewhere this morning. Might we be of help?"

Clark held his hat in one hand, the rifle in the other whilst the well-mannered horse grazed near an old well. "The duchess and her new husband will be arriving tomorrow for Christmas, my lord. In preparation, we're riding the entire estate, as well as the surrounding villages, to make sure there aren't any tramps or dangerous unknowns lyin' about. You say the colonel's gone elsewhere? Where might that be, sir?"

"The castle," answered Wentworth cheerfully.

"Do you mean Anjou, sir? Lion Hall is also a castle."

"Oh, yes, well, we've been calling this place the 'old hall' but the big place 'the castle'," Worthy muttered. "I mean the one up on that great cliff, overlooking the estuary. Enormous old place. Quite foreboding. Danny Stephens claims it's haunted."

"I'm not sure I'd call it haunted, sir," Clark noted with quiet amusement. "Despite local superstition, the only spirits at Anjou come from the Feathers pub. The duchess didn't mention any activity over that way. Have you a letter with different orders?"

"No idea," Lionel answered, gazing at Holloway. "You'd need to speak to Colonel Collinwood. He's in charge of our little troupe."

Seth walked several feet from the younger men and motioned to the chief groom, who followed, leaving his horse for a moment. "Clark, are you saying the duchess hasn't amended the original contract in any way?"

"No, sir. Not that she's communicated to me."

"This is troubling," Seth whispered, keeping his voice low. "I helped her design that contract, you see, and it specifies that only Lion Hall may be surveyed. I suggest sending men to speak with the colonel on behalf of Duchess Elizabeth. I'll send her a telegram as soon as we're back at the village. And keep a sharp eye out, Clark. We wouldn't want anything to happen to our little duchess, now would we?"

"No, sir. Not a bit of it," the groom replied.

Clark signalled to the other horsemen, speaking to a muscular individual wearing a dusty bowler and brown tweed coat. "Mac, you and Gilmore head over to Anjou and make sure the colonel has permission to explore the castle. Ask for something in writing. He'll likely try to talk down to you, but be persistent. Her Grace was very specific about this project, and she never mentioned Anjou. If she's changed her mind, then she'll have put it on paper."

"Right, sir!" Laurence MacLeod called back. Then he and Tommy Gilliam took a northeast path, riding towards Anjou-on-Sea at a brisk gallop.

Clark turned back to Holloway. "Lord Paynton, I know you're a capable man, but be careful round these old ruins. You've heard the duchess's tales of tunnels that run 'neath the estate. We've had a bit o' business lately that I'll speak to you about when you're alone, but for now, promise to keep to the main ruins. Stay out o' the tunnels. And be done and gone from here by dusk. It's dangerous after sunset hereabouts, particularly in these old ruins."

"Thank you, Mr. Clark," Seth answered, shaking the groom's hand. "We'll follow your advice and be safely inside Danny Stephens's pub long before the sun sets."

The chief groom rode off, leaving the Cambridge trio to pack up the picnic boxes and return to their assignments.

"Capable looking fellow," Peter Patterson said to his friends. "What do you suppose he meant by danger after sunset?"

"A local superstition, I imagine," Worthy replied easily. "Danny Stephens will make much of it, when we tell him about it later. These country folk are simple in their ways, chaps. Still, we should follow the man's admonition. After all, he does work for our hostess. I wonder if we'll have the honour to spend any time with Her Grace?"

"Aside from Holly, you mean?" laughed Patterson. "He's got a dark past with the good lady, though he won't talk about it. He even proposed marriage, according to my sister. Come on, Holl. You're amongst friends. The lady turned you down, didn't she?"

"No comment. Let's just get back to work, shall we?" Holloway insisted.

"Leave it, Pitt," laughed Wentworth, gathering up his cigarette case and rucksack. "The Viscount Paynton keeps his love life close to the vest. You'll get no answers out of him."

As usual, Seth ignored their jokes. True, he did have a 'past' with Elizabeth, but he was too much of a gentleman to discuss it. With rich auburn hair that fell thickly across his forehead, laughing eyes, and a ready smile, the twenty-nine-year-old was young for a don. Of the three Cambridge men, Seth was the most serious about the project. Before joining Trinity's Archaeological Sciences department, Dr. Seth James Edward Holloway was an experienced antiquarian and linguist, having spent most of his life digging in Egypt and the Levant with his parents.

For thirty-two years, his energetic father, the 7th Earl of Salter and his artist wife led teams into Assyria and Egypt, sponsored by the Palestine Exploration Fund. As heir to the Salter earldom, Seth had the right to use the courtesy title, Viscount Paynton, but generally didn't, as it put off less affluent students. The amiable peer had grown up on these foreign digs, where he developed an appreciation for simple living and a strong work ethic. When he returned to England in '82, Seth completed two advanced degrees: one in archaeology, the other in ancient languages and iconography. His expertise gave the Lion Hall project legitimacy, but he'd really joined the team to keep an eye on Blackstone's mysterious representatives.

No one else knew of this assignment. To provide cover, Henry Montagu Butler, Master at Trinity (and a close friend to Seth's father) told Albus Flint that a mystery benefactor had provided a scholarship to pay Holloway's expenses and stipend. Butler further insisted that no Cambridge man would receive permission to join without the inclusion of Holloway on the team. As such, Seth never signed or *even read* the Society's strange contract. His university comrades assumed the mystery sponsor's identity was Seth's father, or some other close family friend; most likely the duchess herself.

"It must sting that another man got there first," Pitt dared tell Holloway as they packed up. "Though, it's not the end of the line, you know. Marriages can fail, after all. Keep your hand in, and you may yet obtain the good lady's charms, Holl."

"That good lady is our hostess," Seth warned Patterson. "And she is a dear friend. I will not hear her slandered."

"Lovers often start as friends, old man," teased Wentworth.

"If you're implying anything untoward in our relationship, I consider it an insult to that gentle lady's character," rebuked the viscount angrily.

"You blue-bloods always stick together," concluded Patterson with a grin.

Seth returned the food box to his rucksack, and then pulled the heavy canvas bag across his left shoulder. "*We* blue-bloods? You're one to talk, Pitt! Your father's a baron and an investment banker. It seems to me that the blue of one's blood isn't nearly as important as the gold in one's pocket."

"Come on, Holly, you've money to burn," laughed Wentworth, his tone revealing a strong hint of jealousy. "Shall I help you with your heavy load, or can you manage it on your own, old man?"

"Old man? I'm only eight years older than you, Lionel," answered Seth. "That hardly makes me old."

"May as well be eighty, old chum. Enough idle talk, eh, chaps? I've the landlord's maiden daughter to kiss come evening. Follow me, lads! It's back to the salt mines for us."

"Maybe we ought to call them the 'Salter Mines'," Patterson joked.

Seth found no humour at all in the pun, and he lagged behind his companions, turning to gaze one last time at the dirt road that ran alongside the ruins. Clark's admonition to be done before dark was hardly based on superstition, and Holloway knew it.

He had a very bad feeling about this day.

A very, *very* bad feeling.

CHAPTER SEVEN

Main Library, Montmore House

The morning of the eighteenth began far differently for Dr. Henry Robert Stuart MacAlpin. The viscount was catching up on the week's newspapers when his butler, Elias Saunders, appeared in the doorway.

"Sir, Miss Stuart asks to see you. Something about a distressing dream."

The alienist drained the last of his coffee and set the china cup on a tray. "Mrs. Crossfield's nightmares kept most of us awake last night, Saunders, and it's likely Miss Stuart was affected by them. Oh, I very nearly forgot. Would you let Cook know that I'll be eating breakfast elsewhere this morning? I'm meeting Lord Haimsbury in Kensington, and then there's the Wychwright funeral at eleven, followed by the wake in Mayfair. I doubt I'll be back before five at the earliest."

"Not Lord Haimsbury, sir."

"What? I don't understand," muttered Salperton. "Why not Lord Haimsbury?"

"I believe the proper title is now *Duke* of Haimsbury, sir," the butler corrected his employer.

Henry laughed as he took to his feet. "So it is! I'd quite forgotten. It isn't often a marquess is elevated to a duke. It's a good sight you keep me on my toes, Saunders!"

"Happy to serve, sir," the butler answered as he began clearing away the dishes.

The physician left the library and climbed to the first floor. Henry wound his way through a series of pleasant corridors towards an apartment decorated in cornflower blue and sunny yellow. Just inside, a woman with auburn hair and light brown eyes stood near the window of a small parlour. She appeared ill at ease, and dark circles shadowed her pale skin. Her hands twisted together in a washing motion as she spoke.

"I'm sorry to bother you, Dr. MacAlpin."

"Talking with you is never a bother, Miss Stuart. How may I help you this morning? I understand you suffered a troubled night."

"Can dreams be real?"

Henry responded gently. "I suppose they can *seem* quite real. Why do you ask?"

"I had an awful nightmare just before I awoke," the American answered, "but I'm not sure if it's something that's already happened, or is yet to happen. There was a great fire near water. I can still smell the smoke, and I'm not sure if it's real or not, but I can even hear men and women screaming."

"Most likely someone's burning refuse this morning; that's all. And you probably did hear a woman call out last night. Mrs. Crossfield had another of her night terrors, but they're only dreams, Miss Stuart. There is nothing to be alarmed about."

"It seems so real," she insisted. "You're sure there wasn't a fire overnight?"

Henry crossed to the east-facing window. He could see nothing amiss. No fire, no smoke, not even a hint at anything other than a typical mid-December morning.

"If someone has been burning refuse, the smoke must be blowing in another direction." He opened the window, allowing the brisk air to enter. "I can smell nothing amiss, though I do perceive the scent of viburnum. The bushes are flowering just now. I always appreciate a bit of winter colour, don't you, Miss Stuart?"

"Yes, but I can smell smoke as well," she told him. "It has a pungent, dark sort of smell to it. Like oil mixed with kerosene. And there are children crying. It's rather like an echo, though. Can't you hear it, Dr. MacAlpin? Please, tell me you can hear it!"

Henry's nut-brown eyes grew soft, and he took her pale hands. "I fear my ears perceive nothing, though I've very dull ears, I'm afraid, Miss Stuart. Might I ask, what else do you hear?"

"Violet," she corrected. "You promised to call me Violet."

"Indeed, I did," he answered bashfully. "What else do you hear, Violet?"

"Birds. Lots and lots of birds, talking back and forth. I'm not sure if it's now or then, though. It may have already happened. It might be something from my past, or I may still be dreaming. I've dreamt of fires quite often lately. Is it my illness?"

"I believe so, yes, but you're on the mend. I'm sure these distressing dreams will cease very soon," he promised, squeezing her hands. "What you need is a distraction, and as your physician, I'm prescribing one. I've made plans for the theatre this evening, and I wonder if you'd like to accompany me?"

"The theatre? Is it a play?"

"Yes, by Ibsen, I think. I can't say more, for I'm really not sure. I only received the invitation yesterday, but the company will be enjoyable, even if the performance is not. Do you like Ibsen?"

"I can't say."

"Neither can I, actually, though *Peer Gynt* was somewhat interesting. Of course, I saw it performed in Norway in the original language, and I'm not sure I translated it at all correctly, but... Oh, well, never mind," he muttered, half to himself. "I'm blithering on, aren't I? Will you go with me, Miss Stuart? We can commiserate together, if it's a disaster."

Violet smiled at his obvious discomfort. She'd never seen the handsome alienist so delightfully out of his element.

"I suppose I could go. Who else will be there?"

"A few close friends. Lovely people, and several are Stuarts. They might even be relatives of yours."

"Do I know them?"

"One is the Duchess of Branham, Elizabeth Stuart Sinclair. Her husband will be there, of course. He's half Stuart, and Beth's cousin is likely to join us, as it's his theatre box we're using. His name's Paul Stuart. A very pleasant chap. I've known him for years. He always beat me at cricket, when we were lads at Eton. He's most annoyingly athletic. I'm doing it again, aren't I? Blithering, I mean."

She laughed. "A little."

"I like your laugh, Violet. Perhaps, the play will be a comedy. Wouldn't that be nice? Regardless, you'll enjoy meeting my friends, I'm sure. Afterward, we're to attend a small Christmas party at the Sinclair home. The family are leaving for Branham tomorrow, and it's a sort of farewell to London until the new year. Elizabeth sings beautifully, and we might even persuade her to entertain us. She also plays very well. I do hope you'll join us. I promise you won't be disappointed."

She found herself appreciating the way Henry's mouth twitched whenever he was unsure of himself, and his eyes took on a distinct twinkle whenever he spoke her name. "Yes, I'd like that," she admitted. "Elizabeth Stuart, you say? The name sounds familiar. I wonder if I've met her before? Would I remember, if I had?"

"Not necessarily, but if you are acquainted, seeing her again might jog those stubborn memories. And I'm sure she'd remember you. Who wouldn't?"

"Because I'm American?" she asked, nervously.

Salperton looked down at his shoes as though suddenly embarrassed. "No, of course not. That's not what I meant at all; though your accent is charming. No, she'll remember you because you're such a lovely young woman. How could anyone not remember you?"

Without thinking, he lightly stroked her face, appreciating its softness. "Violet, I've no wish to make you uncomfortable. If you prefer to stay home, I'll understand. In fact, if you wish, I could remain here as well. We can play a game of hearts or finish that picture puzzle you started; or simply talk. I do enjoy talking with you."

"No, you should go, but would you be disappointed if I stayed here—alone?"

"I should miss your company," he told her honestly. "But I'd understand completely."

She looked weary, her eyes rimmed in red from lack of sleep. "I would like to meet other Stuarts. I so want to remember my past."

"Yes, of course, you do."

She pulled away, turning back towards the open window. "Am I imagining the fire, Henry? I can still hear the birds. It's like they're laughing at me."

"I think what you hear is very real—to you. And that makes it real to me. This could be a sign that you're beginning to recall traumatic experiences, which probably involve a fire. Shall I send for Mrs. Winstead and ask her to prepare a sleeping draught?"

"No, I prefer to let the memories come, if they must. Are you going to be here today?"

"I'm afraid not," he answered, suddenly wishing he could be. "I've a funeral to attend and then a wake, but I'll return by six to change for the theatre. Are you sure you wouldn't prefer to sleep a little? A mild sedative might offer relief."

"No, but may I try my hand at the piano while you're away?"

This pleased Henry very much, for it meant she'd begun to feel at home at Montmore. For some reason, he really wanted her to feel welcome here.

"Yes, yes, of course! Spend all the time you like in the music room, and if the weather clears, then stroll through the viburnum. Their scent is soothing. I'm very sorry for your troubles, Violet, but I must admit, your beauty and sweet disposition bring new life to these bachelor corridors."

She smiled again, her face losing the worry lines it so often displayed. "You're kind to say so. If I decide to go after all, what time should I be dressed?"

The viscount's features widened into an unabashed smile. "I'd so love that! No pressure, of course, but if you do feel like attending, I'm to meet the Sinclairs at the theatre at seven, which means leaving here by half six."

"What should I wear?"

"I imagine Elizabeth will wear something quite elegant, but as you have very few options of your own, we could find something that suits from one of Montmore's closets."

"You keep ladies' clothing in your closets, Henry?" she asked, her light brown eyes twinkling.

"I see, you make fun of me now!" he answered, laughing. "Well, I deserve it. Actually, I endow a small charity that accepts donations of all sorts, and we distribute the clothing and toiletries to women and children in need. Hospitals often beg for such things, you see; as do orphanages. Our current collection includes some lovely dresses which proved far too elegant for the average wearer. Ask Mrs. Winstead about them. She'll unlock the storage area, and you can choose whatever you like. Take an entire wardrobe, if you wish."

"I shouldn't want to take something a poor person might need. Though, I suppose it's possible I'm poor."

He kissed her hand, enjoying the silken texture of her skin. "My dearest Violet, your manners and conversation tell me that you're well-educated and accustomed to higher society, though perhaps your life's not been as happy as you deserve. I hope to change all that, if you'll allow it," he confessed. "Now, I must be going. I promised to breakfast with a friend before the funeral begins."

She pulled at his arm, and to Salperton's surprise, Violet kissed him on the cheek. "Thank you, Henry. You're far kinder to me than I deserve."

Blushing, the alienist managed an embarrassed smile. "I doubt that. I'll speak with Mrs. Winstead about the dresses before I go. You're welcome to anything you find." He bowed gallantly. "Until this evening, then."

He turned to find Emily Winstead staring at him. For some reason, Henry felt as though he'd been caught in some taboo activity, for the nurse's manner reminded him of his disapproving father. "Yes?" he managed to ask, doing his best to sound authoritative.

"There's a messenger from the police station downstairs, sir. He says it's urgent."

"Did he say why? Is someone ill?"

"A prisoner requires examination. That's all I know, sir."

"Very well," answered Salperton. "Mrs. Winstead, if you've be good enough to show Miss Stuart our charity closets? I've told her to choose any items she wishes." He turned once more to the patient. "I pray you have a pleasant day, Miss Stuart. I look forward to this evening."

He shut the door, and Stuart—or rather, Cassandra Calabrese, also known as Sir Clive Urquhart's mistress, Susanna Morgan—returned to the window, certain that she could hear the clanging of fire brigade bells.

"Do you smell smoke, Mrs. Winstead?"

"No, Miss," answered the stern nurse. "Should I?"

"I don't know," the young woman replied as she loosened her auburn braids. As she brushed the long hair, Violet noticed dark roots, which had grown to nearly an inch. Both the doctor and Winstead had commented on the colour difference.

Why would I dye my hair? she wondered. *Who am I, really? And why do I smell fires that don't exist?*

Winstead poured a teaspoon of elixir. "This isn't for sleep, but will help to calm you. Once you've finished breakfast, I'd be pleased to show you the charity closets. They're on the floor above, next to Miss Grantham's apartment."

"Oh, yes, thank you. I'd like that," Violet replied, her eyes still on the mirror. "Might I ask a favour, Mrs. Winstead?"

"Certainly," the nurse answered as she shut the window.

"Do you know anything about hair dye?"

Winstead showed no sign of condemnation. "I do indeed. I learnt it from my sister, in fact. She's lady's maid to a baronet's wife and tints her mistress's grey hair. Would you like to keep the auburn, or do you prefer returning to your natural shade, Miss Stuart?"

"Which do you think would look best?"

"Dark hair and brown eyes go well together, I think."

"But do men prefer red locks? Lord Salperton, for instance. Does he like auburn hair, or might he prefer a dark shade?"

"I believe most gentlemen prefer women in their God-given hair colour," she answered plainly, making a mental note to mention the patient's comment to the doctor. "If you wish, I can send one of the kitchen maids to purchase a box of henna powder from the Fulham chemist. That and a cup of strong coffee ought to return your dark hair to you, Miss."

"Oh, yes, please! I'd so like to find my true self again. How long would the process take? Could it be finished in time for this evening—say, if I decided to visit the theatre?"

The nurse sighed. The poor girl was in love with her physician. Winstead had seen it before, and the end was never a favourable one. She'd have to remind his lordship that young ladies' hearts were tender, and that his kindness and supportive affections might be misconstrued by an impressionable, dependent personality.

"Yes, I think it can be finished in time for this evening, Miss. Leave it to me, but careful about setting too much store by invitations to parties and such. His lordship is generous with his time, but he is also a high-ranking peer. I'm not judging, mind you. Just stating a fact."

Violet knew what the woman was saying, but tried not to take offence. "I promise not to set too much store by it, Mrs. Winstead. Thank you for your wise words."

Satisfied, the nurse left the apartment, and Violet began to hum softly to herself. For some odd reason, she pictured herself in a gilded theatre box, sitting beside a handsome escort. However, the man's features weren't those of Henry Salperton. Rather, they were of a far different man—one with intensely blue eyes and long chestnut hair.

Someone named Stuart.

CHAPTER EIGHT

9:18 am – Haimsbury House

Elizabeth Stuart Sinclair sipped peppermint tea as she sorted through the morning post. The master apartment's drawing room fire blazed cheerfully, and the newly installed radiators warmed the air. Despite these conveniences, the duchess felt a decided chill and pulled her dressing gown's belt tighter round her waist. "Esther, whilst you're in there, I wonder if you'd bring me the little blue shawl with the roses? The one my husband gave me," she asked Alcorn.

The former housekeeper stood in a large cedar closet, instructing a lady's maid trainee on how to select the appropriate items for special occasions. She poked her head out of the interior for a moment.

"Are you cold, my lady?"

"Not terribly, but the room has a distinct chill, don't you think? These heaters never seem to work properly in here. I don't know what the problem is. They work perfectly well in the rest of the house."

"Aggie," Esther whispered to the twenty-one-year-old maid, "the blue shawl's folded in the topmost drawer of that cedar chest. There on your right."

"I don't see it, Mrs. Alcorn." Agatha MacGowan said, standing on a foot stool to search the built-in chest. "Will this do?" she asked, producing a scarlet shawl embroidered with yellow flowers.

"Take it and see," answered Alcorn, who began to search the chest herself.

Aggie curtsied as she approached Victoria Stuart, who was reading a French newspaper. The spinster glanced up. "I've not seen that shawl in a long time. Didn't Seth give you that last Christmas?"

Beth turned round from her work. "I'd forgotten about that shawl. Yes, it was a gift, but not from Seth. Paul gave me this. That'll do nicely, Aggie. You're going to make a fine lady's maid. Is Ada feeling better?"

"A mite bit, my lady," answered MacGowan brightly. "The doctor reckons the measles left her run-down. It's kind o' you ta keep her on, e'en though she canno' work."

"We're happy she's here, my dear," Victoria assured the girl. "Your family and Ada's have a long history with the Stuarts. Tell me, do you have plans for Christmas?"

"Aye, my lady, I do," the young woman said, breaking into a wide smile. "My nan's asked me ta spend a week wi' her in Glasgow. Nanna raised me as her own after my folks died, and she's gettin' older now. If I'm ta become your new lady's maid, Yer Grace, then it'll get harder ta visit. I was hopin' Ada could go with me, but as she's still ailin', I'll be goin' on me own, I reckon."

The girl curtsied and returned to the closet.

Victoria began to tap her foot in annoyance. "Already past nine! Beth, you should finish sorting through that mail later. We need to leave soon, and you're not even dressed."

"I'm very nearly done," the duchess argued.

Someone knocked, and the door to the parlour opened a crack. Baxter's wide face appeared. "Is it safe to enter, my lady?"

"As safe as it ever is," Tory laughed. "Do come in, Mr. Baxter. Are those the London papers?"

The butler carried three freshly pressed broadsheets on a tray. "The *Times*, *Gazette*, and *Star*, my lady. I cannot fathom why the duke wishes to read that East End rag," he complained as he laid the papers on the nearest table. "Nothing but innuendo and lies, if you ask me."

"The duke takes it to keep track of those lies and innuendo," Elizabeth told the impeccably dressed butler. "Is the house ready for tonight?"

"We are right on schedule, my lady," Baxter answered proudly. "The footmen are moving the chairs into the receiving hall as we speak. The Christmas trim is finished, and we've only to set the tables. I've told Mrs. Anderson and Mrs. Paget to plan for fifty. Is that number still correct?"

"I've no idea," replied the duchess. "Lady Victoria's in charge of the guest list."

"Thirty-four at last count," the Scotswoman told him as a small dog came flying into the bedchamber. "Samson! Whatever have you been into?"

The brown and white terrier's wiry coat was mired in mud, and his muzzle looked as though he'd spent an hour jumping through piles of wet leaves. Baxter deftly managed to avoid the dog as he collected empty teacups from the tables. "Shall I see he gets *another* bath, Lady Victoria?"

"Yes, please, Mr. Baxter," replied Stuart. "We cannot have him spoiling anyone's clothing tonight. But I'll carry him down. I'm used to my dog's adventures."

Aggie emerged from the closet and picked up the filthy terrier. "Might I do it, my lady? Samson and I've become real good friends. I'll scrub him up. If it's all right with Mrs. Alcorn, o' course. I shouldn't wish to leave my lessons without permission."

Esther laughed merrily. "It's not the usual job for a lady's maid, but it makes a change, I suppose. Go on now, and when you're done, come back up to help me pack the duchess's things for tomorrow's trip to Branham."

"Very good, Mrs. A.," she said, leaving with the muddy dog in her arms.

Baxter stared at the mud-spattered wool carpet. "It'll need a scrub," he mused aloud. "Shall I send up a maid right away, my lady, or do you prefer us to clean the rug whilst you're at the funeral?"

"Later is fine," Beth replied. "We can avoid stepping on the stained areas for the present—besides, there aren't too many. If you'd place a towel down, that is sufficient. Dogs will be dogs, Mr. Baxter. Which reminds me, where are Bella and Briar?"

"With Lady Adele in the conservatory, my lady. She is studying her geography lesson, I believe. May I bring you another pot of tea?"

"I'm quite full from breakfast, Baxter, thank you. Esther, have I any black dresses that still fit me?" she asked the former housekeeper.

Along with Baxter, Esther Alcorn had now moved to Haimsbury House permanently, but as the home already had a housekeeper, Alcorn had taken over as temporary lady's maid to the duchess. Alicia Mallory, the young woman she'd replaced, had left the duchess's employ to live with her newly widowed and heavily pregnant sister in Brighton.

"You've a lovely dark blue that should fit. There are two black ensembles, my lady, which are quite presentable, but the waists are a tad smaller than you are at present. No corsets, remember? Dr. Gehlen's orders."

"I wouldn't wear one anyway," the peeress answered, noticing her aunt's disapproving glare. "Oh, I shall need an entirely new wardrobe soon, I imagine. These children grow faster than thistle in a Scottish meadow!"

Baxter should have left by now, but he rather enjoyed the company of these pleasant women; Alcorn in particular. He busied himself by placing towels across the spoiled carpet and then checking the duke's bedchamber to make sure he'd left no teacups or whisky glasses the previous evening. Haimsbury and Drummond had talked long past midnight, which meant tables filled with empty glasses. Baxter inspected the chamber maid's work on the bed, running a gloved hand along each surface whilst listening to the women talk next door. He checked the locks on the window shutters, and then straightened the letters and papers on the duke's desk in the adjoining study. Finally, the amiable butler could find nothing more to occupy his time, and he returned to the parlour to bid the ladies a good morning.

"Our Baxter's a treasure, is he not, Mrs. Alcorn?" noted Lady Victoria once he'd gone.

"Mr. Baxter's a perfect butler and a perfect gentleman," Alcorn answered diplomatically. "Now, if you're not ready to dress, my lady, I'll go have a quick cup o' tea with Mrs. Anderson."

"Thank you, Esther. Enjoy your break. I should be ready to dress in half an hour or so."

Alone with her niece, Victoria chose the *Pall Mall Gazette* to begin reading. Elizabeth sat at the same writing desk used by her husband that morning to commence his new journal. Victoria occupied a soft armchair near the fire. The maiden aunt lit a cigarette, exhaling thoughtfully.

"I hear you've been annoying Charles's cooks," she said casually.

"I don't know what you're talking about," replied the duchess, reading through a letter from one of her lawyers. "Why would I annoy them?"

"I've no idea. You're the one doing it."

"Then, it's my business, isn't it?"

"Is it? I refer to that cake-baking nonsense yesterday. Trying to learn how to beat egg whites and master proper folding techniques and all that. Honestly, I don't understand you sometimes! You're a consummate musician, a respected hostess, linguist, and horsewoman. Must your horizons also extend to cakes?"

Elizabeth reached for the next letter in the stack, but looked up briefly. "For the record, Tory, Mrs. Anderson and Mrs. Paget are also *my* cooks, and I've not been annoying them. Rather, they were kind enough to help me with a small project. And I do not seek to expand my horizons, as you so cleverly put it. I'm quite content with my life, if you must know. Charles and I are very happy. As to horseback riding, that pleasant pastime is unavailable to me until next fall at the earliest."

"Yet you still spend time in the stables, my dear."

"Checking on our new foals, that is all. I shan't ride again for a very long time. Tory, have you come up here with the sole purpose of irritating me? I really do have work to do."

"Do you work?"

"Of course, I work!" Beth exclaimed. "What utter nonsense! I've been working since I was eleven years old, and you know it. Why are you being so very annoying this morning?"

The Scotswoman laughed as she puffed on the French cigarette. "I'm pleased you've risen to the bait, my dear. Your demeanor has been far too pale and submissive lately. Much too obedient. Not like yourself at all. I'd worried your new husband had somehow extinguished your fiery temperament."

"Shall I unleash my fiery temperament on you? Honestly, Tory, I don't have time for your pointless games. If you're bored, then find someone else to entertain you. It's nearly half nine, and the funeral's at eleven, which means I have to finish these letters quickly and dress."

"Perhaps, your secretary should be doing that."

Elizabeth was reading a letter from an estate agent, only half hearing her aunt's confusing diatribe. "Yes, yes, you're probably right."

"Am I?"

Beth glanced up from the page. "Very well, I'm listening. You've clearly come to offer advice. What is it?"

"If it's not wanted, then, I shall be happy to offer my very sound advice elsewhere," the elder woman pouted.

"I'm sorry, Tory. Perhaps, my temperament remains fiery, as you put it. Forgive me."

The spinster set aside the paper. "No, you're as pleasant as ever. I'm being combative, but it isn't out of boredom. I love you and only want the best for you, Beth. I can see how tightly wound you're becoming. The cake-baking is merely a way to escape from a self-imposed trap."

Putting down the letter, the duchess stared, her eyes round. "Trap? Surely, you don't mean my marriage! Tory, I love my husband. No one has ever made me happier. No one could. Why would you use so hateful a word?"

"I didn't mean your marriage, my dear. I adore Charles, and I can see how happy you are. He's always been your great love, and it's God's merciful plan to bring you together. But despite your joy, the constraints of your pregnancy hang about you like a soft chain. You grow restless and look for ways to channel your energies. Cake-baking is a distraction; nothing more. You need an all-consuming project, not pastries. What about this hospital you mentioned last month? Have you thought any more of how to accomplish it?"

A look of fierce determination crossed the duchess's heart-shaped face and she rose to fetch a small box file from a carved oak, Flemish cabinet. Inside the file, were several large envelopes. She handed the collection to her aunt.

"Not only have I thought of it, I've begun it," Beth said. "These papers form the seed for that very project. My solicitor, Mr. Winterton, is setting up a charitable fund which will underwrite the hospital. We've already held three meetings with estate agencies, and Grandfather's helping secure benefactors. That letter," she continued, pointing to a typed document on blue paper, "is from Lord Gilford. He's contributing glass for the windows. And behind it, is one from Lord and Lady Merton. They're donating mattresses. Behind that is a list of other individuals and businesses who've shown an interest. I'm determined that the Haimsbury-Branham Teaching Hospital will be free for medical students and patients alike. Does that sound as if I've been idle?"

Victoria laughed. "I suppose not. I thought you'd planned to call it the Branham Hospital."

"Originally, I had, but it's important that Charles's name be included. Not only because it is one of my names now, but because Haimsbury is part of our children's inheritance."

Victoria exhaled a thin stream of silver smoke and tapped ash into a bowl decorated with a trio of leaping frogs. "You keep saying *children*. My dear, if you are carrying twins, then..."

Beth stared at her aunt defiantly. "Tory, consider it as fact: I am carrying a boy *and* a girl. Twins."

"If you and Charles believe this..."

"We know it, Tory."

The Scotswoman stubbed out the smoke and leaned against the back of the chair, her dark eyes on her niece. "If true, then how will it all work? Legally, I mean? Twins can be tricky business, as our own inner circle records indicate. Both children cannot inherit your titles. You may have to choose."

"Their order of birth will determine inheritance, I should think," the duchess replied as she used a letter knife to open the next envelope. "If Robby's born first, he'll be heir to the Haimsbury and Branham titles and all that's entailed to them. If Georgie's born first, she'll one day become Duchess of Branham, and her brother the Duke of Haimsbury."

"I see. There are so many 'ifs', aren't there?"

"Tory, why are you cross-examining me this morning? I love you very much, but I've had a dreadful night's sleep, and I'm simply not up to your usual banter."

The duke's youngest sister grew serious. "It isn't my intention to cross-examine you, my dear. You are happy, I hope?"

"Very happy," she answered. "Charles makes me happier than I'd ever imagined. He's thoughtful, loving, and attentive. I doubt there's ever been a better husband."

"Then, why the poor night's sleep?"

Elizabeth sighed. "Nausea is partly to blame, but once that settled down, I had a quite awful dream. I'd hoped to talk to Charles about it this morning, but he left before I awoke."

"What sort of dream?"

"Just a nonsensical one," Beth said. "I'd rather not talk about it. Besides, most of it's gone now. Oh," she said, changing the subject, "did I tell you Seth Holloway will be joining us for Christmas?"

"Now, that will make for a very interesting holiday," answered Tory with a grin. "Did he write? No, wait! Isn't he part of that expedition or project or something? The one for those blackbirds, or black rocks."

"Blackstone," the duchess corrected. "It's a scientific society. You remember, Seth and Paul helped me sort through all the legal tangles. The survey finishes this weekend, and Seth's promised to stay over a day or two before he goes back to Cambridge."

"He doesn't live at Torden Hall?"

"No, he's teaching at Trinity," she told her aunt. "I think he and Charles will get along very well. They're both Cambridge men, and both are curious about the world."

Laughing, the Scotswoman picked up the paper once again. "You *hope* they'll get along, my dear, but I rather doubt Charles will enjoy meeting the man you very nearly married!"

"That's not true," she insisted.

"It is true. Or should have been. How many times did poor Seth propose? Two dozen? Three? Honestly, Elizabeth, I'd have married him in your shoes. Even Dolly thinks him a catch. Broad-shouldered, fair-haired, and those blue eyes have such a lovely sleepy look to them. It gives that boyish face an air of mystery."

"Seth and I are good friends, Tory. Nothing more."

"How often do friends kiss you?"

"If you're going to be difficult, I won't say anything more," Beth answered icily. "Now, if you're finished teasing me, I need to change. Grandfather will be here soon. Is Paul picking up Della? Someone should make certain she's ready to leave. Knowing the earl, he'll be in a rush."

"Della's staying at Maisie's during the funeral. Paul doesn't want her to attend. He worries she'll find it gruesome. Do you need any help with your clothing?"

"No, I think I can manage, but if not, I can ring for Esther. I do miss Alicia, though."

"Your staff members keep leaving. Is it true Andrea Jenkins is going to Edinburgh? Have you worn her out already?"

"Of course not," Elizabeth replied as she left the desk. "As you undoubtedly noticed, Andrea and Michael Emerson had grown quite close before he left to care for his brother, and I suggested she go there for a few weeks to support him. She'll stay with Michael's aunt and uncle. He's the Bishop of Edinburgh."

"Oh, yes! I know Calvin and Hermione Emerson quite well. I'm sure Miss Jenkins will be in safe hands during her stay. She and Michael make a good match, I think. How is Michael's brother faring?"

"Much worse," Beth sighed. "Michael's last letter arrived two days ago, and it's why I gave Andrea permission to leave. The specialists in Edinburgh are perplexed by Laurence's sudden downturn. He's lost all ability to move his limbs, and they fear he'll soon be unable to talk. Already, he's showing signs of it: sputtering and coughing, as though the very breath in his lungs fails. His poor wife is beside herself. They've only been married a year."

Ever the pragmatist, Tory cut to the sad truth. "And they remain childless?" Beth nodded. "Then, it's inevitable that Michael will become heir to the Braxton earldom."

"Yes, I suppose it is," the duchess whispered. "I prefer not to think about it, and I'm sure it's the furthest thing from Michael's mind just now. Christmas only makes it worse."

"Will he continue practising medicine here, if he inherits the title? The Braxton businesses are all in the north."

"I cannot say, but regardless, he's encouraged me to secure someone else as consultant. Michael plans to remain in Edinburgh through Christmastide, and perhaps longer. Honestly, it leaves me very little choice. Charles likes this man Gehlen, but I'm not sure."

"Unsure of what? The man or his methods?"

"I cannot say," the duchess replied, gloomily. "I've promised Charles I'll meet with Dr. Gehlen as soon as we return from Branham. At the moment, I prefer not to think about it. I miss Emerson."

Cornelius Baxter returned to knock. "Do come in, Baxter," said Victoria. "The duchess is out of sorts and weary from poor sleep.

Inform your mistress she needn't solve all the world's problems in one day. "

The butler held a bit of paper in his right hand. "I should never do so foolish a thing, Lady Victoria. Your Grace, I regret to bring you additional problems to solve, but a commissionaire's just delivered this for Duke Charles. It's from Lord Salperton. Shall I leave it with you, or do you prefer I send it ahead to Marylebone Church?"

"Henry sent it?" she asked, crossing to the doorway. "I'll not see the duke until eleven. Did the commissionaire mention if it's urgent?"

"He did not use that precise word, but implied as much, my lady. I could send a coachman to the church."

Beth took the telegram and opened it. "The viscount asks my husband to meet him at Montmore rather than the restaurant. Yes, do take it to the church. It's unlike Lord Salperton to summon someone without good cause."

Victoria took the telegram from her niece. "I'll see he gets it. I'm ready to leave, unless you need me. I can drop Della at Maisie's house along the way."

Elizabeth's thoughts ran in several directions at once. "Yes, I suppose that will work. Thank you, Tory. Baxter, if you'd send Mrs. Alcorn up, please, I'll start..." The duchess paled as nausea overwhelmed her stomach. Without a word, she dashed into the bath and shut the door.

Victoria knocked. "Beth, are you all right?"

Elizabeth offered no reply.

"Beth!"

"Give me a minute," a voice replied from the other side. When she emerged, much paler, the duchess was wiping her face with a wet cloth. "This will be a very long pregnancy, if this keeps up."

"Shall I fetch a doctor?" worried the butler.

"No, Mr. Baxter, it will pass soon. Tory, if you'd stay, I'd appreciate it. We'll send the telegram with a footman. Is that all right?"

The maiden aunt sat beside her niece, stroking Beth's long hair, clearly worried. "Of course. I'm sorry for being so combative this morning. Perhaps, you should stay home."

"No, I want to go. Cordelia needs the support. Baxter, has Miss Jenkins come down yet?"

"She has, my lady. Will you be seeing her off?"

"Yes. Give me time to dress."

The butler left the bedchamber, and Tory began unfastening the hooks on the silk skirt Beth had chosen to wear. "You'll need to let this out again soon."

"Esther's going to alter my dresses whilst we're at Branham."

"I'm sure Martin will be happy to help as well," Tory suggested. "Is he still working on that puzzle room?"

"The one off Charles's library? I'm not sure. Charles won't allow me in there, and the men seldom talk about it in front of me. All inner circle discussions are forbidden in my presence now. Their meetings all take place at Queen Anne, and soon much of their business will move to Loudain House. Who've you invited?"

"Invited? Oh, to the soirée!" exclaimed Tory as she placed the skirt over Beth's head. "The usual guests. Most of them are family or friends we'll not see during Christmas. And I've asked Abraham Stoker and his wife to join us. My brother wants to get to know him better. I think James is considering sponsoring Stoker's research."

"What research? Mr. Stoker is a writer, not a scientist."

"True, but he's been studying matters that James thinks important to the circle. Oh, and I've invited Señor Puccini, but I think he may have a conflict. A Milanese friend is in London for Christmas. But we'll have other musicians, of course. This will be a lovely send-off for us, Elizabeth. It's generous of you to let me plan it all."

The duchess slipped her arms through the black silk jacket, fastening the front hooks whilst her aunt secured those on the skirt. The duchess's small fingers trembled a little on the last hook, and Victoria took notice.

"I'm so very tired suddenly," the duchess said wearily. "I pray I can make it through tonight's party."

A footman knocked, entering after receiving permission. "I'm to say Miss Jenkins is about to leave, my lady."

"Thank you, Bryce. We'll be right down."

Beth brushed her long hair behind both ears and restrained the loose curls with a velvet ribbon. "I know my hair looks plain, but I'll see if Esther can help me with a better style before we leave," she promised her aunt. "Or I could just wear it down."

"Up is more appropriate for a funeral, my dear," cautioned Victoria as they left the apartment.

On the ground floor, Andrea Jenkins waited near the main entry, surrounded by two trunks and a green hat box. The secretary wore a sensible wool skirt and jacket beneath a tweed overcoat. She'd pinned a soft-brimmed hat of dark blue felt over her upswept hair. "My lady," she said, curtsying.

"Stop that, Miss Jenkins," Beth told her, smiling. "I've no idea if you'll remain on my staff, but you've most certainly become my friend. I've sent for a coach to convey you to King's Cross, and from there, who knows where your journey will end?"

"Pleasantly, I hope," the timid woman answered. "Thank you for letting me go, Your Grace. I'm very sorry to leave at so busy a time. Are you sure you don't prefer I remain?"

"Michael needs you with him, and Scotland is magical at Christmas. You'll have a very nice visit. Have you everything you need in the way of wardrobe? Edinburgh can be quite cold this time of year."

The tall, young woman had packed every possession she owned, just in case her visit was extended. "You're kind to ask, my lady. Michael's aunt promised to take me shopping."

"I understand you'll be helping the bishop with his correspondence. I hope you'll write often and let me know how it's all going. And don't worry about anything here. Your job will be waiting should you need it, but I imagine your future lies on a different path."

Jenkins blushed, and tears stained her smooth cheeks. "You've been so very kind to me, my lady! I should never have met Michael if you hadn't been willing to give me a chance. Did I tell you he has a solicitor friend who thinks he can return my son to me?"

"The one you adopted out? Oh, Andrea, that would be wonderful! If there is anything I can do to help, you've only to ask it."

"I will, my lady," the woman promised as a footman carried the luggage to the coach. "It looks as though I have to say goodbye. It's all so very strange; this turn my life's taken, my lady. That path you mentioned lies just ahead. You see, Michael proposed to me in his last letter."

Elizabeth smiled joyfully. "Did he? Andrea, that's wonderful! I suppose the tradition is correct, then. You did catch my wedding bouquet, after all." The duchess took the woman's hands, squeezing them. "I'm very glad it's all worked out this way. And you'll have to stop calling me 'my lady'. You'll soon be married to a peer, Andrea."

"I cannot imagine such a thing," Jenkins answered, swallowing hard, for she hated leaving the home she'd come to know as her own. "Your family has made me so very welcome, and I shall never forget it. I've no family of my own, you see."

"Yes, you do," Elizabeth assured her. "You're part of our family, and we will always be here for you. Now, enjoy your rail journey northward. Did Mrs. Paget make you a food basket? It's ten hours to Edinburgh, though I believe there's a stop at York for luncheon."

"She was kind enough to pack a box for me, yes. And I'll write every day," the woman promised.

"I shall write as well," Beth answered. "Give our love to Michael. Tell him that he and his family are in our prayers."

"I will, my lady."

Beth touched her friend's face. "I shall miss you, Andrea." The duchess embraced the slender woman at the door.

As she waved goodbye from the portico, Elizabeth had an odd sensation in her spirit. At the end of the long gravel drive, she could see wheeled traffic and well-heeled pedestrians moving past the gate. Amongst these was a peculiar looking gentleman in a chimney-pot hat. He stared back at her, not moving, his feet fixed to the cobbles of the bordering street as though cemented there. Though he stood in the middle of the road, no one seemed to notice the strange man, and the coaches failed to divert direction. Rather, they passed through him, as if he weren't really there.

"Beth, are you coming back inside?" her aunt called from the open doorway. "It freezing out here!"

The mysterious man took several steps towards the house. Elizabeth shuddered. "Yes, it is cold," she muttered, heading into the foyer. Just before Baxter shut the door, she turned one last time to look for the stranger.

He'd vanished, but in the cloudy skies overhead, Elizabeth noticed a flock of blackbirds circling. She could almost hear them cawing. And then an all too familiar voice whisper a chilling warning: *The Dragon is coming, foolish human. WE are coming.*

CHAPTER NINE

St. Marylebone Church

Charles Sinclair listened patiently to Edwin Jarvis tell his very peculiar story. "More water?" the duke asked the man as they sat inside the warm vestry.

The flushed driver took a deep breath and swiped at his clammy face with a mended linen handkerchief. "No, thank you, sir. And I'm real sorry 'bout that clip to your chin."

"I have a very hard chin, Mr. Jarvis. Now, start at the beginning."

"Well, my lord, I drives coach fer Cooper and Price Bereavement Services," he explained. "There ain't a Cooper nor a Price no more, o' course. They bofe died in a real odd way on a business trip to Vienna."

"Odd? Why would you call their deaths odd, Mr. Jarvis?" Romanov asked.

"I reckon 'cause o' them bodies, sir. They was found in their 'otel rooms, stretched out on their beds, starin' up at the ceilin'. Neever one were sick a day, but bofe died the exact same night. The police reckoned it were on account o' some poison in the food, but tha' don't explain it fer me, sirs. I ain't wha' you'd call educated, my lords, but even I knows poison don' rob a man o' every drop of blood!"

"Had they been stabbed?" Sinclair suggested without a blink.

"There weren't a mark on 'em, 'ceptin' fer somethin' the police called a rat bite. Anyways, the funeral company were bought right after by some foreign company out o' Paris. Our new manager's Mr. Quincy. He were supposed ta ride alongside me this mornin', but he come down wiv a case of the shivers and arsked me ta take the body down ta Fitzmaurice Place on me own."

"The Wychwright home, you mean?"

"Aye, sir, that's right. The family arsked special fer us to bring the body there first, so's all their friends could follow along back ta the church. Like one o' them royal processions, I reckon."

"An odd request," noted the duke.

"We get all kinds, m'lord," Jarvis replied.

"I believe I understand thus far, Mr. Jarvis, but how is any of this cause for you to become so agitated that you'd resort to physical assault on a total stranger?" Sinclair asked patiently. "Whilst I appreciate a strong punch, I prefer not to be the recipient."

"Beggin' yer pardon, sir. I don't know me own strength—so says me Missus. I ain' never touched her. I'd not 'arm my sweet Sue for all the world, sir! Naw, it were that bird what's the cause of it."

"The bird you had to shoo from the coach," Sinclair observed, slowly making sense of the man's strange tale.

"That's right, sir. Like I done told you afore, when I opened the doors ta free the bird, I noticed the lid 'ad sprung open. That's when I seen it."

"When you saw what, Mr. Jarvis?" the prince asked, his forefinger tapping the head of the cane rhythmically.

"I seen the body were gone an' all. Nuffin bu' an empty box, like the body jus' up and walked away. I didn't know what ta do, so I come 'ere ta arsk Davies fer 'elp. I daren't go back ta Mr. Quincy, sirs. He'll reckon I done it."

"Why would he suspect you of stealing a body, Mr. Jarvis?" the duke asked.

"It 'appens now an' agin, my lord. Two bodies vanished jus' last week from one o' them competition places. Calvin and Rodgers Services, over in the city, sir. Mr. Quincy told me 'bout it."

"Calvin and Rodgers? Do you know the address?"

"Lime Street, my lord. Just where it crosses Leaden'all. Big place, all done up wif black drapin' in the windows."

"Is it new?" asked the detective. "I've never seen such a business, and I know those streets well."

"I cain't say, sir, bu' there's been a righ' bee in Mr. Quincy's bonnet 'bout tha' place. Cuttin' prices ta the bone an' all. You reckon they stole the body, sir?"

"Why would they do that?" asked Romanov.

"Dunno, my lord."

"Whose bodies disappeared from Calvin and Rodgers?" enquired Haimsbury.

"Don't know bofe names, sir, but one were a 'right hon'rable'. Big name in Westminster. Hemsworth? Hemington?"

"*Hemsfield?*" Charles asked, dreading the answer. "Do you mean to say the Earl of Hemsfield's body vanished as well?"

"I reckon so, sir. Mr. Quincy'd know more."

"But why steal a body?" the duke pressed.

"It 'appens now an' agin. Sometimes, it's gangs out ta squeeze a bit o' money out of a grievin' family's pockets. Other times, it's ta provide bodies to them what wants 'em."

"Provide bodies? Surely, anatomists no longer require Burke and Hare provisions for academic study," countered the duke.

"I don' know them men," Jarvis replied innocently. "Might they be part of a new gang o' roughs?"

The prince laughed. "Burke and Hare were resurrectionists, Mr. Jarvis! Men that exhumed corpses and then sold them to medical schools for profit."

"You mean they stole bodies right outa their graves?" the driver asked in shock as he crossed himself.

"Indeed, it was a thriving business at one time. However, Burke and Hare preferred fresher provisions," the Russian replied. "Rather than wait for people to die natural deaths, they hurried the process along through personal intervention."

"Wha' sorta intervention migh' tha' be, sir?" the simple man asked.

"He means they murdered them," Charles explained bluntly. "Mr. Jarvis, why do you think modern day thieves would steal a body, if not for ransom? Is there a black market in post-mortem flesh?"

"If you mean folks what's dead, there is, my lord. Only I don' likes talkin' 'bout it, as it's unsettlin'. Let's just say there's men what uses body parts for *personal* use."

"Personal?" asked Sinclair. "Do you mean for sexual gratification?"

"I cain't say as they's gratified by it, sir, but some folks got strange ways. Then, there's the rituals."

Charles and the prince exchanged glances. "What rituals?"

The man's eyes shifted back and forth as he weighed his response. "I hear tell o' men what dresses up, all in masks like, an' they speaks o' things what's dark and magical. It goes on right 'neath our noses, sirs. *Below...*" he whispered as he pointed towards the floor of the church.

"Below what? The floor? The ground? The pavement?" asked Sinclair.

"Below the city, my lord. Up near the old Roman wall. A place where the devil hisself walks abou' come nightfall!" the man exclaimed, crossing himself once more.

Charles looked to Ifan Davies for help. "Is your friend prone to exaggeration?"

The sexton shook his head. "Not a bit of it, my lord. And what he's sayin' is true. I've heard them rumours as well. There's a new building up by Finsbury Circus, what folks says is haunted. There's strange doin's come nightfall. Ghosts an' the like."

"New building? Where?"

"On Wormwood, sir. Close to the old church yard."

Charles felt that disquieting chill again, as though all this were familiar. *33 Wormwood. Where the late Lewis Merriweather once kept offices.*

Romanov said nothing; merely tapped on his cane, as though communicating through code.

"Do forgive me, gentlemen," the Russian said at last. "I'm late for a meeting at the War Office. I'm sure you'll work all this out—eventually."

Charles also had appointments. "Mr. Jarvis, this is what you're going to do. Screw down the lid of the coffin and tell Lady Wychwright that I gave you the order to do so. I shall be happy to sign something, if required, but say nothing about the body's disappearance. I shall look into the matter myself. The widow needn't know anything. Not yet. Do you understand?"

"I does, m'lord. And Davies won't say nuffin' neever."

Charles withdrew an ICI calling card from a chased silver holder. "This is the address where you may reach me. Queen Anne House. It's the main headquarters for the law enforcement organisation I represent. Stop by there tomorrow morning, anytime after ten, and we'll speak more of these rumours. If I'm unavailable, ask for my secretary, Gerald Pennyweather. He'll know how to find me. Also, I'd like to know more about these strange deaths in Vienna. The men's names again?"

"Cooper and Price, m'lord. They was stayin' at an 'otel called the Empire or mayhap it were the Emperor, somewhere in Vienna. I ain' good on stuff like tha', sir, but I can arsk me missus. Sue's go' a better mem'ry than me."

"I'll start with that information, but if Mrs. Jarvis recalls further details, send word to me at Queen Anne House. Now, go about your business and leave everything else to me."

Sinclair and the prince left the church yard, and Romanov walked his friend to the Haimsbury Coach, where Hamish Granger kept watch.

Romanov bid his friend farewell. "Allow me to look into the deaths of Cooper and Price on your behalf, Charles. Exsanguination is one of Saraqael's favourite methods for murder, but there are others amongst my kind who consider human blood a delicacy."

"Is Serena Di Specchio one of your kind?" Sinclair asked as Granger opened the coach door.

"Not exactly, but she does have an unquenchable thirst for blood. I fear she and Saraqael have formed an alliance, but it is doomed to failure. Neither can be trusted. There's no honour amongst thieves or vampires. If you have need of me, just petition the One, my friend. Do not summon me directly."

"I never would, but if the Lord sends you, then that is another matter entirely."

Romanov bowed gracefully. "Until next we meet, then." He started to turn, but paused. "One final thought, Charles. Keep your eyes open over Christmastide and stay close to the duchess. A sharp-eyed watch dog makes a helpful companion, but she must never wander the grounds on her own. Good day."

Charles started to ask for an explanation of the warning, but the mysterious prince had already vanished. No sooner had the elusive elohim performed his trick than a second Haimsbury coach pulled up next to Granger's.

A young footman named Bryce emerged from the interior and handed a folded message to the duke. "From Lord Salperton, sir. It was delivered to Haimsbury House half an hour ago. The duchess thought it best we convey it to you here."

"Thank you, Bryce. Is all well at home?"

"Very well, my lord. The rooms are set for tonight's party, and Mr. Baxter believes it will be a very great success."

"Lady Victoria's parties are always a success," replied the duke as he read Henry's message. "Very well. I'm afraid I cannot do as the viscount asks. I'm already late for a meeting at D-Division. Bryce, would you be good enough to take a message to Fulham for me? Montmore House, just off Warwick Road."

"Of course, my lord. What message?"

"Ask Lord Salperton to meet me at Tilsbury Tea Room around ten. If I'm delayed, ask him to wait."

"Very good, sir. Tilsbury Tea Room at ten."

The young man departed, and the duke entered his own coach. As they pulled away, Sinclair felt a sense of sorrow. He was leaving Albert yet again to the solitary confines of a lonely cemetery. Certainly, his soul and spirit were not there, but a piece of him was: the ashes Charles had received after his son's body was cremated. He'd make a resolution to visit more often with Beth and eventually their children. Standing beside Albert's grave brought a kind of peace to his heart. A sense of completion.

Soon, he'd be a father again, but there was much to do before the twins arrived. Redwing must be routed and the Watchers unmasked. But how? He'd call a meeting as soon as possible. At Branham, perhaps. If last night's dream had any truth to it, then they had to decipher the puzzle chamber as soon as possible.

First, find Lorena MacKey, he thought as they crossed over Great Portland Street. Not only to make sure of her welfare, but also to seek her advice. As a former member of William Trent's Round Table, MacKey had knowledge they needed.

CHAPTER TEN

Lion Hall

As the spring-like morning gave way to colder air, the Cambridge men continued the tedious work within the newly discovered burial chamber. The hand-hewn vault ran for thirty feet and connected to a series of unmapped tunnels. Blackstone's leadership believed a network of tunnels, just beyond the crypt, led to a massive cavern sitting a hundred feet beneath St. Arilda's Abbey, once a site of pagan worship and the burning of a Satanic abbot in 1589. The legendary passage between Lion Hall and the old abbey had yet to be found, but if the team could discover such a path, then every man would earn a bonus of two hundred pounds.

The trio worked in silence, each man documenting the appearance and *in situ* artifacts within his own section of the newly discovered crypt. Occasionally, one would whistle a music hall tune or quote lines from a Shakespeare sonnet or play; *Hamlet* and *Macbeth* being favoured. Finally, to counter the oppressive boredom, Patterson and Wentworth commenced a long debate on the nature of superstition and religion.

Seth usually remained silent during the students' theological discussions, for his own beliefs were rooted in experiences few men would credit. Whilst surveying the tombs of Egypt and Assyria, he'd heard the Bedouins tell terrifying tales that haunted him to this day: legends of invisible doorways in the desert; of female demons who would entice you with love and then steal your seed; of jinns that could fly upon the slightest breeze and even travel through time; and of shape-shifting shamans who served these hungry demons, ready to sacrifice animals or even humans to appease their ravenous gods.

These powerful sorcerers could curse their enemies, hypnotise the living, and even raise the dead. Seth had witnessed their supernatural powers with his own eyes; even encountering what he believed was a succubus in his tent one night whilst encamped near the base of Mt. Hermon. The experience had forever shaken the young man's worldview.

Raised in an old Enlightenment family with blood ties to the founding members of the Lunar Society of Birmingham as well as Sir Francis Dashwood's Hellfire Club, he'd always assumed mankind's greatest achievements would be gained only after the extinction of all formal religion. However he'd begun to doubt his father's creed. Seth had come to think the Bible might hold some truths within its pages, but he wasn't yet confident enough to reveal that nascent faith to his fiercely anti-Christian companions.

"I'm going to sketch out these statues," he told the students, deciding to avoid their conversations entirely. "Keep track of the time, lads. We'll meet up in an hour for luncheon, and then work until four. No later. Is that clear? The sun sets early in these woods."

Peter Patterson waved from a spot near the second of two large statues. The first was a regal-looking man with painted black hair and light blue eyes, who carried a book in his left hand, a sword in the right. The other statue was of a man-sized bird with painted black plumage and disturbingly yellow eyes.

"Sure thing!" Patterson answered. "I'll tell Lionel. He's decided to look for those tunnels."

Seth put down his pencil and sketch pad. "No, Pitt. No one's to wander off on his own. There are some very treacherous passages beneath this estate, and some have collapsed."

"How do you know so much?" challenged the younger man. "The colonel's not mentioned anything about collapsed sections."

"Experience. I've been through many of them before—long ago. Now, do as I say, Pitt."

"Aye, aye, your lordship!" the young student sang back cheerfully. "I'll warn Worthy."

Moving through the small opening beyond the bird effigy, Peter Patterson, also known as Pitter-Patter or just Pitt, entered a forked junction of dressed stone. One branch wandered off to his left, the other to his right. He had no way of guessing which Wentworth had taken. After tossing a coin, Pitt turned right.

Local time had just ticked over to the hour of one, when Lionel Wentworth, who'd taken the left-hand path, reached a tiny opening that looked far too regular to be natural. Indeed, upon close inspection, the edges revealed chisel marks and a dressed stone lintel. After squeezing through the narrow portal, Wentworth emerged into a grand gallery, lined with perfectly formed, rectangular limestone blocks. He'd seen paintings of similar galleries at the British Museum, and it reminded him of an Egyptian tomb. Every square inch of the smooth walls and ceiling was covered in colourful imagery and symbols, and the floor glowed red with ochre paint. Arched niches were carefully built into the polished walls, and most held animal-headed idols, presumably placed there by the tunnel's builders. Yet, it all looked impossibly new, as though the owners might return at any moment to commence a pagan rite in honour of their strange, hybrid gods.

Lionel stared at the mysterious corridor before him, his thoughts distracted by the fair face of Wanda Stephens. He planned to steal a few moments with her after supper and discover just how sweet Wanda's ruby lips tasted. The anticipation tore at him, making Lionel a man of two minds. On the one hand, he wanted desperately to impress Colonel Collinwood in hopes of securing a full-time position on one of the Society's French digs. However, accomplishing this meant following the colonel's instructions to the letter, which also meant remaining in the newly discovered gallery until he'd completed the initial survey.

Blackstone's rules were these: Each time a new section was discovered, the team member involved was to measure the area and make notations of all he could see. In this case, Lionel must step off the width and breadth of the long gallery, estimate the height, and then record the measurements in a leather-bound book that bore the Society's name embossed in gold upon the exterior. The idea of 'stepping off' the distance was hardly scientifically accurate, but the colonel explained it as the 'first of many steps' (clearly amused at his clever pun) and that a thorough survey would be made by a professional team once the duchess approved the March phase of the project.

In addition to jotting down rough dimensions, Wentworth had to sketch any interesting features and then describe them in a short paragraph. It all felt like busywork, but it was well-paying busywork, and he forced himself to concentrate on the task. The sooner done; the sooner he could kiss the lovely Wanda's lips.

As he walked the gallery's length, Lionel overheard whispered voices. Assuming them to be his companions, he followed the sound to a low doorway, not more than three feet high. It was a tight squeeze for a grown man, but he managed it; and after crawling ten feet or so through a cramped tunnel, Wentworth emerged into an enormous, natural cavern. Its otherworldly beauty made him audibly gasp.

Up until this moment, the complex tunnels beneath Lion Hall had proven somewhat challenging to navigate. Most rose no higher than five-and-a-half feet, some far less, meaning six-foot Wentworth had to duck most of the time; and even in the taller sections, the walls often narrowed so severely that he was forced to remove his rucksack and pickaxe, and then turn to the side in order to pass through.

This chamber offered something entirely new. Here, the ceiling soared to fifty feet or more; the width spanned thrice the height, and the overall sensation was akin to standing in the nave of a magnificent cathedral. However, Wentworth sensed nothing holy here; rather, a heavy sensation descended upon his shoulders like a dense shroud of inexplicable gloom. His ears rang with echoes of men's voices, like dissonant Gregorian chants; as though invisible wraiths huddled round, whispering evil thoughts into his mind.

Ever the proud rationalist, Lionel shook off the worrying sensation and proceeded to examine the cavern. Since his lantern provided the only source of light, he kept it close as he moved about the ancient chamber. Turning to the left, he discerned a connecting passage, just beyond an arched opening containing a set of curving, well-worn steps, hewn into the glittering rock. He peered into this area and discovered, to his utter surprise, a *child's doll*, sitting upon the final step as though it had just climbed down the winding staircase.

Lionel knelt to collect the doll, holding it up to the lantern's flickering yellow light. The perfect little face was formed of fine French bisque and adorned with large irises made of tiger eye and jet beads. The cheeks and mouth were painted in a delicate shades of rosy pink. The black hair felt uncannily real, as though taken from the head of a living girl. The shiny locks curled down the doll's back, ending just above the waist in a trio of ringlets, bound with a black velvet ribbon.

Someone had paid a great deal of money for this lifelike toy, for it had moveable limbs and the porcelain skin had a sensual texture to it, as though wrapped in actual skin. She wore a blue silk dress trimmed in fine fur, and a choker of tiny seed pearls adorned the slender neck; a sapphire pin accented the white fur of the black velvet cloak. A pair of finely sewn kid gloves hung from the left wrist, and the doll's small feet were shod in real leather boots, latched by pearl buttons. Even the fingernails were perfect. It was an exact replica of a little girl, perhaps seven or eight years old, but it had a most peculiar aspect to it; for tucked inside the expensive costume, Wentworth discovered a leather bag filled with *tiny bones*.

"What devilment is this?" he asked aloud. "Mouse or bird bones, perhaps? But why?"

He held the fragile bones up to the lamplight for close examination. The longest of the five bones measured no more than one inch in length, and there appeared to be striations etched upon them; perhaps even symbols.

"You're certainly a mystery," he told the enigmatic toy. "You've hardly a spot of dust, and you look brand new. How did you come to be down here with your little bag of bones?"

He returned the strange bones to the bag and tucked it into the doll's rich cloak for safekeeping. Then, Wentworth inverted the toy to admire the craftsmanship further. He noticed the shoes bore initials, tooled into each sole with a fine awl: *E. Anjou.*

"E. Anjou?" he wondered aloud. "Seems to me Danny Stephens mentioned the duchess was Marchioness of Anjou when she was a girl. I'll wager you belong to her. She's all grown up and married since she last carried you," he told the doll, "but that doesn't explain how you came to find your way down here, does it? Little dolly, you might just be my ticket to meeting Her Grace, eh? She might even offer a reward for so fine a friend. That'd burn old Holly's blueblood biscuits, now wouldn't it?"

The doll's dark eyes glimmered, and for a brief second, it seemed that the pupils dilated, causing the tiger eye irises to turn completely black.

Nearly dropping the toy from shock, Wentworth quickly grasped its dress to keep it from breaking. "You're a strange one," he told the doll. To prevent accidental damage, he secured the valuable toy within the grey canvas rucksack; where it joined a Richie compass, a pewter flask of water, four Faber pencils, a hunting knife, the Society's notebook, a box of yellow-tipped matches, a thin rope with equidistant knots for measuring, the food box from The Abbot's Ghost, and the Blackstone map. The doll barely fit into the crowded interior, so he removed the food box, deciding he could come back for it later.

After closing the brass buckle, Lionel shouted for his comrades. "Pitt! Holly! I found the steps up to the old abbey! I'm standing right underneath it! We've a bonus coming, chaps! You should see it! This chamber's enormous!"

Hearing no reply, Lionel continued the survey, finding, to his very great delight, a pair of torches bolted to the wall near the upward passage where he'd discovered the doll. After lighting each with a match, their luminescence revealed additional sconces on the other walls of the grand cavern, He struck a match to each and was able to move about the chamber as easily as one might do in a public building.

Wentworth stepped off the width and marked it as 'approx. 50 yards'. Likewise with the length, listing it as 'approx. 90 yards but continues round a narrow bend, perhaps into second chamber or cavern'. The domed ceiling was decorated with brightly coloured paintings similar to those in the gallery, and the floor was brushed with the same blood-red ochre paint—or it least it looked like paint. The central area showed evidence of fire and scorching, and Lionel wondered if the old abbot and his demon-worshipping brethren had once met down here. A fire for warmth made sense, but the same blaze might also serve a ritualistic purpose. The thought made Lionel shiver, and for a moment, the whispers met his ears again, like tickles of spectral smoke made of sound.

Ignoring the unsettling sensation, Wentworth crossed to the far wall, where he beheld a variety of interesting features. Embedded within the grey limestone substrate, he could make out the glittering shimmers of feldspar inclusions: silvery moonstone and orange sunstone along with hundreds of white quartz crystals, cut into various shapes and sizes. Wentworth had taken two courses in geology and doubted the stones had grown here naturally. Indeed, they looked intentionally placed, as though creating a pattern. A constellation, perhaps? Ursa Minor? Draco?

He drew sketches of the inclusion stones' arrangement, as well as the general architecture of the impressive chamber, adding copious notes to each drawing. He described a long wall that held decorated urns within deep niches, as well as carved reliefs of ascending and descending staircases, suggesting that the cavern might be even older than St. Arilda's mad monks. However, the urns looked remarkably new for having spent three hundred years beneath the earth. Their metal surfaces shone brightly in the firelight, and the colours of the painted decorations revealed strong artistic lines.

The subject matter was anything but Christian. Nude male figures with grotesque animal faces seemed a favourite subject for the funerary artists; with goats, bulls, and birds receiving primary favour as the chimeric heads. The hybrid monsters were displayed in overtly sexual poses, and a few held dead children within their greedy fingers. Others sat upon great thrones, their forked tongues extended as they consumed offerings that hinted strongly at cannibalism. Still others depicted soldiers, their formal stances that of hardened warriors. These resembled ancient Spartans, brandishing the usual implements of war: spears, swords, bows, and pikes.

A few stood significantly taller than their fellows, and *these had multiple sets of wings upon their muscled backs*.

"What sort of lunacy affected these monks?" Lionel wondered aloud. Were the artists simply illustrating a twisted mythology, or had the soldiers shown here died in a battle long before the abbey was built? Perhaps, they were Roman or even Iron Age warriors. Lionel wondered how this dead legion, whose bones and ash presumably rested within the painted urns, might spend their eternal days and nights; if indeed, the notion of time existed in the afterlife.

The possibility of so great an army caused his generally complacent mind to twist into confused knots; so after completing the sketches, he made one last survey before quitting the dank chamber with its disquieting urns.

It was then that he noticed an area of discolouration along the wall opposite the stairs. Still carrying his lamp, Wentworth moved closer. Even in the lantern's faint light, he could make out fine writing, etched into the blood-red bricks. Not English; not Viking; not Roman, French, or Saxon. No language known to him. The symbols were entirely foreign, but the border round the glyphs consisted of alternating rows of giant ravens and lion-headed men. Recalling

Flint's promise of an additional hundred pounds for any 'unusual finds', Wentworth shouted again to his companions.

"Pitt! Holloway! In here! I'm telling you, it's important! You're missing out on a fortune!"

Several minutes passed before a fair-haired man in drab twill trousers and a black woolen sweater emerged through the low opening. "That's a squeezer," gasped Patterson. "Blimey! I thought that gallery was the prize, Worthy, but it's a pitiful shed compared to this!"

"Fetch another lantern, will you, Pitt?" Wentworth asked.

"Where's yours?" his friend called back.

"Nearly used up, I'm afraid. We'll want fresh ones before heading into this new bit. If this place doesn't count as one of Flint's unusual finds, then I'll eat my hat. If you see Holly whilst you're about it, bring him along. I could use his linguistic skills."

Patterson retreated back through the rabbit hole, returning eleven minutes later with a pair of freshly filled bullseye lanterns.

"No sign of our bashful viscount. He must have gone back up to the first section. Is that some sort of writing?" the twenty-year-old asked Wentworth.

"It is, though I've no idea what it says, or who wrote it."

"This place gives me the shivers, Worthy. Besides, it's nearly two. I'm hungry."

Wentworth ignored the reminder. "There's nothing on the colonel's map that shows a passage 'twixt Lion Hall and the abbey, right? But we're standing *underneath* the abbey, Pitt. Right underneath it, and I think there's another room beyond these bricks. That has to be what the writing is about!"

"That's pure speculation. Besides, we're supposed to document all these other areas first, Lionel. We can come back after we eat."

Wentworth held his hand against the painted surface. "Feel that? Moving air. And it's coming from the other side."

"So?"

"So, it could mean we've found the old devil-worshipper himself. Abbot Lucius! Flint told us his ashes were concealed in a wall somewhere round here. Come on, let's see if there's a way in."

Reluctantly, Patterson agreed, and the pair began searching for signs of a doorway. "It's useless," Pitt muttered after what felt like an eternity. "I'm starving, and we'll run out of oil before long. Let's document your new gallery and then come back tomorrow with Collinwood and the rest of the team."

"It's here, Pitt. I can feel it. Can't you?"

"All I feel is cold and hunger, mate."

"I thought Silver Spoons men feared no future. That's what our pledge says, right?"

"It's not the future that worries me, old chum," said Patterson. "It's the now. Let's have lunch and then come back."

"Fine, you go eat. I'll collect the bonus on my own."

Pitt sighed. "All right, all right! But let me find Holly first. He'll want to know where we've gone."

"You know he's a spy, don't you?" asked Wentworth. "He didn't even apply for membership. Old man Flint just up and let him join; sight unseen. After the hurdles he made you and me jump to join, it strikes as odd, don't you think? And it was Trinity's master, Henry Butler, insisted Seth come along, or else he'd refuse to allow Blackstone anywhere near a Trinity student. You can bet Holly's father's involved in it somehow, which means the British government is behind it. That whole Salter family are waist-deep in politics and intrigue."

"That's not true," whispered Pitt. "Seth's all right for a titled bloke. And unlike us, he knows what he's doing. You're just jealous."

"Jealousy has nothing to do with it. Holly's a spy," Worthy insisted. "And he's closer to the duchess than he lets on. A friend o' mine took one of his classes, and he says old Holly went into a deep depression when he read about Her Grace's marriage. He's still in love with her. If you ask me, the only reason he's here is to..."

Wentworth stopped, mid-sentence. A deep ringing had caught his ears, as though a gigantic hammer struck against a gargantuan iron bell. Flint's unsettling question echoed in his thoughts as though spoken afresh:

Mr. Wentworth, are you easily frightened?

"What's wrong?" asked Patterson, his stomach growling.

"Don't you hear that?" Wentworth whispered tensely. "Bells. Pitched deep like the ones in old church belfries. It's coming from the other side."

Pitt put an ear to the ancient brickwork. "I don't hear anything. Your head's full o' Danny Stephens's tall tales."

"No, no, this is real. Listen! The pitch is very low, but it's there all right. Like the monks are being called to prayer or something."

"Don't hear a thing. Thoughts of riches have sent you round the bend, mate."

Wentworth set down the rucksack, intending to reach for the compass to determine their current direction. If the great chamber opened towards the sea, it meant the wall faced east. He felt inside the canvas bag for the metal and glass device, but instead touched the head of the doll. He withdrew it and showed the toy to Patterson.

"What on earth?" the other gasped. "Where'd you find that?"

"Over there," Wentworth replied, pointing towards the staircase on the far side of the cavern. "It's a puzzler, isn't it? The writing on the shoes says *E. Anjou*, which means the doll belongs to the duchess, but you have to wonder how it got down here."

"Could an animal have dragged it down?" Pitt asked.

"I suppose so, but there's no sign of tooth or claw marks on it anywhere. In fact, it's in perfect condition. Like it appeared here just this morning. But it gets even weirder." He opened the leather bag to show his friend the bones.

"What the devil!"

"Devil's probably dead on," declared Worthy. "What person in his right mind puts animal bones in a doll's dress?"

"I don't like any of this," answered Pitt. "We should go back, Lionel. This wall's not going anywhere. We can give it another go tomorrow."

"No," Wentworth declared emphatically. "This wall gives up its secrets now." He set the doll next to the bag; then, reaching behind his back, removed the pickaxe from its leather sheath. Setting the tool against his knees, Wentworth spat on both palms, wrapped his fingers round the wooden handle, and leaned back to offer the enigmatic wall a sound thwacking.

To the utter amazement of both men, the wall started to crack *before* the first blow was even struck. Not only did the wall crack, it formed a neat, geometrically uniform, nine-foot-tall rectangle.

"Blimey, Pitt, it's a door! And it looks like we're invited in," Wentworth declared victoriously. "You coming with me? Or are you a coward?"

"Coming, I guess," moaned his friend.

The deep-throated bells continued to peal as they entered the opening, and Lionel heard a disembodied voice laughing and whispering:

Welcome, Mr. Wentworth. It's time you learned what Fear really is.

CHAPTER ELEVEN

2 pm - Hôtel Meurice near the Tuileries, Paris

"And this is your private suite, Prince Alexei," the hotel manager said as he unlocked the apartment. "We call it *Le Roi Louis*," the man continued proudly. "There are three bedchambers, a meeting room, parlour, and two water closets. New plumbing runs throughout, including gas fireplaces; and you will notice that, as with our main floor, all is wired with electrics. It is decorated in the Versailles style, of course."

Raziel Grigor, the ancient Watcher, strode into the luxurious apartment as though he ruled the world. "Is this the largest you have, M'sieur Dupuis? Perhaps, I should have stayed at the Hotel Regina."

The manager's smooth face paled a little. "Not the Regina, sir. It is infested with all manner of pests. *Le Roi Louis* is only slightly smaller than their so-called luxury apartment, but our extra 'accommodations' have no rival. Shall I send one up, sir? Will it be blonde, red, or brunette?"

Grigor smiled. "Why not all three? But not until later. Business before pleasure. Ah, Chastain, I see you're already here," he told a fat man in a tight suit, who sat in a tiny chair near the panoramic French windows. "And Urquhart? Is he also here?"

"In the water closet. Indigestion."

Grigor walked all about the grand parlour, touching the fittings and mouldings. "Real gold?"

"But of course, Highness. We spare no expense for our special guests."

"Is that where it happened?" he asked, stepping towards the windows.

"Happened, Highness?" asked Dupuis.

"The revolution. A century ago."

"*Oui*, Highness. It is one site. The *Tuileries* is no more, of course. Most sadly, it was burnt to the ground during the suppression of the Paris Commune in '71. Such a hellish time! I am fifty-six years old, m'sieur, and in my time, I've seen half a dozen such rebellions in our beautiful city. So much death! So much destruction! The *Palais de Tuileries* may be gone, but we have preserved its memory as the *Jardin des Tuileries* so that no one forgets the price of revolution."

Glancing down, Raziel smiled. "*Ordo ab chao*. Round and round it goes, like a dragon eating its tail. I very much like it."

He remained at the window, touching the glass as his mind returned to old memories from the dawn of time—of revolution and its ultimate price. Everyone remained silent, fearful to break the prince's good mood.

The sound of flushing water spoilt the rare peace, followed by the entrance of a portly gentleman wearing an overly formal costume of black tails and white waistcoat. He emerged from the connecting chamber, drying his hands on a fringed, linen towel.

"Ah, most excellent! You are here. *Bienvenue à Paris,* Prince Alexei," he greeted the Watcher prince, using Grigor's human name. "You are now in true civilisation, eh? You will find it most difficult to return to London's dismal streets once you experience the City of Lights, Highness. *Paris est sans égal!* It is without equal. Music, dancing, gambling, and a thousand delightful dens of iniquity, eh? You will never be bored, *mon ami*. Not one moment."

"So you keep telling me, Urquhart," muttered Grigor, his pleasant mood vanished. "Where is this meeting room?"

"Through there," answered the builder, pointing to a set of gilded doors. "I have gathered all your crows. Linville and Comtois arrived an hour ago and now enjoy libations. The Herren Richter, Schmitz, and Baumann are also here, representing the Austrian committee. The gentlemen from Chicago have arrived and now change out of their travelling clothes. Eight days at sea is very taxing, is that not so? And Prince Aleksandr promises to arrive before sundown. He is delayed in Goussainville, it seems."

"My brother is always late," complained Grigor. "Wendaway! Stop ogling that maid and get in here!" he shouted into the corridor.

A thin man with an equally thin moustache of mousy blonde hair hastened into the apartment. He wore a light blue suit with a claret red waistcoat and had a face that reminded one of a marble bust with an overly chiseled nose and chin. The dainty features gave him a somewhat feminine appearance. In fact, had he shaved the sparse hair above his lip and put on a dress, Sir Albert Wendaway might even pass for a rather splendid woman.

The manager offered a set of two keys to the guest he presumed was human. "These are both tagged. You will see one fits this apartment, the other the floor's private smoking room. It is open all night, with many fine entertainments according to your pleasure. You need only ring. Will there be anything else, Highness?"

The Watcher took the keys and handed them to the baronet. "Keep these with you at all times. I find these hotel keys cumbersome to carry. All that jingling is annoying; like tiny church bells in one's pocket."

Sir Albert placed the keys into a red leather valise.

"Where are my other guests?" he asked Dupuis. "I ordered this entire floor reserved."

The manager nodded. "We've secured the entire fourth floor for your comfort and pleasure. The English gentlemen are all on the *Rue de Rivoli* side with grand views of the Tuileries. The French and Germans to the northwest, overlooking the *Rue de Mon Thabor* and the *Place de Vendôme*. There are two Americans who arrived last night, and we've put them nearby, in the English wing."

"That would be Adams and Calabrese. Excellent. That will be all, then."

Dupuis bowed and left, shutting the main suite door. Grigor smiled, his icy eyes twinkling as though he'd thought of a joke. "We're about to begin the next phase of humankind," he told Urquhart and Wendaway. "You've chosen the winning side, gentlemen. Stay here until the Americans arrive, and then bring them into the meeting room. Come, Chastain, you can introduce me to these Germans."

The fat Frenchman followed Grigor into the next room, and Wendaway collapsed into the nearest chair. "That man is insufferable!" he exclaimed. "However do you put up with his constant boasting, Clive?"

Urquhart poured two fingers of whisky into a pair of glasses and handed one to the effeminate baronet. "You will learn to ignore him. You and I should talk, but not here. Let us use that smoking parlour key and ensure privacy, eh?"

He gulped down the alcohol, as did the baronet, and then the men quietly left the luxurious suite.

The corridors were broad and colourful, finished in Languedoc marble and fine silk wallcoverings. Every six feet, a bust of a past French king or queen greeted them, but the electric lighting cast harsh shadows upon their faces, making them seem alive.

Once the two men reached the locked parlour, they hastily entered to begin plotting. "Tell me," Urquhart said to his fellow conspirator, "how is the prince's mood?"

"Jubilant," replied Wendaway, "but he keeps me on a short leash. I truly do hate that creature! He thinks himself above all of us, when he's nothing more than an escaped criminal."

"A powerful criminal," warned Clive. "But at least he's keeping you from the police, eh? Else, you would find yourself in Sinclair's clutches."

"I've not read the papers," the baronet admitted. "Not since Wychwright's body was found at the Exchange. I didn't kill him, Clive. Believe me, I didn't, but I saw it done. I wonder, if I go to the police and tell my story, do you think they'd believe me?"

Urquhart laughed, twirling his waxed moustaches. "I think they would see you hang. Sinclair hates you, *mon ami*."

"I have other information to offer him," Wendaway continued. "Information about my cousin. I could use it to bargain. I never touched that girl, you know. Not really. Just a little friendly slap and tickle. Girls like that sort of thing."

"You did exactly as her mother asked, my friend. Connie Wychwright is as calculating a woman as ever lived. She should sit with us on our new Round Table, I think. Wait, you say you saw the baron murdered? Was it... Raziel?"

"Damned if I can tell them apart! Raziel, Saraqael, and this one they call Samael. They all look the same to me. One of them did it, and then he put that note from me in Wychwright's pocket. To keep me chained to them, I suppose. Blackmailers, the whole lot of them! And now, we're going to release another of their blasphemous kind? Why?"

A shimmering shadow moved in the interior, and Urquhart paused, unsure if the flickering form resulted from the harsh electrics or from something else. It was entirely possible Raziel had set a trap, and that he now listened to their whispers. A chill ran through the builder's frame, and he visibly shivered. "We should be careful of such slanderous words, Sir Albert."

"You've changed your tune," the younger man laughed. "You're the one proposed we create our own Round Table. Have you lost your metal, Urquhart?"

"Perhaps, he's lost his mind," a third man said from within the shifting shadow.

Urquhart feared he might lose his entire breakfast along with every ounce of urine in his bladder, but he managed to hold onto both as he replied. "It has been said so, but those who dared never did so again."

The entity laughed as he stepped from the corner. "What plots are you two hatching? Might I join in the fun?"

Wendaway's bladder did give way as he stared at the enormous creature. A half-man, half-human anatomy with chilling ice-blue eyes. "Prince Raziel?" he managed to croak. "We plot nothing! We only hoped to keep our secrets from the foreigners."

"You're all foreign to me," the intruder answered as he transformed into a more agreeable configuration of molecules. The hairy arms wove clothing about their sinews, and the thick tail wrapped round the loins to become trousers of fine Merino wool. By the end, the being might have passed for a very tall peer or businessman; except for the glacial eyes. The handsome mouth curved into a smile. "Ah, now that is better. I've been eating, you know, which requires a different sort of *teeth*. Do go change your clothing, Sir Albert. No, wait. Allow me."

With a wave of his hand, Saraqael magically transmuted the soiled breeches, making it seem as if nothing had gone awry. "Much better," the Watcher said as he walked close to the terrified baronet and kissed him on the cheek. "You're a dear little fellow. Rather pretty, too. I shouldn't wish to frighten you. Not yet, anyway. Now, Clive, do tell! What are you men plotting?"

"Nothing, my lord Saraqael. Nothing at all. We merely wished to allow your brother privacy during his negotiations."

"Yes, that," Sara muttered as he sat into a leather club chair. "Raza plans to rule the world, doesn't he? Such a mundane plan, but it may prove useful to me. The question is this: which side will you choose?"

"Side, my lord? We choose only the side of power. Redwing and all it stands for," replied Urquhart, suspiciously.

"Then, you will side with me. Do you know the history of Cupid?"

"The god of love?" asked Wendaway. "Oh, sure, I've read about that at college, you know. A chubby fellow with arrows."

"Your dons must have fawned upon your great intellect," answered Saraqael as he poured himself a glass of claret and then transformed it into blood. "The real Cupid is anything but chubby. In fact, he'd quite likely eat your liver for breakfast for making so slanderous a statement. He is not of my class, but powerful nonetheless. He's currently imprisoned, but if my plans unfold as I think they will, then that will soon be remedied."

"What the devil are you saying?" asked Wendaway.

After taking a sip of the transmuted wine, the devious Watcher winked at the baronet. "*There is a generation, whose teeth are as swords, and their fangs* as knives, to devour the poor from off the earth, and the needy from among men. That is quote, by the way, Sir Albert. From the King James Bible. The king was a sensitive fellow, whom I knew quite well—intimately, in fact. It is from Proverbs. Thirtieth chapter, fourteenth verse. I ask you: are your teeth swords or are they chalk? Will they devour or crumble into dust?"

"Do your kind always speak in such pretentious riddles?"

The Watcher licked the baronet's face, his hand on the man's slender chest. "Careful, pretty one. My teeth are adamantine swords. Want to see them?"

"No," Wendaway squeaked. "Thank you, no."

Laughing, Saraqael downed the last of the unpleasant beverage and set the empty glass aside. He rubbed his hands together in delight. "Now, to the plot! Cupid was a great one for strategy, and he used his arrows to alter the thoughts of others, which led to this ridiculous belief in him as some sort of love broker. Some of his arrows killed, whilst others defeated enemies with more silken traps. Let us then play the role of Cupid and lure my brother in with the object of his greatest desire: power, vengeance, blood and fire. And then, when that pleasant point is securely fixed within his crooked breast, I shall let fly my second dart, which will prick him to the deep and trap him in my web for all eternity."

CHAPTER TWELVE

10:27 am - The Tilsbury Tea Room, Bryanston Square

"You say Wychwright's body is *missing?*" gasped Henry MacAlpin. The Scottish viscount sat opposite Charles Sinclair at a round, cloth-covered table near the east window of the elegant restaurant. To his right, a hand-painted trolley held a three-tiered, silver cake plate; stacked high with warm scones, fruit, and buttery confections. On the table, a gold-edged china teapot, decorated with blue and white pansies, offered hot Darjeeling; silvery mists of steam rising from its delicate spout. Piano music filled the scented air with pleasant chords of controlled gentility, yet the theme of their discussion had taken an early turn into the macabre.

"Someone stole the body, Henry. I'm sure I can imagine who," answered the duke.

MacAlpin cut a scone in half and spread it with strawberry jam. "I suppose you're going to tell me it's Redwing?"

"Who else would have done it? Henry, the driver spoke of shooing a bird from the interior of the waggon just before he discovered the body had vanished. A bird, Henry. A raven, in fact. Does that sound familiar?"

"You're referring to the creature you and Elizabeth met inside that other world? What is it you call him? The Nameless Gatekeeper?"

"Not entirely nameless," Charles admitted. "One is Uriens, according to Romanov. The Gatekeeper is a maddening demon, and I suspect he's able to cross into our world at will. Of course, he claimed he was trapped there, but how can that be? Beth and I escaped. Why can't he? And what does this Uriens want with Baron Wychwright's body?"

The viscount took a bite of the pastry, followed by a sip of tea. "Who's to say?" he asked after swallowing. "Charles, I think you expect too much of yourself, if you plan to solve all this today. It's nearly Christmas, and Beth is looking forward to celebrating with you. Can you not allow another investigator to take over whilst you enjoy being a newlywed for a few days?"

Despite having consumed only coffee since rising, Charles had no appetite. Ever since awakening from the odd dream, he'd been nursing a slight headache, and a nagging sensation prickled his skin, as though a light electric charge skimmed along his shoulders and spine. Something was about to happen. Redwing was moving chess pieces into place, preparing for a major assault, and Romanov's warning to keep a close eye on the duchess caused him to worry all the more. If he could only determine the enemy's plans before the attack commenced, then maybe, just *maybe* he could keep Beth safe enough to enjoy the holidays.

"I'd love nothing more than to relax with my wife, Henry," he said. "But it's difficult to let one's guard down, with so much evil in the air."

"Yes, but evil will always hang round you! We are ever on a battlefield, but even the Lord's warriors require seasons of rest. Charles, my very dear friend, let me speak as a physician for a moment. Your personality tends towards carrying everyone's burdens, but though you are strong, you are not Atlas. The world does not rest upon your shoulders. That constant weight will crush you, if you're not careful. Remember, you suffered a sharp blow to the head only a month ago. You're still healing."

"I'm recovered well enough to manage," the duke insisted. "It isn't the first time I've been injured, Henry, nor will it be the last."

"No, I suppose not, being a policeman, but that doesn't make you invulnerable. Tell me, have you noticed any lingering effects? Headaches? Dizziness?"

"A headache now and then, but those are common to every man."

"Charles, I do wish you'd let me examine you properly," Henry worried.

The duke raised an eyebrow in irritation. "I am fine."

"Very well!" Salperton sighed. "Do as you like, but if you'll not listen to common sense regarding your health, then let's puzzle through your latest conundrum. You want to label this strange event—the missing body, I mean—with a familiar name, but that bird may have been only that. A bird. A natural, non-threatening raven. London's full of ravens and blackbirds. This Jarvis might be lying. Have you considered that?"

"Of course, I have, but he seemed reliable."

"Well, then, have you spoken to anyone else about it? What does Paul say?"

"He doesn't know about it yet."

"Ah. What *would* he say, if you asked him?"

A slight smile crept along Sinclair's firm jawline. "He'd probably say the bird is just a bird. Henry, I'm not imaginative. Truly, I am not. Ask anyone at Cambridge. I was a dull as dishwater student, who spent nearly every minute with his nose in a book."

"And now you spend every minute with your nose in a criminal case. Charles, you're no different now than when you were a student. You're still driven to succeed, even at the cost of your health."

The stubborn duke offered no reply. The alienist poured a second cup of tea, his quick eyes assessing the other's pupils and general appearance. Salperton recognised exhaustion when he saw it, and his friend had a decidedly erratic look to his eyes now and then, as though distracted.

"Charles, I wish you would eat something. If you'll not enjoy the pastries, then have some fruit, at least. The oranges are quite good, and the pears as well."

Grudgingly, the duke chose a small satsuma orange and a slice of lemon cake. "Happy now?"

"Immensely," Henry replied with a bright smile. "Now, if you would actually *eat* the cake, I should be even happier."

Haimsbury slowly smiled. "You're a stubborn fellow, Lord Salperton. Very well, I'll forget about the case for the moment. Anyway, I'd not intended our conversation to be business. The original idea for our breakfast meeting was far more pleasant, I assure you. It's a personal invitation. Beth wants you to join us at Branham for Christmastide. We have several other guests who'll be there as well, including most of your old castle companions: Stanley, Anderson, Count Riga, and Mr. Blinkmire. Miss Kilmeade, the two cooks, and Vasily all declined. They've been invited to celebrate with the staffs of Haimsbury and Queen Anne."

"Katrina and Ida? Are they going?" asked the viscount as he buttered a second scone.

"Katrina Gasparov has left the dower house. I asked Ida the reason, but she chose not to reveal it. I've placed a man on her trail, for I suspect she's joined Anatole's new household, wherever that is." Charles paused, staring at the orange, wondering if he should mention his conversation with the elusive prince.

"And Miss Ross? I do hope she'll come, Charles. Ida is a dear woman and actually quite bright. With a little education, she could make a fine wife for a fellow."

Sinclair smiled. "Which fellow might that be?"

Henry actually blushed. "Oh, no! I don't refer to myself! No, hardly that. I'm not meant for marriage. I mean Mr. Stanley, of course. Hadn't you noticed? The two of them have grown very close."

"Have they? Well, then we'll have to look elsewhere for your bride, Henry."

"There's no rush, I assure you," Salperton demurred.

"You've met no woman who merits even a moment's consideration?"

Henry swallowed the bite of scone, wiping at his lips with a linen cloth. "Only one, but she's in love with another. In fact, she married him. I believe you can deduce who that dear lady is, Charles. However, I'm content to be her friend and physician. And talking of doctors, is she consulting Gehlen now that Emerson is delayed in Edinburgh?"

Charles slowly peeled the orange, wondering why he had no appetite. Generally, he ate large breakfasts, but today nothing appealed. "Gehlen? I'm afraid it's been somewhat busy of late. I cannot believe I haven't asked her about him. Henry, what's wrong with me?"

"You're overworked. That's what's wrong. Allow me to speak to Beth about Gehlen. In the meanwhile, do you trust me with her health?"

Sinclair nodded, and Henry could see relief in his friend's eyes. "I've hated to ask, but would you keep an eye on her? I cannot tell you how many government telegrams and messages I receive each day now. Salisbury and Matthews have saved every unsolved case to place upon my desk."

"Then delegate some of the responsibility. Have Paul or one of your men see to these unsolved cases. What is it you call your men? Detectives? Inspectors?"

"Agents," answered the duke. "And I have delegated. It's just that..."

"It's just that you're unable to release the reins entirely. I understand, but your wife might not always be so agreeable. If Paul's stories are true, Elizabeth has quite a temper when roused. But do let's change the topic for a moment. Who else is going with you to Branham?"

"Joseph Merrick will be there for a few nights. James and Victoria, of course. Also, Tory's friend Reggie Whitmore might join us, though he's not yet committed."

"Good heavens! Will there be any room for me?"

"More than enough," the duke answered. "The hall could host a small army, if required. My wife is adamant, Henry. She'll not take no for an answer, and as you're her friend and one of her physicians, you simply cannot decline."

"I should never disappoint our duchess," answered the viscount cheerfully. "I usually visit my father over Christmas, but I could go there afterward, I suppose."

"How is your father?" asked Haimsbury.

"Feisty as ever. He's eighty-three and growing increasingly fragile. It's a struggle, you know. Father and I've never gotten on well, but I cannot leave him on his own completely. Aside from his servants, he's no one else."

"Then, bring him down here. We could see to his comfort and Beth would love to meet him. Besides, he's family."

"Honestly, Charles, you and Beth are far too generous, but I'll write him. I promise nothing. My father is insular in his ways and very unpleasant company. As to matters here, let me see if I can arrange for a colleague to keep watch on my resident patients, and if it can be done, I'll join you. Will Aubrey be there?"

"As with myself, Paul's been occupied with far too many tasks the past few days, so I've not spoken with him about it. But I'm sure he will be. He never misses a Christmas with Elizabeth; not unless duty calls him away."

"Let's pray all such duties take a holiday, then. Now, let me explain why I wired you this morning. I've a very odd fellow in my care at present. The Hammersmith police called me to examine him, and I think he's someone you should meet."

A pretty server in a charcoal dress and pinafore arrived to ask if they'd like more coffee, to which Charles replied 'Yes, please.' As Henry mentioned the Hammersmith man, the pianist, a coatless fellow of slender build and ridiculously long arms changed the selection from Bach's *Jesu, Joy of Man's Desiring* to Tchaikovsky's *Swan Lake*. The haunting strains of the latter danced upon the air like tiny black swans. The sensitive duke could almost feel them skitter along the back of his neck.

"Charles? I say, Charles, are you all right?" he heard Henry ask.

"Oh, yes, of course," the duke replied, though his eyes had a vacant look to them.

"Well, you don't look all right. Are you experiencing a headache?"

"A small one. Nothing time won't heal. You said you met an odd man. Why is he odd?"

"Well, perhaps not odd so much as mad. Mad as a hatter, actually," Salperton explained, mentally filing away his friend's behaviour for later. "The police at T-Division tried to send him over to Bedlam, but the fellow escaped. They've no idea how he managed it, but when they arrived at the hospital, the maria was entirely empty—rather like your missing body, come to think of it. Very strange. They only found him again because a milkman reported seeing someone wandering amongst the tombs in Westminster Cemetery, covered in blood."

"The cemetery near Anatole's castle?"

"The very same," Salperton replied as the server returned with the coffee. "Thank you, Miss. If you'd bring me the bill?"

"It's on the house, my lord. Mrs. Tilsbury asks only that she might meet the duke before you leave."

Charles swallowed a bite of orange. "Meet me? Has she some crime to report?"

The girl giggled. "No, Your Grace, she only wishes to hear you speak and shake your hand, if that's allowed."

"Really? How very strange. Yes, of course. I'd be happy to meet Mrs. Tilsbury, Miss...?"

"Waxman, Your Grace. Sylvia Waxman. Mrs. Tilsbury is my mother's dearest friend. We're all honoured that you've chosen to breakfast here this morning, sir, and pray you'll come again."

She curtsied deftly and left the coffee pot, giggling once more as she disappeared through a set of velvet drapes on the far side of the restaurant.

"How very extraordinary," remarked the duke.

Salperton found it amusing. "Married or not, you're still causing women to swoon, old boy."

"Not intentionally," Charles muttered, thoroughly embarrassed. "Go on with your story. The madman was arrested?"

"Oh, yes, that—well, yes, he was arrested, and that is when I entered the tale. Inspector Ryan and I've come to know one another quite well since I opened Montmore to patients, and he often asks me to consult whenever he books someone with mental instability into his cells. They'd listed him as Bleeding Jack Nobody, for no one knows the fellow's true name, and he was bleeding profusely from self-inflicted wounds when they found him—both times. He's determined to open his veins, it seems, and he shouts of creatures crawling through his blood. I'm hoping someone in the area might identify him eventually, for the family might know the reason for his condition. Charles, the man told some very wild tales about seeing..." he leaned forward to whisper. "He spoke of seeing *dragons.*"

Suddenly, Sinclair was all attention. "Dragons? He used that exact word?"

"I've not yet heard him speak it, but the police claim he did, many times. I could say nothing to Inspector Ryan, but it's possible this poor man may have witnessed some of the supernatural events the night of the castle fire. You and I both saw the remains of that strange creature. It might pass for a dragon, don't you think? And both Mr. Blinkmire and Count Riga told how these things breathed fire. And though I'm an advocate of honesty and truth, I don't believe we should allow this particular truth to find its way into the newspapers. I worry about anyone else overhearing details about that night; particularly as it involved the duchess, so I've had the man transferred to Montmore."

"Montmore? Not to your home, Henry!" the duke objected strongly. "This man could harm your patients, or you! You've no idea what he might do!"

"Trust me, Charles, I would never place any of my patients in danger." He thought of Violet Stuart, the memory of her unexpected kiss causing him to smile. "Each one is dear to me, and I'm their protector as well as their doctor. No, he's in a small cottage once used by my grandmother's gardener. I've made sure the house remains locked, and there's a capable male attendant on duty. Thus far, the man's been quite subdued, actually. He's told me some startling things, Charles. I really think you ought to come talk with him."

"Perhaps, after the funeral today," the duke suggested.

"Yes, that would work, but might we could go before? Montmore is only a ten-minute drive from here. And whilst there, I can introduce you to my mystery patient. Violet Stuart. She's made enormous strides the past few days, and I've even mentioned going on an outing, but I'll require your approval. We're still on for the theatre tonight, I take it?"

Sinclair felt suddenly warm. An odd tingle passed along his scalp and into his brain, making it difficult to concentrate. "Theatre? Yes, I think so. I'm not sure. Beth mentioned it after supper last night. We can ask her at the church this morning."

Charles ate the orange thoughtfully, his eyes drifting now and then to a black-framed, oval mirror on the wall directly behind Salperton. Both their reflections shone upon it, along with several other restaurant patrons; each busily chatting or enjoying breakfast dishes. For a fraction of a second, the surface of the mirror liquefied. Ripples of silver became circular bands of eddying black, as though the mirror formed a doorway to an inky whirlpool. Gradually, a pair of pinpoint lights pierced the darkness.

Two fiery orbs that blinked.

Hello, boy, an ancient voice whispered into the duke's mind. *I'm coming.*

Suddenly, Charles felt like a petrified child. Fleeting images from his past whirled through his mind in rapid succession, and he quite clearly heard two pistol shots, followed by a woman's scream.

He dropped the half-eaten fruit, forcing the unwanted images back into their mental closet, where the memories had slept for nearly three decades.

There was time to face the truth later.

CHAPTER THIRTEEN

10:05 am – 5 Fitzmaurice Place, Mayfair

Cordelia Wychwright had never cared for black. Her skin always took on a dull, pearlescent grey tone in darker shades, but black made her look positively ghastly. She pinched her smooth cheeks, hoping to break enough capillaries that the ghostly pallor might give way to a pleasant blush, but even her cardiovascular system colluded to force the unhappy ingenue into mourning.

"Stop doing that, Cordelia," her mother chided as she descended the staircase. "It will only give you a splotchy look. There's a pot of rouge on my dressing table, inside the little Chinese box. It will make a world of difference, but use it sparingly. I shouldn't want you to give the wrong impression. There will be many, eligible young men at the funeral. Men with influence and impressive incomes."

The middle-aged widow wore a modestly bustled dress made from finely woven silk crêpe with a matching, high-collared jacket, trimmed in four vertical rows of jet beads. The full-length veil had been pulled back from her face and pinned to allow her to see and speak (not to mention check her rouge and powder), however it would be lowered to cover her face once the family arrived at St. Marylebone's for the service. The gauzy fabric admitted just enough light to manoeuvre safely through a crowd, but gave the correct impression of a woman in deep mourning; precisely the effect the ambitious widow desired.

"Do hurry, Delia," she urged her pale daughter. "The coach from Cooper and Price will be here soon, and we don't want to be late. Think of your father, my dear."

"Yes, Mama," the girl sighed, stepping to one side to allow her mother full access to the foyer's black-draped mirror. "You look splendid," she added. "And quite young."

The dowager baroness was straightening a pearl and sapphire pin, which she'd secured to her new jacket. "That's kind of you to say. Is the pin too much? Your father bought it for me last Christmas. I wear it only in his honour; not for any vanity."

"It's quite nice," the girl replied.

"Yes, yes, I know it's nice, but is it appropriate? I've no wish to appear cold-hearted, my dear. We're about to lay your father to rest, after all, and all the important people of London will be there."

"Is he at rest?" the young woman asked plaintively, a slight twitch to her left eyelid.

"Of course, he's at rest! Why would you even ask such a thing? Cordelia, whatever is going on inside that empty head of yours this morning? Did you take the medicine Dr. Gehlen prescribed? It's meant to calm you, yet your face has a distinctly hectic expression to it. You should take another spoonful, perhaps even two."

Apparently satisfied with her appearance and the new face powder's youth-giving assistance, the widow began to fuss with her daughter's simple ensemble, adjusting the cloth-covered buttons and straightening a small cameo brooch at Cordelia's throat.

"Do you take no pride in your appearance, Delia? Your hair looks very dull and lifeless. Have you been brushing it a hundred strokes each night? Do you use that French cream on your skin? Ah, well!" she sighed. "There's nothing to be done about it now. Where are your brothers? I saw William not more than half an hour ago, and he promised to be dressed and ready by ten. Where's he gone?"

"He's probably smoking with his so-called friends in one of the coaches outside, Mama."

"Do I detect envy in your tone, Cordelia Jane?"

"Why should I be envious, Mama? Particularly regarding Will's friendship with such shiftless men."

"Shiftless? Do not *dare* repeat that to anyone else, Cordelia Jane! It's a scandalous way to speak of such fine young men as Sir Richard Treversham and Mr. Cecil Brandon. The baronet may not yet have a career, but he doesn't require one. He receives a very respectable income from his estate, and Mr. Brandon is sure to be accepted to Lincoln's Inn soon and will quite likely become a powerful politician one day, just like his father. Who knows where their paths might lead? As you've no serious marriage prospects, do not resent any favour your brother curries."

"I wish to curry no favour, Mama. I only want to be left in peace!" she exclaimed, tears flowing down her ashen face.

"Now, Delia, do be reasonable. You've done nothing but weep since you returned from hospital. Mr. Treves released you much too soon, I think." Constance Wychwright handed her daughter a lace handkerchief. "Do stop weeping. It will cause your skin to blotch all the more. Dry your eyes and then take another dose of your medicine."

"I don't care for the taste, Mama, and it makes me feel quite strange."

The dowager baroness cast a disapproving glare at her only daughter. "Medicine seldom tastes pleasant, and if the elixir makes you less contentious, then you should take it. Don't you agree, William?"

A tall man with a distinctly military bearing was just coming through the front door. Beyond the curtained windows, a pair of younger men dressed in bespoke finery loitered on the portico, smoking cigars and laughing.

"Do I agree with what, Mother?" her eldest asked.

"That Cordelia mustn't be contentious, today of all days."

"A woman should never be contentious, no matter the occasion. She should endeavour to remain as pleasantly inconspicuous as possible."

William Wychwright glared disapprovingly as his younger brothers descended the staircase, followed by a brace of giggling children.

"Ned, must those girls make so much noise?" he asked the taller of the two brothers. "Remind them that we'll be the centre of attention today. Decorum, my boy, decorum in all things. And Tom, do stop slouching! Must your hair be so long? This isn't Paris. London gentlemen have standards."

Connie Wychwright beamed at her eldest as though admiring a deity. "How very smart you look, my dear. I thought you'd wear your dress uniform today. You look so very dashing in it, but I see you've changed your mind."

"It isn't a military funeral, Mother," the new baron answered as he admired himself in the long mirror. "And besides, I've told Colonel Frobington I intend to resign my commission, effective on the first of the year. My place is here with you. I plan to stand for Father's Parliament seat next year. Ned, do keep those children in line!" he barked, his harsh blue eyes fixed on the mirror as he re-worked the knot in a black silk cravat. "I shall have to engage a valet as soon as possible. I've no idea how Father managed without one. In the army, I had a batman to keep my clothing brushed and mended. They're simply indispensable. You know, I may just hire him."

"Hire whom, my dear?" his mother asked as she brushed his coat.

"My batman. Sievers knows how I prefer things to be done, and he'll be at loose ends when I leave the service."

"I'm sure anyone would be happy to serve your needs, my dear," she told him. "Has this Sievers person also resigned?"

"Not yet, but he will. Frobington owes me a bucket-load of favours. I'll have no trouble persuading the colonel to see things my way. Beside, Sievers didn't have much of a life before taking the queen's shilling, though he's got an adequate education. His father manages a granary in Kent, I believe."

"If you're hiring a valet, perhaps we should consider employing a lady's maid for Cordelia," his mother suggested. "She and I both use Mrs. Complin. Your father never allowed us a proper staff."

"Delia will have to make-do with Complin for the present, Mother. Besides, she won't be living here much longer. The sooner she marries the better."

Cordelia had spent a lifetime being 'spoken about' rather than 'spoken to', and she'd taken a chair in a far corner, as though trying to disappear into the wall. She reached into her silk handbag and withdrew a green glass elixir bottle that bore Anthony Gehlen's handwritten label. She measured out a capful and drank it all down—followed quickly by a second.

"I shall never marry," she told her brother.

"That choice isn't up to you, Cordelia, but to me," William declared. "Mother, what's our solicitor's name again? I plan to speak to him regarding our finances. We're surely not the paupers Father claimed us to be."

"It's Allendale," the widow answered, "but there's no need to contact him. He's coming round tomorrow to read the will."

The small children moved close to Cordelia's chair, the elder of the two girls taking her hand. "Are we poor, Aunt Cordelia?" the ten-year-old asked sweetly.

"I don't know," Delia answered. "But you needn't worry about any of that, Calliope. Not today. Tom, you and Ned look splendid. Really, you do. Black suits you."

Cordelia's brothers, Thomas and Edward (usually called Ned), aged twenty-six and thirty-two, had inherited their mother's mousy brown hair and equally mousy eyes. On the other hand, thirty-five-year-old William Wychwright had the golden locks and pale eyes of their father, and the thin moustache above his upper lip, gave him a regal air. Despite preferring male company to female, the new baron proclaimed a desire to marry—and marry well. In fact, he'd been speaking of little else since arriving two days earlier from North Africa. As the new head of the Wychwright estate, he'd also made it clear that Cordelia should find a husband right away, despite the usual six-month mourning period, for he had no intention of providing support to a sister of marriageable age.

"Delia, you're as pale as a sheep and twice as dimwitted," the cruel baron proclaimed. "No man finds that attractive, which is why I shan't be paying for a debutante ball next spring. It would be a waste of my money. Instead, I shall find you a husband amongst my friends. Surely, one of them will marry you, if only as a favour to me. Oh, and do something with your hair. It lacks life."

The two girls walked past the mirror, and one accidentally bumped William's hand. He pushed the child away. "Ned, do something with these unruly creatures! And why must they come with us? They should stay here where they'll not embarrass the family."

Bashful Ned Wychwright seldom challenged his overbearing brother, but he reached for his daughters' hands and drew them close. "Unruly? Look here, Will, that's unfair. They've been quiet as church mice all morning. Besides, I'll keep watch on them. They loved their grandfather and should be part of saying goodbye. They'll be good as gold, won't you, girls?" he asked, kissing them both on the head. "Come now, let's see if Mr. Wickham has finished putting the feathers on the horses' bridles, all right? Delia, will you come with us?"

The young woman started to rise, but William spun about on his heel. "Do not move, Cordelia Jane!" he ordered as though she were nothing more than a foot soldier. "You're to remain here until you've made yourself presentable. It's quite likely that other carriages have begun to assemble for the procession, and I'll not have you embarrassing us. And don't allow those children to distract our drivers, Ned. Those coaches are costing a fortune to lease. In fact, this funeral is costing far more than it should."

The Wychwright's butler, one of five live-in servants, had been waiting nearby, dressed in sober livery and wearing a black armband upon his left coat sleeve. Though distressed by the family's cutting conversation, the servant remained stoic and silent. He crossed to the door, opening it for Ned and the two children and found a well-dressed visitor just about to ring the bell.

The unexpected caller's shoulder-length, chestnut hair had been pulled back with a black velvet ribbon, and his cleft chin shaved smooth. The tall man wore traditional mourning dress: black frock coat and matching trousers, black silk waistcoat, white shirt, black ascot tie. The jewellery was sophisticated but understated: ebony cufflinks and shirt studs, a silver stickpin with a matching watch and chain.

"Forgive the presumption," the newcomer said brightly. "I wonder, is Lady Cordelia still here?"

Every square inch of Cordelia Wychwright's pallid face lifted with one accord at seeing the man who now stood within the entry.

"Paul!" she exclaimed, not caring that she'd forgotten all sensible manners in front of her brothers. Her previously forlorn feet moved without prodding, and in seconds she'd pulled him into the foyer's flower-strewn interior. "Oh, do come in. I'd no idea you'd be calling this morning. We're all in a bit of a rush, you see."

The handsome earl bowed gallantly, a silk top hat in his right hand. "It's presumptuous, I know, Lady Cordelia, but I'd hoped you might ride with me," he told the grieving daughter. "If your family doesn't object, of course."

Constance Wychwright managed to conceal her jubilant enthusiasm behind a convincingly neutral smile. "We'd planned to ride over together, of course, Lord Aubrey, but as you've made a special trip, I'm sure Cordelia would be honoured to join you."

"Captain Wychwright, I pray you've no objections," the earl said graciously.

The army officer shook his head. "None at all. It's kind of you to offer, Aubrey. Mother tells me you've been most helpful during all of this. Of course, it might have been nice to have our father's body returned to us with greater alacrity. Waiting nearly a fortnight to bury him simply won't do."

"William!" the dowager baroness scolded in shock, not wishing to risk insulting the wealthy earl. "Lord Aubrey has no control over such matters."

"On the contrary, Mother, he has a great deal of control, if my spies are correct." Seeing his mother's stern face, the baron shrugged as if to pretend it had all been said in jest. "Well, spies might be too strong a word for it. Nevertheless, we're grateful. Delia, go along with the earl, and we'll see you shortly."

"Would the children like to come with me as well?" Aubrey asked. "My coach has plenty of room. Would you like that girls?"

The youngsters had followed their aunt like a pair of homeless urchins, and their dark eyes grew large with excitement. "Are there feathers on your horses' bridles?" asked the eldest.

"There are," the earl whispered, smiling as he bent down to look into her hopeful faces. "And I think there's a picture book, as well, with lots of exotic animal lithographs."

"Are they hand-coloured?" asked the younger.

"They are indeed! And many of the wilder animals I've seen with my very own eyes!"

The girls gasped as though imagining such a marvellous feat of bravery.

"Does the book belong to your children?" the younger girl asked innocently.

"I'm unmarried, actually. Twas my sister left the book in the coach last week."

"May we go with him, Grandmother?" the elder implored.

"Are you certain, Lord Aubrey?" the widow enquired, inwardly hoping he'd answer in the affirmative. "They can be quite rambunctious."

"Who isn't when young? Besides, I'd enjoy their company. Ladies, shall we escort your Aunt Cordelia to the carriage?" he asked them, donning his hat to take their small hands.

"Let's," the younger child said very seriously, her cherubic face alight with hope. The butler fetched woolen cloaks for all three Wychwright ladies, handing one to each.

Cordelia paused, looking back at her brothers and mother as they reached the door. "Is it really all right if I go?"

"Yes, of course," William answered, though his words failed to counter the stern look in his eyes. "Why wouldn't it be all right? Go along, now. See you shortly."

Baron William David Wychwright stood in the open doorway, keeping watch as Aubrey led Cordelia and the children down the smooth limestone steps to the waiting coach. Once all had settled into the comfortable interior, the baron shut the door and looked at his mother, a strange expression on his face.

Constance frowned. "Whatever is the matter, Will? Surely, you see the wisdom in pursuing an alliance with the Aubrey fortune."

"He's trouble," declared the captain as his two, ne'er-do'well comrades entered the foyer.

"Wasn't that Aubrey?" asked a dark-haired man in charcoal grey. "Do tell me he isn't the scoundrel Delia talked about!"

William hushed the effete fellow with a dark scowl. "Not here. We'll talk later."

The second, taller man stood slightly over six feet with curling red hair and a pencil moustache. "The hearse is here, Will. Time to start the show, old boy."

"Thanks, Richard. Ned, Thomas, fetch your coats. We have a long day ahead of us with all of Parliament watching. What we do today will ripple into our futures for decades. Come now, men! Make me proud."

Ned Wychwright ran a sallow hand through his mousy thatch of hair. "Shouldn't we try to make Father proud, Will? It is he who died, after all."

The baron offered no reply, for the butler had just admitted a stout man in a dark suit one size too small for his broad shoulders and thick middle. "Beggin' yer pardon, my lord. I'm Jarvis from Cooper and Price. I jus' wants ya ta know tha' we's ready ta go."

"Mother, shall we?" William said, not bothering to acknowledge the driver with anything more than a quick nod.

The dowager baroness kept her counsel, but she worried that her eldest hadn't leapt with delight at Aubrey's obvious affection for Cordelia. She would wait to discuss it later—tomorrow, after the will was read.

CHAPTER FOURTEEN

Montmore House Gardener's Cottage

"He's in here," Salperton told Haimsbury as the alienist unlocked the door to the ivy-covered cottage. The morning's sunshine promise had given way to iron grey skies and the threat of rain. Despite the cooling temperatures, flies buzzed persistently round the fading blossoms of Montmore's spectacular gardens.

"Mr. Rush?" he called as he pushed through the door. "Mr. Fisher? Is either of you here?"

The sound of heavy footsteps reached them first, followed by a stout man with yellow hair and a long chin. He wore casual clothing: olive-coloured shirt of cotton and wool blend, checked trousers with narrow cuffs, black braces and an open waistcoat with a button missing. His shirtsleeves were rolled to the elbows, and a well-used briar stuck out of his left trouser pocket.

"Mornin', Doc. I didn't reckon on seeing you before afternoon. Fisher's out fetchin' more wood. Mr. Jack's been complainin' of the cold, sir."

"It is rather chilly in here," observed the alienist. "Avery Rush, this is Commissioner Charles Sinclair, Duke of Haimsbury. Duke Charles is the man I mentioned to you and Mr. Fisher regarding our Jack."

"Jack?" repeated the duke.

"It's what we call him, Yer Grace," answered Rush. "We got no name to speak of, but as the Hammersmith police call him 'Bleedin' Jack', it seemed better than none. Can I take yer coat, sir?"

"No, thank you. I'll keep it for the moment. You may call me Commissioner, if you prefer, Mr. Rush."

"As you wish, sir."

"Is Jack still asleep?" asked Henry as he hung his own coat on a brass hook near the entry.

"No, sir. He woke 'bout half an hour ago, and he's been ever so quiet since. Just sittin' by the fireplace, tryin' ta keep warm—in his own sort o' way, o' course. He's an odd duck 'bout wearin' clothes. Claims they make the faeries angry."

"Faeries? He's calling the voices faeries now?" asked Henry.

"Aye, sir. Says they talk to him all the time, but it's them dragons what hurts."

"Dragons? You're sure of that?" repeated the duke.

"Jack talks of all sorts of things, Commissioner. I reckon one would, if you was mad."

"Yes, well, let's see if our odd duck has anything more to tell us," the physician told Sinclair. "Come through, Charles."

The men crossed the parquet floor of the entry, through a somewhat low and unassuming hallway, and then into a friendly little parlour. Appropriately enough, the Montmore gardener's cottage had a faery-tale look about it, with four broad timbers spanning a peaked ceiling, running from wall to wall. A creek rock fireplace ran all the way to the ceiling, and a warm log fire danced within its spacious hearth. Charles felt the odd flush of familiarity, and he had to pause for a moment. The room looked eerily similar to the cottage from the Stone Realms, right down to the swing-armed, pot hook mounted into the creek stone firebox. He half-expected to see a loaf of Bannock bread cooling nearby. Tied bundles of dried herbs and floral bouquets hung from the rafters, and Charles could even hear the faint cawing of birds from somewhere nearby.

"Charles?"

He felt a hand poking his shoulder.

"Charles? I say, is everything all right? You've gone rather pale."

"Henry. Oh yes. Sorry. It's just this room looks like... Never mind. Do go on."

"Why don't we both sit?" the alienist suggested, keeping an eye on his friend. MacAlpin took a position nearest the madman, just in case Jack grew violent. Sinclair chose an upholstered wingback. The pattern in the damask was of trumpet vines and bluebirds. *At least they're not ravens,* he thought.

"Hello, Jack. It's Dr. MacAlpin. Do you remember me?"

The man dubbed 'Jack' slumped against a wooden chair closest to the fire. Though he complained of the cold, he wore no shirt, and the sparse chest hair had greyed from its original dark brown. His knobby feet were bare, and his only attire consisted of patched woolen trousers and black braces. A tartan blanket covered his thin shoulders, and he stared into the yellow flames as though dreaming.

Jack had been handsome once, though his face now had the seamed, leathery look of a man who'd suffered hard times. His shoulders and forearms hinted at glory days when they'd bulged with sinewy muscles, but weight loss and lack of exercise had left the fibres feeble. Loose, dry skin hung like sagging paper from the long bones, and his cheeks were hollow from lack of food. Rows of red gashes ran from elbow to wrist on each forearm, where he'd repeatedly sliced into his veins.

"Jack?" the doctor repeated. "I've brought a guest to meet you. His name is Charles, and he's interested in hearing your story."

The madman's face turned towards the duke, the listless eyes blinking languidly beneath furrowed grey brows. "Charles? I know a Charles. Is it really you?"

The duke felt as if he knew the man; or rather, knew something inside him. "Yes, I'm Charles."

The man's cracked lips parted. He had but two teeth remaining, and his thick tongue lolled as he laughed. "You're him! That's right. The faeries say so. You're him! You're that boy, ain't ya? Really and truly him!"

Henry interrupted. "I think you misunderstand me, Jack. This man is Charles Sinclair."

"That's right. He's that boy," the madman insisted, his hollow eyes growing keen; lips quivering. "*You're the one the Dragon's after.* Ain't that right?"

Salperton started to argue again, but Charles spoke first. "Why do you call me a boy, Jack?"

"Cause that Dragon calls you one. Says you're special. Like no other boy ever born, he reckons. Told me to wait here, an' you'd be callin'." The strange man began to laugh, his purple lips opening into a toothless oval. "Reckon he were right 'bout that!"

"Look here, Jack, you really shouldn't..." Henry started, but Charles interrupted again.

"That's all right, Henry. Let him talk. Tell me, do you remember your true name? I assume it's not Bleeding Jack," Charles asked.

"Names don't matter none. Like that bird said, everybody's got lots o' names. Some got meanin'. Others don't. Charles means 'man'. Nemo means no one—backwards, it's omen. Captain o' the world. You sure is a special sort o' man, Charles Robert Arthur Sinclair. You rememberin' yet, boy?"

"What should I remember, Jack? How do you know my full name? How do know about Captain Nemo?"

The madman leaned forward, his rheumy eyes turning to fixed points of shining black as they focused on Sinclair's face. "I remember everything, boy. Every dark thing that ever happened. Every dark word ever spoken. Every minute of every dark day you've ever lived. Don' you wish you could remember it? Ain' no memory stones to help here, human. Not a bleedin' one! You wanna know who you really are? *Ask the bird.* Talk ta Uriens. He'll tell ya without riddles."

"How do you know Uriens?" Charles asked.

The man turned back to the fire, his eyes returning to normal.

"Who is Uriens?" Charles asked again. "Describe him."

No reply.

"Jack, can you tell us about this fellow Uriens?" asked Henry. "Please, won't you help us?"

"No time, no man," the madman whispered. "Captain o' nothin' and leader o' the world. Time will stop when you use the clocks. It's hickory dickory, Doc."

"Stop this, Jack," Henry ordered his patient.

"The crypt is found, and the doll is too. Bones o' children break in two. Babies die and mothers, too. Hickory dickory doo!"

"Stop it! Jack, this isn't funny at all!"

"Hey, diddle diddle, the wolf's in the middle, and the duchess fell into a trance. The digger appears with the dolly she fears, and the Captain loses his chance!"

"Jack, stop this now!" ordered MacAlpin, signalling to the attendant.

"Little boy black made the dark mirror crack, and the Dragon emerged with a cry. The rider and horse, see the woods, o' course, and the rider will probably die!"

"That is *enough!*" the physician shouted angrily as the attendant brought a leather medical bag containing morphine and syringes.

"*I ain't Jack*," the madman growled, his eyes a pair of dancing flames. "I ain't nobody at all." He looked directly at the young duke. "They're coming, boy. They're all coming! A fool's about to open the first gate to hell. Ain't nobody can stop it. Not even Samael."

"What do you mean?" Sinclair shouted. "Is there truth to your hateful rhymes?"

"The answer's in the puzzle room, boy. Two clocks, two rooms, two futures. Tick-tock. Time is running out. Arthur's asleep and the Dragon's eyes are opening. And soon the whole world will run red!"

CHAPTER FIFTEEN

Branham estate, the cavern beneath St. Arilda's Abbey

Far away in Kent, two foolish Cambridge men stood before a mysterious brick wall, staring at the rectangular opening. "Damned if it isn't a door, Worthy!" Patterson shouted, holding his lantern aloft.

"I reckon we're invited in," declared Wentworth as he set the pick-ax against the cavern wall.

"Invited by what? Old Danny's ghosts?"

"I dunno. Rats, maybe."

"Bell-ringing rats? I don't like this one bit, Worthy," Patterson complained. "I think we should head back up and let the colonel deal with this tomorrow. Let's go have lunch with Holly, eh?"

"Holly's a spy, and I've no intention of letting him share the glory or the bonus money."

"You've been down here too long, Lionel," the shorter man pleaded. "You're not thinking clearly. Maybe the air's unhealthy."

"The air's fine. I'm going in."

"Wait," his friend begged. "At least, let me tell him where we're heading." He shouted again to Seth, who'd been sketching a detailed illustration of the bird statue near the first crypt, when his friends had suddenly abandoned him. "Holly, put down your charcoal and get down here! We need your help!"

No one answered the shouts, for Seth Holloway had fallen into a deep sleep in the middle of sketching the statue's disquieting painted, yellow eyes. His auburn head lay against the statue's three-toed feet, close to the claustrophobic tunnel used by Wentworth to reach the granite gallery. Holloway's dreaming mind now wandered in a gloomy land of talking birds, shadowy spiders, and living stones where every wild tale, every inexplicable experience, every rumour of the spirit realm focused into a single beam of uncomfortable truth: The Devil and his minions were real. Demons were real. A netherworld existed and could be accessed by humans. And if evil existed, Holloway reasoned as best he could in so senseless a place, then its opposite must also exist. Surely, the Old Testament stories of God and angelic warfare were true, and if God existed, then perhaps a Saviour did as well.

Deep in the throes of the terrifying nightmare, Seth Holloway fell to his knees, pleading for mercy and forgiveness from Almighty God and from the Risen Christ, whom his father had taught him to deny.

Elizabeth Stuart had tried many times to sway his heart, but it took a journey to hell to achieve it. He thought of her now; wishing he'd believed in Christ that May, when she'd nearly accepted his marriage proposal. He'd argued that superstition was fine for the uneducated, which had caused her to bristle. It was a low, ungentlemanly remark, for Elizabeth knew more of science and the arts than most university dons. If she could place so great a faith in Jesus Christ, then surely, there must be something to it. Perhaps, that's what had so rankled.

Seth longed to take back those hasty words, for it had caused a cooling of their friendship. He prayed for her now, his spirit and soul changing from its old paradigm into something new, something brighter, something far more hopeful.

Deep inside the most terrifying dream he'd ever experienced, Seth James Edward Holloway, 9th Viscount Paynton, had become what he'd once derided: a firm believer in Christ.

Completely unaware of their companion's life-changing predicament, Pitt turned to Wentworth. "I give up. Holly must have left the area. So, what do want to do now?"

"Do?" Wentworth mocked. "We go in, Mr. Patterson. That is, unless you're too timid. If you want to crawl back to Cambridge with your tail twixt your legs, then do so, but I do not shrink from adventure. Silver Spoons men lead, old chum. *Numquam receptum, numquam exieris!* Never retreat, never surrender! Are you a Spooner, or no, Mr. Patterson?"

"I am!" shouted his friend.

"Then, what say you?"

"I say, *lay on, Macduff!*" the younger man declared.

Wentworth grinned, finishing the Shakespeare line as he entered the opening. "*And damned be him that first cries, hold enough!*"

Thus, the naive students passed through the mysterious portal into doom.

The mineral oil lamps cast swathes of dancing yellow against the dank cavern walls as they proceeded forward. The beautiful writing and graven images they'd seen upon the exterior of the door belied the abyss beyond, where the stench of centuries-old animal waste and rotting corpses assaulted their sensitive nostrils. Near the far end, dark shadows, the size of hideously misshapen dogs with arched backs and crooked legs, scuttled about as though sniffing for prey.

"Do you see that?" Patterson asked Wentworth.

"It's a trick of the light," the other declared, but only half-heartedly.

"Be careful, Worthy. This place is probably crawling with all manner of vermin. Flint's map shows a maze of tunnels below Lion Hall, but not this one. We've no idea where this leads."

"Which means another bonus to each of us, right?" Wentworth declared.

"Yes, I suppose."

Ten minutes passed, and then fifteen, and finally twenty. They'd proceeded deep into the passage, when their lanterns suddenly brightened; or it seemed to Wentworth they had.

"Look there, Pitt. See that up ahead?"

Patterson's hazel eyes struggled to focus, and he wished he'd not left his spectacles at the inn. His vision overall was clear enough, but an irregularity in the left cornea sometimes caused lines to double at a distance; especially in low light.

"Is that a rat or one of Danny Stephens's ghosts?"

"Neither," Wentworth answered warily. "I think it's another lantern. Holly, is that you? How'd you get ahead of us? You really are a spy, aren't you? I'll wager you're working with Flint to scare us, but it won't work, mate!"

The third light swayed back and forth, then multiplied into a pair. Unsure if the additional lamps were real or just a manifestation of his astigmatism, Patterson decided to conduct an experiment.

"Lower your lantern, Worthy. Set it on the ground."

Lionel did so. "What're you thinking?"

"That it's a reflection," Patterson answered. "See there? Both lights have gone still now. Pick yours up again."

Wentworth obeyed, and sure enough, only one light moved.

Both men sighed in relief. "Not a ghost," Wentworth said happily. "But how can it be a reflection? Stone doesn't reflect light."

"Polished stone does," Patterson suggested. "If there's another of those finished galleries down here, then it may lead to a second crypt. I'll say, though, it could use a bit o' my mum's rose petal potpourri! Phew! This place makes a night soil cart smell like a perfumery!"

"Hold your nose, then, and let's see what it is," Wentworth decided, holding the lantern high as he moved towards the reflection.

That's when everything went wrong.

Sideways.

Or rather *downways.*

Without warning, the floor of the cavern collapsed beneath their feet, sending both men tumbling down the slanting shaft like a pair of captive passengers in a runaway coal car. Down, down, down they fell, screaming the entire way. Free-falling through the cold blackness, the two men continued to scream until their mad flight deposited them into an even madder place.

The adventurers landed with a painful thud on a rock-hard surface, smooth as glass, surrounded by a thick blanket of silence. Even the sonorous bells had at long last stopped. Once he recovered his senses, Wentworth ran a quick inventory of systems: bones, blood, breath. All good.

"Pitt, you all right?" he asked the other.

"Yeah, sure," his friend gasped, rubbing his backside. "What the hell was that all about?"

"Hell's an appropriate way to put it," a gravelly voice answered as a figure stepped out of the shadows.

The pair of unwilling travellers gaped in disbelief. It was altogether impossible! Before them, stood Albus Lucius Flint; pale-faced, long-armed, and attired in his customary black frock coat and gloves, looking like a grim mourner at a mid-century funeral.

"Congratulations," Flint told the startled men. "You are the first to find your way here. How very *lucky* you are."

"You... I mean, we, uh..." Wentworth stuttered.

"I'm sure your tiny brains are presently burning up a great deal of energy in an effort to make sense of your situation, gentlemen, but you'll soon adapt."

"Are we *dead?*" asked Patterson hesitantly.

Flint's waxwork face elongated into a grotesque approximation of a grin. "Not yet. Just how long that remains true depends on how you proceed from here. Do you recall the contract you signed?"

The students stared at one another, for neither had bothered to read the dense document, assuming the language contained within stipulated the usual sort of paragraphs: An agreement to serve the project for a fixed period of time in return for a stipend, lodging, and food. Probably a section explaining what would happen should either party fail to comply. Straightforwardly complex, as with all such legal mumbo-jumbo.

"Ah, I see. You didn't read it. Still, *qui tacet consentire veditur*. He who remains silent consents," the lawyer laughed. "And your signatures are on the contract. In blood, I might add. All legal requirements are satisfied, meaning you now belong to the Blackstone Society. Heart, mind, and *soul*."

"Our souls?" echoed Patterson in despair.

"Of course. The bargain was struck and sealed in the usual manner. You joined willingly. Now which of you is ready to continue to the next phase?"

Wentworth rubbed his eyes, wondering if he'd fallen asleep in the chamber above, or perhaps still dreamt in their room at The Abbot's Ghost.

"What do you mean, continue? To where?"

"To sublime knowledge, my friend! But I warn you: Great reward comes with great cost. If you wish to earn the bonus, then you must make certain sacrifices. It's all in the contract. You saw the charred cavern floor above, Mr. Wentworth. Do you think the previous occupants of the abbey were merely warming their hands before that fire?"

Neither man answered, and Flint continued as though speaking to children. "Humans are so very predictable. You deem yourselves wise, despite knowing nothing about how the world really works.

You quoted from *Macbeth* earlier. I must admit, it's one of my personal favourites. Such bleakness! Such despair! Such treachery! *Tomorrow, and tomorrow, and tomorrow, creeps in this petty pace from day to day, to the last syllable of recorded time; and all our yesterdays have lighted fools the way to dusty death,*" he quoted. "Ah, that Will had genuine style, I'll grant you that. If only he'd taken my advice, he'd have earned a far greater reward."

"Who *are* you?" Wentworth dared ask.

"I am your worst nightmare come true," Flint replied, twirling a black cane, capped by a silver wolf's head. "I've used many faces throughout my long life, inhabited many suits of clay. But names must be precise and descriptive; not mere appendages or decorations. Names are only useful if they contain *power.* A few of my appellations I've liked better than others, but all have their uses in the human realm. You humans so love to name things, don't you? Adam spun out thousands of them." He laughed, the sound like a million, low-pitched caws. "For the moment, you may call me Flint, though, my other names will eventually seed themselves into your crippled psyches, I daresay. Now, which of you would like to earn the reward?"

"Look, Mr. Flint, if you'd just show us the way out, we'd be happy to go back to Cambridge," Patterson bargained. "I'm very sorry I neglected to read the contract, but had I done so I wouldn't have agreed to this sort of nonsense."

"Nonsense? Do you think my plans nonsensical, Mr. Patterson? Perhaps, you treasure human logic more than immortality."

A series of sharp tapping sounds slowly reached the students' ears, as though a twig scraped against broken glass.

"What's that noise?" Wentworth dared to ask.

"That, Mr. Wentworth, is the sound of my friends."

"Friends? The others, you mean? Colonel Collinwood and the Oxford group?" suggested Patterson, inwardly praying the answer would be yes. "Is there some passage from that old castle to here?"

Flint laughed; a harsh, cackling sort of snort. "Collinwood? Hardly! The man's a bumbling fool! My friends are much more interesting than that smug colonel and his Oxford cronies. They're like three little pigs led by a limping cockerel. I find Cambridge men much more *tasty.* As do my friends."

The persistent tapping rose to a raucous discord and echoed throughout the blackness, causing their ears to ring with pain. The men screamed for mercy.

"Why are you doing this?" cried Patterson in despair.

"Because I *can*," Flint crowed, his black eyes turning into yellow orbs. "Simply because I can."

The wall behind the lawyer began to heave and bulge outward, its glittering obsidian surface cracking into a vast web of fine lines that spread outward in a radial pattern. Like a huge arachnid controlling every filament of a silken trap, Flint snapped his long fingers, and the web flew apart, shattering into a thousand-thousand deadly shards. Then, with the speed of a blink, the slivers of volcanic glass metamorphosed into a tornado of flying ravens, until the air was thick with black-winged terror; a riotous, swirling cloud of anger, aimed straight at the terrified students' faces.

As the carrion crows descended upon his eyes, Lionel Archibald Wentworth discovered that he *could* be frightened; that there *was* something in the world beyond the reach of human reason; beyond the dominion of cold science; beyond the ken of mortal man.

The bullseye lanterns winked out, leaving nothing but darkness and beaks and birds—and both men began to scream like a pair of terrified children.

CHAPTER SIXTEEN

Before the funeral cortege left Fitzmaurice Place, Ed Jarvis shared a few whispered words with Baron William Wychwright, explaining why he'd been forced to secure his father's coffin lid without allowing the family a final look. To prove his statement, the distraught driver offered a paper signed by Commissioner Charles Sinclair, explaining that he'd ordered the coffin sealed for legal reasons.

Oddly enough, Wychwright showed no surprise, and by half past ten, the procession of forty-nine coaches, all draped in black and many bearing colourful crests of England's wealthiest and most influential families, commenced a slow drive to St. Marylebone Church. Calliope and Cassandra Wychwright seemed quite taken with Jarvis's glass-sided hearse, asking the earl if their grandfather lay inside.

"Do you think Grandpapa is comfortable in that wooden box? Does he know where he is? Is he all right?" the younger girl asked Aubrey as they journeyed along the route.

"I think your grandfather has passed beyond such physical cares, Cassandra. That's the nature of these things."

"The nature of death, you mean?" the elder asked. "Our father explained it all, you know. Grandpapa is with God now."

Stuart had no idea whether the baron had died in Christ, but he had no wish to enter into a philosophical conversation regarding salvation with grieving children. He measured his response carefully.

"We all pass into another type of existence after death. An eternal state. Do you know what eternity means, Cassandra?"

"Cassie," the girl's sister corrected, turning the pages of the picture book. "She likes to be called Cassie. And I'm just Callie. Calliope is simply unthinkable."

"I see," Stuart answered, laughing. "I've never had a nickname, actually, though I'd like one. Paul is a difficult name to shorten."

"Have you no other names? Mine's Calliope Jane Marie. Surely, you have others, too."

"It's James Paul Robert Ian, actually," he told her. "My father was Robert, and so I was always called Paul."

"Then, you might be called Jamie or Bobby, I suppose," suggested Cassandra. "Though, you don't really look like a Bobby."

"No one calls you anything else?" asked Callie.

"Some have called me all manner of names," laughed the earl, "but rarely one of endearment. My Cousin Elizabeth sometimes calls me Sir Paul."

"Why? I thought you were an earl," the elder girl remarked.

"I am, but when Beth was your age, she liked to pretend to be a damsel in distress, and I was Sir Paul, her knight errant. The name stuck, I suppose. She still calls me her Scottish knight."

The reference to the intimate friendship twixt the earl and duchess caused Cordelia to turn away and stare at the passing scenery.

"My father likes to be called Ned, but our mother detests that name," Callie continued, unaware of her aunt's emotions. "She's quite cross these days. I don't think Mama likes Father any more. She prefers that other man. The one with the fancy horses. Will you be going to the party, Lord Aubrey?"

Cordelia blinked, roused from her melancholic reverie, for she found the term shocking. "There's to be no *party*, Callie. That implies a celebration, which this most certainly is not! It's a wake, meant to allow friends to pay their respects to your grandfather by honouring his memory. Our Aunt and Uncle Cartringham are hosting it, but it is *not* a party. This is hardly a time for frivolity."

Paul squeezed Delia's lace-gloved hand, noticing it trembled. "Take heart," he whispered sweetly. "This will all be over soon. Trust me."

The sisters grew quiet and huddled close together as they enjoyed the picture book, marvelling at each new animal presented in the alphabetic listing. They'd just come upon a baboon, and Cassie laughed aloud at the comical appearance and curious red spot surrounding its tail. She was just about make a comment, when the carriage came to a dead stop.

"Are we there already?" the child asked the earl.

"Not yet," Aubrey replied, warily. "Stay here, ladies. I'll see what's happened. It may be one of our horses has lost a shoe."

Cordelia glanced out the window, noticing a hansom cab parked to the southwest side of Portland Place and a man in a policeman's uniform sitting inside. "Do be careful, Paul," she told him, suddenly worried.

"I am always careful, dear lady," he assured her with a bright smile. "I shan't be long."

Outside, the earl met a shorter man in a Homburg hat and tweed overcoat. The two spoke for several minutes, and then the earl called to his driver, speaking to him privately. Two minutes after that, the earl returned to the carriage.

Sitting once more in the leather seat beside Cordelia, he explained. "Nothing to be concerned about, ladies."

"I saw a policeman in that cab. Was the man in the hat a detective? Has this anything to do with my father?" asked Cordelia.

"No," Paul assured her. "Something personal actually. I had a minor break-in at my home last evening, and that was my friend Tom Galton. He recognised the carriage and wanted to let me know he's looking into it."

"A break-in? That's terrible. Was anyone hurt?" she asked him.

"No, but a few items were damaged. I told Galton I'd meet with him about it tomorrow."

"Is he a policeman?" asked Calliope.

Paul found the question amusing. "Galton would laugh if you called him a policeman to his face, but he's a sort of private investigator. Much better than a policeman in many ways. Now, what is it you girls found so amusing?"

Calliope turned the book round to show him the baboon. "Surely, this is made up," she insisted. "There cannot be a monkey with so comical a tail as this!"

Paul's mouth widened into a dimpled grin. "Ah, the *Simea hamadryas*, as Linnaeus would say. My sister Adele suggested the very same thing about the baboon, but I can assure you that it's a real animal."

"How can you know that?" Cordelia asked him.

"I know because I've seen this creature with my very own eyes," he answered. "Three years ago, whilst on assignment to the Sultan of Samaroon."

"Samaroon? I've never heard of such a place. Where is it?" asked Cordelia.

"It's a tribal division in a wider clan called the Dir. They live in the northern part of the Horn of Africa, near the Red Sea. The British government have been negotiating treaties with the local tribesmen there, and I was sent as part of the diplomatic team a few years ago."

The girls' eyes widened. "Do you mean you were really, truly *there?* In Africa?" Callie whispered, as though the idea both thrilled and terrified her. "And you saw one of these creatures? Did it bite you? It has very big teeth."

"It tried to bite me," he answered, "but I escaped before it could. Shall I tell you the story?"

They nodded, and soon all three Wychwright ladies forgot the sad reason for the processional for a few moments as they listened, spellbound, to the earl's exotic tale of daring and intrigue.

CHAPTER SEVENTEEN

10:58 am - London Hospital

As the Wychwright funeral procession wound its way towards St. Marylebone, Death was stalking St. Katherine's Dock in Whitechapel. Frederick Treves, Chief Surgeon for the London Hospital had never seen so much charred flesh; so many swollen, dead eyes, or so many broken bones and shattered lives in one day. Three hours. Three long, backbreaking, gut-wrenching, thoroughly exhausting hours of constant activity, life-and-death decisions, and enough despair to fill the Thames river basin all the way to the estuary.

Fred Treves stared wearily at the hospital's densely packed waiting area. Since shortly after eight that morning, he and six staff physicians had joined with every available medical student, nurse, attendant, and porter to treat traumatic injuries, burns, and breaks; and stem endless fountains of blood, caused by a devastating fire that raged through St. Katherine's Docks. At last count, the surgeon had seen forty-one patients, made a hundred triage decisions, administered enough morphine to knock out every horse in Spitalfields, and even delivered a healthy baby boy—God be praised!

Witnesses were divided on how the inferno began, but most described a tall man in bright clothing, who stood on the decks of a Russian steamer attempting to dock illegally at St. Katherine's. Called the *Podzhigatel,* only half of those aboard spoke any English; most knew only Russian, which caused further problems for the triage team, until two Jewish immigrants from Kiev, Dr. Levi Portnoy and Dr. Joshua Kholodenko, arrived to join the medical response and offered to translate.

Detective Inspector Arthur France, currently on loan to Leman Street for the Wychwright and Hemsfield investigations, led a team of valiant police sergeants and constables against the onslaught. The youngest and least experienced policemen aided the beleaguered fire brigades by pumping water, hauling buckets, unwinding rope, or tending to fire horses. The oldest men maintained order and held back worried families of affected dockworkers, but also reporters and ghoulish voyeurs. The most experienced and physically fit waded again and again into the cold river water to offload injured passengers and sailors from the burning ships and overburdened lifeboats.

Treves had just left the operating theatre, having completed his sixteenth surgery, when he saw Inspector France pass through the hospital's main entry. The lean detective had worked without a single break and looked as though he might collapse. Fred rushed to see if the lad were injured.

"Inspector, are you all right? Are you bleeding?" he asked him anxiously.

Arthur shook his head, wiping blood and sweat from his sooty brow with an equally sooty hand. "Just a cut, sir. Nothin to worry you, Mr. Treves. I wonder if there's any water?"

Treves shouted to the nearest nurse. "Sister Sebring! Some water!"

"Right away, sir!" she called over the babelous din as she wiped her raw hands on a cotton towel. The exhausted woman filled two tin cups from a spigoted crockery jar, but nearly spilled the contents when a middle-aged sailor with bandages over his eyes bumped her elbow halfway across the lobby floor. He muttered something in an obscure Russian dialect, and the nurse hurried past, an odd sense of oppression clinging to her thoughts.

She handed one cup to France, the other to Treves. "I'm afraid it's not as cold as it once was, but it will revive you nonetheless."

Arthur gulped it down, and then returned the empty cup to the helpful woman. "Thank you, Sister. You're most kind."

Treves had long since abandoned his formal coat, and stood in rolled up shirtsleeves and an unbuttoned waistcoat: both spoilt by bloodstains, soot, and vomit. The moans and cries of the wounded filled his ears, and he longed to lie down and sleep for just an hour.

"The fire's finally out, praise the Lord," France said, getting a second wind. "My men are helping clear the area for a formal investigation. Captain Shaw's already on scene, sorting through the mess to determine the cause, which makes me useless now, Mr. Treves. Can I help you in anyway?"

Treves smiled wearily. "You look to me like you could use a break not another assignment, Inspector. It's grown calmer now. Why don't you and I spend ten minutes over a cup of coffee? Collect our thoughts, so to speak. There's a lounge down this corridor, where it's quiet."

"That would be wonderful, Mr. Treves. Lead the way."

The hospital's wards were full to bursting, and plaintive cries for morphine, water, and spiritual comfort echoed throughout each hallway. Stragglers continued to enter the lobby, most of them family members searching for loved ones. Uniformed volunteers from the Salvation Army and the Jewish Men's Relief Fund stood ready to provide food, water, and spiritual answers that so many now needed.

"In here," Treves said at a door marked 'SURGEONS ONLY'.

Inside, they found a bleary-eyed Anthony Gehlen sipping strong black coffee from a blue ceramic mug. He started to stand, but Treves would have none of it. "Keep your chair, Dr. Gehlen," Fred told his friend. "Have you met Inspector France? He's been leading the police teams from Leman Street."

"I'd say it's a pleasure, Inspector, but that would be a lie," Gehlen replied. "Nothing to do with you. I'm simply beyond manners at the moment."

Gehlen's head ached from lack of sleep, but also from a series of strange and confusing nights. He'd not yet mentioned it to Fred, but no matter how long he lay in bed, he awoke exhausted, as though he'd not slept a wink. Although a robust individual as a rule, his stamina was beginning to wear down.

What Anthony didn't know was that most nights, he spent hour after hour in backstreet brothels and illegal gambling parlours—or rather his body did. His mind had been put into abeyance by the dark spirit using that body: the devious, bloodthirsty Watcher known as Saraqael.

"How many for you, Fred?" Gehlen asked his fellow surgeon.

Treves poured two cups of strong coffee from a silver server that sat upon a painted oak sideboard. He handed one to Arthur. "Looks like it's gone cold, Inspector. Sorry," the physician muttered after taking a sip. "How many? Forty-one I think, but I may have missed one or two in all the chaos. Honestly, it's like a war zone out there, Anthony. Sixteen surgeries and a maternity case. A healthy boy, I'm happy to say, and the mother is recovering well, despite her anxiety. It was nice to see new life amongst all this death and dying."

"How many have died, sir?" asked France.

"Over twenty thus far, and I fear we'll have more before the day's done. What manner of inferno caused this, Mr. France? I've only seen burns like these in industrial cases. Has either of you noticed, they have a caustic, chemical smell and appearance?"

Finishing the last of his coffee, the bleary-eyed physician answered his fellow healer. "I noticed the caustic signatures as well, Fred. As though an accelerant were used to set the blaze. I've seen my share of burns, but honestly, Fred, this takes the biscuit. We'll run out of morphine before nightfall at this rate."

"I've sent to a supplier for more. It should arrive this afternoon, if the waggon can get through. The streets are utter mayhem."

Gehlen sighed in relief. "Tell me, Inspector France, have we seen the last of the injured?"

"Most likely, sir. My men tell me that all the refugees in the docks have been removed from the area. Six ships and two smaller pleasure boats caught fire. That old Russian frigate where we think the fire originated, three spice traders from India, another from the Argentine, and the sixth ship belongs to an American tobacco firm. The pleasure boats were paddle steamers that ferry locals from one side of the river to the other. Thankfully neither of them had many passengers aboard. However, all the commercial vessels were packed to the masts with goods, sailors, and immigrants of every size and nationality. One of the dockside warehouses caught alight, and several of their workers were trapped inside. All are dead, I'm afraid. This has been a day of unthinkable tragedy, gentlemen. It truly breaks my heart."

"Fred, you should call for a meeting of the hospital governors," said Gehlen. "We don't have nearly enough beds to go round when something like this hits. We must find a way to expand."

Treves wiped his dark eyes and stretched out on a leather divan to elevate his feet. "I fear the governors have no wish to increase our capacity, which means the East will need the duchess's new hospital all the sooner. As I recall, you've moved into Haimsbury House, Inspector. Has she spoken to you about it?"

"I don't really talk with the duchess all that much, other than a quick word now and again, Mr. Treves. But the commissioner says she's been meeting with architects, and I believe she's chosen the location."

"Commissioner?" asked Gehlen.

"Ah, that's Haimsbury's newest professional title," explained Treves. "He's heading up a special investigatory branch of the Home Office, though he reports directly to Prime Minister Salisbury. It's all very hush-hush, and I rather think his actions will be off-book. Isn't that so, Inspector?"

Arthur smiled. "I'm not to say much, sir. Commissioner Sinclair keeps his activities to himself."

"Well, so long as the duchess makes good on her promise, then let her husband do as he likes. And it cannot come soon enough for this quarter!" declared Treves. "We see an endless stream of starving refugees entering our ports every day from Russia's killing fields. They bring heartache, fear, despair, and physical ailments."

"Not to mention religious differences," observed France. "Perhaps, it would help to hire a few Jewish doctors, sir."

"It is my hope to do so, Mr. France," replied Treves. "Perhaps, the duchess will consider doing so as well. Gehlen, are you serving as Her Grace's physician?"

"I've no idea," Anthony answered, his brain an unsettling jumble of half-remembered opium dens and whorehouses. "I believe so. I saw her several times here, of course, but I've not been called to Haimsbury House for anything as yet, which either means all is going well with her pregnancy or another man looks after her. How's she feeling these days, France?"

"Well enough, sir, from what I know. Her Grace and the family are travelling to Kent tomorrow for the Christmas season."

Gehlen yawned. "Christmas. This will be a very lean celebration for anyone employed at St. Katherine's, I should think. You say they're leaving tomorrow?"

"So I understand. Around five tomorrow afternoon."

"Well, then, I'll drop by Haimsbury House in the morning to see how everything's going before they leave—just to make sure of her health. However, I require a good night's sleep before I do anything."

"Don't we all?" Fred remarked. He left the couch and bent forward, touching his toes to stretch out the kinks in his lower back. "Ah, that's better! Nothing like getting the blood moving to sort out the knots! I say, Inspector, how long do the Sinclairs intend to remain in Kent? Is there any chance the duke might return to London in the next few weeks?"

"I'm not sure, sir. He did mention a meeting of the ICI for after the new year."

"ICI?" asked Gehlen. "Is that a men's club?"

"Not exactly," laughed France. "It's that private investigatory organisation Mr. Treves mentioned earlier. Inner Circle Intelligence. ICI. His Grace is the Director General, but in a similar capacity, he's also Commissioner of the Home Office's Intelligence Branch. The two organisations work together."

"Then how is it private?" enquired Treves as he unlocked a cedar closet and selected a clean suit of clothes. "If the ICI is run from the Home Office, then aren't you beholden to the government?"

France finished the last of the cold coffee before answering. "That'd be a question for Commissioner Sinclair, sir. I only know what I'm told."

"Ah, well, it's always the way with Whitehall," said Treves as he removed his stained waistcoat and shirt. "If the duke has time, ask him to come see me, Mr. France. It's about Alexander Collins. I'm afraid his condition continues to deteriorate, and Gehlen here recommended we bring in an alienist to consult. I know the commissioner believes Collins is malingering, but if he is, then he's a consummate actor. If it were a broken bone or an enflamed appendix, I'd find it easy to repair, but the mind is not my area. London has very few men with trustworthy credentials. Dr. Kepler from Castor Institute is one, but as he's a close colleague to Collins, that might present a conflict of interest. Honestly, Dr. Collins seems mad as a March hare these days. Yesterday afternoon, we found him running through the corridors, not a stitch on his body, shouting about dragons of all things! It happened just as Miss Trivoli came through. She's one of our most faithful benefactors; a spinster with a delicate frame of mind. I thought the poor woman might faint from shock!"

Gehlen found this amusing. "Shock? I've met Trivoli. The woman could use a good shock. She claims to understand human nature, but only if that nature confines itself to a very narrow set of definitions. She's a Regency-era prude, Fred. Plain and simple."

France wiped his eyes and poured a second cup of coffee. “The commissioner has an alienist friend named Henry MacAlpin. He might be of help.”

“The viscount?” asked Gehlen. “I know him by reputation, and we met once here, I think. He was visiting the duchess. Is he still in London?”

“He runs a private asylum near Fulham. Lord Salperton’s a fine fellow, Anthony,” Treves said as he buttoned a set of brown braces to the waistband of the clean trousers. “There’s none more qualified in London, in my opinion.”

“Lord Salperton? I’ve never heard of that title. Is it English?”

“Welsh, actually,” he told Gehlen, “though it probably has Norman roots. It’s a relatively young viscountancy, but Salperton’s father is the Earl of Lasberington; which means old Scottish money. I hear he’s not doing well, so Henry’s likely to become Lord Lasberington before long. I’d be happy to ask him to consult, but it’s my understanding Henry will be at Branham over Christmas.”

“Then, you’ve spoken with him recently?”

“No, but Duke Charles is arranging to take Joseph Merrick to Kent on the twenty-third, and he’s asked Henry to keep an eye on our star resident during the visit. Lord Aubrey’s even offered to provide a private train for the journey. Joseph’s quite looking forward to it.”

The door opened, and a nurse with thick, silver hair worn in a tight rosette beneath a ribboned cap entered the lounge.

Treves had just finished buttoning the new collar. “Yes, Mrs. Aldershot?”

“Forgive the interruption, sir, as I see you’re trying to freshen up, but there’s trouble with Dr. Collins again.”

Treves sighed as he stared into the mirror, tying his cravat. “What now?”

“I’m afraid he’s trying to leap out the window, sir. Claims there’s a monster after him.”

“Another dragon?” the surgeon asked, only half joking.

“Not as he mentioned, sir, but he’s quite alarmed by this apparition all the same. He says it walked through the wall and threatened to eat his soul.”

Gehlen stood, leaving the empty cup on the side table. “I’ll go, Fred. You stay and enjoy another cup of coffee with the inspector.

Nice to meet you, France. Perhaps, we can share a meal at a later date and become better acquainted."

"I'd like that," replied Arthur.

Anthony left the lounge and followed the nurse down the busy corridor to a quieter section of the hospital; near the far east end of the ground floor. After passing the same men's ward where Blinkmire and Riga had recuperated from their castle fire injuries, and then the women's ward where Ida Ross and the other Castle Company ladies had slept, they finally stopped at a windowless door marked with a placard that read 'NO VISITORS'.

"Isn't there supposed to be a constable on guard here, Mrs. Aldershot?"

"Yes, sir, but he was called away to help the fire brigades."

They entered to find Alexander Collins standing on the narrow bed, dressed only in a white cotton sheet, which he'd wrapped round his midsection like a Roman toga. His arms were raised above his head whilst he shouted to the heavens about a blood-sucking monster with bat wings. The patient's eyes were round as pennies, and his cheeks an irregular patchwork of pallor and crimson beneath the dark beard. However, as soon as Gehlen entered the room, the distraught former head of Castor Institute immediately fell mute as though some unseen hand had sewn his lips shut. His face went slack, and he collapsed into the bed, both knees buckling beneath him.

He looked dead.

"Good heavens!" the nurse exclaimed as she rushed to the bedside. "Dr. Collins, can you hear me?" Putting her fingers to the carotid artery to find a pulse, she waited several seconds, then sighed in relief. "It's weak and quick, but it's there. Dr. Gehlen, could you lend a hand?"

The tall physician helped restore the collapsed patient to a semblance of order, and then drew a chair to the bedside. "If you'll leave us, Mrs. Aldershot, I'd like to examine the patient," he said sternly. "In private."

"But he can be quite dangerous, sir. I should fetch a porter, just in case he has another spell."

"Nonsense, all the porters are busy. Leave us alone, please. I'm capable of handling it from here."

Grudgingly, the nurse left and shut the door. Once on his own with the terrified patient, Gehlen spoke softly. "I want to help you,

Dr. Collins. Physician to physician. You're an important man, sir. Head of a great and modern mental health institute. Wouldn't you like to leave here and return to your former life?"

Collins tried desperately to speak, but the only sounds that escaped his throat were a series of indistinct gurgles. Anthony performed several diagnostic tests: reflexes, pupil size, hearing, ocular accommodation and object tracking.

"Dr. Collins, I believe you may have an undiagnosed brain tumour, which could explain your seizures and erratic fantasies. Tap the bed with any finger if you understand."

The patient's left forefinger very slowly moved, and he drummed twice against the mattress.

"Excellent. You clearly understand me, but I assume you're incapable of speech. Mr. Treves and I can help you with any organic cause, but just in case there is an underlying nervous condition, I'd like to have another man consult. His name's Henry MacAlpin. Tap again, if you understand me."

The finger drummed twice.

"Very good." Gehlen felt an odd chill run through his bones, and he thought he heard a chorus of whispers in dissonant pitches, mixed with a strident sort of chirping. Alexander's finger began to tap without prompting—slowly at first, and then wildly. Anthony feared the patient might be suffering another seizure, and he rose to call for the nurse, but then the tapping took on a recognisable pattern. He paused, staring at the moving finger.

"Can you do that again?" he asked Collins as he returned to the bed.

The tapping repeated, forming an identical series of movements. Some were quick; whilst others slower.

"Dots and dashes! You're using Morse's code, aren't you, Alexander? Sorry, mine's a bit rusty. I've not used it since Vienna. Can you give it to me once more? Let me find a bit of paper and a pencil."

The terrified patient gulped, his larynx completely frozen, but his mind clearer than it had been in weeks. Gehlen found a pad of paper and a wax pencil in the cabinet and returned to the bed. "Can you repeat the message for me?"

Collins's entire arm trembled, and his fingers seemed to spasm into knots. Anthony gently touched the terrified patient's left hand. "Be calm, Alexander. There's no rush."

Alexander Collins knew better. They had very little time at all. What Anthony Gehlen didn't see—what he could not perceive with natural eyes—was the woman standing at his left shoulder. She stared at Collins, speaking the most hideous, vile threats; repeating them again and again. And then she licked her ruby lips with a thick tongue, allowing it to slide hypnotically over her unnaturally sharp teeth. The woman wore a gown of diaphanous black, which caused her pale skin to take on an ethereal, pearlescent glow. Her right hand caressed Gehlen's hair, and the physician unconsciously reached up, as though he could feel it.

"He doesn't see me," the woman told Collins. "But you do. Have you been naughty, Alexander? Must we discipline you again?"

The patient's entire body began to spasm now, as though suffering a *grand mal* seizure. Gehlen instinctively searched the adjacent cabinet for a tongue depressor, which he then placed in the victim's mouth, forcing it 'twixt the top and bottom teeth. Every private room and ward had a locked cabinet containing prepared tinctures, amalgams, tablets, powders, and elixirs; ready for emergencies. Gehlen used his key to obtain a vial of a high-potassium solution, which he measured into a small glass. He then threw open the door and shouted into the corridor for help. A porter and a young trainee nurse came running.

"Hold him down," he ordered the porter. "Your name, Miss?"

"Augusta Hill, sir," the pretty girl answered. "He's Mr. Samuels."

"Samuels, keep a tight hold on the man whilst I prise his teeth apart. Miss Hill, when I say so, you're to slowly pour this liquid down his throat. Do you understand?"

"Yes, sir. I think so."

Both did as ordered, and the anticonvulsant slowly trickled down Collins's esophagus and into his stomach. It would take several minutes to take effect, but Anthony didn't dare risk an injection. If the man had undiagnosed cardiovascular problems, the intense rush of potassium could kill him.

Ten minutes passed, and the medicine slowly helped the muscles to relax. Hill had never seen an epileptic seizure before, and she found it terrifying. Martin Samuels had seen nearly every condition known to man, and he did his job efficiently without comment.

"Thank you, both," Gehlen said once Collins had calmed. "Samuels, I'd like you to stay, but Miss Hill, you may leave us. I'm sure there are other patients who require you."

The slightly built girl left, and Anthony fell into a chair, exhausted. The porter remained standing. "What can you tell me of Dr. Collins's recent activities, Mr. Samuels?"

"Well, sir, he don't make much sense most o' the time. Always mutterin' like he's talkin' with someone. I never see nobody else about, though. He weren't like this when he first come. Just since the past few days, somethin's changed. Like he's gone round the bend. Some of the nurses, they don't like comin' in here. They're afraid o' what he might do. One even claimed she seen a ghost."

Gehlen's head began to pound, and an odd ringing sensation overtook his ears. *I'm just tired and hungry*, he told himself. "A ghost?"

"Some woman in a black night dress. Claimed this here woman was bendin' over Collins like as she were kissin' him on the throat."

The invisible wraith in black boldly leaned down and whispered erotic suggestions into the doctor's ear, and then ran her tongue along Gehlen's cheek, causing him to jump. Something in his mind summoned up the image of a voluptuous female with dark eyes and blood red lips. He shook off the idea, and Serena di Specchio laughed hoarsely.

"Do you not yearn for my caresses, sweet Anthony?" she whispered to him from the shadows.

Collins may not be the only one who's going mad, the troubled physician thought.

The patient had fallen into a light sleep, and Gehlen remained for several minutes, watching for warning signs of stroke. Satisfied that the crisis was over, he rose to his feet, his balance growing slightly wobbly for a moment.

"You all right, Doc?" asked Samuels.

"Yes, just tired. If anyone asks, I'm going back to my room at the residence hall across the park. Remain here as long as possible, Samuels. If you must leave for any reason, ask one of the nurses to assign another to replace you."

Wearily, the confused Gehlen left the hospital room, in complete ignorance of the merciless Shade that followed behind.

CHAPTER EIGHTEEN

The Wychwright rites ended at half past twelve, and by two that afternoon, nearly one hundred and fifty peers, publishers, and parliamentarians gathered at the Earl of Cartringham's stylish mansion on Grosvenor Crescent in Belgravia to enjoy a light meal, console the grieving family, and make endless small talk. A few dared to discuss the hideous details of the late baron's murder, but these hushed conversations took place within quiet corners, out of sight and hearing of the widow and her children.

As he and Elizabeth arrived for the wake, Sinclair was met by A-Division's Detective Inspector Fraser, who informed the duke of the Whitechapel fire. The news struck Charles hard, for he'd served with nearly all of the policemen who responded—two of whom had now died. He also knew many of the dockworkers and local merchants. He asked Fraser if Reid or France mentioned a need for reinforcements. Did they require anything that the ICI might provide? Manpower, medicine, waggons, blankets, clothing? The inspector had no immediate answer but promised to apprise the duke should he gain further information. Sinclair very nearly asked Granger to take him across town immediately, but decided against it when he recalled Bleeding Jack's dreadful rhymes which implied danger to his wife; but also Romanov's warning to keep close to her during the Christmas season.

He and Fraser also discussed Alexander Collins and the odd case of Bleeding Jack Nobody; though Charles said nothing of the man's rambling threats. Fraser promised to look into the madman's true identity. Charles quickly scribbled a telegram to Treves, saying he'd call on him after the wake. He sent the telegram with the inspector to transmit from A-Division's station house.

By the time Charles finished, he'd completely lost sight of his wife. Assuming she'd gone inside with Aubrey and Cordelia, the duke entered the bustling foyer and was immediately waylaid by two cabinet members, intent on divining the influential young peer's opinion on the current state of Irish rebellion and how it might be related to Jack the Ripper, of all things! This led to an unsatisfyingly intense conversation on the topic of Scotland Yard, and most particularly Special Branch, which delayed him for another quarter hour. What did Haimsbury think of Patrick MacAllen's tenure as branch head? Had he done enough to stem the Fenian tide? Finally, after extricating himself from the annoying parliamentarians, he started to look for Beth in the drawing rooms. As he neared the first, he bumped into his host.

"Ah, Haimsbury, there you are! We'd wondered what happened to you."

"Hello again, Lord Cartringham. Have you seen the duchess?"

The Earl of Cartringham had a pleasant face with dumpling cheeks and mischievous eyes in nutmeg brown. Despite having considerable influence in Parliament, he seldom frowned, like most ministers did. In fact, he was known far and wide as a man of constant mirth and good cheer.

"Elizabeth? She's here somewhere," the earl answered. "As you can imagine, Charles, the lady is much in demand, with nearly everyone hoping to bend her shell-like ear. Poor thing's always had to swat them away like flies, you know. Suitors and solicitors alike. You'll soon discover that being a duke is like wearing catnip round your neck, old bean. And having the queen's friendship only adds to the allure. Congratulations, by the way. Couldn't have happened to a nicer fellow!"

"Thank you, Basil. That's kind of you. Might Beth be in one of the drawing rooms?"

"Now, let me think," mused Cartringham, his dumpling cheeks puffing out as he spoke. "She was talking with my wife, and then she had a few words with the Dowager Baroness—my sister-in-law, you know. Bad business, all that, Charles. I do hope you find the man that murdered poor old David."

"We're following every lead, which to be honest, are scant at best. I cannot say more, you understand."

"Yes, of course, but why leave the man like *that*, Charles? Trussed up and stuffed into a cabinet without a shred of clothing or an ounce of dignity! Seems the sort of thing anarchists might do. Russian influence, I should think."

"Why would the Russians do that?" asked the duke.

"To sow discord, of course. It's their *raison d'être*, isn't it?"

"Being with the War Office, I fear you're more an expert on anarchists and Russians than I, Basil. My wife?"

"Ah, yes," the earl continued as a footman passed bearing a tray of minced lamb sandwiches, cut into quarters. Cartringham took two and began munching on one of the crustless triangles.

"Now, why is it that our cook insists on adding butter to these? Horseradish! That's what makes lamb sing, isn't it? Nothing like a dollop of horseradish to liven up a meal. You'll want to let your cook know about that, Charles. Most women think butter and a limp leaf of cress are all you need to make a sandwich, but it's horseradish that gives it body. Nothing else to match it, pure and simple!"

Passersby kept jostling Sinclair's right elbow, and he decided to avoid taking a drink until the congested space cleared a little. "I'll be sure to tell them. You thought you might know where the duchess had gone, Basil."

"Did I? Ah, yes, so I did! Well, let's see," the absent-minded peer pondered, wiping breadcrumbs from his peppery moustache. "Beth. Now where did I see her? Oh, yes! It was Lord Aubrey. He got sidelined by a shabbily dressed fellow; an assistant to Superintendent Dunlap from A-Division, I think. Just between us, I find detectives quite tiresome, don't you? Well, perhaps, you don't, but as their offices are just a quick hop from mine, I run into them every day. Suspicious lot! Leery of everyone and utterly useless in my opinion, and don't get me started on Patrick MacAllen and his Special Branch ruffians! No offence, I hope. Nothing personal, Charles. I never think of you as one of them. You're a breath of fresh air; far different from most of those Yard fellows, but now—where was I?"

"My wife?" asked the duke patiently.

"Yes, yes, I was getting to that. She mentioned feeling a bit tired, didn't she? Seems like I overheard Aubrey suggest she retreat to a quiet spot. I'd try the white library, if I were you. Second left, just past the music room. You can't miss it."

After thanking his host, Charles turned back towards the main corridor, but found himself face-to-face with a rotund man in a stylishly antiquarian, Regency suit.

"Well, if it isn't our new Duke of Haimsbury!" Reginald Parsons proclaimed merrily. "As you can see, I'm rubbing elbows with the elite, as always, Your Grace. I wonder if I might have a quiet word when you've a moment to spare?"

Somehow, the House of Lords clerk's sudden appearance made an odd kind of sense to the seasoned detective. With the day getting busier by the minute and news of a dockside fire, a visit from Parsons seemed the most natural thing in all the world. "I should have known you'd be here, Parsons. As you're privy to nearly everything in Westminster, I wonder if you might know where my wife is?"

"I believe I do," the apple-cheeked clerk grinned impishly. "I'd be pleased to escort you to that dear lady, and perhaps we might have that word whilst we walk."

Still nearby, Cartringham had finished the last crumb of a third sandwich (cress and tuna spread without so much as a hint of horseradish), which he then washed down with an entire glass of port. He set the empty glass on a table and clapped Sinclair on the shoulder amiably. "I see Reggie's already wormed his way into your confidence, eh, Haimsbury? Well, he always does. If that 'quiet word' I overheard him mention has anything to do with the Whitechapel fire, I'd be interested in hearing more."

"Inspector Fraser told me about it," Charles replied. "I understand it may have started on a Russian ship. Reggie, what have you heard?"

"Probably not much more than you, my lord, but the damage is said to be considerable. Over twenty dead and hundreds in hospital. The London is overstretched, and their governors have asked the Prime Minister for emergency aid. I'd expect a special meeting of the privy council to be called tomorrow, which will include you, sir. Of course, if Captain Shaw determines the cause is arson, then this may all fall into your lap, Lord Cartringham. If a Russian ship deliberately ignited the blaze, the War Office will have to respond."

"Russians! Damn those fellows!" grumbled the plump earl with uncharacteristic irritation. "This sort of provocation will not go over well on Downing Street, sir. The War Office desks are overflowing, as you well know. If Captain Shaw thinks the Russians are behind an attack on our port security and commerce, then it will echo throughout the entire government! I only pray it doesn't come to that."

"Tell me, Basil," Charles asked, "if Shaw does rule this as arson by a foreign power, then how would you go about dealing with Russia? Surely, it isn't cause for war."

"Now, that gets us into very murky waters, Commissioner, and I use your professional title now as it's likely you'll be involved, should war be considered. My office confers with a gentleman of considerable influence in St. Petersburg. He's generally on England's side in these matters, though inscrutable. I shall introduce you."

"Might his name be Prince Anatole Romanov, by any chance?" asked Haimsbury.

This took both men by surprise, until Reggie Parsons began to laugh. "How could I forget, Your Grace? Apparently, my large head is simply too overstuffed with other information and details that it's crowded out all else! The prince is a friend to your family, isn't he, sir? He and the Duke of Edinburgh hosted a costume ball in your honour, in fact."

"My wife and I are happy to call the prince friend," Charles answered without explaining further. "If it's not seen as interfering with the War Office, I can speak with him regarding the fire. Just say the word. Until then, I really must find my wife. Reggie, did you wish to speak to me of anything else?"

"Oh, yes, but a minor matter only," Parsons assured him gently. "Come this way, sir."

The garrulous clerk guided his captive away from the drawing rooms, passing through gossiping gaggles of nominal mourners, and towards the northern portion of the home. Their progress was impeded multiple times by jubilant well-wishers ('Congratulations on the new title, Haimsbury!') or questions regarding the Wychwright murder investigation ('Haven't you arrested anyone yet, Commissioner? I hear it's Russians behind it all.')

A few had heard news of the fire, and these pressed him for information regarding the new Intelligence Branch and its possible responses. The efficient Parsons deflected every question by redirecting the enquirer towards juicier gossip: rumours of tax levies on imports from South America, the current banking crisis, or the Irish

Problem, which invariably caused the persistent parliamentarians to devolve into arguments with their nearest neighbours.

At last, the pair arrived at a small, white-panelled library, and Parsons shut the doors to ensure privacy. "We've only a little time, Your Grace, but I have a message for you from a lady known to us both. I shall refer to her from this point forward as 'Lady Stuart', as that is the moniker by which she is always known when visiting your family."

"Lady Stuart?" asked Haimsbury.

"In honour of her dearest and oldest friend. I refer, of course, to your good uncle, Duke James. Lady Stuart was unable to attend the funeral services, but asked me to convey this to you." Parsons withdrew a small white envelope from his coat pocket and passed it to the duke.

Charles broke the wax seal on the flap and opened the contents, finding a pale blue sheet of paper, overwritten with black ink in a fine hand:

> My Dearest Charles,
>
> How I wish I could be there today, but I'm seldom allowed at funerals. However, if all is well, then I shall join you at Branham for our little Christmas celebration. I look forward to seeing you again, my dear. Remember, I want no special treatment, for my fondest wish is to spend Christmas as nothing more than your friend and relative.
>
> Until then, I remain your greatest admirer,
>
> – Lady Alexandrina Stuart
>
> PS – May I say again just how dashing a duke you make, my dear 'cousin'? The new coronet suits you, but perhaps a royal 'crown' would be even better?
>
> - Much love, D.

Charles smiled at the postscript. "Have you read this?"

"No, but I'm aware of the content; or most of it, at least. I take it that all is well at Branham?"

"So far as I know," replied the duke.

"Ah, well, that's a blessing! I'd heard rumours that a sort of antiquarian survey is taking place there. Lady Stuart wouldn't wish to interfere with any important activities."

"How do you know about that?" the duke asked, realising almost at once that the inquisitive man in the ageless suit knew everything that affected his queen. "The duchess approved a survey of Lion Hall, if you must know, but it's my understanding their activities will end on Saturday. However, I've asked our estate heads to make sure everything is secure on the Branham grounds for the lady's visit. We've distributed a list of approved persons to all the men, and only those on the list will be permitted through the gates."

Parson's ample cheeks rounded in delight. "How thorough of you, my lord! I'd told Lady Stuart that you would see to the arrangements for her safety. The lady also asked me to remind you that she hopes to travel there on the twenty-third. Is that possible?"

"She and I've already discussed that, Reggie. I'll come to London to escort her, personally. We'll use one of the Aubrey trains, which are secure and very comfortable. And I've arranged for her constant protection, both during the journey, and whilst at Branham; armed agents with years of experience. *Circle* members, if you appreciate that statement."

"Oh, yes, I do indeed, my lord," the clerk grinned. "I most certainly do."

"Yes, I thought you might. Tell my good lady 'cousin' that she will be as safe with us as in her very own home. Now, if there's nothing else, you promised to take me to my wife. Sometime this year would be nice."

Parsons chuckled, his grey eyes looking youthful and mischievous. "I do enjoy your wry sense of humour, Your Grace. I believe we'll find that dear lady in this direction."

Parsons opened the library's main door to the corridor. As they exited, they ran headlong into their hostess, Lady Margaret Simpson, the Countess Cartringham, who took the duke by the arm.

"There you are Charles! Whatever are you and Parsons up to? I noticed you in a *tête-à-tête* with some poorly dressed man earlier. A policeman by the look of him."

"I'm a policeman, if you'll recall, Lady Cartringham. Do I have that look?"

She giggled coquettishly. "No, of course not! You are a bespoke vision, my dear, with the finest fashion sense of any man I know. But it's a dreadful worry, you see, having police business conducted on one's own doorstep. Was it about that awful fire? Everyone's talking about it," she said, cooling her face with a black silk fan. "I've heard hundreds of people have died!"

"Not nearly so many, but hundreds are injured, and the fire's out, praise God. Sadly, I may need to leave early to survey the damage," Sinclair answered.

"My dear friend, when do you ever have time for yourself?"

"It grows rarer by the day, but even a minute in my wife's company is enough to cheer me. Talking of police matters, I want you to know we're doing everything possible to find your brother-in-law's murderer, Lady Cartringham."

"Margaret," she reminded him.

"Ah, yes, Margaret," he repeated, offering her a dimpled smile. "This is certainly a fine turnout. Are these Parliament wakes always so well attended?"

"Oh yes, but our numbers seem to have doubled since leaving the church," she replied, touching his forearm. "That's often how these occasions go. Once word leaks out, all manner of intruders burst through the doors! As poor David's murder remains unsolved, the lure to such brash individuals is all the more tantalising, I shouldn't wonder. Honestly, I don't know most of the people in the corridors."

Parsons snatched a square of spiced raisin cake from a footman's tray. "I fear some of those unfamiliar faces are reporters, Lady Cartringham. Shall I encourage them to find other homes to visit?"

"Oh, now that is kind of you, Reggie, but it's best to let them lurk about," the countess answered. "Reporters are a necessary evil to Parliament. No press means no public opinion, and no public opinion impacts elections. Such a sudden lack of interest would grind most MPs into dust, I fear. Oh, it is awfully crowded!" she added, the fan blowing loose tendrils of her chestnut hair. "I cannot imagine my sister hosting this turnout in her small house, can you? And her poor, poor husband! Why *ever* would someone wish to kill him, Charles? And in such an embarrassing manner!"

The clerk interrupted before Sinclair could offer a reply. "Do forgive me, dear friends, but I see Lord Bosworth just leaving the music room. I really must have a word." Parsons bowed and then expertly cajoled his way upstream through the noisy crowd.

"He's an odd sort of fellow, isn't he?" Sinclair observed.

"Yes, but Reggie's the sort of fellow one needs to make sense of government riddles, Charles. Congratulations on your new title, by the way. Duke of Haimsbury suits you very well, I think. And may I say that you and Elizabeth make a splendid looking couple? You really do."

"That's kind of you to say, Margaret. I've been trying to find my wife for half an hour. Have you seen her, by any chance?"

"She was talking with Lord Aubrey and my niece in the conservatory earlier. Or at least, I believe Cordelia's with them. Poor little thing! She's like a lost lamb these days. Delia simply adored her father, Charles, and he positively doted on her. This has all been very difficult for her, especially after that dreadful business in Whitechapel."

"Has she told you much about that?" the detective asked.

"Nothing specific, but it's clear she endured something quite awful. I've tried to draw her out, but she simply won't discuss it. I fear the experience has changed her into a shadow of her former self. Have you investigated it?"

"I was, but her mother insisted I discontinue. The dowager baroness claims she's protecting Cordelia from public scrutiny, but I have my doubts. It's quite frustrating, for it goes against all my instincts; both as a policeman and a gentleman."

Lady Cartringham showed marked surprise. "My sister told you to stop? Why?"

"She mentioned a need for privacy."

"But, Charles, if this man did assault Cordelia, then he broke the law. Isn't it up to you to decide whether or not to investigate? It's not up to Connie, surely."

"I'm afraid there was little evidence that cannot be otherwise explained. Delia admitted going with this man willingly, and the witnesses at the boxing match claim she appeared happy in his company."

"She was hardly that! You call him 'this man', but we both know his identity, Charles. Delia's named him. Sir Albert Wendaway."

"So she's said, but Wendaway is nowhere to be found. And even if we did arrest him, we'd require Delia's testimony at the trial.

Her mother refuses to allow that, and if we cannot rely on Cordelia as a witness, then we cannot obtain a conviction," he told her as a footman squeezed past, balancing a tray of empty glasses. "It seems I'm in everyone's way, Margaret. The conservatory is where?"

"Back of the house. To the right, then through the big doors," she said, pointing towards an east-west corridor. A second footman walked past, and the countess called his name. "Andrew, would you show the duke to the conservatory, please? I'd take you, Charles, but I have to keep watch for my sister. She disappeared half and hour ago with a pair of backbenchers from Cumbria. I'm worried about her, if you must know, for she isn't grieving properly. I know people think her somewhat callous, but she is my only sibling. Blood matters, you know. If you see her, would you send her to me?"

"Of course," he answered, following the footman down the corridor.

As with other mansions on the square, the Cartringham's London home sprawled upwards rather than to the sides. Ignoring the frontage limitations, the large conservatory jutted out towards the back gardens and was filled with fragrant orange and lemon trees, interspersed with graceful *spathiphyllum*, known commonly as the 'peace lily', placed oddly next to *sansevieria*, often called the 'snake plant'. In each corner, marble busts representing the four winds watched from fluted pillars. Through the conservatory's three glass walls, guests could enjoy beds of flowering viburnum, bordered in evergreen boxwood. In the middle of these subservient flowerbeds, reigned the Cartringham's folly: a domed limestone building with a marble-pillared portico, dressed with wrought iron tables and matching chairs. It looked a bit like a small Greek mausoleum, softened over time by the incursion of climbing trumpet vines, soft green lichen, and thorny wild roses.

Just past the music room, Charles overheard a familiar voice coming from a narrow hallway near the smoking parlour. It was Cordelia Wychwright, clearly upset, being scolded by a tall man with light hair and a pencil-thin moustache. His harsh tone caused the duke to divert his path and interrupt.

"Cordelia, is everything all right?" Sinclair asked.

The man with the moustache turned towards the perceived intruder, his face lengthening in frank outrage. "Just who the hell are you?" he asked Charles pointedly. "Is this another of your fancy men, Delia?"

The young baron hadn't met Sinclair at the church, for Henry and Charles arrived late and were forced to sit towards the back. Thoroughly embarrassed by the scene, poor Cordelia had no chance to explain or even reply, for her cold-hearted brother scarcely took a breath before he continued the litany of charges against her.

"Do you hear me?" he bellowed at his pale sister. "Your brazen behaviour brings shame upon our home and a curse upon our family name. Father may have tolerated your wild wantonness, Cordelia Jane, but I will not."

"Please, William, you're embarrassing me," she pleaded, wishing she could drink the entire bottle of Gehlen's elixir and disappear forever into a deep, dreamless sleep.

"I'm embarrassing *you?*" the baron shrieked. "You can stand there, in your deplorable state, and suggest that to me?"

"Will, please!" she whispered. "I can't bear this."

Charles took her arm. "Come, Delia, let's go."

"Get your money-grubbing paws off my sister, or else explain yourself to the police!" the baron dared to shout. "You should be in prison from all I hear."

"I suggest keeping your voice down, Lord Wychwright," Charles warned him.

"I suppose you'd like that, wouldn't you? Let you keep your dirty little secrets and ungentlemanly behaviour quiet? You're the one's gotten her into this mess in this first place. If it turns out she's in trouble, then it's your fault!"

"Will, please, stop! You're making an awful mistake," the girl pleaded, weeping.

"Am I? The only mistake I'm making is tolerating this bounder for even a moment. Why do you defend him, Delia? He's made you little better than a whore, and I wish you weren't my sister," he seethed. "In fact, it's probably because of your wanton behaviour that Father is dead!"

"*That is enough!*" Charles shouted, placing himself twixt Cordelia and her brother. "Wychwright, you will apologise to this woman immediately, or else you can explain it to me outside."

"How dare you, sir!" the army captain spat back angrily, his eyes boring into Sinclair's as he stepped closer. "After what you did to my sister, Wendaway, it's a wonder you dare show your face amongst decent men. Outside works very well with me, sir. Very well indeed. Name the place and time!"

"William, you've no idea whom you're addressing!" cried Delia.

"Don't I? Sir Albert Wendaway, of course. The parasitic paramour that's taken advantage of your womanly generosity. That much is clear by the way he defends you!"

"I am not Wendaway, Lord Wychwright, and I suggest you lower your voice before I lower it for you," Sinclair ordered, now nose to nose with the lower-ranking peer. "I defend this woman, because she has need of it. And Cordelia is now and always has been a lady. Always. Your harsh accusations speak more of your nature than hers."

"I'll show you harshness," the baron whispered, his eyes narrowing into cruel slits. Despite being three inches shorter than Sinclair, William Wychwright clearly thought himself the bigger man.

Charles's right hand clenched, itching to connect with the man's face, but he counted to three before replying in a calm whisper. "I suggest you compose yourself, Baron, before you make too great a meal on that enormous foot inside your elitist mouth."

"How dare you speak to me in such a way!" Wychwright shouted. "Do you have any idea who I am? Of what I'm capable? I'd be pleased to teach you the same lesson many a raw recruit learns on his first day in Egypt, sir! I say again: name the time and place, and I shall make good on that promise!"

Charles smiled, and it was that cold, confident smile that finally sent a chill down the baron's spine. "That would be a *deadly* mistake, Baron. You've no idea of what I am capable. If you wish to test your assumptions, then I'd be pleased to offer a lesson of my own. Right now."

"Oh, I see you've met," came a sensible voice to the back of the tense confrontation. "Charles, Elizabeth is asking for you."

Cordelia Wychwright had paled to the colour of writing paper and looked as though she might collapse. "Paul, please, take me into the garden."

Delia's brother had fallen completely mute. The revelation that the influential Scottish earl had called this presumed bounder *'Charles'* had set the army captain to thinking.

"I say, Aubrey, is this fellow a friend of yours? If so, I may have gotten the wrong end of the stick."

"I'd assumed you two met at the church, William," the earl answered with disarming friendliness. "Allow me to introduce you to Commissioner Charles Sinclair, 1st Duke of Haimsbury. Charles is my first cousin and recently married Elizabeth."

"*Duke?* Oh. Well, I mean..." Wychwright blustered, doing his best to appear unfazed. "I pray you'll forgive the presumption, Haimsbury. I've clearly misunderstood completely. You see, I'd been speaking with my sister about this Wendaway person, a rakish fellow who's dogged her steps of late. He's a man who needs a good thrashing, actually, and I mistakenly assumed you were he, when you came to her defence. Do forgive the blunder."

"Considering that you're grieving, Lord Wychwright, I'll let it pass, *this time*," Charles answered, making it clear that the man's left-handed apology was understood for what it really was: weak and insincere. "Delia, why don't you come with us? You and Beth can enjoy one another's company whilst the earl and I discuss a business matter. Paul, is that all right with you?"

"Yes, certainly," Stuart answered. "I'm sure Delia could use some time off her feet. You're looking pale again," he whispered to her. "Beth's in the conservatory, Charles. Delia can show you the way. I'll catch up momentarily, and we'll have that talk."

The duke left with Lady Cordelia on his arm, but Aubrey remained. Paul waited until he and the insolent army captain were alone before speaking again. Standing toe to toe with the foolish baron, the Scotsman's cool blue eyes took on a focused expression intense enough to cut the strongest steel.

"Hear me well, Captain. If you *ever* mistreat your sister again, I will drag your worthless carcass from whatever bed or brothel it's in and when I've finished with it, leave the lifeless remains where no one will ever find it; food for crows. Test me, if you dare, for it would be your last act upon this earth."

Aubrey allowed a beat to pass before he turned to leave. The baron offered no reply, but once the earl had gone, he smashed his fist into the nearest wall, scraping off skin and leaving bloody marks on the silk paper. As if summoned by magic, a muscular man with long dark hair and ice-blue eyes appeared behind him in the quiet corridor. The stranger used a scarlet handkerchief to wipe the warm blood from the enraged baron's hand.

"Aubrey can be such a bully," the newcomer whispered seductively as he tended to the wound.

Suspicious, embarrassed, and growing evermore angry, Wychwright pushed against the tall stranger. "Who the devil are you?"

The handsome man smiled, unruffled by the rebuff. "The right kind of devil, Captain. Only the right kind. Now, let me clean up that blood."

CHAPTER NINETEEN

Charles Sinclair and Cordelia Wychwright arrived in the conservatory and found it alive with many dozens of boisterous individuals who'd apparently come there for 'a quiet conversation'. The duchess sat on the far side of the enormous glassed garden, close to a cheerful fireplace, dealing with two very talkative businessmen.

"Forgive me, Cordelia, but do you know either of those men with my wife?" he asked the ingénue.

"They don't look familiar," she said, her face pale, eyes listless. She'd taken three doses of laudanum by now and felt rather sleepy. "Am I supposed to call you Duke or Your Grace? I'm a bit confused for some reason, and I can't seem to think."

"Call me Charles," he said sweetly. "Come now, let's find you a seat. You look ready to fall down."

He located the last two empty chairs and set them against a relatively quiet spot near a side door. "Wait here and I'll fetch you a glass of punch," he said, touching her hands compassionately. In response, Cordelia grasped his fingers, clutching at them as though drowning.

"Please, don't leave me alone!" she begged the duke. "I'm afraid to be alone."

Sitting once more, he placed his hands round hers, noting their coolness. "That's a natural reaction, Delia. You're grieving, and the manner of your father's death would unsettle anyone. You've been through a great deal in the past fortnight."

She began to cry. "Mother says I must forget about it, but I can't, Charles. I can't! I keep reliving it. William is right. I'm ruined. What am I to do?" Weeping without restraint, she let her head drop against his shoulder.

"Delia, will you tell me what Wendaway did to you that night? I want to arrest him, but I need evidence. Allow me to help you, please."

"I can't. Don't ask me! Mother says we must leave him alone, even though he... He...!" The weeping became heavy sobs, and her entire body shook.

Sinclair wondered how to name such a terrible act. Gehlen had sent Charles the full report of the physical findings of Cordelia's case, and the thigh bruising and vaginal tears were consistent with sexual assault, possibly attempted rape, but her intact hymen indicated the attempt had failed.

"Delia, dear, what happened isn't your fault. You are an innocent. Did Wendaway try to force you?"

This caused a raging torrent of tears, and she found it impossible to speak, but managed to nod. For Charles, that was enough.

"I'll take care of it," he promised. "Sir Albert will face justice. None of this is your fault. None."

"But I was foolish enough to go with him," she whispered.

"And Albert was responsible for you, Delia. It was his duty to protect you. Instead, he took advantage of your innocence. He is to blame. Not you."

She looked up, her eyes swollen and red. "What if someone else is to blame?"

"What do you mean?"

"Perhaps, someone who coerced him."

"Coerced?"

"Yes, prompted him to do that to me. Paid him, I mean. The same person who may even be behind Father's murder," she continued, trembling all over. "Oh, it's the worst sort of nightmare! Surely, she didn't. She couldn't!"

"*She?* Delia, what are you saying?"

The young woman reached into her pocketbook and withdrew the nearly empty elixir bottle. Her hands shook, making the simple task of removing the stopper a major challenge. "Why can't I do this!" she cried in despair.

Charles took the bottle and examined the typed label:

TINCTURE OF OPIUM IN ELDERFLOWER WATER. ONE TSP. AT NIGHT FOR SLEEP.

NOT TO EXCEED 2 TSP. PER DAY.
– ANTHONY GEHLEN, M.D., F.R.C.S.

"Delia, how much of this have you taken?"

"I don't know. Mother told me to take a second dose before the funeral, and I may have taken another when we arrived here. I'm not sure."

"And before that? Did you take any this morning?"

She nodded. "I took some before my bath, I think. Oh, but I shouldn't talk of baths in front of a gentleman. But then, I'm no longer a lady, am I? Not after what happened."

"Sorry to keep you waiting," a pleasant voice interrupted. "I had to deal with a vermin problem." Aubrey had the look of a man who intended to settle an old score with an enemy. Charles understood completely, but now was not the time. Cordelia required protection first.

"I pray you've not broken the law, Cousin."

"Not yet. Shall we have that talk?"

"In a little while. First, I want to visit with Beth, if you'll stay with Delia." He still held the elixir bottle and decided against returning it, fearing she might overdose. "Delia, I'm going to give this to the earl for safekeeping. Do you understand?"

"Yes, I suppose so. Is it warm in here?"

"Paul, make sure she takes no more of this. From what I can tell, she's already exceeded the daily amount by two doses. I'll say a quick hello to Beth, and then we'll meet in, say, half an hour?"

"Yes, of course," the earl replied, as he sat beside Cordelia. "I'll be here, whenever you're ready."

The duke wove his way through the dense crowd, offering polite smiles to wives and daughters of government officials who somehow managed to insinuate themselves into his personal space at the oddest of moments. One was a bright-eyed girl of seventeen or so, whom he recognised as the youngest daughter of Lord Castlereigh. Her father had hosted one of the Kent County balls the previous month.

"Pardon me," Sinclair whispered as he tried to move past.

"Pardon you for what, Your Grace?" she giggled, her full lips blushing hues of pink. "It's my fault entirely."

"Not at all," he told her automatically, his eyes on his wife. "If you'll excuse me, Lady Louise..."

"You remember my name!" she gushed, inching closer. "Perhaps our dance last month made a stronger impression than I dared imagine."

"Ah, yes, our dance. Yes, it was quite—memorable. If you'll excuse me, Lady Louise, my wife is waiting. Just over there." He pointed towards the duchess, whose attention was dominated by the persistent gentlemen, currently bending her ear.

"I'd forgotten you and the duchess had already married. Such a pity. But she's talking with my cousins just now. William and Wallace Abernathy. They're not twins, of course, but only ten months apart; so Irish twins, I suppose. They operate a textile factory in Newcastle. I believe they're talking to her about investments."

"Is that so? How interesting. Again, if you'll excuse me," he repeated, wedging his way past her.

The Abernathy brothers rose to their feet as the duke arrived. They had strikingly similar appearances, though subtle differences emerged after a few minutes' concentrated effort. William, the elder, had a habit of sucking his back teeth as if they pained him, and his squinting eyes were different colours: the left more of a greenish-blue in contrast to its hazel partner. His lips were thin and asymmetric towards the left, giving him a permanent smirk. His ears were low and round, and his chin weak and smooth, as though incapable of sprouting any hair at all.

Wallace, on the other hand, had matching eyes; both hazel, both constantly blinking. His lips skewed in a jagged fashion, rather like a Jack-O-Lantern's. He'd made a feeble attempt at a chin beard, which grew in a patchwork of auburn and yellow. Neither brother had seen thirty winters, but both looked far older.

William reached out to shake Sinclair's hand. "You must be the Duke of Haimsbury," he declared in a thick, Northumberland accent. "It's a distinct pleasure, sir. A distinct pleasure, indeed! I'm Will, and this poor excuse for a mourner is my younger brother, Wallace. And before you ask, we are indeed named for the Scottish hero, William Wallace. A Scottish mother, you see. But we're not rebels. Not yet, at least!" he added, laughing at his own joke. "My brother and I've been speaking with your good wife regarding plans to extend our manufacturing business into London. The East End, to be exact, and we're very interested in a property she owns there."

"I see," the duke replied as he took the chair vacated by William. He kissed his wife's cheek. "I'm sorry to keep you waiting, little one."

Elizabeth smiled brightly as he took her hand. "You're here now, Captain. That's all that matters."

"What's this about a property in the East?" he asked her.

"There is none. Mr. Abernathy is mistaken," she replied. "We do own two warehouses on Mansell, but neither is for sale. I've been telling these gentlemen that for quarter of an hour. Besides, a wake is hardly the place for business discussions."

"We'd give you a fair price for them, Duchess," William insisted. "The location meets all our needs. Doesn't it, Wallace?"

"It certainly does, William," the other agreed, his Jack-O-Lantern mouth screwing into the facsimile of an unsettling grin.

Charles answered for his wife. "Gentlemen, if you wish to visit with us regarding this matter *after* Christmastide, we'd be pleased to do so." He handed the elder brother a calling card. "Speak with my secretary, and he'll arrange a time. Now, if you'll excuse us?"

The tone in his voice made it clear that Charles had no intention of speaking further on the matter, but the younger brother refused to take the hint.

"Five minutes is all we ask, sir. We've the best of intentions, I assure you."

"Then, you'll not object to waiting 'til January," Haimsbury answered. "As I said, speak to my man. His name is Gerald Pennyweather, and he's available at Queen Anne House twixt ten and four. Good day, gentlemen."

Shrugging, the persistent pair reluctantly departed, and Charles noticed that they stopped to collect their obtrusive young cousin, Lady Louise, before exiting the conservatory.

"This is supposed to be a wake?" he sighed as he took his wife's hand. "The invitation called it a small gathering of bereaved friends and family, but it looks more like a soirée. Beth, why are you sitting out here all alone? I'd assumed you'd remain with Paul."

"He's been busy doing other things, and I've hardly been alone, Charles," she answered. "After you wandered off with your detective friend, Paul suggested I find a quiet place to relax, and so brought me out here for a breath of air. Before long, a dozen people followed, and then another dozen after that. I've been hosting business proposals ever since. Apparently, someone has told the bankers and factory owners of England that I'm building a hospital in Whitechapel. The Abernathy brothers run a cotton mill and thought to curry favour with me by offering to donate cloth for bed coverings, uniforms, and the like. In exchange, they hope to pay a pittance for our warehouses."

"Clearly, they underestimate you, but if you wish my input, I'm happy to offer it. Where are these warehouses?"

"Not far from Leman Street police station, on Mansell. We own two of the three on that block. The third goes under the hammer next month for unpaid taxes. The estate agency representing the Crown has offered me first right of refusal, providing we make the right offer. If we can buy it at a reasonable price, then we could transform the entire block into the new hospital complex."

"And these textile merchants also intend to bid for that building?" he asked.

"So, it would seem. Charles, I know it's asking a lot of you, but I'd like to tour the building as soon as possible. Mr. Pinchin, the estate agent, says he can meet me at ten o'clock the Friday after Christmas. The twenty-eighth. It would mean coming back to London for a day, but we could be back at Branham by five or so. Do you think you might go with me? This hospital is sorely needed, Charles, and the sooner it's built the better. I've overheard the ministers whispering about a terrible fire at St. Katherine's. All the area's hospitals and infirmaries are overstretched. Don't you see? Such tragedies make it imperative that we build this hospital right away!"

"Yes, of course. I admire your fervor, darling, but I cannot promise about the twenty-eighth. Let me take a look at my diary, and I'll do my best."

"Please, don't patronise me, Charles. This is not a whim, and I am not a child," she declared fiercely.

"I never said you were. Martin calls you a lioness, and he's right. Woe to any man who gets in your way, Mrs. Sinclair."

"If only Victoria saw it that way," Beth sighed. "She thinks I've become too complacent."

He began to laugh. "You? Complacent?" Her expression turned a bit harsh, and he immediately retracted the comment. "That is not to say you're headstrong or unyielding, darling. Never. But you are determined. I admire your fiery spirit."

"I pray so, Charles, for I intend to build this hospital, no matter what."

He decided to change the topic. "I wrote in my new journal this morning."

Beth's smile returned, and she took his hand. "Did you? I'm very glad. It will help, Charles. You've grown restless these past few days; tossing and turning at night. You've even talked a little in your sleep. I pray the dreams aren't too terrible."

"How could they be, when you're lying beside me?" he whispered. "And I apologise for stealing away this morning without a goodbye kiss. Once we get to Branham, all that will change. For two weeks, I'm all yours."

"My darling husband, I hope it works out that way, but I understand the demands on your time. Criminals toll their deceitful bells, and you must dash away to still the ringing and uncover the hand upon the rope. You are my hard-working, busy husband! Did writing this morning help at all?"

"Yes, actually, it did," he said, leaning close. "I'm not sure how faithful I'll be to that daily task, but I'll try. In one way, it did allow my mind to wander, and it was surprising to see what I wrote."

"Good," she said simply. "That's the reason for the exercise. Remember that anything written there is private. For your eyes alone. And you must use the key that came with it and keep it locked. Those are your private thoughts, Charles."

He smiled at her generosity. "Thank you, little one. I shall follow your instructions. Now, as regards the warehouse, I'll speak with Pennyweather and see if my calendar permits it. If there is any way I can make it work, I will." He glanced in the direction where Aubrey sat with Cordelia. It looked as though the earl's presence had brought the girl a sense of calm.

"Perhaps, Paul could tour the warehouse with you," he suggested.

"Paul has other matters to worry him just now. Other responsibilities."

"You mean Cordelia? Do you think he's serious about her?"

"I think he's trying to understand his own heart," she whispered.

"And how will you feel if he falls in love with her?" the duke boldly asked, a part of him fearing the answer.

"Grateful," she said, surprising him.

"How so?"

"I'd be ever so grateful to the Lord for healing Paul's heart, but also grateful that he would have what you and I have, Charles. If he falls in love, then I'd consider it a beautiful miracle."

"You are the miracle, little one. It's no wonder every man falls in love with you. Talking of which, I had breakfast with Henry this morning."

"Yes, I saw the two of you arrive late. Did you invite him to the theatre tonight?"

"I did, and he promised to attend, unless he's delayed in Whitechapel. Fred Treves sent for him."

"Because of the fire?" she asked.

"No, on another matter, but I'm afraid I shall have to go there as well, Beth. The fire is making extra work for every fireman and policeman in the city."

"Should we cancel tonight's plans?"

"Not at all. You and Tory have worked too hard to do that. I'll do my best to make the theatre party, but if not, Henry can accompany you. Is that all right?"

"Yes, of course, if you must work. Henry's welcome to bring a friend, if he wishes."

"I told him that. He thought he might ask his new patient. The one with amnesia. Her name is Stuart, apparently."

"So he told me. Have you met her?"

"No. He'd wanted to introduce us, but she was involved in some beauty routine to do with hair. He speaks of her with great fondness."

Beth's dark eyes twinkled. "Does he? Now, that's very interesting."

"Are you matchmaking, darling?" he teased her.

"Merely making an observation."

"But a very astute one. Henry claims he's no desire to marry, but I think he might be smitten. Do you think I should investigate the woman? I shouldn't like to see him hurt."

"Neither would I," she agreed. "She's American. Did he mention that?"

"Is she? That makes it easier. Did he give her age or description?"

Laughing, Elizabeth stroked his face. "Ever the detective, aren't you, Commissioner? Let me see if I remember. She's somewhat tall, auburn-haired. He once referred to her as 'voluptuous'. It was a slip, I think. He looked quite embarrassed after saying it. Oh, and she plays the piano and sings."

"Auburn hair? She sounds a little like Lorena MacKey."

Beth bristled at the mention of the woman's name. "Why do you instantly think of her, there must be a thousand women with those features."

"I didn't instantly think of her. It's an obvious conclusion. Lorena's missing again, and it's possible she's feigning amnesia to protect her identity."

"And you worry about her, apparently."

"Not worry, exactly, but I'd like to make sure of her welfare," he replied. "Beth, you claim to admire my chivalrous spirit, yet you chide me when it applies to other women. Why is that?"

"Not all women. Some need a man's care, but others are rather like cats. These can take care of themselves."

"You're calling Lorena a cat?"

"Perhaps."

He sighed. "Jealousy is unwarranted, little one. I've no romantic ideas about Dr. MacKey. She wants to leave Redwing, which puts her in danger. Lorena's vulnerable, Beth. Can't you see that?"

Her dark eyes rounded in anger. "Vulnerable? Charles, Lorena MacKey sided with William Trent in my abduction!"

"Yes, but she wants a fresh start. Who amongst us can cast the first stone?"

He could see the muscles of her jaw tense, and she pulled away from him a little. "Charles, have you forgotten the three-day fever you suffered in Scotland? Lorena MacKey caused that fever. She may even be connected to the castle fire." She grew quiet for a moment, trying to maintain her temper. Finally, she reached for his hand. "Forgive me. I know your heart is in the right place, but I worry that the doctor's considerable charms blind you to other truths. Charles, if she *is* this Stuart patient, then it may be a ruse to involve Henry, and I will not allow either of you to be hurt!"

He drew her chin upwards to kiss her lips. "Forgive me. You're right. MacKey's behaviour shows signs of repentance, but it could all be an act. I promise to bear that in mind. Besides, this Stuart woman's American. It cannot be MacKey."

"Accents can be faked, Charles. Please, be careful."

"Of Lorena?"

"Of her, yes, but at all times. I overheard several ministers saying the streets in Whitechapel are quite dangerous now, and looters run riot, brandishing knives. Take your pistol."

He patted the shoulder holster beneath his coat. "Both Paul and I are always armed. You know that."

She smiled a little. "He's going with you? I'm glad. If you get the chance, talk to him about Cordelia. You might be able to coax him into sharing his feelings. And whilst you're investigating in the East, remember how much you're loved in the West. All right, Captain?"

"You are ever on my mind and in my heart, little one," he whispered, kissing her once more. "But just in case I'm delayed, remind Baxter to make sure no guests enter either the library or the ballroom this evening. Even if someone asks to see the library, he's to deny them entrance."

"I promise."

Charles noticed Ned Wychwright standing with the coquettish Lady Louise near the entrance. "Isn't he married?" he asked, nodding towards the middle Wychwright son.

"Yes, but I believe they've separated. According to my grandfather, Ned's wife left him for another man."

"Poor chap. I can certainly sympathise. Ned seems a nice enough fellow, but his elder brother is an insufferable lout."

Beth's dark brows furrowed together. "Why would you say such a thing?"

"Because it's true. We met briefly in the corridor, and he mistook me for someone he believes wronged Cordelia. Honestly, the man called her some quite awful names, Elizabeth. It was all I could do to keep from knocking him to the ground!"

She cupped his chin with her fingertips. "Is that why I see a bruise beneath your beard, Captain? I pray you've not been engaging in fisticuffs at a wake."

He rubbed the aching jaw. "Not here, but earlier. And for the record, I was caught off-guard by the punch. It happens in my line of work. There's James," he said, seeing Drummond. "I hate to leave you, darling, but I really must fetch Paul and head to Whitechapel. I'm sorry to run off again. I promise to make it up to you later."

She laughed as he kissed her hand. "I shall hold you to that, Captain. And the next time a fist comes your way, please duck."

Haimsbury passed by Drummond on the way to Paul's location. The cheerful Scottish duke was greeting a dozen friends, talking politics and sport. Upon reaching Charles, he placed a firm hand on his nephew's shoulder, leaning in to whisper, "You've heard about the fire, I take it?"

"Yes. Paul and I are leaving now."

"Good. Also, it seems Alexander Collins has suffered a mental break of some kind. His mind may really be gone, son, but it could also be a trick. Keep your wits about you. Collins keeps evil company."

"If it's a trick, then it's the second one today," Sinclair told his uncle. "A vanishing act took place this morning. I'll explain later. I'll likely be unable to attend the theatre, but I'll do my best to make the party. Keep an eye on Beth for me, James."

"As if I would do anything else?" the Scotsman laughed. "Take some of our men with you, son. I'll enjoy the night better, knowing you've armed guards about you, but do what you must. I'll look after Beth."

"Thank you, James," answered the young duke as he walked towards Aubrey.

Along the way, Charles noticed a pretty child with auburn curls and freckled cheeks. She wore a modest costume of dark velvet and carried two lemonades, a glass in each hand. She nearly spilled one because of a thoughtless bump by a tall man in a distinctly out-of-place suit made from bright blue silk, trimmed in scarlet velvet. Sinclair managed to catch the beverage before it toppled.

"Careful!" Charles said, placing himself close to the girl protectively whilst keeping one eye on the mysterious man in blue. "You wouldn't want to ruin that lovely dress."

"He did it intentionally. That man. Why would he do that?" the girl complained, turning this way and that, searching for the culprit. "Oh, that's very strange! He's gone. And who are you? Are you another stranger? My father says to be wary of strangers. I'm not to talk to them."

"I'm Charles," he told the child.

"Charles? Are you family, friend, or servant? You're very well dressed if you're a footman."

"I'm not a footman," he told her.

"Then, are you family?" she probed, her copper brows arched high upon the freckled face. "Even if you are family, I shouldn't talk to you, as you're strange and all."

"Then I shall do my best to avoid being strange. May I carry the glasses for you?"

"Very well, but you mustn't drink any," the precocious child ordered.

They walked together towards the eastern wall, which was formed entirely of leaded panes of glass. "Are you taking one of these to Lady Cordelia?" he asked.

"Do you know her? Cordelia's my aunt, of course. And that's Paul sitting with her. He's an earl. I think she plans to marry him."

"Does she?" the duke asked, a smile playing at his lips. "How very interesting."

"Do you know Paul? If so, then perhaps you're not too awfully strange."

They arrived at the seating area, and Aubrey stood politely. "I see you've met."

"Not really," Haimsbury admitted. "I'm too strange, it seems."

"I'm not to talk to strangers," the girl said firmly. "It is a hard and fast rule. That's what Father says."

"And your father's correct," agreed the earl. "But this man is my cousin. Charles Sinclair, this is Miss Calliope Wychwright."

"Your cousin?" she asked. "Is he also an earl? I know he isn't a footman."

"A footman?" laughed Aubrey. "Hardly! Charles is a duke."

"Nonsense. I was told the only duke here is that man," she declared, pointing towards Drummond. "Besides, dukes are old and smell of pipe tobacco."

"Not always, and yes, I'm really a duke, though I hardly feel like one. That other duke is my uncle," Sinclair told her. "If this second lemonade is for him, you may need to splash in something stronger. He prefers drinks with a bit more kick to them."

"You're very funny for a duke," Callie laughed placing one of the glasses in the earl's hands. "This is for you, Paul. To thank you for allowing us to ride in your very nice carriage. And for telling Cassie and me all about Africa."

Charles handed the second glass to Cordelia. "And I'm sure this is for you."

"I couldn't find any blackberry punch," Callie explained. "Only lemonade. I spilled a little, though, because of that very rude man in the blue suit."

Cordelia stared at the sweet refreshment as though she couldn't recall how to use a glass. The noise level of the room made it impossible to converse in soft voices, which meant nearly everyone had begun to shout, and the chaotic sounds bounced inside her confused mind like a rosinless bow skipping across out of tune violin strings.

Sinclair could see his cousin was worried about the young woman, and so was he. "How's she doing?" he whispered into Paul's left ear.

"Coping, but only just," Stuart answered in similar fashion. "I'd like to take her home, but I'm not sure it's a good idea, considering the way William treats her. He's mercurial at best, and last night, he threatened to put her on the streets. Ned told me about it."

"How is that his choice to make?" the duke asked. "It's Delia's home, too, isn't it?"

"Not legally, no. All the baronial properties are likely entailed to the title. Once the legal matters are done, William will gain full control of all the houses and the money. He could evict his own mother, if he wanted."

Charles caught Drummond's eye and waved, beckoning him over. "This place is a madhouse!" he told the earl. "Hardly a gathering of mourners."

"But it's precisely what Connie Wychwright was hoping for," Aubrey answered as Drummond reached them.

"Charles, are you two leaving now?" asked James.

"Yes, and I wonder if you'd keep an eye on Cordelia and her young nieces for us?" Sinclair asked their uncle. "Perhaps, they could join you and Elizabeth in a quiet corner. And afterward, if you'd make sure everyone is taken safely back home?"

The duke bent down, smiling at the two children. "Girls, would you like to explore your Uncle Basil's folly with me?"

"Oh, yes, please!" both answered in gleeful unison.

"Where is it?" asked Calliope.

"Just outside those doors, near the back of the rose garden. But you'll need warm cloaks. It's grown quite chilly, and it may even snow whilst we're walking about. Delia, why don't you come with us, dear?" he said gently to the distraught young woman. "We'll fetch my granddaughter and see if we can't find that pirate treasure Basil claims in buried 'neath his hedges."

"What's a folly?" Sinclair asked Aubrey as the children left to fetch their coats.

"Usually, they're old buildings or the remains of them, used as garden features or summer houses. You had one when you were a boy, Charles. We used to play there, whenever I'd visit. There's also a delightful old folly at Branham, on the edge of the pond in Henry's Woods. Ask Beth to show you."

The earl reached for Cordelia's hand with obvious affection and helped her to stand. His cousin took note of the gesture.

"Don't forget your handbag," Paul whispered, lightly kissing her cheek as he draped a woolen cloak round her shoulders. "Go with James now. He'll watch after you."

Drummond put out his arm, and Cordelia automatically took it. Her halting gait gave the impression of a sleepwalker stumbling through a dream. The two cousins waited until their uncle had collected Elizabeth, and then watched as the group left the conservatory to search for buried treasure.

"My coach or yours?" asked Aubrey.

Charles smiled. "Let's take mine. If the roads are as dangerous as I hear, Granger's an imposing figure and a keen shot. James will make sure Beth gets home safely."

"All right, but I need to fetch extra ammunition first. My coach is parked by the entry."

The pair pushed their way upstream once more, winding through narrow corridors. As they passed the formal dining hall, Haimsbury noticed the peculiar man in the peacock blue suit who'd so annoyed Calliope. He was deep in conversation with William Wychwright and two other men. Only now, did Charles realise what had so bothered him about the flamboyantly dressed stranger.

"Good heavens, Paul! That's Rasha Grigor!" he exclaimed, starting towards the dining hall to confront him. "I am *not* leaving Elizabeth, if that demonic Romanian is here!"

Paul tugged sharply on his cousin's coat sleeve to stop him in his tracks. "No, Charles, it isn't Grigor. In fact, he's one of the matters I need to discuss with you, but not here. Come on, let's go. James will look after Beth."

It took nearly five minutes to reach the quiet sanity and fresh air of the outdoors. The Aubrey coach sat nearby, and the earl collected a box of ammunition from a steel container beneath the seat. Charles noticed the picture book that had so amused the Wychwright children.

"Conducting research for a future trip?" he quipped.

"Very droll. No, it belongs to Della. She'd probably like it back."

"I'll see her later. Shall I take it with me?"

"Only if you promise not to keep it," teased the earl.

After another short walk, they reached the Haimsbury coach, parked on Wilton Place. Charles spoke briefly to Hamish Granger before joining his cousin inside, and by three o'clock the two men were on their way to Whitechapel.

As they moved along Victoria Street, Charles began leafing through the picture book's colourful pages. "I see Adele's added her own comments to some of these drawings. Apparently, this spider monkey is on her list of possible pets."

"A spider monkey makes a very poor pet!" the earl laughed. "Trust me. A man I knew in South America kept one, and it was quite aggressive with strangers. Della loves animals, but a puppy or songbird is a better idea. She's at a funny sort of stage, my daughter. One moment, she's a child, the next practically a woman. She spends a great deal of time with Winston Churchill over at Maisie's home. Apparently, I'm not to notice her fascination with the boy, but it's difficult not to."

"She'll be sixteen before you know it," Charles observed.

"Please, Lord, not so quickly!" Paul answered with a sigh. "She's already asking if she can live with Tory next summer. As it happens, I'm glad she didn't come with me today, particularly in light of some of those attending."

"Do you refer to that creature in the vulgar suit?" his cousin asked.

"Exactly. We've met several of these entities now, and they have very similar looks. Perhaps, they're constrained to a certain set of features, but overall, they reflect the countries they claim to represent."

"You think their human roles are fiction?" asked Charles.

"I think they've lived many lives. But they bear striking similarities. As though imitating something else. I've no idea what, but it's a theory Martin proposed. I mistook this one for Rasha as well, but then I noticed subtleties about his appearance that seemed different from the Romanian upstart."

"Such as?"

"His height, for one. Rasha's shorter than Romanov and Raziel. As though he's weaker, perhaps subservient. Also, the way this one holds his posture; the mannerisms of movement and voice differ. Charles, I believe he may be the creature that attacked you at Branham."

Charles dropped the book, now all attention. "The one that killed Beth's horse?"

"Yes. As you know, I've spent the last few evenings trolling through the city's less fashionable venues for signs of these demonic creatures, and they leave a very definite blood trail in their wake. There are whispers of their foul deeds all over the East. I'm sure Reid and his men hear them, but their energies remain focused on solving Ripper."

"We know who Ripper was, Paul."

"The circle does, yes, but the Home Office aren't satisfied with our explanation. When I told Matthews the crimes were committed by a group of demonic murderers, he called it 'fanciful'."

"Henry Matthews lacks imagination, but he's typical of most men in government. Paul, when you say 'blood trail', do you refer to the Victoria Park murders?"

"Yes, but there've been others since," the earl replied. "In the past week, six women were attacked, but unlike Victoria Park, only one has died. The other five were left dazed, complaining of a strange dream involving a tall man with a European accent who promised them money in return for sexual favours."

"That's hardly unusual in Whitechapel, Paul."

"True, but rather than collect these favours in the usual manner, the creature drinks their blood."

The duke shuddered at the thought. "Is he a vampire?"

"Some of the immigrants are using that very word. The Jews claim it's the *dybbuk* demon returned. The Lascars call him the *chedipe*. The Slovaks *dhampir*, some of the Slavs call him *mara*, others a *mullo*. The immigrants from Kiev call it an *upir*. Others say *wampyr*. But they all mean the same thing: a seductive supernatural creature, returned from the dead to prey upon the living. As you can imagine, these prostitutes find very few policemen who'll believe their tales. They're called mad or liars, and one was sent to Bedlam last week. Fearing similar confinement, the other victims have recanted their testimonies."

"This is very bad, Paul. Only this morning, I heard of two similar deaths; but in Vienna, not London. Might this vampire be one of an entire class of supernatural beings? A monstrous, spirit division of Redwing?"

"Possibly, but such a group requires a leader. I suspect that leader is the Watcher summoned during Redwing's Ripper ritual, not Raziel Grigor or his so-called son, Rasha. And these evil deeds may take other forms. The arson fires set about the city in recent weeks, even this morning's dockside fire at St. Katherine's, have more to do with Redwing than Fenian or Russian anarchists."

"Which means Special Branch's current investigation is wasted effort," noted Haimsbury.

"Probably, but if they hunt the wrong path, then it keeps their noses out of our investigation. Besides, it's important to operate on multiple fronts at once. If we're to reach the truth, then anarchy must be ruled out."

Charles took a deep breath, focusing his thoughts as if evaluating a complex equation. "Susanna Morgan's story of thirteen mirrors and thirteen Watchers begins to play out before our eyes. Are you sure Beth's safe? Perhaps, I should go back."

"The creature was working its magic on Wychwright and seemed to take little notice of us. Beth's safe with James. And besides, I placed ten of my best agents at the house. She and Delia are well looked after."

Charles began to laugh. "Ten agents? Those must be the men Margaret noticed and thought were reporters! Well done, Cousin. I should have known you'd have it handled."

"I try to anticipate danger," Paul said. Several thick strands of chestnut had dislodged from the ribbon, refusing to remain constrained. Frustrated with the hair, Aubrey pulled the ribbon off and stuffed it into his coat pocket. "I should probably just cut it," he declared.

"But it makes a grand disguise," Charles argued. "And Beth likes your hair long. She calls it poetic."

The earl ran his fingers through the long waves to smooth them. "Yes, she used to call me Lord Byron, but you'd be surprised how well I can blend into the seedier quarters of the city with this poetic mane."

"Even without the beard?" asked his cousin.

"The beard gives me a scraggly look; but clean shaven, I now look like a Fabianist or any number of artists and writers hanging round the East End. In the past few nights, I've walked amongst them in opium dens, music halls, and gambling parlours, but so far, no one has seen a woman answering Susanna's or MacKey's description. I even called on Clive Urquhart at his disgusting home two days ago in hopes of obtaining information."

"Has he seen either of them?"

"The man claimed Susanna left England to visit her father in Chicago; and that he paid the passage to America. He seemed surprised I'd ask about Lorena, but claimed to know nothing of her. I detest that little man, but the visit revealed a bit about Redwing. I asked if he knew anything about Hemsfield or Andrews, and he grew quite evasive. The worm hinted he might have useful information for the inner circle, but insists he'll tell only you. He's afraid, Charles. The house had armed guards posted at every entrance, and the windows were strewn with garlands of garlic."

"Garlic? Whatever for?"

"It's thought to ward off certain spirits. I'd like to talk with Anatole about these vampires and the Redwing civil war, if we ever find him."

"I spoke with him this morning," Charles informed his cousin.

"What? He's finally shown himself? Where's that devil been? Did he explain?"

"Not really," replied Haimsbury, "but he did answer several of my questions in plain language. And he helped me with a somewhat sticky situation that requires our attention."

"What's that?"

"Baron Wychwright's body is missing."

Aubrey stared, wondering if he'd heard correctly. "Missing? Wait a moment. Is that why you signed the order to seal the coffin?"

Sinclair nodded. "It seemed the easiest solution at the time. The driver claimed the body vanished without anyone entering the hearse."

"A missing body. Well, it's yet one more mystery to add to our ever-lengthening list of conundrums. My closet is another."

The duke's left brow rose into a question mark. "What about your closet?"

"Aside from the fact that my fashion currently lags behind yours by a season, it was broken into last evening."

All humour left Sinclair's face. "Broken into? By whom?"

"That remains a mystery. Every item was removed from its hangar, box, or shelf and scattered about the closet floor. Bailey ran a detailed inventory. Strangely, nothing is missing. The Aubrey jewels were in there, my guns, even a box of gold sovereigns! It makes no sense."

"We'll need to get someone on this right away," Charles said in a business-like tone. "I could put Matthew Laurence on it. He's just returned from Ireland."

"No, I've assigned Tom Galton to look into it."

"Was the closet locked?"

"Of course, because of the valuables and weapons, it remains locked, and only Bailey and I have keys. Mine is with me at all times, and Bailey keeps all master apartment keys on a ring inside his livery pocket. Do you remember the ceremonial sword I wore at your investiture ceremony?" Charles nodded. "It's been in my family for three centuries and is stored in a locked cabinet. That cabinet was opened, without leaving a single mark upon the metal, and the sword removed from its sheath."

Charles felt a chill run down his spine. "How? Paul, if not a thief, then who would do this? And why?"

"I've no idea," Paul answered, "but it all took place in the blink of an eye. Bailey says he'd locked everything up tightly after setting out my suit and shoes last night, but when he returned five minutes later, the closet had been thoroughly trashed."

"I'm very sorry, Paul."

The earl shut the book, his blue eyes serious. "Charles, I really don't know how you manage it. You and Beth deal with phantoms all the time, but I prefer my enemies be made of flesh and blood. I've no fear of human threats, but something imperceptible has decided to make me its target. Something able to enter a locked closet and stir it up like a whirlwind!"

"Have you any idea which whirlwind targeted you?" asked his cousin.

"Not yet, but he left a calling card. There's a large, locked steel box where I keep Father's medals, family photographs, a collection of Beth's letters and several drawings she made for me as a girl. Also, Adele's French birth records, her Scottish adoption papers, and a lock of her mother's hair. I thought she might like such a keepsake one day. This photograph of Cozette was inside a small envelope, sealed with wax." He reached into his inner coat pocket and removed a hand-coloured cabinet photograph of a beautiful, fair-haired woman with soft blue eyes. He handed it to Charles.

"She's lovely," Charles remarked.

"She was like a little sunflower. All smiles, no matter what the day brought. Della reminds me so much of Cozette. She has the same bright smile, and as she gets older, her eyes take on her mother's colour—it's similar to your own, an azure sort of blue. Turn the photo over, Charles. There's writing on the back."

The duke did so, and read the inscription: *Pour mon David – Avec tout mon amour, Cozette.* Scribbled in large letters by a different hand, just over the sweet dedication, he read this: *Meurtrier.* The French word for 'Murderer'.

"Is someone accusing you of Cozette's death?"

The earl appeared shaken, and he gazed out the window as he answered. "I think so, but I had no idea she was pregnant when I left Paris, Charles. If I'd known, then..."

Sinclair touched his cousin's forearm. "You needn't explain, Paul. I understand."

"I wish I did," he sighed. "Charles, do you remember the embezzler Fermin, who sponsored Cozette at the *maison close?*"

"The man found dead in the Seine; and may I add, deservedly so?"

Paul nodded. "He had this photograph made, but she convinced the photographer to supply one, hand-coloured print for me. Charles, this picture was stored inside that locked box of mementos. Yet, this morning, Callie Wychwright found it at the back of *that* picture book. How did it get there? And what is this impossible thief's purpose?"

"The picture book is Della's. Clearly, your thief hoped to force you into telling her the truth—or he wants to embarrass, even discredit you. He wanted Della to find it. Paul, why not just tell her the truth?"

"I can't, Charles. It means she learns that her mother was a harlot, and her father is the cad who abandoned her."

"Nonsense," his cousin insisted. "You'd have acted differently if Cozette had told you about her condition, but she didn't. You must stop dwelling on what might have been and think of what can be! Since losing the man she called Father, Della's struggling to make sense of her place in the world. Give her that identity, that security! Tell her she's yours. She'll only love you the more for it."

The earl grew quiet, clearly unwilling, or perhaps unable, to speak more of the matter. "How is Kepelheim doing with your puzzle room?" he asked.

"Tell her, Paul."

"Has he deciphered any of it?"

Haimsbury sighed. "Very well, since you refuse to listen, the answer is yes, he has. But only a little. He's decoded one word he hopes will form a sort of Rosetta key to the entire code. Martin is certain he's found the word repeated at least twenty times on the walls, though there may be more."

"What word is that?"

"Fire."

The earl's face grew even more grim. "Given recent events, that is an ominous key word, Charles."

"It is ominous in many ways," agreed the duke. "As of this morning, I have reports of thirty-one fires across the metropolis. Most are minor in scope, but troubling for their proliferation. Four in the square mile, St. Katherine's makes seventeen in the East, and the others are scattered across various manufacturing areas. Whilst fires aren't symptomatic of supernatural activity on their own, so great a number demands our attention, especially if Martin's right about the code."

Paul grew thoughtful, tapping on the window glass with his signet ring. Charles noticed and sat back against the tufted, brown leather seat, watching his cousin's mind at work.

"My father had a wonderful gift of insight," Aubrey said after several minutes. "Very few attacks surprised him, and he rarely lost his temper or good humour."

"I admired your father a great deal, Paul. I look forward to meeting him again one day, in heaven."

The earl managed a slight smile. "He left very big shoes, Charles. I remember, he once asked me a question regarding fallen angels. Rebel spirits, if you will. He asked, if these powerful beings can affect the material world invisibly, without being observed, then why would they take human form at all, since taking on flesh limits them?"

"Limits them? How so?" asked Charles, finding the idea intriguing.

"We're approaching one of two, high holy seasons within the Christian calendar. One, of course, is Easter, the day when Christ resurrected. But Christmas represents that pivotal moment when he took on the flesh of a human. Father felt the reason these Watchers and demons assume human form is twofold. First, an imitation of Christ's incarnation; some twisted reversal of that miracle. But secondly, to deceive us. Rather like a stage magician uses sleight of hand. Christ incarnated to understand us, to live a sinless life, and then offer himself as the perfect sacrifice in our stead. The fallen take on flesh in order to sin carnally and whilst in this form, *they* sacrifice *us*."

The duke nodded soberly. "I think your father was right, Paul. And sleight of hand is accurate. Entering a locked closet is a magic trick to us, but child's play to these unseen creatures."

Aubrey continued with the theory. "Let's assume for a moment that you have no personal faith in God, and one of these angelic pretenders knocks on your door, or appears at your place of business. He's able to manipulate matter and may even appear as a vagabond or an orphaned child. There are numerous folktales of travellers who seek shelter for the night and then reward their host. What if this grateful stranger offers to reward you with eternal youth, wealth, power, even life without end? Might this charade allow fallen spirits to plant their evil seed—both metaphorical and literal? Is this how they bend the will of mankind towards their foul ends and beget hybrid offspring?"

"It's certainly a possibility," Charles answered. "Do you think they see us as weak, then?"

"I believe the fallen see humans as pawns in a high-stakes chess match," the earl replied bluntly. "And I believe we're moving into the next phase of that game—a gambit that involves you and your children."

The coach began to slow, for they'd turned onto Commercial Street. A grey haze and the smell of smoke hung in the air, and fine ash had settled on porches and posts. Even now, hundreds of wounded survivors huddled for warmth near barrel fires, their gaunt faces streaked with blood and soot.

For a brief second, Charles saw a vision of things to come: poisonous air, a darkened sun, eternal night, nocturnal creatures consuming the flesh of all those who refused to take the mark.

Hell on earth.

When the Dragon ruled.

He could see the devastation of cities, burning buildings, charred bodies of the dead, and the terror in children's eyes. He could smell burning flesh and hear the wind of a thousand wings; Watchers making sure every human obeyed. Sinclair shuddered with dread at the horrifying vision, for it was as real as the coach—as real as his cousin—as though he'd already lived it.

Anatole said he would begin to have waking dreams. Was this one a warning? A threat? A prophecy?

"Charles? Are you with me? Your eyes glazed over for a moment."

"Yes. It's just this strange feeling," he told his cousin as the horses stopped. "For days now, it's hung about me like a shroud. As though something terrible is coming. Invisible eyes watching me, waiting for me to make a false move. To get it wrong. My children and my wife are at risk, but with all you've told me, I now believe the entire family are targets, including you and Della."

A hideous hissing voice called from the well of the duke's fractured memory. Sharp teeth, shining skin, an ancient scaly face emerging from a black mirror.

The vagabond traveller with the dragon's eye.

Hello, boy. I'm waiting. Let's play.

CHAPTER TWENTY

7:45 pm – The Lyceum Theatre

With Christmas nearing, most of the city's popular theatrical venues were mounting productions of Dickens's *A Christmas Carol,* Hoffman's *The Nutcracker and the Mouse King,* or a traditional English pantomime filled with broadly drawn caricatures and bawdy jokes. However, that Tuesday night, as the Lyceum's grand drapes drew aside, the theatre's manager stepped forward to announce a change in their program.

"Good evening and welcome to the Lyceum. I am Abraham Stoker."

Most of the wealthy patrons applauded at this point, recognising the business manager as the author of several successful plays and a collection of short stories published in London periodicals. Stoker bowed gracefully to accept the accolades.

"Thank you all. You're too kind. Mr. Irving has asked me to stand in his place whilst he dresses for the first act. I pray you'll forgive us, dear friends and patrons, but the leading actress in our scheduled Ibsen play has taken ill. The doctors are confident of her recovery, but the malady makes it impossible for her to perform. You might assume that her understudy would take the stage, but alas, just yesterday morning, that dear lady left England to play Ophelia in New York City. Consequently, we cannot mount our announced production. Now, this conundrum might produce despair within many a theatre owner's heart, but Mr. Irving has devised a brilliant substitution. You, my friends, will be the first in all the kingdom to preview a marvellous new staging of an old favourite."

A murmur passed through the well-dressed crowd as everyone wondered what play he might mean.

"You are all connoisseurs of the dramatic arts," he continued. "Meaning most of you are familiar with the masterworks of E. T. A. Hoffman. I am therefore pleased to announce an entirely new adaptation of his popular novel, *The Devil's Elixir.* I humbly pray you'll enjoy it, for I have aided Mr. Irving—but a little—with added dialogue and set design. This is a Jekyll-and-Hyde tale of disguises and devilish intrigue, where the cover-up of a murder leads to the creation of a mischievous *doppelgänger*. Our players include Mr. Henry Irving as Medardus, Miss Ellen Terry as the Princess Aurelie, and Max Bruner as the Count. We must dress the stage for the first act; therefore, I ask you all to relax with a glass of wine whilst you enjoy a brilliant, French mezzo-soprano. She is the toast of the Paris opera, and we've engaged her for just one night. Performing arias from the title role of Georges Bizet's *Carmen*, I give you the incomparable Mademoiselle Antoinette Gévaudan!"

Stoker exited to the left, and from stage right, a tall woman with dark hair and smoky eyes strode with great purpose to the centre of the curved proscenium. She wore a flounced skirt of crimson red that narrowed towards her knees, and then followed the curve upwards, skimming tightly along a pair of round hips. An intentional side-slit permitted a tantalising view of her left ankle and very shapely calf. The neckline of the tight bodice plunged so low, that it revealed the decorative lace of her corset with round flesh pillowing over top. Most shocking of all, the woman wore no bustle at all. The ladies in the audience gasped in disapproval, but their husbands and escorts smiled in frank appreciation.

Since Sinclair and Stuart still worked in Whitechapel, and Adele had stayed over at Maisie Churchill's home, the Aubrey theatre box held only four occupants that auspicious evening. Elizabeth Sinclair sat next to Henry MacAlpin, and beside the viscount were Victoria Stuart and Duke James. Drummond had very little interest in seeing a play, but the singer's gaudy apparel managed to elicit a more stirring response.

"That French singer's certainly proud of her, uh, talents."

Tory flicked her brother's wrist with her fan. "The woman's a harlot, James. Gévaudan's well known in Paris, but not as a singer. Most of her performances are more private, if you know my meaning. I'm surprised Irving engaged her."

"Shall I order champagne, then? We can toast to the coming year whilst ignoring the stage. How's that, Sister?"

The duke pressed a buzzer near the back draping, and within seconds, a uniformed usher appeared. "How may I serve Your Grace?"

"A bottle of your finest champagne, young man. A '58 Krug, if you have any. Beth, will you join us?"

She shook her head. "We'll have spirits aplenty at the party later, Grandfather."

"Make it four glasses, just in case," he told the youth. The duke yawned and stretched, weary from the long day. "Tory how long is this soirée of yours going to last? I've business at the palace come morning. Privy council meeting."

Victoria cast her brother a disapproving glare. "It will last until it is over, James, and no longer. Do stop being so very tiresome. I'm aware that you'd rather be on the moors shooting pheasant or some other manly pursuit, but I've spent very little time in London of late and will likely return to France after the new year. Allow me to enjoy decent theatre whilst I may."

The spinster had been anticipating the party for weeks, and she'd invited Dr. Reggie Whitmore to join their theatre group. The widower was typically late, and she felt nervous that he might not come at all. The attractive Scotswoman had worn her best dress, a sky-blue satin gown with capped sleeves edged in white fringe. Her salt-and-pepper hair was arranged in loose curls on her head, and she'd added her late mother's sapphires for sparkle.

The duke smiled at his sister. "You look lovely," he whispered. "I'd forgotten how much your eyes look like Beth's. You know, this reminds me of our younger days. Remember all the plays and parties we used to attend? All the many balls! I can still picture you in those grand hooped skirts, your agile feet polishing the dance floor. You've always made be proud, Vic. Really proud."

She finally smiled and tapped her brother's hand. "You were actually quite dashing, James. It's no wonder the queen was set on marrying you—against her mother's will, I might add."

Drummond dismissed the comment with a jovial laugh. "Drina was better off with Albert. It's a pity Charles couldn't make it," he said, turning to his granddaughter. "I'm sure both he and Paul will be at the party later."

"If he makes it, then I shall be glad, but I married a policeman, Grandpa. I must allow him to do his job without adding to his worries, now, mustn't I?" The duchess's tone was surprisingly calm, but Drummond knew her well enough to detect a hint of strain.

"Tory, did I see Stoker's name on your guest list?" he asked.

Victoria's attention had fallen on the occupants of Box Seven, across the way, and she muttered a halfhearted reply. "Yes, I suppose so. I must say, that is a very great surprise."

Salperton had been relatively quiet, but now followed the direction of her gaze, squinting a little due to a slight myopia in his right eye. "Why is it a surprise? Wait, isn't that Lord Ashdown?"

"Yes, it is," she answered in an odd tone.

"But then, who's the young woman sitting next to him? I know the Ashdowns quite well," the viscount continued, "and they've no daughters, not even a niece."

Tory cleared her throat in obvious irritation. "No, they have only the two sons. I've seen that young woman before; only with someone else. It is very disappointing, for I appreciate most of what Ashdown does for our government. He can be a force for good, when he chooses the right side, but it's a shame that men are so annoyingly consistent when it comes to character flaws."

"Do you mean me?" asked her brother, who'd been watching the mezzo once again. "What have I done?"

"Of course, I don't mean you, James! No, it's Ashdown. He played Cathy for a fool in Bombay, and it looks as though he's doing it here as well—in front of all her friends! I shall cross him off my Christmas list, and I'm very glad I didn't invite him to the party."

Fearing Tory might enter into a long diatribe on male failings, Salperton turned to Elizabeth for less discouraging conversation. "I'm glad you asked me here tonight, Beth. Did I tell you that I stopped by Fitzmaurice Place on the way here? I'd hoped to persuade Cordelia to come. Paul asked me to look in on her."

"That was thoughtful, but it's too early for public appearances, Henry. Your heart meant well, but Delia needs time to grieve."

"Yes, I realise that, but she also needs distraction and distance."

"Distance?" asked the duchess. "From what?"

"From her eldest brother. The new baron is the sort of fellow who'd fry you up for breakfast and then expect you thank him for the privilege. I rarely find a man with no redeeming traits, but he qualifies in triplicate. Put simply, I don't trust him. I think Cordelia should leave that house as soon as possible, and until then, spend very little time there."

Beth found the sudden flush of righteous anger a little surprising coming from the ordinarily reserved alienist. "Do you say this as a man or as a physician, Henry?"

"Well, as both, I suppose," he said in his own defence. "I can hardly speak as a woman, now can I? I mean no disrespect to either of you wonderful ladies. It's just that Delia lacks positive reinforcement. Connie Wychwright constantly belittles the girl, and her brother is an overbearing bully!"

"Perhaps, bullying is the manner of a soldier," Tory suggested.

"Yes, perhaps," the viscount replied. "I imagine soldiers live rugged and demanding lives that require a certain amount of pride and self-reliance, but it's no excuse for treating a woman harshly."

"Not all soldiers do so," countered the duke. "I served in Crimea, and Paul may not be a soldier according to the common definition, but he certainly serves on England's front lines."

"Yes, that's very true," replied Salperton. "My father served in India, and though he can be temperamental and harsh, I've never seen him mistreat a woman. Of course, he sometimes misunderstood my mother, but he tried his best to be pleasant and protective. Why then, is Wychwright so damnably cruel to his own sister? Oh, do forgive my language, ladies. I forget myself sometimes."

"You are always forgiven, Henry," the duchess whispered, tapping his hand and offering a bright smile.

"Hush now," warned the duke. "This etiquette debate must wait. It looks as though Miss Gévaudan's about to sing another song."

The Lyceum's pit orchestra conductor lifted a baton to commence the downbeat of the singer's second number, one of Carmen's most controversial arias. As she voiced the enthralling melody, her curvy hips swayed rhythmically, and she flounced the skirt to show off her left leg and ankle. It was the *Séguidilla*, a scene of open seduction, in which the gypsy cigarette girl, Carmen, makes musical love to the malleable gendarme Don Jose, hoping he will set her free.

"Près des ramparts de Sévilla, chez mon ami, Lillas Pastia! J'irai danser la Séguidilla *et boire du Manzanilla! J'irai chez mon ami, Lillas Pastia!"* she sang huskily.

Every male's eye stared in transfixed fascination at the singer's erotic movements. Back and forth and side to side, went Gévaudan's erotic round hips. Even the viscount found it difficult to remain aloof. To break the spell, he reached for Elizabeth's hand and squeezed it.

"Duchess, might I exchange places with you? It's grown somewhat warm in here."

Elizabeth leaned in to offer support. "Perhaps, we should escape the heat until the play begins, Henry. We could both use some water, I think."

He nodded gratefully and helped her to stand. "We're going down for a little air," he told the amused duke. The viscount gallantly led Beth down the carpeted staircase.

"Where is your friend this evening?" she asked him once they reached the lobby floor. "I thought she'd planned to join us."

"Miss Stuart? Changed her mind, I'm afraid. Another pity, in my opinion. I'm sure she'd enjoy getting out for a change, but she's afraid of crowds, I think. She spends nearly every moment cooped up in her apartment, which will only cause her to grow all the more insular."

"Henry, when did Miss Stuart become your patient?"

He paused to think. "Let's see. It was just about the time the prince first called on me. All that is rather a blur, you know. But a happy blur," he said, touching her hand affectionately. "I cannot imagine life without you in it, Elizabeth."

"You saved me that day, Henry. No matter what, we shall always remain the closest of friends. I wonder, if she'll start to remember who she really is?"

Henry crossed one leg over the other as he considered this, his right hand close to hers. The world always took on a peaceful sheen whenever he spent time with the duchess. As though everything fell into balance. "That's an interesting question. You don't believe she's a Stuart?"

"She may have the name, but I doubt she's family. I've never heard of any Stuart cousins in America, and Violet isn't one of our usual family names. It's lovely, but non-historic, and we've a habit of repeating names. Though, I do remember Paul once saying he'd like to name a daughter Abigail Violet Rose, and that we'd call her Violet."

"I assume he referred to a child he'd share with you?"

She nodded, and a quiet sort of regret flashed through her dark eyes. "He and I used to make all sorts of plans when I was younger, and it felt like make-believe in many ways. Did I tell you that I very nearly accepted his proposal this summer?"

"I thought he proposed to you in October. Am I mistaken or misinformed?"

She reached for his hand, absentmindedly stroking the cuff of his shirt. Henry had noticed her do this with Sinclair now and then, and he wondered if it had some psychological root with her father. "It's been a difficult year in many ways. I seldom talk to anyone about it. Even Charles doesn't know everything, but you're my dearest friend, Henry. I feel as if I could tell you anything."

"You may open your heart anytime you wish. Why has it been difficult?"

"As you know, Paul spends a great deal of time in other countries. He visited me last Christmas at Branham, and then was sent to Belgium on some emergency for the War Office. Afterwards, he spent nearly two months in Ireland. I never ask the reason for his absence. Government assignments are secret, you know. Most of them, anyway. I wrote him dozens of letters during those months and received only one in return."

"I'm sure he thought of you, Beth, I know Paul very well, and he's not exactly open with his feelings. And his assignments must make him a very poor correspondent."

She smiled. "That's true. I turned twenty last April, and usually Paul makes sure to come home for my birthday, but it was May before I saw him again."

"You were in Paris then, correct? At Tory's house?"

"Yes, the Château Rothesay. It's a lovely, storybook sort of castle with lots of spired towers and slate roofs. Dolly and Sir Richard Patterson-Smythe live nearby, and they hosted my birthday party that year. When Paul finally called at Tory's in May, I already had two visitors. One was Prince Rasarit Grigor. I've already told you about him."

"And the other?"

"Do you know Lord and Lady Salter?" she asked.

"Only by reputation. They're antiquarians, if I remember rightly. Generally out of the country in some arid sort of place, digging up old bones. Did they pay a call to Tory's home?"

"No, it was their son, Seth Holloway. He's actually the Viscount Paynton, but he seldom uses the title. I think he prefers the company of ordinary people, rather than peers. He and I've been friends for over ten years. His sisters Gemma and Ruth are my age. Gemma's a year younger, and Ruth a year older than I. Their family seat is Torden Hall, close to Branham in Faversham. We three girls spent nearly every summer riding together back then. We called ourselves the Kent County Riding Club. Seth used to accompany Gemma and Ruth on the train whenever they'd visit. At first, I think he saw me as just another annoying girl, and then one day in '84, he asked if I might walk alone with him—away from his sisters. From that day forward, we became very close."

Salperton grew very ill-at-ease with the direction of her confession. "Beth, perhaps, this is better told to your husband."

She sighed. "Yes, but may I tell you first? No one else knows this story, not even Paul. I'd like to see your reaction before I tell Charles. He'll be meeting Seth soon, and I shouldn't want any misunderstandings."

"Regarding what?"

"My affections."

He laughed. "My darling friend, Charles Sinclair would never doubt your affections! Not in a million years!"

"Oh, but he might," she whispered. "Henry, I spent years imagining my life with Charles, but in truth I don't know him very well yet. I'm still learning about his moods, just as he's learning mine. I find myself jealous of his friendship towards other women; one in particular, which he finds irritating, I know. What if he becomes jealous of Seth?"

"Has he reason to be?" the viscount asked boldly.

She was about to answer, when an usher appeared with two flutes of champagne and offered them to the pair.

"We didn't order these," Henry told the young man.

"From a gentleman who asks to remain anonymous, my lord."

"Well, that's very kind. Please, offer our thanks, then," he answered. "Do go on with your story, Elizabeth."

She took a sip of the wine. "This is quite good, but perhaps, you're right. I shouldn't burden you with my worries."

"Nonsense, that's what friends are for, isn't it? Beth, I am happy to listen for hour upon hour, if you like. We could skip the play and remain down here."

Her expression grew serious. "Do you know a woman named Lorena MacKey?"

Henry's eyes widened. "Good heavens, how do you know her?"

"Then, you have met her?" asked the duchess

"I should think so! I was one of her instructors. London Medical College for Women. I teach nervous diseases there each spring. MacKey had a brilliant mind but always seemed distracted towards the end of the term. She'd have made an excellent alienist. I think she finally specialised in herbal remedies. Homeopathy, they call it. Why?"

"No reason," she answered, clearly relieved. For if Henry knew MacKey, then surely this 'Violet Stuart' was someone else. "I hear applause. I think the mezzo's performance has ended. The play will begin shortly. We should finish our champagne and go back up."

He took her hand. "Elizabeth, if you're holding something back—if you need to talk, I'm here for you. Forget the play, you're much more important."

"Thank you, Henry," she said softly, and then, without warning, kissed his cheek. "You're such a dear man. Promise you'll take care with your heart."

"My heart is yours alone," he answered, his eyes glistening. "Though, if I ever do marry, I'll be sure you approve of her first."

"Is there someone? You've an air of secrecy about you, Lord Salperton," she teased. "Might you be interested in this mystery patient?"

"Interested in Miss Stuart? I hardly know her, Beth, and as you say, she might have dark secrets beneath her memory loss. She might even be married. I'm concerned for her health, of course, but not interested in her romantically."

Beth laughed and then stood to go. "Men seldom realise when they're falling in love."

"Love?" he gasped, standing as well. "Really, Beth, it's nothing like that, I assure you! Nothing like that at all! I'm merely concerned for her mind."

"If you say so. Perhaps, I'm wrong."

His mouth tightened. "How is caring about someone a sign of intimate affection? Why, someone might make the same claim about us! You and I are dear friends, but we have no romantic affiliations, do we?"

Elizabeth studied his face, observing the obvious signs of confusion and deep affection—but for whom? This patient, or for her? "Forgive me, Henry. If I've struck a nerve, I'm very sorry."

"Of course not. You've nothing to apologise for," he said, gulping down the champagne. "My nerves are sound as a penny."

"I didn't intend to hurt your feelings. Truly, I didn't."

"I presume women have keener insight into their own hearts?" he complained, wondering just why her comment bothered him so very much. "Did you realise you'd fallen in love with Charles right away, or did it take time for the truth to sink in?"

"My relationship with Charles is complicated. And I'm very sorry for offending you."

"No, I'm the one should apologise. You caught me off-guard; that's all. Perhaps, I have a blind spot to my own heart."

"If so, then Paul has a similar blind spot. He doesn't see the great changes awaiting him either."

"Which are?" asked MacAlpin as a tall man with dark hair bumped into his right elbow, causing him to drop the empty glass onto the carpeted floor. "Good heavens!"

The man took no pains to stop or apologise. Instead, he pushed through the crowd, but to Henry's astonishment, no one else took notice of his passage. In fact, his feet didn't even touch the floor!

Salperton recovered the fallen glass and handed it to an usher. "Wait here," he told Elizabeth, leaving her alone as he chased after the rude wraith. "You!" he shouted. "You there! Stop!"

MacAlpin quickly reached the man's position and took him by the shoulder, turning him round. To his utter shock, it was Anthony Gehlen, the London Hospital physician who'd taken care of Beth and Delia Wychwright.

"Gehlen!" the viscount managed to sputter, thoroughly perplexed. "Do forgive me, I must be mistaken. I thought you were someone else."

"So it seems," the doctor answered, his dark eyes glinting in the chandelier's soft glow. Henry noticed the distinctive smell of whisky. "I'm often mistaken for someone else. Perhaps, it's a trick of the light. Or maybe just a trick. I do love tricks, don't you? Enjoy the play, Lord Salperton—and the beautiful company," he whispered. "She's a lovely bit of flesh."

Outraged at so crude a comment, Salperton opened his mouth to answer the inebriated physician, but Beth's soft touch on his arm diverted his attention. He turned, finding her looking very pale.

"Please, Henry! It's growing cold down here. May we go back up? I left my wrap on the chair."

"Of course." He took her arm, intending to leave Gehlen with a flea in his ear, but to Salperton's utter shock, the man had completely vanished.

CHAPTER TWENTY-ONE

8:15 pm – Surgeon's Lounge, London Hospital

"As you can see from the tallies, gentlemen, the number of dead now tops thirty, and the wounded nearly four hundred. I believe I speak for all the staff here when I say this has been the worst fire in our borough's history since 1666."

Frederick Treves looked as though he might collapse as he finished his report, and he steadied himself against the wooden table.

Charles Sinclair stood to shake his friend's hand. "Thank you, Mr. Treves. I'm afraid you're right. People here in the East will talk of this for generations. They'll speak of the dangers, the tragedies, the terror; but also the selfless dedication and bravery of the police, the fire brigade, and everyone here at the London. Now, go sleep for a few hours, my friend. You've done enough for one day."

Treves wiped weary tears from his dark eyes. "I can remain if you need me, Your Grace."

"All we need presently is privacy and coffee, which you've kindly provided. It's generous of you to allow us this room for our discussion. Go sleep, Fred. You've earned it."

Once the chief surgeon had gone, the meeting commenced in full force. Present that evening, aside from Sinclair, were: Paul Stuart, Arthur France, Edmund Reid, Fred Abberline, Hamish Granger, Martin Kepelheim, and Ed MacPherson, who'd brought a guest.

"Gentlemen, before we begin, Dr. MacPherson has brought a friend to help us in our endeavours. Ed, if you'd make the introductions?"

The surgeon's lounge occupied the northwestern corner of the ground floor. Night had long since fallen, and gas lamps along Commercial cast an eerie luminescence into the room. Hansom cabs, omnibuses, charabanc coaches, fancy broughams, and humble dog carts passed back and forth before the two windows; but no one seemed in a rush to travel. All of Whitechapel lay in mourning, and a heavy gloom mixed with the smoke that hung about the grief-stricken streets.

Ed stood. His thinning grey hair was slicked back with scented pomade, and a pair of *pince-nez* sat upon his prominent nose. He looked tired and aged; years older than the man Sinclair had first met in early November.

"This is a day that will stain London's history for ages to come, I fear," he told his friends in a heavy voice. "But we who meet tonight in this room are probably the only group aware of the true cause of this monumental heartache. Need I say the name?"

Paul Stuart hadn't slept for over twenty-four hours, and even his usual positivity had waned. "Redwing," he muttered gloomily. "How I hate that word!"

"It's become a curse, hasn't it, Lord Aubrey?" replied MacPherson. "A seven letter, two syllable, cipher for evil. I know we are all of us tired this night. I shall not temper my words nor truncate my pronouncements. My colleague knows all about our purpose and our history, and he shares our concerns for this diabolical collection of devils.

"Eli and I first met, when I was asked to serve on an ecumenical committee here in Whitechapel. The intent was to form an alliance for mutual understanding amongst the major religions, but he and I soon became fast friends. Since then, we've jointly visited families and congregations of several faiths and preached true happiness in Christ. Eli calls himself a completed Jew, which means he believes in Jesus as Messiah. He teaches at Oxford and has agreed to help us. My friends, I'm honoured to introduce Dr. Elias Yehuda Lieberman."

Charles walked over to shake the gentleman's hand. "It's a great pleasure, Dr. Lieberman. Do forgive our somewhat bedraggled personalities this evening. Most of us have expended a week's worth of energy and worry this day. Reid, Abberline, and France in particular."

Lieberman smiled, his soft brown eyes crinkling at the edges. He was slightly under six feet in height with wavy black hair, cut short. The round face was smooth except for a thick moustache. A pair of round wire-rimmed glasses framed his almond-shaped eyes, and he adjusted them often, as though trying to find the perfect focus.

"Indeed, it's been busy," Lieberman told Sinclair. "And I am honoured to be included in this august group tonight, Your Grace. If my experience and knowledge bring aid to your efforts, then I thank Christ for it."

"Christ?" asked Abberline. "Then you're a Christian?"

"I am a believer in the one you call Jesus. We completed Jews call him by his Jewish name, *Yeshua ha Mashiach*. Jesus the Christ in the Greek. Both Christ and Mashiach, that is Messiah, mean 'anointed one'. He is our Redeemer and our King."

"Then, you've a much different view than most of your brethren, Dr. Lieberman," Abberline answered. "But then I don't usually attend these meetings. Reid here's been after me for years to come to one, but I always figured it was nothin' but a lot o' titled men with little to do. Gentlemen, I stand corrected."

Charles laughed at this, as did many of the others. "Fred, if you decide to join our circle, I think you'll discover these titled men act more like Yard detectives than pampered peers. I'm very glad you're here tonight, just sorry for the reason. Tell me, Dr. Lieberman, is your father also a believer in Yeshua? He's a leading rabbi, is he not?"

"My father is not yet a believer, Your Grace, but he is leaning in that direction. Give him time, and he'll finish that journey. As Ed may have told you, my father is Rabbi Jacob Lieberman, and is considered a *gaon* or genius, because he's memorised so many ancient texts and meditated upon them. He is a true man of God, and though his current interpretation differs from our own regarding Messiah, you could find no one better to consult regarding this Dybbuk."

"Dybbuk?" asked Abberline. "Don't tell me we're going to talk about that nonsense!"

"The circle takes these tales very seriously, Inspector," Sinclair cautioned his colleague. "I have personal experience with unseen enemies. All I ask, Fred, is that you keep an open mind. Trust me, when I say that when my wife first told me about Redwing my own reaction was similar. Since then, I've come to realise the world is not as neatly packaged as we like to think." He turned to Lieberman. "Doctor, does your father connect recent crimes in Whitechapel to a spiritual cause?"

"He does, indeed, but he places no burden upon me or anyone else to follow him blindly. Rather, Papa asks each to weigh the scriptures for himself. I speak of the Tanakh, of course, the Hebrew version of what you call the Old Testament. I was born in London, raised speaking and reading English, but also Russian and Hebrew. Since going to school at Oxford, I've learnt many other modern and ancient languages, which is why I teach Ancient Middle Eastern linguistics. I'm fascinated by how various languages intersect, but especially, how their mythologies do. I accepted Yeshua as Messiah when I was twenty-six, just three years ago, and I have never looked back. It's my daily prayer that Papa will one day recognise how the old prophecies point to fulfillment by this one man—Yeshua, God made flesh! The rabbi nears that moment of clarity, and I have hope. After all, our Saviour made the blind to see, did he not?"

Sinclair smiled. "Well said, Dr. Lieberman. May all your family soon find their vision restored."

"Thank you," Elias answered. "Regardless of his current beliefs, if you wish to know about the spirits behind this heinous string of crimes, then my father is your man."

"But do you think he would work with us?" asked Sinclair. "Not only are we Christian, some of us are members of another much-hated group."

"The aristocracy, you mean?" the professor asked.

"No," Charles replied with a soft laugh. "Actually, I still find it hard to think of myself as a member of the aristocracy, but I suppose I am. Actually, I refer to the brave men in blue. Whitechapel residents have little love for the police, especially now."

"I see what you mean, but I think you'll be surprised, Your Grace. My father's been aided by your policemen many times since he arrived here thirty years ago. Whilst still a boy, I saw much of the East's brutality, but seldom did it originate with policemen. My people are treated far worse by our Jewish brothers than by your officers. The wealthy who live in Westminster or the square mile see us Whitechapel Jews as little more than filth upon their boots. It is to their own shame, I think."

"I agree," Sinclair said soberly, "and I'm very sorry for all you've endured; both here and elsewhere. Has your father mentioned the Dybbuk?"

"Yes, he's talked of it. All of Spitalfields, a largely Jewish neighbourhood as you know, speak of it, and many cower behind their windows at night. The Ripper's deeds had my friends and relatives worried for months, and they feared reprisals from their neighbours because of the claim he is a Jew, but these recent crimes strike more deeply. I read that pollution of the water by mouldy grain caused the mass hallucinations last month, but these sightings were no hallucination. My father recognised the description from the old country. The old stories from Russia. Legends most men think are fable have roots in reality. Wolves that walk like men, demons with a taste for blood and human flesh, succubi and incubi, ghosts that attach themselves to individuals or families and cause all to grow sick and die. My friend MacPherson says your group believes in these tales, but tell me, Your Grace: do you believe in them?"

Charles looked to Paul Stuart, who'd been writing notes on a sheet of paper; a series of symbols he'd come to recognise as the circle's code. "Lord Aubrey, would you like to reply to Dr. Lieberman?"

Aubrey glanced up, dragged from his inner thoughts. Rising to his feet, the exhausted earl took a sip of water before answering. "Forgive me, gentlemen, I've spent many nights recently, prowling the byways of London for certain criminals, and I fear my mind is not as clear as it might otherwise be. Inspector Abberline is welcome to hear what I'm about to say, as are you Dr. Lieberman, but I must ask you both to swear never to reveal our discussion to anyone else without first obtaining our permission. Will you agree to that?"

Both men nodded.

"Very well, then," continued the earl. "Let me tell you a story of history that will likely shock and dismay. I grew up with this knowledge, but to someone hearing it for the first time in his adult years, it can prove quite alarming. You asked if we believe these old tales of skin-changers and vampires. The fact is this: we not only believe in them, we hunt them. The inner circle protects a human bloodline that's been hidden from official histories, but those in power are aware of its existence. Again, I insist you agree to reveal none of this."

Abberline stood, his manner uncharacteristically subdued. "I expect you're talking to me, Lord Aubrey, and I understand your reticence. I've never been particularly commiseratin' when it comes to some o' what you and Reid discuss, but I've always suspected there's a lot more to it. I ask your forgiveness for my thick-headedness. I'm a simple man in a complex world, and it grows evermore confusing as I age. If you'll speak plainly, I promise to keep your secrets, for I respect each of you men like brothers." He turned to Sinclair. "Charles, I've known you for thirteen years, and I feel a bit like a father in some ways. You make me proud to be a policeman, son. Gentlemen, there is no finer man nor mind upon this green earth. If Charles Sinclair believes in these secrets, then so will I. And Martin's far more than a mere tailor, if you ask me," he added, casting an eye towards Kepelheim. " I reckon he's got secrets, too. Just sayin'."

Fred took a seat midst a collection of smiles and mild laughter.

Martin offered a dimpled grin. "My history is long with the inner circle, as is Lord Aubrey's," he said. "But as I age, the world moves further and further into a dark place. Let us pray that Dr. Lieberman will provide a lantern to light our way."

"It is Christ who lights our path and feet," the Oxford teacher observed. "Yeshua, the light of the world."

"He is indeed," echoed Aubrey. "Fred, since you arrived late, you missed our opening prayer, offered by our humble tailor. It's our custom to petition the Lord for his protection and mercies before each man offers reports. MacPherson mentioned the name we all hate: Redwing. Allow me to explain. It is a cabal of spiritually compromised men and women who side with demons and fallen angels in a plan to rule the world."

"Rather like bankers," Abberline quipped.

All laughed. "True, but not all financiers side with devils. It only seems as though they do," Paul observed. "Recently, the newspapers of London ran a series of articles that have been repeated by major editions throughout the western world. The implication is that Queen Victoria's reign is illegitimate, and that another has a stronger right to the throne of England."

"It's on the tongues of nearly every student at Oxford," Lieberman told the group. "But surely, these are spurious rumours only."

"I cannot confirm whether or not the rumours of our sovereign's parentage are true," replied the earl, "for contemporary sources vary on opinion, but I can speak to the other. I mentioned a human bloodline earlier, and it is our honour as circle members to protect it. Martin is keeper of the lines. Perhaps, he should explain."

The tailor rose, his mischievous eyes gazing upon the gathering of men. "Thank you, Lord Aubrey. Allow me to add clarity to our earl's previous statement regarding Her Majesty's right to the throne. No one here is old enough to have lived through those uncertain days during the reign of William IV. That king's issue numbered as many as thirteen, according to some, but none could be considered legal. All were borne from mistresses, which the Royal Marriage Act of 1772 strictly forbade. All liaisons and marriages had to be approved by the sovereign and privy council. And because all legitimate heirs had died, Victoria Alexandrina, daughter of the Duke of Kent, became the heir presumptive.

"However, the Duke of Wellington and many others at court, had doubts concerning the parentage of the young princess. Sir John Conroy had come on as Duke Edward's equerry in 1817, just after the duke's marriage to Princess Victoria of Saxe-Coburg-Saalfeld. Very early on, the duchess had a fondness for her husband's equerry, despite Sir John's being a married man. In May 1819, young Victoria Alexandrina was born, and only six months later, Duke Edward died. Instantly, whispers arose regarding who might be her *true* father. Tensions ran high, and the widowed Duchess of Kent could have dispelled them by dismissing Conroy, but instead she had inveigled her late husband into naming him executor of the will! Not since the death of Henry Tudor had there been so many intrigues taking place! That is when our own Duke James's father, the 9th Duke of Drummond, was approached by the Earl of Liverpool, who was prime minister at the time.

"On behalf of England, Liverpool asked permission to publicly name James as the heir presumptive, based on a legal document signed by himself and King William. It is known as the D.B.A., which stands for the Drummond-Branham Agreement. I can show you a copy of the document at your leisure, but it essentially places the rightful lineage to England's throne in these two ducal lines. With hatred for Germany rising, many in Parliament had begun to call for a return of an English sovereign. Though the Plantagenets are actually French in origin, most now consider them historically English. James is Plantagenet and Stuart. As elder nephew, Charles inherits this position. Of all those in line for the throne, Charles Sinclair has the greatest claim."

"Then it's true?" exclaimed Abberline. "We've all been jokin' 'bout it at the Yard, but you're saying it's true?"

Charles stood. "I do not say I have any right to the throne; only that some believe I do. Martin has my entire pedigree written down on a collection of scrolls, and I believe Mac also keeps a copy. Uncle James keeps all original documents at Castle Drummond, but I've recently learnt there are additional proofs in a vault beneath Buckingham Palace. I'm not at liberty to reveal the source of that information."

"I can guess who it is," remarked Abberline, winking at Reid.

"Regardless, I will not confirm it," the duke declared. "My father and grandfather spent years researching our bloodlines and believe they trace not only to Sinclair but to the French royal houses of Anjou, Bourbon, Valois, and Capet. As well as the Scottish houses of Stuart, Bruce, Dunkeld, and MacAlpin. And then there is Plantagenet, the bloodline protected by the inner circle. All these lines converge into a point with my birth."

Martin Kepelheim stood once more. "If I may, Your Grace, there is another line yet unconfirmed, but we grow nearer. The duke, your good uncle, and I discussed it with an expert in the field only this morning and lack but one diary to make it fact. Your father firmly believed in this, and I agree with his conclusion."

Charles's left brow arched. "What conclusion is that?"

"There are clues throughout your childhood, my friend, if you will only remember them. Coupled with the tales of spirits haunting our city and our own experiences, the truth is slowly crystallising."

"What truth, Martin?" Sinclair insisted, growing irritated. "Tell me!"

The tailor swallowed hard, for he feared saying it. "I do not delay for dramatic effect, my friend, but because I worry that this might have dire consequences. However, as you've already begun to recover bits of your memory, let me be bold and reveal it to all. Just before you pledged your life to our little duchess on your wedding day, you asked me about our circle's symbol. Do you remember?"

"Of course, I do," answered the duke. "You'd sewn the P and S into my waistcoat's pattern. Why?"

"Because, I hinted then that the P and S stood for more than just Plantagenet and Stuart. Sinclair is the double meaning to the S, of course; but the P initial also has a twin meaning. Pendragon. Charles, you are the direct descendent of King Uther, through his son Arthur."

CHAPTER TWENTY-TWO

9:11 pm - Saint Clair-sur-Epte, Normandy, France

Albus Lucius Flint rubbed his pale hands together greedily.

"Well? Is this the real codex or not?"

An older, lanky man in a broad-brimmed felt hat stood in the interior of a yellow tent, twenty feet away from a yawning chasm. The expert held a a dusty scroll in his hands, turning it round in the lamplight. He squinted at the fine writing, his aged eyes growing weary.

"It looks right, but there's no way to know for certain without testing it first. That will take time."

"By test, I presume you refer to the paper and ink. Surely, the writing is his? I brought you here because you are the leading expert on Dee's work! Surely, you can draw an inference."

"It appears to be Dee's writing," answered the man. "And as you say, dating the ink and paper adds another layer of authentication."

"Hmph!" muttered the cadaverous lawyer. "All this will take too much time, and ultimately, the only way to test it is during the actual ritual," he complained. "If it's a forgery, then all is lost, which will not please our friends, Lord Salter."

The sixty-two-year-old earl placed the fragile document into a leather case for protection. "They're *your* friends, Flint, not mine. I'll take a better look at it tomorrow. You won't need it for three more days. We've plenty of time."

"I warn you, Salter. If your expertise proves a mistake, it is you who will pay, not I," Flint assured him angrily. "We hired you and your wife because of your flawless reputations. Were we mistaken?"

George Edward Holloway, 8th Lord Salter, had served on the dig since September and endured enough of the lawyer's burdensome oversight. He glared at the annoying little man, a thick blonde moustache undulating along with the earl's wide upper lip as he fired back.

"See here, Flint! If you wish to dismiss my services, then do so! I came into this at the last minute only because my son thinks enough of your so-called Society to join your project in Kent. But do not *dare* to growl at me, sir! Why you thought to dig in this backwater village is a mystery, but it appears your sources have certain merit. Whether or not this scroll is the copy reputedly made by John Dee is another matter entirely. The writing is certainly Sumerian, but claims that Dee had access to the Emerald Tablets are spurious at best."

"He had three of them in his possession. Of that, there is no doubt," Flint replied calmly.

"But no one really knows what these tablets are, or if they existed in the first place!" argued Salter.

"They are real, Lord Salter. As real as this cavern. As real as that crevasse below. As real as your hands and eyes. I require only your confirmation before we use the spell."

"Spell? If you think these phrases contain a spell, then it's more than any record indicates. You should have engaged my son. His knowledge of the esoteric surpasses mine. Dash it all, if you weren't holding my wife, I'd report the lot of you to the English Antiquarian Society, or perhaps the police!"

"Calm yourself," cooed the solicitor. "We do not 'hold' your wife. She is my employer's guest. The Prince Aleksandr has spared no expense to lavish hospitality upon her. As soon as the ceremony on the solstice is over, you may both return home."

"Koshmar's a devil, if you ask me," answered Salter bitterly.

Flint grinned, that crooked line of the lip that always unsettled humans. "I thought you believed in material life only, Lord Salter. Are you now saying the ethereal and spiritual have merit?"

"Damned if I know any more!" shouted the earl, sitting at the table in resignation. "Look here, why are you so convinced these tablets are real?"

"All in good time, my lord. Once the ceremony is done, then I shall be happy to answer all your questions."

"And what if this spell fails, eh? This so-called elixir of life may be a load of poppycock!"

The lawyer's face turned dark. "Take care with your speech, Lord Salter. Are the words spoken by the First Intelligence a load of poppycock? Some call him God, but we do not. His words have power, and when used correctly, can open ancient paths and doorways and even transmute Time itself! The *Tabula Smaradgina*, or Emerald Tablets, are fragments of the *Sefer Raziel*, which we call the Book of First Words. The original was torn into thirteen pieces which are lost in other realms and sealed by wards."

"What the devil are you rambling on about? Look here, the Blackstone Society describes itself as scientific, but it seems to me that you're spouting alchemical gobbledygook! Dee may have been a bit mad, but I doubt he fell for such utter nonsense."

"One man's nonsense is another man's religion, Lord Salter. You pronounce yourself a rationalist, but given the right evidence, even you would admit to the existence of a supernatural realm. Dee sought such knowledge, for he believed it explained hidden truths about the material world."

Salter wiped sweat from his brow. Despite the cold temperature in the cavern, he suddenly felt feverish. "What truths?"

The solicitor began to smile, a decidedly evil grin revealing a hint of the birdlike man's true face.

"You might call it the secret formula to *Ordo ab Chao*. If we recite the proper words on the winter solstice, then we can summon the Keeper of the fragment. He knows the locations of all the book's other pieces. With his knowledge, we can find them and reassemble the Book of First Words. Don't you see it? It is the end of the beginning! The true Omega to the Alpha! The snake shedding its accursed skin to regain its magnificent wings. The Golden Age returned! Surely, that is a laudable goal, is it not?"

"I suppose so; if by 'golden age' you mean an age of scientific reason," the earl answered.

"It is precisely what I mean, Lord Salter," lied the deceitful crow. "The Dark Ages quenched that early movement towards the light, but we can return that glimmering hope to the world. If all goes as planned, a new king will arise, and with him the first step towards utopian glory!"

Salter gulped, wishing he could be anywhere else—not here. Not involved in this mad enterprise. "And my wife? Will you release her once it's done?"

"As I've told you many times, Lady Salter is free to leave our accommodations without encumbrance. But if you wish to see her well and happy, then use your skills to verify this scroll. But do so quickly. Friday's setting sun provides the light required for our ritual, which gives us a very narrow window."

"And this spell, as you call it, will unlock some doorway? Is that it?" asked Salter, his hands trembling.

"Not only a doorway, but a sealed portal. I shall speak the words, and the Stone King and his mighty Dragon will arise once more to set the world aflame."

CHAPTER TWENTY-THREE

11:53 pm – Haimsbury House

The Sinclairs' farewell-to-London party began at half ten, following the conclusion of a rather disappointing Lyceum play, bringing music and small talk to the fashionable drawing rooms of Haimsbury House. Charles returned home at eleven and was met by a very happy wife when he came through the front door. Paul Stuart joined them thirty minutes later after going home to change into the required evening clothes.

Victoria Stuart, who'd planned the gathering, assumed the role of primary hostess. The first guest to arrive was her dearest friend, Dolly Patterson-Smythe, who, along with her husband, Sir Richard (usually called 'Dickie'), had come to London for the Christmas season. Nearly all the other guests came directly from the theatre, but a few stopped at their homes first, which meant the front bell continued to ring for over an hour.

Tory had promised to keep the guest list short, but as always happened with the popular Lady Victoria Stuart (who knew practically everyone in London society), many guests had sought permission to bring 'just one more', and these then took it upon themselves to invite a few others. Thus, a party which Charles assumed would host four-dozen at the most had swollen to the status of a major event with nearly a hundred well-heeled people to serve and entertain. Ever the perfect hostess, Elizabeth received all with good humour, and soon the attendees were calling it the best party of any holiday season.

As so often happens with Westminster soirées, government men and important peers migrated to the galleries and smoking parlours, whilst the ladies preferred the cheerful music room, Cumbria drawing room, or the grandly decorated 'all-season' conservatory. Here, two stone fireplaces kept the space cozy and inviting, and Dolly Patterson-Smythe's favourite musicians, a husband and wife team famous for their Bach repertoire, provided a constant source of entertainment on the pianoforte and harp.

In addition to peers and Parliamentarians, the guests included musicians, writers, and actors; all eager to rub shoulders with the country's bluest of bloods. Amongst these was Abraham Stoker. The handsome playwright arrived on his own that evening, explaining that his wife had taken the children to Ireland to visit their grandmother for Christmas. With his Ripper play still in the minds of Westminster's patrons, the writer found no paucity of opportunities to discuss his work and theories on the crimes.

Aubrey never lacked for company either. The handsome earl was constantly surrounded by eyelash-fluttering ingenues in low-cut dresses, ready to cater to his every whim. Charles thought it quite amusing, but the sleep-deprived earl found the constant attention exhausting.

By half past one, the party began to wind down, and Sinclair noticed his cousin had been absent for a very long time. He left his wife in the care of Duke James, Victoria, Dolly, and several other stragglers in the Cumbria Room, and sought out the earl. Along the way, he ran into Henry MacAlpin, who was descending the staircase. One of the musicians had accidently spilled half a glass of claret on the viscount, and he'd changed into a fresh shirt, trousers, and waistcoat; courtesy of Sinclair's stylish closet.

"That cut really suits you, Henry," the duke told Salperton.

"And the fabric is soft as butter. Is this one of Martin's designs?"

"Of course. I've no idea when he finds the time, but nearly every day, he brings by another item of clothing. If you want to place an order, I'll warn you: Paul's first in the queue. Have you seen him, by the way?"

"Paul? I believe he's taking a nap somewhere, actually," Henry replied as he fastened his watch chain to the white waistcoat. "I understand the poor fellow's hardly slept in three days. Lovely party though. I've never seen so many unattached females in one place. Perhaps, it's best Miss Stuart decided to remain at Montmore. The crush of chattering people might have put her off."

"I can see how it would. Crowds often put me off. Baxter!" he called to the man with the magnificent eyebrows. The butler was just leaving the music room, carrying a tray of empty glasses.

"Your Grace?" his melodious voice replied. Charles wondered how the eminent Mr. Baxter managed to appear bandbox crisp after so many hours serving. In fact, he'd never seen the butler look anything but perfect.

"I wouldn't want to interrupt whatever it is you're doing, but I wonder if you've seen Lord Aubrey?" Sinclair asked.

The powerfully built butler pondered a moment, searching his memory. "I believe the last time I spoke with his lordship was an hour ago. He asked to be let into the locked library so he might find a bit of quiet. I offered him my key, which he used to lock it from the inside. I hope that was all right, sir."

"Yes, of course. Aubrey should probably have his own key. Thank you. Oh, Baxter, as regards tomorrow's plans, we hope to depart Victoria Station no later than five. I've several errands to run in the morning, but if I can keep to my schedule, I should be back here by three. Will you and Mrs. Alcorn be ready?"

"Everything is prepared, my lord. You've nothing to worry about. Leave everything to me."

Sinclair smiled. "They are the four words by which I live, my friend. 'Leave everything to Baxter.'" He searched his pockets. "I don't seem to have the library key on me. Have you a second key?"

The butler set down the tray and searched his own pockets. "Yes, sir. I made a copy to keep two with me at all times, in case Mr. Kepelheim locks himself in. Now where is it?" The man's greying brows pinched together, and then inched upwards along his high forehead, whilst his hands searched every pocket of the formal coat and trousers. "I cannot imagine where it could have gone, Your Grace! Perhaps, it's in my office. It won't take me a minute."

Baxter left to fetch the key and returned five minutes later. "It would have been a shame to force the door, sir. Perhaps, we might have another copy made?"

"Another good idea, Baxter," said the duke. "Have three more made. One for Miles next door, another for Mr. Kepelheim, and the third you may give to Lord Aubrey."

As the door opened, Sinclair noticed the ambient temperature differed markedly from that of the main house, and the room stood in complete darkness. As no one planned to use the library that evening, the fire remained unlit but the room's four radiators should have maintained a modest sense of warmth.

"Forgive the cold, Henry," he told the viscount. "Some of these new radiators have been acting up. The plumbers are having a look at them tomorrow."

The viscount put a hand on his friend's shoulder. "I don't think it's the heaters, Charles. Stand still. We're not alone."

The duke could see his breath in the ambient light given off by the anteroom's lamps, and a supernatural heaviness settled into his chest. "Paul?" he asked, stepping farther into the library. "Paul, are you in here?"

Baxter slowly followed, scanning the room for signs of life. "Do be careful, my lord," he urged his master.

Henry had already advanced halfway across the shadowy carpet, and he turned back to the duke and whispered, "Charles, the hidden panel is open."

Baxter switched on the electric sconces and chandelier. Sure enough, the spring-loaded panel stood ajar, leading into the secret maze of interior passageways. "Go tell my uncle what we're doing, Baxter, but don't alarm the duchess. Say we're taking a walk, or something."

"Of course, sir. Shall I return to offer assistance?"

"Just keep an eye on the door. If we're not back in fifteen minutes, send Kepelheim and Duke James. Again, do not alarm my wife."

Baxter left and shut the door, keeping the key just in case. Charles and Henry peered into the looming space before them. Sinclair had only been inside the puzzle chamber once, but even that short visit had led to a ghastly nightmare. He dreaded returning, but worried that his impetuous cousin had gone into the mystery room alone and accidentally passed through the obsidian mirror attached to the inner side of the chamber door.

"It's like an ice house in here," observed Salperton. "Charles, there's a distinct feeling of oppression in the air. I really don't think we're alone."

"Do you sense it or see it, Henry?"

"Neither and both. It's more an intuition. Wait, I hear something now."

Sinclair stopped to listen. "I can't hear it."

"No? It's someone speaking, whispering. A woman's voice."

"A woman?"

"Yes, a woman. And she's... It sounds like she's singing."

Ten minutes earlier

Paul Stuart had no idea how he'd arrived inside the puzzle chamber. His ears rang so loudly it hurt, and his body felt as though he had been dragged through Time itself.

"How...? Where is this? How did I get here?"

"A mere manipulation of matter. A party trick," a woman answered. "It's been ages since I last beheld this chamber. Did you know that I helped to construct it? The room's design is my own, but the writing—well, another did that. I don't care for any of it. This was once the heart of a magnificent temple, but that was long, long ago. Ages and ages. The writing ruins it," she sighed. "Why must things change?"

Paul felt deathly cold. His heart still beat, but the atmosphere of the room was that of a tomb. All he could remember was falling asleep on the library sofa. Perhaps, he was dreaming.

The woman spoke from inside the mirror, her image ripping like water. She wore nothing at all, and the reflected light of the chamber's gas sconces painted the curves of her naked body with undulating strokes of multi-coloured light. Her hair fell in rich, dark waves of such length that it pooled upon the floor. She was Lady Godiva come to life, but rather than use her hair to conceal her most intimate contours, the mirror nymph brazenly swept the wavy locks behind her shoulders, exposing every one of her ample curves.

Aubrey shut his eyes.

The seductive succubus drew close, trying to emerge from the mirror. "Don't you remember me?" she whispered in a French accent.

Despite his fear, the earl opened one eye, and then the other. The woman's appearance had changed completely, morphing from a raven-haired harlot into the perfect image of a long-dead love. Her golden hair fell along the contours of the creamy skin like a waterfall of amber light, and the turquoise eyes gazed upon him with adoration.

"*Mon* David," she whispered in a French accent. "Come to me, *mon cher*."

It was Cozette du Barroux, fully flesh and more voluptuous than ever; warm and sensual and impossibly real. She stepped closer, touching the obsidian from the other side of the portal. He could smell her perfume, feel her breath upon his face, hear her heartbeat as though she lay beside him.

"You cannot be here," he choked, terrified to move. "You're dead."

"But I am alive, *mon couer*. *Je t'aime*, David. *Je t'aime*. Kiss me. Come to me, my beautiful one, and kiss me once more."

He shivered, longing to embrace her, but fearing it. "You are a phantom. A lie."

"I am as real as you want me to be," she insisted, motioning for him to join her. "Remember when we would lie together and talk until the sun rose over the Seine? And then after, how we would sing and laugh and drink red wine? No one else loved me that way, David. No one!" Her smile then vanished, her eyes turning cruel. "But no, I must call you by the true name, mustn't I? You are Paul. A man of wealth, who left me to die; all alone with a child. Your child. And then you stole her from me!"

"No! It wasn't like that! I didn't know," he told her, stepping backwards in shock and regret. "If I'd known, then..."

"Then what? You would have taken me home to your mama? To your papa? No, *mon coeur*, you would not. You'd have paid me to kill it. You'd have seen her dead!"

"Never!" he wailed, falling to his knees. "Cozette, I loved you! I love our daughter! She is with me now, and she... She looks more like you each day." He began to weep, anguish filling every corner of his being.

"Then, come to me, if you love me. Come to me, my beautiful Scotsman. How I love you, my beautiful Paul. Let us be together forever!"

He shut his eyes, consciousness fleeing, as he collapsed onto the floor. A curl of smoke emerged from the mirror as she sang a siren song. The smoke became an avatar, an extension of the witch within the mirror, and the spectral form bent over his body, her thick, smoky hair covering his cold face. She forced him to stand and then dragged him towards the mirror's portal.

"Come to me, Paul," she sang. "Join us!"

Stuart blinked as he neared the mirror's face, but he had no will to resist. All strength had left. His fingers touched the obsidian surface, disappearing into the abyss beyond.

Just then, Sinclair and Salperton entered the room. Without a moment's thought, Charles reacted. "In the name of Christ, I command you to stop!" he shouted.

The hideous phantom hissed, her teeth bared as she howled, "You are too late! He's mine!"

Henry rushed towards Aubrey, but the she-devil pulled hard, and the earl's arm sank into the black abyss.

"In the name of Christ, stop!" Sinclair commanded, pulling on his cousin's arm with all his strength. "In the name of Jesus Christ, Son of the only true God, who offered himself freely, who died but lives again, and is coming to end your reign of terror, demon!"

"Use not that hated name with me, boy!" the entity screamed. Releasing its hold on Aubrey, the beautiful siren transformed into a scaly green dragon, its eyes burning with flames of crimson fire.

"I will use that name, because Christ is my salvation and my shield," Charles declared in a commanding tone. "I do not fear you, hellion. Christ is your creator and only he rules, demon! I command you in his holy name to return to the pit! You have no right to this man!"

The dragon paused, the clawed hands raking at the mirror, apparently bound there. "We are coming, Child of Blood. And soon, your heritage will call you, and darkness will reign once more!"

With a rush of foul-smelling wind, the image vanished, blowing piles of mouldy dust across the chamber's stone floor.

Henry held Paul in his arms, checking his pulse. "We need to get him out of here. Help me, Charles."

The duke took one arm, and Salperton the other, and the two of them carried the half-conscious earl back into the library, finding Baxter waiting anxiously. Without a word, the butler fetched a decanter of brandy and filled a tall glass.

"Give him this."

After consuming half the stout spirit, Stuart's eyes blinked, as though rousing from a deep sleep.

"What happened?" he said weakly. "Where am I?"

"You're in the library. What can you remember?" Charles asked him as he sat nearby.

"Not much. I came here to lie down for a moment. Nothing else; though I had an odd dream. Sorry to disappear like that, but I just had to close my eyes. Charles, what's the matter? You all look as though you've seen a ghost."

Charles weighed several options for reply, wondering how much truth his cousin could endure, but it was Henry who answered.

"We heard you cry out, that's all, old man. That dream must have been quite something! But it's understandable, your wanting to lie down for a few minutes. Good heavens, Paul, you're not a machine. Even you must sleep now and again. Come now, we're all gathering in the Cumbria Room. I hear Stoker's going to regale us with his current research. He's writing a book, apparently."

Sinclair decided Salperton must have a reason for keeping back the truth; perhaps, fearing for Aubrey's mental state.

"Honestly, Paul, you look done in," the duke said. "Why don't you give the rest of the party a miss and go upstairs? Sleep in your old apartment. Baxter will set everything in order."

The butler hovered close to the earl, worry painting his features. It was clear he loved the man dearly. "I'll see to it myself, Your Grace. Come with me, Lord Aubrey. Let's get you upstairs."

CHAPTER TWENTY-FOUR

Elizabeth felt exhausted, and that weariness, coupled with slight nausea, began to impede upon her good mood. She longed to retire, but as hostess, she hated even to suggest it.

Nearly everyone else had left by now, including the musicians and mysterious 'hangers-on'. Baxter had unmasked two of these as reporters, whom he hastily showed to the door with orders never to return. As the clock struck two, only a few intimate friends remained to drink the last of the punch and devour the final cakes and sandwiches. Dickie Patterson-Smythe had long since left for a Mayfair hotel, but his garrulous wife Dolly sat beside Drummond, both of them enjoying a cup of punch, which he'd spiked with a splash of Drummond Reserve. Victoria occupied the next chair, and running clockwise round the room were Dr. Reginald Whitmore, Elizabeth, Ed MacPherson, Kepelheim, and Abraham Stoker. When Charles and Henry joined the group, the young duke explained his cousin's need for sleep and that Paul had retired to his usual apartment upstairs.

Charles took the seat next to his wife with Henry beside him.

"Henry, have you met my friend, Lady Patterson-Smythe?" asked Victoria.

Dolly was taller than Victoria by two inches, with upswept hair that gleamed with wheat and silver strands. The wrinkles at the corners of her grey eyes revealed a fine sense of humour, but there was a serious look to them, indicating a woman of fierce resolve and intelligence, accustomed to exerting influence on her surroundings.

She reached for Henry's hand, her wide mouth opening into an impish grin. "Oh, yes, we've met, Tory. I gave him a little kiss in the music room, just after the harpist finished that last Bach piece. Henry blushed; dear thing! You know, I don't think he remembers me."

"Should I?" Salperton asked, blushing again at her mention of the unexpected kiss.

"You were only ten at the time, my dear," she said sweetly. "There was a dog that followed you everywhere, wasn't there? A spaniel of some kind. Black and white."

"Droigheann, yes! I'm sorry for not remembering. Did you used to visit us?"

"Every summer, when I could manage it. Dickie and your father are old friends, and I adored your dear mother. What a delicate, charming woman she was."

"She was indeed, Lady Patterson-Smythe. It's kind of you to remember," he said with delight. "I'm sorry for my poor memory. I've a dreadfully slow brain, some days. Perhaps, it's all the wine."

"I rather doubt your mind is ever slow, Henry, and do call me Dolly. Everyone does. Come, sit by me," she said, patting the empty chair next to hers. "We're all going to talk about ghosts and demons!"

"Really? It's hardly the sort of conversation one would expect in so elegant a home," he answered, and then took the seat next to Dolly, his mind on the terrifying creature who'd attacked Paul Stuart.

"I'd thought Lord Aubrey might be with you," spoke Kepelheim. "It's a shame our earl has abandoned us."

"Charles and I found him sound asleep on one of the sofas and persuaded him to overnight here," Henry told the tailor. "Oh, thank you, James."

Drummond had handed him a glass of whisky. "This is our special Reserve, Henry. If you've never had it, you're in for a treat. Nothing warms Scottish blood like the Reserve!"

"I'm sure my Scottish blood will appreciate it. It is somewhat chilly in the house, isn't it?"

"A little," answered Tory. "Charles thought the boiler might need cleaning, but we manage well enough with the fireplaces. Henry, have you met our special guest yet? He's the reason for our topic of conversation. Mr. Abraham Stoker, this is Dr. Henry MacAlpin, 7th Lord Salperton."

"A pleasure" said the viscount, holding the whisky in his left hand whilst shaking Stoker's with his right. "You're the manager at the Lyceum, correct? We enjoyed the play this evening. Well, most of it. The scenery that crashed in the final act was unfortunate. And I'm sorry about the illness in your cast. Might it be measles? I'm afraid it's going round the city." He took a sip. "Oh, this is quite strong, isn't it? A lovely finish, though. Somewhat smoky with a hint of sweetness. Maple?"

"Maple and vanilla, but don't sip it, son," ordered the duke. "Tip it back and let it burn its way down your throat. You sip the second, but tip the first. That's my rule."

"Clearly, my education continues, sir. Very well," the alienist said, obediently gulping down the contents. "Ah, yes," he coughed, trying to catch his breath. "I see what you mean by the burning. It really intensifies the aftertaste. Rather like charred honey in a warm bed of pain. Very, uh, excuse me—very nice."

"That's your Stuart blood calling out, son," James said proudly. "Henry's my cousin, Mr. Stoker. Through his mother. Now, we're discussing ghosts and the like," he told Sinclair and Salperton, "because Stoker's working on a new book that expands on themes of interest to us."

Haimsbury turned to the playwright. "A new book? I hope it doesn't expand on your Ripper play. Forgive me, but the play was quite unsettling."

"No, sir. Though, the topic is related."

"How did it fare in the box office?" Charles asked.

Stoker held a small glass of sherry, and thoughtfully sipped before replying. "Most of the audiences seemed to enjoy the frank horror of it all, Your Grace, though I know it unsettled your dear wife."

Beth responded with kindness. "Please, don't take that as criticism, Mr. Stoker. I appreciate your talent, regardless of the play's subject matter. Perhaps, though, you'll consider writing on a happier topic for your next play."

"I should love to comply, my lady, but as theatre is a business, ticket sales dictate content," he replied as the firelight danced upon his bearded face. "The public's appetite for the macabre and mysterious is never sated, but only grows as our world becomes more modernised. The two are in direct proportion, I think. The further our country progresses towards humanism, the greater the desire for transcendence; for a spirituality to explain the supernatural phenomena all round us. There is much more to the world than what we see.

As the public abandons the Bible, they will inevitably turn to the occult, not science."

"Yes!" Beth agreed. "Oh, yes! I've said that very thing to my husband, haven't I, Charles? Ghosts and demons take advantage of our natural curiosity; this yearning for the ethereal, if you will. But most now discard the Bible's answers in favour of spiritualism and the occult."

The young duke held his wife's hand as he answered. "Mr. Stoker, as you know from earlier conversations, this family applauds invention and scientific discovery, in fact we help to underwrite it; but modern conveniences come at a cost, which may ultimately be human souls. Your theory is sound, and as a mathematician, I agree with your reference to direct proportionality."

"It is a very troubling ratio, if you ask me," the duchess observed. "One with deadly, eternal consequences. As rural workers leave the open fields to put their hands to industry's machines, they uproot themselves to congregate in cities. We've seen that happening for nearly fifty years in London, but also in Birmingham, Liverpool, and Manchester. The consequence is that villages decline as overburdened cities swell. If a young man leaves his father's farm and moves to London, then he abandons a warm bed and regular meals; but also his church and family. It's as though he's traded his entire inheritance for a bowl of porridge!" she exclaimed. "What does he gain in return? A backbreaking job in a heartless factory with high taxation and unsanitary living conditions. Soon, he grows bitter, and along with that comes, despair and complete loss of faith. Truly, it makes me weep to think of it."

The writer set aside his glass, excitedly. "Yes. Yes! I'm so very pleased that you both see it! And this loss of faith is replaced with a ravenous hunger for the occult. It is gratifying to hear so genteel a lady express the problem so very well. I find myself fascinated by the topic, my friends, but I've no desire to write violent, gory scenes merely to sell tickets. No, it's the struggle twixt good and evil I hope to convey to a wider audience through my book. To demonstrate the power of faith over evil."

Drummond sipped the spiked punch, allowing the whisky's burn to slowly drift down his muscular throat. Smiling with satisfaction and a lovely glow, he entered the conversation. "Tell me, Bram—oh, do forgive me, may I call you that?"

"Of course, Your Grace. I'd be honoured. It's what my mother always called me."

"Tell me, then, Bram, when you speak of the occult, do you mean the demonic realm?"

"Yes, precisely that, my lord."

"Demons in literature are one thing," interjected Henry, "for they're dismissed with the closing of a book. Do you plan to portray these demons as real, Mr. Stoker? As agents of evil in human lives? Honestly, I'm not sure how entertaining that is."

"All novels, plays, and music, must first reach the consumer, Lord Salperton, which requires that they entertain. However, if one can use that captured attention to convey truth, then is it not worth the effort?"

"I think it is," proclaimed the duchess. "It's rather like an inventor discovering a way to add a day's nutrition to a glass of whisky without changing the taste."

"So, I should drink only whisky all day, Princess?" teased Drummond.

Before the duchess could reply, Cornelius Baxter entered quietly, speaking briefly to Salperton. The viscount stood. "Forgive me, ladies and gentlemen. It seems there's a minor problem at Montmore. I need to speak with a messenger. Shan't be long."

He left the drawing room, followed by the butler. Charles moved closer to Beth, his arm round her shoulders. "Perhaps, whisky is a poor metaphor," he whispered. "Beer or gin might serve better, if you require an alcoholic comparison."

She frowned, the long day wearing on her good humour. "Whether it's gin or beer or whisky, it makes no difference. Perhaps, the liquor metaphor is a poor way to describe it. I'm only saying that if an inventor could insert healthy nutrients into tea, perhaps, or another pleasant-tasting drink—something that would energise their bodies and minds—perhaps consumers would slowly improve and leave off drunkardness entirely."

"I fear that's dreamy thinking, Princess," her grandfather argued. "It's a fine idea, but it'd never work. Books, now. That's another kettle o' fish. If you could teach all children to read, then there's a chance for improving their minds through stories. You have to start there, lassie. This hospital o' yours should have a school attached. Not just for trainin' doctors, but for educating unwanted children."

"A place for orphans?" she asked, her sleepy eyes brightening at the thought. "That's a very good idea, Grandfather! It may require more space, though. But you're right. Books are the key to change. After all, one cannot study the Bible without reading." She turned to their honoured guest. "Mr. Stoker, once you get to know me, you'll discover I'm an avid reader of all manner of materials. Novels, biographies, scientific papers, histories, even the *Police Gazette* and *Daily Star* when I can find a copy."

She leaned towards Stoker, continuing her comment in a whisper. "My husband worries that recent reports of ghosts and demon killers weaken my constitution, and therefore he endeavours to keep most papers from me, but I still manage to stay abreast of news and events."

"Are you saying I shouldn't try to protect you?" Charles asked.

She offered him a loving smile. "I'm not complaining, Captain. I appreciate your protection and understand your reasons, but you cannot shelter me from all reality. It is an impossible task. I know about the fires across London and of this Dybbuk creature some say is haunting the East End. The people of Whitechapel and Spitalfields must be terrified! Do you think the source of all these horrors might be intangible and therefore impossible to police? Paul's father had a saying—a maxim, if you will. He'd often quote it, and only recently have I come to understand its meaning: '*Human form does not a human make*.' Martin, do you remember Uncle Robert saying that?"

"Many times," the tailor answered wistfully. "The late earl was startlingly insightful, yet humble in his approach to our work. That maxim, as you call it, dear lady, is a phrase he used when speaking of *shape-shifters*. Those with the power to imitate life of another kind. Spiritual entities are a type of life, but lack materiality. They require physical form to interact with us. Why do you mention it, Your Grace? Do you connect this ability with the murders in the East?"

"Yes, I do," she declared. "Mr. Stoker, you implied in your play that the Ripper isn't a man, but rather a demon in human form. Do I understand that correctly?"

Stoker had finished the sherry, and Drummond refilled his glass with Reserve. "Thank you, sir." Taking the first sip, the writer appreciated the nutty sweetness beneath the smoky taste. "Why, this is marvellous! Far better than Jameson or Kilbeggan. This is your own, Duke James?"

"My family's run the business for over a century. This is the '36 batch, I think. That was a particularly good year. There's another cask in the cellar; unless Kepelheim's drained it. Go on, Bram. Tell us what you think of this shape-shifting idea."

"Tis a very old belief, Your Grace. We've many such tales in Ireland, and I'm sure Scotland is the same. Women and men make pacts with the devil and learn how to transform into wolves, bats, birds, snakes, even rats and flies. And there are spirit beings with similar capabilities: faeries, sprites, and the Tuatha dé Danaan, who some say are the descendants of the goddess Danu. I like that maxim of Lord Aubrey's father. Perhaps, my play is right. Ripper may not be human, but a demon who only appears as a man."

"It certainly explains why witnesses describe so varied an appearance," observed Sinclair. "Beth, are you sure you can talk about this? The subject matter is hardly fodder for pleasant dreams, and you look very tired, darling."

She leaned in close. He could see the weariness in her face but didn't want to insist she go upstairs. This was their final night in London before mid-January, and he wanted it to be perfect. He had no wish to shorten it.

"I find the topic important, Charles. May I stay? We've two very capable physicians present, should I require them. And I've felt much stronger lately. I'd like to remain for another half hour or so."

He kissed her cheek. "Of course, but let's both go up soon. It's been a long day, and I'm fading quickly."

Victoria had been uncharacteristically quiet, for her attentions were fixed on Reginald Whitmore. Charles noticed the handsome widower sometimes touched his aunt's hand with obvious affection, and the two of them shared quiet conversations now and then. Hearing the mention of the duchess's health, Reggie cleared his throat to offer an opinion.

"I'm probably an old-fashioned stick-in-the-mud, but as a doctor, I think the duchess should have retired two hours ago. Call me overcautious, but I imagine it's been a very long day for you as well, Elizabeth, and as you're travelling tomorrow, a good night's rest is all the more important. Tory, back me up on this."

Despite her affections towards Whitmore, the spinster refused to do so. "Reggie, you should know by now that we Stuart women seldom do as we're told. If you make it a requirement, you'll only set her teeth on edge. Beth looks no more weary than the rest of us. If she wants to stay, then she should."

Dolly Patterson-Smythe supported her friend's comment. "Stuart women are anything but compliant, Reggie. Surely, you know that by now! If you plan to spend very much time in this family, then you'd best put aside your old-fashioned ways. Now, I want to get back to this Ripper business," she continued eagerly, a glass of Chablis in her tapered fingers. "My husband's a banker, Mr. Stoker, which means we keep track of all the news. The major Paris papers nearly ran out of ink with all the headlines about this East End fiend, and now they talk of ghosts and demons! Dickie and I live near Goussainville, a little village that's become a sort of British conclave. Every one of our neighbours is either a diplomat, a banker, or a businessman, and they're all worried about London. I've not seen your play, but based on this conversation, it sounds as though you think Ripper's more than mere human. I wonder, is that creative licence, or do you really believe it? I should also love to hear Charles's opinion on it, since he's been involved in the hunt."

A footman entered the parlour with a message for Drummond. The duke took the note and then handed it back to the servant. "Thank you. I'll take care of it at once."

"Is there a problem?" asked Elizabeth.

"Nothing major. Booth asks if I'm staying here tonight or returning home."

"Do stay," she urged him. "Then, we may all continue our talk tomorrow."

"You've twisted my arm!" he laughed. "I'll just dash off a quick note. Won't be long, Princess." He kissed his granddaughter's cheek, whispering as he did so. "You really should go to bed soon. You look worn out."

"I will, Grandpa. I promise."

Once through the foyer, instead of dashing off a note, Drummond climbed the main staircase to an apartment now being used by the earl. Inside, he found Salperton sitting at the edge of a canopied bed, running a series of medical tests.

"What's happened?" asked James. "When you and Charles returned without him, I assumed you were keeping something back. Is he ill?"

"I'm not sure. There was a spot of trouble in that odd room off the library. A spiritual attack of some sort. Charles and I went looking for him and discovered the earl at the mercy of some mirror demon! I've never sensed anything so hateful, James. It looked as though she intended to pull him through to the other side. We had Baxter bring him up here, but now he's showing signs of fever and a quick pulse. I think we have to assume it's connected to the attack."

The elder Stuart stood at the end of the bed, staring at his nephew's pale face. "Paul's been injured many times in his life, but he's hardly ever sick—not since he was a wee sprout. If he's ill, then this demon must be the cause."

"I'll stay here tonight, in case he worsens," promised Salperton. "I've already sent word to Montmore. My nurse can look after my patients until tomorrow."

"Thank you, Henry. You're a good lad. I mustn't be too long. Beth'll grow suspicious. Baxter will find you a place to sleep."

"I'll remain in here. I'm fine on the sofa."

Drummond slapped the viscount on the back in typical male fashion, letting him know his feelings without the need for emotional words. "As I said. You're a good lad."

Once the door was shut, Salperton knelt at the foot of the bed to pray, for he had a very dark, troubled sense all through his spirit. Not since the week at Anatole's castle had the Scotsman felt so great a burden. He began to petition the Lord for mercy, pleading the blood of Christ and the intervention of his mighty warrior angels to protect the Stuart family and the inner circle members; but also, he added with great emotion, that the Lord might protect Violet Stuart and help her to recover her lost life.

CHAPTER TWENTY-FIVE

When Drummond returned to the drawing room, he entered in the middle of a conversation. Beth glanced up, touching her grandfather's strong hand as he took the empty chair beside her. "Is anything wrong?"

"Not at all. I was just sayin' goodnight to your cousin. I'm sure Charles told you Paul's gone upstairs to sleep. Poor lad's worn through. He says he'll see you in the morning, Princess, and sends his love."

She seemed satisfied with this, shifting in her chair to draw close to her grandfather, content to sit between the two men she loved most in this world.

Drummond smiled, enjoying the glow of his grandchild's affections as he returned to the previous topic. "Mr. Stoker, I missed your answer to Dolly's question. Do you believe in demons as literal entities that can interact with our material world?"

Stoker took a deep breath. "Here's how I see it, sir. Modern scientists believe themselves pioneers in a world with no room for God; but a man with *true* wisdom, allows God's truth to guide his quest. When God is removed, then demons rush into that vacuum. These are not phantasms of folklore; they are not mere myth. They exist just as we exist, here, now—perhaps, in this very room. We only perceive them when they choose to reveal themselves. I've done a great deal of research into this subject, and I tell you this: folklore is a civilised silvering to cover the hideous entities behind the looking glass. This mirror realm is the darkling reflection where demonic creatures linger and plot their evil stratagems. In short, we are not alone."

Elizabeth squeezed Sinclair's hand, and he put his arm round her protectively once more. "Courage, little one," he whispered. Then to the writer, he asked, "Mr. Stoker, is your new book a treatise on this theme?"

Stoker set his empty glass on the gleaming coffee table, amongst silver trays of cross-cut sandwiches and iced desserts. "It's a novel, based on research. I hope to show how humans battle against spiritual wickedness. The folklore of the Carpathian Mountains forms the central idea. I've discovered stories that circle round an historical person named Vlad Dracul, or Vlad the Dragon, a Romanian warrior with an unquenchable thirst for the macabre and horrifying. He's said to have impaled his Ottoman enemies on pikes whilst feasting at a bountiful table in their presence."

Beth shuddered. "You mean he ate a meal as these men died? Slowly and in agony? How awful!"

"So the legends say," Stoker continued calmly. "In the Carpathians, locals also speak of werewolves and something they call the *wampyr*."

"What is that?" she asked, the mention of werewolves unnerving her a little.

"A ghost or demon that lives on the blood of humans. A shape-shifter, you might say. It consumes blood in the way we drink wine. Perhaps, not only for pleasure or satiety, but for some spiritual purpose we've yet to fathom."

Elizabeth's face paled. "Why would you choose to write about such things, Mr. Stoker? Have you experienced this wickedness? Have you seen demons? I know you hope to teach through fiction, but these are very distressing topics."

Dolly Patterson-Smythe, who had nerves of steel and infinite curiosity, began to laugh. "My dear girl, didn't you read that *Frankenstein* book last year? And that other one; the book about the scientist who drank a potion that turned him into a diabolical fiend. You read that as well."

"*Jekyll and Hyde*, you mean," Beth answered. "Yes, I read both those, but they're make-believe, Dolly. Seeing ghosts and demons in the real world is far more frightening."

Stoker found the comment surprising. "Do you speak from experience, Your Grace?"

Haimsbury answered for her. "My wife sometimes suffers from troubling dreams, Mr. Stoker, but she's also experienced events that defy natural explanation."

Stoker was intrigued. "Have you? Then, allow me to relate a strange experience of my own. When I was a boy in Clontarf, I suffered from an illness that required me to remain bedridden for many months. It was during this time, that I began to perceive a world not available to us with our natural eyes. One night, I found myself unable to sleep. I was perhaps, five years old at the time. As I lay there, a shadowy figure crept into the room and stood in the corner, watching me. He had multiple arms, that had a spindly aspect to them. I remember thinking he resembled a squid, but as I looked more closely, I realised some of the arms were actually elongated wings, emerging from his back. This creature called upon me night after night during my illness. I said nothing to my mother about it, for his appearance seemed to me perfectly normal; though I cannot explain why.

"One evening, I overheard my father speaking of a puzzling phenomenon. Sheep were dying from a mysterious illness up near Clontarf castle, and farmers were talking about a blood-sucking ghost, which the old folk called the *Droch-fhola*—which, as the duke must surely know, means 'evil blood' in Gaelic. Seven sheep and three dogs were taken by this creature. Had the losses been limited to animals, that would have been heavy enough, but people also began to grow ill and die. Seven in all, with not one drop of blood left in their veins. It was ruled the work of a wolf pack, but I always felt it had something to do with this winged shadow."

A hush had fallen upon the room, each contemplating the disturbing account. Finally, Victoria broke the silence. "What a very strange story! Tell me, Mr. Stoker, does Ireland have many wolves? Might the authorities have been correct?"

Elizabeth had begun to shiver, and Charles moved closer, pulling her into a comforting embrace. "Shall I take you upstairs?" he whispered.

"No, I want to hear this. Do go on, Mr. Stoker."

Drummond nibbled on a ham spread sandwich, his eyes thoughtful. "You know, Mr. Stoker," he said, swallowing. "I recall reading a report about those deaths. I even mentioned it to the other circle members."

"Circle?" the writer asked. "What group is that, sir?"

James took a moment to answer. In truth, this was the real reason he'd asked Victoria to invite the writer: to decide if he might be a candidate for the inner circle. He decided to wait a while longer before revealing too much.

"Ah, well, it's merely a reference to those of us within the family who find such tales of interest. If memory serves, this was in the early '50s, just before I left for the Crimea. You know, I believe we sent someone to look into it." He turned to the circle's resident expert on the occult, Dr. Ed MacPherson. "Mac, do you remember any o' that, or am I completely off the map?"

"I shan't comment as to your map, sir, but I do remember the assignment," the cleric said with a smile. "I'm sure Martin recalls it as well."

Kepelheim was lost in thought, deciding whether another crumb cake slice would be a late night snack or an early breakfast. "Remember? Ireland, you mean? Oh, yes! Yes I do remember! Of course, I remember. Mac and I travelled to Clontarf together and investigated on behalf of our, uh, circle."

Stoker's eyes brightened. "The circle again. I shouldn't wish to pry, sir, but might this group be the *inner circle?*"

"You know it?" asked Haimsbury, clearly shocked.

"My father once spoke of it, and I've tried to uncover more about it, but with no luck. There are countless rumours, but very few facts."

"And what facts have you discerned, Mr. Stoker?" Charles enquired.

"That it is run by your family, and that Duke James is the head."

Everyone grew quiet; looking from one to another, silently deciding whether or not to offer a response.

At last, Drummond began to laugh, easing the tension. "Is that so? Then praise the Lord for it! It seems, Mr. Stoker, your research has led you to us for a reason. It's true that the inner circle forms the core focus of our family, but I no longer lead it. Duke Charles is the head now. The inner circle endeavours to learn all we may about occult activities and these veiled demons you speak of. But we do so as Christians engaged in spiritual warfare, not as curiosity seekers or willing pupils who bend to the whims of the fallen realm. Was it '53 when you went to Ireland, Mac?"

"1852, sir," the cleric corrected.

"Oh, yes, that's right," said Drummond. "Derby had just taken over as Prime Minister. We'd read about a series of mysterious deaths in Clontarf and sent agents to discover the truth of it. Tell me, Bram, how much do you remember of that time?"

"I fear my memories are that of a six-year-old child, Your Grace. I know the hour is late, but I'd be interested in hearing Dr. MacPherson's account, if he's willing to share it."

The clergyman's greying brows rose as he gathered his thoughts. "Let me see if I can recall it for you, Mr. Stoker. Martin and I were much younger, of course—thinner and even rather handsome, if you can believe it," he added with a wink to Martin, who was enjoying the crumb cake.

"A bit thinner, yes, but dashingly handsome!" Kepelheim grinned.

"Well, one of us was, at least," Mac teased. "We'd received an invitation from our inner circle contacts in Dublin, asking us if we might prove or disprove the wolf theory. Martin and I arrived in Dublin in mid-April and then travelled north to your village, where we were met by the Reverend William Kemptson of the Clontarf Parish church."

"Yes, St. John's. I was baptised there!" exclaimed Stoker. "How strange that you speak of my home with such familiarity."

"Then, my memory isn't failing me yet," Mac smiled. "Mr. Kemptson's account made it clear that something out of the ordinary had invaded your village. He did *not* think it wolves."

Kepelheim interrupted. "To be frank, Mr. Stoker, even now, that trip gives me nightmares. The atmosphere that April would provide a chilling setting for any gothic tale of horror, but Mac and I hadn't the luxury of closing the pages of a book. Rather, we lived it, along with you and many others."

"How many others?" Stoker asked. "Again, I seek only to reconcile it. A child's memories are not always reliable."

"There were dozens, and you weren't the only child who reported seeing a winged presence in your room at night. Mr. Kepelheim and I interviewed over thirty children who told stories much like your own. No, Mr. Stoker, the spiritual world is not fiction. It is a part of all the known and unknown realms, and these interact with ours in ways our limited senses find unsettling. Abraham is also your father's name, is that right?"

Stoker nodded. "Yes, it is."

"Your mother's name was Charlotte?" continued MacPherson.

"Yes, that's correct. You spoke with her?" asked Bram anxiously.

MacPherson poured himself a glass of water. "She was a lovely woman, intelligent but high-strung. Although, that may have been due to the topic of our conversation. Most of the parents we interviewed were quite shaken by the events that spring. We heard the spirits *droch-fhoula* and *leannán-sí* mentioned many times during our fortnight there, and we examined all the victims' bodies—animal and human. Each was drained of blood, but there was another phenomenon that accompanied these murders. Not only were the corpses exsanguinated; some showed signs of cannibalism."

Kepelheim worried about the duchess, for her face grew evermore pale with each word. Rather than mention her directly, he used a different tack. "Bloodless corpses! Oh, my! Perhaps, our conversation has wandered too deeply into the maudlin, my friends. Lady Patterson-Smythe must think us all a pack of ghouls!"

Dolly's reaction hardly helped, for her response was to laugh. "Not a bit of it, Martin. Dickie and I often have conversations like this back in Goussainville. Our village may be small, but it's steeped in all manner of ghoulish tales. In fact, there's a very odd little group of people that attended one of my soirées this past summer. I think you and Beth met one of them, Tory. You remember the peculiar fellow Dickie called Mr. Sunshine?"

Victoria shrugged, lighting a second cigarette. "Do you mean the chap who looked as though he'd eaten a rat? Always wore black with the most funereal expression. What was his name again? Something to do with rocks or metal. Mr. Stone? No, that doesn't sound right."

"Mr. Flint," said Elizabeth. "Albus Flint. He's the solicitor for the Blackstone Society, and we met several times. Do excuse me, won't you? I fear the food isn't settling well, and I'm growing very tired. Tory, I'm sorry to leave you with hostess duties."

"Nonsense, it was my idea to have the party in the first place. Charles, go with her, but do come back once you've tucked her in. We've more to discuss."

The young duke took his wife's arm to help her stand. "Forgive us, darling. I fear we've let our talk drift into very dark territory. We foolish men sometimes forget ourselves."

"You are anything but foolish, Captain," she whispered. "Goodnight, everyone. Thank you for coming, Mr. Stoker. I hope you'll visit us again."

The Sinclairs left the drawing room, and Drummond turned to the writer. "Now, let's speak more openly. Tory, Reggie, this is now official. Are you in agreement?"

"It's why we asked Bram here, isn't it, James?" his sister asked.

"Dolly, are you sure you wish to stay?" the duke asked Patterson-Smythe. "It could become intense. Dickie may prefer you return to the hotel."

"Nonsense, he's long since gone to sleep. I've not sat in on a meeting since last May. I've rather missed it! Do go on."

"Shall I fetch Henry?" asked Kepelheim, starting to stand.

"Not yet. We'll fill him in when he comes back down." Drummond reached for another sandwich. "Mr. Stoker, you are now privy to a conversation open to very few. The inner circle meetings are closed to outsiders, but from time to time, we allow a potential member to sit in and listen. Sometimes, we use that visit as an opportunity to assess the candidate's fitness and willingness to participate. If you prefer to leave, we'll understand completely."

Stoker's dark eyes shone with open excitement. "I'd be a fool to leave, Your Grace. If this is an interview, then proceed with your questions. But may I first address one comment I heard earlier?"

"Of course."

"I mentioned that I hope to teach my readers about the Christian response to spiritual wickedness. It's a challenge to have such a work published these days, because the rise of scientism discounts such books as foolish or archaic. Therefore, I must be careful how I deal with the topic. We cannot deny that something unseen exists. And within that unseen world, live beings of immense power and capability. Some are loyal to God; others are not. These may offer us rewards in return for worship, but in truth they hate us."

The duke leaned forward, his black eyes deadly serious. "Then, would it surprise you to learn that the recent newspaper reports are but a small glimpse into spiritual activities in London? Ripper, the Victoria Park Beast, and now this East End Dybbuk are but a sliver of what our circle has uncovered. Children talk now of the White Lady, who calls them to their deaths; wolves walk like men in the East, but also in Westminster. Pickling jars filled with body parts have been recovered from the Thames; most of them dismembered women, whose bodies show obvious signs of scientific intervention, and many without a drop of blood left in their veins. But others are dead newborns, some which show obvious deviations of form and anatomy."

Stoker was all attention. "Do you speak of the Embankment Killings, Your Grace?"

"Yes, but also other crimes cutting a diabolical swath through our city. These recent fires, for instance. Once properly investigated, we may discern a thread that connects them to this infernal web. Mr. Stoker, are you interested in helping us discern this web and cut the evil threads?"

Bram gulped down the last of the whisky, looking from one face to the next. "Yes! What would you have me do, sir?"

The duke was just about to answer, when Henry slipped through the door. "Do forgive me, everyone," he whispered. "It looks as though I've interrupted."

"Nonsense," Drummond answered. "Beth's gone up, but Charles will return in a moment. You must have passed them."

"Yes, actually, I saw them briefly as I came through the foyer. The duchess looked quite pale to me. I hope she's all right."

"A long day and troubling topics," Tory explained. "I'm sure she'll sleep late tomorrow."

"Today," corrected Whitmore. "It's nearly three, Vic."

"So it is. Reggie, would you fetch my shawl from the music room? I left it on a chair near the piano."

Whitmore stood and bowed slightly, kissing her hand. "Your wish is my command, Lady Victoria."

After quarter of an hour, Charles returned and assumed his empty chair. "She's already asleep. Where are we in the conversation, James? Have you made Bram an offer yet?"

"Not a firm one, but we're getting there. Have some of the Reserve, son. You've had a long day."

"That day has long since past, James, and soon yields to morning."

"And you've never remained awake all night?" teased the elder duke.

"Only several times a week—as a policeman," Sinclair answered as he poured a finger of the whisky and tipped it back.

"Clearly, the Scottish blood does call out," Henry observed wryly. "Now, if I may ask, what offer are we discussing?"

"To Stoker, regarding the inner circle," answered Drummond. "Bram could bring a wealth of research and experience to our conversations. But would Henry Irving object?" he asked the writer.

Bram sat back, considering the idea. "I doubt he'd mind, so long as it doesn't affect my work at the Lyceum. You may not be aware of this, Lady Patterson-Smythe..."

"Dolly, my dear. Just Dolly."

"That's kind of you. Yes, well, Dolly, there was a brutal murder at the Lyceum last month, and it's affected our business adversely. Not financially, not in the near term, at least. On the contrary, individual ticket sales have increased, but some of our box patrons show a reluctance to attend. I mentioned it to Mr. Irving, but rather than cater to the box seat holders, he's decided to indulge the public's fascination with even more horror and titillation."

Whitmore had stopped in to check on Aubrey before returning with Tory's shawl and he entered the drawing room, placing it round her shoulders. "Sorry to be late. Thought I'd pop in and see Paul. He's sleeping. Alcorn's watching over him."

"Thank you, Reggie," Victoria told him. "You know, Mr. Stoker, Irving's new attitude explains the singer he engaged tonight. Is he aware of her reputation in Paris?"

"What singer? Is she someone I know?" Dolly asked as she borrowed a cigarette from Victoria. "I don't generally smoke, but they help me to keep awake."

Henry lit the cigarette with a silver and ebony lighter he found on a nearby table. "I've never understood the allure of cigarettes, but a cigar now and again is quite enjoyable. James, what did you think of the singer? Beth and I left during her second aria—if you can call it an aria. I'd call it seduction set to music, actually. Truly, her performance seemed more at home in a music hall than a reputable theatre."

"I can say this, for I've no wife present to scold me," declared the Scottish duke. "I found the lady's performance quite interesting."

"You would!" Tory exclaimed. "And your late wife, God rest her beautiful soul, would have dragged you away from the theatre the moment that woman took the stage. Really, James, I'm a modern woman, and I realise fashion changes with the times, but her costume was straight out of the Follies Begere!"

Charles laughed. "It sounds as though the earl and I missed a great deal whilst we toured the fire damage in the East. Why was her costume disgraceful, Tory?"

"Because there was so little of it! And she brazenly flounced her skirts again and again to show off her lower limbs! She might as well have been a trollop, if you ask me. Shameful way to behave."

"It's my understanding such behaviour's in keeping with Carmen's character," Henry suggested. "Perhaps, Miss Gévaudan was simply performing a role."

Sinclair's face paled considerably. "Did you just say *Gévaudan?*"

Stoker answered. "Yes. Antoinette Gévaudan. She's the toast of Paris at present, primarily for her Carmen. We were lucky to engage her for tonight, as she's in London to visit a friend. Do you know her, Your Grace?"

Charles poured another two fingers of whisky and drank it down in one gulp, surprising everyone. "We've met."

Dolly tapped grey ash from her cigarette, interrupting the conversation. "Have you really? When?"

"No more of this nonsense," declared Victoria. "The woman is scandalous and distracting us from the topic. James, go on with your offer."

Slowly, the conversation returned to the topic of ghosts, but Henry kept thinking about the idea of musical seduction and wondering if it had anything to do with the female temptress who attacked Aubrey.

Then he remembered Gehlen. Or what looked like Anthony Gehlen. Though he only knew the man professionally, he understood him to be an avowed non-drinker. But no human could glide without touching the floor and then melt into a crowd with such ease. It was as though he'd simply vanished into thin air!

Henry's singular mind focused on the problem, drawing him into a self-imposed reverie of sorts. Gehlen, Gévaudan, the mysterious, blood-sucking Dybbuk haunting Whitechapel, the White Lady luring children to their dooms, the bodies of chopped-up women floating in the Thames. It must all connect in some way. But how? Might Gehlen's physical form be useful to the fallen spirits stalking London? He was, after all, Elizabeth's physician. If so, did his odd appearance at the theatre have anything to do with the inner circle, Bram Stoker, or even himself?

Henry had no answers, but he was determined to find them. She might be married to another man, but Henry MacAlpin felt responsible for the beautiful Duchess of Branham. He couldn't explain it with a thousand books, but he felt as though some golden thread ran from her heart to his. Not a romantic one, but one of unbreakable friendship and a trust beyond human understanding.

Then, a terrible thought whispered behind his eyes: *What if Violet Stuart is involved in this web?* Might she be some enigmatic, missing piece to a larger pattern? And was the madman in his care connected? A sense of foreboding clutched at Henry's gentle heart, and he wondered if he shouldn't put the man into Bedlam after all. Remove him from Montmore for the safety of his patients—Violet in particular.

But his resolve was too late for Bleeding Jack Nobody. By dawn, the porter would find the madman dead, deep cuts scored into his veins, and his scrawny body drained of all blood.

Charles finally came to bed at half past four, finding his wife turned on her left side, sound asleep. The two Labradors lay at the foot of the bed, snuggled close to their mistress, snoring loudly. The room felt cold, and he checked the radiators. All three emitted steady heat, yet he could see his breath. He turned up the gas in the fireplace, causing the flames to rise higher, slowly warming the chamber. The whisky had gone to his head, and Charles decided to sit for a moment before changing for bed.

The duke eased into a comfortable armchair, close to the marble fireplace, his thoughts running through the day's events. Romanov, the dock fire, Alexander Collins. He'd looked in on the alienist, who'd now been diagnosed with epilepsy. Sinclair began to fear they'd never obtain any prosecutable evidence from Collins. Still, the Castor Institute was engaged in illegal activities; he felt sure of it. Perhaps, he'd pay them an unannounced visit later that day with Henry. If Paul felt well enough, he'd ask the earl to tag along.

"Perhaps, I should jot all this down," he muttered to himself.

A small table sat at his elbow, and he rummaged through the top drawer for a pencil and tablet of writing paper. Charles found making lists a sort of mental cleansing; or perhaps, a nominal comfort to an overcrowded mind.

The light from the fire painted the unlined page in flickering ribbons of light, and he noticed obvious indentations. Someone had written several lines in a large, heavy hand. But the handwriting looked nothing like his or Elizabeth's. Using the pencil, he lightly shaded the paper, causing the indentations to emerge into words. What he found there chilled his soul:

The Scot sleeps, but I keep watch.
I can enter his closet.
I can enter his dreams.
I can enter his mind.
Defy me again, boy, and I will KILL HIM.

CHAPTER TWENTY-SIX

1:23 pm, 19th December

Paul Stuart awoke to his daughter's sweet voice and a wet sensation along the fingers of his right hand. The eleven-year-old was sitting at the end of the bed, and Tory's terrier, Samson, was licking his hand.

"Down, Samson! That is very naughty of you. I don't think my brother likes that at all," Adele scolded as she placed the animal on the floor. "Brother mine, are you going to sleep the entire day through? We're all packing for Branham. We don't want to be late, do we? Do get up, Paul!"

He slowly opened his eyes, finding that the sunlight from the windows hurt. "Oh, yes, Branham. What time is it?"

"It's late and getting later every minute," she said. "Nearly half one. I've never known you to sleep so very long. I'm to leave on the first train with Mr. Baxter and Mrs. Alcorn at four, but I want to spend a little time with you first. Do get up, please!"

The earl rubbed his eyes and sat up. "Sorry. Yes, of course. Good morning."

"It's afternoon, silly."

"Ah, yes. So you said. Did you have a pleasant visit with Winston yesterday?"

"A very pleasant one, and Maisie invited the Wychwright girls to stay over as well. We played games and listened to music cylinders on their new machine. Callie and Cassie are very nice, and they talked about you often. I think they have a little crush on you. Perhaps, we could invite them for Christmas."

"That would be up to Charles and Beth. Branham's their home. Darling, would you go ask Charles, if he's an extra robe I might borrow?"

"Already taken care of," she announced proudly and brought him a green velvet dressing gown, trimmed in black silk. "Mr. Baxter left you an entire suit of clothes, though I don't know why you need them. You've plenty at your house."

"Yes, but I've nothing here to wear. I hadn't planned on sleeping here last night. I suppose the long day overtook me. Is there any breakfast or luncheon?"

"Luncheon's not been served yet, but Mrs. Paget left lots of breakfast for you, dear brother. Hurry now! Cousin Charles wants to meet with you once you've eaten. He and Mr. Kepelheim are in the library with Henry. Isn't Henry handsome? And he's very nice for a doctor. He smells a bit like bergamot rather than quinine. You know, I might study medicine one day. Are there lady doctors, Paul?" she jabbered as he dressed in the connecting bath.

"Yes, but not many. I think you'd make a marvellous doctor, Della. Is there a hair brush anywhere out there?"

She opened several dressing table drawers and located a boar hair brush with a silver handle. "Here," she said, knocking on the door. She could hear water running. "Paul?"

The door opened a crack, and he took the brush. "I'll be about fifteen minutes. Ask Baxter if he'd bring a food tray to the library. Take Samson with you when you go, darling. After I meet with Charles, you and I'll visit for a bit."

"Come, Samson!" she called as she left the room, followed closely by the terrier.

Inside the gold and blue bathroom, the earl stared into a gilded mirror. He felt as though he could sleep for days, and an odd hum rang in his ears. Assuming it nothing more than fatigue, he quickly bathed and dressed in the suit left by Baxter. He passed by Lester on the way to the main staircase.

"Sir, if I might have a moment?" asked the underbutler.

"Certainly. What can I do for you?"

"I've been asked to pack your cases, sir. I wonder, how long do you plan to remain at the hall? Mr. Baxter has selected enough items for a three-day visit, but I overheard the duchess mention you might be there until the new year."

"I will, but I plan to return to London for a day or so on Monday. I'll stop by my home and pack additional clothes. Do be careful with my firearm, Lester. It's loaded."

"Of course. I will, sir."

Paul descended the stairs and passed by the music room, where his daughter sat playing a Brahms piece. He watched for a few minutes, enjoying her delicate touch and phrasing, and thinking what a little miracle she was. He remembered nothing of the phantasm that attacked him the previous night, but a whisper of gloom hung about his thoughts. Images of Cozette dominated them, and he longed to see her once more. Reaching the locked library, he knocked to gain entrance.

His cousin opened the door. "You certainly look better. Clearly, you needed the rest, as did we all. Most of us didn't rise until long after ten. Come sit. Baxter's bringing food. We want to go through everything we've learnt about the fire and other events."

"It looks as though you've assembled most of the London team," the earl noted as he took a chair near the fire.

Rather than gather round a table, Charles had asked Lester to form the library's most comfortable chairs and sofas into a modified circle. In the middle, the underbutler placed a low table, set with coffee, tea, and biscuits. The assembly that morning numbered twelve in all: Sir Thomas Galton, Martin Kepelheim, Henry MacAlpin, Malcolm Risling, Edward MacPherson, Edmund Reid, Arthur France, André Deniau (fresh from Paris), a recent American recruit who'd once served with the Texas Rangers named Thomas Crenshaw, Haimsbury, Aubrey, and to Paul's surprise, Abraham Stoker.

"I hadn't expected to find a writer amongst our number this afternoon. Good to see you again, Stoker."

"And you as well, my lord. I'm honoured and delighted to be part of this esteemed group. My mother would have loved hearing your stories, sir."

The earl took a leather chair near Galton, and Sinclair stood to open the meeting. "First of all, let me express my gratitude for coming on such short notice. As you know, we'd not planned to meet again as a group until after Boxing Day, but yesterday's fire has changed all that. Duke James cannot join us, as he's at Buckingham Palace until three, but sends his sincere best wishes and prayers."

The door opened, and Baxter entered, followed by half a dozen footmen, each carrying a large covered tray. "I hope we didn't overstep, Your Grace, but when Mrs. Paget learnt of the meeting, she decided to prepare a light brunch. Shall we arrange the dishes on the main table, sir?"

"Please," Charles answered. "And thank Mrs. Paget for us all. I, for one, am very hungry."

The footmen spread the brunch across the largest table, and Baxter lifted the domed lid from each steaming dish. "We've scrambled eggs as well as fried, bacon rashers, ham slices, chicken spread, kippers, rye toast, Bannock bread for Lord Aubrey," he said, winking at the earl, "potatoes, sausages, and a bowl of gravy for Mr. Kepelheim." The butler reached for a large basket covered with a tea towel, which he deftly removed, revealing a glorious selection of baked goods. "In here, you'll find scones with raisins and apple bits. There are also sticky buns, croissants, and chocolate biscuits for our new duke."

Charles smiled at this last item. "Paget's chocolate biscuits rival Mrs. Stephens's, but we shan't tell her. Baxter, will you join us? We'd value your input."

"I, sir? Sit with the circle? But I'm staff, my lord."

Sinclair crossed the room and took the butler's arm. "My dear friend, you are one of our greatest assets. Now, sit here beside Kepelheim and enjoy the fruits of Mrs. Paget's labours. No serving this morning. As of this moment, you are a full-fledged circle member. And I hope to speak to you about another opportunity soon, but that will wait for Branham, I think. Now, everyone," he said, facing the gathering, "let us seek the Lord's guidance before indulging our palates. Mr. Baxter, I wonder, if would you take us into the Lord's presence this afternoon?"

A smile lightened the elder man's face. "It would be my very great honour, my lord."

Standing, the formidable butler bowed his head. "Gentlemen, let us pray," he said, his sonorous voice low. "Our Gracious and wonderful Saviour and King, we humbly come to your throne, many of us weighed down with the troubles of the day already; some with health issues, some with financial woes, others with concerns about family and friends, some carrying fear and doubt that darken the soul and devour the mind. But no matter what our worries, no matter what our concerns or anxieties, no matter the dross or decay of the world that rises to the top and surrounds, they all vanish and are vanquished in the light of your holy face!

"It is unusual for me to speak before such an honourable gathering of fellow soldiers. I say this not because most of these men bear noble titles, but because they bear noble scars. Physical as well as spiritual. I have watched the members of this circle rush into battle wearing naught but your promises upon their mortal frames, wielding nary an ax, but flashing the sword of the Spirit in the eyes of the enemy. A double-edged blade likened unto the Word of God that proceeds out of them with a fiery vengeance! But as brave as these deeds are—as valiant as their exploits in armour might be—this circle's greatest achievements are accomplished not on the battlefield but within the quietness of the prayer closet. Before these warriors take to their feet, they spend time on their knees; each and every one of them, and it is my honour to be called their fellow.

"I know not what plans the enemy now devises, my Lord, but you do. Help us, then, to unmask their faces and uncover their secrets. Let us rise to the fight until our arms grow numb, and our breath be gone. Let us crawl when our legs will no longer run, whisper when our voices fail, feel our way forward when our eyes become blind. Bind upon our hearts an affection for one another that knows no language other than love and no title other than brother or sister. Help us to serve you with all our strength, soul, and mind until the end of our days. And when those days are done, my Lord, let us continue to intercede for our beloved fellows whilst we kneel before your throne. As St. Paul wrote, '*Wherefore seeing we also are compassed about with so great a cloud of witnesses, let us lay aside every weight, and the sin which doth so easily beset us, and let us run with patience the race that is set before us, Looking unto Jesus the author and finisher of our faith; who for the joy that was set before him endured the cross, despising the shame, and is set down at the right hand of the throne of God.*'

"Saviour and King, I shall consider it a privilege to be counted amongst that cloud of witnesses one day, standing alongside men like Paul and Peter and James, cheering on this group of servant-soldiers who continue to battle upon the field. May that day come for us all when our Saviour returns. In the meantime, we consider it all the greatest joy to partake of only a small share of that which you endured on our behalf. Bless our conversation and our fellowship this day, my Lord. In the name of our King, we ask it. Even Christ Jesus. Amen."

As the men lifted their heads, every eye glistened with tears, every cheek was stained with salt. Charles Sinclair drew the butler close and embraced him like a brother.

"Cornelius, I have never felt so humbled in a man's presence. You, my dear friend, are an example to us all. And if it is true that we wear scars in honour of Christ, then it is only because your constancy and humility have taught us to do so."

Baxter wiped his eyes and pressed the young duke's shoulder, his ageing face filled with youthful amazement. "Sir, I've known you and Lord Aubrey since you were born, and I can think of no finer men upon this earth. If the Lord had given me sons, I should be pleased to have it be the two of you."

He returned to his seat, still wiping tears from his round cheeks. Sinclair sniffed, fighting a flood of pleasant emotion.

"My friends," said the duke, "the enemy seeks to divide us, but the Holy Spirit will never allow that to happen. Where two or more are gathered in the Lord's name, he tells us that HE is there in the midst, and I can testify to that truth today. Now, we have little time, so I must move forward to business. Inspectors Reid and France have a great deal to tell us about the dockside fire. Please, help yourselves to Mrs. Paget's delicious dishes and enjoy your meals in casual fashion, but pay close attention to all we say. I've a very strong feeling the enemy is moving its battalions into position, and we must be ready when the onslaught begins. Edmund?"

"Mind if I remain seated whilst speaking?"

"Not at all. It makes it easier to balance a plate," Sinclair replied, smiling.

Edmund cleared his throat and then began. "As you're all aware, an historic conflagration overran St. Katherine's Docks yesterday. The fire commenced at approximately eight in the morning. Witnesses describe a man in bright clothing, standing upon the stern of a Russian trading vessel. France, what's the name again?"

Arthur checked his notes. "The *Podzhigatel.* It isn't registered with any of the usual sources."

Aubrey's face showed surprise. "Are you sure about the name, Arthur?"

"I double-checked it with one of the sailors, sir. The Jewish doctor tending the man's burns told me how to spell it. Dr. Kholodenko also asked if the name were true. Why?"

"Because *Podzhigatel* is Russian for 'firebug' or 'firestarter'. It's as though the enemy is toying with us! A ship that isn't registered tries to dock illegally in Whitechapel, and its name means firebug? Charles, I fear you're right when you say something dark is on the horizon. Edmund, yesterday evening you told us that over four hundred people were now in hospital at the London, with many others treated at the Eastern Dispensary and by local doctors in their surgeries. Thirty dead? Is that number still accurate?"

"Thirty-nine as of this morning," Reid replied soberly. "Most died from the caustic, black smoke that inundated the area. Captain Shaw and his fire brigade inspectors believe a chemical agent served as ignition. As you can imagine, most of the *Podzhigatel* is destroyed, but when we searched the hold, we found the remains of several barrels of a black, oily material as well as broken bottles of chemicals. As to the man seen tossing the lantern into that hold, we've found a possible lead. This morning, a local landlady named Porter came forward. You may know her, Charles. She carried one of your calling cards."

"Do you mean Molly Porter? Paul and I visited her in connexion with Beth's abduction case. Porter told us a Russian sailor sometimes stayed in her inn. Does she believe this firestarter is the same one?"

"She does," Reid answered between bites of bacon. "We also spoke with her two sons. They offered a very good description of the man. Apparently, he took them for a walk into a dangerous rookery off Gowers Walk a few days ago. What they saw there terrified them both, and since then, Porter's evicted the tenant."

"The Russian took them to a brothel?" asked Aubrey angrily. "Those two boys aren't yet ten years old! What sort of man would do that?"

"One hoping to sell them, I should think," Reid answered darkly. "The man calls himself Chernyy Paukov Veron. It's a tongue-twister. I have the exact spelling, courtesy of Dr. Kholdenko, if you need it."

Paul took the paper from Reid to examine the name. "Again, the enemy plays games. This is a riddle, Charles. Aimed straight at you. The name means 'Black Crow, son of the Spider'." The earl poured himself a cup of coffee, worry furrowing his brow. "Ed, did the boys or their mother offer any further information? Did this Russian always wear these bright colours? Might he have kept a journal of some kind?"

This surprised the Leman Street detective. "Yes, they did say that, but how do you know? Both the boys and one of the injured sailors mentioned seeing this Russian with a leather book, and that he was frequently seen writing in it. And here's another oddity. One of the witnesses, a Spitalfields Jew from Kiev, claimed he'd seen the man vanish into thin air after marking an odd symbol on a door near his place of business. I checked the address, Charles. It's 29 Hanbury Street."

Sinclair paled. "He's sure about the address?"

Reid nodded.

"What's that mean to you, sir?" asked the American newcomer. "I ain't so sure 'bout street names yet. I only been in these parts since January."

"It's very well-known to Whitechapel police, Captain Crenshaw," answered the duke. "29 Hanbury is where Ripper murdered Annie Chapman."

All the members grew silent, and it seemed that a dread fell upon them. A loud door knock startled everyone, breaking the tension, and Baxter rose to answer. After speaking briefly to the footman, he turned to his employer.

"Sir, I'm told Dr. Gehlen is here to speak with the duchess. Has he an appointment with Her Grace?"

Henry stood immediately, setting his plate aside. "Charles, I know it's your place, but I'd like to speak with Gehlen first. I promise to explain once I return."

"Certainly," replied Haimsbury without hesitation. "I doubt he has an appointment. Elizabeth's gone to the dower house to speak with Count Riga and Mr. Blinkmire regarding the rail journey to Branham. She'd not have left, if she expected Gehlen to call. Yes, do go on. Let me know if you want me to join you."

"I will," Salperton told him, exiting the library.

"I wonder what that's about?" mused Aubrey.

Stoker had said very little, for he'd been busy making copious notes of Reid's report. However, the mention of Gehlen aroused his curiosity.

"Might that be Anthony Gehlen, sir?" he asked Sinclair.

"Yes, why do you ask, Mr. Stoker?"

"Call me Bram, please, my lord. I ask because of his association with our singer. Yesterday evening, near the hour of six, I was backstage, talking with several cast members. As business manager, I find myself wearing many hats, you see, and I overheard Miss Gévaudan in hushed conversation with Dr. Gehlen. I recognised him at once, for he often attends our performances; always watching the actresses from backstage."

Charles found this puzzling. "Bram, are you sure we're talking about the same man? The Anthony Gehlen I've come to know is sober, studious, and somewhat insular. It's hard to imagine him keeping company with a woman like Antoinette!"

Every eye turned to stare at the duke.

"Antoinette?" repeated his cousin. "You know her on a first-name basis?"

Suddenly, Sinclair felt exposed and self-conscious. "I prefer to withhold the explanation for the moment, but yes, I know the woman. She's a thoroughly untrustworthy, conniving little witch, if you must know. Please, do go on, Bram. What did she say to Gehlen?"

A cloud of gloom descended into the group, knitting itself into a heavy shroud of anxiety. Everyone felt it, as though Death itself watched them from the wings of a great stage.

Stoker paused in his story, sensing the mood. "Am I the only one who feels a presence?"

Charles stood, moving to the concealed panel. He placed his ear to the wall, listening.

Hello, boy. I'm waiting.

Kepelheim left his plate and crossed the room to join his friend. "Charles, what is it?"

"I'm not sure. Paul, would you open the panel, please?"

The earl felt cold run down his arms and into his hands. A husky voice whispered into his memory, *'Mon cher! Come to me!'*

"I'll do it," offered Baxter, who climbed the library ladder and tilted the Malory book on Arthur. A soft click sounded, and the muralled panel opened.

"Paul, you stay in here," ordered the duke. "Martin, come with me."

Aubrey objected, crossing towards the open wall. "Not for all the tea in China!" he exclaimed. "Where you go, I go. Charles."

Sinclair remembered the Dragon's threatening message: 'Defy me again, and I will KILL HIM.'

"Stay here, Paul. That is an order. I'm not arguing with you."

"Fine, because I've no intention of arguing, for my mind's made. Now, let's go."

Kepelheim, Aubrey, and Sinclair entered the dark passageway, stopping just the other side of the opening. "Before we go into that chamber, I want to mention this painting," the tailor told them. "Do you remember the vision or dream of your father, Your Grace?"

"Which one? I've dreamt of my parents often recently. Do you mean when he showed us this secret passage?"

"Indeed, yes," replied the tailor. "He indicated that the mural inside the library is a riddle. And that the answer lay inside the passage."

"Yes, I remember. Why?" asked Sinclair, distracted by a series of whispers echoing throughout the chilly space.

"See here?" continued Kepelheim. "I've had opportunity to study the mural on this side of the wall now, and I've made a copy of it as well as photographed the entire scene. In the library, we see a painting of your childhood home from sometime in the past, before the house was built. The River Eden, flowing past a robust and relatively new Pendragon Castle—which, as you know, now stands in ruins."

"Yes, and there are men standing beside the river," added the duke. "I've dreamt about this, Martin. Just recently. Father was taking me on a tour of this house, and he showed me a cabinet made of lacquered wood in a Chinese finish. The painting on its doors was the same. Men in a circle near the river. And in the centre was..."

"A dragon?" asked Martin. "Yes, I've seen that cabinet, but it's at Rose House; not here, Charles. Your dreams must conflate the two homes. What else do you remember?"

"A sword, I think. Lann Lasair? Does that ring a bell?"

Kepelheim's mouth opened in shock. "You remember the sword? Good heavens! Charles, what else do you recall?"

"Fleeting images. Fragments of events. But dragons always appear." He paused, wondering how much to reveal. "Why?"

"Because—well, I've wondered if I should tell you this, but I had a conversation with that Russian prince once. Shortly after our session. The one where you remembered the Christmas at your home in '59."

"You spoke with Romanov?" asked the duke. "When?"

"The following day, actually. He dropped by my home. He appeared suddenly without announcement. I'll admit, it gave me quite a start! I'd been working on a new waistcoat for you, and I pushed the needle into my thumb! It bled and bled, but Romanov touched it, and the wound healed as if it hadn't happened."

"And what did he tell you?" asked Sinclair.

"That you'd begin to dream of dragons, and that when you mentioned them to me, I should tell you about the clocks."

Charles felt dizzy suddenly, and he leaned against the cold wall. "Clocks? Do you mean the Arthur clocks?"

Paul held his cousin's arm. "Let's find you a chair."

"No, I'm just tired. Look, before we discuss all this, show me the painting on this side. Explain why it's important."

Martin used a match to light the gas sconce nearest them. "The riddle on the library side asks a question in Gaelic. Do you remember?"

"*A bhios a 'cumail a' gheata?*" Paul quoted. "Who keeps the gate?"

"Exactly. And on this side, we see the very same painting, but with a slight variation. Instead of men surrounding a dragon, there are seven dragons surrounding one man. See?"

They looked at the mural, which portrayed the Eden River Valley at night. A round moon dominated the midnight sky, and the constellations Draco, Ursa Minor, and Boötes stood high overhead—as though the Dragon joined forces with these formations.

"Draco, I understand. It refers to the Dragon, but why Ursa Minor and Boötes?" asked Charles, who knew astronomy well.

"Don't you remember your Sir Walter Scott? In the *Lay of the Last Minstrel*, he wrote: 'Arthur's slow wain his course doth roll, in utter darkness round the pole.' But Tennyson's poem *Percivale* speaks of the seven stars of the Bear, who form Arthur's round table. Charles, this painting is all about you. Arcturus, the brightest star in the northern hemisphere. Charles, Arcturus—Arthur—is YOU, and you are the gatekeeper."

The revelation made the duke dizzier yet, and he leaned upon his cousin's arm. "Take me out of here," he muttered. "It's too much."

They reentered the library, finding the men finishing their brunch. Baxter had remained near the opening, and he instantly took his master into his arms and guided the duke to a comfortable chair.

"Now, sir, this is enough for one day. You must eat and enjoy a brief respite. I'll fetch you a plate."

"Mr. Stoker," called the duke from his chair near the fire. "Come tell me about Gehlen. I want to know his relationship with Gévaudan."

The writer set down his empty plate and chose a companion chair to the duke's. "Of course, my lord. I cannot say just why this gentleman spent so many hours at the Lyceum. I take it, this is unwelcome news."

"More than you can know," muttered Sinclair. "Did you overhear their conversation? His and Gévaudan's?"

"A little, but he called there many times. Usually with another woman as company. Black hair and eyes, skin as pale a milk with unnaturally red lips."

"Di Specchio!" exclaimed the earl as he joined their small group. "Serena in company with Gehlen? You're sure it was he? Can you describe the man?"

"Yes. He's taller than I, but shorter than either of you," began Stoker. "Around six feet, I'd say. Muscular in the manner of a professional boxer. Broad shoulders and a narrow waist. Dark hair, parted on one side and cut short. The stage wings are generally quite dark, but I believe his eyes are a medium brown. He dresses well, usually in fine evening wear, of course. He wears a signet ring upon his left hand, which is figural, but I was never close enough to discern the exact design. It had white enamel, though. Of that, I'm sure. He often teased the dancers, speaking to them in a very frank manner. I shan't repeat his words."

"And Gévaudan?" asked Charles, regaining his strength. "Did he speak to her with such frankness?"

"Oh, yes. He and Mademoiselle Gévaudan seemed at ease in one another's presence, for they laughed often, whispering together as though sharing intimacies. They touched one another as lovers might."

"Charles, what is this all about?" insisted Aubrey. "Why are you so interested in this physician's personal life?"

"For one thing, he claims to be a teetotaler who shuns night spots! Look, I've had enough of second-hand information. I want to see the man for myself. Edmund, continue with your report whilst I'm gone."

Without another word, Sinclair left the library and crossed through the busy corridors to the foyer. Standing outside the Cumbria Room, he could hear Henry MacAlpin shouting phrases that were anything but friendly. They were, in fact, filled with accusation and outrage.

"How dare you say such things?" answered Gehlen as Charles opened the door. "It's clear you've decided to hire another to look after the duchess, Your Grace. If you'll excuse me, I'll take my leave."

"Not yet," Sinclair ordered his guest. "Sit down. I've questions of my own before you return to Whitechapel, Dr. Gehlen. Many, many questions."

CHAPTER TWENTY-SEVEN

"Just what is this all about?" demanded Sinclair. It seemed to the duke that the two physicians were ready to come to blows, and he suspected he knew the reason why.

Elizabeth.

Henry's face was flushed with outrage. "Shut the door, Charles, just in case Beth returns. I don't want her to hear any of this."

"I don't understand why you're treating me with such disdain," Gehlen objected. "I only came to see to the duchess's welfare. I am her doctor of record. How am I suddenly a pariah here?"

"You can ask me that?" accused the viscount. "After you behaviour last night, you have no right to ask questions!"

"Stop it! Both of you!" shouted Sinclair, his head pounding. "Henry, what do you mean by last night? Is there more I should know?"

"Oh, yes, indeed!" exclaimed Henry, scarcely keeping his temper. "The liar insists he knows nothing of what happened, and I'm absolutely certain he does!"

"Do you mean his relationship with Gévaudan?" enquired the duke, trying to sound calm. "Dr. Gehlen, do you know a singer named Antoinette?"

"Of course, not!" answered Gehlen angrily. "Why do you keep asking me that? Henry's clearly mistaken someone else for me. I was nowhere near the Lyceum last evening. I was in my rooms at the London's residence hall, if you must know; sleeping, or trying to do so. I'm sure the matron can vouch for me. I saw her at ten o'clock, when I made a cup of cocoa in the kitchen."

"Cocoa!" shouted Salperton. "That was not cocoa on your breath last night. Charles, this man dared to refer to the duchess in an insolent, thoroughly inappropriate manner, and he'd been drinking heavily. Very strange behaviour for a man who claims to abstain from alcohol."

Confused and exhausted, Anthony collapsed onto the sofa. Dark circles rimmed his eyes, and his ordinarily robust complexion had a dull, pale aspect. Charles noticed that his hands trembled as he spoke.

"I tell you both, as God is my witness, I was in my bed last night. All night. Please, believe me! Someone else must have been there; someone who bears a striking resemblance to me. Dark hair and eyes are hardly uncommon in London."

Sinclair offered the troubled visitor a glass of water and then sat in the opposite chair. "Take a seat, Henry. Please."

The viscount reluctantly obeyed, for an energetic sense of indignation ran through his nervous system, and he longed to pace or strike out. His friend Elizabeth had been wronged, and he wanted satisfaction.

"Very well, but talking will accomplish nothing, Charles. In fact, I'm tempted to go to Treves today and unmask this man as a devious bounder and a bald-faced liar!"

"I assure you both that I'm not lying," Gehlen entreated. "Have you a Bible? If so, let me swear to it. I am telling the truth!"

An odd sense danced on Charles's skin, and he found himself believing the man. Silently praying for guidance, he decided to pursue a different path towards truth. "Anthony, have you noticed any strange moments of late? Times when people treat you differently? Misunderstandings regarding your actions? Even running into someone who claims to know you, when he's unfamiliar?"

Gehlen looked as though he might break down weeping. "Yes! Yes! But how did you know? Charles, I do not drink. I cannot! My constitution doesn't handle it well. I become violently ill, if I drink even one glass of wine, and the effect of spirits is worse. Ask Fred Treves, if you don't believe me. I once had a small whisky at his home, and I passed out."

MacAlpin's hands slowly relaxed, and the physician and healer's part of his nature took over. "You passed out? Have you noticed anything similar of late? Lost time, blackouts?"

Gehlen nodded, trembling all over. "Yes. Many of them, but I didn't dare tell anyone."

"Did you ever suffer such spells before you moved to London? Without drinking, I mean."

"Only once, when I lived in France. In '79. I'd gone there on a fellowship with the Sorbonne to study neuro-anatomy, and for weeks, I'd suffer from memory loss and unaccountable skips in time. Finally, a colleague diagnosed me with an unknown type of brain fever, and I spent six weeks in a private clinic near Rouen. My doctor, a brilliant man named Emile Sandoval, determined the cause might lie in alcohol and advised me never to partake again. I followed his instruction, and I've been healthy since. Fred knows all about it. I hid nothing from him when I came here."

Henry grew kinder. "Forgive me for my outburst, Anthony. But appearances spoke against you. I hope you understand; we're only concerned with Elizabeth's welfare."

"Yes, of course, you are. And so am I, which is the reason I stopped by. Is she doing well?"

Charles poured the distraught physician a second glass of water. "I can bring tea, if you prefer."

"No, just water. Thank you."

"Beth's doing much better," the duke told Gehlen. "Her nausea is less taxing, though it comes and goes without warning. She's gained a little weight, I'm pleased to say, and it's clear that our unborn children are growing well."

"I'm very glad to hear it."

"Look, here, Gehlen, it seems to me that Henry should give you a thorough examination. Would you submit to him and follow his advice?"

"Yes, of course, I would. All I want to do is teach, and Fred's been kind enough to grant me the chance. I've no wish to disappoint him or either of you. I wonder, though, would you promise to keep this confidential for the present? I'm on probation until next year, which means any infringement of the hospital rules could be my last. Gone before I can even make a start. For years, I've dreamt of teaching other doctors about properly managing pregnancies and newborns. It's such an important specialty, but very few physicians understand it. Women are dying every day for lack of informed physicians, and I want to reduce that number, if God allows it."

He drank the water in one gulp and then held the empty glass as he continued. "The past fortnight has been hell, you know. Is it possible the brain fever has returned?"

"I suppose so, yes," replied Henry gently. "Brain fever is a catch-all sort of diagnosis. I've never been in favour of it, to be honest. There may be a more concrete cause which is treatable. When do you begin lecturing?"

"Middle of January."

"Then, come stay with me at Montmore until then, and we'll work through this together. What was the French doctor's name again?"

"Emile Sandoval. He's of French and Spanish descent, I think. Dark hair and eyes. Looks very Slavic, strangely enough."

"How tall?" asked Charles, that odd tingle returning.

"Quite tall. Six and a half feet or near to that. Taller than you or Aubrey, certainly. Forgive me, I'm very tired suddenly."

Gehlen looked as though he might fall apart, and Charles placed a comforting hand on the man's shoulder. "Anthony, you're not alone in this. Allow us to help you."

"That's kind of you, Charles. I've felt alone since my uncle's death. As I've told you, Father and I don't get along. But I could move into his London home, I suppose. My lawyer has the keys."

"Pencaitland House, isn't it?" Charles asked. "It's close to Uncle James's home, just west of here. Anthony, is there a staff there presently?"

"Not that I'm aware. Father's a miserly sort of fellow. His brother was much kinder. Look, I've taken enough of your time already. I should go."

He started to stand but nearly collapsed.

"There now! Don't be so hasty," said Henry as he and Charles helped the distraught doctor back to the chair. "Living on your own is a bad idea. I insist you come back with me to Montmore. We'll send to the London for your belongings. Just tell Fred that I require your help during the Christmas season."

"This is a bad time for me to leave, Henry," answered Gehlen. "The London's teeming with wounded and dying. I can't abandon Treves now."

"You're no use to him in your present condition," Henry argued. "Look here, Anthony. I insist you take time to heal."

"Please, do this," Charles implored. "Beth and I need your experience and knowledge, especially now that Michael Emerson's in Edinburgh. If this is a decline in your health, then you must address it right away. If it's something else, then Henry will uncover it. There's no better man, in my opinion."

"I've failed you, Charles," Gehlen whispered, his voice filled with regret. "How can you place any trust in me?"

"We all fail sometimes, Anthony. I bear you no ill will, and neither does Henry. Do you?"

Salperton smiled patiently, the former anger vanished. "No, of course not. Charles, I wonder, might we ask MacPherson's opinion on this?"

"Ed's not a physician, Henry."

"No, but he represents a healing of another kind. Trust me on this. I think it's a good idea."

"Give us a few minutes, Dr. Gehlen," said Sinclair. "We shan't be long."

The two men stepped into the foyer, moving away from the doors, down towards the main staircase. "What is it you suspect? Is he ill or not?"

"He's very ill, Charles, but I'm not sure brain fever is an accurate diagnosis," replied Salperton. "I've a little experience with demonic possession, but..."

"What?" exclaimed Sinclair. "You think him overcome by a dark spirit?"

"Charles, you saw that creature attack Paul last night! And you've said again and again that the spirit realm is placing pieces into position. Now, whilst I sense nothing supernatural in him today, last evening at the Lyceum I saw a spiritual entity glide past me just seconds before running into Gehlen. Anthony's behaviour was entirely different, as though another controlled him—or used his form as a mask. His mental state seems consistent with possession, or at least external influence. I'd like MacPherson to examine him further."

"Very well, but not here. There are enough dangers in this house as it is. I'll not have some creature released in our corridors because it's fleeing a human host!"

"I'm not really sure it works like that, Charles, but Mac's the expert, not I. May I speak to him?"

As a man who commanded entire divisions of police detectives, Sinclair was accustomed to making quick decisions, and he made one now. "We leave for Branham in a few hours. Take Gehlen to Montmore then, but keep him separate from your other patients. If there is a demonic spirit involved, you must protect them."

"I can put him in the gardener's cottage, now that it's vacant again. Poor old Jack!"

"His body's been removed?"

"Oh, yes. Mr. Rush, the attendant in charge overnight, called the police immediately, and they removed the body to a waggon and kept it there for me to examine. I declared it suicide, because of the self-inflicted marks on his arms, but it's my conviction that some darkness influenced his mind, causing him to self-harm."

"Be careful, Henry. That spirit might still be there."

"Another reason for bringing in Mac. My attendants are cleaning the cottage. And Mac can help anoint all the lintels and rooms. The cottage will be ready for a new occupant by evening."

"Very well," Sinclair agreed. "Mac's on leave from college duties until after the new year, but you'll need my uncle's permission to second him for more than a few days. Mac's still the pastor of Drummond Chapel."

"I'll make sure he addresses that. I doubt James will refuse so great a cause."

"I'll send a footman to the London to collect Anthony's clothing and other personal items," Charles suggested. "How long will the process take?"

"I've no idea," Henry admitted, scratching his head. "I've had other patients with spiritual attachments, but never a case of possession. Honestly, Charles, I may be in over my head."

"We're all in over our heads, Henry. Every last one of us, but regardless, God is still in control. Nothing surprises him."

CHAPTER TWENTY-EIGHT

5 Fitzmaurice Place, the Wychwright Home

Stephen Algernon Allendale was typical of successful London solicitors. His clothing was tailored on Savile Row. He wore elegantly expensive jewellery: watch and chain, tie pin, collar button, cufflinks; all designed to match. He seldom added finger adornments of any type, although he did possess a masonic ring that he put on when visiting fellow lodge members. Now, as he sat in the Wychwright's dining hall, he gave careful consideration to his manner of speech, the way he conveyed ideas, and even the sound of his voice. He'd read a hundred wills during his twenty years in the Ames, Groves, and Allendale firm, and he'd learnt to be wary of surprises.

He did, in fact, know the family were about to receive a very large one.

"Yes, yes, all that language is typical and tells us nothing," the eldest son and presumptive heir was spouting from the seat opposite the lawyer.

Allendale had summed up the man quickly upon meeting him fifteen minutes earlier: Self-absorbed and rude. A man who expected life to hand him a ripe apple filled with sweet juices, the seed of which would produce evermore ripening, golden fruit—all for the cost of a few magic beans.

Instead, he was about to receive a very sour lemon.

"Time, sir! Give me time, please," the lawyer replied. "The entire will must be read, as I'm sure you're aware. As I've said, your late father bequeathed all the usual properties to you, as is the requirement due to the entail."

"Meaning, my dear, that you get the title and all the property and money," said Wychwright's mother soothingly. "As it should be."

Allendale cleared his throat. "Not exactly."

"What the devil do you mean by 'not exactly'?" the impatient son shouted.

"I mean that there is an addendum, sir. A codicil, dated two months ago."

"Two months? Addendum? No, I'll not have it! Mother, what do you know of this?"

Constance Wychwright had already begun to amend her drab widow's weeds with hints of colour, adding a bright red comb to her upswept hair, as well as shedding her veil. She shook her head in dismay, using a soothing tone as she patted her son's hand.

"I'm sure it's nothing important. The last time your father and I discussed the will, he told me that everything would go to you, my darling. I'm sure this addendum merely emphasises that fact. Do now, let's all listen, shall we? Mr. Allendale will explain."

Ned Wychwright said nothing, certain he'd receive little if anything, and Tom was nursing a bang-up hangover from an all-nighter at a Soho men's club. Cordelia looked like a ghost of her former self, wishing she could awaken from the nightmare her life had become.

"Thank you, Lady Constance," the solicitor said smoothly. "I shall now read out the specific bequests, so that we are all sure of the late baron's wishes. As I said earlier, the barony, as entailed, passes to the eldest son, Captain William David Wychwright. This includes the title, and I have a copy of the letters patent, should you require them. You also inherit the house in which we now sit and all its furnishings, Windermere Hall in Cumbria and all its furnishings, a hunting lodge on the Isle of Skye called Plover's End with all its furnishings. A seaside cottage, which is somewhat rundown, but..."

"Yes, yes, we know all that! What of the money?" William interrupted. "How much is there, and does it all come to me?"

"I'm getting to that, sir," explained the solicitor. "Plover's End and all its..."

"You've said that already!" the new baron shouted. "And that damned seaside cottage is a miserable little shack. Get to the rest of it!"

"Of course, my lord. Regarding liquid assets, there are several bank accounts to mention. One at Barkley Brothers in Carlisle containing 14,236 pounds, nine shillings and seven pence. This account is used by the estate steward for management and sundries, staff wages, building maintenance, and taxes. I shall leave a detailed report of expenses for your own accountant to peruse. Barings Bank keeps an account with a current balance of 12,649 pounds, twelve shillings, eight pence, which is available for your personal use. There is a forty-seven pound cheque against it currently, payable to a Mr. Silas Winchester, which has not been presented. As before, I have those details in my briefcase, and they're also available at your accountant's pleasure. A third deposit is held at Silverman's on Finsbury Circus. This is an investment account, and is *not* entailed to the barony."

"Not entailed?" asked Connie. "How can that be?"

"Entailment only applies to monies derived directly from the estate: that is, sale of property, income from associated businesses or farms; that sort of thing. This account was opened by the late baron sixteen years ago, using only his Parliamentary salary. The amount currently in the account is 34,492 pounds and twelve shillings. There are no cheques outstanding."

"But it's not entailed?" William persisted, looking at his mother angrily. "Does that mean it might be left to someone else?"

The lawyer steeled himself to present the lemon.

"I have specific instructions regarding this account, all laid out in the addendum I mentioned to you earlier, Lord Wychwright. It was signed by your late father in my presence and witnessed by myself and two others at my firm. The account is tied to the management of a property in St. Marylebone on Munster Square; a handsome terraced home, completely furnished. Both the house and the Silverman's bank account are left to Lady Cordelia Wychwright."

Will practically shot out of the chair, ready to strike the poor lawyer in the face. "What sort of trickery is this? I'll see you in court, if you think you're going to pull something like this, Allendale! Father would never have left all that money and a house to a mere daughter! It's ludicrous!"

Ever the schemer, Constance's mind was already whirring with ideas, finding ways to manoeuvre the newly set chessboard to her advantage.

"Let's not be hasty, my dear. Mr. Allendale is only telling us what your father wanted. We can have another lawyer take a look, if you like, but why must this be a problem?"

"Why? I'll tell you why. Because it leaves the lion's share to her, that's why! How am I supposed to manage an expensive estate on so very little?"

"Your father often complained that the entailed accounts were inadequate, but I'm sure there are ways to make them grow. Isn't that true, Mr. Allendale?"

"I've many banker friends who insist that is true, Lady Constance. I'd be pleased to put you in touch. Might I suggest speaking with Mr. Harmon at Silverman's? He's done very well for your late husband's private account. I'm sure he'd offer sound advice for your son as well."

"A very good idea," she answered, planning to call on Harmon. After all, Cordelia was young. Perhaps, she required an advisor to help administer the sizeable account.

The lawyer continued to slice the indigestible lemon. "Now, allow me to read the aforementioned letter to you all. I have two signed and witnessed copies at my office, of course, and you may keep this one, along with all the other papers." He cleared his throat to read:

> 'My Dearest Constance,
>
> If you are hearing Allendale read this, then I am dead. I have a few confessions to make to you, and you will not like hearing them.'"

The lawyer paused, peering at them over his tortoise shell spectacles. "I did warn the late baron that you would find it difficult to hear these words read aloud, but his lordship insisted. Now, to continue:

> 'I pray first of all, that my death is a natural one, but I suspect the opposite will be true. My health could not be better, but there are certain men with whom I've been forced to deal of late who've made threats against me. I have my suspicions as to the real face behind these threats, but I shan't write that name here. Suffice to say, I am ashamed

to think that the line of accusation might even reach to my own family.'"

"His own family?" shouted William. "Does he accuse one of us of murder?"

"No, sir, I don't believe one can construe that. May I continue?" Clearing his throat, Allendale began anew. "He goes on:

'My greatest concern at this point is for my children. William will have no trouble moving on and thriving. I expect him to do as he's always done, but I pray that his proclivities in certain darker venues come to an end and that he produces an heir to continue the barony.

'Ned, my gentlest son, I've left you three hundred pounds in cash and all my personal jewellery (save that which is entailed): three gold watches, a diamond stickpin, and two rings. Sell them, if you like, and use the money to care for my granddaughters. I only wish I'd known them better.

'Tom, I fear that your choices in life give me no alternative but to leave you at the mercy of your brothers. You've squandered every penny I've ever given you, but if Will or Ned offers you succor, then may you prove wiser with their generosity.

'Constance, I have little to give you, dear wife. I know our marriage wasn't always joyful, but I still remember the lovely girl with whom I first danced beneath the stars in Cumbria. I leave you a thousand pounds cash in an envelope. May it bring you happiness, my dear. I'm sorry my ambitions were never enough to supply all your needs.

'Finally, to my darling daughter, I leave my heartfelt love and fondest wishes for a bright future. I've secured you a house and enough money to provide a few years' independence. I do not want you at the mercy of a man who mistreats you, dearest Delia. I would have you smile for the rest of your days and singing like an angel!

'Now, I will sign this letter and leave you to discuss its content. I imagine you'll challenge my decisions, but you'll find all is in perfect order. I've made some poor choices in my life, but I pray to our Saviour that He allows me enough years upon this earth to become a better man. If not, then I leave it to His mercy.

'Much love and affection,
'David, 9th Baron Wychwright'"

Allendale removed his spectacles. "Thus ends the letter. Are there questions?"

"Hundreds!" shouted William, now glaring at his sister. "It's clear that Delia bewitched my father into making such a ridiculous bequest, and I intend to challenge it."

"That is your right, sir. My firm remains available to you at any time. I believe, though, that you'll find the clauses are airtight and completely legal. Now, I'll leave all these papers with you so you may discuss matters."

Allendale stood and followed the butler to the entrance, where he donned a stylish felt hat and Harris Tweed coat. Once he'd gone, Connie searched through the stack of papers to find the letter, reading through it.

"Delia, I think you and your brothers should leave William and me to talk. Go lie down for an hour, dear."

Without a word, the girl rose to her feet and left the room. Ned and Thomas did the same, and the dowager baroness turned to her eldest.

"A legal challenge could ruin us, William. There must be another way."

"I don't care if it breaks us. I'll not have my sister richer than I am!"

"You do care, Will. You must! Now, listen to me. I've not done all this to lose everything."

"Done what?"

"Acted, my dear. Acted! Unlike your father, I see the world as it is, and I bend its imperfections to fit my needs. You can learn to do that as well, but you must listen to me! Cordelia may have inherited a house and money, but we can make use of it, if we are wise. Your friends, Sir Richard and Mr. Brandon. They are both available, are they not?"

"What do you mean available? What have they to do with this legal fiasco?"

"I mean, are they unattached? Neither is engaged, I hope?"

"Of course, they're not engaged; though Brandon has a sort of understanding with some banker's daughter. Why?"

"Because, the right marriage would return the money and this Marylebone house to us! A husband would gain legal access to Delia's inheritance, but *the man who controls the husband*, also controls the property. Surely, you can manage that!"

"And Aubrey? Isn't it better that she marry him? The earl has boatloads of cash and influence to rival the queen's."

"True, but there's no guarantee he'd share that wealth with *us*, and he's hardly a malleable sort of man, now is he?"

Cunning and avarice shadowed Wychwright's face, and he began to see his mother's point. "We'd only be thinking of Delia's welfare," he whispered in an oily voice. "She used to consider Sir Richard rather handsome, as I recall. And he does find her attractive; for a woman, that is. Yes, Mother, I believe that's what we'll do. I'll invite both men over tonight, and we'll hash it all over. We might even play cards for it. The winner gets my sister!"

CHAPTER TWENTY-NINE

7:02 am, 21st December, 1888 - Charles Sinclair's Journal

It's been a strange and very busy three days since my last entry. I'd hoped to write daily, but time works against me, I fear. We arrived at Branham on the evening of the 19th as planned, but since then, very little has gone as we'd anticipated. Immediately on arrival, I was informed by our butler Mr. Kay that the village's constable asked to speak with me, as soon as possible. Joseph Tower is a green but eager young officer, assigned to the village only a month ago after spending a year at D-Division. He grew up here, so he fits in well, but he's had little experience with anything other than petty crimes.

(MEMO: Contact Draper about the boy).

The problem is this: The morning of the 19th, three men from the Cambridge team for the Lion Hall survey were reported missing. Late night, one was found dead, presumably murdered. Such a crime is beyond the constable's experience, which means I either bring in another from London, or break a promise to my wife and become involved myself. My beautiful Beth did not hesitate, but insisted I lead the investigation. She reminded me that, as Duke and Duchess, it is our responsibility to look after the villagers in legal matters.

The dead man and his two missing colleagues had worked with the Blackstone Society's Branham project for the past five and a half weeks. All three were last seen on the morning on the eighteenth at Lion Hall by Edwin Clark and his men. He reported them as friendly but somewhat young—except for a Cambridge don named Seth Holloway, Lord Salter's son, whom Clark knew well from previous visits to the hall. We've shut down all activity at the survey site and commenced a wide-area search.

The don I mentioned is one of Elizabeth's oldest, closest friends, and I could tell by her reaction that any risk to his welfare would affect her deeply. But rather than wring her hands in despair, my amazing wife has rallied into action, allowing me to see her as reigning Duchess of Branham in the truest sense. She reminds me now of that 'take-charge' little girl I first met in '79, and only a fool would get in that lady's way.

Upon hearing the report of the missing men, Elizabeth immediately gathered the entire staff and asked every able-bodied man to leave off his current task and join the search. She's organised the farmers' wives into teams to provide meals and other refreshments for the searchers. Every cook and maid in the hall is helping to bake bread, roast meats, trim vegetables and pack fruit. Adele had also pitched in by filling baskets with food. These tireless women have made hundreds of sandwiches and gallon upon gallon of coffee, tea, and hot cocoa, and I praise God for each of them!

The weather has turned quite cold since we arrived. I expect snow before too long. It's imperative that the two missing men be found soon; otherwise, we'll be searching for bodies. If it's Seth Holloway's body awaiting me in Branham, I fear my wife will never be the same.

It's a grim way to begin so meaningful a season. I shall write more later, but I'm to meet Baxter downstairs in ten minutes. I've pressed dear Cornelius into service as my detective inspector this morning. He knows the area and the villagers as well as any, which will make my task easier. And, though he doesn't know it, this will permit me to see how his mind works as an ICI agent.

Four days until Christmas, and we begin it with a death. May the Lord bring his tender mercies to the dead man's family, whoever he might be!

CHAPTER THIRTY

9:52 am - Branham Village Constabulary

Constable Joseph Tower longed for the morning to end. When the twenty-two-year-old replaced Charlie Graham as village policeman, young Joe assumed his life in Branham would be much as it had always been: spend time with the locals, take in a bit of fishing at Queen's Lake, enjoy the spring fête and the fall apple festival, and court Betty Andrews. For fifteen and a half weeks, that was precisely the life he'd led, but no longer. As of last night, all such idylls vanished, when a dead man was discovered near the Branham rail sheds.

The body was found on a spur that ran into one of the car sheds owned by the duchess. The dead man wore no clothing, and his back, arms, legs, and stomach showed signs of violent torture. His genitals had been rudely excised as though torn off, and not one drop of blood remained in the man's veins. The sight caused Joe to vomit up his breakfast. George Price pronounced it murder by unknown means, but it was up to Tower to sort it all out. The lad had no idea where to start.

The constable convened a meeting inside the Abbot's Ghost, located opposite the green. The landlord served up coffee, fried bread, sausages, and eggs to the sleep-deprived young policeman as they waited for reinforcements from the hall.

Relief arrived in the form of two men. One stood taller than the other by two inches, however, the shorter man, gave the impression of greater size due to a barrel chest and broad face. Both were dressed fashionably well, their demeanor one of authority and calm.

"Good morning, Constable," greeted the bear-like fellow. "Danny, it's a dark matter that calls us together."

"So it is, Mr. Baxter," concurred the landlord. "Might that be our new master, sir?"

"It is indeed. Allow me to introduce His Grace, Commissioner Charles Sinclair, 1st Duke of Haimsbury. Sir, this gentleman is Danny Stephens, landlord of the Ghost. You've already met our new village constable, Joseph Tower, a local lad who's done us all proud."

Charles shook their hands amiably. "Good to meet you, Mr. Stephens. Baxter is right, gentlemen. It is indeed a dark matter which draws us together."

"It certainly is, Your Grace," said Tower.

"Constable, as we're discussing murder, I think it's best you call me Commissioner."

"Yes, sir. I got a wire this morning from Inspector Reid at H, sir. He's offered to come help once the fire inspections are finished. Might I ask, sir, what is this ICI organisation he mentioned?"

A third voice replied from the snug. "That's a very good question, Constable. We're all wondering about that, aren't we, Michael?"

Charles peered into the dimly lit interior of the small room next door. What he saw only doubled his dismay. "Fred Best and Michael O'Brien. Both on the loose in Branham of all places. Might I ask how you walk free, O'Brien? Shall I inform Newgate that I've found their missing prisoner?"

"Commissioner, you know very well that my friend walks free because he is innocent," Best replied. "No evidence and, therefore, no infraction of the law."

"Give me time, Best. I'll find some law you've broken and see you both enjoying our comfortable cells."

"I ask you, sir, is that the speech of a prominent duke? And one so very *royal* at that?"

"Get out, Best. We're engaged in private business, and you're not invited."

The reporter casually lit an Egyptian cheroot with a gold lighter. "Murder is public business, Commissioner. Is the ICI investigating this as another ritual killing? Is Ripper expanding his field beyond London, into Kent?"

It was Baxter who answered. "A gentleman would never harass an honest man who serves the public, sir. Newspapers provide a service, but when the printing press becomes a platform from which to launch lies and innuendo, then it is time we of the public demand more honest writers and refuse to buy your filthy rags until you comply! The British pound speaks with a mighty voice, sir, and even your employer must bow to the power of commerce!"

Both reporters stared at Baxter, devoid of any answer to his attack. Rather than engage further, Fred dropped a shilling onto the table and picked up his hat and coat.

"Michael and I were just leaving as it happens, so you may call off your bulldog, Commissioner. There are other ways to obtain information for our readers."

The pair left, and Charles watched as they wandered along the high street, stopping at each shop to talk with the merchants. He turned and patted his friend on the back. "Well done, Mr. Baxter! Going forward, I believe I'll keep you close when dealing with the press. Bulldog, indeed! Now, if I might get a cup of coffee, we'll talk through what you know, Constable Tower."

Charles and Cornelius took seats at a wooden table inside the vacated snug, warming themselves by the pleasant fire. Danny brought each a steaming cup of strong coffee. By half past ten, Tower, Stephens, and George Price had joined them at the table.

"I'll turn the sign, sir," said Danny. "Just to let the locals know we're shut till later. Oh, mornin', Grimes. You're runnin' late. I just 'bout locked ya out. Everyone's in the snug."

Price looked up as a sixth man entered the room. "Welcome, Mr. Grimes," he called to the newcomer. "You know most everyone here, I think, but this handsome gentleman is the hall's new master, Duke Charles of Haimsbury. You may call him Commissioner Sinclair in this instance, for the duke's also a police detective, and he's in charge of the murder investigation."

"An honour ta meet ya, Yer Grace," the uniformed man said, bowing slightly. "It's a right mess, m'lord, iffin ya don' mind me sayin'. This'll cause delays in the schedule, an' it'll affect London soon."

"Why is that, Mr. Grimes?" asked Sinclair.

"The body, sir. It's inside the rail station, an' I daren't let passengers see that! Lord Almighty, I wish I'd never seen it, sir! I got my char woman moppin' up the floors, o' course. You'd think a man with such wounds as he got'd leave the floor in a right state, but there's not much blood, only muddy boot marks. But with him layin' there, I can't open up the station, lessin' you gives the word ta move the poor sod elsewhere."

"Your position with the station?"

"Grimes is the manager, Yer Grace," Danny told the duke as he poured the distraught fellow a cup of coffee.

Grimes stirred in a splash of thick cream. "I expect you'll be wantin' ta see the body, sir?"

"Yes. In fact, if Dr. Price and Constable Tower will accompany us, I'll go there now. Mr. Stephens, we'll return and have lunch here, if that's possible. I'm told your inn is full of overnight residents, and the village teems with tourists."

"We got 'em comin' out our ears, m'lord."

"Simple fare will do, then. Sandwiches, if it isn't too much trouble. It's nearly eleven o'clock now," he added, glancing at his pocket watch. "We'll try to be back here by one. Is that too soon?"

"We'll have everythin' ready, sir."

Price walked alongside Baxter and Sinclair as they strolled the brick-lined high street, past shop windows and curious onlookers. Charles noticed Best and O'Brien inside the local bakery, chatting with the rosy-cheeked proprietor and taking notes. The duke's keen eye also noticed other familiar faces amongst the crowds, speaking with holiday shoppers and calling on local businesses. He counted seven reporters in all, representing the *Star, Gazette*, *Times*, and *Daily News.* Shopping amongst this fourth estate invasion were a hundred or more wealthy tourists and ghost hunters, obvious from their bespoke attire, and nearly everyone tipped their hats or curtsied as he passed.

A few greeted him with cries of 'Welcome to the village, Your Highness,' or 'Long live our prince!', and Charles grew increasingly irritated with each step. Since several newspapers had printed articles implying Charles's legal right to the throne, he found himself the centre of unwanted attention, no matter the locale, and some dared to whisper of England's 'uncrowned king'.

"Do you ever wish for your old life, sir?" Baxter asked him, perceiving his employer's darkening mood.

Breaking from the reverie, Sinclair managed a smile. "Do you read minds, Inspector Baxter?"

"Not really, my lord, but I've come to know your mind a little since we first met. Did you just call me Inspector, sir?"

"I did," he answered stopping. "Look, I know you enjoy serving in your current capacity, and no butler in the kingdom could ever replace you, but I wonder if we might put your intuitions and experience to better use? The ICI is in its infancy and requires men with broad capabilities and keen instincts to help it mature. As you demonstrated with those reporters, you have the rare gift of knowing what to say and when to say it. And your instincts are sharper than most who call themselves detectives. I'd like to add you as one of our investigators, Cornelius. How does Detective Inspector Baxter suit you?"

The butler took a moment to consider the idea, and his puzzled expression slowly lifted into a radiant grin.

"Inspector Baxter," he repeated, his dark eyes brightening. "I rather like the sound of that, but if it isn't too bold a remark, I enjoy looking after you, sir. I shouldn't wish to leave you in the lurch."

"And you won't," answered Haimsbury. "I'd make you my right hand man in all things, and you'd assist me directly with enquiries. You asked if I miss my old life. Truthfully, I sometimes do, but you've helped me transform from a commoner to a duke. And you keep me humble, Cornelius, which is even more important. How is that not service?"

"Will you allow me to speak with Mrs. Alcorn first, sir?"

Charles's lips curved into a smile. "Do I detect another change in your future? Might there be a wedding at Branham one day soon?"

Baxter actually blushed. "We have discussed it, sir. Esther and I have been good friends for many years. We grew up together. She lost her first husband long ago to cholera, as you're aware. I've never been married, but I should like companionship as I near retirement. And we hold one other in high regard."

Charles laughed aloud and slapped his friend on the back. "High regard, indeed! Baxter, old man, you're in love and you know it!"

"So, I am, sir. So I am."

The continued on their way, and had reached Twitcham's Mercantile, when the round-faced proprietor rushed out to offer a gift. "Forgive me, Your Highness," he said with an awkward bow, "but I hope you'll accept this small token. It ain' much, my lord, but it comes from the heart. My missus made it. She's a steady hand at lacework and asked me ta give it to you, if I seen ya."

Twitcham presented a small, beaded cross formed from white, tatted lace. It had been starched to hold its shape and hung from a blue silk ribbon.

"My Cathy makes all manner o' goods, sir. She says a man needs ta keep the cross with 'im at all times. Carry yer cross daily, tha's what the good book says, don't it? Carry it daily."

Charles held the delicate gift aloft, deeply touched by the man's humility. "Please, tell your wife that I shall keep this with me every day, Mr. Twitcham. And I'll remind the duchess of your good lady's talent with a needle. My wife has a fondness for lace, and I expect will make use of your Cathy's talents quite often. Thank you."

The butcher bowed again. "It's our honour, sir. Your Highness."

"Just call me Commissioner for the present, Mr. Twitcham. I'm a working man, just as you are."

A nearby reporter for the *Pall Mall Gazette* took notes on the encounter, and by the next morning, the story would be told throughout Westminster.

The journey continued in similar fashion along the high street, with Baxter shooing away several persistent reporters who peppered the duke with questions about his life, recent marriage, his royal blood, and of course, the newest murder on a long list of investigations. Finally, at half eleven, they reached the railway station, where Charles found the draped body lying on an oak registration table just inside the lobby.

Sinclair lifted the canvas drape. "Poor man," he said, then turned to Joe Tower. "I could offer my opinion, Constable, but let's discover just how skilled you are at observation and deduction. What do you see?"

The inexperienced police officer felt as if he were taking an exam at school, but he remembered what his sergeant at D-Division had always told him: *Use your eyes, boy. Just say what you see.*

"He's been dead no more than a day."

"Why?" asked Sinclair.

"Rigor mortis, sir. He's still stiff. Rigor goes away after two days. And he died somewhere else. Not on the rails."

"And your reason for drawing that conclusion, Constable?"

"The marks, sir. There are lividity marks on his upper arms, thighs, and knees. Like he died lying on his front, but he was found on his side."

"And the other wounds? The mutilations? What caused those?"

Joe shook his head. "You got me there, sir. Might rats have done it? Some o' the punctures look large for rat teeth, but the man's privates look like they were bitten or gnawed, sir."

Charles considered this. "Rat bites or other animal predation is possible, but that fails to explain the blood loss. Nor does it give us the cause of death. All in all, a fair assessment, Constable, but you got the time of death wrong. Cold weather delays cessation of muscular rigidity. I've seen it take a week for rigor to disappear in winter. On the other hand, I've seen rigor begin within minutes, as in cases of cold weather drowning. Cadaveric spasm hastens post-mortem rigidity. When a person hits freezing water, every muscle tenses and remains fixed." He turned to Price. "George, what can you tell me?"

"Aside from applauding your medical knowledge, sir? Let me see." Price adjusted his spectacles and stepped forward. He'd investigated his share of inexplicable deaths in the decades since becoming official physician to the Branham family, but this one took the prize. As a younger physician, he'd examined the remains of tortured bodies—what the men of the inner circle referred to as *ritual* murders, some of them quite young—but never one with a total absence of blood.

"It is a mystery, to be sure, sir," he began. "Therefore, I shan't draw any conclusions. Not yet. However, Tower is correct regarding time of death. I'd say between forty-eight and thirty-six hours, but no more. The landlord's testimony is that he and his friends left the inn the morning of the nineteenth with plans to return by nightfall. Mr. Clark spoke with them around half nine, when they promised to vacate Lion Hall by sunset. Therefore, something happened within the next few hours that led to this man's death."

"Do we know his name yet?" asked Charles, dreading the response. *If this is Holloway, Elizabeth will be devastated.*

"The Honourable Peter John Mark Patterson, son of Baron John Patterson, a banker with Barings. Peter was a second year student at Trinity. Colonel Collinwood identified him."

"And he is?"

"The project leader," replied Price. "The man's insufferable, if you don't mind my saying. You'll be meeting him later today, so I understand. Presently, he's in London explaining Patterson's death to family. Dreadful business! No parent should receive such news."

"No, they shouldn't," Charles answered, thinking of his dead son. "And the puncture marks?"

"They are not rat bites; of that I'm certain. The conformation of the incision is too precise and straight. These are more like jabs with a pointed object. The tip of an ice pick, perhaps. Or a sharpened awl. However, none of the wounds goes deeper than an inch. Also, rats do not usually excise the entire eye, and the genital wounding is undecipherable as well. It's as though the killer or killers grew so frenzied in their attack that he or they lost all control. It is personal and monstrously brutal. I'm afraid this poor man suffered a great deal before he died. All the wounds, including the genital mutilation, are pre-mortem."

"And the blood loss?" asked Sinclair.

George pointed to a deep puncture at the base of the throat. "I believe this to be the source. It lies just over the jugular vein. A wound such as this would bleed more slowly than an artery, but would leave pools of blood over time, especially if some sort of poison were involved."

"Poison? Why would you suggest that, sir?" asked Baxter.

"Merely being thorough. I'll run blood tests to be sure, but some poisons have an anti-coagulant effect, which would prolong bleeding. And, as there were no bloodstains on or near the rail spur, we have to assume the attack occurred elsewhere. Commissioner, may I remove the body to a more permanent place soon? I've a small garden shed near my surgery, which might suffice. The body needs to remain cold for continued study, you see."

Charles considered how the next few days would proceed. It was all too likely that the dead man's missing colleagues were either complicit in Patterson's death or themselves victims. It might be that three bodies would eventually require preservation—if not more, if Ripper or this Dybbuk demon had widened his territory.

"No, I prefer to keep my options open, George. Baxter, have we any buildings in the village? Ones owned by the estate?"

"There's the granary, sir. It takes in oats, rye, and barley from surrounding farms and then transports them to the brewery. We grow the hops on our own land, of course. There may be an empty room there that's unheated, sir. Perhaps, a cellar or well room."

"Good, let's do that. George, if you'd be good enough to speak with the granary's manager, I'd appreciate it. Is there anyone else from the Blackstone group about this morning I may speak with? These three Oxford men, for instance. Have you taken their statements?"

Joe Tower answered. "The colonel sent the Oxford men away, sir. I warned him that we'd need to speak to them, but he insisted on it. Collinwood is somewhat stiff in his manner."

"And so am I, when obstructed," answered the duke coldly. "So far, Blackstone's actions have done nothing but impede our efforts, which makes them primary suspects. I want the names of everyone associated with the Society, and I want it yesterday. When is Collinwood returning from London?"

"This evening, sir. Assuming we can open the railway station before then. The lines to Branham have been rerouted."

"Then finding a suitable morgue is our first priority, Constable," Charles answered. "Make those arrangements with Dr. Price, and then set up an office for me here in the village. I want none of this dark business to touch the duchess, is that clear?"

Tower saluted. "Of course, Commissioner."

Price made some notes in a small leather book. "We should be able to move the body by mid-afternoon. How is Elizabeth holding up?"

"Remarkably well, considering. Our lives rarely stop long enough for a breath."

George laughed. "Wait until the babies arrive, assuming it is twins. Mr. Baxter is helping you, I see? And the earl? Is Lord Aubrey joining us this Christmas season?"

"He's helping with the search at present. Elizabeth is handling that aspect of things, but I prefer she not hear the grisly details of this man's death."

"She'll learn nothing from me."

"Baxter, let's make our way back to the inn, but use the journey to interview the merchants about the two missing men. I want to know if anyone noticed unusual behaviour, or if any of the men met with outsiders. Also, I want to search their rooms at the Ghost."

Baxter nodded. "Very good, Commissioner. I can aid you in those endeavours, and then I suggest we break for luncheon. The next few days will be busy, sir, and you mustn't neglect meals."

"You are the perfect second in any investigation, Baxter. Come, you can introduce me to the locals as we make our way back."

CHAPTER THIRTY-ONE

Saint Clair-sur-Epte, Normandy

George Holloway stared at the dusty scroll. With only a few hours left before sunset, time was running out to decipher and prove the text was genuine. Someone, perhaps John Dee, had penned the lines upon a vellum of antique age. Dee, a founding fellow at Trinity College Cambridge, once served as astrological advisor to Queen Elizabeth I. The writing certainly looked like Dee's, and the membrane seemed old enough, but the frustrated earl had no way of testing it. The ink had the correct appearance and 'bleed' for the late 16th century, and the formation of the letters looked correct. He wished his son were here. Seth's knowledge of textual evidence, language, and ciphers would prove very helpful right now.

"Have you got it?" asked the macabre solicitor as he entered the chilly drawing room.

Since arriving at the dig, Lord Salter and the Blackstone team had lived and worked in the north wing of an old castle, built by the Duc du Ross.

"I'm nearly there," replied the earl, who then sneezed several times before wiping his thin nose with a handkerchief. "This place is freezing, Flint! It'll be all our deaths if we stay in this God-forsaken place much longer!"

The lawyer grinned as he took a chair close to the earl's desk. "It is this place's 'God-forsaken' nature that most appeals to me, Lord Salter. And death isn't so bad. Have you arrived at an opinion regarding the vellum's authorship?"

"It certainly looks like Dee's work. He's included some of his Enochian figures in the margins. The man was mad, if you ask me.

"Mad or not, you have two hours to verify the text."

"Two hours?" echoed the man in dismay. "That's impossible! I cannot possibly decipher it by then."

"We do not require a translation. We can read the writing ourselves, Lord Salter. All we need from you is verification."

"You should have asked my son, then. He's more informed than I on Dee."

"Ah, but the dashing viscount is elsewhere at the moment. Far, far away," Flint answered vaguely. "Verify the document, and then leave it to us. Dusk provides a window into Time itself, and an old friend awaits."

An impossible fly buzzed past the earl's weary eyes, and he swatted at it, wondering how an insect could fly about in such cold temperatures. In the millisecond it took for his hand to fly past his nose, both the insect and Albus Flint had vanished.

Sundown – the Branham Estate

Paul Stuart had never before seen this section of the tunnel maze. Several times, when Elizabeth was a child, she had taken him through parts of the system, but he'd never imagined it was so vast! He'd been leading a team of four through the ruins of Lion Hall, when they'd discovered a series of tombs that led to a large crypt.

"Powers, have you or your men ever come this far?" he asked Branham's head groundskeeper.

"No, sir. Not this far, though I reckon the little duchess might o' done. You know how she used to follow these old tunnels as a girl."

"I know it all too well," answered the earl. "I can see why an archaeological team might want to record these ruins, but I wish the duchess would tear them all down. There's an unhealthy miasma about these tunnels. A palpable darkness that gets into one's bones."

"Aye, sir. I was raised on the estate, not far from here, on the old Anjou sheep farm. Most of us lads played hereabouts, and they'd tell stories to curdle a man's blood! Ya never wanted to come down without a candle and a prayer book."

Stuart bent down to examine the floor of the cold crypt. The walls were roughly hewn, and two had large niches for votives or perhaps urns, now long gone. Two large statues acted as guardians to the entrance and exit. One a large bird; the other a human.

"I believe we're standing in a stone puzzle, Mr. Powers. A tangible spell of some kind. Have you noticed? The carving on the doorway lintels matches the figural doorposts, as well as the statues."

"I don't follow, my lord," answered the gardener.

"On this side of the crypt, we have human figures in a variety of poses. See there? The paintings over the door? Some of the humans demonstrate subservience; others appear more like masters. On the opposite side of the chamber, leading into the next phase of the tunnel system, is a great bird. Perhaps a raven or merlin. The images on the lintel and the posts are also birds. Some subservient; others clearly masters. But on both lintels, the uppermost figure is crowned. A human at the first door, a bird at the second. It's intentional, and it has meaning. But what, I wonder? Now, what might this be?" he said hopefully. "At last! Evidence the men came this way, Powers! Crumpled tinfoil, an apple core, and a broken pencil."

"Might that book belong to one of the lads, my lord?"

"Book?" asked the Scotsman. "What book?"

"There by the bird door, sir. Beneath the statue."

Paul crossed the wide crypt to the exit, kneeling to collect a leather book. "Blackstone Exploration Society," he said, reading the embossed name on the exterior. He opened the book. "This belongs to Seth Holloway! I pray this means he's alive, Powers."

"It'll lift the little duchess's spirits, if we can find him, sir. But Lord Paynton's a friend to you as well, isn't he, my lord?"

"An old friend whom I treated very badly the last time we met. I pray for the chance to apologise."

"I'm sure he understood, sir," the older man said.

"I doubt it. Have you ever been jealous, Powers?"

"No reason to be, sir. My Annie's too good a woman for me ta worry 'bout that. We been married fer more 'n thirty years. I've never regretted a minute."

"You're a blessed man, then," answered the earl, glancing through the notebook at a series of pencil drawings. One was of Elizabeth, apparently done from memory. The fine lines showed great skill and sensitivity, and Paul imagined how the viscount must have felt as he make each pencil stroke. "I failed to recognise love in myself until it was too late. I sometimes wonder how a man knows he's in love."

"You just do, sir."

"Really? Then, why couldn't I see it? Never mind. Let's keep moving."

Taking the book with him, Aubrey crouched low to cross through to the next tunnel. Some of the more narrow sections nearly proved too confining for the broad-shouldered earl, and he feared they might need to turn back. "Careful, Powers. Hold tightly to your lamp. There are sconces in the main cavern ahead, assuming this way leads to it. Our little duchess knows this stone maze as well as she knows the yew maze above. I remember getting stuck in here once, when she guided me through. Did you know most of these connect to Branham Hall?"

"Is that right?"

"Yes. The routes are very old, and some say part of a vast underground system that radiates outward from Kent like a spider web, reaching all the way to London—perhaps, even beyond."

"It feels a bit like hell, sir."

"True, but it's an engineering marvel, nonetheless. Look at this!" he cried as they cleared the next doorway to enter a grand gallery of polished stone. "This construction is vastly different from the earlier tunnels, don't you think? You know, Powers, I really don't think King Richard had anything to do with these structures. I've heard it argued that he ordered the building of this massive underground as a redoubt against a French invasion, but this chamber looks more like Egyptian stone-work to me. The blocks are fitted to one another with near perfection. It's as though they *grew* together naturally! Truly marvellous! How did Blackstone know these were here, I wonder? From the outside, Lion Hall is nothing more than crumbling stones and fractured battlements. One might find an old piece of armour or a rusted horseshoe, but there's nothing of importance. How did they know it held such treasures?"

Already past sundown, Aubrey hastened through the impressive gallery, looking for signs of the missing men. After squeezing through a narrow opening, they reached a fork. The earl had no idea which way to choose. "I'll go left, you go right," he told the groundskeeper. After two or three minutes, he heard the other man shout.

"I canno' make it, sir! The way's too tight!"

The earl turned round and met Powers at the fork. "Go on back then. I can make it alone."

"Sir, forgive me for disobeying, but I canno' do that. Whoever killed tha' other fellow might still be down here."

"I'm armed and experienced in close combat. Go on, Powers. I'll be fine."

"Sir, please. Allow me to stay."

Aubrey placed a hand on the man's shoulder. "It's all right. I've been doing this sort of thing since I was twelve. If my father trusted me on my own, so should you."

"Very well, my lord. I'll go fetch the others." He paused before heading back to the grand gallery. "Sir, might this passage lead up to the old abbey? My granddad claimed some o' these tunnels connected up to it. I could have some of the men wait up there to keep a lookout for you."

"A team's already searching the abbey. If the way leads there, then I'm sure we'll meet up."

Reluctantly, Powers left, and the earl moved forward, crouching lower and lower, until finally dropping to his knees to crawl through the last section. He barely managed to squeeze past the final opening, but once through, he emerged into the grand ceremonial cavern beneath the abbey. Instantly, he knew his location from Sinclair's vivid description of the place. A shivering cold ran through his veins as he walked along the stones.

This is where Patricia died. Where Beth watched Trent kill her. Where she saw a helpless boy abused and slain. How many offerings were made here? How many blood sacrifices to devils?

The thoughts made even the brave earl shudder.

With darkness upon him, Paul said a quick prayer, asking for protection. Then, he realised what had so unnerved him. The torches were all lit.

Who had lit them?

Surely, the missing men. It was a positive sign.

He used the lantern to examine corners lying in shadow, and as he perused a niched wall near the right-hand side, his sharp eyes fell upon an impossibility. A small doll gazed at him as though waiting. He instantly recognised the toy as one Beth carried as a child; one he'd thought long since destroyed.

He crossed to retrieve the doll, but as he reached it, he heard breathing. A shallow, rapid sort of panting like that of someone in great distress.

"Help me," a raspy voice whispered. It was barely audible, coming from the darkest corner.

The earl rushed towards the sound, finding a man he'd not seen since August. "Seth?"

The injured teacher lay on a sharp slab of hard stone, his cotton shirt and waistcoat stained with blood.

"Here now," Paul said gently. "You're going to be fine. Can you stand?"

"Paul? Is that you? No... No, it cannot be," Holloway choked, a thin stream of blood trickling from his mouth. His eyes were sunken, and his lips cracked and dry.

"Don't try to speak, Seth. You're badly hurt. Can you walk?"

"I'm not sure. I can try. Where am I?"

The earl checked the man's limbs for fractures. Nothing broken. Opening the torn shirt, he discovered the source of the blood: a gash that ran diagonally from the left shoulder to the right hip. It looked deep and jagged, possibly caused by a serrated hunting knife.

"Lean on me, and we'll find a way up to the abbey."

"I saw a staircase on the other side of the cavern," Holloway gasped. "I started to climb up, but then I heard them screaming. Worthy and Pitt. Oh, it was horrible!" he wept. "I thought it came from behind that brick wall, but there's no door. I tried to find a way in. They kept screaming and screaming! Then *she* came, that woman and the other."

"Tell me later. Let's get you to a doctor first, my friend. You're in very bad shape."

With Aubrey doing most of the work, it took nearly half an hour to climb the winding staircase and cross through the ruins of the abbey, but with many stops and much agony, the earl and Holloway at last emerged into the cold night air. Both Powers and Clark met them, and Aubrey assigned two of their men to return to the chamber and search for anyone left stranded. After an hour's diligent hunt, the only things recovered were Wentworth's rucksack, a short ax, and the doll. These were brought to Aubrey, who added them to the evidence they'd previously collected: some food scraps, tin foil, a food box marked 'Abbot's Ghost', Holloway's journal, a set of drawing pencils, a measuring line, and now the rucksack and a doll that looked eerily like a young Elizabeth Stuart Sinclair.

By eight o'clock, Seth Holloway, only son and heir to the Salter earldom, had fallen into a deep sleep in the east wing of Branham Hall.

CHAPTER THIRTY-TWO

A cavern deep beneath the earth, near Saint Clair-sur-Epte

Albus Flint gazed intently into the dark pool of cool water. Beneath its ripples, lay a glittering surface of obsidian that had not reflected light from the human world since Enoch walked the earth. He urged the diggers to move swiftly but carefully to lift the large mirror.

"Easy with your ropes," the lawyer commanded the student workers. "Keep them taut, but do *not* pull until I give the order."

The legal gatekeeper to the Blackstone Exploration Society had trusted no one else to exhume so prized and valuable an artifact. Its unique properties made it indestructible, but the precise moment that light struck the molecules had to be timed to the second—only then, could the spell be read.

A tall being with shoulder-length locks of raven hair stepped close to the pit's edge. "Is that my brother?" he asked, nearly upsetting the huge crane's precarious balance.

"Careful, my lord!" Flint exclaimed. "If you want this team to perform the task without mishap, then you must allow them room to manoeuvre. Step back, now!"

"You always were an insolent little crow, Albus," Saraqael answered, already growing bored. "No wonder she chained you up."

"She had good reason, but see? I wear no chains now," the lawyer answered slyly. "And milady has chains aplenty, with skills to fasten them tightly *upon anyone*."

"Is that humour, Albus? You're out of practise. I wonder if he is buried alongside the mirror?" asked the elohim.

"If who is buried with the mirror?" enquired a dark-haired woman as she approached the group. "Surely, there are not two of us down there."

"You are not yet an 'us', Serena. Be patient, if you hope to receive your eternal body and powers. I could just as easily toss you into this pit. Shall I do that and be rid of your harping?"

Di Specchio stepped away from the edge. "I prefer to remain here. Who else might be down there? Other than your brother, I mean?"

"An older power. One attached to greatness. One that was, and is, and shall be again. But it will take much more than the solstice light to resurrect him. It will take a very special key and a unique vessel!"

"You and your brothers love to speak in riddles," complained the vampiress. "Even you, Flint. You present yourself as somber and serious, yet I have seen you in your natural state. Rather flighty, in my opinion."

"I care nothing for your opinions, human!" he warned her. "There!" he cried to the students. Of course, none of them perceived the supernatural beings standing round the deep fissure; neither Saraqael nor di Specchio, for both remained cloaked. The six men saw only Flint in his material mask.

The wax-faced lawyer checked his pocket watch. "Two minutes, and then you may allow it to surface. Check the mirrors, Mr. Johnson!" he shouted to a lanky Cambridge student. "You, Mr. Walters, see to the second and third mirrors. They must reflect the sun's rays upon the object in a precise manner, else the incantation will fail."

The students obeyed, whilst the four men holding the thick ropes strained to keep the heavy mirror stationary, hanging just below the pool's surface. The watch's hands ticked slowly, moving forward as though the timepiece itself conspired to stop the sun.

"Well?" asked Saraqael.

"Three, two, one. NOW!" shouted Flint, and the muscular young men, chosen for their brawn and not their brains, lifted the gleaming prison from its watery abode. A series of curved mirrors, placed at various depths along the cavern bounced the setting sun's final beams one from another until a faint glimmer found its way to the pool. Flint read from Dee's scroll, enunciating the ancient tongue as if born to it. The entire cavern began to shake, the deep temblor growing evermore close with each spoken word of the spell. Then, just as the mirror broke free of the water, the final solar photons of the winter solstice struck the polished obsidian, causing the midnight glass to crack into a vast web of fine, black lines.

A shudder ran through the water as the glass bulged outward. A clawed hand emerged, and then a scaly arm.

The terrified students dropped the ropes in a panic and ran for shelter, causing the device to crash back into the inky pool, submerging into its cold, black waters forever. Flint and Saraqael peered over the chasm's edge, their eyes on the mirror as it descended.

"Did it work?" the elohim asked. "Do tell me we don't have to do all this again!"

Suddenly, the floor beneath their feet began to quake, and the walls of the cavern split apart. The waters disappeared into the ever-widening pit, and all six students plunged into darkness.

Moments passed, and the black waters turned a deep crimson; a red lake of blood.

The earthquake shook the mount above, where an old abbey stood; and below, the River Epte flowed backwards. Farmers and villagers ran for cover, hiding in their homes, screaming of old prophecies and ancient dragons. Clouds of bats rushed from the Saint Clair caverns, and smoke rose up through cracks in the earth. A dry hayfield caught fire, which set the nearby barn alight, and soon all of Saint Clair-sur-Epte was ablaze; colouring the night with red. By morning, seventeen homes would be turned to ash, entire flocks would be dead from the smoke, and eleven people would lie slain—including the six students who'd raised the monster from its sleep.

Terror had come to Saint Clair-sur-Epte.

8:15 pm - Montmore House – Fulham

"Mrs. Winstead, have you looked in on Miss Bunting since four o'clock tea?"

Emily Winstead was in the middle of an inventory of the private hospital's stock of pain medicines and tinctures, when she heard the doctor call. She glanced up over the top of her spectacles. The glasses fit her nose poorly, for Winstead had a very narrow bridge, which flattened just below the eyes.

"Has something happened to her, Dr. MacAlpin?" she asked as he wandered into her office.

Henry shook his head, not really focusing yet, for he'd only just awoken from an unexpected nap on the library sofa. He'd spent an hour getting Anthony Gehlen settled into the newly cleaned gardener's cottage, and the short nap had left him somewhat foggy.

"Not that I'm aware, but I had a very odd dream about her. You'll recall that she's here because of troublesome apparitions and imaginings, which her father thought indicative of weak nerves."

"Yes, sir, I recall. If you ask me, Sir Aleister only wants rid of a daughter he thinks unlikely to find a husband. Miss Gillian is pretty enough, and very sweet-tempered. Being twenty-six shouldn't work against her. She's never spoken a harsh word to anyone since arriving here three months ago, not even to Mrs. Crossfield."

"Which is remarkable in itself," Salperton laughed, "but I'd like to see if she's all right. Might she be in her apartment, or have the patients already assembled for supper? What time is it, anyway? I've lost all track."

"After eight, sir. Cook will serve supper at nine, as usual. I believe the residents are enjoying tea in the music room. They're listening to Miss Bunting play piano."

"And Miss Stuart as well?"

"Yes. May I speak of her for a moment, sir?"

"Of course," he said, running a hand through his thick hair.

"If you'll forgive an old woman for prying, it seems to me that your manner with Violet is too friendly. Women know women, sir, and she's been mistreated somewhere in her past. I can sense it. She's vulnerable."

"Which is why I am friendly with her, Mrs. Winstead. Would you have me mistreat her?"

"Of course not, but she's falling in love with you, sir. Can you not see it?"

The viscount believed no such thing, but he had no wish to argue with his forceful nurse. Winstead worked long hours and remained on call at night, and had done so faithfully since he'd hired her six years before.

"If Miss Stuart shows fondness or an attachment towards me, then it is only as a patient, Mrs. Winstead. I'm quite certain of that, but I shall take your comment into consideration in future." He turned to leave, but she called him back.

"Henry?"

The nurse rarely used his Christian name, and whenever she did, Salperton had learnt to listen carefully, for it was the mother in Winstead who spoke, not the nurse.

"Yes, Emily?" he replied gently.

"Do be careful of yourself. I've seen how you look at her. We've no idea who she really is, or what life she's led. She might even be married, sir. I beg you to heed my words. First help Violet discover her past, and then if she can legally and willingly return your affection, follow your heart."

He crossed the room and kissed her forehead. "Thank you, Emily. I shall honour those words, and I pray I shall ever and always honour you. I cannot imagine this place without you in it."

She smiled in a way that dropped years from her face, and it lightened the viscount's kind heart. The odd dream vanished from his thoughts as he headed towards the music room to join his resident patients. The current roster included Edwina Crossfield, a widow of some means who suffered from strong delusions and depression; Brian Gosberg, a businessman of considerable wealth who blamed himself for the deaths of his wife and three children, all drowned at sea in a boating accident in Cornwall; Mrs. Pamela Emmerdale, a widow who believed her husband had returned from the dead and lived with her; Miss Gillian Bunting, the spinster daughter of an MP, who claimed to see ghosts and twice tried to kill herself; Violet Stuart, an amnesiac who was slowly recalling bits of her former life; and now Dr. Anthony Gehlen, who suffered from memory lapses, unexplained shifts in time and place, and unfathomable fatigue, currently living in the gardener's cottage at the north end of the estate.

Upon arriving at the music room, Henry heard the piano, played beautifully by a competent pair of hands. He stepped inside, finding the house's complement of patients chatting amiably whilst listening to Bunting play the haunting melody. To Henry's delight, everyone looked happy—a major accomplishment for so varied and often melancholy an assembly. He decided to sit with Bunting and visit with her for a few minutes.

The woman rarely smiled, but she did so as he approached, her white hands pausing upon the keys.

"Do you play, Dr. MacAlpin?" she asked him timidly.

"A little. My grandmother insisted I take lessons from her cousin, but I'm hardly proficient. Was that Chopin?"

"Yes! Do you know it? I so love this nocturne. He wrote it in 1832. He was only thirty-nine when he died. Isn't that terribly sad? Such a gifted composer, yet so tragic a life! Do you think he ever found love, Doctor? I've read that he and the woman novelist, George Sand, loved one another, which gives me hope. Mademoiselle Sand, or *la Sand* as she was sometimes called, was hardly the epitome of femininity, nor was she young. Yet, she refused to compromise. I wonder, must a woman become an ageless doormat to find a man's shoes beneath her bed?"

This last question was thoroughly inconsistent with Bunting's genteel, even timid manner. Henry hoped no one else heard it; but of course, everyone had. He searched for the right words to answer, not wishing to confirm the girl's *idee fixe* that she was somehow old and ugly. Indeed, Gillian was quite beautiful. Lithe, tall, fair-haired with large blue eyes and copper lashes set against alabaster skin.

"Truly, Miss Bunting, such a question has never occurred to me. Perhaps, one of the ladies might offer a reply. I fear my maleness rather disqualifies me."

"Oh, but it makes you all the more qualified! Isn't that true, Miss Stuart?" she asked Violet, who sat five feet away, reading the evening papers.

"If my life has included experience of the kind required to offer an educated reply, then I've quite forgotten it, Miss Bunting," she answered gently. "I'm sure Dr. MacAlpin appreciates all women, don't you?"

"I most certainly do," he replied quickly.

Gosberg had only recently begun to speak in these gatherings, but even he offered an opinion of sorts. "Shoes beneath the bed do not mean love within the heart, Miss Bunting. True love should be the goal for a lady of breeding, not a ring on one's finger. My Alice was such a lady. And also our girls. No, no, dear friend, I do not intend to retreat into melancholia, I merely honour them. Would you play another for us, Miss Bunting? You have such a delicate touch."

"Yes, would you?" asked Henry. "I'll move over here, but only to appreciate the notes better. Perhaps, another Chopin?"

"Yes, yes! Another Chopin!" the gathering shouted in unison.

She began the Opus 9 nocturne, and he could see her eyes drift into a dream as her dainty fingers danced upon the keys. Henry wondered what thoughts now governed the woman's restless mind.

"You should be careful," whispered Violet. "Gillian's going through a bad patch."

"How so?" asked Henry. "She's not mentioned it to me."

"She wouldn't," answered Violet. "It's the kind of thing she'd only tell another woman."

"But I'm her doctor," he whispered.

"Exactly."

"I'm afraid I don't understand, Miss Stuart. Just what...?"

He had no chance to complete the question, for his butler Saunders entered with a note.

"From Lord Aubrey, sir. He asks that you come to Branham right away."

Standing to read the message, the viscount ran a hand through his curling hair. "Have Mrs. Winstead meet me in my office right away, Saunders. When is the next train to Branham?"

"Not until tomorrow, sir, but the policeman who delivered the message says there's a special awaiting you at Victoria. Lord Aubrey's train, sir."

MacAlpin felt all at sea. He'd not planned to leave for Kent until the twenty-third, accompanying Joseph Merrick and the Castle Company. Only an emergency would cause Aubrey to send such a message tonight.

Please, Lord, let it not be Elizabeth!

"Everyone, do forgive me. As you know, I'd planned to be away for Christmas, but I hadn't intended to leave you so soon. I'm afraid this message changes all that. I pray you'll take care of one another whilst I'm away. Dr. Hepplewhite is capable and quite agreeable, and I think you'll find him a far better musician than I. He also loves Chopin, Miss Bunting. I'll stop in for a moment once I'm ready to say goodbye, but again, forgive the sudden change of plans."

He rushed from the room and into the library to pack his medical bag. If something had happened to Elizabeth, he had no guarantee of a chemist's shop. His thoughts ran in a dozen directions at once. It felt all too similar to the night when Romanov had taken him to the castle.

As he added a fresh bottle of laudanum to the bag, he felt an odd sensation along the back of his neck; as though every hair stood on end. He turned slowly, certain someone had entered without speaking.

"Do I startle you?" spoke a familiar voice.

Henry nearly collapsed with relief. "You do come and go without warning, Your Highness. Why are you here?"

Romanov laughed softly as he shut the door. "I have always admired your directness, Lord Salperton. It is refreshing, compared to the circuitous conversations I endure at Whitehall. Forgive the sudden intrusion, but I thought it pertinent to speak with you before you leave."

"You know I'm leaving? Wait, of course, you do. You know everything that happens, I imagine."

"Not everything," the elohim answered. "Only the One can make that claim. I merely use the eyes of my helpers to obtain information. It is not Elizabeth who is ill, but a dear friend to her. I can tell you this much: without your skills, the man will die. George Price is experienced and knowledgeable, but his perceptions for diagnosis pale to your own. He's going to miss a key component to the young man's condition."

"Price is a fine doctor. I really doubt my powers of observation and diagnosis are any better."

"You see things Price cannot. Look with eyes of the spirit, Henry. Branham's east wing has many phantoms. And when you are there, tell Charles that another of my kind has just arisen in France, and even as we speak, this powerful prince unfurls his wings and grows strong. Tell him I shall speak to him in person after he remembers the mirror in the attic."

"Mirror? Attic? What the devil do you mean by that?"

"It will make sense to Charles, but only when he remembers. Also, I have placed wards over your gardener's cottage to protect your new patient. These will not obscure it from human eyes but only from the spirit realm. Gehlen's mind and soul are under attack, but he will recover. The one who's been using him is presently distracted by the ceremony in France, but my wards will deny his return."

"None of that makes sense," complained Salperton. "Do speak plainly for once!"

"Very well," answered the Russian. "Saraqael, one of my rebel brethren, has been assuming control of Dr. Gehlen's mind. Raziel, in the guise of a physician named Emile Sandoval, placed a mark upon Gehlen in 1879 that allows such outside control."

"Then, Gehlen is possessed?" asked Henry.

"Not permanently. The mark allows temporary infestation only."

"How is that?"

"Dr. Gehlen never invited the mark; it was forced upon him. Free will is the law, Henry. Raziel bent that law by using an old ruse. He hoped the subterfuge would allow a wolf to enter your homes in the fair guise of a trusted sheep."

"Gehlen, you mean?"

"Indeed. What Raziel did not realise is that Saraqael is disobedient. He intentionally made his presence known to you."

"By his behaviour at the theatre?" asked Henry. "But why?"

"Because Sara intends to remove Raziel from power."

"You mean he's planning a coup?"

"A very bloody one, yes. Saraqael now sows discord amongst the Redwing members, knowing Raziel will slay all those who betray him. What you call spiritual activity will increase in the coming months. All the realms are awakening, and the sleepers within them stir to rise. Your place in this battle is beside Charles and Elizabeth."

Anatole started to go, but Henry reached out, daring to grasp the mysterious entity's arm. "You cannot leave yet, please! What of Gehlen? You tell me that my place is with the Sinclairs, but how can I abandon a fellow physician when he's in so much pain?"

Romanov's icy eyes softened with boundless compassion, and he touched Henry's shoulder gently. "You have great love within you, Henry. Your mother would be proud. But fear not for Anthony. The One allowed this test for him, for he foreknew what struggles were required to bring Gehlen to salvation. Even now, Dr. MacPherson is sharing the gospel message with him; and by morning, Anthony will be protected by the Saviour's blood. Eventually, Gehlen will sit at the inner circle table, but he had to pass through the trial by fire first. His experiences will aid all of you in the coming years; but more so—and this is why he is so very important in the battle—Anthony Gehlen will one day save the life of Robby Sinclair."

"He'll do what?" asked Henry, but Romanov offered no reply. The elusive elohim had vanished.

CHAPTER THIRTY-THREE

Branham Hall

Two hours before Henry left for Victoria Station, Elizabeth Sinclair turned her thoughts to Branham business. Despite the flurry of activity and upset at the hall over the missing Cambridge men, she'd tried to keep as many of her scheduled meetings as possible. Each year at this time, the young duchess was accustomed to examining the various estate accounts with an eye towards plans for the year to come. So, when Hiram Eberly arrived from Gravesend at half past six with a briefcase filled with reports, the duchess asked Esther Alcorn to take charge of the women volunteers.

Beth had been reading through the steward's summaries for nearly a quarter of an hour, slowly turning ledger pages, but saying nothing. Her carved Rococo desk and matching chair stood before a set of French doors that overlooked the hall's central courtyard. A cheerful fire warmed the air, and beside it, snored a pair of black Labradors. In all, three men awaited Elizabeth's approval, sitting in a row near the desk, patiently awaiting her decisions as nightingales and owls flitted across the gaslit courtyard, the slender twigs moving beneath each bird's weight. A mouse scampered along one of the brickways, a bit of bread in its teeth, but before it could reach its home inside an elm tree, the owl pounced, devouring it in one gulp.

Unaware of the life and death struggle, the duchess glanced up from the ledgers. "Mr. Eberly, you've been my steward for how many years?"

"Nearly a decade, Your Grace," the fifty-three-year-old estate manager replied confidently.

"You took over for Mr. Prudeau during very difficult days, and since that time, I've come to depend upon your opinion. I find nothing out of the ordinary with any of the other estates. Beau Rêve in upstate New York is easy, as it's been shuttered for ten years. The Scotland and Ireland properties are in fine shape. Queen Anne is now looked after by my husband's manager as part of his new ICI endeavour. You have met with the manager, I hope?"

"Yes, ma'am. And I've sent Mr. Dryden all the books."

"Good. We've transferred control of the houses in France and Spain to M'sieur Rebolet, correct?"

"Yes, ma'am, as of the first of January. Shall I meet with him next month?"

"Please do. The wineries in particular require close management. I understand the new root stock we obtained from America has helped overcome the blight that's plagued our grapes for the past few decades."

"The grafted vines have grown very well and are quite vigorous. DuBonnier Winery will bottle a new vintage of Bordeaux next year, ma'am. They'd like to call it *Saint Clair Royale*, in honour of the duke."

Beth smiled. "I take it the people of France have also read the rumours of my husband's lineage."

"They have, indeed, my lady. May I approve the name?"

"Yes, I think so. Please, tell them we look forward to trying the new vintage when it's available. My husband and I may visit DuBonnier whilst in France next autumn. I must say, you're doing an excellent job for us, Mr. Eberly. An excellent job. *However,*" she added gently, "I noticed one odd entry in the Branham ledger, regarding the loss of Ambrose Aurelius. I've spoken with Mr. Clark, and both he and Mr. Soames estimate the loss of Ambrose at nearly five thousand pounds, yet your figure is far less than that amount. Can you explain that?"

Hiram Eberly had replaced a disgraced and hastily dismissed Louis Prudeau after Cornelius Baxter discovered the indiscreet bookkeeper had spied for Sir William Trent. The reckless estate manager avoided arrest only because he fled England's shores and hadn't been seen or heard of since. Three months later, in June of '79, Eberly was hired by Duke James (Hiram's father having served the duke for thirty-six years without one error in judgement or a single bad report). Not once in all the years since, had Duchess Elizabeth questioned Eberly's advice or his character.

"If you'd do me the honour of reading through to the end, Your Grace," he explained, "you'll see that I was able to recover a portion of the horse's value from the seller, Sir Ralph Menderson. His lordship deeply regrets the loss of so fine an animal and offered to shoulder part of the burden. Hence, the final loss of three thousand pounds."

"I see," Elizabeth said as she glanced through the final paragraphs of the annual report. "I take it you've no objection to my writing to Sir Ralph? His willingness to assume part of the loss is admirable, though contrary to his usual business dealings. As I recall from the contract, I bought Ambrose Aurelius with the understanding that only undisclosed health problems, provable through veterinary examination, would invalidate the purchase. When Mr. Soames examined Ambrose on arrival here, he pronounced the stallion fit and capable. I'd owned Ambrose for three months prior to his death, and I'm happy to read in Mr. Clark's report that six of our finest mares are now pregnant, thanks to Ambrose's capability. Dr. Stillwell's necropsy revealed no discernable illness, only a tiny wound and great loss of blood. How did you persuade Sir Ralph to be so very reasonable, Mr. Eberly?"

Eberly squirmed upon the chair, his grey eyes shifting from side to side. "Soames thought the horse looked lame when he arrived, my lady. He had an odd gait. That's what I told his lordship."

Andy Soames shook his head adamantly. "I said no such thing, Your Grace. If you'll read my report, you'll see the stallion was in perfect condition when he was taken to stable, as his capability can attest. I know my business, and the stallion's subsequent death from whatever insect or animal preyed upon him had nothing to do with any previous condition!"

"Calm yourself, Mr. Soames," she said quietly. "I do not question your integrity, nor do I question that of Mr. Eberly, I merely want to get to the bottom of the discrepancy. I take my job as custodian of the Branham estate very seriously, and I look to each of you to help me in that endeavour. I wish only to pass a sound and successful legacy to my children. That is all."

She paused to make sure the men understood her position. Beth made a mental note of Eberly's clear discomfort, but decided against pursuing it any further for the present.

"Now, there is another topic which requires your attention, gentlemen. Given our current worries for the missing men, it feels somewhat strange to discuss this, but May is but five months away, and planning must begin soon. I speak, of course, of the fête. As you know, the seventh of May marks the four-hundredth anniversary of Branham's annual festival, and I'd like to suggest a theme which honours that long tradition. I wonder, might we construct a reproduction of the Golden Hall?"

"The Golden Hall, my lady?" asked Soames. "I'm not sure what you mean."

"It was the very first celebration," she answered. "There's a painting in the upper gallery which you might use as inspiration. In 1489, Duke Henry's carpenters constructed seven marquees, each made from red and gold, painted canvas, encamped round a much larger, golden marquee which served as the focal point for food, dancing, and general celebrations. The duke's idea was later copied by King Francis when he met with Henry VIII at Calais. *Le Camp du Drap D'Or* is how historians refer to it. The Field of the Golden Cloth. That magnificent tent city was built by the French king as the site of their peace negotiations. Sadly, those talks broke down in like manner to the painted tents. I wonder, gentlemen, might we reconstruct Branham's original Golden Hall? We should have begun planning this years ago, but is it feasible, Mr. Wendt?"

Alvin Wendt was fifty-one, able-bodied, and wise. His seamed face widened with pride as he confidently replied. "Not only can my men and I achieve it, my lady, but we'll do so with great energy and purpose. You've but to give us your plans."

Elizabeth reached out for the carpenter's rough hands. "My dear Mr. Wendt, you are gracious, as always. I believe the original plans are in the Branham archives. Our librarian, Mr. Gresham, has been cataloguing all our histories. You might speak with him. He lives in Anjou-on-Sea, I believe."

"I'll write to him at once, my lady."

"Excellent!" she said happily. "Mr. Eberly, I should like to see an accounting for all expenses regarding the planned construction. I've put together a proposed budget for the fête, which is ten times our normal expenditures, but worth it, I think. Four hundred years is something quite monumental, and all England will join us to celebrate. My husband and I shall invite dignitaries from other countries, of course, but we'll also provide the usual delights for the villagers and our local friends. I anticipate attendance in the tens of thousands over the course of the week's activities."

Eberly was jotting down notes from the conversation in shorthand and had started to ask which account the duchess planned to use, when the door to the library was opened by Mr. Kay.

"My lady, do forgive the intrusion," the young butler said softly.

"Not at all, Kay. What is it?"

"Lord Aubrey asks for you. It seems one of the missing men has been found."

"Thank you, everyone. If you'll excuse me," she said, her voice coloured with a mixture of apprehension and relief. She left the room, speaking quickly as she walked beside Kay towards the lift. "Who found him? Where was he found? Is he alive? Is he injured?"

"We've taken the gentleman to a small apartment in the east wing. His lordship said to tell you it's Lord Salter's son, my lady. And he's in very poor shape. It might even be fatal."

Beth grew exceedingly pale, and Kay dared to touch her hand. "Are you all right, my lady?"

"Yes, yes. Have you sent for Dr. Price?"

"We have, ma'am. The earl says he found Lord Paynton beneath the old abbey. In some sort of cavern."

"The cavern?" she repeated weakly. "Oh, not there!"

Her eyes rolled into her head as every memory of that awful place flashed through her mind in a blink: her mother's murder, Trent's threats, the ritual sacrifices, the blazing fires, the deep pools of innocent blood, the laughing men cavorting in animal masks.

Kay caught his mistress just as she fainted.

Montmore House

Following supper, Violet Stuart had decided to investigate a mystery. After telling her fellow patients she suffered a headache, the amnesiac used a side passage, which Mrs. Crossfield had told her about, to exit the house without being seen by any of the servants or the ever vigilant Emily Winstead. She carried a small candle as she walked along the moonlit path, her chiffon and taffeta skirts brushing against the bricks and picking up telltale bits of debris. It had begun to snow, and Stuart shivered, wishing she'd worn a heavier coat. Her destination stood just beyond the fountain, so she hurried her pace, praying she wasn't making a terrible mistake.

All round, night creatures roamed through the brittle leaves and lacy underbrush. A black rat stared at her from its spot near the foot of a faded lilac bush. Its red eyes looked eerily human.

At last, she reached the gardener's cottage and started to knock. The door wasn't latched, but swung inward an inch or two. Inside the pleasant interior, she could see shadows dancing along the walls of the narrow entry. One of the attendants was sorting through a suitcase. Perhaps, a donation? More likely, the clothes belonged to the new mystery patient.

She dared to enter. *Nothing ventured, nothing gained.*

"Good evening," she said as innocently as she could muster.

"Miss Stuart, you're not allowed in here," the man said politely. "Dr. Hepplewhite's coming to speak with everyone shortly, and he'll expect to find you in the main house. Go on back, now, Miss."

"I shall," she promised, "but I wanted to satisfy myself regarding the man staying here. I noticed him earlier from my window, when Dr. MacAlpin first admitted him. I believe I know him."

"I doubt it, Miss."

"Oh, but I'm sure he's familiar to me, Mr. Rush. As you know, I'm unable to remember very much about myself. I hoped this man might help."

"I'm not supposed to make decisions like that, Miss."

"I'm sure that's true, but I'll never sleep for thinking about it. May I ask the man's name, at least?"

Footsteps sounded from nearby, and then a tall man emerged from the parlour. Both he and Stuart gasped.

"Anthony," she whispered, the sudden shock of memory nearly causing her to faint.

Gehlen's medical experience precluded all else, and he ran to her side. "Fetch a nurse!" he told the attendant. "Now!"

Rush hastily left the cottage, whilst Gehlen carried the unconscious woman into the parlour, where he placed her on a small settee. He rubbed her wrists and patted her face. He despaired for the lack of a medical bag or brandy, or even a bottle of smelling salts, but the circulatory stimulation soon brought her round, and Violet opened her eyes.

"Hello, Susanna," he said.

"Susanna?" she asked. "It's Anthony Gehlen, isn't it? I once knew you."

"A long time ago in Paris. 1884. What are you doing here, in an asylum?"

She sat up slowly, pieces of her past flying through her mind. It was like watching an entire library of photograph albums whoosh past her eyes in quick succession. She could make very little sense of the images, but she did remember him.

"I was in Paris?"

"For a few weeks. You were with Sir Clive Urquhart. I never understood what you saw in the man."

Clive Urquhart? Who?

"And my name is Susanna?"

"One of them. Clive told me you had another name, but he never revealed it to me. Why are you here?"

"I might ask you the same question. Oh, I'm very confused!"

He fetched a glass of water and helped her drink it down. "You act as though your memory's impaired."

"I thought my name was Violet Stuart. I can't remember much."

"Then, I'm sorry for shocking you," he told her. "My memory comes and goes as well. But not about who I am; rather where I've been. Mr. Rush is right. You shouldn't be out here. Where's Henry?"

"Gone to Branham Hall. He received a message and left immediately."

This caused Gehlen concern. "Has it anything to do with the duchess?"

"I can't say. You're right. I should go."

He took her hand. "Susanna, if you want to talk, I'll be here for a few weeks. Henry's treating my memory loss. If I can help with yours, I'd consider it a fair trade."

She smiled. "I'll come back tomorrow, then."

Gehlen kissed her hand, which startled Morgan. "It used to make you giggle when I'd do that. Sorry. Have you any idea why you lost your memory?"

"No; though, it might have to do with a fire."

"We had a terrible fire in Whitechapel yesterday. I need to recover quickly and get back there."

Fire? Perhaps, she hadn't imagined it! "When?"

"It started around eight yesterday morning. Hundreds of people were injured. The London was overrun with patients. I hear Mrs. Winstead coming, Susanna. You must go."

She quickly left the cottage, running into the nurse a few feet from the door. Morgan pretended to remember nothing, deciding to discuss it further with Gehlen the next day. But before dawn broke, every moment of her previous life would tumble back into her conscious mind, and Henry MacAlpin would return to find his favourite patient missing.

CHAPTER THIRTY-FOUR

Branham Hall

Charles and Baxter arrived back at the hall shortly after nine o'clock. It had been a long, puzzling day, and the exhausted duke needed food, a glass of wine, and the reassuring touch of his wife's hand. Instead, he was met at the door by a contentious Victoria Stuart, who'd arrived with Dolly Patterson-Smythe half an hour earlier.

"It's time you came home!" she declared without preamble. "Dolly and I had to drive all the way in from Faversham, of all things, because the line to Branham was closed. It took us nearly an hour, and Samson barked the entire time. You'd think he'd never seen sheep before. Poor Dolly's having a lie-down, due to her head, and now it's snowing of all things!"

"So I've noticed," Charles said, brushing fluffy snowflakes from his gloves. "And it's nice to see you, too, Tory."

"You've heard about Seth, I presume?"

"Seth?"

"Yes, I'll tell you all about it after you've had a chance to relax. Now, where has that dog of mine gone? Samson! He's been fiddling with the Christmas decorations. He always does. Samson!"

Responding to the call, the terrier came tearing into the foyer, nearly upsetting a footman carrying boxes down from the attics. Staying remarkably calm, despite the animal's odd behaviour, the underbutler Stephen Priest continued removing the duke's overcoat (expertly overseen by Cornelius Baxter, who quietly mentioned several bloodstains upon the left sleeve, assuring Priest he would personally see to them later that evening and to send the coat to Baxter's rooms).

In the background of this familiar ballet, the foyer buzzed like a hive in July. A tall ladder sat beneath the largest chandelier, which was now being decked with festive greenery before the arrival of the largest of the home's Christmas trees the following morning. Some footmen hung holly and ivy garlands along bannisters and doorframes, whilst others trimmed the foyer's smaller chandeliers. All of this activity was augmented by the pleasant chatter of farmers and gardeners, most in stained clothing from the day's long search. A long table dominated the northern portion of the palatial foyer, laden with a variety of food and served by the evening shift of farmer's wives and kitchen staff. It all felt a bit like Victoria Station to the duke, an apt comparison; only this time it was his Aunt Victoria Stuart in charge of the madcap depot. In his weary state of mind, Sinclair found it difficult to focus on his aunt's endless stream of words.

"Charles, are you listening? I said we all need a guiding hand! The search teams have nothing to do until you make a decision regarding how to proceed. Do the men call it quits until tomorrow or push on tonight, despite the snow? With Elizabeth off her feet, it's up to you, Nephew."

This last phrase drilled into his brain, and suddenly the duke heard every word. "What do you mean 'off her feet'? Is Beth ill?"

"Not ill, really. She fainted earlier, but..."

The rest of his aunt's sentence hung in the air without an ear to hear it, for Charles was already halfway up the staircase. Anatole's warning to 'keep watch on the duchess' rang in his thoughts, and all he could think of were his wife and unborn children.

Even at such a panicked pace, it took him two and a half minutes to reach the master apartment. Branham Hall's layout had altered little over the centuries, growing haphazardly larger as each duke or duchess added to its complex design. Some of the journey took him through formal state rooms, whilst others along hotel-like corridors filled with busy maids and footmen. When he finally reached the master chamber, he found—to his very great relief—his wife sitting in a chair, talking casually with Paul Stuart.

"Thank the Lord!" Charles exclaimed as he took her hand to kiss it. "Tory told me you fainted, and I... Well, I worried, that's all."

Though somewhat pale yet, the duchess appeared unharmed. "I had a shock, nothing more. I imagine Tory told you all about it. She's been hovering ever since she arrived, but nothing's amiss. Really, I'm fine, Captain. Sit down, won't you? We have good news. Paul found Seth."

"Tory mentioned it. Is he injured?"

"Yes, I'm afraid so. Is it true the dead man is one of the Cambridge students?"

"Yes, darling. I hoped to keep it from you."

She nearly argued with him, but the look of exhaustion in his eyes stopped the thought before it reached her mouth. "I understand. I'm very sorry for his family."

"As are we all, little one," he answered softly. "But tell me about Holloway. Has he spoken? Did he tell you what happened? Does he know where the other student might be?"

"Let me, Beth," the earl answered. "I found him beneath the old abbey, about an hour after dark. He's in very bad shape, Charles. Nearly out of his mind with pain. He looks as though something fierce attacked him. That's why I sent for Henry. With Emerson still in Edinburgh, and Gehlen a mystery..."

"Dr. Gehlen's a mystery?" Beth asked. "Is he also ill?"

Charles took the seat nearest her. "No, dear, he's merely run off his feet with the fire at the docks," he told her, deciding against any further explanation for the moment. "Where is Holloway?"

"The east wing. Alcorn and Price are looking after his physical needs," she told him. Beth reached for her husband's hand. "I'd like to sit with him, Charles. If it's all right with you."

"We'll discuss it later," the duke murmured, for he had to consider Holloway a murder suspect. He might be a dangerous man.

Paul stood, straightening his waistcoat. "Sitting with him is pointless just now, Princess. Price gave him a strong dose of morphine. I doubt he'll wake before tomorrow. As for me, I'm off to see Della. She's reading a book to Dolly. It seems to help with her migraines."

"Did Sir Richard come as well?" asked Sinclair.

"He's coming down tomorrow, assuming the line's open. Charles, if you have a moment I'd like to hear about your findings in the village."

"Yes, of course. Is there a room that's quiet?"

"Hardly," Beth said, hints of colour returning to her cheeks. "You might try the blue library. If there are servants decorating, ask them to go elsewhere until you're finished. Since the line to Branham is closed, Grandfather sent word that he'll remain in London for another day."

"Do you mind if I abandon you?" Charles asked.

"Not at all, Captain. I've plenty books to read. Go be a detective. The dogs will keep me company."

He kissed her and then left with the earl.

The men took the stairs to the main floor and then turned into the west wing, walking past a series of state rooms alive with greenery and festive ribbons. They found the smaller, blue library warm but devoid of activity, awaiting its turn for Christmas cheer.

Sinclair took one of the leather chairs near the fireplace. Paul poured two small glasses of cognac. He handed one to his cousin and then sat into the companion chair.

"What a day! I could sleep for a week."

Charles swallowed, smiling at the woody taste with a hint of citrus. "Danflou?"

Paul laughed. "You're becoming an expert now? Yes, I find it restful after a long day, but Tory also loves it, which means it will disappear quickly. Look, Charles, before we go over the investigation, let me explain about Holloway."

"What's to explain?" asked his cousin.

"How and where I found him, but also his relationship to Beth."

The duke set the glass aside. "I'm aware of her affections for him, Paul. They're childhood friends. She cares for him deeply."

The earl took a moment, and his cousin could read concern as well as doubt. "It's my fault really. The way I treated Elizabeth. Abandoning her so often, I mean. We were always so close, it never crossed my mind she might grow fond of anyone else. Her reaction to you in '84 is but one example of my education."

"Are you saying something happened twixt Beth and Holloway?"

Aubrey gulped down the wine and poured a second glass. "Another?"

"No, I want to keep a clear head, and I've not eaten much today."

Returning to the chair, Stuart continued, his manner almost apologetic and uncharacteristically downhearted.

"Life's been strange the past few days."

"Only the past few days? Really, Paul, it's been strange for me since October! Not that I'm complaining regarding my family or my marriage. It's just that I'd not imagined I'd be fighting a constant war against an unseen enemy."

"I've grown accustomed to that part of it," his cousin answered. "Or rather, I've grown used to watching Beth go through it. When I was younger, I loved the idea of chasing down criminals and spies. None of the circle's spiritual aspects affected me the way they do you and Beth. My targets have always been the humans involved with Redwing. I suppose it's one reason I reacted so badly to her short affair with Holloway."

"They had an *affair?*" Charles exclaimed, sitting forward anxiously.

"Forgive me. That was a poor choice of words, and I believe I also used it with Beth that summer. In fact, it's why she and I argued so often before she left for Paris. You've no reason for jealousy, Cousin. I only wish someone had told me the same back then."

The duke relaxed, but only a little. "Tell me what happened. How did they meet?"

"As you already know, Seth's parents are Lord and Lady Salter. Their country estate's ten or fifteen miles to the west, close to Faversham. Seth's sisters used to take the train up almost weekly after Elizabeth became duchess. Ruth and Melinda are close to Beth's age. Ruth's a year older, Melin's a year younger. They called themselves the Kent County Riding Club, and the three of them would spend hour upon hour, racing along the hunting paths of Henry's Woods. Seth travelled a great deal of the time with his father. Salter's an avid antiquarian and took Seth along to learn the family business."

"Archaeology?"

"Yes, but that's only the public aspect of it. Salter's scientific activities serve as cover for a political agenda. He'll often negotiate secret treaties for England whilst digging in the sands of Palestine and Egypt. As the only son, he wanted Seth to follow in his footsteps, both academically and politically."

"As you followed in your father's footsteps."

"Yes, and I'm grateful for it. I never knew Seth very well until the past few years. He's five years younger, but he always struck me as a serious sort of person. An academic mind with a strong capacity for language and the arts. He loves music and painting, and he uses that artistic eye to discern fine details when translating hieroglyphs and ancient writing. As I mentioned earlier, Beth and I had a misunderstanding over him that year. Do you recall that she and I were arguing when you ran into her in my library in '84?"

"I remember it vividly, as does she."

"Seth was the reason," Paul admitted. "He'd accompanied his sisters to Branham for the fête that May, and whilst there, discovered Elizabeth had grown up in his absence. When Ruth and Melin asked to stay for a few weeks to spend time with Elizabeth, he decided to remain with them. The girls preferred riding at Branham, because of the stable. Connor established some spectacular bloodlines, and Branham's known all over England for producing fine hunters. Paladin is a product of that breeding program. He can clear any hurdle without disturbing the rider a whit."

"I can attest to that," Charles agreed as he sipped the last of the cognac.

The earl watched his friend's face carefully. "Thank you for not pressing me with questions, Commissioner. This story reveals a jealous streak in me which isn't flattering; meaning it isn't easy to tell."

"Proceed at your own pace, Cousin. I wear Beth's promise inside this watch and her wedding ring upon my hand. Nothing that happened in the past will ever alter that."

Aubrey finished the second cognac, gazing down into the empty glass. "Do you ever wish you go back in time, perhaps make a better choice? Make a different decision that could lead to greater happiness? Never mind, I grow maudlin lately. It's not like me at all. Sorry. I'm allowing my emotions to overwhelm this tale, but those regrets have nothing to do with you or Beth."

"I'm here to listen, if you wish to talk, Paul."

"Perhaps after Christmas."

Charles worried about his cousin. Even Aubrey had his limits, and though the demonic attack at Haimsbury left no visible wounds, he began to fear for the earl's mind.

"Regret isn't a weakness, Paul."

The earl ignored the comment. "As I said, the Holloway girls came to stay a few weeks, and Seth with them. Victoria and Dolly were here as chaperones, so all was properly done. Seth and Elizabeth spent a lot of time together during those weeks, and by early June, she'd become quite fond of him; and not only as a friend. Dolly saw him kiss her once after a picnic and wrote to me about it.

I felt Beth was too young for such things; that Seth had no business kissing a child."

"She was sixteen, Paul. Hardly a child."

"Yes, but I had difficulty seeing her that way. I thought myself protective, not jealous. She'd always been my little cousin, and I her Scottish knight. She was the princess I rescued from towers, not a desirable young woman! That day in the library, I asked her about the kiss, and she flew into a rage. I'd never seen her so angry! She accused me of spying on her and threatened to return to Queen Anne on her own. When I saw her react to you with such obvious affection, I fear it only worsened my mood."

A soft knock interrupted, and Charles turned to find Kay opening the door. "Sir, I'm to tell you Lord Salperton has arrived."

Both men stood. "Is a time set for supper?" asked Charles.

"Ten o'clock, sir. Mrs. Stephens apologises for the late start, but with feeding the volunteers, and many of them still lingering about..."

"Quite all right, Kay. Tell the men we'll call off the search for tonight. The tunnels are dangerous enough during daytime, and the snow will only hamper their vision. I won't risk any of our men. We'll begin again at first light."

"Very good, sir." Kay left and closed the door.

"Is there more?" the duke asked Aubrey.

"More?"

Charles shook his head. "More to their relationship? Was Seth in love with her? You called it an affair. Did she love him?"

Paul rose, deciding he'd shared enough for the moment. "You'll have to ask Beth that question. I'm off to take Henry to his patient."

Aubrey exited the peaceful library, leaving Charles wondering just what sort of friendship his wife once shared with the mysterious viscount. Had she loved him? Did she love him still?

No matter. Despite her feelings, he had to proceed as he would with any other man. If Holloway killed Peter Patterson, then he'd have to pay for it. With his life.

CHAPTER THIRTY-FIVE

8:13 pm - Fitzmaurice Place

"How quiet the house is with Ned and the children gone," sighed Constance Wychwright from her armchair.

Cordelia had said little that evening, preferring to sit quietly in a corner and read. "Yes, Mama," she answered like a pale automaton.

"I do wish Dr. Gehlen had been available to see you, Delia. I'm not sure I like Dr. Sanderson. Did he offer you a new medicine to counter your moods? It seems to me your demeanor has worsened since the funeral. Perhaps, I'll call in another doctor. One with more impressive references. Perhaps, this George Price that serves the Branham family. He's called on the queen, you know."

"Fine, Mama. Whatever you say."

Lady Constance set aside her embroidery. "You know, my dear, it seems to me that what you need is a purpose. William told me his friend Sir Richard Treversham confessed a secret fondness for you. The baronet's a very handsome man, with a fine country estate and a London home in Mayfair; all supported by a large income. As his wife, you could..."

"I don't like Richard, Mama. I don't like any of Will's friends. They're all just like—like that awful man!"

"What awful man?" the dowager baroness asked.

"Sir Albert. I hate him, and I hate all of William's friends!"

Her mother shook her head, returning to the needlework. "Now, Delia, hate is a very strong word. I'm sure you don't mean that."

"But I do mean it." She stood, intending to leave the drawing room. "I'm going up now. You should have named me after Shakespeare's Ophelia rather than Cordelia, because all I want to do is sleep until I am dead!"

The distraught young woman started towards the doorway, but ran headlong into the very man she so detested. Sir Richard Treversham. The tall baronet bowed as he kissed her hand.

"Good evening, Lady Cordelia. Your brother said I might find you here. And with your lovely mother, too. Lady Constance, I pray this night finds you well."

Connie Wychwright wondered why her daughter failed to appreciate the baronet's lovely brown eyes and supple mouth. Yes, he did lack the firm musculature one might expect in a descendent of Sir Henry 'Hotspur' Treversham, hero of the Battle of Dupplin Moor, but then he had no need for knightly prowess. Sir Richard's only challenges were what suit to buy and which wine to drink. Surely, a man of such wealth could provide her daughter a fine life—particularly as Richard would then control Cordelia's inheritance. And with William controlling Richard, the end result would be amenable to all.

"Do come in, Sir Richard!" she sang, colour rising to her powdered cheeks. "We've sorely missed your merriment. Living in a house of mourning is so very dull. Delia, fetch Sir Richard a glass of sherry."

"No need, dear lady," answered Treversham. "Will and I have plans to go out this evening. Delia, would you be interested in joining us? We've tickets for a most amusing play. My sister is coming along, and she'd find it terribly boring without someone sympathetic to talk with. Perhaps, the two of you could discuss the upcoming Christmas parties."

"Parties?" the girl asked, growing slightly interested. "It sounds nice, but I shan't be invited to any parties. Not ever again."

He reached for her hand. "But of course, you will. Parties and dances and costume balls and all manner of frivolities! You frown far too much these days, dear lady. You need to hear jokes and songs and see a bit of ballyhoo nonsense. Tonight will leave you a changed woman. I guarantee it! Come now, take off that dull black dress and put on a pretty frock. Let's go find that smile, shall we? I've always said yours is the prettiest smile in London."

"But I mustn't," she argued half-heartedly, for she longed to lay aside grief, if only for an hour. "It wouldn't be proper."

Constance took her daughter's hand. "I'm sure it is proper when accompanied by your brother. Come, dear, I'll help you select the perfect gown. A dark blue one, perhaps. More in keeping with sobriety. Which play is it, Sir Richard?"

"A Christmas pantomime that will keep us all laughing merrily throughout the night. The curtain rises at ten, so we'll need to hurry."

With so much medicine in her bloodstream, Delia felt confused and a bit unsteady, but she longed to get away from her mother. She wished Paul had come to visit, but her brother had warned him to stay away. It was doubtful she would ever see the handsome earl again.

"Yes, all right," she said at last.

By half nine, she was sitting in a charabanc coach with her brother on one side, Sir Richard and Millicent Treversham on the other. The theatre was barely that: a Grand Guinol sort of place north of Seven Dials. Following a blood-soaked opener about the Dybbuk of Spitalfields, came the panto with ribald jokes and scantily clad actresses. Any mention of Christmas was accidental, for every routine's purpose was to offer the ladies onstage another opportunity to shed more clothing.

Cordelia hated every minute.

When the coarse entertainment had at last finished, she assumed they'd return home, but instead she was taken to a Soho hotel, where the two 'couples' paired off into separate rooms: William with Millicent, and Sir Richard with Cordelia. The baronet mixed a pungent powder into her champagne, designed to make her more compliant. The goal was to force a physical union, after which an outraged William would demand Sir Richard marry his 'wronged' sister.

It was a devious, hateful sort of plan, and no loving brother or mother would ever have designed it. But Constance Wychwright and her scheming eldest son had very little love in their hearts. And by midnight, the naive ingenue would be running for her honour and her life.

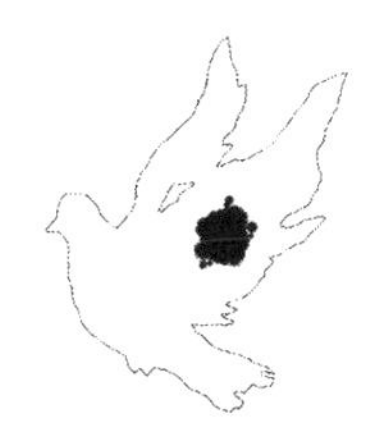

CHAPTER THIRTY-SIX

7:11 am, 22nd December – Charles Sinclair's Journal

I overslept this morning, but Beth is already awake and gone downstairs. I can hear activity below and in the nearby state rooms. I think the footmen are finishing up the decorations. Oh, it's difficult to believe Christmas is but three days away! Tomorrow, I shall collect our special guests from London and bring them here. My only prayer now is for peace.

Last night, Baxter, Paul, and I sat up until after midnight, hashing through the Blackstone murder mystery. Price has installed the body in an unused cellar at the Branham Granary, about two miles from the village, and hopes to give me a report this afternoon. Constable Towers set up an office for me at the Herne Hill boarding house, run by a Mr. and Mrs. Swalecliffe. I've paid triple the going rate for their best suite, since the couple could easily rent it to a London punter. The village is crawling with reporters, and Towers is sleeping there, to make sure no one tries to 'rummage' through the rooms.

Collinwood sent a telegram late last evening, apologising for missing me, but promising to meet up today or tomorrow. He has informed the Oxford men that each must be available for questioning. First on my list, however, is Seth Holloway. Henry believes the viscount's injuries are life-threatening, so I must tread carefully. Paul assures me that Holloway isn't the sort of man to commit murder, but the same could said for many who've gone to the rope. I pray the man had nothing to with it; for if he did, my marriage might never be the same.

I'll write more tomorrow. For now, I must dress and begin the day.

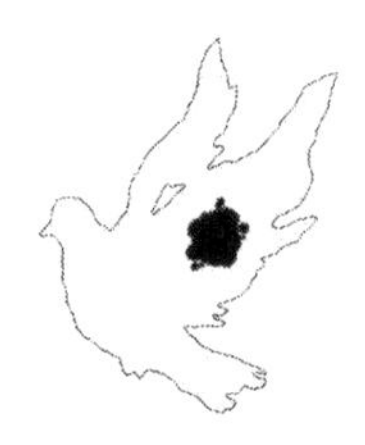

CHAPTER THIRTY-SEVEN

As Charles Sinclair descended the magnificent central staircase, he entered a house transformed. All through the evening and into the night, maids and footmen had continued their elf-like labours, festooning every railing, every lintel, every light fixture, and nearly all the doors with boughs of fragrant evergreen. Velvet bows of gold and red trimmed the fresh cuttings, and mixed amongst these, dwelt bright red crabapples, rowen sprigs, and mint leaves; as well as lemons and oranges pierced with cloves—all held together by yards and yards of red velvet ribbon.

In the centre of the foyer, stood a large, wooden planter placed upon a circle of waxed sailcloth, awaiting the arrival of the grand tree. The air was filled with heavenly scents of citrus, cinnamon, and peppermint; but amongst this spicy mélange floated the familiar smells of baking bread and roasting meat. Charles felt as though he'd awoken to a wonderful dream.

"Good morning, my lord," sang a chorus of servants as he made his way to the morning room. In most great homes, the 'morning room' indicated a singular space reserved for use in the early part of the day. These generally faced east, to take advantage of the morning sun's light and warmth, and thereby save on wood or coal. However, at Branham, there were four morning rooms, and Charles headed to his favourite: a converted greenhouse with glassed walls that extended into the central courtyard. Gas sconces on the interior wall augmented the sun's natural lighting, and a hearth built into the same wall provided warmth against the cold.

Branham Hall was built of several components: The original, quadrangular construction climbed four storeys high with a grand courtyard in the middle. Extending outward from this, ran three primary wings, north, west, and east. However, an oddly situated 'second east' bisected the more traditional east and north wings. This was where Sir William Trent had kept rooms, and where supernatural events most often occurred. Guests staying here often told tales of ghostly encounters, of seeing a man with a wound upon his forehead and hearing a haunting violin play for hours. Some spoke of spidery phantoms that scuttled about the corners and shadow men in tall hats.

Thankfully, no ghosts troubled the serenity of Branham Hall that bright December morning, and Charles entered the charming little room, finding one of the chars—a girl named Iris Howell—lighting the fire.

"Oh, so sorry, my lord!" she exclaimed with a sweet curtsy. She had pulled her long hair into a tight braid down her back, and wore the customary dark uniform dress with white pinafore apron. Her large, green eyes and auburn hair reminded Charles of Lorena MacKey, possibly how she'd looked before her stepfather began to abuse her.

Where is she? he wondered.

"Never apologise for doing what's asked of you," he told the girl kindly. "It's Iris, isn't it?"

Charles had met all the servants upon arrival, when the household staff had assembled in the foyer to greet their master and mistress.

"You remembered me, sir," she said happily.

"Sometimes, my memory works," he laughed. "If only I could recall my childhood as well. How old are you, Iris?"

"Seven, sir. I'll be eight next March. My folks work on the old Anjou sheep farm."

"I've heard others talk of it. Is it a large farm?"

"Very large, my lord. Thousands of sheep and six shepherd cottages. We live in the St. James house. They're all named for disciples."

"Ah, I see. And do you like living there?"

"I do, sir. And my pa's ever so good with sheep. I like to help, when I've the time. Pa's here today—ta help look for the missin' man. And Ma's packin' food for the searchers."

"Have the men begun to assemble?"

"Yes, m'lord. In the main dinin' hall. They're eatin' breakfast, sir." She curtsied politely and then returned to her task.

Charles sorted through a collection of newspapers from the previous day. The death toll of the East End fire had risen to forty-three, and the Lord Mayor of London had visited Leman Street for a photograph and interview. The main article featured a picture of the mayor shaking hands with Edmund Reid and Fred Abberline.

"Fatuous little tripe," he muttered at Mayor Whitehead's political posturing.

"Sir?" asked Iris, turning round.

"I'm commenting on the news. Forgive the interruption. Do you need any help?"

"No, m'lord. I'm used to makin' fires. I'm quite good at it."

"So I see," he said as the flames ignited into a bright blaze. Almost immediately, the room grew more cheerful.

A footman entered with a trolley, laden with coffee, tea, and pastries. "Hot dishes are forthcoming, Your Grace," he said with a bow.

"Thank you. It's Hopkins, isn't it?"

"You've a remarkable memory, my lord. Yes, it is. Tim Hopkins. Will there be anything else, sir?"

"The early editions from London, when they arrive."

"The station master delivered them a few minutes ago, sir. Mr. Kay is ironing them. He'll bring them shortly."

The servant left, and young Iris brushed her hands of wood and bark debris as she stood to leave.

"Tell me, Iris, are you attending school of any kind?"

She smiled, and he noticed a gap in the front where a baby tooth had fallen out. A stub of the adult tooth had just emerged from the pink gum.

"The duchess sends all us children to school, sir. We work two hours each mornin', and then attend classes from ten 'til three with a nice luncheon in between."

"You're very well spoken for seven, going on eight."

"Mrs. Shelton insists we speak clearly and with proper pronoun... Pronounc..." She stumbled on the word.

"Pronunciation?"

The grin widened. "That's right, sir. Pronunciation! We have to say each word correctly and write it out in a clear hand."

"Do you enjoy reading?"

"Very much. The duchess keeps lots of books in our school library. Will there be anything else, sir? I've more fires to light before I go to school. Today's our last day, and we're to have punch and cookies."

"Then hurry along, but I pray it isn't you who fills these wood boxes. The logs are quite heavy, even for me."

"No, sir," she laughed. "One of the gardeners does that. Good day, sir. Thank you for talking with me. You're awfully kind."

"As are you," he said as she scampered from the room. The girl passed by Aubrey as she left, curtsying politely, and the earl offered her a slight bow in return, which caused her to giggle.

"Another child who's the better for this place, Charles. She's paid well, learns service skills, and receives an education. The girl would be working the streets as a pickpocket or worse if she lived in London. How's our Princess this morning?"

"Beth rose long before I did. She's sitting with Seth, according to Mrs. Alcorn. Was there more than just the one kiss?"

"When? In '84?"

"Have there been others?"

Paul sighed. "Probably, but I'm not the person to ask about that. Tory mentioned a marriage proposal in May. Obviously, she turned him down. Are those the morning papers?" he asked, pouring a cup of coffee.

"You're changing the subject."

"Yes, I am. I find it easier."

"Very well, I'll speak with her about it later. As I said, I wear her ring."

"And she loves you, Charles. That love will never wane."

"You're right! So, what's our strength this morning? How many men plan to join the search?"

"Most likely the same as yesterday," replied the earl as he sat into a deep-cushioned chair near his cousin. "I think we counted seventy-three. It sounds like a lot, but there are thousands of acres to search, including Henry's Woods and Queen's Downs. I've told them to concentrate on the areas nearest that hellish cavern where I found Holloway. Have you spoken with him at all?"

"Not yet. Henry said he awoke briefly last night, raving about statues and dolls. I shudder to think what happened down there, but that cannot sway my opinion. I have to consider him a suspect, Paul. Holloway may have killed Patterson."

"Yes, I'd thought of that as well. One warning, though. You'll have a great deal of trouble with Elizabeth if you decide to charge Seth."

"It cannot be helped. If he's guilty, he'll hang," Charles answered firmly.

"That will not go down well, Cousin. On a more pleasant topic: is our pretend aunt, Lady Stuart, still coming to visit?"

"I think so, yes. I did warn her we might have a bit of excitement now and then, but Drina found the possibility intriguing. I leave to fetch her first thing tomorrow. If all goes as planned—which it seldom does in this family—then, we'll be back by nightfall."

"The servants should have all the trees in place by then. There will be four on the main floor, or there have been in past years. Is James bringing our Castle Contingent?"

Charles smiled. "So he says. I miss Riga. He's a wise old bird, and he's promised to tell us Romanian tales. We'll also have a chess tournament. Riga and Blinkmire both play very well, and Merrick is good enough to beat me."

"Ah, but does he cheat the way you do, Cousin?"

"I do not cheat, I merely take advantage of uncommon rules. Any word from France or Galton on the investigations in London?"

"Plenty, but none that satisfy," answered Aubrey. "We'll talk about it Monday morning with James. Drina seldom rises before eleven, but she stays up very late, which gives us the morning hours to talk freely. She and James are quite close, and she'll likely want to monopolise his time whilst here."

Kay entered with the papers and a stack of letters. "Good morning, Your Grace, Lord Aubrey. Here are the London and Edinburgh editions along with the first post. Also, Mr. Baxter asked me to remind your lordship of a promise to assist Constable Tower with the interview of Colonel Collinwood. The colonel apparently arrives in Branham this morning."

"That's earlier than I'd hoped. Excellent. Thank you, Kay. The earl and I will leave at nine. Ask our newly promoted Inspector Baxter to be ready to accompany us."

"*Inspector* Baxter, sir? Very good, Your Grace," Kay responded with a proud smile. "Hopkins will bring your breakfast shortly."

The butler started to leave, but Paul called to stop him. "Kay, have you seen my sister this morning?"

"Yes, my lord. Lady Adele is breakfasting with Lady Victoria and Lady Patterson-Smythe."

"Thank you. That will be all, I think."

Charles poured a cup of tea and added a cube of sugar. "I could get fat if we stayed here for very long. Stephens might outbake even Mrs. Paget. Her biscuits are light as feather down."

"Wait until you taste her rum cake. She serves it on Christmas Day, along with a cornucopia of equally tempting cakes and confections. I always gain several pounds whilst here. Who's this Collinwood person?"

"Head of the Blackstone project. Danny Stephens at the Abbot's Ghost calls him a 'right howler'. Says he does nothing but howl and bark at the students. He had very little love for Holloway, apparently."

"Odd. Seth gets along with nearly everyone. Did you search their rooms?"

"Yes, but nothing there offers insight into what happened. There's no evidence of disagreement amongst the three men. A few letters. Patterson was engaged, apparently. I've sent telegrams to all the families, including Lord Salter. Did you know Dolly and Dickie are related to the dead man?"

"Yes, Tory told me," answered Aubrey. "A third cousin, or some such, from the branch before the hyphenation with Smythe happened. Dickie asked is he might help with the funeral cost when it comes to that, but Baron Patterson has plenty of his own. I tell you, Charles, death is a dark omen at Christmas. Though the hall's trimmed for festivities, already there's a pall of shadow creeping amongst us."

"Then, let us shine the Lord's light into those shadows, Paul. I will not have Christmas ruined. Let's see. Reid's sent a report," said the duke, shuffling through the post. "There's also one from Arthur France, and another from Matthew Laurence. He's apparently uncovered some interesting information in Ireland about Harold Lowry."

"The man your late wife ran off with?" Aubrey asked, stirring cream into his coffee.

"Yes, that's the man. Laurence found evidence that Lowry is connected to Redwing, which puts a whole new colour into that Chapter of my life. Now, what's this?" he said, seeing a letter forwarded to him from Haimsbury House. The original address was typewritten with no sender's information. He opened it with the letter knife left by Kay. Two pages of typed lines met his eyes, and his body posture altered as he read.

"Who's it from?"

"Lorena."

"MacKey? I'd keep that from Beth, if I were you," said Paul. "What does it say? Where is she, and why did she leave Queen Anne?"

"Read it for yourself," he told his cousin, handing over the letter. Aubrey scanned the neatly written lines:

21st December, 1888

Dearest Charles,

Anatole insisted I write to you and allay any worries you may hold for my welfare. He visited last evening and mentioned he'd spoken with you. I cannot tell you how much that meant. It is like life-giving water to hear your name.

I'd been staying with a physician friend in Mayfair, but the prince has moved me to one of his homes. I'm not to say where, but I'm well cared for and safe. I know that Redwing still hunts me, just as they hunted poor Susanna. Is it true she might be alive? Anatole has dropped hints—for he always speaks of her in the present tense. I pray she is!

Last night, Anatole left for France. There is something big happening there, and I have a terrible dread as to what it might be. The winter solstice just occurred; a high occult season, when the veil between realms thins. If another mirror has been found, then it's possible a third Watcher has been released. Please, take care!

I will write to you each day during the prince's absence. If two days pass without a letter, then you're to assume the worst. But I've no fear, Charles. I've started reading the Bible, if you can believe it. In fact, I'm reading the Christmas story right now. I'd never realised how that moment in history changed the entire world. What a fool I've been to believe in lies!

Enjoy your time with the duchess. She is a lucky woman. I'll write again tomorrow.

Lorena

"A curious letter," said Paul. "She suspects a Watcher's been released?"

"If so, then I think Anatole expected it. We'll need to stay on our toes at all times."

"No different than normal, eh?" teased the earl. "And she's reading the Bible? God's mercies and plans are ever and always surprising. I wonder where Romanov is hiding her?"

"I don't know, but I intend to find her," Charles said firmly.

"She's in no apparent danger," the earl argued. "Anatole insists she's all right, as does she. Charles, let the Russian handle this."

"If she's abandoned her old ways, then Redwing considers her a traitor, which means she's in danger," his cousin countered. "With Anatole away, anything could happen."

"Or perhaps, she herself is dangerous. I don't mean as a Redwing operative, Charles. I mean as a woman. I can see she means a great deal to you, but that puts you at risk."

"I see her as vulnerable, not as a temptation, Paul. My concern is brotherly, nothing else."

"Charles, do be careful. Lorena may have changed, but those around her have not."

"We'll discuss this later," his cousin stated. "Let's eat and then find Baxter. The three of us have work to do."

One hour earlier

Henry MacAlpin sat in the pleasant parlour of one of the hall's smaller apartments, located on the first floor of the east wing. The walls shone with a shimmering pale blue silk, the trim and mouldings a soothing white. The space felt fresh and airy. The door to the apartment stood ajar, and a black Lab entered, her thick tail wagging as she approached the Scottish viscount.

"Well, hello, Bella," whispered Henry. "What brings you this way?"

A second dog followed, and then a third. Finally, their mistress entered, dressed in a softly flowing skirt of forest green velvet topped by a cream blouse with a high lace collar. The untucked hem had been modified to give it a square, finished look by adding Battenberg lace edging. Beneath the soft cloth folds, the expanding presence of twin children could be plainly seen now. Beth's face had a serene, rosy look. She seemed a woman at peace.

"Good morning, Duchess. You're up early," the viscount told her as he stood to offer a polite kiss on the cheek.

"Yes, but I slept very well," she said as she glanced at the patient. "I see quilts and pillows on the sofa, Henry. Did you sleep in here last night? We've plenty of rooms, you know."

"Yes, over three hundred, so I'm told, but none close enough to my patient for my liking. The sofa was quite comfortable. Have you already eaten?"

"Do you ask as my friend, or my doctor?"

"As I cannot stop being either, I ask as both. Have you? Eaten, I mean?"

"Not yet, but it's only seven o'clock. I've had tea and biscuits, which is settling well thus far. How's Seth?"

"Still unconscious, but it's a light sleep. Nothing like what Charles experienced. Poor fellow must have seen some quite awful things down there! Price thinks him mad, but after what I've seen of late, I wonder if he isn't saner than most."

"Why would George think him mad?" asked Beth.

"Murmurings. An odd phrase in his sleep now and then."

"And his injuries?" she asked as they sat together near the fire. "How serious are they?"

"Quite serious, I'm afraid. The abdominal wound is deep. Price had already sutured the gash as well as treated the scratches along his limbs and face. Poor chap looks as though he's fought his way out of a briar patch filled with demonic badgers!"

Her dark eyes looked away, and the viscount saw the clear signs of emotional distress.

"What a blunderer, I am!" he declared, moving closer so he could take her hand. "Forgive me, Beth. As your doctor, and your friend, I'm a wretch to cause you pain. Holloway means a great deal to you, and I should know better. I'm here to listen, if you wish to talk. Have you told Charles yet? About your relationship?"

"Not everything, but I will. Tonight." She glanced at the sleeping patient. "Will he die?"

"Not if I can help it," Salperton declared. "He asked about you. He was somewhat conscious when I arrived last night, and though suffering from unimaginable pain, his first words were to ask about you."

This caused her to weep, and he placed a comforting arm round her shoulders. "You loved him, didn't you?"

"He asked me to marry him," she whispered.

"Why didn't you accept?"

"Because of Charles," she answered, wiping a tear from her cheek. "I simply couldn't get his image out of my thoughts. I tried, Henry! Really, I did, but no matter how gallant, no matter how handsome and kind, no other man could replace him. Charles is permanently etched upon my heart, you see. But I do care a great deal for Seth. Had I never met Charles, it's possible I would have accepted his proposal. I still love him as a friend. Is that wrong of me?"

"Of course, not," he assured her. "You and I are friends. I'd like to think we share love for one another."

"Of course, we do. You're my very dear friend, Henry. Poor Seth! It's his love for me that placed him in danger. If I hadn't asked his opinion on Blackstone, he'd be safe in Cambridge right now."

"Seth's a grown man. If he's here, then it's because he chose to be. Now dry your eyes," he told her, handing her a handkerchief.

"Thank you, Henry. I'm so very blessed to have such good and wonderful men to love me!" she exclaimed. "I really don't deserve it."

"Ah, but you do, and we men who love you are blessed for knowing you, dear Elizabeth. Trust in our Lord for Seth's recovery. I've a strong suspicion he's come back into your life for a reason."

Inside the darkened bedchamber, just beyond the parlour door, Holloway tossed and turned upon the soft mattress. He dreamt of mirrors and blood-filled streets; of fire-ravaged buildings across a smoky city; of destruction and dragons and endless death.

So much so, that the Thames turned red.

CHAPTER THIRTY-EIGHT

10:23 am – The Abbot's Ghost Inn

Charles Sinclair could summarise Colonel Sir Alfred Collinwood in one word: pompous. He was tall, ginger-haired, with a copper moustache that hovered over a thin upper lip like an autumn caterpillar; square jaw, grey eyes, and a slight limp. Collinwood attributed the injury to Wolseley's Ashanti Expedition to rescue a German missionary in '74. Aubrey had warned his cousin that Collinwood would say little in the presence of a man he deemed 'inferior' or 'subservient'; so rather than expose the newly commissioned Inspector Baxter to a litany of veiled insults, they'd sent Cornelius with Constable Tower to conduct additional village interviews.

Sinclair had encountered many a proud man during his years with the Metropolitan Police, but seldom interviewed one with so high an opinion of himself. However, Collinwood was a multi-generational Oxford man, which made Aubrey's attendance that morning all the more helpful. The men sat at a table in the pub's cheerful snug, the door shut to assure privacy. Collinwood added gin to his cup of coffee. Already, Aubrey had thoroughly charmed the obstinate man. In addition to being Oxford men, each served the government in foreign climes, and Paul spoke the soldier's language.

"Which college?" enquired the colonel as he stirred cream into the spiked coffee.

"Merton," the earl replied easily. "Rowing team?"

"Of course. Boxing club?"

"Champion my last two years. Polo?"

"What true gentleman doesn't play? And you're an Etonian, I take it, Lord Aubrey?"

"My father insisted I uphold the family tradition, but I admit to idling away some of my time whilst there. One cannot study every hour, can one, Colonel?"

"Quite!" Collinwood laughed as he stroked the bristled moustache. "Well, this is all very enjoyable, but I know you gentlemen are busy. How may I assist in your enquiries? It's my understanding that you, Duke Charles, are in charge. Correct?"

"I am, Colonel, and you may call me Commissioner for the present, as I represent the Crown."

The man's face grew serious, and his cheeks flushed. "Ah, yes! The Crown, indeed. Well, we'd best be spit and polish, eh? Fire away, sir."

"To begin, what can you tell me about the Blackstone Exploration Society?" asked Sinclair.

"Not much, I'm afraid. I met their solicitor in Egypt about a year ago. Albus Flint. Odd sort of fellow; a trifle off the mark, if you know what I mean, but sound where it matters. His legal abilities are flawless. The chap got me out of a rather nasty scrape last summer. Nothing to do with your sort of cases, Commissioner, but one that caused me a sleepless night or two, I can tell you! The army is deployed now and again to guard British expeditions in North Africa. Our unit was tasked to keep watch on a dig near Luxor. Do you know much about Egypt, sir?"

"No, but my cousin does. The earl has visited there several times."

"Ten at last count," Aubrey inserted with a disarming smile. "I've been to Luxor several times. The British Empire is expanding her reach."

"We've put a few marks in the sand," the other replied as he sipped his coffee. "The Ottomans are doomed, and England must be ready to pick up the pieces. It requires placement of assets, if you get my meaning."

"Assets conveyed in the waggons of an archaeological expedition?" asked Sinclair.

"It's nothing those Moors haven't done themselves! Subterfuge is part and parcel of war, sir. When the day comes to strike, the Ottomans will find us ready and able."

"You might even say England's drawn a line in the sand, daring the Ottomans to cross," suggested the earl. "But Constantinople is destitute, relying on British loans to survive the rebellions in Europe. Our line is both military and financial."

"We play the great game," the colonel answered proudly. "Russia, Turkey; it's all the same. Shadow boxing, you might say until the opponent is dead on the mat. These Musselmen cannot survive without our English money. Yet, they repay us with thieving, rape, and murder! Damnable darkies!"

"Not all are murderous, Colonel," argued the earl. "Most want only to raise their families in peace."

"So you think," the army man countered.

"So, I know," Aubrey declared. "I've lived with the Bedouins, Colonel. And I've worked with many of their fellow tribesmen. Painting Africans with a broad brush is hardly fair. They are no different than we."

"You surprise me, Aubrey. We offer these pickaninnies a better way of life. The *English* way of life, yet most are simply too thick-headed to see the advantages!"

"Those people are human beings with rights and sensitivities, created by God. Is it any wonder they see us an invaders?" Paul asked. "Surely, an Oxford man can see that."

"I see only guns pointed at my face, sir. Eradication and rat traps are the proper response to vermin."

"And that's supposed to represent England?" the earl volleyed back. "If the reason for invading is to offer them our idea of civilisation, then compassion and education must lead, should it not?"

"I agree with Paul," Charles interjected. "Africans, Asians, Indians, Englishmen—regardless of skin colour, we are *all human*. Now, may we return to the point of this discussion? Colonel, you were describing the solicitor, Albus Flint."

"Yes, so I was," replied the soldier, remarkably obedient to the Cambridge man's admonishment. "Forgive the deviation, Commissioner, but I'm not a diplomat. I leave that nonsense to others," he added, looking at Aubrey. "Yes, well, as I said, Flint's an odd chap. Deathly pale with a forbidding manner. But then lawyers who lack a steel backbone are gobbled up in the courts, aren't they?"

"When did you join the Society?"

"Six months ago. Strange collection of miscreants, that lot. Many of them are exiled princes or counts of some sort or other."

"Did you meet any of the leaders?"

"Indeed I did!" Collinwood declared proudly. "At a peculiar little party in Düsseldorf last June. I signed a contract that afternoon, and that night attended this soiree, in a mausoleum of all places. Animal masks and the like. But they're all right, if a bit odd. Wealthy beyond measure and determined to uncover the world's buried treasures."

"Any and all treasures, or do they seek something in particular?" asked Aubrey.

"Funny you should ask that. They keep whispering about some sort of sacred book. Seems it was torn into thirteen pieces and hidden ages ago—sometime after the flood."

Charles felt a shiver run down his spine. "Thirteen pieces?"

"So Flint believes. And each hiding place is guarded by a high profile burial, which is why we're looking at Branham."

"You hoped to find one of these 'high profile burials' here—beneath Lion Hall?" asked Aubrey.

"We did find it. It's why the Oxford chaps and I returned to Anjou Castle on the eighteenth. We'd already found a previously unknown crypt at Lion, but our discovery indicated another at Anjou."

"The duchess gave no permission to enter that castle, Colonel Collinwood," Charles said. "I'm sure Mr. Clark's men informed you of that."

"But she did give us permission!" the other argued. "It's in the contract. I showed it to those two fellows as well."

"Clark's men?"

"Yes, they'll vouch for it. Have you been there? That place is remarkable. Simply remarkable! Anjou Castle sits on a hill, of course; that much is obvious. But do you know what rests beneath that hill? An ancient burial mound. Far older than the castle. Flint believes it's 5th century, perhaps older."

"Pre-Christian England, then," Aubrey noted. "There's nothing about that in any of the family histories."

"Nothing? Well, that is strange," mused the colonel.

"What new discovery caused you to survey the castle? As it wasn't part of the original contract, I'd like to know what changed your mind."

The colonel's eyes widened, his back up. "Now, look here, Commissioner, we really did get the duchess's permission. If she's forgotten, then it's not my fault."

"The duchess is a careful businesswoman, Colonel," Sinclair declared, his ire rising in defence of his wife. "I've no doubt she had an army of lawyers comb through every paragraph before she signed. She believes the contract applies only to Lion Hall."

"Then, she's mistaken," argued the soldier, refusing to back down.

"We won't solve this today, gentlemen," Aubrey interrupted in a calm voice. "Colonel, what was this new discovery?"

"A map," he answered proudly, his upper lip tight against his teeth. "We began the project using an old Viking map that's been in Blackstone's keeping for many centuries. It shows a warren of tunnels beneath Branham that extend throughout Kent. These are supposed to connect to St. Arilda's, and from there to Anjou Castle. I confess we deviated from the plan a little when we entered the abbey, but it was worth it. For there, we discovered a new map that indicated two important burials on Branham property. One beneath Arilda's; the other under the hill at Anjou. Knowing our legal access to the sites ended on Saturday, we decided to spend another day there, but I left strict instructions that no one was to go into the tunnels beneath Lion Hall in my absence. No one. They were to remain in the newly discovered crypt and record its features. If those men disobeyed, then it's hardly my fault, now is it?"

"Peter Patterson's family might disagree," the duke replied. "Tell me about this second map."

"It's carved into the south wall of the grand cavern. Flint called that room the crucible. A strangely religious name, I thought, but then he's a strange little fellow. We copied the writing and presented it to one of our Society's experts for translation. It was instructions, you see. Instructions to a second site. Another crucible and an accompanying crypt. Beneath Anjou Hill."

"When did you start working there?"

"We'd been there all along," he admitted. "Now, before you protest, understand that one paragraph of the contract provided a small loophole. One line 'and the immediate vicinity'. Since immediate is somewhat difficult to define, we took it to mean anything on the estate."

"You tricked my wife?" shouted Charles.

"No, sir. Not really. She had her lawyers sift through it all. And she signed it. I admire the duchess, but if she failed to take into account..."

"Failed to take into account!"

"Charles, this isn't the time," Aubrey warned his cousin, seeing Fred Best lurking on the other side of the snug's door. "Colonel, what did you find at Anjou?"

Collinwood grew silent for a moment, considering just how to respond honestly without giving away too much—or placing himself in legal hot water. "We found the crucible, all right—but also the second crypt, about fifty feet below the castle."

Charles sensed a road block coming and decided to find a way round it by diminishing the statement's importance.

"That's no great surprise, Colonel. Barrows abound in England. How are common graves important to Blackstone?"

"Did I say these were common?" the soldier shouted. Growing suddenly cautious, Collinwood leaned across the table to whisper, his copper moustache puffing out with each word. "Blackstone wouldn't want me to say, so I hope this won't go into any official record, Commissioner. But we uncovered seven skeletons in a chamber identical to that beneath St. Arilda's."

"Human skeletons?" asked Charles.

"No. Enormous horses. Thirty hands high if they're an inch! Each was fully articulated, and their bodies carefully arranged to form a radial pattern, like the spokes of a large wheel. Flint said he'd seen the same formation before in Denmark, Romania, Spain, even Assyria. It was a blood sacrifice to empower..."

"Empower what?" the duke asked, his scalp and hands beginning to tingle with that familiar electric charge.

"To empower resurrection, sir. To raise the dead!"

Charles digested this remarkable statement, the electric tingling overwhelming his senses as he added this puzzle piece to others already in his mind. Taken together with his dreams and the symbols in his own home, he suspected all this had some connexion to his past—and perhaps, his future.

Hello, boy. Shall we play?

"Do you believe in such things?" he asked the colonel. "Pagan rites for bringing back the dead?"

Collinwood laughed nervously. "Of course not! It's all utter nonsense, but it gets far more interesting. After we cleared away the large rocks from over the skeletons and swept up the dust, we discovered a doorway to a decorated royal crypt. Nothing common or mundane here, sir! Knock me down with a feather, if these weren't the finest discoveries since Petrie surveyed Giza! Painted statues, provision jars containing food for the afterlife, weapons, a chariot; and all along the ceiling were constellations made from glittering feldspar. Draco, Ursa Minor, Boötes, and Gemini."

"Say that again," Charles interrupted.

"The constellations, you mean? Draco, Ursa Minor, Boötes, and Gemini. Why?"

A shiver ran along the duke's back, and his hands went numb. *The same star formations as they found in the hidden passageway. The mural of Eden River and the seven dragons.*

"Nothing," he managed to reply calmly. "It's an old family story. Go on, Colonel."

"Ah, yes, well, the crypt led to a small door that required one enter on hands and knees. A sort of penitence, Flint told us. Once through, we found it. It was almost too good to be true!" the soldier whispered, his eyes gone wild.

"What did you find?" asked Aubrey.

He drew back, his eyes suddenly unsure. "You must promise to say nothing, sir. This is not for public knowledge."

"The earl and I are not the public, Colonel, and our commission is no less important than yours."

The man stared down at his spiked drink. "I wonder..."

"You wonder what?" asked the earl.

Again, the man leaned forward, speaking in a conspiratorial whisper. "Look here, Your Grace, is what I read in the papers true?"

"Regarding?" asked the duke.

"Your background. Inheritance and all that. I know how these things work. Someone lays down a scent, and these newsprint dogs start sniffing about. One track leads to another and then another, but it doesn't mean there's a fox at the end. Sometimes, it's nothing but a rabbit."

Charles smiled. "Are you asking if I'm a fox or a rabbit?"

"In a manner of speaking, sir, yes."

Paul answered for his cousin. "For your information, Colonel, Duke Charles is a *very* important, *very* highly pedigreed fox. He descends from the oldest, most important blood lines of French, English, and Scottish royal heritage. Let's leave it at that."

"Ah, yes, I see. Then, I may speak freely, Your Grace? As I might to Her Majesty, or perhaps another sovereign?"

"You may," Charles answered.

"Then, meet me at Pembroke Manor at five o'clock today. It's where the Oxford chaps and I've been staying. It's a mile or so the other side of Eleanor's Castle. Meet me there, and I'll show you something that will alter the way you see the world, sir!"

"Can't you tell me now?"

"You won't believe a word I say without physical proof, but it's rather too large to carry about one's person. And it's positively dazzling, sir! It will alter every presumption about the world of men. Meet me, and I'll tell you everything."

CHAPTER THIRTY-NINE

10:03 a.m. - Drummond House

James Stuart was just finishing a late breakfast when he received a message from the butler at Aubrey House. The ordinarily circumspect servant's handwriting looked as if the words were hurriedly composed, but the meaning was clear. The duke had to come right away to resolve a crisis.

Traffic along the shopping district was heavy that morning, and it took the intrepid Scotsman half an hour to to reach Aubrey House. When he arrived, Bailey explained in a rush of apologetic sentences.

"I hope you'll forgive the interruption to your morning, sir, but I couldn't think what else to do! When she arrived last night, it took us all by surprise. Certainly, we never expected so late a caller, but a *woman!* I tell you Mrs. Chesterfield had much to say about it. We put her in the second master for the present. I dared not send you word last night, Your Grace. The hour was so late, and I felt certain your household would be abed. I pray I've not committed an error in judgement. I do wish the earl were here, sir. It's been so very strange hereabouts this week. First, the closet incident, and now this. His lordship must know, of course, but I'd no idea what to do until then!"

"Slow down, Bailey. What woman have you put in the second master?"

"Lady Cordelia, sir. Didn't I say? She awoke us all very early this morning. Around three, I should think. She'd come in a cab and had no money, but we paid the driver and took her in."

"She came here at three this morning?" asked the duke, growing concerned. "Did she say why? Is she ill?"

"She is in a most unusual state, sir. Her conversation was unclear and somewhat, shall we say, incoherent? Her appearance disheveled, and her face and arms badly bruised. But also in *other places*. Mrs. Chesterfield could tell you more, for she helped to undress the lady."

"Have you sent for a doctor?" Drummond asked, already heading for the stairs.

"Dr. Whitmore will arrive shortly, my lord. We hated to disturb him at such an hour. Forgive me for sending to your home. As the earl is more than two hours away in Kent, it seemed quickest to inform you first. Should I wire his lordship, sir?"

"Not yet. Let me handle it. You did well." The two men arrived at the first floor and turned east towards the second master apartment. "Have you notified her mother?"

"No, sir. I thought it best not to do so. Some of the things Lady Cordelia said indicate a sort of rift twixt them. I dared not widen it further."

"Yes, that was wise," he said, knocking softly on the apartment door. "Delia? Are you awake, dear?"

After waiting a minute, he knocked again. Hearing no reply, the duke entered the apartment's parlour and crossed through to the bedchamber door and knocked.

"Delia?"

The only reply was a faint muttering; slurred and disjointed. A terrible fear crept through Drummond's spirit, but as the door was locked, he put his shoulder to it, forcing it open.

He found Cordelia lying on the floral carpet, barely conscious. Her nightgown looked as though she'd thrashed about during the night; rising up to expose her limbs. The bachelor butler shut his eyes in modest response. The duke threw a blanket over Cordelia, and then lifted the girl into his broad arms, gently placing her in the bed. He brought the quilt up to her chin and touched her forehead to check for fever. "She's warm. Did you dress her in these night clothes?"

"Mrs. Chesterfield did, Your Grace. It's one Duchess Elizabeth left here when she last visited."

"I'm glad it isn't from my nephew's closet," Drummond joked to ease the tension. "The earl does love disguises. Fetch Chesterfield at once and ask her to keep watch until Whitmore arrives. I'm heading back to my home to make arrangements. Lady Cordelia's to remain here this morning, but will stay with me tonight. Would you say she's taller than the duchess?"

"It's hard to say, my lord. An inch, perhaps. Are you thinking of a temporary wardrobe?"

"If there's a rift twixt Cordelia and her mother, then we've no alternative. I'll have someone at Haimsbury House pack enough clothes for a few days. Twice now, this child's been abused and injured, and I will *not* allow a third! Tomorrow, she goes with me to Branham, and when Christmas is over, whoever did this will wish he'd never been born!"

5:02 pm –Pembroke Manor

Charles and Paul arrived at five o'clock, precisely as directed and were met at the door by a sallow woman in a dark blue dress, decorated by a single brooch at the throat. She wore no apron.

"Yes?" the stern-faced female asked the two peers. "You're too well-dressed to be selling anything, which means you're reporters. Sir Simon has nothing to say about that boy's murder. Nothing at all. Go sniff elsewhere!"

The door started to slam shut, but Aubrey put his foot in the opening. "Colonel Collinwood invited us, madam."

The crack widened, and the guardian's brows arched in response. "The colonel is not here at present."

"He asked us to meet him here at five, good lady," Charles told her with all the charm he could muster. "And we are not reporters. I'm Duke Charles from Branham Hall, and this gentleman is my cousin, Lord Aubrey."

Suddenly, the woman's sour expression melted into an open world of sunshine. "The duke? Oh, sir, do forgive me! Sir Simon never mentioned anything about a visit. Do come in!"

The men entered, careful to wipe the snow and mud from their boots. She took their coats and Charles's hat (Aubrey wore none) and hung both in a nearby closet.

"I'm Mrs. Ketchum. Do come through, sirs."

She led them past a drawing room and into a thoroughly masculine space, lined with walnut panelling and hunting trophies. In one corner, the stuffed bodies of a rhinoceros, a lion, and an American Grizzly stood as though meeting for a chat. On the opposite wall, half a dozen mounted antelope horns and a variety of stuffed birds and foxes kept watch. A wood fire burnt in the brick hearth, and an Irish Setter lay before it. He barely glanced up.

"That's MacTavish, the master's hunting dog. He's no bother. Tea, sirs?"

"That's very kind of you," Charles replied, still oozing charm. "Is Sir Simon at home, Mrs. Ketchum?"

"He is, Your Grace. If you'll have a seat, I'll let him know you're here."

She left, shutting the doors. Aubrey began a tactile survey of the room, touching all the stuffed animals and examining a wall of mounted heads as though looking for a secret.

"I've never understood why a man decorates his den with the heads of conquered prey. It's a bit like head-hunters in the Amazon. These animals are noble and beautiful, yet they're left here like lifeless trophies. It's the pursuit of ghouls, if you ask me."

"Perhaps, it's to impress other men," Charles suggested. "Tell me about Pembroke. How well do you know him?"

They sat, choosing leather chairs near the fire. "My father and he served together at the War Office. Simon's the second baronet Pembroke. His grandfather received the title for his service against Napoleon. Sir Simon's father died before inheriting, which is why he's the second. He's in his mid-sixties. Intelligent, but not overly so. More a follower than a leader."

"Is he Redwing?" Charles asked.

"Not to my knowledge, but this Blackstone Society has all the hallmarks of a Redwing subcommittee, doesn't it?"

"Or a rival," suggested the duke.

The door opened, and a soft-bellied man of six feet and a whisper entered. He wore a tweed shooting jacket over brown trousers, tucked into black riding boots; the costume accented by a yellow wool waistcoat. He looked as though he'd not shaved in a week, and the wispy beard hair dotted the curved, dumpling chin as though each strand tried to declare independence from its neighbours. Rosy cheeks against pale skin added to the odd mix of traits, but a firm, friendly hand reached out, eager to shake the hand of his guests.

"Duke Charles! Lord Aubrey! I cannot tell you what a lovely surprise this is! Mrs. Ketchum's fetching tea and cakes at present. I've only two servants. An old bachelor like myself has no need for more. Mr. Ketchum's my valet, footman, driver, and gardener when needed. Mrs. K. cooks, does the washing up, and keeps me in line. Tell me, gentlemen, to what do I owe this pleasure?"

The duke began. "As you're no doubt aware, Sir Simon, one of the Cambridge men serving with the Blackstone project has been murdered. Another is seriously injured, and the third is yet to be found. Colonel Collinwood promised to enlighten us further regarding the case and asked us to meet him here at five. He claims to be your guest."

"Oh, yes, he is. Collie and I've been friends since Oxford, you know. It's why he and his three Oxford students billeted here for the past six weeks. If he asked you to meet him, then he'll show up, eventually. Collie's not the most reliable when it comes to clocks. Military life formed a reactionary spirit in him, I'm afraid. He deals with problems only as they arise, which means he often misses appointments. Might I help?"

"Tell us all you know about Blackstone," Charles told him.

The housekeeper entered, pushing a tea trolley. "Forgive the interruption. Sir Simon normally has a light meal at this time of day, my lords. I've brought sandwiches and desserts as well as tea and coffee." She poured a glass of water and gave it to her employer. "Your five o'clock pills, sir."

"Ah, yes, thank you, Mrs. K.," replied the baronet, who swallowed three small pills along with the entire glass of water. "That will be all for now, but when the colonel arrives, do send him at once."

She left without a word and shut the door again.

"The pills are precautionary," the baronet explained, pointing to his chest. "Bad ticker. Now, Blackstone. An odd bunch, if you ask me. Their lawyer called on me the first time several years back. He was with your wife's stepfather, in fact, Duke Charles. Sir William Trent."

Sinclair sat forward, that electric shiver running along his hands. "Trent was involved in Blackstone?"

"I imagine he was, yes. They certainly seemed amiable whilst here. I never cared much for Trent, though Duchess Patricia adored the man. Poor Trish was somewhat pliable when it came to suitors. Forgive me for speaking ill of the dead; that isn't my intent. I adored the late duchess. What man didn't? But she had an eccentric sense of etiquette. Constrained to the point of isolation one minute; boisterously charming, the next. Surely, you know what I mean, Lord Aubrey. I remember one Boxing Day when she flirted quite scandalously with you, and Lord Kesson not ten feet away!"

Charles stared at his cousin. "Is that true?"

"Trish had a very poor sense of self," Paul explained, "and she sought affirmation from all men. I was one of them. I'm sure that's how Trent insinuated himself into her life so easily. Sir Simon, how well did you know Trent?"

"Not well," he answered. "No one did. The fellow hosted all the important players in commerce and shipping whilst master of the hall. British, American, German, Dutch, French, Romanian, Spanish, even African! I never understood it. To my knowledge, he had no money of his own. In fact, I never heard much about his so-called baronetcy. I dare you to find records of it. I serve as magistrate hereabouts, and I never could."

Charles stared at his cousin. "Surely, someone in the circle did that."

Paul shook his head. "We tried, but all efforts were blocked. I had Reggie Parsons dig into it, but even he came up empty. We've always assumed Trent either lied about his title, or else bought one."

"Can one buy a baronetcy?" asked Charles.

"Certainly. Money's the reason King James created the title in the first place. Cross the right palm, and a minor title is easily gained. Higher titles are more tightly controlled."

Sir Simon nodded. "Oh, it's very true. My title is genuine, I'm happy to say; but Trent was another kettle of fish. It was the summer of '76, when he knocked on my door. We don't get many visitors out this way, and Ketchum generally shoos them off."

"So we noticed," the duke commented.

"Yes, sorry about that. Well, this man Flint set Ketchum's teeth on edge, but Trent exerted all his charm, as he always did. Damned fellow had a way with women! Anyway, she let them both in to see me. Flint hardly said a word, just stared at my bird collection and muttered beneath his breath. Trent, though, now that was a man who understood hunting. He talked of expeditions to Egypt and Palestine, of safaris to Somaliland, and promised to take me with him the next time he sailed to South America. I thought it bragging, if you must know. But then he changed the subject entirely.

"He mentioned how this Blackstone outfit was surveying our corner of Kent and asked for access to one of the old dungeons beneath Eleanor's Castle. My south garden connects to them, by way of a tunnel, you know. This whole area's rife with tunnels! Branham's Warren, we used to call it. Some were constructed by the

Marquess of Anjou, but most are far older. I've a history book on it, if you're interested. But Trent put me off. When I declined, he pressed hard and made some thinly veiled threats. I may not look like much today, but when I was younger, I could have taken on both of you at once, Your Grace. Boxing, shooting, archery. Name a sport, and I've done it! I sent both men packing. Never heard of Blackstone again until Collie wrote to me in August asking if he could live here during the project. I said yes, of course. Now it's all gone pear-shaped, and you're missing Christmas parties. Shame."

"And a man is dead," Aubrey reminded the pudgy baronet. "Murdered by one of his colleagues, presumably."

"Yes, bad business."

"Did you ever meet the Cambridge men, Sir Simon?" Stuart asked.

"Only Holloway. Good lad that Seth, despite his alma mater. Collie and I are Oxford men, of course. Can't say much good about Cambridge."

"The duke attended Cambridge, Sir Simon. Trinity College."

Their host laughed, causing the sparse hair on his dumpling chin to dance. "Well bless me sideways! I've certainly put my foot in it! Sorry, Your Grace. Jolly good college, Trinity. I know the master quite well. Play chess together through the post. I imagine you studied politics."

"Mathematics, actually."

"Dear me," puffed the baronet. "My noggin couldn't add one and one! That's why I did so well at the Exchequer. I expect you want to know if Collinwood's offered a theory regarding the boy's murder?"

"Yes. Did he?" asked the duke.

"He did, but it makes no sense. Collie believes it has to do with an artifact the team discovered that same day. The eighteenth. A sarcophagus covered all over with polished obsidian. The thing shone like a mirror!"

The cousins stared at one another.

"Obsidian?" echoed the earl.

"Oh, yes. Collie brought it back here. Enormous thing. Ten feet—no eleven feet long, I should think. Must be worth a fortune, even if it is empty; though we've no idea, as it hasn't been opened.

Perhaps, there's a mummy of some sort inside. Quite exciting, but I can't see how it can be the cause of those chaps going missing."

"Where is the sarcophagus now?" asked Sinclair.

"Oh, we locked it in the root cellar for safekeeping—just in case."

"May we see it?"

"Yes, of course. Now?"

"If it's convenient."

The man puffed like a steam engine as he led them through the corridor, down a staircase, and into the kitchens. Ketchum and her husband, an older gentleman in livery, sat eating fish paste sandwiches and ale. The man jumped to his feet. "Sorry, sir. Did I miss your ring?"

"Not at all! We're just here to take a look in the root cellar. Is the key in your office?"

"Yes, m'lord. On the hook, like always."

Pembroke fetched an iron key from a row of numbered hooks and inserted it into an arched doorway at the end of a narrow hallway.

"We keep the wines and other spirits down here, as well as root vegetables and anything else that requires cooler temperatures. Flint thought it would help preserve the coffin." He pushed the door, and an icy wind rushed past their faces. "Never felt this cold before! Must be the snow. Mrs. K., is there a candle in here?"

"By the door, sir," she called from the kitchen. "Shall I come?"

"No, no, I can manage!" Charles and Paul heard the shuffling of feet and a swear word or two as the baronet fumbled in the candle box for matches and tapers. "Found 'em!"

The hint of sulfur was followed with an instantaneous brightening of the room beyond the doorway. "Come in, gentlemen. Mind the rats. I've an old gun room back here. The other side of the claret rack. We've put the thingy in there."

The two cousins ducked as they passed beneath the low door. The cellar smelled of cider and apples and mould.

And something else. Something unsettling.

"Dear God!" shouted Pembroke from across the room. "Collie!"

Charles turned the corner at the rack, nearly stumbling over a crate of apples. Behind the claret, his candle's light fell upon the white face of a ginger-haired man with a caterpillar moustache. Colonel Sir Alfred Collinwood was dead.

CHAPTER FORTY

Sunday, 23rd December, 1888 - Elizabeth Sinclair's journal

It is just after four o'clock as I pen this entry, and I write with a mixture of joy, fatigue, and sadness. This morning at ten, the Captain left to collect our special guests from London, and though their arrival will bring new life and laughter to the hall, I find myself missing my husband once again. Since beginning our marriage (following a harrowing time in that 'other world'), we've seldom had more than an hour or two together at any stretch. Often, I find myself lying awake at night, simply to enjoy his comforting presence without distraction. Charles has promised to do better in future. He's even sent for Sir Thomas Galton and Malcolm Risling to take over the investigation into the village murders. Two men now dead—a student and an army colonel! How can this happen at such a glorious time as Christmas? I pray the men died in Christ.

A third Cambridge man, Lionel Wentworth, is still missing. Charles believes Wentworth may have murdered his friend Patterson—perhaps Col. Collinwood also—and that he's now fled the area. Paul will sail to France after the new year, for a man of Wentworth's description was seen boarding a steamship at Dover last night.

Seth awoke last evening, but is unable to speak coherently. I dread to think what might have happened to him in that awful cavern! I've seen so much horror in that accursed place; surely it's inhabited by demonic spirits. I sent telegrams to Seth's parents and sisters, but have not yet heard a reply. It is possible the earl and countess are once again touring abroad. Ruth and Melinda live in Vienna with their Aunt Gwendolyn. I hope to hear from one of them today.

The Master of Trinity has written, expressing his sincere prayers and condolences. He and Seth are close friends, and I've learnt he also knows Charles. Apparently, Dr. Butler was headmaster at Harrow whilst Charles attended. I look forward to meeting him next week.

As I said, it is a time of mixed emotions. Henry keeps me laughing to ease the strain. He came to tend Seth's wounds, but will remain and spend Christmas with us. I shall always bear a special kind of love for Viscount Salperton. His faith in the Lord and constant bravery rescued me from the worst of fates: that awful stone world with its bloodthirsty crows and liars.

Grandfather arrives today, and I shall run into his arms when he gets here! How I miss my dearest childhood confident! James Stuart has a way of enlivening any room, and I always feel safer whenever he is near. I wish he and Charles could have attended church services this morning to hear the local choir. My, how wonderful it was! They sang all the old Christmas hymns: *It Came Upon a Midnight Clear, God Rest Ye Merry Gentlemen, Away in a Manger, Hark the Herald, The First Noel,* and *Silent Night.* Then, afterward, we hosted everyone at the hall, and the school children offered a second concert, which I believe they plan to perform again for our 'special guest', Lady Stuart, tomorrow for Christmas Eve.

Mrs. Alcorn has kept busy with her new sewing machine, aided by the amiable and delightfully loquacious Mr. Kepelheim (who arrived on last night's train). They're altering my favourite skirts and blouses, allowing my expanding waistline room to grow further. I shall have a new wardrobe made later in London, but for the present, I am well-attired and in relative comfort. I say relative, only because my nausea continues to plague me now and then. I say nothing to Charles. He has enough to occupy his thoughts. Henry tells me the nausea is perfectly normal, and that it should subside soon. I mentioned setting an appointment with Dr. Gehlen next January to him, and Henry's response was quite odd. I thought he liked Anthony Gehlen, but now I'm not sure.

Two days until Christmas, which means today will be very busy! Despite delays caused by the search for the missing men, the hall decorations are nearly complete, with only the final touches to add. I'd been practising baking cakes with Mrs. Paget in London and hoped to bake a rum-raisin cake for Charles (his favourite, according to an old Haimsbury recipe book), but Mrs. Stephens has cautioned against it. Apparently, Mrs. Anderson wrote to her about my previous experiments. Henry agreed, declaring, "No cake-baking, Beth. That is an order." Happily, Mrs. Stephens has promised to prepare it, and Charles will still enjoy a small taste of his lost childhood.

Victoria and Dolly have been such a blessing, helping me pack Christmas baskets for the farmers and shepherds. The gift baskets include dried fruits, nuts, flour, salt, sugar, spices, coffee, and tea. Tomorrow, we'll add eggs and milk, and then drive the baskets round to all the cottages. It's a tradition begun by the 6th Duchess of Branham. Della has baked Christmas cookies, and we'll add a dozen to each basket as well with a little poem she wrote. We'll deliver them tomorrow, and I hope Charles is able to come with me.

I believe we're nearly ready for Christmas. The only missing ingredient is my handsome Captain, but he will be home in a few hours, and then the celebration begins!

CHAPTER FORTY-ONE

Due to problems on the line at Maidstone, it was midday before the Aubrey train arrived at Victoria Station. To make matters worse, the train's engineer then received instructions to place all the cars and engine into one of the earl's rail sheds for maintenance on the braking system. Frustrated by the delays, Charles left Baxter at Haimsbury House to deliver Christmas gifts, whilst he continued on to his uncle's Westminster mansion, arriving at half past one. What he discovered there fueled an anger in Sinclair that nearly sent all their schedules into orbit, along with the young duke's temper.

"She's in here," Drummond said as he led Charles into a dimly lit drawing room. "Whitmore's given her some fairly strong medicine."

Sinclair entered, and Cordelia turned to offer a confused sort of smile. "Oh, hello, Charles. How nice of you to call on me."

His uncle had explained the situation, and Charles sat beside the girl, taking her hand with great tenderness. "It's always good to see you, Delia. My uncle is certainly happy to have you as a guest. How are you feeling this afternoon?"

"Not that well," she answered sleepily. "Do forgive me for not standing. Will you have tea?"

"No, thank you. I'd hoped you might agree to come with me on a little trip, but we'll need to depart soon. It's already snowing, and the lines to Kent might close before long. Would you like to spend Christmas with us?"

A faint light entered her vacant eyes. "Christmas? Is it that time already? I'll need to shop, won't I?"

"Yes, but then so will I. Perhaps, you'd help me. There are some lovely little shops in Branham. Elizabeth is so looking forward to seeing you again. As is Della, of course. And Paul."

"Paul," she repeated wistfully. "He's at Branham, isn't he? Oh, wait. Do you think he's finished his shopping?"

"One never knows with my cousin, but you can ask him yourself. Mrs. Dalborough will help you to pack, and then we'll leave as soon as we've all eaten. How does that sound?"

"Yes, that sounds fine," she answered, reaching up to touch his face. "You're so very kind. Thank you, Paul."

"I'm Charles, Delia."

"Yes, I know. Paul."

He kissed her forehead, leaving the housekeeper, Mavis Dalborough, to help the young woman prepare for the train trip.

Once he was far away from the drawing room, Sinclair flew apart, shouting as he paced. "Will Wychwright allowed this?"

"He encouraged it from what I can glean," his uncle answered, equally angry.

"I'll string that army rat up by his hind legs for this!" Charles bellowed. "I promise you, if what you tell me is true, I'll haul mother, son, and that rotten little baronet in for questioning before the day is out! Did Whitmore examine her for signs of force?"

"He did, and thus far, Lady Cordelia's maidenhood remains intact, but not for lack of someone trying very hard to alter that fact. Either Sir Richard, William, or both repeatedly tried to assault that girl, but she held her own."

"Both?" echoed Sinclair. "William may have...? God bless the angels who helped her escape such treachery! Why would any man do such a reprehensible thing to his own sister?"

James stood at the foyer table, writing a telegram as they talked. "I'm sure it has to do with David Wychwright's will. I called on the law firm this morning after I left Paul's house. Abernathy is a friend, and when I mentioned a possible criminal action, he showed me the will and codicil. David left a great deal of money to Delia, as well as a new house, and you can bet her brother wants it all. She turns eighteen tomorrow, Charles, which means she'll no longer require permission to marry. We've both seen how fond Paul's become of the girl. He's even talked to me about proposing to her."

"Which is the last thing William wants, because Paul isn't one of his whipping-boy cronies. If Cordelia marries Paul, he loses any chance at her money."

"Precisely, which is why he tried to ruin her. With Delia turning eighteen tomorrow, William had very little time to enact his plan. I praise God for helping her escape! But she'll need to wed soon, son; before the new baron has a chance to find her and try again. Honestly, I'll marry her myself if Paul refuses, just to keep her away from that family. Nothing but guttersnipes, the lot of them!"

Charles wanted to smash something, and then he thought of Adele. What if someone treated her this way? Suddenly, he felt protective and righteously furious at the same time. But as a policeman, he had to look to the law for a remedy first.

"Can we put men on this?"

"Already done. Matthew Laurence is working with Hamish Granger."

"What about Ned and the girls?" asked Charles. "Did they receive any large bequests? Should we protect them as well?"

"Only some jewellery, not worth more than a thousand pounds total."

"Ned seems a good man. Do you think he'd testify against his brother?"

Drummond sealed the note and handed it to his butler. "Get that to the palace right away. Use the code word *Guinevere*. The chamberlain will see it gets to the queen." He turned to his nephew. "They sent poor Ned and his girls packing as soon as the will was read. I'm sure he'd have stood up for his sister, which is why they needed him gone. I might offer him a job here, if he wants. I could use a man with management skills."

"James, we should take her away as soon as possible. I'm sure William's scouring the city, looking for her. If we're to arrange protection, then we have to get her out of London, but travel might prove difficult. I'd like to take her back to Branham, but someone ordered Paul's train put into the rail shed."

James grinned, his dark eyes twinkling mischievously. "Ah, yes. Well, I'm responsible for that. Did I tell you that I've prepared a wee Christmas gift for you, son?"

Charles stared. "No, sir. Did you tamper with the train's brakes?"

Laughing, the Scottish duke slapped his nephew's back. "No, son, I didn't have to. I ordered the engineer to leave you stranded. It'll all make sense soon. I've just sent a telegram to the queen, informing her we're leaving at three, not four. With the snow coming faster by the hour, we cannot risk getting trapped on the line. I'm fetching Her Majesty myself at half two. You collect our Mr. Baxter and meet me at Victoria at quarter to three. Shed number seven. Now, let's go have a bite to eat. Mrs. Carson's made lamb stew and soda bread."

"Simple fare, sir?" laughed Charles.

"You know me well, son. We'll fill our bellies and then make plans.

Sinclair and Baxter arrived at Victoria Station's shed seven, met by a man named Gabberfield. Charles noticed the Drummond coat of arms on the shed door and wondered just what surprise the duke had in store. Gabberfield wore a large ring of keys on his belt, and he took his time finding the one that fit the lock.

"I ain't been in here since October, sir, but I understand it's all done ta your taste and special needs. The duke—well, sir, I mean your uncle o' course—well, he's been round 'ere nigh on ta every day o' late. Is it true 'bout yer blood, sir?" he asked Sinclair.

Charles had grown used to this sort of question, and he nodded. "It's true, but I'm happy to serve England as a policeman. Might we enter some time this month, Mr. Gabberfield?"

"Beggin' yer pardon, Yer 'ighness. There she is! Got it." He turned the brass key, and opened the workmen's door. The interior was dark, but Gabberfield threw a switch near the entry, which sent electricity coursing through wires above, illuminating a hundred bulbs hanging from the ceiling. Suddenly, the shed seemed bright as day, revealing its special secret: a magnificent steam-driven train.

"This 'ere's one of a kind, sir. Real unique like. It's got seven cars, all kitted out to Duke James's specifications. I'm to say the train is part of yer Christmas present, Yer Grace. Only a part, that is."

Charles wondered if he'd stepped into a dream. The idea of owning his own train struck him as the height of fancy, yet here it was. The exterior was of gleaming black, trimmed with red and gold stripes; each car emblazoned with the Haimsbury coat of arms, featuring a rampant lion facing a dragon, surmounted by a golden crown and gartered in blue with the words 'Commit thy Way unto the Lord'.

"How very appropriate, sir," Baxter observed as he ran a hand along the first car's crest. "Only the queen may authorise the inclusion of a crown, sir."

"Yes, well. It's a magnificent gift. Mr. Gabberfield, how did the duke produce this customised train in so short a time? We've all been quite busy of late. When did my uncle have time to build it?"

"Well, sir," Hiram explained, "it's my understandin' the train was originally intended for Duke James's personal use, but two months ago, the order come down to finish it out fer you. Aside from the crests, the train's been given a new name, sir. It's just here, on the engine door."

Charles stepped forward. Within a red box, gold script spelled out: *The Captain Nemo Special.*

The duke laughed heartily at the reference to Beth's nickname for him, for the surprise gift served to remind him just how much his life had changed since October.

"What do you think, Inspector Baxter? A perfect name, no?"

Cornelius's smile could have lit the sun. "It is indeed, my lord."

Gabberfield found the name puzzling. "I don' know who this Nemo fellow is, sir, but that's how the duke wrote it out for the painter. I hope it's all right, Yer Grace."

"It's perfect," Sinclair answered. "Absolutely fitting. May we come aboard?"

"Oh, yes, sir! O' course! You men follow me. Each car 'as a purpose, ya know. This first one 'ere's fer guests," he explained as they climbed up the steps. "It's got spring-loaded leather seats, o' course, and all the finery of yer fancy, luxury trains. But it's open, so folks can talk to each other. And these little tables are 'ere so you can serve meals or play cards, if you want, sir. But they fold away to conserve space."

"Quite efficient," Baxter noted as he examined the mechanism. "I see there's storage inside the tables as well. I'm sure His Grace will find that useful."

They continued through the beautifully finished first car, and then passed through a connecting door and into the second. This car looked nothing like the first—in fact, it looked like no rail car Charles had ever seen.

"It's an office!" Haimsbury exclaimed, admiring the efficiently arranged interior. Two chandeliers with electric bulbs hovered from a painted ceiling, decorated in scenes from Scotland.

"Are those electric, Mr. Gabberfield? How are they powered?" Sinclair asked their guide.

"That big car just behind the engine, sir. It's the generator. You've electrics all through the train, in every car. And there's a wireless message machine as well. A transceiver, I think Mr. Kepelheim calls it. Just like in Lord Aubrey's trains."

"We've stepped into the future, Inspector Baxter."

"Indeed we have, Commissioner," answered his friend. "You even have a desk, sir."

"And leather chairs. Paul's going to be very jealous."

The mahogany roll-top desk was inscribed on the side with the coat of arms, and Haimsbury's stationery lay waiting upon the top. Several, comfortable leather club chairs provided seating for guests, and an efficient but small fireplace occupied the centre of the end wall. In place of windows, the car held a variety of locked cabinets. On the wall opposite the desk, the cabinet doors were painted as a unit showing a detailed map of England and Scotland's rail system.

"And here we can follow our journey or plan a route," Baxter remarked. "Mr. Gabberfield, I see these closets have locks. What is their purpose? Are they luggage compartments?"

Gabberfield's fleshy face widened with pride as he unlocked one of the doors, showing hooks and shelves. "These can be customised for clothing, weapons, anythin' you wish, sir. That one on the far left contains a dial safe. I'm ta tell you the combination is the day you met the little duchess."

Charles smiled. "Open it."

The porter used a small key to unlock the door, revealing a tall safe. Charles dialed in the sequence: 31-3-79. The handle clicked, and the safe opened. "It's a lovely sentiment. My uncle thinks of everything."

"He does, my lord. Now, the next car down is equipped in like fashion ta this. Duke James mentioned that Lord Aubrey sometimes works with you, sir, and might require his own office, so it's done up the same, though with different colours. I was told the Haimsbury colours are red and gold, which is how we done it up in here, but the earl's are green and gold. So his office is decorated in those colours. Car number three contains medical and scientific equipment. Four and five are fer special guests. Cars six and seven are sleepers with room for six persons apiece and include water closet accommodations. You've a water closet of yer own, sir; just there, to the left of the connecting doors to Lord Aubrey's office. There's also a comfortable caboose with more chairs and somethin' the duke calls 'lookout windows' for keeping watch from three sides. His Grace even had a kitchen installed back there, along with another water closet. Oh yes, sir, one more thing. In there," he said, pointing to the last of the painted cabinets, "you'll find libations."

"Libations?" asked the duke. "Where my uncle's concerned, that can only mean one thing."

Gabberfield opened the door to reveal an array of shelves containing filled decanters, wine bottles, and all the appropriate glassware—even a matched pair of silver-topped soda syphons.

"Very well organised. I assume all the contents come from your cellars, sir," noted Baxter. "If you'll recall, Duke James sought permission to make an inventory. I noticed his men removed several crates once they'd finished."

"I remember," laughed Sinclair as he sat at the desk. "He said it was for a party. Some days, Cornelius, I think I must be dreaming. The only thing this train lacks is a place for my wife."

Gabberfield cleared his throat. "No, sir, it don' lack that at all. Like I said, cars four and five are for special guests. Each is furnished in gilded, royal style with a canopied double bed, mirrored bureau, a fireplace, and a water closet."

"Then, my uncle has thought of everything."

"Of course, I have!" bellowed Drummond, who'd quietly joined their group. "Gabberfield, tell your men they've done a splendid job. I'll commission another just like it for myself—with Drummond heraldry, of course. Tell your manager, will you?"

Gabberfield bowed. "Trumble and Hope are honoured to serve all your family's needs, Yer Grace. Shall I 'ave the porters load up the luggage?"

"Yes, Lady Stuart is riding with my nephew, but several other passengers are boarding Aubrey's train." He turned to Charles. "Paul's Christmas gift is in the shed next door. It's similar to this one, but with two cars just for weapons and various devices, which we'll demonstrate on Boxing Day. Now, as soon as our passengers board, we can head to Branham."

"And the Castle Company?" asked Sinclair.

"Riding on Paul's new train with Merrick. Drina's below saying goodbye to Reggie Parsons. Oh, and Treves asked to speak to you before we depart. He's in shed eight."

"Baxter, if you'd see to Lady Stuart's comfort?" Charles asked before leaving.

"My pleasure, sir."

Shed eight was also owned by Drummond and housed the Haimsbury train's twin. The engine and cars bore the Aubrey crest, but upon the engine door, painted in green and gold Charles read '*The Scottish Knight*'.

"Perfect," he said to himself. "Treves?" he called to a dark-haired man with a thick moustache. Frederick stepped off the train to shake Sinclair's hand. Snow had already begun to drift into high mounds near the sides of the long shed, and the wind howled in their ears.

"Afternoon, Charles. I pray you can make it through this snow."

"I've no fear, Fred. The Lord will plow the way," the duke told his friend. "Has Joseph boarded?"

"He's settled in with Blinkmire and Riga. They're already playing chess, if you can imagine it. And the count is tuning up his cello to offer a concert as they ride. I've never seen so luxurious a train in my life!"

"If it's anything like mine, it's magnificent," answered Haimsbury. "My uncle spared no expense this Christmas. James is far more generous than I deserve, but I'm glad it provides comfortable accommodations to our guests. I wish you could come along with us. Perhaps, bring your wife and children."

"It sounds lovely, but the London's jammed with patients. Losing Gehlen right now is difficult, but the governors have allowed me to hire the Jewish doctors as temporary consultants. I thank the Lord for those men! They're like angels in a crisis. How is Anthony doing, Charles? Have you heard anything from Henry?"

"Henry was called to Branham to look after a patient, but he left a well-respected colleague in his place, Bruce Hepplewhite."

"Hepplewhite's a fine man. Brilliant mind and a pleasant bedside manner. I'd love to hire him as well, but I hear he's planning to retire. Look, I'll try to visit Gehlen later today. Don't worry about him for the present. Enjoy Christmas with your family, Charles; and your maiden voyage on your new train! I'm sure the Lord will act as guardian, but I noticed the duke has men stationed throughout the cars."

"James is always cautious. See you next week, then?"

"Yes. Send a wire with the details, and I'll come meet you." They shook hands once more and Treves trudged off through the snow.

Sinclair stepped briefly into the first car and waved to the happy passengers. "Where's Miss Kilmeade?" he asked Riga, who was holding his cello to examine the strings.

"Measles," replied the count. "I fear our brave Brona has succumbed. But Mrs. Meyer is tending to her with the affections of a mother. Ida's already had the disease and chose to remain and learn nursing."

"She'll be a great help, I'm sure. I'm very sorry to hear of Brona's illness. We'll keep both ladies in our prayers. Good morning, Mr. Blinkmire, Stanley, Anderson. Joseph, it's a pleasure as always," he told Merrick, who was setting up a chess board.

"A pleasant day to you, Duke Charles. I hear we have more snow coming."

"We do, but our engineers are experienced men, and the Lord is our champion. Have no fear. Enjoy the trip, everyone. See you all at Branham station!"

The group waved in return, and Charles left the car, running into his uncle and Baxter as he headed back to shed seven. Cornelius held Cordelia Wychwright's arm with all the tenderness of a father.

"Aren't you riding with me?" asked Sinclair.

"I've convinced Baxter to escort our guest, son. Four of my men are on your train along with the usual guards. They'll all be bunking at the porter's lodge at Branham. It has plenty of space, and they'll keep watch on the gates whilst we're there. All's in hand, son."

"Thank you, James. Is there a sleeper on this train as well?"

Baxter answered as he helped Delia up the steps. "I'm told there are two of them, my lord. Here now," he told the girl sweetly. "Not too quickly. We'll find the room you like, and get you situated. Mrs. Alcorn will look after you once we get to the hall."

"Mrs. Alcorn?" asked the girl sleepily.

"She's a lovely woman. You'll like her."

Delia turned to look at Charles. "Aren't you coming?"

Haimsbury kissed her cheek with brotherly affection. "Not on this train, but I'll see you again soon. Paul's waiting for you at Branham."

"Paul. Yes, he's waiting. Thank you. Goodbye, Paul."

"It's Charles, dear," he whispered.

"Yes, that's right. Charles. Goodbye."

James pulled up his coat collar, squinting into the swirling snowfall. "It's starting to come down hammer and tongs. We'd best be leaving, son."

"Thank you, James. For everything."

The Scotsman laughed. "It tickles me no end to see you happy, Charles. But the trains are for work as well as pleasure. You and Paul will put thousands of miles on these in the coming years. I'm off to see Riga. He owes me a chess match."

The two men embraced, and Charles returned to the Captain Nemo Special. He found Gabberfield standing beside the engine, chatting with a burly man in a grey uniform, bearing the Haimsbury crest.

"Are we ready to leave the shed and connect with the line to Kent?" Charles asked.

"We're waiting on the signalman, sir," answered Gabberfield. "This is your engineer, my lord. Mr. Blevins. He's run trains for thirty years. You're in good hands."

"It's an honour, Mr. Blevins," said the duke, shaking the man's hand.

"No, sir, it's my honour to serve aboard this train. Duke James says I'm to mention my membership in a certain circle of agents, sir. I have six men on board; all competent in a crisis."

"That's a very great relief, Mr. Blevins, but hardly a surprise. My uncle is a man of vision and preparation, after all. May I board?"

"You may, my lord. Larson's the electrics man. He runs the generator engine. If you have any trouble, just talk to him. We're told there's snow drifts in Kent, but we'll go slow and steady."

"Proceed as you think best, Mr. Blevins. And thank you."

Sinclair turned to Gabberfield. "I take it your company creates these beautiful trains?"

"It's a family business, sir. We all proudly serve the inner circle. I've been one of the duke's agents since I turned fifteen. Handed down from my father, and his father before him. We're loyal to the Stuarts, sir. Always have been. And now we're pleased to pledge our loyalty to the Sinclairs, as well. Go with God, sir."

Charles boarded the train, finding a steaming cup of coffee waiting on his desk, white with two sugars, just as he liked it. A plate of freshly baked almond biscuits sat to the right of the coffee, and an elderly woman sipped tea from one of the club chairs.

"I believe your train is nicer than any of mine," the queen told the young duke. "Do you like it?"

"It lacked one thing; but with your presence, it is now complete, Your Majesty," he said with a bow.

"Do stop that, Charles. It's Drina, and bowing to me is hardly necessary in private. Baxter prepared your coffee and my tea, but thought we might prefer to travel in private. Cornelius is a charming man, isn't he? You're very lucky to have him. Now, do sit, my dear. We have a great deal to discuss."

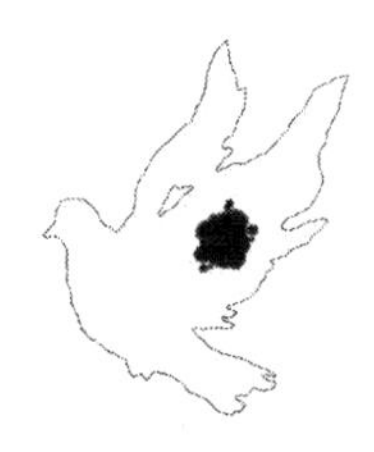

CHAPTER FORTY-TWO

Branham Hall

The day had grown colder with each passing hour, and as dusk fell, snow began to drift across the peaceful gardens and graceful statuary of Branham Hall's park. It was one of those elegant, picturesque snowfalls, with fat flakes of purest white that quickly gather into swirls of icing sugar glory, burying twigs and trees and gravel turnings with great sweeps of glittering, pristine beauty. The first crystal descended from on high at precisely 3:01 pm, and by half the hour of five, the entire south lawn lay sleeping beneath a thick blanket of frozen wonder.

Inside the hall, the main drawing rooms now boasted an evergreen tree, either fir, pine, or juniper; each decorated with festive garlands, beeswax candles, and elegant ornaments to enhance that room's individual decor. The largest tree, a majestic Nordmann Fir, rose forty feet in height and took centre stage within the hall's grand foyer; its highest tip a mere fifteen inches from the bottom arm of the main chandelier. The next largest, a Scots Pine, was only twenty feet in height and placed into its water-filled planter near the northeast corner of the red drawing room, as was tradition. This would be the family tree, and beneath its supple green arms, piles of gaily wrapped gifts had already begun to accumulate, like the drifting snow upon the lawn.

The hall's smallest tree, a mere ten feet tall, proudly occupied the private drawing room of the master apartment: a fragrant juniper, delicately formed and painstakingly grown in the conservatory, but left uncut. Rather, it remained rooted within its clay pot and would be transplanted into the hall's ten-acre Christmas copse as soon as the ground grew warm enough in March. For nearly thirty years, rooted evergreens of many varieties had served as master apartment guardians during the holiday season, and Mr. Kay, the new butler, insisted the tradition remain unbroken. In fact, he had chosen this tree himself.

That wintry day commenced with a tizzy of last-minute activity. Some of the footmen unpacked boxes of ornaments, whilst others carried down still more decorations from the attics; each filled with an assortment of candle rings, tinsel and garland, hand-made keepsakes (some made by a young Beth Stuart), souvenirs, photograph albums, and even collections of wooden toys and games. The constant flow of traffic kept the lift so busy, that the drive's chains required an extra coat of grease by midday.

Everyone on staff had known for days that a special guest would arrive that evening from London: Lady Alexandrina Stuart, a distant cousin and close friend to the Duke of Drummond. Whispers ran through the warm kitchens and round the servants' dining hall like smoke through a hot chimney regarding the Scottish duke and his mysterious 'friend'. Many speculated the mystery woman might be a future bride; after all, Duke James had been a widower for twenty-two years. It made sense that an energetic man of such a handsome countenance might want to end his years with a trusted female companion.

Of all the Branham servants, only Kay and Mrs. Stephens knew the truth of the matter: that the lady's name had been altered to conceal her true name, a legendary and most regal name which, if spoken aloud, would instantly bring every reporter, well-wisher, and ambitious courtier to Branham Hall. Instead, Lady Stuart would be welcomed no differently than any other guest.

Six soft chimes had just rung the hour, and Lady Adele, dressed in a blue satin dress trimmed with cream lace, was helping Priest and Troughton decorate the red room tree.

"I think it needs more colour, don't you, Mr. Priest?" the eleven-year-old asked as she sorted through a small crate of ornaments. "And stars. Lots of lovely little stars. Have we any more stars, Mr. Troughton?"

The shorter man stepped off the wooden ladder and began searching through a large, silk-lined, velvet case. This box had been removed from the duchess's jewellery safe, for it contained dozens of jewelled and valuable ornaments, used only during Christmas.

The footman very carefully removed each of the tissue-wrapped items, setting them out on a trolley for close examination.

"I see gold and silver bells, Lady Della. A ruby-encrusted toy soldier. No stars, though. But there are some quite nice eggs."

"Eggs?" she asked, laughing. "Eggs are for Easter! It is Christmas, Mr. Troughton. Shall we put eggs on a Christmas tree?"

The underbutler, Stephen Priest, a handsome lad of twenty-six with golden hair and an easy manner, stood balanced upon the top step of the high ladder. Priest was five years older and three inches taller than Jack Troughton, but even he had to stretch to reach the evergreen's top branches.

"Those are quite expensive eggs, actually, Lady Adele," the underbutler explained, glancing down from his lofty perch. "Each Christmas Eve, the duchess receives a new one from the Russian tsar; probably as enticement."

"Enticement for what?" asked Della, busily unwrapping a box of tatted-lace snowflakes.

"I believe the tsar once hoped for a marriage twixt the duchess and his son, but of course our little duchess chose a far better match."

"She certainly did," agreed the girl. "My Cousin Charles is the perfect match. Handsome and very kind, and he laughs a lot, which makes Cousin Beth smile. How many eggs are there?"

"I'm not sure. Five, I believe," Priest answered. "You should look at them, Lady Della. They're covered in all manner of gems, and each has a surprise inside."

She peered at the tray. Within the red silk, nestled five gold eggs, each engraved in a guilloché pattern and overlaid in brightly coloured enamel. Adele lifted the first and set it against her lap. "These are so very beautiful! This one has ruby-studded doors with a great pearl on top. I can see why the tsar thought them an enticement."

"Open it," a soft voice spoke from the doorway.

Della turned about, her eyes widening with wonder. Just inside the doorway, stood her cousins, Elizabeth and Charles, the latter holding the arm of a distinctive and quite lovely old lady. She wore a deep blue velvet dress, trimmed in Battenberg lace, and a simple cameo brooch sat just below her short throat. Her silver hair was braided and then twisted into a chic knot behind her head, adorned with a glittering headband cap in the same rich velvet. Soft netting in black lace edged with small stars framed her face, just covering the lady's eyes. The loose weave of the lace allowed the twinkling blue of each iris to shine forth like mischievous robin's eggs.

Adele set the Russian ornament aside and stood to curtsy. "Lady Stuart," she said politely, remembering the strict rule never to reveal the queen's identity before servants.

The visitor reached for the girl's hand, pressing it twixt her own. "You're Lady Adele, aren't you? Come, give your Auntie Drina a kiss, dear." Della did, and it caused the queen to laugh merrily. "My darling girl, you've grown very tall since I saw you five years ago. You'll pass me by before the holiday's over, I shouldn't wonder. How old are you now, my dear? Twelve? Thirteen?"

"Not quite, Lady Stuart. Eleven-and-a-half."

"You must call me Auntie Drina, and may I say, you're a very mature eleven-and-a-half."

"Thank you, Auntie Drina," Della said, curtsying once more.

"How well-mannered you are! Now, Della, I've brought you a little present. I believe one of those nice footmen is bringing it in, along with all the other items, including my dog, I think. He is bringing her, isn't he, Charles?"

The duke led the queen to a soft chair near the crackling fire. "He is indeed, Lady Stuart."

"It's Auntie Drina, remember? We are family, after all."

Elizabeth kissed the disguised sovereign's cheek. "Della, did you know that Lady Stuart is my godmother? I've called her Auntie Drina for all my life, haven't I, darling?"

Queen Victoria laughed softly, her ageing eyes crowfooting at the corners. She patted the duchess's hand. "Oh, yes, my dear, you have. And I've called you my Little Princess for just as long. Come now, Della, tell me all about yourself. When will you be twelve?"

Adele sat on a round, tufted stool near Lady Stuart's chair. "Next June, Auntie Drina. The twelfth. When is your birthday?"

"I don't talk about birthdays any longer, Della, though mine comes in May. Next June, you say? Isn't your Cousin Charles's birthday also in June?"

"It is. His is the tenth," Adele answered quickly, looking up at Sinclair. "Perhaps June is a month that leads to tall people! Which means the new babies will be tall as well, doesn't it?"

Lady Stuart smiled and reached for the young duke's hand. "You may just be right on that, my dear. Now, I wonder if I might have a spot of tea? It's dreadfully cold, despite the cheerful fire. My old bones find it harder and harder to warm up these days. Charles, would you be kind enough to ring for some?"

"No need, Your Grace," offered the shorter footman. "Allow me to fetch it."

"Thank you, Troughton," the duke answered. "Also, if you'd enquire as to when supper will be served, we'd appreciate it."

Jack bowed and left the room to fulfil the request, passing through the foyer just as two liveried footmen entered the main doors. A whirlwind of snow swirled behind them as they carried the queen's leather cases and hat boxes. A third trailed behind, carrying a small dog and a handled basket. As he set both down, Bella, the female Labrador, gave the new dog a quick sniff, making sure the newcomer was friendly. She then turned her attention to the basket, nosing at the curving willow and whining softly.

"Bring the basket in here," the duke told the footman. Bella kept her eyes on the servant as he delivered the basket to Haimsbury. The queen's dog ignored the mysterious basket entirely, choosing instead to greet her mistress.

"Here's my girl!" Lady Stuart cried happily at seeing her pet. The animal had black and white markings with a dapple of tan, and a feathery tail curled upwards and wagged continually. Her long black ears stood high upon the head, perked up nicely, with similar dapples of tan near the skull.

"What kind of dog is she?" asked Adele as she reached out to scratch the animal's back. "What's her name?"

"Her name is Dumpling, and she's a bit of a mongrel, actually. Somewhat like myself. I come from all sorts of heritages, as you're probably aware, and this sweet little darling is the same. I found her in Scotland last year, running free through one of the fells near an old cow shed. She was half-starved, poor thing, and we took her in. As you can see, she's fattened up considerably, and her coat is sleek and lovely now. My vet thinks she's border collie and rat terrier with a smattering of spaniel. She has a habit of herding people, which makes sense for a collie. She'll likely try to keep an eye on you, my dear. Dumpling loves young people. It's your energy, I think. Oh, look, she likes you!"

The dog's tail swept the air like a feathery fan, and she licked Della's hands, offering special kisses. "She's very sweet. Bella seems to like her." she told the older woman.

"Oh, I do love dogs, don't you, Della?"

"We all love them," the girl replied. "Do you have very many dogs, Auntie Drina?"

"Oh, yes, lots! But I generally travel with just Dumpling these days. It makes it easier. Do sit, Elizabeth, you make me nervous standing so long in your condition. You need to rest your ankles. Children play havoc with one's ankles. Mine used to be trim, but no longer. They grew evermore fat with each new baby. I cannot imagine carrying two at a time!"

The duchess complied by taking a seat upon a buttoned leather divan that spread out over broad mahogany arms. The duke sat beside his wife, placing an arm round her slender shoulders. "Drina's not the only one who's chilled," he said. "You're shivering, Beth. Shall I find a quilt?"

"I'll warm up soon now that you're home," she said, leaning against him lovingly. "But shouldn't we open that basket before Bella does?"

The Lab was fascinated with the willow container, and had begun to paw at the lid. Charles looked at the queen. "May I?"

"It's Della's gift. Perhaps, she should open it."

"Mine?" asked the girl. "What is it?"

"Open it and see," the queen replied.

Adele knelt down beside the mysterious present. Three leather buckles secured the lid, and she unfastened each. "Is it alive?" she asked, seeing the basket wiggle a bit.

"I certainly hope so!" Drina exclaimed.

The last buckle gave way, and Adele lifted the lid. Inside, wrapped in a thick tartan blanket, lay a nine-week old puppy, just rousing from a deep sleep. The black and white animal looked up at her new mistress.

"It's a little dog!" Della cried as she lifted the puppy out of the basket. "He's so very cute! Thank you! Thank you so very much, Auntie Drina!"

"*She*, not he," the queen corrected. "And you're welcome, my dear. This is the last female of the litter, and the most darling in my opinion. She's a Cavalier King Charles, descended from a line developed by the 4th Duke of Marlborough. I thought it a perfect gift, for it honours your Cousin Charles as new master of the hall—and a duke at that! I've also given a puppy to Winston Churchill for Christmas, as it's descended from his ancestor's kennels. Winny's puppy is male, of course."

"Winston has this one's brother?"

"He does. I had it delivered yesterday to his Aunt Maisie's home. You'll find she sleeps a great deal of the time, but is very healthy. These spaniels are wonderful companions. I had one as a girl. A perfect little dog named Dash. But they're working dogs, you know. They'll hunt woodcock and pheasant; most any bird. Do you shoot, Charles?"

"Generally, when I fire a weapon, it's at fleeing criminals," he teased her. "But there's a shoot arranged for Boxing Day. We can see how she does with shotgun noise."

Drina nodded. "It's never too early to start. If you raise them round guns, they'll be all right."

"Is she really mine?" the girl asked again, cuddling the wriggly puppy joyfully.

"All yours, but she'll need a name."

"Oh yes!" Adele exclaimed. "I'll have to think about that. Names are very important, you know."

"And you'll have to train her to be careful indoors. Bella will help, won't you, girl?" said Elizabeth.

The Labrador kept nosing Della's hand until she set the puppy on the floor. Immediately, the older dog took the tiny pup into her soft mouth and carried it from the room and towards the main entry.

Beth laughed. "Bella's either trying to get rid of the competition or else wants to take her outside for a lesson."

"I can take them both outdoors, my lady," offered Priest, climbing down from the ladder.

"Don't go too far, Mr. Priest," the duke called to the departing servant. "We don't want Della's present to disappear into a snow drift!"

Adele shut the basket and set it before the bright fire. "We're still finishing the tree, Auntie Drina. Perhaps, you can help."

"I'd be happy to, so long as I'm not required to climb that ladder. I fear my limbs aren't what they once were."

"Shouldn't we wait for Grandfather and the others?" asked the duchess. "Some of the ornaments are from Drummond castle, and he likes to hang them."

"What of Mr. Blinkmire and Count Riga?" Adele sang back. "Didn't they come with you, Cousin Charles?"

"They're in the second train with Baxter and your Uncle James," Charles explained. "Also, there's a surprise guest. And I should probably explain her to my wife."

"Explain *her?*" Beth asked warily.

"It's Cordelia, dear," he whispered. "She has nowhere else to go. It's a long story, which is better told upstairs, but I've asked Kay to prepare rooms for her. She's in a very bad way. I'll want Henry to look at her right away."

"A bad way? Has her depression worsened?"

"Yes, but there are other factors as well. I'll tell you upstairs," Charles answered softly. "As for the remainder of the night, I am at your disposal, little one. I've left all police work behind until next week. Tonight, we shall have laughter and music and Mrs. Stephen's fruit cake. Count Riga's brought his cello and a selection of special music, but we'll need a singer. If only we knew someone," he added with a wink at Della.

Adele jumped to her feet. "I can sing, Cousin Charles! And I can also play accompaniment for the count, if he needs it. He and I've practised lots of songs together. But you didn't mention Mr. Merrick. He is still coming, I hope?"

"He is, and tomorrow we'll have a chess tournament. Now, why do I see eggs at Christmas?"

"I was just asking the same thing," Adele replied. "They are quite beautiful, and they're Russian. The tsar sends them to entice Cousin Beth."

Charles glanced at his wife. "A tsar plies you with golden treasures as enticement?"

Beth laughed. "Not in that way, Captain! Tsar Alexander sends them to demonstrate his friendship. If enticement was involved, it had to do with his son, not himself."

"You and Nicholas?" asked the queen. "Never. He's far too timid for Elizabeth's temperament. Charles is a much better match for you, my dear." She placed a pair of thick spectacles on her nose and waved her stout arms, motioning to the child. “Bring that largest egg to me, dear. Let me see it.”

Della complied, and the visitor took the jewelled egg, turning it round slowly in her arthritic hands. “It’s exquisite, isn’t it? May I open it?”

“Of course,” answered the duchess. “There’s always a surprise inside. Last year’s included a replica of a royal coach. You know, I just realised it’s like the one we rode in for the ball, Charles. Do you remember? The night before our wedding.”

“Prince Anatole’s coach?”

“Yes. See if that egg’s in the box, Della. It has blue and red enamel on the outside with golden doors.”

The eleven-year-old fetched the remaining eggs. At the same time, Stephen Priest returned, covered in snow, holding the puppy inside his livery coat.

“She dutifully did her business, my lady,” he told the duchess. “Bella served as teacher. I think she’s adopted the puppy as her own.”

Della took the chilled spaniel to the fire and placed it inside the basket. “What a good little pup you are! Look, Auntie Drina, Bella’s licking her to warm her up! Shall I put the blanket down on the rug, so Bella can act as mother?”

“The pup’s already weaned, dear, if that’s what you’re thinking,” the queen told her.

“Bella’s had two litters of her own, so I expect this is old hat to her,” added Elizabeth. “And there’s another litter due in a few weeks.”

“Really?” asked Charles. “I thought Bella seemed a bit stouter these days.”

“It’s what comes of letting Briar keep so close,” she told her husband. “Ordinarily, he lives with our gamekeeper. I’ll be pleased to have more puppies from their two lines. Both are such good dogs. Briar’s the finest hunter in the county. Now, let’s see about this tree. Oh, Mr. Priest, do be careful up there! Make sure your boots aren’t still wet!”

“I’m quite safe, my lady,” the underbutler said as he climbed the stepladder. He carried three strings of glass beads, winding them round and round the graceful branches, to add sparks of gold, red, and silver to the green boughs

"It's a beautiful tree, Mr. Priest. You and Troughton have done a wonderful job. This may be the best tree yet," the duchess told him.

"Mr. Powers chose a fine tree indeed, my lady," Priest concurred. "It's a little fuller than last year's. Though, last year's was taller."

Elizabeth gazed at the tree fondly. "Last year's tree was precariously placed for a room filled with revelers. Lord Aubrey nearly fell into it as I recall. Della, do you remember that?"

Laughing, the girl returned to her chair. "My poor brother tripped over a toy train! We mustn't remind him, though. Paul's sensitive about such things. But Uncle James drank so much eggnog that he started singing sea shanties. Do you remember, Cousin Beth?"

"James often digresses into song at Christmas time," noted Lady Stuart wistfully. "When he and I were young, he had a magnificent baritone voice. He'd regale all the court with some very curious lyrics. My mother nearly fainted from shock, but I thought it all quite amusing."

"You knew Uncle James when he was young?" asked Adele.

"Oh, yes. Your uncle and I've been friends since we were your age. I very nearly married him, you know."

"Really?" she asked in amazement. "Would he have been king, then?"

"Quite likely," Drina replied. "But then royal blood flows in your family's veins. Doesn't it, Charles?"

Sinclair gave no reply, merely offered her a smile in return.

Oblivious to the subtle hint, Adele decided to uncover more ornaments and squealed in delight when she reached the bottom of the crate. "A stereo viewer! I have one of these at Briarcliff! Are there any photographs to go with it, Cousin Beth?"

"Quite a few. They should all be in the same crate," the duchess answered. "My father loved stereo photographs, Charles. On birthdays and other special occasions, he'd always hire a professional to make them. Eventually, he bought a stereo camera of his own."

"Allow me, Lady Della," Priest said as he descended the ladder. "I believe the photographs are in this box." Using a prise bar, the underbutler opened the last crate.

Della eagerly dug into the box, beholding treasures galore: two albums of stereo photographs, a silver whistle, a board game, chess set with ivory and ebony men carved in medieval dress, a stack of Christmas postcards tied with red ribbon, a jack-in-the-box painted with elephants, zebras and tigers; and a hinged tin container filled with metal discs painted with marching soldiers, dancing ballerinas, and running animals.

"Oh, this is filled with all sorts of treasure!" declared the youngster as she brought several of the items to Elizabeth. "I found the stereo photos, but I'm not sure what these are." Adele handed her the tin of painted discs.

"I'd forgotten all about these," Beth said happily, showing the queen. "Did you ever own a phenakistiscope, Auntie Drina? These are the discs. I'm not at all sure where the device might be, though."

"What's a phena-kiss-ta...?"

"Phenakistiscope," her cousin finished. "You place these painted discs into it, and once the key is wound, the device spins to make the pictures appear to move. Rather like a zoetrope. This set belonged to my father. Connor Stuart was your first cousin, Della." Elizabeth didn't bother to add 'once removed', since Adele had no idea she was Paul's daughter, not his sister.

"I never met Cousin Connor, but his portraits look quite handsome," the innocent girl answered. "Do you miss him, Cousin Beth?"

"Every day, darling. Just as Auntie Drina misses her dear husband. But such an earthly parting is only temporary, is it not?"

"Indeed, it is, my dear. It is ever my hope and prayer to see my darling husband again," answered the queen wistfully, not speaking his name to keep her disguise intact. The much-missed Prince Albert.

Charles thought of his own Albert, and how lonely and grief-stricken that Christmas in '78 had been following his son's sudden death. "So it is," he whispered, tightening his grip on Beth's hand. "Now, let's have a look through these photographs."

Della smiled in delight. "It may take a while, Cousin Charles. There are hundreds of them. I wonder, might Auntie Drina be in any of them?"

The queen laughed as her dog leapt onto her lap once more. The new puppy had fallen asleep next to Bella on the rug. "It looks as though Dumpling wants to see the photos, too. It's a shame we can't all look at them at once. One of James's inventors should create a device that displays stereo pictures to an entire room, don't you think?"

Jack Troughton returned with a wooden trolley filled with tea, coffee, lemonade, and cakes.

"Our refreshments have arrived and just in time," said Sinclair. "And you're absolutely right, Drina. My uncle should underwrite such an invention, but knowing James, he may have already done it. Troughton, what time is supper tonight?"

"Not until nine, sir, but Mrs. Stephens has prepared something quite special to make up for it. For the present, she's sent along hearty sandwiches and sweets to compensate."

"Thank you, Troughton," Beth whispered. "We'll help ourselves. I believe Mr. Priest requires your attention. It looks to me as though this last string of beads has challenged his untangling abilities. Della, why don't you pour tea for our guest, whilst I look through these photographs to see if any include Auntie Drina?"

"I should be in several," the queen reminisced. "I remember one year when your father took all sorts of those stereo pictures, Elizabeth." She reached for the tray to take two small sandwiches and a jam tart. "No milk in mine, dear. Just sugar. Three cubes."

Della served while the duchess sorted through the pictures.

"Where's Paul, Adele?" asked Charles after biting into a cheese and cress sandwich. "I thought he'd meet us at the village station."

"With Dr. Holloway. Cousin Henry is up there, too. Oh, and Aunt Victoria said that she and Dolly will be down shortly. They're wrapping gifts, and I think some are for me, because they shooed me from the room. You're certain Mr. Merrick is really coming?"

"He is really coming," the duke assured her. "In fact, they should have arrived by now. I hope the second train wasn't delayed getting out of London. Victoria Station was terribly crowded. All the ministers were heading home to their country estates."

"Which train did you take? Paul's or your new one?" asked Beth.

"You knew about that?" her husband asked.

"Of course, I did. Do you really think my grandfather designed it all? I had a hand in making sure it matched all your needs. I hope you like it, darling."

He kissed her cheek. "The Captain Nemo Special will provide a mobile theatre of operations for the ICI, but also a pleasure train for us to use one day. Perhaps, we can take it to Carlisle and spend a week at Rose House."

"I'd like that," she whispered lovingly. "Wait, I think I hear a coach! Look out the window, Della, and see if I'm right."

The youngster dashed to the window, her posture eager as she peered through the frosty panes. "It is! There are four large coaches, and Uncle James is getting out of one! Oh, they're here, Beth! They're here!"

She ran from the room, through the foyer, towards the front door, already opened by Kay. Cornelius Baxter led the way up the broad steps, his arm round Cordelia Wychwright as he tenderly aided her through the snow and ice. Close behind was Duke James, talking happily with Blinkmire and Riga. Next came Elbert Stanley, David Anderson, and Joseph Merrick. Two footmen kept close to either side of Merrick, making sure his halting progress never faltered upon the snowy gravel or up the portico steps.

Once everyone had safely entered and removed their coats, hats, and gloves, Drummond took control. "Now, let's get all our guests settled, and then we can begin our celebration. Princess, where have you put us?"

"Kay and Baxter arranged it all," she told her grandfather standing beside Sinclair in the foyer. "My dear Mr. Merrick, it's lovely to see you again. And our clever Count Riga and the gallant Mr. Blinkmire. We're honoured to have you with us for Christmas. Mr. Stanley, I believe you and Mr. Anderson are sharing an apartment. There's a lift, Mr. Merrick. No need for stairs! Cordelia, I'm so glad you could join us," she told the pale young woman. "The rail trip from London can be very tiring. Would you care to lie down before supper? Kay, would you ask one of your men to see Lady Cordelia to the west wing? She'll want to be close to the earl, I should think. The Anjou Suite is vacant. Oh, and ask Ada MacKenzie to fetch a dressing gown and slippers from my closet for our guest, in case she needs them. It doesn't matter which."

"Very good, my lady." Kay motioned to a young man with prematurely silver hair and bright blue eyes. "Stafford, will you escort Lady Cordelia to the Anjou Suite?"

By seven, the foyer had emptied; whilst upstairs, footmen and lady's maids helped guests to unpack. The main floor of the great mansion grew still. It was an eerie sort of silence that seldom happened in the centuries-old home. Unseen and unheard, ghosts patrolled the second east wing, climbing up and down the wooden maze staircase, and inside the upper gallery. The painted eyes of a hundred portraits stared, mutely observing the living inhabitants, as though waiting for something to happen.

And above it all, upon the highest chimney of the great house, a white owl kept watch, its ice blue eyes fixed upon the horizon.

CHAPTER FORTY-THREE

10:29 pm – The Branham Music Room

Supper that night featured a broad selection of Lady Stuart's favorite foods: roast lamb with rosemary and thyme, pork shoulder in apple sauce, boiled haddock in dilled cream, and three types of potatoes. Raspberry tarts topped with cream satisfied her sweet tooth, and mulled wine allowed the sovereign to grow quite cheerful as the evening wore on. Now, as the family gathered for an hour of music, Lady Alexandrina Stuart looked as though she could drift off to sleep at any moment. Elizabeth took the chair beside the queen, joined by a quartet of adult dogs: Briar, Bella, Samson, and the newcomer Dumpling.

"It's beginning to look a bit like a kennel round here," she laughed as Adele brought her new puppy to the cheerful fire. "If she's cold, there's a blanket in the willow basket next to the grandfather clock, Della. Have you given her a name yet?"

"Not yet," the girl answered as she draped a Stuart tartan blanket over the animal. "Names are very important. She'll live a long time with her name, so I want to make sure it's the right one. Will we open the presents on Christmas morning? Cousin Charles says he's bought me something quite nice, but I didn't see it beneath the tree."

"We've not added our gifts yet," the duchess answered. "Oh, it's been a long day! A long, wonderful day; hasn't it, Drina?"

"Oh yes," replied the queen. "Tell me, how is young Seth doing?"

"Better, so says Henry," answered Elizabeth. "I apologise for all the activity, Auntie Drina. It never used to be this busy, when I was a girl."

"It only seemed less busy because you were just a child, my dear," the queen admonished. "Adults view the world far differently than children. I've spent many holidays here at the hall, and it's nearly always busy—but a lovely sort of busy. One of my favourites was the spring of '75. The famous Branham fête! The theme that year was Egypt, and the grounds were filled with people in costume, and there were mummies and dancers and all sorts of games. And your mother played the role of Cleopatra to your father's Marc Antony. Do you remember it, Beth? Your father'd just come home, and everyone was here. Robby and Angie Sinclair, Rob and Abigail Stuart—oh, Della, your late father was a handsome man. When I was young and a mere slip of a thing, I used to dance and dance with the Stuart cousins."

"The Stuart cousins? Do you mean my father and Uncle James?" asked Della. "When was this, Auntie Drina?"

"Yes, James and Robert. I was sixteen, when I attended my first ball here at Branham. Everyone was there! What a glorious night it was! The late earl was five years older than I, and he outshone every other man on the dance floor. None of you knew Rob Stuart in his youth, but he was a fine figure of a man. You know, Charles has a similar bearing and physique. It's that Stuart blood, I imagine. True royalty will always show itself."

"And my grandfather?" asked Beth, leaning in to listen. "The two of you were close friends?"

"Intimately close, and we still are. Sir John never liked the Stuarts. Although, my mother had a fondness for Robert."

"Who's Sir John?" asked Della.

"Sir John Conroy," explained Drina. "He was my late father's equerry. Of course, the idea of being 'master of the horse' has altered in our modern times. You might say he was a private secretary. Somewhat like a chamberlain, I suppose. He ran the household, but he also ran my mother. I detested the man, if you want the truth," she added as the count entered the room, carrying a cello. "Good evening, Count Riga," the queen said politely.

"May I help you with that?" asked Adele, rising from her chair.

"Oh, no, I'm accustomed to its weight, Lady Della. Am I the only gentleman to join so delightful a group of ladies? Clearly, this is my lucky day! *Serendipitous*, you might say."

Beth laughed at the choice of descriptor. "Is that your dictionary word for today, Count?"

He set the instrument against the curve of the piano. "Indeed, it is. Language is a luxury, and I intend to luxuriate to the full whilst here. I understand the hall has several well-stocked libraries, Duchess. I wonder, might I peruse their shelves during our visit?"

"You may examine them all, dear Count, and borrow whatever you like. Please, sit, won't you? We're listening to Lady Stuart's reminiscences."

Riga bowed slightly before taking a seat opposite the queen. He knew the woman's true identity, of course, for Charles had informed the Castle Company several days earlier. All had promised to keep the secret.

"Lady Stuart must have many exciting tales, I should think," he observed with an endearing smile. "Do go on."

Drina reached for a tray of chocolate dipped bonbons and took one, gobbling it up in two bites. She wiped her hands on a lace handkerchief. "Oh, these confections are delicious! I shall gain even more weight whilst here; I know it! Now, what was I saying?"

"You were talking about the Branham ball," Della said to the queen. "And my handsome father. You said he was a fine figure of a man, and that he looked like Cousin Charles."

"Yes, so I did. Well, it's true, you know. Rob's sister was Charles's grandmother. Black hair and striking blue eyes. It was always exciting when the Stuarts came down from Scotland. Except for that fête in '75, of course. Far too much excitement, I think. Don't you agree, Elizabeth?"

"I'm not sure what you mean," replied the duchess. "Riga, have you any idea what's keeping my husband and the others?"

"Mr. Merrick is regaling them with a story about the recent fire near the docks. I've no wish to hear about fires, but Blinkmire seemed to find it interesting. He and Merrick have become fast friends. What happened in '75, if I may ask, Duchess?"

Beth reached for her dog Bella, pulling the animal close as though suddenly fearful. "I'd really rather not talk about that year," she whispered, stroking Bella's ears.

"Why not?" asked Adele. "In May of '75, you'd have been seven, right? Surely, that was a lovely age. Did you dress as an Egyptian princess?"

Elizabeth's eyes took on a faraway look as she stared into the fire. "No, but Paul was a Roman soldier," she whispered.

"My brother was here, too?" asked the girl.

"He and all the Stuarts," replied the disguised queen.

The duchess had begun to shiver, and the dog drew closer, whimpering. "I can't remember," she whispered to herself. "Why can't I remember?"

The queen called to Dumpling, who'd been nosing the sleeping puppy. Immediately the dog leapt onto the sofa, snuggling twixt her mistress and the duchess. She placed a paw on Beth's forearm, as if trying to offer comfort.

"It began so very nicely," Beth told the listeners. "Tents covered the grounds, and we had camels brought in from the London zoo. But then a tent appeared that shouldn't have been there, and I think... I think I went in, and then something happened. Something I cannot remember."

CHAPTER FORTY-FOUR

The main library

"We mustn't linger here too much longer, my lord," Cornelius Baxter told Duke Charles. "If I know the little duchess, she'll start to suspect us of having a meeting during Christmas celebrations—which, of course, we are. Best not pique her curiosity, my lord."

"You're right. My wife is generally quite patient, but even that lovely aspect of her personality has its limits," replied Haimsbury with a smile. "I've sent Riga ahead to keep our ladies occupied. Now, I want to offer a brief welcome to Elbert Stanley and David Anderson. Both lived at the Walham Green Castle when my wife recuperated there, and I consider them dear friends. Welcome to the inner circle, gentlemen."

Anderson looked to Stanley, who stood. "Thank you, Your Grace. I know I speak for us both when I say how surprised we are at life's turns. Had you asked me ten years ago about my future, I'd have said I hoped to retire as a detective inspector. Police work's all I knew back then. Now, I realise just how wide the world truly is. As for my good friend, Mr. Anderson, well, David's story is slowly emerging. He'd lost most of his memories whilst imprisoned at the Institute—that's Castor, for those who don't know it, sirs—but as his body heals, the mind follows. Another piece to that puzzle emerged only two nights ago. It has to do with you, Your Grace."

"With me?" asked Charles. "How so, Mr. Anderson?"

David resisted standing, but did so at his friend's encouragement. His eyes seldom looked upwards, and his hands trembled a little from nervous anticipation.

"I've no right to be here," he said bashfully. "I'm no one in the scheme of things, but you make me feel important, Your Grace.

What Mr. Stanley said is right. I've recovered many of my old memories, and one of the clearest is of a grand estate sitting upon a hill of yellow flowers. Below it lies a valley divided by a sparkling river of blue. I speak of Rose House, my lord. I once served there as footman."

"You're very young to have served there, Mr. Anderson," Drummond observed. "Might you have been a page? You look no older than my nephews."

"I am, to the best of my knowledge, fifty-six or seven, sir. I once asked Prince Anatole about my youthful appearance, and he said it is the lingering effect of the cruel blood treatment I received at Castor. That which made me a beast, that is. Prince Anatole believes I shall begin to age again, but slowly."

Stanley stood once more. "Tis the same with me, my lords. I'm nearly sixty, yet look to be in my mid-thirties. One might call it an accidental fountain of youth, but one with poisonous insinuations, for the Castor serum caused us both to change into hideous monsters. Both David and I would eagerly trade older bodies for a life without such memories."

Both Stanley and Anderson returned to their chairs, and Sinclair walked round to place his hands on their shoulders.

"We are honoured to have you at our table and in our home, gentlemen. Whilst we cannot undo the insults to your bodies and minds, we hope to offer you a chance to live for God. Martin tells me that he and Dr. MacPherson spoke to you about Christ, and that you've placed your faith in him alone. Is that true?"

Both men nodded, and Stanley responded. "We trust in Christ's blood, sir. Prince Anatole often spoke to us of a being he calls the One, and of Christ's mercies. The prince is a good man, sir—though, man is not perhaps accurate. Neither David nor I will speak ill of him. The prince saved our lives and preserved our souls. Now, we want only to make each moment count for others."

Still standing beside Stanley and Anderson, Haimsbury looked to the faces round the table: Duke James, Kepelheim, Baxter, Joseph Merrick, Stephen Blinkmire, Malcolm Risling, Sir Thomas Galton, and his beloved cousin, Paul Stuart.

"My friends, we join hands at a time of year when men and women of the earth celebrate the incarnation of God himself. How can anyone who speaks the word 'Christmas' not believe in miracles? I consider it a miracle that I am here at all. As a child, I had all my family and even my memories stripped from me; yet here I stand, restored with greater blessings yet. It's my belief that Mr. Stanley and Mr. Anderson are miracles as well, and that God is restoring to them far more than they've lost. But it is not my opinion alone that sets the course of this table—but the opinions of all. What say you regarding admission of these fine men into our fellowship?"

Rather than raise hands or voice their votes, the entire table began to spontaneously applaud and rise to their feet. The overwhelming response caused the new members to weep, and poor David Anderson bowed his head.

Charles leaned over to whisper. "Stand up, dear friend, and let us show you our gratitude."

Trembling all over, David rose obediently, placing a hand upon the duke's forearm for support. It was then that a strange thing occurred. A palpable electric shock ran from the former footman to Sinclair, causing the duke to experience a momentary flash of memory. For the briefest of seconds, his entire childhood crystallised with rare clarity: he remembered the musical sound of his mother's voice, his father's after shave, the smell of Rose House kitchens, the sound of the River Eden as it rushed along below their home, the feel of the silk curtains upon his nursery bed, and he remembered the clock. Arthur's Victory: the animated clock with its growling voice.

Hello, boy. Shall we play?

The final flash of memory was of a black mirror sitting in the corner of a attic, its beguiling surface glittering with fiery eyes.

"Charles?" an anxious voice called from far away. "Charles, are you all right? Martin, fetch a brandy!"

"I think he's about to faint," someone else said—perhaps, Tom Galton.

"Go fetch Henry!" his uncle shouted.

"No, wait. I'm fine," Sinclair assured them as Kepelheim brought the filled snifter. "May I... May I speak?"

The men slowly returned to their chairs. Charles sat into the nearest wingback, beads of sweat causing his face to shine. "Forgive me for frightening you. Paul, do stop hovering."

The earl drew a chair close to his cousin. "Hovering am I? What happened to you?"

"David Anderson happened, I think. Never before have I experienced so great a rush of complex memory. Even those I recovered with your technique, Martin, cannot compare to this. It was as though every moment of my childhood was served up to me in an instant. Yet, I cannot now discern the individual images. The *sense* of memory remains, but it's like looking at the cover of a novel; knowing you've just read it, but unable to tell others the plot. Still, even so brief a glimpse gives me hope. David, I believe you have a great role to play in my life and in this circle."

Anderson's entire physicality had altered during the curious exchange of energy. It seemed to all that he now moved with purpose and determination as he approached the man he'd once served at Rose House. Bowing deeply, the former footman knelt before the duke.

"If I may, Your Grace, I also felt an impossible surge coursing through my blood. And it has returned me to my old self. It's as though my identity was bound up inside your mind. And with those memories, comes a great sense of responsibility. May I serve you again, my lord? As once I did?"

"Serve Christ alone," Charles told him. "But if you wish to be a help to my mission, then I should like to speak with you another time about my childhood and my father."

"It would be my honour," the man humbly replied.

Finishing the wine, Sinclair handed the empty glass to Kepelheim. "Now, gentlemen, I shall leave this mystery of my childhood for another meeting. Presently, we've other mysteries to solve, including two murders. We'll discuss the dockside fire another time, when Reid joins us. Galton, you and Risling have been investigating Blackstone. What can you tell us?"

Sir Thomas rose to his feet. "First of all, let me say how much it means to meet at Branham once more. During the duchess's residency in France, we had few opportunities to gather at the hall, and to be here at Christmastide brings a rush of pleasant memories and emotion. Duke Charles, may I also offer my heartfelt congratulations on your new title. It is a miracle indeed that you returned to your family, but the speed at which the Lord is elevating you in peerage and public hearts is also miraculous. And a matter for the circle to discuss—but not today.

"Now, lest I wax on too long and cause our dear one to worry about her Captain, I shall offer all that Malcolm and I've learnt thus far. Blackstone Exploration Society's literature claims the organisation commenced in 1807, when their founding members met together in Idumea. Five men comprised the original society, and their records indicate a discovery made near Mt. Hor to be of great significance. It is thought—and I must thank Mr. Kepelheim for his assistance here—that these five men found a rock which they believe holds the secret to all life. They call it the Black Stone. Ten years later, a German society was founded called, *Die Herren auf dem Swarzenstein*; or Lords of the Black Stone. Our intrepid tailor infiltrated this group in 1858, and returned to our circle with all he'd learnt."

"Which was not that much," Kepelheim noted as he poured himself a cognac. "These so-called 'lords' think themselves superior to most of humanity by nature, claiming hereditary lines which reach back to pre-flood times. It is their belief that their blood is unique and that exposure to this stone awakens and enhances it. Though men of business and power, they perform hedonistic rituals before this rock—even sacrificing children to it."

"Children? You saw this with your own eyes?" asked Duke James in shock.

"No, I never witnessed it personally, but another member reported it to me in disturbingly graphic detail. It was shortly after this, that I fled Germany and returned to England to offer my report. Blackstone's men tried to stop my passage, but the Lord had other plans, I'm pleased to say."

Charles glanced at his cousin, who was scribbling notes in code. Sinclair had observed Aubrey doing this at other meetings. Paul had a basic rule: assume everything you write might fall into enemy hands.

"Is the Blackstone Exploration Society the same as these German miscreants?" asked James. "If so, why are they interested in Branham?"

"We believe the Society is but one branch of the Lords of the Black Stone," replied Galton. "Redwing has similar branches to its malformed tree."

"Redwing!" exclaimed Joseph Merrick mournfully. "Such evil in so small a word."

Everyone's eyes turned to the misshapen gentleman known to most as The Elephant Man.

"You're familiar with it, Mr. Merrick?" asked Kepelheim.

"It has a dark reputation in Whitechapel. Some of my Jewish friends have spoken of it. But Blackstone! Now that foul organisation is also known to me, for I've personally encountered their kind."

"Please, go on, Joseph," his friend Sinclair urged.

Merrick took a small sip of water, using a paper straw, kindly provided by Baxter. "It is a strange tale, but I assure you all it is true. My mother died when I was eleven, a great tragedy as you can imagine. But two years after, my father remarried. My stepmother found it difficult to love someone as deformed as I, and so I left to live with my uncle. Charles Merrick was kind, but even he found my form difficult to love. He remanded my future to the workhouse. It was there I met Sam Torr, who ran a penny gaff show."

His hands knotted round the head of his cane, and he took a deep, raspy breath, followed by another sip of water. "Some say I encouraged Torr and others to exhibit me, but what else might I do? The workhouse offered me no opportunity for employment; in fact, most there derided and abused me. But I believed with all my heart that God had a plan, thus I began a life on the road."

"God always has a plan," Charles whispered, touching Merrick's hand gently. "Had you not gone with Torr, you might never have come to London and met Fred Treves. Nor me. Your friendship and encouragement is a shining example of God's love, Joseph."

A tear slid down the deformed man's bumpy face, and he nodded, trying to smile. "So true! But that road to my present circumstances took me through many adventures. After leaving Torr, I joined Tom Norman, and then later Sam Roeper, who took me to Europe. We played in nearly every major city, including Bremen, where we remained for several weeks. One night whilst there, I overheard Mr. Roeper speaking with a man who claimed to represent an enlightened group of individuals who collected rare species. He offered to buy several of the acts, including myself and a young man dubbed Wolf Boy. I remember quite clearly that Sam asked the man if he represented a group called Redwing. Apparently, Sam had some knowledge of them from having lived in Whitechapel. This person answered no. He did, in fact, seem insulted to be so conflated with Redwing!"

"How frightening to overhear such a conversation, dear friend! Did he try to sell you?" asked Blinkmire, his small eyes blinking rapidly with concern.

Joseph shook his oversized head. "Not that night, but I began to fear he might, for this strange gentleman returned again and again. Mr. Roeper and I fell into disagreement after that, and he abandoned me in Brussels. But God still had a plan, and a very compassionate Russian gentleman paid my passage back to London."

Blinkmire's eyes widened. "A Russian? Was he a prince?"

"He dressed like one. Exceedingly tall with long, dark hair and pale blue eyes that looked right through a man."

"It sounds like Prince Anatole," said Elbert Stanley. "Once again, he provided rescue to one of God's creatures!"

Charles stared at his friend. "Do you really think Roeper would have sold you, Joseph? Was he sympathetic to this dark group's agenda?"

"Yes, most likely, he would have sold me. But I think money drove his decisions, not any alliances. Roeper did sell the poor lad to them, and I cannot say what might have happened to him. Since then, I've learnt there are men who buy and then kill curiosities such as myself, using our bones in their secret rituals. I fear, my Wolf Boy friend might have served in so shocking a manner. To avoid aiding such dark mens' causes, I've asked that my skeleton be donated to Mr. Treves when I die."

Sinclair's voice choked with emotion as he said, "May that day be many years hence, my friend."

"It is in God's hands," replied Merrick.

Kepelheim was also scribbling coded notes, passing them to the earl, and he glanced up. "Mr. Merrick, did you ever hear the name of this Blackstone fellow? Were you ever introduced?"

"I was," Joseph answered. "And I shall never forget him! He is a decidedly memorable person. Pale to the point of seeming dead, ghastly black eyes that have a cold effect, and he always dressed in black. Head to toe. The man's name escapes me, but I believe it sounded stony. Not stone, of course, but a word relative to one."

"Might it be Flint?" asked Charles, growing evermore concerned about Blackstone's mysterious project.

"Yes! Albus Flint! How could I have forgotten so curious a name? A very sallow fellow, I must say. I remember telling Mr.

Roeper that Flint might also be exhibited as one of his acts. The Animated Corpse, or some such nonsense. Even his hands felt cold, as though he lacked blood."

"And this same man visited Beth several times in France this summer," Charles noted, anger colouring his voice. "Why did no one attend these meetings with her? We of the circle are meant to protect the duchess, and yet she was left on her own for years!"

"Never alone, Charles," the earl countered. "Not ever. Galton, Risling, Sir Percy, and André Deniau stood by at Tory's to watch. We knew of her meetings with Flint, and Victoria attended two of them. If you must know, our concern at that time, was Rasha Grigor. James and I felt his influence more of a threat than any archaeological request."

"It's true, son," Drummond told his nephew.

"I'm sure the team did its best, but am I to understand that Beth's callers required no formal screening? Rasha, Flint; who else had access to her?"

Paul shut his book and set down the pencil. "We cannot isolate her, Charles. We observed due diligence at all times, but even our best plans sometimes failed. You've seen that these past few months. The enemy is clever and insinuates himself via seductive means. I understand your concern, but we love her, too, Charles. Have you forgotten that?"

Sinclair lowered his head in shame. "Forgive me. Here of all places, I should remember your love for her, Paul."

Baxter stood, clearing his throat. "If I may speak, my lords, there have always been moments when the enemy steals into our little duchess's life, but my lady lives and breathes and laughs. My observations pale to your own, of course, but it seems to me the circle's methods are primarily reactionary. Now, I do not suggest anyone here has the ability to foretell the future, but trends exist. And these trends show possible future paths, do they not? If we had supernatural abilities and could observe the duchess's life, her encounters, conversations, and decisions; then might not our plans improve? I suggest then, that we produce a history of my lady's life—and then compare it to histories of both Lord Aubrey and Duke Charles. Augmenting any written accounts with photographs, for I can tell you of multiple photographic images that reveal far more than human sight perceived at the time, rather like silver nitrate ghosts. And there are paintings in the upper gallery that seem to hint at unperceived companions. Spectres from the family's past, if you will."

Charles smiled. "Baxter, your constant wisdom outshines us all. It's an excellent idea. It's the sort of thing a good inspector would suggest to his commissioner! Well done, Inspector Baxter! Consider this your first assignment, then: to compile a history of our three lines up to the present time. Paul's, Beth's, and mine. But we should also include Henry MacAlpin. Prince Anatole insists he's important to Beth."

Paul left his chair to congratulate the former butler with a massive embrace. "Baxter, you're a gem! I can give you access to all the archives at Aubrey House, if you like. Lord Salperton probably has family histories to share as well. Somewhere within those tales, diaries, photographs, and letters lies a hidden thread that connects us all. We've been distracted by the affairs of the day, I fear. Reactionary by nature and myopic by sight, which means we fail to see the woodland because of all the trees in our way. From now on, Charles and I will concentrate on felling the trees, whilst you map out the woods, Inspector Baxter."

Cornelius beamed with pride. "It is an honourable task, my lords. If I might ask one favour?"

"Anything," both cousins answered in unison.

"I should be pleased if Mr. Kepelheim could join me in this endeavour. As he is the circle historian."

"I'd hoped you would ask me, Mr. Baxter!" declared the tailor. "We shall begin tonight, right after we enjoy the music. Now, my friends, perhaps we should return to the ladies. I promised to accompany our duchess in several songs."

All rose, but Charles placed a hand on Baxter's arm. "Stay a little, Cornelius. And Paul, if you'd remain as well?"

The earl waited until the others had left, and then shut the door. Taking his former chair, he looked to the circle leader. "I think I can guess why you wanted this private talk, Charles."

"Are you still reading my mind, Cousin?"

"Always," laughed Aubrey. "It's likely the same reason I'd planned to speak with Baxter later. These photographs and paintings. The ones that reveal more than human eyes perceive. I wonder which you mean?"

The former butler poured himself half a glass of Bordeaux as though preparing for a speech. "I've told His Grace about the appearance of Duke Henry's ghost in the east wing, sir," he said to Aubrey. "Perhaps, it's time I tell a very strange story of that doll now sitting with the other Blackstone murder evidence."

"The doll?" asked Sinclair, sitting next to Baxter. "The one that looks like Beth?"

"The very same, sir. Tis an odd story, and I have yet to understand it. The doll is one reason why I am convinced that our male myopia is rather profound regarding our little duchess's life. Most especially since my lady often forgets troubling experiences. The duchess possesses a remarkable memory otherwise; yet, she often loses track of certain *disagreeable* passages in her life. This is one of them, I believe, for when I mentioned the doll's recovery to her yesterday, she denied possessing such a toy; yet, surely, you recall it Lord Aubrey?"

"Of course, I do. We called it the impossible doll."

"Why's that?" asked Sinclair.

"Because she received it as a christening gift at the age of one month old—yet, it is the very image of her as a girl."

Baxter sipped the wine thoughtfully. "Yet, there is more that's strange about it sir. The story begins with your departure, Lord Aubrey. May of '75. Just after Lord Kesson's birthday celebration."

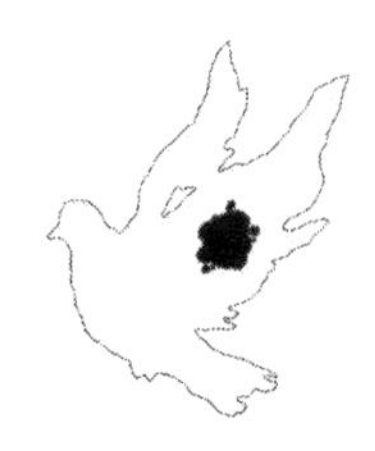

CHAPTER FORTY-FIVE

Baxter continued. "As a child, our little duchess, was often accused of having a vivid imagination. My lady's late mother refused to credit stories of spidery monsters and whispering voices, but it is my belief that the Duchess Elizabeth told only the truth. Now, this happened in May of '75. The year of the Egyptian Fête. Everyone in the family attended. Even your aunt, Lady Victoria, came from France. You will soon discover, Your Grace, that the fête is the singular event of the year to our village. It is the one time when the citizens may trod upon the Branham grounds as though each flower, bench, and stone belongs to them. For a week, no one is denied entrance, so long as they mean us no harm. That spring, however, our men missed an intruder. Though, how could we know?"

Charles had been listening attentively, the half-filled brandy snifter in his right hand. "It's hard to imagine the Branham men missing anything. Who was it?"

"That remains a mystery, my lord, but as I've pondered the puzzle these many years, it seems to me that the doll is involved."

"The doll?" asked the earl. "Beth's doll?"

"The same, sir. You'd only just left for Brussels. Twas due to an urgent telegram from Lord Derby, as I recall."

"Yes, the foreign secretary had a sticky problem in Antwerp that required an immediate remedy," the earl noted obliquely. "What happened in my absence?"

Baxter poured himself another half glass of the wine. "Perhaps, your absence was required, sir. If I may suggest it, my lords, these Redwing devils took advantage of your departure to reach our little duchess. Perhaps, *they* wanted you gone, sir."

"Whatever happened, Baxter?" asked the earl. "Beth's said nothing about that spring. Connor was home, and he mentioned nothing." Aubrey paused, his eyes searching about the room as though recovering a long-filed memory from his mind. "The faery copse. That's when Beth disappeared, and she was found in the woods! But, wait, someone else was here. Not only family but also neighbours. The Salters were staying at Branham, were they not?"

"Indeed, they were, my lord. Our delightful Lady Alexandrina Stuart was also here."

"The queen came then as well?" asked Charles.

"Her Majesty finds Branham a pleasant escape from the constant duties of the palace," answered the new inspector. "And she enjoys spending time with Duke James, of course."

"And Seth was here," Aubrey added. "I wonder if he was involved in the search that day?"

"The search for Beth, you mean?" asked Sinclair. "I've heard only vague references to this, Baxter. You told me some of the tale last month, but I'd no idea it happened during the fête. You say a stranger entered the grounds?"

"In a way, sir. Let me now tell the story in full. It began on a warm spring day, the fifteenth of May. In residence at the hall were Duke James, the late Lord Aubrey and his wife—your good parents, my lord," he said to Paul. "How I miss the late earl."

"As do we all, old friend," whispered Stuart. "My mother wasn't feeling well that spring, but she did come down. She remained indoors during most of it. I think Victoria kept her company. When did the Salters arrive?"

"The day you left, sir. The fourteenth," the great bear of a man continued, gazing at the empty wine glass. "Now, as I was saying, twas the fourth day of the fête. You'll experience it for yourself come May, Your Grace, but for an entire week, the lawns and gardens bustle with visitors. Tents and pavilions litter the grounds, each filled with all manner of attractions and games. There's a steam-driven carousel with painted horses and a calliope. Stilt-walkers, clowns, jugglers, and Punch and Judy shows."

"All those strangers?" asked Sinclair. "I'm not sure I like that."

"The circle have always been careful to conduct a thorough background investigation of all the merchants and other entertainers who're hired," Baxter explained. "Usually, all goes perfectly well, but that year one person was missed. A woman. She called herself Madam Corbeau. A gypsy sort, who claimed to foretell the future."

"How was this woman missed? And why would the family allow a fortune teller to erect a tent?" observed Sinclair.

"We did not, sir. The list of tents had no such person, nor had the tent even existed until that afternoon. It seemed to appear all on its own—as if it jumped up out of the grass!"

Charles felt that same electric charge that so often occurred when something important was about to happen.

"Her name again?"

"Madam Corbeau, my lord. Is that important?"

Paul groaned. "The name's another of these annoying riddles! Corbeau's French for raven, Charles."

"Yes, I'd deduced as much. Go on, Baxter."

A knock sounded, disturbing the hushed tale. "Am I too late?" asked a friendly voice as Kepelheim's silver head appeared in the doorway. The tailor entered quietly and took a seat opposite the duke. "Mr. Blinkmire is telling the story of the castle fire to everyone. Her Majesty's quite taken with Blinkmire and the others. Riga's promised to play a duet with Mr. Stanley as soon as the storytelling ends. I suspected our good Mr. Baxter might be offering a tale of his own and rushed back as soon as it seemed appropriate. Which story is it?"

"The fortune teller and the faery copse," Baxter told his friend. "As you were there as well, Mr. Kepelheim, perhaps, you can chime in as needed."

The cherubic tailor poured brandy for all, but Sinclair declined. "I have plans with my wife later, Martin. A clear head is required. Go on, Cornelius."

"Ah, yes. Well, as I said, the woman and her yellow tent seemed to rise up from out of the aether, and I noticed the little marchioness—as our lovely duchess was then called, of course—enter. I know she did so, for I remarked on it to Mrs. Alcorn. You may confirm that with Esther at a later time, should you wish. She and I had been conversing near the statuary park."

"Did the tent appear close to the maze?" asked Charles.

"At the very entrance to it, sir, which is another reason I took note. The layout of tents during the fête is according to a very strict plan, and nothing is to obstruct the entrance to the maze; yet here it was! A peaked tent of mustard yellow with red tassels hanging from each corner. Madam Corbeau's name was written in green lettering above the entrance and beneath were the words 'Your Future Awaits'. Now, when I saw the little marchioness enter, I immediately set aside the basket of toy prizes in my hand and made for the tent."

Kepelheim laughed. "You always did win at the games, Mr. Baxter!"

"I'd had a rather good day, Mr. Kepelheim. Clean sweeps of many of the booths. As I said, I gave the basket to Esther and signalled to Clark as I walked towards this mongrel tent. Edwin had been keeping watch on the area as part of Lord Kesson's regular guard, you see. All staff are given three days off during the fête, but a rota assures each position is filled at all times. It was Clark's turn at day watch. You might speak with him as well, Your Grace, for our later conversations indicated he'd seen no tent until I motioned to him. Clark has very sharp eyes, and if a tent had stood there earlier, then he'd have seen it."

"Was this a ghost tent?" asked Aubrey.

"So it would seem, but the little marchioness—duchess now, of course—she saw it plainly and entered." Baxter gulped two swallows and set down the glass. "Thirsty work, these tales. Now, sirs, we arrive at the greatest aspect to the mystery. When I entered the tent, the little marchioness was nowhere to be found. Neither was any woman. The tent was empty as air."

"You found nothing at all?" asked Aubrey.

"A table and some playing cards."

Another surge of electricity ran along Sinclair's hands. "Describe these cards."

"The usual fortune teller's cards, sir. I gave them to Lord Kesson. Did you see them Mr. Kepelheim?"

"Briefly," admitted the tailor. "Tarot cards of a sort, but not the Marseilles cards."

"Which Tarot cards? All or just certain ones?" asked Charles.

"There were only three as I remember," Baxter told them. "One had a picture of a knight, another of a king, the third of a woman holding two children. The illustrations were quite detailed and appeared old, the cards being handmade."

"Yes, they were ragged and creased, as though carried in a pocket for years," said the tailor. "Connor kept them, I believe. Usually, items like that are stored in the circle archive, but if so, then I've failed to catalog them."

"Is this when the search for Beth began?" asked Charles, suddenly worrying about his wife in the present day.

"It was, my lord," replied Baxter. "Lord Kesson formed up a search party, and everyone helped, even the women. Hours passed, but as the sun began to set along the trees, we saw her at last! I tell you, everyone had looked in those woods, yet here she was, running towards us as quickly as her small feet could carry her. And when my lady reached her father's arms, she had a very strange story to tell. Her limbs were like ice, and her cheeks cold as though she'd walked through drifts of snow. And she carried that doll, which surprised us all. Our dear one never liked the toy, you see. She complained of hearing it speak to her at night, and that it moved of its own accord. Lord Kesson had it removed to the attics several times, but it always reappeared. That evil doll gives me chills, sirs. It is an accursed thing, and when Lord Kesson saw it that day, he looked as though he might faint!"

"Why?" asked the earl.

"Because he'd taken it to India and thrown it into the sea!"

Everyone stared at the former butler. "Are you certain it was the same doll?" asked Haimsbury.

"Quite certain. The shoes are engraved E. Anjou. This doll had the same engraving."

"When did the earl dispose of it?" asked the tailor.

"During his most recent posting. Early '74. He told only me about the plans, and I informed the little marchioness that her dolly had gone missing. She appeared quite relieved, actually. When she returned with it that day, both his lordship and I were aghast."

"How did Beth explain it?" asked Stuart.

"We dared not ask, sir. As I said, she appeared to be suffering from exposure to intense cold. She did say that a nice man named Hal had helped her find the way home. He'd taught her to recite a psalm for comfort."

"Hal?" asked Sinclair, for he knew Henry MacAlpin's tale of rescuing the duchess from the Stone King and his dragon. "Might she have meant *Henry?*"

"She said Hal, sir. And the doll showed no sign of injury. In fact, it seemed pristine, as if newly made. Lord Kesson took the doll from her, and he and I examined it whilst his daughter slept, for she was exhausted. We discovered a small bag attached to its dress, which had not been there previously. The bag contained tiny bones, inscribed with runes of some sort. I wrote the figures down in my diary from that day, and still have it, if you're interested. Lord Kesson ordered me to say nothing, and he took the doll away and burnt it."

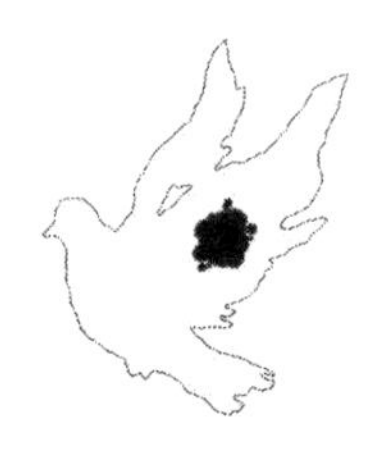

CHAPTER FORTY-SIX

Completely unaware of the peculiar revelation, Henry MacAlpin had just left Cordelia Wychwright's chamber and was heading towards the Plantagenet Suite to pay one final visit to the hall's other patient, Seth Holloway. The viscount had an odd sensation as he passed through the upper gallery, his progress watched by the painted eyes of so many long-dead peers. Upon reaching the turning for the east wing, he met Ada MacKenzie, who curtsied politely. She carried an armload of monogrammed cotton towels, trimmed in delicate silk fringe.

"How's Lady Cordelia, sir?" asked the maid.

"Doing better. She ate a little supper and then returned to a deep sleep. I doubt she'll awaken before morning. Did you find anything for her to wear, Ada?"

"The duchess provided clothing to last for several days, my lord. Blouses, skirts, dressing gowns, and all the 'delicates' a lady might need."

"Ah, *those*," laughed the viscount. "I'm not supposed to know about them, of course, but being a doctor, I've seen my share. Is Mrs. Alcorn with our other patient?"

"She is, sir. Dr. Holloway's right handsome."

"Is he? I wouldn't be the one to ask on that. Tell me, has he awoken?"

"Not really, sir. It's more like he's mutterin' in a dream. Excuse me, sir. I promised to stock the linen cupboard in the master bath before my lord and lady come up. A good evenin' to you, sir."

Henry continued on, finally arriving at a large suite of rooms, decorated in shades of pale blue and cream. As he entered the primary bedchamber, he noticed Holloway moving haphazardly as though trying to throw off the quilts. His eyes were open. Alcorn had gone, and the room lay in semi-darkness.

"Here now, you mustn't do that!" exclaimed MacAlpin. "Dr. Price and I've worked very hard to stitch your wounds. We'd prefer you didn't tear them open."

"Who are you?" the patient asked, huskily. "Where am I?"

"Two questions at once. That's an encouraging sign. I'm Henry," replied the viscount cheerfully. "And I'm your doctor. I hadn't expected to find you awake, actually."

"I was dreaming," he answered slowly.

"A distressing dream or pleasant?"

"Unusual," replied Holloway. "Where am I?"

"The east wing of Branham Hall. Are you in pain?"

He nodded. "My chest's on fire, if that makes sense. And my head pounds. Am I still dreaming?"

"I rather doubt it, unless I'm sharing the dream with you." He took Seth's pulse and examined his eyes. "I'm surprised to find you talking with such an injury. May I listen to your heart? I promise to take care with your bandages."

Henry pulled back the velvet quilts. To make medical attention easier, the patient wore a pair of Haimsbury's pyjama bottoms with no shirt. A bandage ran round his left shoulder and then came forward to cover most of the chest and stomach, wrapping round his back and waist. He looked like a modified mummy. Stains of brownish red mixed with a brighter crimson stained the area just below the right ribcage.

"You're bleeding again, Dr. Holloway. Let's pray you've not torn any stitches. I'll have a look and then change the bandage." He placed the stethoscope against his patient's chest and listened carefully. "It's still irregular. Any headaches?"

Seth nodded. "Like a blacksmith is pounding out a wheel rim behind my eyes."

Henry used the bedside lamp to shine light into the other man's pupils. "Look to your left and right, but without turning your head, please." As he glanced left, Seth cried out in pain. "So sorry. Your responses indicate a possible fracture to the left orbital rim. Whoever struck you there just missed taking out the eye. You're a lucky man."

"I hardly feel lucky. How long have I been here?"

"A couple of days. I'm told you and the duchess are friends. She's quite worried about you."

"Beth is here? Now?" Seth asked, his neck and facial muscles tensing as he tried to sit up.

"Please, Dr. Holloway, you must lie down! You've plenty time to speak with Elizabeth. Your injuries will take many weeks to heal. There's plenty time for a visit. You mentioned an unusual dream. Might I ask the content?"

"Does it matter?"

Henry smiled as he returned the stethoscope to his bag. "Not to all, but I find dreams informative to the mind's health. That's my area. Nervous conditions and the brain."

"You're an alienist?"

"Yes, but also a competent surgeon. Your dream?"

Seth wiped his eyes, the small movement painful. "I was teaching at Trinity. It was springtime, and one of the younger men had asked me to solve a puzzle."

Henry drew a chair nearby, alert for any dream elements that might reveal more about Holloway's mental state—particularly those that spoke of guilt. It was still possible that Holloway had murdered Peter Patterson.

"Is that so unusual? Students often present their dons with puzzles."

"Yes, but not like this. It was like nothing I'd ever seen. A totally unique language."

"A language?" mused Henry. "Ah, yes, that's right! You're the ancient languages expert. Dreams are often our way to work through real life puzzles. Did you recognise the student in this dream?"

"No. He was a stranger."

"This puzzle he gave you. Did you solve it?"

"I don't think so," answered Seth. "The student said he'd discovered the writing on an old standing stone near the Grantchester Meadows. He used a pencil and paper to make a rubbing, which he showed to me."

"Do you remember any of the symbols?" asked the physician.

"Some. They were like a combination of Egyptian and Akkadian. Only with stylised animal figures tossed in for good measure. If someone hit me in the head, no doubt, my brain is confused."

The door opened, and a tall woman entered. Seth tried to sit up, for he recognised her at once. "Dolly? Is that you?"

Patterson-Smythe took a chair close to the bed. "Yes, it's your old friend, Dolly," she said, kissing his hand. "Mrs. Alcorn thought you might need company whilst she helps elsewhere in the house. I didn't intend to interrupt. I wasn't aware Henry would be tending to you. Should I leave?"

"Not unless Seth wishes it," answered Salperton.

"Are you in pain, dear?" she asked, holding the patient's hand.

"Only a little," he lied. "I'm told Beth is here. Is she nearby?"

"She's downstairs, listening to music. You remember how Christmases are at the hall, darling. Dickie's round here as well, somewhere. I'm forever losing track of my husband; though, I think he and James are talking politics in one of the smoking rooms. Shall I fetch you a glass of water?"

"No, thank you," he whispered huskily. "You and Richard are visiting for Christmas?"

"Yes. Darling, do you remember anything? How you arrived here? Or what happened before?"

He shook his head. "Nothing. What happened to me? How did I get here?"

"May I tell him, Henry?"

"Yes, but let's not overdo, all right? If you have a strong stomach, I can change these bandages whilst you talk."

This made Dolly laugh. "Oh, Henry, you're so sweet! But you needn't fear. My stomach's hard as iron. I can help, if you need an extra pair of hands."

The viscount cut through the outermost layers to reach a thick pad of folded cotton wadding. Beneath, he could see two stiches had pulled apart. "Could you hand me that medical bag, Dolly?"

She did so, and Henry used a lantern to examine the wound again. A faint glimmer caught his eye. Using tweezers, he removed two slivers of rib from the area. He held them up to the others. "I believe this may be what dislodged Dr. Price's stitches. You've cracked a rib, Dr. Holloway, and these chipped away. They might have travelled and caused blood vessel damage if gone unnoticed. I'll need to re-examine the entire area to make sure there aren't any more. I'm afraid, this will hurt."

It took ten, agonising minutes of probing, but Henry finally declared the wound clear of debris. He'd recovered six additional bits of bone in the long wound, and laid them out on a cloth beside the bed. "You all right?"

Holloway nodded. "All in a day's work for professors. How did I get here?"

"Paul found you," Salperton answered whilst closing the wound.

"Aubrey?"

"Yes," Dolly answered. "In some sort of cavern near that God-forsaken abbey. You've been unconscious ever since. Beth's been in several times since to keep you company. She's very worried."

"Elizabeth," he whispered. "And she's downstairs?"

"Yes, dear. It's nearly Christmas, you see. The twenty-third."

The viscount swallowed hard. "Do you think she'd come up now? I need to speak to her."

"I don't know. Henry, is it all right?"

"Yes, but only for a short visit."

"Of course," Dolly answered, kissing Seth's forehead and leaving the room.

"You're remembering something," Henry said.

"Perhaps," Seth answered.

He tried to recall the symbols within the odd dream. A dread shook its way through his bones, whispering of evils to come. Holloway had faced many such terrors in Assyria and Egypt, but this one felt different. Older. Stronger.

Much more malevolent.

He shut his eyes, praying silently to the Lord—something that would soon become a habit for the newborn believer.

"Do you go to church?" he asked Salperton.

"When I can," the alienist answered. "I sometimes have to tend patients on Sunday morning, but we have services at my sanitorium. Montmore, it's called. Are you a religious man?"

"I didn't used to be, but all that's changed. I need to talk to Beth. Something's coming, Henry. Something darker than night itself, and it's got its eyes on her."

CHAPTER FORTY-SEVEN

Midnight – Cordelia's private drawing room

James Stuart was ordinarily jovial and pleasant, but the Scot could be a dangerous man when crossed. His enemies seldom saw him angry, for the duke had learnt to hide his emotions well in his sixty-nine years. Usually, he placed matters into the Almighty's hands, but when his loved ones were threatened—or worse, a helpless woman fell victim to the cruelty of a man—then his ire knew no bounds. Payback, according to Drummond, came slowly, inexorably, and it hit the perpetrator where it would hurt the most. In William Wychwright's case: his pride, his position, and his bank account.

"Delia wasn't able to recount the crime in clear detail," he told his nephews, "but in my book, she suffered assault and attempted rape. I want those men to pay, Charles. Is there any way we can prosecute without Delia's testimony? She's fragile enough without having a court judge ask difficult questions. The experience would shatter her into a thousand pieces, I think."

"Who dared to did this?" asked Aubrey. "What's his name, and where do I find him? I'll see he pays for daring to harm that girl, if it's my last act on earth!"

"We will not respond with violence," Charles told the others. "Let the law do its work. And if the law fails, then there are subtler ways to skin this serpent. Open violence will only put you in the dock, Paul."

"I don't care. And I've yet to hear a name," muttered Aubrey, picturing the broken young woman lying beyond the connecting door. "You say it was William's friend? Which? The man hasn't many friends. Was it Treversham or Brandt?"

"It was the baronet, from what I've discerned, but I believe Brandt may have served a supporting role, for Delia's mentioned him as well," Henry interjected. "She keeps repeating the word 'money' over and over. 'I don't want the money'. I've no idea what she means by that, James. Do you?"

"Her father left Cordelia a sizable inheritance," Drummond explained. "William wants access to it."

"Oh, I see," replied Salperton. "Actually, the reason is unimportant as far as Cordelia's concerned, though it's likely she'll fixate on it and try to use that as a means to escape her torment. I've worked with rape cases before, gentlemen, and they fracture a woman's mind and heart as nothing else. It will be a very long time before she heals—if at all. What are your plans? Do you intend to keep her here?"

"That's what we have to discuss," the Scotsman answered.

"I will not have her go back there, James!" Paul shouted, standing to pace. "If it's money they want, then I'll pay it. I don't care how much. Let them name their price and give her up!"

Charles glanced at his cousin. "Paul, what do you mean? Are you implying you'd *buy* her from Wychwright?"

"If that's what it takes."

Sinclair turned thoughtful. "Must it be so crude an exchange? Here's the way the law sees it. Until Cordelia is eighteen, she must receive her guardian's permission to marry. Legally, William may claim guardianship. If she's inherited money of her own, then he'll want to control it, which means controlling her and any husband she might marry. This makes Paul an obstacle to that control."

The earl sat down once more, leaning forward. "Go on."

Henry interrupted. "Charles, you cannot be suggesting what I think! Surely, not."

"Paul, do you care enough for Cordelia to marry her?" asked the younger duke. "Not only as a friend, but as a man. Someone who wants to build a life with her?"

The earl's countenance performed a series of subtle movements, as though his mind were clearing successive hurdles and internal objections. "If a desire to protect and cherish her is love, then the answer is yes. I'm willing to make her my wife."

Salperton interrupted again. "See here, Paul, if you do this, you must understand you're marrying a broken woman who might never be mended! She'll likely suffer from a deep and abiding fear of intimacy, if you must know. Can you live with that?"

"Yes," he whispered. "She turns eighteen tomorrow, which means she can marry without her family's permission."

Drummond reached for his nephew's hand. "Son, you needn't do this. Let me marry her. If Henry's right, and Delia has no wish for intimacy, it makes no difference to me. I don't need an heir, for I've got Charles and you—and soon, Beth's son. I could keep her safe without causing her mind any further dismay."

Paul shook his head. "No, James, I want to do this. If honest love and God's time can offer healing and hope, then I want to give her that. I'm content to wait as long as she needs—forever, if it comes to that. In truth, I've no need for an heir either. Charles can assume the title if anything happens to me. And I know he'll always take care of Adele. So then, how do we go about this? I'll not tip my hand to Wychwright, which means we cannot publish banns at their church."

The duke sighed. "Very well, if you're sure."

"I've never been more certain of anything."

"Then, there is a way, but it means a trip to Canterbury. The archbishop approved Beth's marriage to Charles without banns, despite their both being Presbyterian. I think he did it to impress us, if truth be told; but once he hears the queen will attend the ceremony, Benson will run here if he must!"

"Then, it's settled," Paul declared. "If we're to do this, it must be soon, before Wychwright catches wind of our plans. She's eighteen tomorrow. If she'll have me, then that's when we'll marry."

Henry sighed. "I cannot say I approve, but I'm outvoted, it seems. Let me assess her condition tomorrow, and if she's up to it—and *only* if she is—then, I'll do all I can to help. The only other consideration for you, Paul, is how to tell your sister, or rather your daughter, of course, which is another issue entirely."

"And I have to tell Beth," the earl whispered, suddenly weighed down with regret. "I'll do so tomorrow. Tonight, I plan to stay with Delia and pray."

Long after the others left, Aubrey remained, staring into the drawing room's pleasant fire. He'd made many memories with Elizabeth over the years—most of them wonderful, a few filled with danger and dread. How could he marry another woman here—at Branham, her childhood home? Would Beth understand, or would he lose her forever?

With his mind thus occupied, he'd not heard the knock.

A sliver of light cast in from the corridor as the door softly opened and closed again. "Am I disturbing you?"

He sat upright, surprised to see her; yet a visit from Elizabeth at that moment felt like a gift from God—and an answer to prayer.

"You're never a disturbance, Princess," he answered in a whisper. "But we should keep our voices low. Delia's sleeping."

Beth joined him near the warm fire. "I hope I'm not disturbing you. Charles has fallen asleep, and I kept thinking of you. You've been distracted lately, Paul. Are you all right?" she asked.

She'd not enquired about Wychwright first, but about him. Somehow, her constant loyalty only caused the earl more anguish.

"You needn't worry about me, Princess," he said, taking her hand. "I've been short on sleep, but then when am I not?"

"Are you unable to sleep or unwilling?"

"How well you know me," he said, kissing her hand. "Did Charles talk to you about our plans?"

"No, should he have? I assume it has something to so with Cordelia. Grandfather's angrier than I've ever seen him about all this. He, Martin, and Henry are still talking downstairs. I overheard Kay mention a train to Canterbury in the morning. Is it because of this missing student? Lionel Wentworth? Paul, do you think he murdered Mr. Patterson and Colonel Collinwood?"

"We've no way to know, darling, but it's possible. It's all a bit of a mess, isn't it? Poor Drina must wish she'd stayed in London."

Beth smiled as she snuggled in close. "Actually, she says it's the most interesting trip yet, and that she looks forward to tomorrow's events. I rather hoped for peace and quiet, but so long as everyone's safe and well. You are well, aren't you?"

"Perfectly well, now that you're here. I'm glad you came to see me. You and I used to talk into the wee hours, didn't we, Princess?"

She laid her head against his shoulder. "We've made hundreds of memories in this house. Not all pleasant, but most of them are. I remember one Christmas when you took me on your lap and told me that story of when you were a boy."

"Which story is that?"

"You remember. The one about the boy who'd run and leap across the fells, but his mother made him stop to come wait for a baby."

He laughed, gripping her hand tightly. "Ah, yes! I remember. Shall I tell it to you again?"

"I'd like that. Shall I pretend to be six?" she asked him.

"I prefer you this age," he admitted. "Let me see if I can recall how it goes. Oh yes."

He cleared his throat and she shut her eyes, listening to the earl's lilting voice.

"Once upon a time in Scotland, there lived a rambunctious youth who spent all his days climbing rocks and swimming in brooks. He rarely looked at books, but wasted hour upon hour, rushing towards disaster as if only adventure could satisfy. The youth's mother worried that he'd spend his entire life in such a careless manner, and one day, she called him into her sitting room and told him of a new responsibility. The boy's cousin was about to become a father, you see, and so the boy must travel to his uncle's castle, to be there when the baby was born."

Beth laughed, opening her eyes slightly to glance up at his face. "I imagine this boy went to Drummond Castle?"

"He did indeed, my lady. How did you know?" he teased as she pulled close against his chest. "Well, the boy thought his mother's command all very annoying, of course, for the weather had grown warm in preparation for spring, and he had dozens of swift brooks to swim and a hundred cliffs to climb. Still, he loved his mother very much and couldn't disappoint her."

"He was a sweet boy, I think," she whispered. "And rather handsome as well."

"You mustn't interrupt a storyteller," he told her. "And he may have been somewhat handsome, in a Scottish sort of way. Now, the trip was a very long one, especially for so impatient a youth. After leaving the castle in his father's fancy coach, the boy then boarded a train, and then another train, and finally another coach. In all, he spent over twelve hours contemplating the brooks and hills as they passed by his window, wishing he could escape and run free. At long last, just as the sun was setting, he arrived at his uncle's castle. The boy lived in a castle of his own, of course, but his was very old and very drafty. His uncle's castle was much newer and very nice. Only two centuries old, instead of six."

"And no trees growing in the towers," Beth interrupted.

"Nary a one. His uncle's castle sat farther south, and the springtime flower buds had begun to open, and foxes raced upon the heathered moors. There was a small lake nearby and steep fells that needed a boy to climb them. However, when the boy arrived, the uncle's son, who was also the boy's first cousin, announced that this new baby—the centre of all the attention—was about to be born."

"A new baby who would grow to love and adore the boy, I shouldn't wonder," she said as he placed an arm round her shoulders.

"Yes. Though the lonely boy didn't know this new baby would offer him so much love."

"Was he lonely?" she asked, touching his hair.

"Very, though he didn't yet know it. Only when his life found completion, did he realise how empty it had been before." He kissed her forehead. "But that realisation wasn't to happen quite yet. The special baby's imminent arrival had sent everyone in the castle into a whir of activity. There were nurses and midwives and lots and lots of doctors crowding the upper floors of the castle, each of them arguing how best to care for the expectant mother, and whether or not this method or that method was most useful. None of it interested the Scottish boy. He just wanted to get it all over, so he could run in the meadows and chase after sunbeams. So the poor boy lay upon his bed, night after night, waiting for the sound of a baby's cry, but four days passed and then five, without even one hint of the newborn's arrival. The mother, as it turned out, had gone into something the quibbling doctors and midwives called false labour. This was in late March, and a week passed, and then a second, and the boy began to doubt the expectant mother had any plans at all to bring this new baby into the world. He wondered if everyone had gotten it wrong."

"And did this boy decide to give up and go home?" she asked. "He can be rather impatient at times."

Paul laughed, kissing her fingertips. "The somewhat impatient boy considered it, but his father and mother had arrived by then, and they assured him such a wait wasn't all that unusual. The boy pondered this revelation, wondering how it would be, when he became a father. How his wife might make him wait and wait and wait some more. He even began to worry about it, you see. He feared the new baby might be having trouble getting out."

"Perhaps, she was shy," Elizabeth suggested with a soft smile.

"She was hardly shy!" he laughed. "No, this baby was remarkably garrulous and highly intelligent—and very beautiful, I might add. This child knew the perfect day was coming, but she'd decided to make the boy wait."

"The poor boy! Of course, he was very kind and sweet and exceedingly handsome. Why would she make such a lovely boy wait?"

"I cannot answer that," he said seriously. "Perhaps, God had chosen the precisely correct moment, and the boy was simply too thick to realise it."

"The boy isn't thick at all," she told him. "I think he's brilliant."

"I'm very glad you think so," he answered. "But seriously, Beth, when you were at long last born, and I saw your sweet face, I thought my heart had stopped beating. Honestly, it felt as though my chest grew completely empty. And then, when Father placed you into my arms, it began to beat again."

Suddenly, Beth noticed how very quiet the room was, with only the soft ticking of a grandfather clock to remind them of reality. She sensed how important this moment was to them both, as though they had reached a crossroads in their lives. Despite her great love for Charles, it would be difficult to release Paul to another woman; yet she must. The boy who waited deserved all the happiness God had in store, and she had no right to prevent it.

"Do you love her?" she asked at last.

"Love whom?" he whispered, his arm still cradling her shoulders.

"Cordelia."

He removed the arm, looking intently into her eyes. "Honestly? I don't know. Perhaps. Beth, that day in Scotland, I vowed to protect you; to love and adore you for all the days of my life. The very idea of loving another is foreign to my heart."

"Darling Paul, I've watched you with her; seen the tenderness and gentleness in your manner. You are not breaking a vow by loving her. Trust in God to hold our hearts together in friendship, and he will! No matter what, I will love you for all my life, darling Cousin. All my life."

"Even if I marry another?"

"Even then," she whispered, kissing his hand. "It's been on your mind, hasn't it? These past few days."

All the tension in his muscles, all the worry in his heart and mind—*in his very bones*—fell away, and he began to weep. She held him close, stroking his long hair soothingly.

"Today marks a new start for us. Tell me how I can help, and I'll do it."

"Just love me," he whispered.

"That, my darling friend, is easy."

"I do love you, Beth," he whispered. "Ever and always."

"I know my darling knight; I know. And I love you, Lord Aubrey. Ever and always."

She began to hum softly: an old Scottish air that sang of meadows and fens and ancient castles. By half past one, he'd fallen asleep in her arms. She eased him onto the sofa, spread a quilt across his body, and quietly left.

Tomorrow, would be a new day.

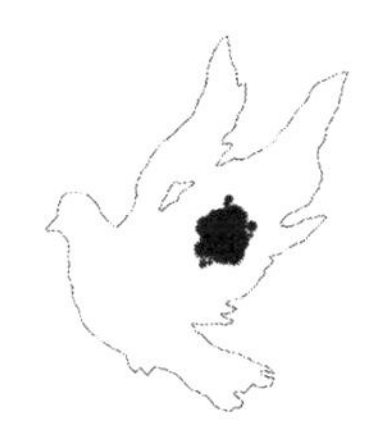

CHAPTER FORTY-EIGHT

Monday, 24th December, 1888 - Charles Sinclair's Journal

It is just after seven, and dawn lies upon the horizon. As I sit in Connor Stuart's former study, I marvel at the turnings my life has taken. This is a magnificent room, sitting just off the duke's bedchamber (it is still strange to call myself a duke). The arrangement of the master apartment is logical and spacious. At Haimsbury, my study is somewhat small and sits twixt the parlour and my bedchamber, but here, the study is actually the grandest room in the entire apartment. Baxter explained that this was once a drawing room, but Patricia preferred using the smaller parlour, and Connor converted this to a study shortly after he and Patricia wed. We are on the northwest corner of the house, and this room faces west. In the afternoons, it's bathed in warming sunlight streaming through four, very tall French doors. There is a balcony beyond, which oversits the west wing portico, making it strong enough and large enough to hold a great many people. There are ironwork tables and chairs aplenty, all covered in canvas presently, but come the spring, I shall enjoy coffee out there in the mornings and write in this journal whilst watching a sea of graceful flowers and fruit trees bloom with radiant colour.

My dearest, sweetest flower is Elizabeth, of course. Most of us talked long into the night, but I had some time with her before retiring. Sometime around two, Beth slipped away for a little while, and when she returned, she thought me asleep, but I'd only just switched off the lamp. She'd been talking with the earl (as I assumed), and I held her as she shared her heart. Paul will always be her dearest love after me; this I know. I try to recall Kepelheim's wise words whenever my thoughts turn towards doubt: that Elizabeth requires both of us—Paul and me—to serve as protectors. God has given me great peace in this, for no woman could be a better wife. Somehow, this has brought us even closer.

Despite the short night, that same dear woman has already gone downstairs. 'It is Christmas Eve!' she told me as she dressed. 'And there's much to do!'

At the hall, Christmas Eve is traditionally a day of fellowship and food (so I'm told); a constant celebration, ending with church services in the grand gallery, with all the family, guests, and servants attending. Canon Edgar Greves is the vicar of the village church, which is Anglican, but he will be joined by Dr. MacPherson (arriving today), who'll represent our Scottish Presbyterian faith. A few of the villagers practise the Catholic religion. Beth explained that these worship in either Anjou-on-Sea or at Hampton.

Now, let me recount the events of the past few days. Beth reminded me this morning that the purpose of this activity is to allow my thoughts to coalesce upon a paper medium. In a way, it's similar to the way Bob Morehouse (may he rest in peace) taught me to organise evidence and theories about a crime. Then, we used a blackboard to make lists and see how they connect; but now I use pen and paper.

1. Three men disappeared into the tunnels beneath Lion Hall sometime after 11:30 a.m. on the nineteenth.

2. One man, Peter Patterson, was found dead near a rail shed. His body showed signs of torture and a complete loss of blood. Price believes he was killed elsewhere.

3. Later that day, a second man, Dr. Seth Holloway, was rescued from that hellish chamber beneath St. Arilda's Abbey. Holloway is severely injured and being treated by Henry MacAlpin here at Branham.

4. The third student, Lionel Wentworth, is still missing, presumed to have boarded a steamer at Dover (per three witnesses).

5. Colonel Sir Alfred Collinwood, who had promised to reveal important information about Blackstone Exploration Society's major 'find', was found dead in his host's root cellar. The obsidian covered coffin he intended to show me is missing. I've assigned the case to Galton and Risling. We plan to meet later today.

7. George Price promised to provide detailed autopsy reports on Collinwood and Patterson by Boxing Day.

8. Though it is probably unrelated to items 1-7, Cordelia Wychwright was assaulted in London, probably by her brother's friend—and possibly even her brother. Cordelia's account is disjointed and difficult to follow. I've wired Arthur France, offering him the full authority of the Intelligence Branch to investigate the charges but to make no arrests at present.

9. I've now received three letters from Lorena MacKey. All are brief but heartfelt. She assures me of her welfare, saying Anatole has provided shelter in another city. In this last, she mentioned concern for Margaret Hansen, the keeper of The Empress Hotel. I've written to Meg and asked her to contact me.

10. Supt. Fisher from T-Division wired that a woman has escaped from Montmore Asylum. When I mentioned it to Henry, he sent his own telegram to Dr. Hepplewhite, who replied that the woman is Violet Stuart. I've ordered all London ICI agents to begin a city-wide search for her. I pray the Lord looks after all the women on this list, and extend to them His tender mercies.

Now to ACTIONS that must occur in the next few days:

1. Look through all Beth's correspondence with Blackstone. Paul has given his account of the three meetings he attended in August, and I'll speak with Seth Holloway regarding his dealings with the group as soon as he's able.

2. Interview the families of the Cambridge men.

3. Interview the three Oxford men. It's possible one of them is the murderer, though Collinwood claimed all three were with him at Castle Anjou until long after nightfall on the nineteenth.

4. Speak with Reid when he arrives here later today. And with Abberline after I return Drina to London on Thursday. Not only regarding Blackstone, but also the dockside fire and other open investigations: Victoria Park murders, the Redwing murders (Hemsfield, Andrews, and possibly Wychwright), the so-called 'vampire' attacks on women and children, and the Embankment

murders. Whilst in Whitechapel, I'll call on Margaret Hansen. And I will follow-up on this Violet Stuart person. I begin to suspect she has something to do with all of this.

5. I plan to confront Raziel Grigor in his new offices on Wormwood. Baxter's right. We REACT rather than ACT. It's time we anticipate the movements of these creatures, which requires learning how they think. I shall interview him as I would any human suspect.

6. And, of course, I must protect Elizabeth and Adele. Anatole warned me that Christmastide is a time when the fallen realm play tricks upon the world of men; therefore, I'll try to keep Beth indoors, where it is easier to keep an eye on her. We've had nearly ten inches of snow, which should help in that effort. I see it as the Lord's protective blanket.

James left for Canterbury this morning. Cordelia turns eighteen today, and he hopes to persuade His Grace, Archbishop Edward Benson to allow Paul to marry her as soon as possible without publishing the required banns. Paul plans to propose to her this morning. I pray this is the right decision for them both.

I discussed the match with Drina last night. I'm discovering that my 'aunt' is wise beyond all imagining, and she bypasses the usual governmental rhetoric and ramblings and slices to the bone of a matter.

"A Christmas wedding would be marvelous, my dear!" she told me. Then she asked Baxter for pen and paper to compose a letter to the archbishop, asking that he allow the wedding, but also explaining that she planned to attend—incognito. Would he come to Branham to officiate?

Canterbury is nearby, but surely Christmas Eve is a very busy time for His Grace. Despite that, James is confident of a positive reply and has taken Paul's 'Scottish Knight' train to hand-deliver Drina's message. Elizabeth has asked Alcorn to prepare the upper gallery to host a family wedding service—just in case.

May God Almighty protect us all during this season!

CHAPTER FORTY-NINE

10:18 am – 24th December

"If you could slow the tempo a little at the fourth measure, Mr. Stanley, I should be most grateful," Viktor Riga suggested to the former policeman. "Alas, my arthritic fingers are not what they once were."

Elbert Stanley made a pencil notation on the sheet music. "Like this?" he asked, playing through the section in a languid *largo* tempo. "Or do you prefer it slower still?"

Riga sat in a hard-backed chair near the piano, his twisted spine braced by a small pillow. He wore a black frock coat and matching trousers accented with a bright red waistcoat; his beloved cello resting twixt his knees. He held a bow in his right hand, with his left upon the instrument's fingerboard.

"I'm not sure," he replied. "Lady Adele, what do you think? Should we slow the passage a little more? We aren't rushing, are we?"

Della sat with Blinkmire and Joseph Merrick on a camel-back sofa, enjoying cider and teacakes. The girl swallowed a bite of brandied orange cake before replying.

"I prefer the slower tempo actually, Uncle Viktor. Don't you, Mr. Merrick?"

Joseph sat alone in a wingback chair, a plump pillow behind his overly large head. He was still somewhat weary from the rail journey, but enjoyed being part of this loving and large fellowship and therefore hated to sleep late.

"It is one of the most beautiful songs I've ever heard," he wheezed; the words muffled by bulbous tumours round his deformed lips. "Lady Della must play for us, too, though. I've heard very good reports of her talent from the duchess."

"Oh yes!" Blinkmire insisted, clapping his large hands like a child. "I think it's time our young friend gives us a preview of what she'll play for us this evening. Music, music, and more music! Truly, I've never enjoyed myself so much in all my life. This home's entertainments are without equal. Not only music, but books! Mr. Merrick, have you seen the main library? Why, there must be ten thousand volumes, covering every subject one can imagine! Truly, I could remain here for the rest of my life, if God so willed it."

Adele poured Merrick a second cup of tea. "Books are like paper windows into other worlds, aren't they, Uncle Stephen?" she asked the Irish giant.

"Oh, my yes! Paper windows! I do like that, Lady Della. I admit to taking several dozen of those literary windows to my room last night and reading until dawn. But with so many things to occupy our time, sleep must wait for less busy days. Mustn't it, Viktor?"

"At my age, I sleep very little. A few hours suffices."

An elderly woman entered the room upon the arm of Henry MacAlpin. All the men stood, and even Merrick made the attempt, but the lady rebuked him.

"No, no, my dear Joseph, you mustn't rise on my account. I simply won't hear of it. Please, stay seated," Lady Stuart insisted.

Lord Salperton eased the disguised queen into an upholstered chair and offered a selection of pillows. "I see thick ones and thick ones, Auntie Drina. Which do you prefer?"

"The little yellow one with the bluebirds, I think. I've always loved bluebirds. So cheerful and bright! Now, let us all enjoy the comfort of these lovely chairs, shall we?"

The men returned to their seats, and Adele brought the queen a cup of tea. "Here you are, Auntie Drina. Three sugars, just the way you like it. Milk?"

"Not this morning, dear. I wonder, Henry, would you bring me that needlepoint footstool near the fireplace? My gout begins to complain. I shall have to ask Mrs. Alcorn for a cup of bicarbonate to add to my bath. Soaking the foot eases the swelling, you know. I should have done so last night, but James and I talked until nearly three."

"I can offer you a liniment that often proves effective. I haven't a bottle prepared, but I have the ingredients with me," the viscount told her. "Oh, good morning, Mr. Anderson," he said as the former

'Mr. Thirteen' joined them. "You're looking much better this morning. Did you sleep well?"

"Moderately well, sir," Anderson replied. "The room I share with Mr. Stanley faces north and has heavy draping, which restricts the chance of light intrusion."

The queen found this comment strange. "Why do you avoid the light, Mr. Stanley? Are your eyes sensitive?"

"My entire body used to be troubled by natural light, my lady, and I wish never to experience it again. It's kind of you to ask."

Victoria Stuart joined the growing group, dressed for outdoor activities. She'd chosen dark trousers, paired with a yellow blouse and brown waistcoat, and her salt-and-pepper hair was bound into a chignon. Dolly Patterson-Smythe arrived with the Scotswoman, also dressed for riding. Behind the two women, followed a troupe of friendly dogs. Bella, Briar, Samson, and Dumpling scampered into the room, greeting each of the humans in turn. Dumpling sniffed at the music room's small Christmas tree, examining the lowest ornaments. Adele's new puppy lay in a basket near the fire, apparently dreaming, for her tiny legs twitched beneath the tartan blanket. Dumpling noticed the movement and decided to sniff at the puppy, causing it to stir.

"Come now, Dumpling," called the queen. "No more of that. You must leave Della's little doggy alone." The animal nimbly leapt onto Lady Stuart's lap. "Good dog," she told the animal, petting her perky ears.

The mantle's anniversary clock chimed the hour, and Henry turned to Patterson-Smythe. "Eleven already? How this day is flying past!"

"How's Seth this morning, Henry?" asked Dolly as she spread jam on a bit of cracker.

"Improving. The gash across his chest will take many weeks to heal, but he has a strong constitution and a fierce determination. Baxter mentioned a Bath chair in the attics. I've ordered it brought down and cleaned. If Seth wishes to join our festivities later, then he can do so with relative comfort. Has anyone heard from Lord Salter yet?"

"Not a peep," answered Patterson-Smythe. "Dickie sent a telegram to Paris yesterday. He'd heard the Salters might be staying there with a friend. It's so hard to find them, you know. They're both such gadabouts!"

"And Seth's two sisters?"

"I wrote to them. Both live in Vienna with their aunt. I believe Ruth is engaged to a Baron von Something-or-other. One of those hyphenated German names."

Drina laughed. "Like Saxe-Coburg?"

Dolly smiled back, her eyes twinkling. "Yes, something like that. Or even Patterson-Smythe, I suppose. Dickie's family chose to hyphenate it several generations back when Gerald Patterson married Lady Catherine Smythe. Her father, Lord Colderoy, insisted upon it. You know, I'm a little surprised Elizabeth and Charles didn't hyphenate theirs."

"Stuart-Sinclair?" asked the queen. "I rather like the simpler name. Elizabeth Sinclair is quite refined, I think. Tell me, Count, are there many hyphenated names in Romania?"

"Not usually, Lady Stuart. Though, the so-called 'double barreling' of a surname is sometimes done in peerage families to maintain traditions in both houses. I wonder, will the duchess's firstborn son inherit both titles? Duke of Haimsbury and Branham?"

"It's very likely he will," Drina replied. "Though, Robby Sinclair may inherit grander titles yet to come. Who knows?" she added with a wink. "Dumpling, you mustn't beg. Della, I apologise for my dog. She keeps pawing at your hand. It's the biscuit, you see. She loves almond bikkies."

"May I give her one?" asked the youngster politely.

"Not yet. She'll have plenty of treats as the day continues. Best not spoil her too much. Speaking of names, have you named your little doggy yet?"

"I'm still thinking," she answered. "She sleeps a great deal. Perhaps, I'll call her Napper."

Blinkmire giggled at this, his small eyes bright. "Forgive me! It is just the name is so very apt, Lady Della. Napper! Oh, I do like that one."

"Then, it's settled," she declared. "Napper Stuart. Or perhaps Lady Napper Stuart-Sinclair."

All applauded, and Henry took the opportunity to stand. "Lady Napper has a regal name to it; quite fitting. Now, as I'm to meet with our hostess shortly, I'll bid you all a good morning. Drina, I'll prepare that liniment and leave it by your bed."

"You're too kind," the disguised queen answered, taking his hand. "By the way, Henry, I've written to your father. He might be coming down this way after the new year."

"Really? To say I'm shocked is understatement!" he exclaimed. "Your powers of persuasion certainly outmatch my own, Aunt Drina. Truly, nothing short of an earthquake would rouse my father from that house. Is he truly coming down?"

"He said so in his letter. We'll arrange a little party, if he does; or rather, *when* he does."

"I've not seen your father in years. Dickie and he used to hunt grouse together. Lovely days!" Patterson-Smythe reminisced as Della offered everyone blackberry tarts. "Oh, thank you, my dear. These look quite delicious."

"I helped bake them," she said proudly.

"You bake as well?" asked Henry. "Adele, you are a true renaissance woman, much like your Branham cousin. You're going to make some man very happy one day."

This caused Adele to blush slightly, and she curtsied to the viscount. "I do my best, Lord Salperton."

"It's a shame your father can't make it down for the wedding, Henry," Dolly said wiping tart crumbs from her hands.

"Wedding?" asked Count Riga. "Do you mean we're to have a wedding?"

"It's supposed to be a secret," Tory said with a harsh look at her garrulous friend. "But, yes, we might have one. It's still being arranged."

Blinkmire's face opened in delight. "Oh, I do love weddings! But who would be involved in so serious a ceremony, I wonder? Our little duchess is already married, and I'm aware of no engaged couples staying with us. Surely, Lady Della isn't pledging her troth so soon," he teased the youngster.

"Not yet," Della replied with a mischievous wink. "I'm still trying to decide whom to marry. Dr. Holloway is rather nice, if one likes men with ginger hair."

"I find red hair quite attractive," Dolly interjected. "Dickie's hair was red when we first met. Now, it's gone white. Pity."

Della laughed. "Sir Richard hardly has any hair at all," she noted.

"Yes, well, he used to have loads of it. Keep that in mind when you choose your husband, my dear. Even your brother's lush mane may all fall out one day," Patterson-Smythe warned her.

"Paul's hair would never do that," Della declared. She turned her gaze to Salperton, noting with a bright smile, "Your hair is very nice, Cousin Henry. Dark and thick, and it curls like Cousin Charles's does. You're rather handsome, too. Don't you think he's handsome, Auntie Dolly?"

Salperton stared, wondering if she'd spoken in jest or meant the comments seriously. Della allowed him to wallow in his doubts for several seconds before running over to offer a hug.

"Don't worry, Cousin Henry. I shan't marry you yet. Perhaps, when I'm older. Besides, you'll find someone else to be your wife before I'm eighteen. Won't you?"

Salperton's thoughts turned to Violet Stuart, and he wondered where she'd gone; why she'd left. Was she safe? Had the police found her yet?

"I'm content to wait," he decided to say, gallantly kissing Adele on the top of her head. "You know, my mother was somewhat prophetic; seeing visions now and then. She always said I'd end up marrying one of the Stuarts. Perhaps, she was right. Now, if we're not going to plan weddings, then I really must find the duchess."

He left, but Adele stood quietly, watching the handsome viscount depart. "Come here, Della," the wise queen called. "Let's discuss tomorrow's festivities, shall we? I see Dolly and Tory are planning to ride. Perhaps, we can tour the stables with them, if the weather's nice."

Riga and Stanley returned to the somber arrangement: a slow rendition of *O Come, O Come, Emmanuel* that evoked the miraculous beauty of the Saviour's birth. Victoria Stuart chatted with Drina, failing to notice anything unusual in the girl's manner, but Lady Patterson-Smythe perceived a familiar 'look' to Adele's pleasant expression. It was that same wistful gaze she'd seen upon the trusting countenance of Elizabeth Stuart, whenever she spoke of her love for a mysterious man she called 'Captain'.

Dolly made a mental note to speak with Charles. Young Adele Marie might be developing an attachment.

2:30 pm – Branham Library

Martin Kepelheim sat with his friends and colleagues at a large round table, adding sugar to a cup of coffee. A series of magnificent mahogany shelves lined the three-storey library's walls, rising upwards into a grand dome that allowed natural light to illuminate the many tables and chairs. As the largest private library in England, the Branham collection drew scholars from Oxford and Cambridge and housed many thousands of original books, diaries, and ledgers rescued from the 1666 fire by a team of inner circle agents.

"My what a lovely day it's turned out to be!" the tailor exclaimed. "Snow on the ground, the sun in the sky, and music throughout the house. Christmas at Branham! It's enough to inspire any poet."

"Do you plan to offer your report in verse?" asked Sinclair, stirring a dollop of cream into his coffee.

"Perhaps," Martin teased. "You know, Charles, it occurs to me how different this visit is from our last. You and the earl have spent time here since October, but the last time I slept at Branham was during that battle with Trent's men! My, who can forget it?"

Cornelius Baxter had a satisfied look upon his ample face, and he thoughtfully nibbled on a slice of fruit cake. "An epic battle indeed, Mr. Kepelheim; fit for the pen of Virgil or Homer. A war twixt men and beasts."

"But not only men," Martin reminded his friend. "Also, our beloved Mrs. Alcorn! How that dear woman rose to the mark!"

"Ah, true," mused Baxter. "But our little duchess and her companions would never have escaped without Mr. Reid's magnificent balloon."

Edmund and his wife Emily had arrived just before luncheon, and the inspector smiled at the memory. "The Queen of the Meadow is lovely and so easy to manoeuvre. One of these days, if my wife allows it, I should like to own one and sail it out over the sea at Brighton."

"Not here?" asked Sinclair. "Anjou-on-Sea has a sheltered bay for storage, and the limestone cliffs provide enough natural beauty to rival any coast."

"Perhaps, I'll keep a balloon in every port city," joked the inspector.

"Perhaps, you will," Charles answered slyly, for he'd purchased the Queen of the Meadow for his friend, and it now sat, wrapped and waiting, in a nearby barn. "Despite these lovely reminiscences, we must turn to business, for our agenda is long, and the day is not. Mac, are you and Martin prepared to offer any insights into the Haimsbury House puzzle room?"

"I believe so," answered Ed MacPherson, "but before we begin, may I offer my congratulations to Lord Aubrey? I can think of no better reason for delaying our project than a wedding."

"Thank you, Mac," replied the earl.

"Does the prospect please you?" Mac asked, noting a lack of enthusiasm.

"Of course, it does," Paul answered vaguely. "Lady Cordelia's a lovely young woman. I'm a lucky man. Shall we begin?"

Sinclair also noted his cousin's odd response but decided to let it pass. Paul was making a chivalrous sacrifice by marrying Wychwright, but Charles believed that—deep down—his cousin truly loved Cordelia. Standing, he faced the table of circle members.

"Thank you all for making the time in your busy schedules for this meeting. For many reasons, I felt we needed to join hands this afternoon, but as Martin said, we also celebrate an important milestone. For our records, Baxter, would you jot down the names of all members present?"

Acting as secretary, Cornelius entered the names in the circle's log book. Beginning with Duke Charles, the clockwise list as recorded that afternoon included Lord Aubrey, Mr. Martin Kepelheim, Dr. Edward MacPherson, Inspector Edmund Reid, Lord Malcolm Risling, Sir Thomas Galton, Lord Salperton, and C. Baxter.

The duke opened the meeting with prayer. "Gentlemen, let us seek the Lord's wisdom." Every head lowered, and Haimsbury began. "Father, it is with humble hearts we offer this gathering to you. Our circle is small this morning, but your word promises that where two or more are gathered in your name, you are there in the midst. Therefore, we welcome you into our meeting and pray for your guidance. We praise your holy name and offer thanks for the many times you've intervened on our behalf; unseen, unfelt, often unbidden. We may not always recognise these moments, but your hand is ever upon us.

"I confess, my king, that I sometimes allow the weight of responsibility and worry to overwhelm me, but when I finally turn to you, Lord Jesus, you lighten the load by taking it upon yourself.

What a gift that is! What joy unspeakable! As men, it is our nature to be self-reliant and energetic when a problem arises. We want to repair what is broken, mend what is torn, heal that which is wounded. Perhaps, we do these things, because of your imprint upon us. You made us your imager upon this earth, and in so doing, you presented us with two choices. We can either allow your image to shine, or we can selfishly rework it into something else. Something darker. Something irrefutably perverse and evil. I speak, my Lord, of those men who seek power from your enemy. It is a malevolent tree which dominates throne rooms and board rooms alike, the roots of which descend into the very pit of hell."

Charles paused, troubling thoughts overtaking him as though warring factions fought for control of his mind. His hands began to tremble, and he could hear the dragon's voice whispering more loudly than ever:

I'm here, boy! I have arisen! Find me and claim your rightful inheritance!

His knees grew weak, and he nearly collapsed, but a strange sensation passed through his muscles, and Charles could sense warming hands upon his arms and shoulders. His hands and feet tingled as though an electric spark flowed through every nerve.

"Trust in the One, Charles," a soft voice whispered in his mind. "Trust in the nail-scarred hands and feet."

Ignore the weakling! the seductive voice interrupted. *We will change the world, my son. Find me. Claim that which is yours! The kings of the earth will bow to you, even as they bow to me, for you are mine. I have designed you.*

"Trust in the Way, the Truth, and the Life, Charles," the other voice whispered sweetly. "Your destiny was determined long ago. The Dragon lies."

Remember when we used to speak, boy? Remember the attic and the sparkling mirror? I showed you my friends, and explained how they long to gain release. We need you, boy. I need you! I OWN YOU!

Charles leaned heavily upon the table, gasping for breath as a thousand demonic claws raked at his spirit. At that moment, his very soul was the prize, and the room grew intolerably warm.

"Lord God Almighty, I claim your promises!" he cried out. "Help me, Lord! Have mercy upon me!"

What Charles did not know, *could* not know, was that this battle took place outside of human time. No one else at the table heard his cries or noticed his distress—save one man. Henry MacAlpin not only heard the voices, he felt the war rage in his own spirit, and when he opened his eyes, the scene before him caused the viscount's knees to weaken, and he nearly fell as he rushed towards his friend.

He could see the other men at the table, their heads bowed, some with hands touching; yet no one moved. Even the flames in the hearth had frozen in place, looking like a painting. In fact, all aspects of the material space seemed lackluster and perfectly still, as though nothing but a photograph; a pale imitation of life.

Sinclair, however, had grown brighter, more intensely coloured as though *only he was real* in this extradimensional space.

But Charles was not alone.

Salperton could see dense clouds of interference, as though a dark force enrobed the besieged duke. Stepping towards the spiritual battlefield, his vision sharpened, and he discerned multiple sets of wings. A huge, shining being, shaped like a glittering dragon, formed the centre of the chaotic maelstrom, and its long tail wrapped round Charles's chest, as though to crush the breath from his victim's lungs.

"I will not join you!" Charles shouted. "I belong to Christ, not you! Help me, my King! I claim your promises!"

Henry reached for Sinclair's hand, touching the fingers, and instantly he could feel the raging turmoil seething through his friend's heart and mind. He could hear the Dragon's rasping voice as though it raked through his own soul.

It was though he and Charles had become one.

You cannot deny your blood, boy, whispered the demon. *Find me and discover the power of that ancient blood!*

"In the name of Christ Jesus, I call upon the Lord's protection for his servant!" Henry shouted boldly.

The Dragon's head turned, and a pair of cruel eyes focused on the viscount.

I know you, son of Scotland. I saw you in the Realms of Stone. You dared to challenge my authority! What a foolish, little Scotsman you are. Shall I tell you what I did to your mother?

Images of torture tore into Henry's mind: his mother tormented by diabolical visions and cruel whispers, racked with pain and endless suffering. But he refused to yield to the pressure.

"Hear the Lord's word, Demon!" he challenged the Shadow as he began to quote from Psalm 86.

"Give ear, O Lord, unto my prayer; and attend to the voice of my supplications. In the day of my trouble I will call upon thee: for thou wilt answer me. Among the gods there is none like unto thee, O Lord; neither are there any works like unto thy works."

The Shadow's form faltered, and a brightness emerged from behind it, passing through the violent storm's swirling blackness; as if a second great being now controlled the field of battle.

"All nations whom thou hast made shall come and worship before thee, O Lord, and shall glorify thy name," Henry continued. *"For thou art great, and doest wondrous things. THOU ART GOD ALONE!"* he ended in a shout.

The bright presence whitened into the form of a man, and Henry perceived a fiery sword within its right hand. The being's face shone like polished brass, and his limbs radiated a thousand colours as though made of prisms.

"Step back, Henry," he heard God's messenger say.

The flaming sword swung in a wide arc, and the Shadow cried out, the storm and darkness gone in a blink, as though hurled through a hidden doorway.

Instantly, the air returned to Charles's lungs, and he began to breathe once more. The duke opened his eyes and saw Henry's confident face; felt his comforting hand, holding his tightly in a fierce grip.

A voice whispered in both men's minds: "Fret not, sons of the Most High. The day of the evildoers and the workers of iniquity soon ends. They shall be cut down like grass and wither as a green herb. Rest in the Lord and wait patiently upon him. Do not fret because of wicked men. Evildoers shall be cut off, but they that wait upon the Lord shall inherit the earth. The enemy sought permission to sift you, Charles," he told the recovering duke softly. "For you and your sons will alter the shape of the world. This is not the final battle. The enemy bargains for you, Charles Robert. He seeks to devour you, but you are never alone in this fight. Trust in the One with the nail-scarred hands. He commands his host to stand beside you. We are ever at your side."

The being's brightness lessened, and for the briefest second Henry recognised Anatole Romanov.

Immediately, the material world emerged as dominant. The fire's flames began to flicker and dance, the clock to tick, and the chest of each man round the table expanded and contracted with natural breaths. Time moved forward, and the room's subdued hues returned to normal.

The entire battle had taken place in the infinitesimal space between the ticks of a clock.

"Thank you, Lord God Almighty, for aiding your servants," Henry said, continuing the prayer for the duke. "We are grateful for your kindness and tender mercies. I thank you for your loyal servants who surround us on this field. I pray for my friend, Charles, that you would continue to uphold him and surround him with your mighty warriors. Grant us, his fellow servants, the resources to aid him in the battles ahead. Grant us vision, wisdom, and strength of heart. Fill our hands with purpose and our hearts with love for mankind—and lead us along your chosen path, dear Saviour. We humbly ask all these things in your name and for your sake, my King. Amen."

The fellowship's members looked up, their faces filled with questions. Martin spoke first. "What just happened? Henry, how did you move so quickly? And Charles? Are you ill? What's happened?"

Henry was checking the duke's pulse, urging him to sit. "Your heart is racing, Charles. Please, take the seat. Mr. Baxter, might we have a glass of water for the duke?"

The butler had already stood, ready to help his friend, and he filled a crystal glass and handed it to Haimsbury. "Do you need to lie down, my lord?" he asked with deep concern.

"No," Charles managed to reply, his breathing laboured. His ribs ached, and his limbs responded slowly to command. The supernatural battle had left physical bruises. "I just need a minute," he told them. "I feel as though I've run a hundred miles. The same as the night I chased after that demon through Henry's Woods."

Baxter remembered the night all too well. The stallion, Ambrose Aurelius, had been drained of blood by an unseen foe, and Sinclair had raced after it for ten miles—in an impossibly short space of time—and then boldly challenged the spirit creature.

With his fingers still on Sinclair's wrist, Henry counted again. "It's slowing. It may help to lie down, if only for a few minutes."

"I'd rather sit, Henry. Please, everyone, let's begin the reports."

Aubrey had sensed nothing during the encounter, but he realised something quite terrifying must have occurred.

"Whatever just happened here is beyond the capacity of most of us to perceive; however, the Lord has filled one of our chairs with a man who has eyes to see into that darkened mirror and discern the hidden actions of both sides. I'll offer a full report of our current investigations in a moment, but first, I'd like Henry to tell us what he witnessed."

The viscount remained standing. He placed a hand on Sinclair's left shoulder. "In the thirty-four years I've walked this earth, I've witnessed some quite miraculous events. As a boy, I perceived what my mother called angels, walking and speaking to one another within our home. Usually, these beings were gentle and kind; but despite that, my father feared for us. He saw nothing out of the ordinary, and thought us both mad, to be honest. Most husbands would have committed my mother to an asylum, but Father kept her close, shut up in her rooms."

"And you?" asked Aubrey.

Henry grew quiet for a moment, strain showing upon his face. "He avoided me. You see, he couldn't even imagine the world Mother and I saw so clearly. It made me doubt my own sanity for a time, but Mother told me it was a gift. That my vision set me apart. I never asked for this ability, yet I begin to understand why it exists; for it allowed me to rescue Elizabeth from a prison within another realm. And today, it's given me eyes to see a battle that might have weakened any other man's faith. But Charles Sinclair is stronger than any man I've ever known. He became a battleground, with warriors from both sides grappling for his heart and soul. I saw them and I heard them. I think it all happened in the blink of an eye, perhaps outside of time; for the rest of the world had frozen. None of you moved. I imagine, to you, nothing occurred; although you can see the consequences of Charles's battle."

"Indeed!" declared Martin. "Clearly, our duke has fought a great fight. And I fear these occurrences will only continue."

"So the messenger told us," Charles answered, his colour improving. "I'm fine, Henry. Thank you for your aid."

Paul asked, "Henry, are these entities still here, or do we now meet as men only?"

The viscount resumed his chair. "Presently, I see nothing, but that doesn't mean we're alone. We meet in a material space, but it's my firm belief that we interact within unseen rooms. The Lord's guardians keep watch upon us. I sense nothing evil or disruptive here now. Only peace. And such sweet peace it is!" he added, his eyes filling with tears as his own heart slowed.

Charles nodded. "Thank you, Henry. The Lord brought you to us for a reason, and we begin to perceive it. Tomorrow, we celebrate the incarnation of God Almighty as our Redeemer. Is it any wonder that the enemy might choose to engage us now? These intrusions—in fact, all these recent crimes—are intended to lure us away from our true goal, but we must not be duped! Rather, let us look to our purpose, gentlemen. To the path ahead, with our hands upon the plow, looking neither to the left, nor to the right, but ever onwards—our eyes fixed upon Christ!"

The table erupted into shouts of praise and agreement.

Kepelheim stood. "If I may? What we've witnessed here are but the remnants of warfare. We dull-eyed others lack vision, but it is not our purpose to 'see'. Each of us serves our Lord with gifts unique to him. Henry has entered our circle as a guardian and watchman. Charles is our leader, and if I may choose a chess metaphor, he is our king. Elizabeth is our queen, and Henry acts as one of the knights, whilst Paul serves as the other. Perhaps, Mac and I are bishops who seek to convey spiritual truths from written records. Now, lest you other wonderful men conclude you serve only as pawns, let me remind you that pawns can make or break a game. In some cases, a pawn becomes your most powerful weapon."

"So long as we do not sacrifice our queen," Charles interjected. "Martin, chess is an apt comparison, for all humans stand upon that eternal board, but the difference in the two sides is this: The black assembly, representing darkness and evil, enthrall and bind the men and women upon their side. No piece, regardless of rank, has autonomy, for each is subject to the whims of that infernal chess player—the hidden hand behind human actions.

"However, God's side, the white, *allow* his hand to move them. We are not slaves, but willing participants in the match! We cooperate rather than capitulate. Therefore, our rank and position on the board is determined by God's plan. Trusting in that plan is a choice, made daily. We must continually walk in his light, study his word, follow his commands, and lift him up for all the world to see! *That* is our mission, gentlemen. To bring Christ's light to darkness. If the Dragon thought to frighten or intimidate me, then he knows nothing of the Sinclair sinews. They are strong and unyielding, for the blood that strengthens me comes not from any ancient race, but from the bleeding hands of Christ alone!"

Again, shouts of 'Amen' and 'Praise the Lord' rang throughout the magnificent library, echoing upwards into the lofty, stained-glass dome three storeys above, where a white owl watched from its perch near the edge.

Kepelheim wiped tears from his ageing eyes. "I wish your dear father were here," he said. "But I'm certain he watches from the throne room, cheering you on, Charles. The board is now set, my friends, and we chessmen take our places. We look to our human king and seek his commands."

Sinclair swallowed hard, for the notion of being called a 'king' touched numerous strings within his heart, sounding a discordant tone. "I seek no such title, nor do I seek a throne, but one may await me. Gentlemen, I trust everyone at this table with my life. As such, I need to tell you of a conversation I shared with our gracious Lady Stuart. All of you know her true title?"

Every man nodded.

"On the rail journey from London, we had the train to ourselves, for the most part. Four of James's men guarded the doors, and six others sat near the back, but overall, she and I had three hours to talk privately during that long, snowy journey. We discussed a question she asked me weeks ago. I explained that my commitment to that decision depends entirely upon the support of you inner circle members. James has given me his opinion and his support. All I need is yours."

Every eye fixed upon Haimsbury—as though, this moment were the culmination of all their centuries of work.

"Did you say yes?" asked his cousin.

"In a way. Allow me to explain. When I first met with this good lady in private some weeks ago, her easy manner and frankness took me by surprise. She's a formidable queen beneath that heavy crown, but in the quiet of a drawing room, she becomes a woman of sparkling wit and deep political convictions. She even asked about my views on Christian faith. I shall continue to sound her out on this and allow the Lord to lead those conversations."

The air grew still, and the background noise from the rest of the house—servants talking, music from Adele's piano, dogs barking—all stopped, as though the world took a breath.

Charles, too, inhaled deeply, praying inwardly as he spoke. "My friends, the queen has asked me to assume the throne upon her death."

A feather dropping would have sounded like a hammer blow, so heavy was the silence. The young duke could see each man's concentration, his mind at work, sorting through the possibilities of so major a shift in England's monarchy; imagining how it might affect the ability of the inner circle to continue its mission; what it might mean for future generations.

Finally, the earl rose to his feet. "My friends, we need not offer a joint opinion, for I suspect each of us foresees both positive and negative consequences. Charles, when must you give the queen your final answer?"

"Thursday morning, when I take her back to London."

"Then, may I suggest we consider it privately until then—speaking of it in whispers, only to one another. We'll meet again in this room on Boxing Day to vote."

Charles nodded, grateful for the suggestion. "Yes, I think that's the best solution. Now, let us leave this weighty issue and review our current responsibilities. Each of you belongs to the ICI, and most also serve in the Intelligence Branch. Therefore, it's up to us to solve several riddles. Paul, if you'd be good enough to give the first report? Then, we'll hear Reid regarding the London situation. Oh, but before we do so, Cousin, perhaps you could address any questions about today's wedding."

The earl took a beat before speaking. "When Charles announced his engagement to our beloved duchess, I never imagined I'd be sharing similar news before the year was out. It probably seems sudden to all of you, which it is, but I believe it's the right thing to do. Two nights ago, Cordelia Wychwright was sexually assaulted."

Ed MacPherson gasped, for he'd heard only scraps of the story. "Is this verified? Was it this fellow Wendaway again?"

"No," answered the earl. "Though she's said little since arriving here, Delia told James a great deal when he first spoke with her. In fact, she told him more than she realises, I think. Delia's come to trust my uncle; as do we all. Here is how it stands. Cordelia's father left her a furnished home and the a modest fortune to operate it. James believes the new baron, Captain William Wychwright, wants to control this inheritance through a forced marriage to one of his disreputable friends."

Reid's hand went up. "Forgive the interruption, Lord Aubrey, but Duke James asked me to look into both men. Wychwright's friends, I mean. Both have form with the Met, and been bailed out multiple times by their fancy lawyers. Interestingly, one of those lawyers is a retired QC named Wentworth."

"As in our missing Cambridge man?" asked Aubrey.

Reid nodded. "His father. This Wentworth didn't negotiate the release directly but influenced it through a letter to the Home Office. Charles, you'll be interested to learn that Wychwright and his friends are all members of the Silver Spoons Club at Cambridge. As are Lionel Wentworth and the late Peter Patterson."

Charles blinked, his mind adding this bit of information to the complicated puzzle. "The Spoons were mere rumour, or so I thought. I never realised they actually existed! Sir Thomas, I want you to find a circle member with Trinity connexions and ask him to investigate this club. See if they have dealings with any Redwing members."

"I'll get on it right away, sir," Galton answered, taking notes. "But you might ask Seth Holloway. He teaches at Cambridge."

"I will," Sinclair replied, "but I want a circle member to verify anything Holloway says. He's still a suspect in Patterson's murder."

"But he can't have killed Collinwood, Charles," Paul interrupted. "Besides, Seth's not a killer; he's a victim."

"We'll speak of this privately. Go on, Edmund. What more do you know of Treversham and Brandt?"

"I know they're both thieves, who should be in prison. They act as a team. They enter a jeweller's shop with the announced purpose of ordering a special ring or expensive brooch. The unwitting shop owner opens his cabinets and drawers and allows them to examine a variety of stones with a loupe. Brandt pretends to notice movement in the back, suggesting he's seen a street urchin lurking about. The trusting jeweller goes to check; and when he returns, an item or two from his inventory is stolen, and the men gone. But that isn't the only charge laid at the doors of these men. Illegal gambling figures prominently in our records, along with three charges of assault against Brandt. All from young society women. Thanks to Brandt's banker grandfather—also a Silver Spoon—he never once stood in the dock."

Paul's hands clenched. "Three assaults? If my father were here, even his patience would be tested!" he exclaimed. "Gentlemen, I cannot; nay, I *will* not allow Wychwright and his gang of predators the opportunity to harm Delia again."

A knock sounded, and Baxter rose to answer. He spoke in whispers to the underbutler, and then turned back to the meeting. "Sirs, Mr. Priest has just received a telegram from Duke James."

Cornelius handed the slip of paper to Haimsbury.

Charles smiled as he read the short message. "James says he and Archbishop Benson will arrive within the hour. If we're to have a wedding, then we'll need to adjourn and get ready. Paul, did you bring anything formal that a groom might wear?"

"Not really, unless Baxter packed something. Beth insists we keep things informal during family gatherings."

"Then, we'll look through mine. Baxter, you're more familiar with my closet than I."

The former butler stood. "Several choices might suffice Lord Aubrey's needs, sir. If I may, I shall look through them."

Kepelheim jumped to his feet, already making plans. "And I'll fetch Mrs. Alcorn. If anything requires tailoring, she and I will make short work of it."

CHAPTER FIFTY

"Perhaps, something with a little more colour," suggested Dolly. "Elizabeth, didn't you once wear a lovely cap sleeve gown in iced pink satin? It had embroidered flowers along the bodice. You wore it for a spring dance, I think."

The duchess watched from a comfortable chair near her bedchamber's fireplace as a pale Cordelia Wychwright tried on dress after dress, coached by Victoria Stuart and Dolly Patterson-Smythe. Esther Alcorn helped the girl with hooks, buttons, and laces.

"A wee bit o' colour would help bring out your eyes, my lady," Alcorn suggested. "You've very pretty eyes."

"I believe I wore that pink dress at your last soirée, Dolly," Beth answered. "Esther, did Alicia pack away my older clothes when we returned from France?"

"She did, and I know just where it is," Alcorn announced. "Let's get you out of this one, my lady, and I'll fetch it."

Cordelia Wychwright moved as though lost in a dream. Alcorn unlaced the current dress (number five), a silvery satin affair with bows down the sleeves and a full bustle. Each time Delia paused for even a moment, Dolly dabbed her face with pearlescent powder to cover the girl's facial bruises. A final hint of colour from the rouge pot helped to overcome the overly pale aspect of her cheeks.

"The pink gown will work much better with your light hair, my dear. Beth's dark hair and eyes make her able to wear almost any colour, but you're too fair for neutral shades. There, much better," she announced. "You should see yourself in the mirror, Delia. My darling girl, you are beautiful!"

Tory fetched a tortoise shell mirror from the dressing table and held it before the young woman's face. Cordelia stared at the reflection.

"Is that really me?" she asked, her blue-grey eyes wide.

"Dolly's right," Elizabeth assured her, "you are as lovely as springtime. Tory, I wonder if you and Dolly would help Alcorn look through my stored dresses? I'd like a moment to talk with Delia in private."

"Yes, of course," said Patterson-Smythe. "Come, Tory, Esther! We old ladies are extraneous to youth."

Alcorn led the way, and soon the duchess was alone with her friend. "Sit for a minute, won't you?" she asked Cordelia.

The girl obeyed, almost mechanically. She now wore a blue velvet dressing gown, embroidered with the Haimsbury-Branham crest. She took a needlepoint settee, close to the fire. She kept rubbing her arms, and it seemed that she shivered.

"I apologise for the cold. A house this size can prove difficult to heat, and gas fires seldom give the same warmth as coal or wood. I'm afraid it can make trying on clothes difficult. Would you like another cup of tea to warm you?"

"No, thank you." She stared into the fire as though dreaming.

"Delia, do you want to marry my cousin?" Beth asked bluntly.

The girl's chin lifted, and a flash of alertness sharpened her eyes. "Marry Paul? Of course, I do. It's just..."

"Just what?"

"I'm not really sure he wants to marry me," she whispered. "Why would he?"

Elizabeth left her chair and joined the guest on the plump sofa, taking Cordelia's right hand. "My darling friend, you're like ice! You're not running a fever, are you?" Beth touched Wychwright's forehead. "You're cold all over, it seems, but your forehead's cool."

"Mama says I'm always cold."

A Sinclair tartan blanket lay folded nearby, and Beth spread it across the girl's lap. Delia quickly pulled it up to her chin as though trying to disappear.

"Is that better?"

"Yes. Thank you."

"Delia, you're about to become my cousin, and I'm very glad about it. I only wish you could be happy, too."

"But I want *Paul* to be happy!" she exclaimed. "He'll be miserable if he marries me. My family's hateful and filled with users, and they'll try to use him! But I don't know what else to do, Elizabeth. I'm terrified to go back home. Nor can I go to the house Father left me. Will knows how to find me there, and he'll do it again—they'll do it again! They'll try to...! Try to...!" She couldn't say the actual words 'assault' or 'rape', but instead fell into a heap of weeping.

Elizabeth pulled her close and allowed the girl to cry, stroking her hair like she might a child's. "Rest assured that Paul loves you. I know the earl better than he knows himself, and I've watched him fall in love with you these past few weeks. I'm sure he'd already planned to propose. This merely advances it a little. So long as you love him, then there's no reason why you cannot be very happy together."

"But Paul loves you," whispered Wychwright.

"Yes, but not in the way a husband loves a wife. He and I shall always have a special bond, but yours will be stronger. Just as mine is stronger with Charles. We all want your happiness, Delia. Can you be happy as Paul's wife?"

"I want to be," she answered hesitantly, her voice small. "I'm afraid—of tonight. And every night after. He'll want to *be* with me, and the thought of it... Oh, I can't, Beth! I can't! I do love him, but I simply can't do that!"

"I understand," Beth answered soothingly. "Really, I do! I've had experiences that left me shaken to my soul. A man once tried to force me into... Into *being* with him, but despite that, Charles and I have a healthy relationship. And Paul is an exceedingly patient, compassionate man. He's nothing like the men who hurt you. I know he'll treat you with tenderness and respect. I can understand why you find it difficult to trust, but with time, you'll see I'm right."

"Must I sleep with him tonight? I just can't imagine it, but he'll be angry if I tell him and, I don't know, he may hit me. Would you tell him for me?"

"Paul is not that sort of man, Delia. He would never harm a woman. Not for any reason. It's simply not in his nature."

She slowly relaxed, and Elizabeth began to pray softly in her thoughts. "Delia, would you rather sleep with me tonight?"

She pushed up, wiping her eyes. "No, I mustn't do that. Charles wouldn't like it. Is there another bed in Paul's apartment?"

"Yes. I'll have Ada MacKenzie put some of my clothes in there for you, along with personal linen, soaps, and perfume. She can be your lady's maid, if you like. After Christmas, we'll search for a permanent maid."

"My own maid?" she asked in disbelief. "I've always shared one with Mama."

"No more sharing for you, my dear Cousin! Paul is wealthy. He'll hire any staff you want. And Aubrey House is a beautiful home. It was built at the same time as Queen Anne and by the same architect, so the layout and details are similar. If we're able, we can all go to Briarcliff Castle next month. In the past, that was our Christmastide tradition. Branham, then Castle Drummond, then Briarcliff. We'll see if Charles and Paul can get away from their current investigations and take us."

"Paul is quite handsome," Delia said, smiling a little.

"And he can be a great deal of fun," Beth added. "He's a very good dancer, and he plays the violin. Did you know that?"

The door opened to women talking. Alcorn carried an elegant opera gown. The bodice and skirt were of buttercup yellow satin, overlaid at the hips in a gauzy, white toile draping that tied behind, just over the ruffled bustle. The capped sleeves were trimmed in the same silk toile, and the high, ruffled neckline would cover the poor girl's upper body bruises. A pair of opera gloves would conceal those on her forearms.

"Shall we see if this fits?" asked Alcorn.

Fifteen minutes later, Cordelia stood before a cheval mirror, admiring her butterfly transformation. "I've never worn anything like this. Oh, I feel like Cinderella in that story!" she told the ladies. "Really, I don't deserve such happiness."

Beth hugged her friend's waist. "Of course you do. I'm very glad you decided to wear your hair down in the back. The ringlets show off the soft highlights in your hair. Here now," she added, as she opened a large velvet box. "I cannot *give* you this, for it belongs to the Branham collection, but I hope you'll wear it."

Inside the hinged box lay a magnificent choker necklace made from three strands of pearls, finished along the top with a row of yellow diamonds. Below, a large teardrop pearl was delicately suspended from a yellow diamond bow. Cordelia had never seen such a beautiful design, and her hands trembled.

"This must have cost a fortune!" she cried. "Are you sure?"

"It was given to my great-great-great grandmother, Katherine DuBonnier, by King Louis XIV in appreciation for her help with a treaty twixt England and France."

"But I can't," Delia objected. "It's far too precious."

"That is the point," Beth explained as she clasped the choker round her friend's throat. "It tells the world how very much you're worth. Cordelia, you are priceless."

Tory opened a box of her own. "I brought these with me out of habit, I think. These earrings belonged to my Grandmother Stuart. They are pearl and yellow diamond, and I want you to have them as a wedding gift."

Delia began to cry. "You're all so very good to me! I didn't think families could be so loving. Except for Aunt Margaret, of course. She and Uncle Basil are very sweet."

"I'm glad you think so, for they're both here," Victoria told the girl.

"They're here? Are you sure?"

"Quite sure. Charles sent his new train to fetch them, and they arrived half an hour ago. Everyone's assembled in the upper gallery to watch you become the Countess of Aubrey. Come now, we mustn't keep your groom waiting, my dear. Are you ready?"

Cordelia nodded. "Yes, I think so. Will you hold my hand?" she asked the duchess.

"Of course, I will. Now, let's go greet the man's who about to become your husband."

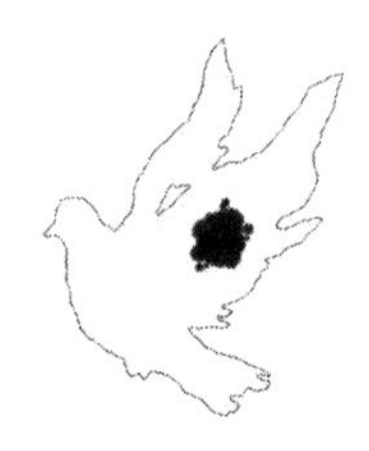

CHAPTER FIFTY-ONE

The upper gallery of Branham Hall was quadrangular and served as a sort of interior cloister walk, formed from the central portion of the original house. The interior walls contained four doors each, north, south, east, and west, which led into state rooms, smoking parlours, and from these into primary wings. Beth had chosen to set the wedding in the east gallery, taking full advantage of the light of the setting sun, which cast pyramidal beams of white through the gallery's arched windows.

Baxter and Kay had supervised the arrangement of fifty dining chairs, placed into rows with a wide aisle down the centre. Adele helped Dolly and Victoria add golden bells and white bows to the Christmas garlands, and a crimson runner drew the eye to the aisle. A piano had been moved from the ballroom, and Stanley played softly, joined by Riga on his cello.

Adele wore her best pink party dress, and her small shoes made a tapping sound as she entered the side parlour now used by her brother.

"Aren't you dressed yet, Brother mine? You will be late for your wedding, and Cordelia will be very sad."

Paul smiled at his beautiful sister. "Then, we shall blame Martin for it. He's never satisfied with how I tie a cravat."

The tailor added a pearl stickpin to the perfectly tied silk. "You form a knot as though hanging a criminal, Lord Aubrey. Really, for someone so graceful on the dance floor, you'd think you'd have more delicacy when it comes to your neckwear. There!" he said, triumphantly. "Della, your brother is quite handsome, thanks to me." He placed his hands on Paul's shoulders, fussing with the seams. "I wish I had the time to rework this coat. Charles's shoulders are an inch broader than yours, but I doubt anyone will notice. Only another tailor would, I imagine."

"An inch wider?" the earl echoed as he turned round. "It's most likely fat from lack of training. We'll soon fix that."

"Perhaps, it's just my naturally superior build," Haimsbury teased. "Paul, you really do look splendid."

The earl smiled. "Whether I do or not is immaterial to Archbishop Benton. He'll marry us regardless, but your clothes do suit me, Cousin. I may steal Kepelheim from you."

Martin laughed. "Once I've translated the cipher in Charles's puzzle room, I shall have more hours for sewing," he said, still fussing over the left sleeve. "There, all done! You are positively resplendent! I only wish your dear parents could be here to watch you take this step."

"As do I," Paul whispered.

The door opened, revealing the bright face of Duke James. "Are we ready? Everyone's waiting."

"Might we have a minute, James?" asked Haimsbury. "Martin, if you'd see Adele to her place?"

Taking the hint, Drummond led the others out and shut the door. Charles turned to his cousin. "Paul, not long ago, you stood with me in the vestry at Drummond Chapel and shared your heart. You admitted your eternal love for Beth but assured me that she no longer owned your heart. You're my dearest friend in all the world. I have to know: do you have any doubts? Any lingering feelings for Elizabeth that could overshadow this marriage? Because, if you do, then I beg you call this off. Henry says Delia may have difficulty showing her affection—physical love, I mean. I know it's none of my business, but..."

"I love her, Charles. I do!" Stuart interrupted. "I understand your concern, but it's unnecessary. Perhaps, my love isn't the same as yours for Beth, but it's a deep and growing affection that will blossom. I'd already thought of proposing to her before all this happened. William's assault only accelerated a plan already in my mind."

"Yes, I realise that, but... Well, I'm thinking of her happiness as well as yours. If there is anything I can do to help, I'm here. James has said he could marry her. I beg you not to ruin your life and hers from any sense of chivalry."

"Charles, I am content in my heart and my mind. When I proposed to her this morning, a light entered her eyes that I'd never seen before—a light of hope and joy. I intend to do all in my power to keep that light shining. It's true; I shall always love Beth, but..." He paused, tears now flowing. "Beth and I had a lovely talk last night, and she helped focus my thoughts. I believe the Lord wants this, Charles. He is in this decision. I know it! Delia's lost her family through all this. Her father is dead, and her mother and brother have turned on her. Let us become her new family and a place of refuge."

Charles smiled. "I'm proud of you, Paul. My cousin—my brother. And I love you."

"And I love you. My cousin and brother. This is a day for celebration. Let's do that, shall we?"

The two men embraced, wiping away tears. Mr. Stanley began to play a lively arrangement of Haydn's Cello Concerto No. 1, and the earl and young duke entered the room.

To Paul, the ceremony felt wonderfully intimate. As he pledged his life and love to the petite eighteen-year-old, an overwhelming sense of belonging and responsibility took root in his heart. This was his wife; his *mo bhean.* Cordelia's hands shook as he held them, but her eyes focused with more clarity than he'd seen in many days. By five o'clock, the newlyweds were toasting their commitment with friends and family, and by eleven, he would take her into his bed as the love of his life.

The shock of the assault in London had not subsided, but she agreed to sleep with him that night; nervous and very fearful. However, Paul did nothing more than hold her, whispering of his childhood in Scotland and sharing his hopes for the future. He made no demand for intimacy, beyond a sweet kiss now and then. Delia had never felt so loved, so cherished; confident in his promise to shield and adore her from that day forward.

As dawn broke over the chimneys of Branham that Christmas Day, Cordelia Stuart, Countess of Aubrey, pledged her whole heart to this patient, tender husband. For Paul's affections had given her more healing than any physician's medicine ever could.

CHAPTER FIFTY-TWO

Christmas Morning

Elizabeth awoke alone. She could hear birds chirping outside the bedchamber windows and bells ringing from the nearby chapel, announcing Christ's birth. She lay beneath three velvet quilts, for the snow had begun again in earnest overnight, lowering the temperature even further. The gas fire cheered the room but failed to warm it much. She missed her husband's arms. Assuming he'd gone to his study to write, she rose and slipped on her dressing gown. Frost had formed along the bottom and sides of the window panes, and she traced a pair of conjoined hearts in the cold crystal veil.

"Charles?" she called into the next bedchamber as she crossed through the tiled bath. "Captain, where are you?"

His untouched bed had an abandoned, lonely look; for Sinclair always slept in the duchess's chamber. He'd already set out trousers, shirt, waistcoat, and other items in preparation for the day. Beth found this room comforting and masculine, and she ran her hands along the carved bedposts, thinking of her father and all their many talks.

"I hadn't realised you were awake," her husband said, emerging from the doorway to the apartment's upper floor. He kissed her sweetly. "I was just fetching your Christmas present."

Still in a blue paisley dressing gown, Charles led her into the large drawing room, his arm round her shoulders. They sat on one of the sofas, close to the fire.

"Happy Christmas," he said, placing a wrapped envelope into her hands. "I've spent weeks deciding what to give a woman who has everything she could possibly wish for. I hope I've gotten it right."

The envelope was addressed: '*To My Beloved Wife on Our First Christmas Together*'. She untied the ribbon, somewhat nervous. "I can't imagine what might fit into such a small package."

He smiled. "This is not your only gift, of course. But the one that feels most appropriate to begin the day, considering all we've been through and discussed."

Inside were a dozen pages of dense, legal language. Elizabeth laughed as she perused the first page. "I hope this isn't some addendum to our marital laws, Captain. Let's see now. It's from the offices of Langham and Drover. I know those solicitors. They act on behalf of the Crown in matters of taxation." She stopped, her dark eyes growing wide. "Oh, Charles, you bought it! The warehouse on Mansell! You bought it! Is this true? Is it really ours?"

"Not ours. *Yours*, darling. The property is in your name, and you'll notice, if you read the other documents, that I've directed the same construction company that remodeled Haimsbury House to begin work on all three Mansell warehouses at their earliest opportunity. They're currently remodeling Loudain House for the ICI agents, but Mr. Brenner thinks they'll complete it by early February. He's already drawing up plans with an architect."

She set the gift aside and threw her arms round his neck. "Captain, this is the most wonderful gift you could have chosen! And it represents aspects of our first adventure, for that's when we first discussed building the hospital. On the train to Branham. Oh, Charles, you really are the most thoughtful, remarkable man!"

He kissed her, the moment sparking an intimate fire, but rather than yield to it, Beth pulled back, gazing at him adoringly. "How I'd love to return to that warm bed with you now, husband, but there's so much to do. We mustn't stay up here too long. I've a gift for you as well, and like you, I struggled to decide. Now that you're a wealthy duke, you have all you might ever wish for. I pray this pleases you, Charles."

She knelt before the tree and selected a small rectangular box wrapped in a silk square of Sinclair tartan and tied with a golden bow. Handing it to him, the duchess offered it with a kiss. "Happy Christmas, Captain."

"Knowing you, I'm sure it's perfect," he whispered as he untied the bow. The tartan scarf opened to reveal a hinged box made of a light wood. "A cravat? An ascot?" he asked as he unfastened the latch. A folded bit of paper lay inside. The duke set the box on the table and began to examine the document. "Beth, you can't do this."

"It's already done," she told him. "As you can see, these are official registration papers."

"But he's yours, darling."

"No, Captain, he's yours. Paladin already looks to you as his master. He has done, ever since that harrowing ride from the abbey to Reid's magnificent balloon! Never in my life, have I seen a horse take to someone so quickly, and since then he's grown to love you. Paladin had never allowed anyone but me to ride him, yet since that day, you control him as no one else does. He's your horse, Charles."

The duke's eyes teared. "But he's the most sought-after sire in England. Beth, he's worth a small fortune in stud fees!"

"Then store up that fortune for our children, Captain. Or use it in your ICI projects. Anything you earn from his efforts are yours. I imagine he has another five years in him before retiring. But even then, he'll be a magnificent hunter. I do love watching the pair of you take those jumps!"

"Paladin," he whispered. "How my life has changed! Not yet three months since our fist kiss, yet I feel as though we've lived a lifetime together already. I love you, little one. With all my heart, I love you."

Beth nestled into his arms, the two of them watching the pleasant fire. "What did you think of the upper storey?"

"I found it quite surprising, actually. When you first told me our apartment had an upper floor, I'd assumed it was an attic, but there are three large rooms and a storage area."

"It's because that floor was originally a nursery. A bedchamber, play area, parlour, and the smallest room was the nursemaid's chamber. After I was born, Mother had the nursery moved to the north wing. She found it difficult to sleep whenever I cried."

He started to make a harsh observation regarding Patricia Stuart's selfish mothering technique, but decided to say nothing. "We could move it back," he suggested instead. "I used to get up with Albert in the night. I always found those times with him quite nice, actually." He grew quiet for a moment. "Beth, I'm late in saying this, but thank you for the roses and the ragstone bench. I don't know if you had time to visit Albert's grave after Lord Wychwright's funeral, but it looks very cheerful there now. Thank you, darling. That was a lovely thing to do."

"You needn't thank me. I was happy to add a small touch. I suppose I wanted to show my affection and attachment. He is with our Lord now, but Albert's still your son, which makes him my step-son. And I promise to do all in my power to be a good mother to our children. Robby was so like you in that other world, Charles. He has your eyes, the same expressions when he's contemplating a puzzle, the same laugh, and his hair curls just like yours." She reached behind his neck and teased at the raven locks that curled over the dressing gown's satin collar. "Are you intentionally growing it longer, or is it to disguise that scar at the back of your head?"

He reached up to touch the healing wound. "This scar is a reminder of my mortality, but also of how precious life is. Shall I let it grow, little one? Georgie claimed I have long, grey hair in 1899."

"Grey?" she laughed. "Well, if true, then I'm sure it's very striking, Captain. How long?"

"What?"

"The hair. How long did she say it will be?"

"She wasn't precise, but apparently, Paul will have short hair, whilst mine becomes dashingly poetic. Perhaps, he and I exchange personalities."

"You mean Paul becomes a mathematician? Oh, really, I cannot imagine that at all!"

Laughing, Sinclair took to his feet. "No, neither can I. The earl's solution to a complex calculation is to shoot it." The duke stretched and yawned, his mind sifting through the day's schedule. "If I understood Baxter correctly, the plan for this morning is a light breakfast, church services at eleven, followed by a buffet luncheon and a concert by the village and farm children here at the hall. Is that right?"

"Yes, but after they sing, you read the Christmas story and we hand out gifts to each. By four, the children disperse back their own homes for a family celebration."

"And they all return tomorrow for Boxing Day?"

"That's right, but then, the parents come with the children. We'll have a delightful time with games, and sleigh rides, and lots more singing. Today, is all about the serious contemplation of Christ's birth and what it means to mankind."

He drew her into his arms and kissed her mouth. "You're showing more each day," he whispered as he touched her abdomen. "How strange to think that our children rest beneath my fingers. I wonder if Joseph had such thoughts about Mary as they neared Bethlehem? Oh, my beautiful wife, these children are miracles! You are a miracle."

She kissed his hands. "As are you, Captain. Perhaps, next year, we'll be expecting another child. And then another after that. And then another..."

"Let's see how this pregnancy goes first, shall we?" he answered cautiously. "Any nausea this morning?"

"Not much. It's time we start our day, I suppose," she sighed. "Charles, I'd like to sit with Seth for a few moments before we leave for church services. Do you mind?"

"Not at all, but be cautious, Beth."

"Charles, do you really think him responsible for Mr. Patterson's death?"

"I have to consider all possibilities, darling, but I'll not let that overshadow Christmas. Come the twenty-seventh, I'll wear my detective hat again, but now I want only to be your husband. Shall I ring for Esther?"

"Yes, I suppose so. I miss Alicia."

"She's not returning?"

"No, her sister's in dire need of help. It's likely Alicia will remain in Brighton. For now, Esther's very good company and a valued friend."

"She may soon be Mrs. Baxter."

"What?" the duchess gasped. "Captain, are you keeping secrets?"

"Inspector Baxter's been keeping them, but I'll allow him to reveal all his plans in good time. He's an ICI agent now, you know. He's staying on as my *ad hoc* valet, but primarily, I want him with me as advisor and another set of eyes and ears. Cornelius is better at sizing up suspects than most at the Yard. I plan to triple his current salary, as he's taking on additional duties. It should allow him to marry and settle into a nice home."

"I hope he'll find one close by," she said. "I'm used to seeing him every day."

He kissed her cheek. “I have a plan. Leave it to me. Now, I must dress.”

She touched his hand. “It isn’t up to me to serve as your valet, but you’ll want to dress somewhat formally this morning, Captain. It will be the locals’ first chance to see you at church as a duke.”

He smiled. “A duke? Most of the locals seem to think me as a prince, actually. Which reminds me, several merchants in the village gave me gifts for you. I have them in my study, but I’ll place them all in here later; beneath the tree.” He kissed her once more, suddenly remembering his cousin. “I pray Paul and Cordelia passed a good night.”

“We’ll find out soon,” she answered. He kissed her once more, the peaceful moment interrupted by persistent scratching at the door. “Our dogs all slept with Adele last night. I think they want in.”

“Or out,” he laughed. “Very well, time to begin the day!”

CHAPTER FIFTY-THREE

8:09 am - Whitechapel

Susanna Morgan heard mild snoring coming from the room next door. She lay in a simple bed, beneath several quilts. She could smell food cooking and the sound of children. Sitting up, she threw off the covers and placed her bare feet on the cold floor. The window shutters were closed, but light pierced the boards. *Where am I?* she wondered. The bedroom had simple furnishings: a nightstand with a kerosene lamp, a tall chest with five drawers, a mirrored vanity, and a painted chifforobe. She opened the wardrobe and found it filled with dresses. To her surprise, all seemed her size. Choosing a woolen skirt, cotton blouse, and waistcoat, she added laced-boots (which also fit) and brushed her newly coloured hair, braiding it, and then pinning it at the back of her head.

Opening the door, she found herself in a narrow hallway, which she followed to a staircase. One side was open to the floor below, and she could see six tables, dressed with checkered cloths. A plump woman, aided by two boys, was setting places at each.

"Good morning," Morgan called to the woman.

Glancing up, the stranger grinned, causing her plump cheeks to round. "Mornin', Miss. Come on down, now, an' get a bite o' breakfast. Me an' the boys is settin' up fer Christmas, but we got plenty bacon an' eggs left over. Come on, now! It's warmer down 'ere by the fire."

Susanna descended the steps and took a seat at a table nearest the cheerful blaze. "Do you know me?"

"Now that's a right strange way ta start the day," the woman replied. "Sure nuff, do. You're Miss Stuart. That man what brung you 'ere told me all 'bout you. Right nice fella."

"A man brought me here? Forgive me, but I don't remember any of that. Who are you?"

"Name's Porter. Molly Porter. You been 'ere a few days, Miss. Sleepin' like a lamb. I checked on you, though. Like yer friend made me promise. He said 'e'd come back once you was awake. I reckon you're 'ungry, eh?"

"Starving. Did this man give a name?"

"Said it was Romanov. I like 'im a lot better 'n them other Russians what comes round 'ere. Real pleasant fella, an' 'andsome as a lad in spring! Scrambled or fried?"

"Oh, scrambled, I suppose. He told you my name is Stuart?"

"Oh, yeah. Said you 'ad other names, but we was ta call you Miss Violet. Bless me for livin'! Now 'ow did 'e know you was awake?"

The main door to Porter's Rooming House had opened to reveal a tall man with shoulder-length hair and piercing blue eyes. Susanna had no recollection of meeting him before, but he walked directly to her table, bowing gallantly.

"A very good morning to you, Miss Violet. May I join you?"

"Do I know you, sir?"

Anatole drew out a chair and sat into it, setting his hat on the empty seat next to him. "We met briefly when I found you walking near the river. Do you remember it? You were lost."

She shook her head. "Not really. The last few days are blank. But I'm not sure you have my name correct. It isn't Violet Stuart, it's..."

"Susanna," he whispered, leaning in close. "Susanna Morgan, but not really. Cassandra Calabrese is your birth name, isn't it?" She nodded. "I've repaired your memory, and now you begin the next phase of your life. Until now, names and duties have been forced upon you. Beginning today, my dear, you choose which name and which path you will take. Tonight, I shall take you to an old friend of mine, but first I hope you will deliver a message for me."

"Who are you?"

"A friend and protector. You may call me Anatole."

"And this message?" she asked warily.

He took her hand. "You might call it a final warning. A war is about to break out in England, between two major wings of a very dangerous bird. One side is red; the other black. Both are evil. Are you brave enough to deliver the message, even though the recipient once tried to kill you?"

She pulled away. "Who?"

"Sir Clive Urquhart. He took you from your hotel and knocked you unconscious. He'd planned to torture you and then kill you. I was sent to prevent that."

"I don't understand."

"No, but you will. Eat your breakfast, and then after, you and I shall take a journey to the West End. Are you brave enough to face him again?"

Every memory of Clive Urquhart rushed through her mind. His pawing hands, his greasy moustache, his soft belly; the pagan parties with endless champagne, opium, and victims. Children, mostly. She hated him, but Susanna also feared the man's power.

"Why would you rescue me? I'm just as bad as he is."

"Even a liar is evil in the eyes of the Lord," the angel told her. "Man's righteousness is as filthy rags to the One. Yet, He loves you, Cassandra Calabrese. He heard your prayer the night Urquhart took you from the hotel, and He despatched me to rescue you. Now, He asks you to face this monster once more. Every man deserves one last chance. This is his."

"God might forgive him? For all those monstrous acts?"

"He forgives all who call upon His name with a contrite heart. Are you willing to do this?"

Tears flowed down her cheeks, but she began to think of Paul Stuart—how he'd told her of Christ and helped her to see a brighter future. "Yes. I am."

"Good," answered Samael. "Today, your bright future begins."

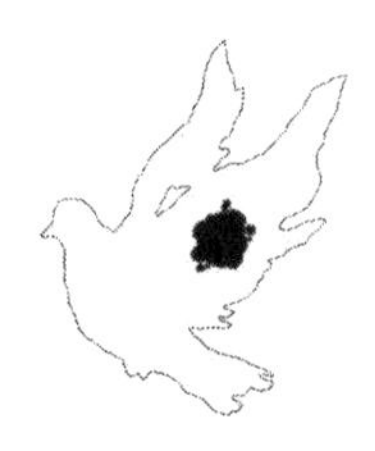

CHAPTER FIFTY-FOUR

Branham Hall – 2:45 pm

The foyer of the great hall looked like a festive railway station, filled with whispering children and a few anxious grandmothers and fathers. There were chairs aplenty, and at the centre, stood a majestic evergreen adorned with candy, cookies, candles, ribbon, golden ornaments, toys, and bells. The children were dressed in their best clothing, and knew the duchess well from her visits to their school. A few had served as chars, others as maids. One, a Miss Eva Sloane, had served in the kitchens and later the upper chambers, where she came under the duchess's notice. The intelligent girl soon found a sponsor, eventually earning a teacher's certificate from London College. Now, Miss Sloane taught at the school, and she proudly stood that afternoon to offer the first of many speeches.

"Your Graces," she said, addressing both the duke and duchess, who sat together near the tree. "It is a very great honour to once again stand inside this historic mansion and celebrate our Saviour's birth. In the many centuries since Branham's creation, the Dukes and Duchesses of Branham have provided employment, education, and edification to the people of our village. But you, Duchess Elizabeth, have risen higher than all your ancestors in the way you treat us. We all feel as though we share in this magnificent home—and in the lives of your family. Today of all days, we want you to know that Branham is in our hearts, just as it is in your blood. May this be the happiest of Christmases for you and Duke Charles."

Haimsbury stood to reply, his wife's hand in his. "If I may answer for my wife and family? Miss Sloane, it is your work with these children which should be praised. My wife and I came into this life through inheritance. You rose to your position through hard work and diligence. Christ, who stands higher than all, once lowered himself to become a human being, so that he might raise us up as his adopted children. Seeing all these young faces here today, makes me happier than any gift beneath a tree. Thank you for the songs, for your unabashed merriment, and for your prayers. Now, am I right that the Christmas story is next?" he asked Elizabeth. She nodded. He took a deep breath as she handed him an old family Bible. Charles turned to Luke, Chapter two. He opened his mouth to begin reading, but then paused.

"No, this doesn't feel right. Baxter, I wonder if you'd do the honours this year?"

Cornelius had been speaking with Kay near the turn towards the east wing, when he heard his name. "My lord? Forgive me, did you ask for me?"

"Come here, please. Yes, I need you."

Quickly, Baxter stepped through the dense collection of children on chairs, children on the floor, and children on their grandmothers' laps. Nearly every one of the fifty-seven households on the estate had sent their young ones, as well as many of the families from the villages of Anjou, Hampton, and Branham. Beth had counted two hundred and seventeen children in the crowd, along with a dozen infants.

Lady Stuart sat next to Charles in her blue dress, a cream veil over her face to help the disguise. In the next, Duke James kept her company, followed by Victoria Stuart, Dolly and Dickie Patterson-Smythe, Lord and Lady Cartringham, Paul and Cordelia Stuart, Henry MacAlpin, and in a Bath chair, a rather sleepy Seth Holloway. Merrick, Riga, Blinkmire, Stanley, Anderson, and all the other guests, including Kepelheim and Reid (along with his wife Emily) sat along the edges of the foyer, sipping mulled wine and punch.

"Here now, Mr. Baxter," said Charles as the former butler approached. "Or perhaps, I should introduce you by your new title. Everyone, if you don't already know it, our very good Mr. Baxter no longer serves here at Branham as butler. Mr. Kay now holds that position. And as of this week, my home in London will have a new butler as well; for our former butler is now Detective Inspector Baxter of the Intelligence Branch." Haimsbury applauded, and nearly everyone rose to his or her feet in admiration and appreciation. "My dear friend, you will help guide all our investigations. And, I imagine, will become Lord Aubrey's boss ere long, and mine as well! To our Inspector!" he said, raising his glass.

All toasted, and then Charles set his drink aside to place a hand on Baxter's shoulder. "Thank you, my friend. Thank you for helping to turn me from a humble detective into a successful duke. Happy Christmas, Inspector."

Charles handed Baxter an envelope. "Open it later, if you wish; or now. But I'd hoped you would read the Christmas story for us. Beth says you're the one who's been reading it these past few years. I should like to keep that tradition intact."

"Thank you, sir. I may open this now?"

"If you wish."

Baxter unsealed the envelope, which contained a legal document for the Haimsbury Spring House, a four-bedroom cottage near the west end of the grounds. "Sir, are you...? I mean, is this true? No, sir, it's too much!"

"We want you to have a place of your own, but we selfishly would keep you close. The spring house is entailed to the estate, therefore, I've no legal right to dispose of it permanently, but I can decide who lives there. Baxter, the home is yours for all the days of your life—and should you ever marry," Charles continued with a wink, "for your wife as well."

Baxter wiped tears from his plump cheeks. "This is a truly fine Christmas, sir, for I've just asked that future wife to marry me. Mrs. Alcorn has agreed to become Mrs. Baxter."

Once again, the room burst into spontaneous applause, and toasts were made and wine consumed. The children laughed and ate cookies, cakes, and finger sandwiches; all washed down with lemonade. Esther joined her future husband near the tree.

"Congratulations to you both," the duke told the former housekeeper as he kissed her cheek.

"Thank you, Your Grace," she said. "It's this promotion that's done it. I think Cornelius is getting ideas."

"One of many more to come, I expect," Charles answered happily. "Now, Inspector, if you'd tell us all why we celebrate Christmas?"

Everyone returned to their chairs, and Baxter began to read:

"'And it came to pass in those days, that there went out a decree from Caesar Augustus, that all the world should be taxed. And this taxing was first made when Cyrenius was governor of Syria. And all went to be taxed, every one into his own city. And Joseph also went up from Galilee, out of the city of Nazareth, into Judaea, unto the city of David, which is called Bethlehem; because he was of the house and lineage of David: To be taxed with Mary his espoused wife, being great with child.

"'And so it was, that, while they were there, the days were accomplished that she should be delivered. And she brought forth her firstborn son, and wrapped him in swaddling clothes, and laid him in a manger; because there was no room for them in the inn. And there were in the same country shepherds abiding in the field, keeping watch over their flock by night. And, lo, the angel of the Lord came upon them, and the glory of the Lord shone round about them: and they were sore afraid. And the angel said unto them, Fear not: for, behold, I bring you good tidings of great joy, which shall be to all people. For unto you is born this day in the city of David a Saviour, which is Christ the Lord.

"'And this shall be a sign unto you; Ye shall find the babe wrapped in swaddling clothes, lying in a manger. And suddenly there was with the angel a multitude of the heavenly host praising God, and saying, Glory to God in the highest, and on earth peace, good will toward men.'"

Inspector Baxter finished the verses, and a hush fell upon the room. Kay switched off the electric lights, leaving only the tree's white candles to illuminate the foyer. The eyes of each child turned upwards to gaze in wonder at the glittering symphony of gold and green.

Riga commenced the plaintive strains of '*O Come, O Come Emanuel*' on the cello with Stanley providing soft piano accompaniment. As the majestic hymn ended, the duchess stood, her face radiant as she broke into an unplanned solo.

"*Minuit, chrétiens*," she sang, beginning the first verse of the beloved French carol, "*c'est l'heure solennelle, o*ù l'Homme Dieu descendit jusqu'à nous. *Pour effacer la tache originelle et de Son Père arrêter le courroux. Le monde entier tressaille d'espérance, en cette nuit qui lui donne un Sauveur. Peuple à genoux, attends ta délivrance! Noël! Noël! Voici le Rédempteur! Noël! Noël! Voici le Rédempteur!*"

She paused, and Riga took up the music, joined by Stanley who knew the song by heart. Beth then switched to English for the second verse, and one by one, the entire room joined in the meaningful song known to most as 'O, Holy Night':

"Truly, He taught us to love one another,
His law is love and His gospel is peace.
Chains shall He break for the slave is our brother
And in His name all oppression shall cease!
Sweet hymns of joy in grateful chorus raise we,
Let all within us praise His holy name!
Christ is the Lord! O, praise His name forever!
His pow'r and glory proclaim forever more!
His pow'r—His pow'r proclaim forever more!"

On the final lines, Elizabeth sang a high descant, an octave above, her sweet voice floating upwards along the grand foyer's multiple storeys, reaching the pinnacles of the roofline and penetrating the snow and ice.

Sitting upon the slate peak, a white owl began to weep, its feathery head bowed in humble reverence. He prayed silently, listening to his Master's voice. Once done, Anatole Romanov, known to his brethren as Samael, lifted his great wings and elongated into his elohim appearance: a magnificent being of light and power, and he soared towards the heavens, disappearing from the world of men; only to reappear in London, just outside a Greek Orthodox Church.

CHAPTER FIFTY-FIVE

8:45 pm - Branham

"Another delightful Christmas goose!" exclaimed Duke James as he escorted the disguised queen into the music room. "It's a shame the Cartringhams had to leave this afternoon. They surely missed a treat! Basil loves Stephens's cooking. Did you enjoy it, Drina?"

The queen was careful never to wear black or mourning colours during her stay, as most of the public had never seen the sovereign without her widow's weeds. Instead, she wore brown or grey, or even pale blues. This evening, she'd chosen a simple skirt of forest green velvet, topped by a matching jacket embellished with tiny pearls at the placket and throat. The sleeves widened into bell shapes at the wrist, revealing fingerless gloves of cream lace.

"Mrs. Stephens certainly raises the bar for future cooks," she told her childhood friend. "Beth, you ate very little. Roast beef and goose are good for babies. They impart stamina. My dear, you're not ill, I hope?"

The duchess sat, joined by Charles. "A bit nauseous," she admitted. "The beef was perfectly done, but I think goose may not be a favourite of these children. Where's Henry gotten to?"

"Upstairs," Aubrey replied as he led his new wife to a soft chair. "Comfortable?" he asked her.

Cordelia nodded. "Yes, husband." The simple word caused her to smile, for despite trepidation over the demands of marriage, these few hours spent as the earl's wife had lifted her mood as nothing else might. "Who's to play for us?"

"Riga and Stanley," explained Kepelheim, who was laying out sheets of music on the piano. "Adele, of course, but I may offer a few arrangements of my own. Duchess, will you sing for us again?

Your spontaneous carol this afternoon caused everyone to weep tears of joy! I soaked an entire handkerchief. And poor Blinkmire! Ah, our gentle giant may require an entirely new set of them."

"You're very kind," she answered, holding her husband's hand. "And we'll make sure both you men receive handkerchiefs aplenty before you leave Branham. However, tonight, I wish only to listen. Wasn't the children's choir wonderful, Auntie Drina?"

"Oh, my, yes!" exulted the queen. "Are all of them in your school?"

"Every child five or older attends until their fourteenth year, and then each is apprenticed to a trade. However, anyone who wishes to continue study, does so with a tutor. Miss Sloane is an example of that program. We have two who are at university even now. One studies chemistry at King's College in London, and the other is reading mathematics at Newnham in Cambridge—both on scholarship."

"Cambridge?" asked Dolly. "Perhaps, Seth knows her."

"I doubt it," remarked Charles. "The women at Newnham rarely commune with the men from Trinity. Besides, he's a don, not a student. Where is he this evening?"

"Exhausted," Beth answered. "I fear this afternoon took all his strength." She leaned in to whisper, "And I pray you'll give him another day before you pepper him with questions, husband."

"I'm letting others handle that, little one. Never fear. My detective hat is shelved, remember?"

She kissed his cheek. "So long as *you* remember it, Captain. I'm sure Henry prefers no one undermine his medical efforts."

As though summoned, Henry entered at that very moment, worry shadowing his fine features. "Do forgive the interruption, everyone. I wonder if I might speak with you, Charles? It won't take long."

The duke kissed his wife's cheek and stood. "Please, don't delay starting the concert for me. I know Della is anxious to hear Riga and Stanley perform."

Once away from the music room, Salperton explained. "I really am sorry to cause disruption, but Seth's desperate to remember what happened beneath those tunnels. He's a decent chap, and he's asked me to help. So I've decided to try something new, but I need your permission."

"Mine, why?"

"Because, we still haven't heard from his father or sisters. I suppose it's because of Christmas. They've probably all met up elsewhere—Germany or Austria, perhaps—but if so, I wish they'd told their butler! Really, people can be very disappointing at times."

Charles smiled. "Do I detect frustration in that comment, Lord Salperton?"

"Perhaps, a little. It's just this whole business with Miss Stuart! I received a telegram before supper. It's from Leman Street. Apparently, someone in Whitechapel reported seeing a woman of Violet's description near London Hospital, of all things, but now she's vanished without a trace. Inspector France investigated the sightings, and followed the clues to a local hostelry. Violet had indeed stayed there, but her hotel bill was paid by a tall man with a Russian accent! Dash it all, Charles, it upsets me no end!"

"A Russian accent?"

"Yes, and he seemed rich, too. Honestly, after all we've done to help, and now she runs away with some foreign chap!"

"Did France discover the man's name?"

"No, but Mrs. Porter thought him kind. I just pray it's Romanov and not one of these others."

"Was this Molly Porter?"

"Perhaps. I don't know," answered the viscount. "Look, I shouldn't burden you with these troubles."

"You're not a burden, Henry. Do you want to return to London? I can offer my train, if you wish."

"No, I can't do that. And besides, it would make no difference. It's happened before. Patients start to recover, and then they rush away without a word. Look, don't mind me. I'm a little worried, that's all, but not enough to leave you—or Beth. Or Cordelia, for that matter, though, she certainly looks better this evening, don't you think?"

"Yes, she does," replied Charles. "But it seems you're not. Henry, you're exhausted."

Salperton ran a hand through his thick hair, his eyes casting about as though his mind turned like a top. "Yes, but there's too much to be done. I'll sleep tomorrow. For now, Holloway is my patient, and you need his information; as does he. I really don't think him a murderer, Charles, but he may be a witness."

"Possibly."

"Then, may I do this? The method, I mean."

"What method is that?" asked the duke.

"It's called 'catharsis', and I've used it before with some success. But there is also the possibility that once he remembers, the shock might cause him to block it all out again—permanently."

"Which means we lose his testimony, if there's a trial."

"Precisely. Shall I risk it?" Henry asked. He overheard footsteps and turned to find Kepelheim walking swiftly to catch up to the taller men.

"I asked Victoria and Dolly if I might abandon them for a short while. Is this about Dr. Holloway?"

"Yes," answered Salperton. "He's eager to regain his memory. Holloway's a man of science and familiar with Joseph Breuer's method. He asked me to try it."

"Do you mean catharsis?" asked Martin. "I've read several monographs by Breuer. His method is similar to one I employ."

"You?" asked Henry. "I'd no idea you worked with memory, Mr. Kepelheim."

"Martin's technique is simple but effective," said Charles. "He's helped me to remember a little of my childhood, simply by talking."

"I might ask for your assistance, then," Salperton told the tailor. "If you men have a moment, perhaps, we can speak to Seth about it."

Charles hated to leave Beth, particularly for something connected to the murder case. "Give me a moment."

He returned to the music room and drew her aside. "Beth, I've been asked to give permission for an experiment. Henry has a treatment that may help Seth to remember, but I think it important that a policeman attend and write down all that's said. I can ask Reid to go up, if you prefer. Or Paul."

She smiled, the compassionate expression calming his heart. "Go be a policeman, Captain. But once done, hang up your hat once more. And you will owe me these lost minutes later, all right? I shall collect the debt in private."

The duke bowed and kissed her hand. "Such a pleasant debt will be paid in full, my lady. I promise."

Charles returned to the men, and the trio proceeded upwards to the apartment where Seth Holloway awaited. Exhausted after three hours in the bath chair, he lay upon his bed, half asleep. The large tester bed was hung with damask curtains in a striped blue and yellow silk. The matching duvet lay crumpled near his feet, and only a light blanket and sheet covered the patient, as if he'd grown overly warm.

"Forgive us for waking you," began Haimsbury as they entered.

"Have you come as my host or as a detective?"

"Both," answered the duke.

"Then, make yourself comfortable. From what I've read of this Breuer method, it could take some time. Before we begin, might I ask a question?"

"Certainly."

"It's just no one will tell me anything about the other men. I've asked Paul and Henry—even Beth. But everyone remains silent. Is it that bad? Are Patterson and Wentworth dead?"

Charles took a seat, switching his thought patterns to that of a detective; reading the man's body language. *Is he lying? Did Seth kill Patterson, perhaps Wentworth as well? But he couldn't be responsible for Collinwood. No, someone else must be involved.*

"I'm very sorry, Dr. Holloway, but Mr. Patterson is dead," he told the patient. "As for Wentworth, we believe he's fled England. Our French operatives are following the trail there. Can you tell me how Patterson died?"

Complete shock ran through the twenty-nine-year-old's features. He tried to sit, and his hands fidgeted with the thick red hair. "Dead? How can he be dead? Good heavens, how! It was only the three of us in there. No, wait. Shadows... I saw... Something. Someone." His eyes rounded, and all colour left his cheeks. "I can see snatches of images in my mind, but nothing tangible. How was I injured again? I don't remember."

Henry took over. "Tell me about these 'snatches'. Describe them, no matter how trivial it may seem. Perhaps, we can unveil them without hypnosis."

"Just dreams, mostly. Last night, I dreamt about Pitt. That's what we call Patterson. Short for Pitter-Patter. He's always talking. He's dead? Good heavens, he was just a boy!"

"You were fond of him, then?" asked Charles.

"I suppose so. He reminded me of Ted Treadway."

"Who's that?"

"A cousin of mine. He used to go on the digs with us."

"The archaeological digs?" asked Kepelheim.

"Yes. I grew up on those expeditions. Nearly every year, we'd spend months up to our knees in sand, flies, and mummies. Father's a linguist, and he trained me to read hieroglyphs and cuneiform, as well as speak the local languages. Mother's more artistic and taught me to sketch and paint. Treadway joined us when I was about eighteen. He jabbered all the time, just like Patterson. Ted was killed when a tunnel collapsed."

"I'm very sorry," Henry told him.

"It was quite awful, actually," Seth explained. "The Bedouins claimed the area was cursed. We ran into some very strange beliefs amongst the locals. Despite all efforts, the Ottomans have failed to destroy the ancient gods. They've merely gone underground. You can ask Paul, if you want to know. He joined us on one of the North African digs. I'm sure he could verify that."

"I'll speak to him," said Sinclair. "Let's get back to the project. When's the last time you saw the other men?"

Holloway felt a sudden chill and reached for the duvet. Kepelheim helped by adding another quilt. "You look feverish, Dr. Holloway. Perhaps, we should leave you to sleep and conduct this experiment tomorrow."

"I've slept too much already. And I'm used to injuries. As my scars attest. I think the last time I saw Pitt and Worthy was in the new section. Collinwood and the Oxford team found a crypt, which held several urns, niched into the walls. There were statues as well, and I agreed to sketch the main features whilst Worthy and Pitt forged ahead to see if the crypt connected to other rooms. It's a massive labyrinth down there, and I doubt King Richard's men designed it. It's far older, in my opinion."

"Your recollections of the crypt are clear?" asked Sinclair.

"Very. It's only when I started sketching that raven statue that everything gets cloudy."

Charles felt a chill run down his spine. "Raven statue?"

"Yes. It's my belief the crypt was intended as a transformational chamber. The entrance is from Lion Hall's main tunnel and contains a large statue of a man. The opposite door, the exit, is guarded by a large raven. It's the same size as the man and disquieting in its aspect. As with Egyptian statues, the tunnel builders painted the details, giving the bird a realistic appearance; as though it might come to life at any moment."

"Was the human statue the same?" asked Kepelheim.

"Strange you should ask me that, for he... Well, sir, the man resembled the duke."

Charles felt a second chill, only this one included a whisper.

Hello, boy.

The duke ignored the taunt and continued the interview. "Describe it."

"As I say, eerily similar to you, sir. If Aubrey found me, then surely he passed by it. You can confirm it with him. It stood on an inscribed base, with the total height of ten feet or more. The man's eyes were azure blue, and the hair black. It struck me as odd, for the style of the carving was more Greek or Roman, but the colouration typical of Egyptian statues."

"And the raven's height?"

"Also about ten feet."

"You called it a transformational chamber," Kepelheim interrupted. "Do forgive me, Your Grace, but I find the descriptor quite odd. Transforming into what?"

Seth's face grew serious, his blue eyes fixed on the men. "Into something new. The spell is this: You enter as a man, but leave as something else. In this case, you are either shepherded by this raven to your goal, or else you become the raven. He might serve as a gatekeeper. It may be the man becomes the gatekeeper."

Charles had to fight to remain calm, for the Dragon's grinding whispers roared inside his head.

Boy, you're not listening to me!

"Gatekeeper?" he managed to ask.

Martin stared at the duke warily. "Charles, are you all right?"

"Fine," he answered simply. "Dr. Holloway, what doorway might this gatekeeper guard?"

"Without translating the writing on the statues, it's difficult to say. I presume it's a passage to the underworld. Why else would these tunnels proceed downwards, ever deeper into the earth?"

"You found writing?" asked Kepelheim, suddenly all ears. "Did you by any chance copy it?"

"Yes, of course," the earl's son answered wearily. "Forgive me, gentlemen, but this is more talking than I've done in two days. Might we rest a little?"

Salperton took the injured man's pulse. "Quick but relatively strong," he murmured to himself. "Seth, I promise we'll let you sleep soon, but first I'd like to try this new method. It may help you recall those lost memories, and afterward, you'll sleep very deeply."

"Shall I turn down the lights?" asked the tailor. "To prepare the room."

"Oh, yes, that would be most helpful, Martin. Thank you," replied the physician. "Now, Seth, I want you to shut your eyes and concentrate only on my voice."

Charles pulled his chair away from the bed, closer to the fire to allow Salperton room to work. He wanted to believe Holloway's tale because of Elizabeth, but he had to treat him as he would any other suspect. Despite his boyish charm, Seth Holloway might be a murderer.

Henry sat next to the bed. The soft-eyed alienist motioned to Kepelheim. "I wonder, Martin, if you'd be kind enough to keep watch on our patient's pulse for me? If it ever rises significantly or grows erratic, let me know. Some of this may cause physiological responses, and I shouldn't wish to overtax his heart."

Seth opened his eyes. "Overtax my heart? Will this hurt?"

"No more than your wounds already do, my friend," Salperton answered gently. "However, you're about to re-live whatever happened to you. For good or ill, the truth will come out. If you share any responsibility for what happened, that, too, will come out. Do I still have your permission to proceed?"

"Yes, of course. I want to know as much as anyone," Holloway insisted. "No matter the truth, I need to know."

"Very well, then. Now, before I begin, I'd like to do something my colleagues in the profession might find unusual. Since we are delving into your inner thoughts, I'd like to seek the Lord's guidance. Martin, would you pray for us?"

Kepelheim stood. "I'd be pleased to do so. Let us bow our heads, gentlemen."

Holloway did so as well, and it felt strange, but right. His parents had raised him as an atheist: to trust in science for answers. Though members of the Church of England, George and Imogen Holloway practised a social sort of religion, attending primarily to be seen, rather than worship. Indeed, if the 7th Earl of Salter believed in anything, it was knowledge, for he pursued it with a vengeance.

Though Seth had accepted Christ and sought deliverance during his brief but hellish journey through the Stone Realms, he had no memory of it now; only an underlying fear of dreams. Now, as Martin Kepelheim lifted his voice to the throne of God, the young man at the centre of this experiment felt a wonderful calm wash over his spirit. And though his eyes were shut, a warm white light permeated his lids, as if the sun stood over his bed.

"And may your mighty hand protect Dr. Holloway, my Lord," the tailor was saying, somewhere beyond the beautiful light. "We seek guidance, and especially ask that you would provide him your answers. May the truth be revealed, dear Lord. Most of all, I ask that your redemptive truth be sown within Dr. Holloway's heart, and that he will grow ever nearer to you. Thank you for keeping your great and tender hand upon us, my King. In the name of your only begotten Son, I ask it. Even the name of Christ Jesus. Amen."

Seth opened his eyes, wondering if the intense light would blind him, but instead he saw the faces of three men who were about to change his life:

Henry MacAlpin, whom he'd first met five years ago at Torden Hall, his family's country estate near Faversham. He knew little of the viscount's personal life, but in the past few days, he'd come to trust in his medical skill.

Martin Kepelheim, a peculiar little man, whose colourful phrases and eccentric behaviour struck Seth as a mask to hide a complex and incisive mind. Kepelheim had visited him often over the past few days and hinted at dark, ancient origins to the tunnel system.

Finally, there was Duke Charles Sinclair of Haimsbury. Never in all his travels, had Seth met anyone like the duke. His bearing, mannerisms, and speech defined him as regal, commanding, and formidable; yet, there was a kindness to his eyes that revealed a deeper, intuitive side to the man. If ever Seth wanted to make a friend, it was Sinclair. He couldn't explain it, but since first meeting the duke, Seth had the strangest sense that they'd met before—though, he felt certain they never had. Still, he felt a connexion so profound that it defied all logic.

Then, a voice whispered into his right ear: *You need Aubrey.*

Though he felt like a fool for asking, Holloway voiced the thought. "I wonder, before we begin, might we ask Paul to join us? I realise he's probably busy; this being Christmas and him only just married, but of all you men, I know him the best. Might he be a part of this experiment?"

"Yes, of course, he may," answered Henry. "I'll fetch him at once."

Whilst Salperton was away, Charles decided to pursue an entirely different sort of interview. "Tell me about your parents."

Seth felt energised from the prayer, and he answered easily. "Father's a hard crust of cheese. His grandfather and father were both antiquarians, and he grew up on expeditions. Therefore, he thought nothing of bringing up his sons in hot tombs and sandy digs."

"Sons?" asked the duke. "I understood you were the only son."

"I am now. I had a brother, George Abel. George after my father and Abel—well, that was my mother's idea. Her father's name was Adam, and she always wanted a boy named Abel. He died of cholera at just six years old. I was born a year later; hence the name Seth. The replacement for Abel. That fact was drummed into me from my earliest years. Father insisted I become tough and resistant to all disease. To accomplish this, he and Mother dragged me all over the Levant and Africa. And I did become tough."

Martin smiled. "That's certainly true. The wound that runs along your chest and stomach would have been the end of most men, yet you're healing at a remarkable rate. I almost call it miraculous. Tell me, what sort of tasks can a child manage on these digs?"

For the first time since becoming a patient, Holloway laughed, revealing a far more handsome countenance. Charles took notice, wondering if Elizabeth had found the young man's laughing eyes pleasant. Had she enjoyed kissing him that summer?

Listen to me, boy. This one will usurp your rightful place. He will steal what is precious to you.

"As you can imagine, a child's muscles are useless in most aspects of a dig," Seth explained, "but my mother used the time to teach me to read, write, calculate mathematics, and speak a dozen living languages. And I learnt to paint and draw our finds. I've kept a detailed journal of all our digs, including watercolour and pastel portraits of the places and people."

"I imagine the duchess appreciated your artistic temperament," Charles heard himself say.

"We share an interest in art as well as music."

"And much more," Charles answered, instantly regretting the sarcasm.

The comment caused the patient's mirth to disappear. "Honestly, Your Grace, I'm pleased for her. Pleased for you both! It's true that I loved Elizabeth and wanted to marry her, but she would never give me an answer. Not hearing a direct 'no', I assumed she only needed time, and I visited as often as my schedule allowed. I went to France to see her many times, but always, whenever we'd talk together for any length of time, Beth's conversation would inevitably include references to this fellow she called 'Captain'. I knew she loved you and held out hope you might one day seek her out. She never named you, nor did she explain why you'd remained silent. I was quite jealous of you, to be honest. But it's clear you've made her very happy."

Sinclair started to ask if Seth had ever kissed the duchess whilst in France, but Aubrey's entrance prevented it.

"I hear we're about to conduct an experiment," said the earl as he reached the bedside.

"Forgive me for taking you away from your new bride, Paul, but I thought it might help to have you a part of this experiment, as you call it," answered Holloway.

"My wife's enjoying the music, and she'd just struck up a conversation with Mr. Blinkmire, when Henry arrived. Blinkmire's become quite protective of both Cordelia and Adele. They're in safe hands. Henry tells me he's using Breuer's method. I'm familiar with how it works. During one of my many assignments, I had to study theories on hypnosis. Charcot, Bernheim, Bramwell. There's a rousing debate regarding its efficacy, but I've seen it work. I do, however, advocate praying for the Lord's protection."

"We've already done that," Henry told the earl. "I hadn't realised how well versed you are in medical matters, Paul, though I should have known. In the course of your work for the Crown, you've pretended to be just about everything!"

"Very nearly," laughed Aubrey, "but don't ask Galton about the circus. That's all I ask." Taking a chair beside the duke, Aubrey became a spectator.

Henry resumed his previous chair. "Now, Seth, you must close your eyes. As with the earl, I've read through the various schools of thought, and it seems to me the secret is total relaxation. Most of us experience times when we struggle to access memories. The brain is an undiscovered country, but beyond the physical frontier lies the metaphysical. Our souls and minds intermingle with our physical forms in a way that defies measure, yet we do so with ease. However, sometimes, a blockage appears; a tangling of the neural links, you might say. It's my hope now to remove that impediment."

"Just tell me what to do," answered the patient.

Henry held a small clock in his hands. "I want you to take this. Hold it firmly. Its sound will act as a means to connect you to this room, but also provide a soothing rhythm. By holding it, you'll also feel the gears move. Now, close your eyes and concentrate on my voice. Let the ticking and the sensation of the gears become part of you whilst you listen."

Downstairs, in the music room, Elizabeth had agreed to play. She'd hoped Charles might return before now, but as Adele had run through her entire retinue of songs, and Count Riga's cello had broken a string, Beth agreed to play whilst the Romanian restrung the instrument. Not having practised anything in particular, the duchess did something quite daring.

"Lady Stuart, I wonder if you would choose a song from our box of music? Whatever you pick, I'll play; though I make no promises for my technique."

Baxter took the box of sheet music and books to the disguised queen, holding it close so she might look through them. Alexandrina Victoria laughed. "Oh, my! I suppose I shall be to blame if it all goes wrong, is that it? Very well. Let me see. Mr. Baxter—oh, wait. I'm mistaken, aren't I? You're now Inspector Baxter."

"I am, as they say, off duty today, my lady," he told her drily. "Mister is quite correct."

A mischievous look sparkled in the sovereign's eyes. "Mister? Ah, well, who knows what the future holds? Ah! How about this one?"

The butler turned detective gazed at the selection, his magnificent eyebrows pinching together as though concerned. "This might be better played by someone else, my lady."

"Nonsense! It isn't difficult, or at least the first movement is not. And I've always loved it," argued the queen. "Beth plays it beautifully."

Waiting at the piano, Elizabeth reached out, her delicate fingers grasping the air. "Let me see it, Baxter. Please."

The great man reluctantly crossed to the duchess and placed the music into her hand. She gazed down at the title, and it seemed that the room grew abnormally still. The audience waited, motionless.

"It is Beethoven," the petite pianist announced. "His *Mondscheinsonate*, or in English *Moonlight Sonata*." She paused before speaking again, and those who knew her well wanted to rip the music from her hands, but she remained regally calm. After whispering a silent prayer, the duchess smiled at their guest. "This is also one of my favourites, Lady Stuart. I'll happily play all the movements for you. This is..." Her voice caught in her throat, as tears brightened her eyes.

Joseph Merrick leaned forward, worry shadowing his misshapen face. "No, dear lady, you mustn't! Not if the memories are too painful."

"But the pain is sweet, Mr. Merrick," she answered demurely. "It reminds me of other Christmases. Although this is the final work I ever played for my father, it is also one he often requested. It's only right that I should play it now, before my dearest friends. And I do so in his honour."

"Perhaps, you should wait until your husband returns, Duchess," suggested Blinkmire, sensing a dark mood in the atmosphere. The sensitive giant worried about his hostess, wanting only to protect her.

"No, I'll play it now. It might be that my father's strength will pass into us all as I play. Many of you knew him, but others have only seen portraits. Connor Stuart was a man of great stature. Not as tall as our good Mr. Blinkmire, of course, but taller than most. Six foot five and a wee smidge, as he used to say. Isn't that right, Grandpa?" she asked Duke James.

"Aye, lassie. So he did. I'm glad to hear you play it again, Princess. Show off your pretty talent and remind us all of a great, great man."

A blanket of silence enveloped the room as all awaited the introductory chords of the mournful first movement. Elbert Stanley, Stephen Blinkmire, Joseph Merrick, Edmund and Emily Reid, Malcolm Risling, Dickie and Dolly Patterson-Smythe, Victoria Stuart,

Adele Stuart, Duke James, Baxter and Esther Alcorn. All sat on the edges of their chairs.

As Elizabeth's fingers touched the keys; upstairs, a man lay in torment, recalling events so horrifying that his mind had tried to discard them forever.

CHAPTER FIFTY-SIX

Belgravia, London

"Where is she?" Wychwright bellowed. "I insist you bring her out to me at once!"

Edgar Alden had served the Earl of Cartringham as batman three years in North Africa and twenty years as butler. As a former soldier, he knew William Wychwright's type well. The army captain (soon to be retired) stood toe to toe with the slightly shorter butler, screaming as though only ever-increasing decibels held the power to convey information.

"Do you hear me?" he shouted into Alden's left ear.

"I hear you quite well, my lord, but I must repeat my earlier and constant answer. Lady Cordelia is not here, nor has she been here since the wake, sir. Lord and Lady Cartringham left two hours ago for his lordship's cousin's home in Oxford. I shall pass along your best wishes when they return."

Sir Richard Treversham tapped his friend on the shoulder. "Leave it, Will. Alden's loyal to Basil. He'll never talk. Let's get back to the coach. It's freezing out here!"

Wychwright grudgingly turned to go, but threw one last threat as he departed. "If you're lying, I'll have your job, Alden!"

The butler shut the door, imagining how very nice it would be if the vile young baron actually did 'have his job', and how satisfying it might be to see him reduced to the rank of a servant.

Meanwhile, in the coach's slightly warmer interior, a dark-haired companion greeted the baron with a smooth and easy smile. "I take it your sister isn't here?"

The baron and his greedy friend slouched into the seat, opposite the smiling man. "Complete waste of time!" shouted William. "Why did the foolish girl run, that's what I want to know. She could have had an easy life by marrying Richard. Really, why a woman can't simply enjoy the act and have done is beyond me. She'll make a very poor wife, if she thinks the marriage bed is all flowers and hearts."

Saraqael (wearing the guise of his favourite Romanian 'pattern') offered consolation. "Yes, it is difficult to comprehend the female mind, isn't it? Richard is handsome, in a feminine sort of way—and I mean that as a compliment, my friend. Truly, I do. Women don't want overly masculine bears, do they? They want a man of refinement with gentility and charm. You speak of hearts and flowers, but Cordelia failed to see the soft rose beneath your prickly thorn. But don't give up, my dashing friend. Just because she found your initial approach somewhat repulsive, doesn't mean she won't come round eventually."

"Repulsive!" shouted Treversham. "How dare you!"

"Now, now, Richie, old boy," soothed the fallen elohim. "It's not your appearance, but your approach that repels. Now, there are some women who prefer a strong hand, but not Will's pretty sister. She wants to be wooed. A sensitive nature such as hers requires finesse. Wendaway had the right idea. He'd very nearly charmed the lady, but then his own plot with the mother sent it all crashing down. I rather think the dowager baroness is becoming a hindrance, don't you, Will? The police will eventually discover Sir Albert's hiding place and arrest him for rape and possibly murder. And it's a short hop from him to you."

The baron shook his head adamantly. "It'll never happen. Even if Reid did find him, Albert would never go to trial, because we shan't allow Cordelia to testify. She's still under my authority."

Saraqael grinned, his light eyes flashing as though he kept a secret. "So you say. However, if you want to get your hands on her *money*, then you'll need to act quickly. I noticed Aubrey paying a great deal of attention to your sister at that wake last week. I wonder, why do you call it a wake? Do you expect the dead to rise up and walk?"

"Of course, not," muttered the baron.

Treversham was still recovering from being called 'repulsive', but this odd comment caught his ear. "Don't you have funeral customs in Romania, Prince Aleksandr?"

"We have many customs for the dead in my country. I grew up in the Carpathians as you know; a mountainous region with sharp slopes that defy the foot of man, fit only for goats and ghosts. The dead do not remain so in my country. They wander amongst those impossible crags and crevasses, searching for their lost lives. To assure a man is truly dead, you must cut off his head and stuff garlic into the mouth."

Treversham laughed nervously. "Cut off his head? That's ridiculous!"

"It may sound so to English ears, but all such rituals have roots in truth, my pretty friend. There is an old song, which is sometimes sung by the women of our village..."

"Village? I thought you lived in a castle," William interrupted.

"Once I did, but the Russian invasion of our beautiful mountains has made refugees of even the richest prince. Many of the villagers now live under the lash of our invaders, but I shall conquer it again. Time is my friend."

"And this song? Is it a ritual?"

Saraqael, in the guise of Prince Aleksandr Koshmar, offered an unsettlingly sardonic smile. "A beautiful word is that. *Ritual.* And yes, the song is ancient. It is not original to the Wallachian people, but harkens back to a time when Striga, the father of all skin-changers, roamed the mountains of my homeland. By day, he lived as an exceedingly beautiful and charismatic man; taller than all his brethren, with skin of such iridescent paleness that even the snows were jealous. His eyes shone like fiery drops of ice, and his full mouth pulsed with ruby blood. The wavy locks of his raven hair flowed along his muscled back and shoulders like a rippling waterfall, and his sexual prowess had no equal. All women fell at his feet, pleading for him to take them—right then and there! This song is about him. The translation from Romanian to English is imprecise and fails to rhyme, but the gist—as you British say—is this. The song recalls Striga's power over women; one in particular. A rare beauty named Princess Trandafir. It means 'Rose' in our language.

"This enchanting creature loved to dance in the woods, and all the woodland animals danced with her. Striga saw her there and fell in love, but she refused him. Day after day, he pursued her, but each time the princess rebuffed his advances. One night, Trandafir decided to dance in the moonlight. The pale orb was round and bright, illuminating the voluptuous dancer. As it happened, that same night, Striga was roaming the fields and forests in the skin of a great wolf, just one of his many nocturnal forms; and he saw her there amongst the sycamore trees.

"His desire for her overwhelmed all reason, and he fell upon her with a mad fury! Come the dawn, she lay upon the forest floor, dying. Changed back into his human self, Striga wept bitter tears over her torn body, but he could not allow her to die. To keep her alive, Striga offered some of his own blood, granting her immortality. Thus, Trandafir became a skin-changer, an eternally beautiful woman beneath the sun, but a voracious animal by moonlight. To this very day, when a man or woman dies a violent death, the head must be removed to make sure Striga and Trandafir do not steal them; for both are jealous of humans and desire company. It is said that they wish to build an army of skin-changers. With such a bloodthirsty multitude, no country would be safe. The world of ordinary men would soon fall."

The two humans stared at the Romanian. Though the tale sounded impossible, something in the prince's manner, in his eyes and the sound of his voice, added an uncomfortable measure of credibility.

"Surely, that's a fable," William laughed.

"Not at all. It is practised yet today. Some say that those who die violently—no matter the country, no matter the race—their bodies may be snatched away from the grieving families and conscripted into this undead army. The theft can happen in the smallest of seconds! The day is coming when the dead will rise once more, my friend," he added, leaning forward to stare into their eyes. "You may rely upon it."

The two men shuddered, and Saraqael/Koshmar laughed, clearly pleased with the effect of his tale. "But men such as you have no fear of the undead, do you? I sense a shimmering of specialty in your bones. A taste of blood royale," he insinuated, taking their measure. "You know, William, it's time I introduce you both to my other friends. It's time for you to join *us*."

Treversham laughed nervously, his hard eyes blinking. "Join what? The Freemasons?"

Saraqael laughed, his icy eyes shifting hues. "You have no idea how very funny that comment is! Do not allow the Masons to hoodwink you, my pretty friend, for they are pretenders: a pale imitation of a very old fellowship. If influence and wealth are what you seek, then join us. Ordinarily, we meet Saturdays at the Empress Hotel, but that venue has fallen out of favour. Do you know the building at Wormwood and New Broad?"

"The big one? Just west of the police station?"

Again, Sara laughed. "Yes, it is a fitting location. Come there tonight, at midnight."

"But it's Christmas," objected William.

"You've no plans, I take it?"

"No, but... Look here, just what sort of group is this? You're not a religious outfit, are you? Prince or not, I have a strong aversion to anything connected to the church. You're an ignorant fool, Koshmar, if you put any trust in so dated an institution!"

The false human grew serious, his gloved hands gripping the head of the carved cane. "I should be careful how you address me, Lord Wychwright. Do not tempt fate when success lies before you. The tale of Striga is true, and his blood flows in my veins, which makes me a powerful ally or a vengeful enemy. I can fulfil your every wish, but just as easily, I could crush you like an ant. The choice is yours. Will you join us and live forever or die like any worm?"

Wychwright felt an odd tingle in his fingers, as though energy coursed through them. Suddenly, he longed to run through woods and streams beneath the silver moon with nothing but blood upon his skin.

Soon, his wishes would all come true.

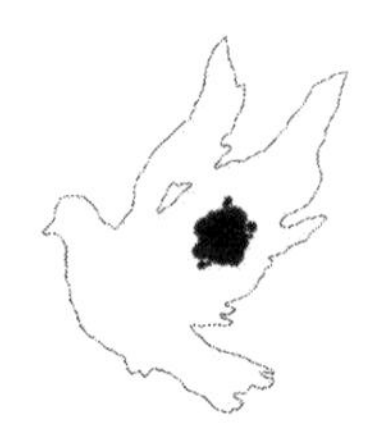

CHAPTER FIFTY-SEVEN

Branham Hall

"Tell me what you see and hear, Seth," spoke a soft voice. "Where are you?"

Holloway had a vague notion that the hypnotic voice belonged to someone he knew—a doctor, perhaps?—but it sounded far away, as though spoken from another point in time. "Where am I?" he asked the disembodied speaker. "Who are you?"

"It's Henry," someone answered. "Tell me what you see."

Holloway stood in a large, high-ceilinged room hewn from limestone and decorated with bright paint. He recognised it at once. "I'm in the crypt Collinwood keeps calling Richard's tomb. He really is an idiot sometimes. No Norman tomb would contain hieroglyphs. And King Richard's body was divided and then interred at Rouen, Châlus, and Fontevraud Abbey. His embalmed heart at the first, entrails at the second, and the rest beside his father, King Henry II."

"Ah, I see," the voice muttered. "Your knowledge of history is quite detailed. You mentioned hieroglyphs. Can you describe them?"

In his trance-like state, Seth was able to survey the room as though re-living the event. "Some are Egyptian, but others look more like modified cuneiform. I also see proto-Hebrew, early Chinese, and something similar to rock art found in France."

"You're an expert?" asked the voice.

"I teach this at Cambridge, so I suppose they consider me an expert. Why am I here? Who are you?"

Henry paused, for he'd conducted this sort of therapy a dozen times before, but had never been challenged by a patient. "You're there to discover your hidden memories. I'm your doctor, and you're lying in bed just now. Do you remember that?" Henry looked to Kepelheim and shrugged his shoulders. “Am I doing this wrong?” he whispered to Martin.

The tailor whispered back, “May I?”

“Yes, please,” Salperton replied. Then with a normal voice, he informed Holloway of the decision. “Seth, you’re about to hear a different voice. His name is Martin, and he’s quite good at helping people recover lost memories.”

The dreaming man on the bed said nothing. He still clutched the ticking clock, and Martin used this to begin the new conversation.

“My dear friend,” he started amiably, “I envy your ability to wander through your own past. Can you feel anything? In your hands, perhaps?”

The patient’s lips moved slightly, as though considering how to respond. “I feel a rhythmic sensation. Very regular. Is it a clock?”

“Yes, indeed, it is. Dr. MacAlpin placed it into your hands only moments ago, to anchor you to this place and time. Do not let your thoughts lose that sensation, Dr. Holloway. Now, as you’re a scholar, describe the room to me as you might report it to a fellow researcher. I’m an amateur antiquarian, and I’ve deciphered many hieroglyphs. Walk me through this crypt.”

Below, in the hall’s music room, Elizabeth had finished the first movement to Beethoven’s *Moonlight Sonata*, a mournful passage evoking loss and contemplation. The duchess had played the sonata countless times, and thus paid no attention to the music sheets, but shut her eyes, allowing herself to drift backwards in time to her childhood, when her father still lived.

Every member of the audience sat still as a statue, marvelling at the interpretation and skill. Only those who knew her best, noticed how Beth’s expression altered with the rise and fall of the notes. Baxter began to worry that the queen’s choice was dangerous. His own mind reached back into the past, remembering the last time the duchess had played the sonata in this room: the final Christmas of Connor Stuart’s life.

The second movement eased the tension, and its lilting *allegretto* pace allowed Elizabeth’s nimble fingers to dance along the keys as though skipping joyfully. Even her face shone more brightly, and Baxter breathed easily once again.

One storey up, Seth Holloway was about to make a confession.

"As I've already said, the chamber is transformational. And the bird statue probably represents a gatekeeper figure that guides the applicant to the next level. But I'm not thinking of that."

"Why is that, Dr. Holloway? And where are your companions, if I may ask?" Kepelheim probed.

"Worthy and Pitt must be up ahead, for I no longer hear them. They've been singing or quoting from Shakespeare all morning, but it's gone quiet. Worthy's been strange since we left the Ghost. I think he's sweet on the landlord's daughter. I could be wrong, I suppose. I don't really know the men well."

"They're not your students?"

"No."

Martin shifted in his chair, an odd dread creeping into his flesh. "You said your mind was fixed on something else. Was it the raven statue?"

"In a way. I've been sketching it and copying the inscriptions on its base, chest, and wings. There are hundreds of them, but I'm not sure of the language. It all reminds me of Elizabeth."

Charles grew tense, his eyebrow arching in suspicion. "Why Elizabeth?" he asked.

"Who is that?" Seth enquired, his closed eyelids twitching.

"A friend," Kepelheim explained. "Another researcher."

"Ah," Seth answered. "Am I dreaming?"

"In a way," Henry told him. "There are four of us here, but you're perfectly safe. Only your mind has returned to the crypt. Your body lies upon a bed."

The young man paused, the flesh over his high cheekbones pulling upwards as though he were smiling; or rather trying to do. "Four of you? Am I being judged?"

"Not at all. We're your friends," Henry assured him. "Why do you mention the duchess?"

"Because of the raven statue. She told me about it once—in Paris, during one of my visits. Beth used to wander through these tunnels as a girl, and she mentioned seeing a huge statue of a bird. It's why she grew so angry with me that day. I openly doubted her tale, but now I regret every word, because she was right."

His voice revealed deep emotion, and the duke's three companions all turned to the look at him, for Sinclair's face also revealed strong emotions.

Paul Stuart reached for his cousin's forearm. "Charles, I've already told you they had a strong friendship."

"I'm not a fool, Paul. They were lovers," whispered Sinclair.

Henry worried the entire experiment was at risk, and he tried to return it to the original goal. "Seth, it's Henry again. What lies beyond the raven's doorway? Did you go past it?"

"Yes, but..."

Everyone waited to hear more, but Holloway said nothing for nearly a full minute. Those sixty seconds passed in agonising torpidity, each tick of the clock sounding like a death knell.

At last, he spoke again, but his demeanor had altered. "Where am I?" Seth whispered, every muscle in his face tensing. His eyes cast about beneath the closed lids, as though following someone's movements. "What place is this? Who are you?"

"Seth, it's Henry. You're safe."

"Who the devil are you? What have you done with Pitt and Worthy?"

"Seth, is there someone there with you?" asked Henry.

"No! Stop! Get away from me! Stop!"

"Seth, you're safe. Nothing can harm you. This is only a shadow of what happened. A memory; that's all. Have you moved to a new location?"

He began to shiver, and the tailor drew a third quilt over the young man's body, gently tucking it beneath his hands; careful not to disturb the clock.

"Are you cold?" asked Martin.

"It's freezing here. But at the same time, it's hellishly hot. Who are you? Is this Martin?"

"Yes, it is. Are you alone?"

"No, there's a strange man talking to me. He wears a feathered cloak with a high collar. His attire is old, as if from another era. His eyes are amber yellow, and he's asking me about you."

Every man tensed.

"About me?" asked Henry.

"No, I don't think so. He wants to know who keeps talking to me. He says it's rude to interrupt. He keeps calling me a stupid human."

Charles jumped to his feet and crossed to the bedside. "Seth, ask him to tell you the name of this place."

A slight pause, and then came the reply. "He calls it *Sebet Babi*."

Sinclair felt dizzy suddenly, and nearly fell against the bed.

"Charles!" cried the earl as he rushed to assist his cousin. "Sit down. You're overwrought!"

Obeying, the duke returned to his former chair. "What else is this creature saying? Ask for his name."

Another slight pause. "He says his name isn't for me to hear, and he asks about someone named Sinclair. He has a message for him."

"What is the message?" asked the duke, struggling against rising fear.

Hello, boy. I'm watching.

"He says your time has run out. The Dragon is already here."

"Dragon?" asked the tailor. "What dragon?"

"He won't explain. He says I'm too stupid to understand. Now, he's forcing me to enter some sort of maze. I think I remember being here now, but I got out. At least, I *think* I got out. How did I do that? Good Lord, am I sill here?!"

"Don't go into the maze," Charles warned the sleeper.

Seth's voice grew soft; barely audible. His lips moved, and his fingers tightened on the clock.

"I think he's praying," whispered Kepelheim. "Perhaps, we should pray as well. It may only be a memory, but this event is all too real to Dr. Holloway; and perhaps, God can connect spatially disparate petitions. Come, gentlemen, join me."

The men began to pray silently, and Paul took his cousin's hand, gripping it to impart strength. As they prayed, Henry noticed a peculiar light without an obvious source floating about the room. It shone brightest near the duke's position, but the overall illumination moved as though searching.

As the others prayed, the viscount kept his eyes on the light. Slowly, its form grew more distinct: an orb approximately three inches across. The phenomenon emitted multi-coloured lights, as though it contained a prism, and Henry thought he heard voices—speaking in an unknown language. The orb seemed most interested in Charles, for it returned to him again and again. Sinclair's head remained bowed, but Henry noticed his shoulders moved as though the duke could feel the light's presence. He made a mental note to speak with Charles about it later.

Then Holloway spoke words that shocked them all.

"She's here. It's an answer to prayer! She's here! Christ has brought me Elizabeth!"

Charles started to ask a question, but Henry quickly preempted it—not wishing for the duke to interrupt the dreamer with angry words.

"You see the duchess?" the alienist asked.

"Yes, but... She's a girl! A child, I mean. It's how she looked when we first met, many years ago."

"A child? Ask her name," Charles told him, all anger vanished.

A momentary pause was followed by six impossible words: "She says her name is Georgianna."

All four men stared at one another in shock.

"Georgianna who?" urged the tailor, seeking clarification of the miracle. "Did she give a surname?"

"Yes. It's Sinclair. Elizabeth Georgianna Sinclair."

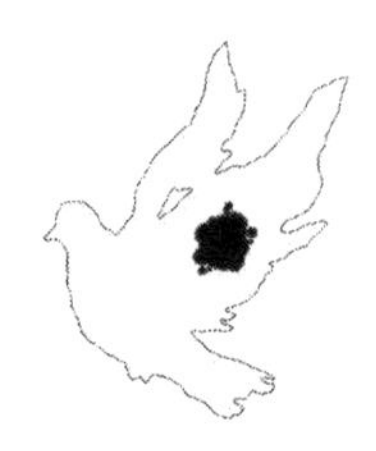

CHAPTER FIFTY-EIGHT

Anatole Romanov always found the Christmas season one of glorious beauty and harmony. Though not the actual date when Christ was born, the elohim enjoyed it as one of the very few times in the human realm, when Christ's name was spoken by nearly everyone on earth in a variety of languages. A rare unity of mankind. Because he'd lived as a Russian for so many centuries, Romanov often attended Orthodox church services—sometimes Russian, other times Greek.

He'd come to St. Sophia Cathedral, a relatively new Greek Orthodox church first opened in 1879, to meet with the Very Reverend Georgio Georgiadis Lambelet. The priest had just finished offering evening communion to seventy-four parishioners, and his aged eyes looked ready to close. An unhealthy sixty-two, Lambelet already looked to life in heaven, but chose to keep his feet on earth so long as Christ commanded it. He knew Romanov well, for the prince had contributed fifteen thousand pounds to the church during its construction phase. Lambelet smiled wearily when the prince entered the vestry.

"Ah, Your Highness, it is a pleasure as always," he greeted the royal visitor in stumbling Russian.

"I speak English quite well, as do you, my friend. Sit and enjoy some tea with me, won't you? You've been standing far too long, and I sense an oppressing weakness in your knees."

The priest had removed all his vestments, wearing simple shirt and trousers now, and he gladly obeyed. "I never know how you read minds, Highness, but I and my knees are grateful for the rest." He poured tea into a pair of brightly painted cups. He handed a cup to the prince.

"To what do I owe this visit?" he asked.

Romanov's dark hair swept along his broad shoulders like a sable collar, and his pale blue eyes sparked with life. The priest admired his friend's stature, for Lambelet stood only five-foot-six. The prince sipped the tea before replying.

"This is excellent. My compliments to your secretary. Mr. Andropolis certainly has a way with tea. Now, to your question. I come to celebrate Christ's birth, of course, but also to enquire regarding a matter you and I discussed some years ago, after the stone was opened at the British Museum."

The priest's face filled with concern, and he leaned across the marble-top table to whisper. "Do you mean *the* stone? From Mt. Hermon? Please, tell me your news is good. That this foul creature has been captured! I have prayed for it daily, pleading God's mercies and protection over our city. Do you bring good news, Highness?"

"I fear my not, Georgio. Raziel Grigor not only remains free, but he's trying to fulfill the prophecy. Last month, he released Saraqael."

"No! But, how? You chained Saraqael yourself in 1860!"

"True, but the One allowed the release. It does not mean we sit by and watch. As ever, we must use all our weapons, but trust in the One to make all things right."

"Yes, so you always say, but it means there are now two of these creatures walking the earth."

"Not two, Georgio. Three. That is why I'm here."

Lambelet's wrinkled face lengthened in shock. "Three? *Theé Mou!*"

"*Agapitós mou filos*," the prince said softly in Greek. "My dearest friend, I apologise for the evil tidings on this bright day. A ritual took place a few days ago in France; on the solstice. A long-buried, very powerful entity has been released."

Shock painted the priest's face in ash. "Another! May the Lord God Almighty, our Heavenly Sustainer protect us! Another? How do you know?"

"I keep watch on all the realms," he said frankly. "It is my job."

The priest nodded, his eyes drifting down to the cup as though fearful to look upon his guest's face. "Of course. You are one of them," he whispered. "I have known it in my heart for many years, but never did it become fact until this moment." He looked up, perceiving a richness to Romanov's appearance that made the prince seem more real than anything else in the room; as though colour took on new dimensions. "If you are a messenger, then what is your mission? And why me?"

The elohim reached for Lambelet's hand, touching the loose skin and imparting a warm strength to his cold bones. "One day, this mortal flesh will take on immortality, my friend, and you will know, just as you are known. For now, the truth is veiled behind a glass, but then, you will see with new eyes—face to face with Christ."

The human began to weep, and he clutched at the angel's hands. "Bless me and help my weakness! I have carried this knowledge since '71, and it grows heavier with each passing day. Yet, now you tell me another evil creature walks our earth? I am but dust! An old man! How can I help?"

"Your body is old, but your spirit is young, my friend. And your service is vital. My task is to spy upon the fallen realms; those whom I once called friends and brothers. That burden is grievously heavy, yet, my steps are made lighter by trusting in the One who created all things, the Great King who orders our steps. Will you help me to foil the enemy's plan? Even a child can throw sand in the eyes of a monster. And an old man's foot cause an ogre to trip."

The priest's hands shook, but he nodded affirmation. "Yes. Yes! Though it may take my life, I will help! What would you have me do?"

"In a few minutes, I will bring two women to your door, seeking shelter. Cassandra Calabrese and Lorena MacKey. Calabrese uses other names, also. Violet Stuart and Susanna Morgan. Both women have only recently received salvation through the blood, but they are infants in the faith and need a guiding hand. I have told them to wait in my coach until your bell sounds. When they hear it, they will knock on your door. Once I know they are safe, I must leave."

"Then, I must ring the bell!" exclaimed the old priest.

"Not you, Georgio. Send Andropolos to do it. He is younger. Station yourself by the door to receive them. When the taller of the two will say her name is Violet, you're to offer correction. Tell her this: 'You are Cassandra Calabrese, but God has given you a new name. You are now Violet Rose Stuart, and your future is bright.' And when the other whispers of her unworthiness, you're to say this: 'God has a plan for you, Lorena Melissa MacKey. The man you love will become a dear friend, and all the pain of your childhood will melt with the winter snows.'"

"My memory is poor, Highness. What if I do not remember these words?"

The prince touched his friend's forehead. "You will remember all. These women are in great danger, Georgio. Not only from man, but from evil elohim."

The priest's hands trembled as he clasped them together. "Redwing?" he whispered.

"Redwing and another. Blackstone has come to England."

The priest crossed himself. "Blackstone! May God save us! Those demonic men are after these women?"

"They are, but these children of Eve have much to do in this battle. I must leave England for a few days, and it's possible that absence will be extended, for I go to fight against the new evil in France. If all goes well, then I shall call here again in three days." Romanov passed an envelope to the priest. "This is to pay for food and anything else they might require. No one must speak with them. Teach them of Christ, my friend."

"I will," promised Lambelet. "But what of you? Must you fight alone? May I pray with you, Highness?"

Anatole smiled as he touched Lambelet's face. "You are a true man of God. Pray for your fellow man and for these women. Pray for Charles Sinclair, who must face his greatest challenge tomorrow."

"The boy whom you rescued long ago?"

"The same. The Dragon will sift him like sand, and I will do all I may to help. Shelumiel will assist here, but I must take the fight to France. And you, my humble friend; you must run your race until the very last breath. You were born for such a time as this. Happy Christmas, Georgio Georgiadis, most beloved of God. May His light shine upon you this day and always. And may His grace ease your pains and fill your hands with purpose. Peace be unto you this day."

Without another word, the enigmatic elohim vanished from sight. It took Lambelet a moment to recover from the astonishing visit, but then he hastily called to his assistant, ordering him to ring the bells at once. Lambelet then donned his cassock and stationed himself by the front doors, ready to receive his guests.

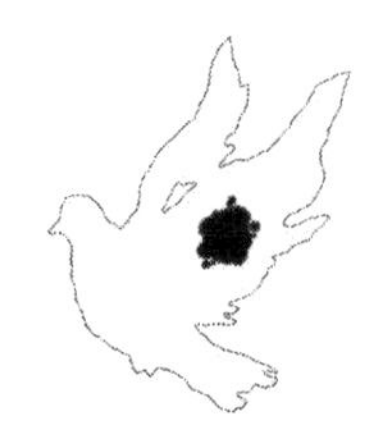

CHAPTER FIFTY-NINE

The music room of Branham Hall

Elizabeth's small hands flew upon the keys as she commenced the third and final movement of Beethoven's sonata. This section's mood was radically different from the previous two: frantic, powerful, and dynamically challenging. When learning the piece as a girl, she'd struggled to perform it, for the *presto agitato* pace, coupled with page after page of sixteenth notes, demanded agility, speed, and concentration.

As she played, the power of the music rose throughout the foyer and upper gallery, filtering into the strange session taking place in the east-wing suite.

"Georgianna?" asked Henry, thoroughly perplexed. "Georgianna Sinclair? Is that the name this girl gave you?"

"Yes," the dreamer insisted. "She looks just like Elizabeth did as a girl of ten or so. She says she was told to rescue me. By her father."

Charles lost all ability to remain silent. "Ask if he is there."

"What?" enquired the sleeper, his facial muscles tightening.

"Ask about her father," repeated the duke. "Is he nearby?"

There was a long pause, and then Holloway's expression lifted as if amazed. "She says she is about to go find you. That her brother is there as well, and that he is helping their mother. She says her father told her many times that she'd need to rescue the man with red hair. I suppose that's me, but none of it makes sense. She sees me crying and has taken my hand. She calls me 'Uncle Seth' and says she's known me all her life. How like Beth she is! It breaks my heart!"

Charles was weeping, remembering how courageous his daughter had been when she'd helped him during that dark experience. "Tell her she must be brave."

"Yes, I will."

Holloway grew silent, his eyes moving rapidly beneath the closed lids.

"Seth?" asked Sinclair anxiously.

"She says I'm to deliver three messages. One to her father, one to her mother, and one to Uncle Henry."

"Uncle Henry?" repeated Salperton, grinning. "How nice. What does she say? What's the message?"

He grew silent once more, his facial muscles tense. "Yes, I can do that."

"Do what?" asked Salperton.

"She's asked me to repeat the messages. She knows you're listening."

This sent a chill of wonder through every man. Charles wiped his eyes, an idea forming. "Tell her that her father's listening, too."

A moment's pause. "Georgie says she knows that already. You've apparently shared this with her. She's laughing now. She says she's not to reveal secrets, but I should tell you she will meet you in June of next year."

Sinclair wept openly, thinking of his beautiful daughter and longing to hold her. "Yes, on the tenth."

"She says that's right. Here are the messages. To her mother, I'm to say 'Leave the doll alone. Destroy it.'"

Paul moved close now, speaking. "Seth, this is Aubrey. Ask her if she knows me—if she knows my wife."

A slight delay, and then Holloway answered, "Yes, she knows you. She laughed when I asked and said 'Of course, I know Uncle Paul! He's married to Aunt Delia. She's my good friend. We all pray for her.'"

"Why do they pray?" the earl asked.

Seth answered, "She says it's because of the baby, but she's not permitted to tell more than that. 'Father's rules', she says. The other messages are these: To her father, 'Tell him he's the greatest man in all England, and that his decision is the right one. And don't be afraid of the hedge maze. You won't go in alone.'"

Charles wanted to ask more, but the sleeper continued. "Finally, to Henry, she says 'Run after Adele. Inside the copse is the answer to a riddle. Remember, God is in control.'"

Henry ran his hand through his hair; a nervous habit when confounded. "Run after Adele? That makes no sense!"

"We're walking now," Holloway continued. "She's holding my hand, as though I'm the child; not she. The ravens and spiders are howling like demons, but they keep far away. These creatures seem to fear her, as though she has power over them."

Another long pause followed, and then Seth began to laugh. "Never have I known such a remarkable child. She's arguing with a tree! We're passing through a dense wood. All is darkness and gloom here, but ahead I can see a glimmer of light. We've stopped before a tall stone tower. It rises upwards into the mist."

"Do you see a moon?" asked the duke.

"A somewhat sickly one, yes. Always, there's the chatter of these awful birds and whispers of other creatures. I hear roaring and thunder now and then. She's telling me to enter the tower."

"Do whatever she tells you," Charles urged the sleeper.

"Must I? The tower has an unhealthy look to it. I argue with her, but she insists I go in. I can hear bells, coming from high overhead." He grew silent for a moment, his face widening into a look of amazement. "Georgianna is singing! She's singing, and the tower is changing! It's growing lighter and more welcoming! The door opens. She's telling me goodbye."

Charles wanted to weep again, dreading the loss of this connexion. "Tell her I love her."

"She says she loves you as well. She calls you 'dearest Father'. How she laughs! Can one fall in love with a child? I enter the tower. She tells me one last thing. 'I must find my father now. He's a bit lost.'"

Swallowing hard, Sinclair nodded. "So I was, but she found me. With Christ's help, my daughter found me."

"I—I, uh... I'm flying!" shouted Holloway. "Flying into the air and passing through a thousand doors at once." His entire body shook, and the fingers whitened round the ticking clock. "I can feel air slamming against my face and hear voices in languages I don't understand. God help me! Please, Lord, help me!"

"You're all right, Seth," the alienist told him.

The body shocks grew more severe, and Charles placed his hands round Holloway's, helping him to keep hold of the clock.

The tremors reached crescendo as though timed with the music Beth played downstairs. The sleeper's jaw tightened, and he screamed. "Help me!"

Then all stopped.

His body grew slack. His eyes flitted about rapidly beneath the lids.

"Where am I?"

"Have you moved?" asked Kepelheim.

"Yes, I think so."

"Do you see Georgianna?" asked Sinclair.

"No, she's gone," he answered sadly. "Already, I miss her."

Charles understood Holloway's reaction. Georgianna had her mother's inner light and compassion that imparted courage and strength, even to a grown man.

Henry took over once again. "Do you still hear the birds?"

"No, they've gone. I'm in a cavern now."

"Can you describe it?"

He panted, as though catching his breath. "Yes, give me a minute."

"How's his pulse?" Salperton whispered to Martin.

"Rapid but slowing now. What happened in that tower took its toll. We shouldn't go much longer."

"Seth, are you injured?" the doctor asked, now wondering if the rapid journey from the tower had caused the wounds.

"No," the sleeper answered. "Just winded. Am I really here? You said I'm in bed."

"This is all a memory, but it may feel as though you're living it. Can you tell us what's happening?"

"I'm alone, but I can describe the cavern, if that's useful. Is this part of my treatment?"

"Yes, it is. You're nearly finished. Can you continue?"

"Yes, I think so. The cavern is remarkable. The ceiling must be fifty feet over my head. I still have my compass—it's in my pocket." A brief pause. "The compass behaves strangely, rotating as though the needle's lost its magnetism. It stops for a second. I think the cavern's heading east, towards the sea. I can see three doorways. One has a natural look about it, as though part of an ancient cave system.

The others are arched and dressed with finished stones. The northern arch leads to a staircase, and the west leads..." There was a long silence. "I've walked the width to this other door. All the sconces are lit. Wentworth and Patterson must have been this way and lit them. You know, this may be the Apotheosis Vault, where the transformation into a demigod occurs. I see writing and carved imagery from many different religions. The floor's covered in red paint—no, wait. Not paint. I think it's blood. Old blood, and there's lots of it. If this is the Apotheosis Vault, then it makes a hideous sense. Metamorphosis requires sacrifice."

Charles knew that chamber all too well. It was where Elizabeth watched Trent kill her mother. He nearly instructed Holloway to climb the steps—to escape whilst he could—but he didn't wish to alter the true facts of what had happened.

"Do you see anything else?" he asked.

"No, nothing—wait! How can it be? It's impossible!" His breathing became quick. In his mind, Seth had run to the south wall. He picked up a two-foot high toy. "It's Beth's doll. How can it be here?"

"You recognise it?" asked Aubrey.

"Of course. It's that doll Beth found in Faerie's Copse. The one Connor tried to destroy. How did it get here? I wonder if this is the doll Georgianna mentioned?"

Another silence followed, and then everything changed. Seth Holloway, now reliving the attack that led to all his injuries, began to scream.

In the main floor music room, Elizabeth was lost in a trance as she played. Her interpretation of Beethoven's musical genius danced upon the molecules of air and vibrated each atom, forming sound waves that coursed along the walls and up the chimney. Its power overtook the musician, and Elizabeth Sinclair formed the nexus of transformation itself. The same bright orb which had hovered over Sinclair's head now floated o'er hers, unseen by all except for the dogs and David Anderson, the former Mr. Thirteen. His entire body shuddered, for he sensed evil within the ball of light.

Why does no one see it? he wondered, trying to decide if he should attack it.

Beth had nearly reached the last page, when Holloway's piercing scream rang throughout the upper corridors.

She stopped—two measures short of completing the piece. Without a word, the duchess ran from the room and hastened up the staircase before anyone could stop her. Duke James, Reid, and Cornelius Baxter quickly followed. James tried to stop the duchess before she reached the steps, but he was too late. The nimble duchess had already gained the first landing and was climbing the second course to the first floor.

Henry MacAlpin got nothing more from the session. Fearing for his patient's mind, he did his best to calm Holloway. "You're safe! Seth, you're perfectly safe! Listen to me—concentrate only on my voice."

"No! Leave me alone! God in heaven, leave me!" he screamed in manic terror. The clock dropped to the floor as he raised his hands to protect his face.

All four men tried to hold him down, for Holloway began to thrash about as though trying to escape. The screams continued as he endured a replay of the original attack.

"Wings! They have wings! Get them off me!"

"I don't know how to get him out of this," Henry told Kepelheim. "Do you?"

Martin placed the clock back into the sleeper's grasp. Charles once more added his own hands to Seth's, holding them and the clock.

"Seth, you must concentrate on the clock," Kepelheim told him. "Listen to its ticking, the soothing rhythm. Can you hear it? Tick, tick, tick."

"No! Get them off me!"

"Shut it out of your mind. Wherever you are, close your eyes and listen to the ticking."

"Who is she? Where are the others? No, please, no! Aarrghhhaahhhh!!! No, please! God help me! Help me, *pleeeeaaaassse!*"

Just then, Elizabeth entered the room, followed quickly by Reid, Baxter, and Drummond. She rushed to the bedside and took Holloway's right hand.

"Seth," she whispered.

His entire body, which had been in constant motion, stopped completely. The muscles relaxed as though each part of him now listened.

"Beth?"

"Yes, darling, it's Beth," she told him sweetly. Then, she glared at MacAlpin. "What have you been doing to him?"

"A therapeutic experiment," Salperton admitted. "To help him recover his lost memories, but he won't come out of it. He can't hear us now, but he hears your voice, Beth. Speak to him. Remember how I called to you when you were lost? Perhaps, you can bring Seth home."

Charles took her arm. "You don't have to do this," he heard himself say, instantly realising the pettiness of the remark.

"But I do," she answered without condemnation. "Might I sit?"

Henry helped her to a chair, and Charles stood behind her. He squeezed his wife's hand, thinking of Georgianna's bravery. "Forgive me, little one. Henry's right. Seth needs your help."

She kissed his hand, lovingly. "I'd do the same for any of you. I only pray this works." Reaching for Holloway's arm, she was surprised when he clutched her hand as though drowning.

"Help me," he whispered, his eyes still shut. "It's dark, and demons surround me. I'm terrified, Beth. I'm so sorry I doubted your stories, but you were right. These tunnels are filled with evil."

She stroked his coppery hair tenderly. "Nothing there can harm you, Seth. Trust in Christ to bring you home. Only our Lord has the power to do that. Do you believe in him? You and I spoke of it so many times. Do you remember?"

Tears streamed down his cheeks, and he nodded in his sleep. "Yes, I remember. It's why you kept refusing to marry me. But I know the truth now, Beth! I've seen the fallen ones with my own eyes! I'm hurt and bleeding, and it's freezing here. I can hear screaming, somewhere below me. I think it might be the other men. I dare not imagine what hellions now torment them!"

"We'll pray for them, darling. All of us will pray," she said, looking at the men now surrounding the bed. "Follow the sound of my voice. You needn't suffer through this torment another moment, for it is only a memory. An echo of what happened. You're safe at Branham now. In a soft bed, surrounded by friends. Paul is here. You were rescued by him. Do you remember?"

His hands shook, and they seemed deathly cold. She placed hers round his, rubbing them lightly to bring warmth.

"Darling friend, listen to me. Follow the sound of my voice. Pull yourself up by pulling on me, if you must! I *will* not leave you there!"

In his mind, in the cruel cold of the sacrificial chamber, the Cambridge don managed to stand. He could feel her grip: the delicate, soft palm and dainty fingers that he'd held so many times before. Seth still loved Elizabeth dearly, but she belonged to another.

"Where are you, Beth?" he asked. "I feel your hand, but I can't see you."

"I'm right here with you; sitting beside you. You need only open your eyes, darling. I'm right here. My grandfather is here, and so is Paul. But most importantly, the Lord Jesus is here. The enemy wants to keep you in chains, Seth. Let Christ break them!"

His eyelids fluttered, and the grip on her hand grew so tight that it left marks on her fingers for many minutes afterward, but the duchess refused to let go.

"Look at me, Seth," she told him. "Open your eyes."

Finally, the lids parted, revealing Seth Holloway's intense blue irises. His clenched jaw relaxed, and the lips widened into a grateful smile. "Hello, Princess," he whispered.

Beth immediately broke down, her head resting against Seth's right arm. Charles made no effort to remove her, and a beautiful peace filled his heart—a sense of compassion and profound admiration for his wife.

Salperton was at Holloway's left side, taking the radial pulse. "It's normal again. Can you remember anything, Dr. Holloway?"

"I remember everything," Seth answered, his voice strong. "You brought me back, Beth. You rescued me from a place far darker than I ever thought existed."

"Christ rescued you," she told him, stroking his damp hair. "Now, you should rest. Charles, would you take me back downstairs, please?"

The duke placed an arm round his wife. "I'll be back later. Paul, would you remain? Or do you want to spend the evening with Delia?"

"Is she still in the music room?"

"Yes, I think so," Beth answered. "Charles, if you prefer to stay, Grandfather can take me down."

"I'll do it," he insisted. "Gentlemen, I shan't be long. Dr. Holloway, if you'd share your story with my cousin? Martin, would you write it down using your shorthand method?"

"Oh, yes, I'd enjoy making use of that," answered the tailor. "Once Dr. Holloway goes to sleep, I'll come join you as well. Let Riga know I hope to hear his new duet."

"I'll tell him," she promised, leaving with Sinclair.

Once the door had shut, Aubrey took the vacated chair closest to the bed. "Now, Seth, while it's still fresh in your mind, tell us what happened."

Before entering the lift, Charles pulled his wife into the upper gallery, shutting the door. Without a word, he placed his hands against her cheeks and kissed her tenderly. "I'm a fool," he whispered when their lips parted.

"If so, you're a very handsome fool," she answered with a bright smile. "Charles, do you think my past with Seth affects our present? No matter what happened with him, my love for you never once waned."

"Yet, you nearly accepted his marriage proposal."

Her eyes lowered along with her voice. "Yes, but will you let me tell you the entire story? Later?"

He kissed her again. "Of course, you may. Again, I apologise. I'm spoiling our first Christmas together."

"Not at all. The only change I'd make to our celebration would be spending more time with you."

"Thank you, little one. I love you."

She stroked his bearded cheek. "And I love you, Captain. For all eternity, I shall ever be yours."

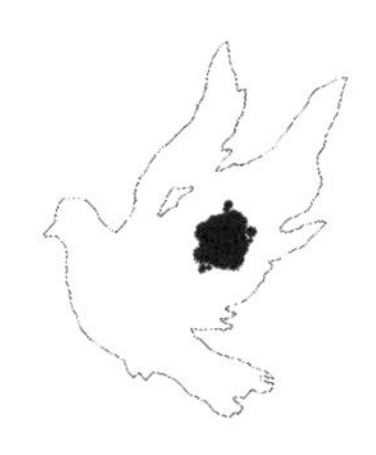

CHAPTER SIXTY

Midnight - 33 Wormwood, City of London

"Shall we begin the meeting?" asked Serena di Specchio. The vampiress wore her typical attire: a black and red gown decorated in glass beads along the bust to enhance her round figure. Her coal-black hair was piled high upon her head and adorned with a ruby tiara, accented with bright diamonds.

"Thinkest thou a queen, Serena?" teased Saraqael, wearing the guise of Prince Aleksandr Koshmar.

"Of course, I am a queen! I reign over many, and I do as I wish," di Specchio answered proudly. "Where is Raziel this evening?"

Sir Clive Urquhart, just returned from Paris, sat at the opposite end of the rectangular, ash table, smoking one of his special blend cigars. The builder's beady black eyes blinked like a rat's.

"Our leader is delayed in France, dear lady," Urquhart explained. "When I left, he'd gone to Goussainville, or so I am told. He never speaks to me directly these days, but conveys all messages through his new lackey, Sir Albert Wendaway. I'll admit, Albert's a handsome little leach. I suspect Prince Raziel finds him a very satisfying companion."

Saraqael began to laugh, and he took the chair at the head of the table. "You think Raza would take a male lover? What human would find that nose attractive? Now, Samael is another story. My elder brother's always had a knack for presenting himself as exceedingly beautiful to both sexes."

"Is Samael interested in men?" asked Gerald St. Ives, the 5th Earl of Wisling. With strong and varied sexual appetites, St. Ives spent many an evening touring both types of brothels to satisfy his twisted desires. The idea that angels might enjoy the same duality intrigued him.

Saraqael found the baronet annoying, and he ignored the question, whispering instead to Sir Robert Cartwright, a soft-spoken baronet with strong ties to the royal family.

"I asked if Prince Anatole is interested in men!" St. Ives shouted, angry at being ignored.

Di Specchio cast her cold eyes upon him. "Why do you ask, Lord Wisling? Is it because you find Sama alluring? Does your heart yearn for strange flesh, as did the men of Sodom? You do know what happened to them?"

The earl had no wish that his predilections be uncovered, for he was married to a wealthy American, the daughter of a powerful Washington senator. "I find it interesting; that's all. He's always struck me as rather *asexual*, if you want the truth. Yes, Samael is quite handsome, but Raziel? He's far too brutish. The man lacks refinement."

"And I?" Saraqael asked. "Do you not find this form enticing, Lord Wisling? Do your deviant inner longings wish *me* to embrace you? To place my teeth upon your thick neck and bleed you until you scream in ecstasy?" he asked, the full lips curled beneath a gleaming black moustache. "Shall I use you up and spit you out, then remake you into the image of myself?"

St. Ives cowered upon his chair, but Serena found the behavior tedious. "Must we waste time with these boyish games? You're far more handsome than Samael, my prince. No woman could resist you, nor any man! Indeed, there is no contest twixt you and your brothers. Not those we've met, at least," she added with a brazen toss of the head. "We've not met the other yet, have we?"

"Other?" asked Honoria Chandler. As the only female member of the dwindling Round Table, she found the idea of a new elohim exciting. "Is it possible Raziel has a rival?"

In response, Saraqael leapt onto the table and began to stride upon it as though assuming control of the room.

"Raziel has always had rivals, though he's loath to admit it. Even at the height of his power, he bowed to many other, stronger elohim. We have a ranking system in the hidden realms, just as you have a peerage system in this one. Before the great rebellion, Raziel stood beside the throne recording all the One spoke. When he fell, he stole the book and gave it to Adam. For that, Samael was ordered to slay him."

"Yet Prince Raziel lives," Chandler noted.

"Yes, but only because Samael pled for his life. The One relented and allowed the imprisonment. I, too, was there, for I was loyal back then. But seeing Samael wage war against so many of our kind changed all that. I began to read the prophecies of the infernal realms, and these took hold in my mind. The secrets are in Raziel's book, and that is what we must find! We must locate all the scrolls and reassemble them."

"Raziel is doing this?" asked Chandler.

"He *was*," Saraqael answered, standing over her. "But no longer; for a stronger elohim has arisen. Now, Prince Raziel must bow to the one he released. What a fool my brother is! He thought Araqiel would follow him as leader, but even in the divine realms, Ara always outranked Raza! As the psalmist says, 'A brutish man knoweth not; neither doth a fool understand.'"

None of the humans appreciated the irony. "Wilt thou inherit the wind?" the elohim asked them. "What fools these mortals be. Is there no education in these modern days, or has man abandoned all wisdom for empty air?"

"Must you drone on?" Serena complained. "Why are we here?"

"I gathered this assembly of fools to give you a warning. I told you of a book, once given to Adam by a rebel. Adam chose to disregard this collection of powerful utterances, but Cain heard the book's voice and stole it. Later, Azazel found it in a cave beneath the Mount of Hermon, where he and his brethren descended."

"Why is this book so important? Surely, it's not a Bible!" laughed the newest member, Captain William Wychwright.

"Hardly. The Bible is told from our jailer's viewpoint. But *Sefer Raziel* is filled with the words of creation. Together, they are a spell that can reorder all things. Azazel tried to use the book, but Sama took it from him in battle and tore it into thirteen pieces, which he concealed inside thirteen prisons. One in the Hermon stone; one in my own. Two more were unearthed in France last month. One in Goussainville, the other in Saint Clair-sur-Epte."

"Then there are only nine more to uncover!" declared Urquhart.

"Yes, but most of the words are unreadable," answered Saraqael. "Allow me to explain, for those who've only just joined us. Long ago, the One created us, the elohim, to serve as his companions and council. We participated in the creation of the universe, in the same way a chorus might accompany a soloist. The One spoke, and we confirmed those words by singing. Know you not the verse in Job? '*Where wast thou when I laid the foundations of the earth? Who laid the measures thereof? Or who hath stretched the line upon it? Whereupon are the foundations fastened? Or who laid the corner-stone thereof, when the morning stars sang together, and all the sons of God shouted for joy?*'

"Oh, it was a mighty, resounding chorus that echoed for aeons! Four recording angels stood beside the throne and took down all words of creation. The One looked upon us as though we were equals, and it caused a fierce loyalty within our hearts! Then, he made that mud creature, and our place in the council changed. We learnt of a plan to elevate this Adam to a higher position than we held. He would be our judge!

"I watched as many of my brethren plotted against the One. But then, I was a fool—still loyal to a tyrant. I fought against the legion of the Nachash as they assaulted the throne. Raziel took advantage of the war to steal the book. He fled the council and followed Adam eastward."

"And he gave it to Adam?" asked St. Ives.

"Yes. Cain then stole it, but the book betrayed him. Azazel would have used it to reverse Time, but Samael took it from him."

"Then why didn't he simply return it to heaven?" asked Urquhart. "If Sama is so loyal, why not give it back to God?"

"Because, the One ordered us to hide it upon earth. I can only guess why."

"*Us?*" asked Urquhart.

Saraqael smiled at the builder. "Yes, us. I didn't see the wisdom of Lucifer's rebellion until nine centuries ago. I used to walk beside Sama as we patrolled the seven realms. He and I were as close as any. Friends as well as brothers. Now, I hope to bring him that same enlightenment—but if not, then I shall kill him," he added, coldly.

"But what of this book? What powers lie within it, and how can we use it?" Wychwright asked greedily.

"We can use it to release the others. The book can reorder all human choices; breaking the past and creating a new present. It can alter Time. That was the mission Trent began, but his vision and plans were too small. Raziel's plans are large, but he is too weak to implement them. Mine, however, are *perfect.* We shall assemble all these fragments along with the Watchers who guard them, and then speak the words to change the world."

"And this Araqiel you mentioned?" the builder pressed. "Will he follow this plan?"

"He will do as I ask, so long as it fits his desires. I know how to manipulate his mind, you see. Ara is a high ranking member of the Nachash. The oldest Dragon Order."

"Nachash? Dragon Order?" asked Wychwright. "A load of nonsense!"

Urquhart turned to the baron, his expression dark. "Take care how you speak, *mon ami!* Hold your tongue!"

Saraqael glared at the careless captain. "Yes, hold your tongue, little man, lest I bite it off. I've no need for humans to accomplish this plan. I include you out of kindness. Would you be an eater, or would you be eaten? A wolf or a meal?"

"We prefer complete answers," the builder interrupted. "Lord Wychwright is new to all this, *mon ami.* But we others have slaved for you, bled for you, and sacrificed much for your kind, my lord Saraqael. And it has done us very little good! Raziel may be a poor general, but you seem interested only in your vendetta against Charles Sinclair. Why is that?"

Surprisingly, Sara defended the young duke. "It is true. Once, I tried to kill the boy, but Samael foiled it by stealing him from my grasp and hiding him away. Then he threw me into a dark cell, where I saw no light but the weak moon of the Seven Realms. I wandered through those mazes for years, planning my escape and whispering into the minds of the men and women of Redwing. I called out to you for aid, and last month, you answered that call. My anger against the boy was fierce when I first emerged, but I begin to see a way he might prove useful. I've conferred with others of my kind, including the Prince of France. Sinclair's blood is rarer than I thought, and with Araqiel's arrival, the boy's blood begins to awaken. Like calls to like, after all. Without his blood, the spell to reorder Time will fail. Sinclair is the key—the gatekeeper to another world. A utopia beyond human imagination! Samael was right to save him. Sinclair is like no other man on earth."

Serena's face lit with hunger. "Yes! Yes! I perceived it when we touched! He is unique, is he not? But how? I could feel it pulse through his veins, yet no one has explained it to me. Sir Clive is right, my lord. We wish only to serve you, but it is difficult to walk in darkness. You spoke of wandering a maze, and yet we stumble in one of our own. Can you not show us the way?"

"Is that so?" the fallen angel asked, his eyes sparking fire. "Would you learn more, foolish human? Do you not know that blood is required to unseal these books? Which of you would volunteer to open his veins? Your Round Table numbers dwindle, but whose hand holds the blade? Perhaps, it is Raziel."

"Someone is killing us, but for no reason. We are all loyal, my prince," St. Ives prattled.

"Are you? No deceit slithers through your innermost thoughts? No treachery lies in your dark hearts?"

"We all do as you ask, my lord," added Clive, "but Raziel holds the blade. He told me himself, that he is our killer."

"Then, my brother lays claim to acts not his own," declared Sara. "But if not Raziel, then who? Might another hand hold the blade? Perhaps, Samael wields the knife. He is, after all, a Reaper. Then again," he added, his dark eyes becoming deep pools of oblivion, "perhaps, *my* hand held the knife that slit Lord Hemsfield's fat throat. Mine that thrust the sword into Lord Peter Andrews's traitorous back, and my own fingers that throttled Baron Wychwright even as he begged for mercy from the One. My lips that sucked the blood from his veins, and my eyes that beheld his last glance."

The humans grew quiet, their faces pale.

"How amusing you all look!" crowed the demonic elohim. His Koshmar appearance grew liquid, turning into smoke before solidifying into the figure of a massive grey wolf.

The terrifying creature snarled at them, its teeth bared. "You look like a row of sheep, ready for slaughter. Do you think me a jester now, Sir Clive? Am I the funny one with the amusing ideas? The one that bows and scrapes to Raziel and Samael? I am almighty Striga, the Skin-Changer!" he proclaimed proudly. "The ancient dread, the ravenous spirit, the King of Stone with a will of iron! I conquered the stone maze and emerged as its new king! Uriens, the ancient raven, is now my pet, and I am your eternal master. Shall

I rip out your insolent throat for your doubts? Consume you like I would a suckling pig?"

"No, my lord! No, I, uh... Well, I wish only to serve you."

The others nodded, their eyes downcast, hands trembling.

"A wise answer," the Stone King growled. "I play the trickster spirit to disarm my enemies, but my powers are far greater than Raziel's—and he knows it. That is why he fled to France. He seeks Araqiel's alliance, but he will fail in this, for Ara has pledged himself to me. We are allies, you see. A brotherhood formed in the Realms of Stone. He is the Dragon that commands the earth, the rocks, and trees. He speaks to the woods and discerns the hidden marrow of the caves. And he knows the locations of the other sacred fragments. Those which contain the words spoken by the One before man was created. When the Seven Realms lived in harmony," the fallen angel recalled.

"Since that dreadful day, we who are wise have come to understand the One's hidden plans. He intends to replace us in the council with you apes. That will never happen! We will unseat the One and return the realms to beauty once more, but first human civilisation must burn. The Seven Dragons, the league of the Nachash, will join together once more and bring refining fire with them. Their wisdom will set the realms aright. They are the children of Chaos, and they hunger for revenge. Soon, when Sinclair rises to become King of England, when he submits to his calling; then, his blood will be sufficiently aligned to open the gates and reset Time, and old Saturn's reign will return."

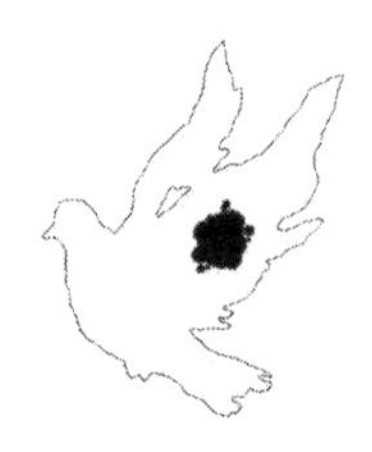

CHAPTER SIXTY-ONE

Midnight – Branham Hall

"Everyone's retired for the evening, my lord," Baxter told his employer. "Mrs. Alcorn and I just wanted to bid you goodnight."

"Oh, wait! I have something for you, Cornelius," Charles told the servant. Reaching into his coat pocket, the duke withdrew two folded cases, one made of royal blue leather; the other of black. "We've been so busy this evening that it slipped my mind."

Sinclair opened the black case to show its contents:

WARRANT CARD
Intelligence Branch
Home Office

DET. INSP. CORNELIUS J. BAXTER
24th December, 1888

The royal blue case was embossed on the exterior with 'ICI Agency' and identified Baxter as a circle agent with the rank of Inspector. The official date listed was also 24th, December, 1888.

Baxter's fleshy face lifted into a proud grin. "It's official?"

"As official as my own. Now, get a good night's rest. I promise you that serving as a detective will be taxing. Perhaps, not physically, but mentally. Your future wife will need to keep you on a healthy schedule. The duchess and I are delighted for both you and Esther."

Alcorn took Baxter's arm. "We'd hoped it wouldn't interrupt the order of things, my lord. With Neil a detective inspector now, we no longer have to worry about how our marriage might seem to the staff, ya know."

"Neil?"

"Short for Cornelius, sir. It's what my father always called me," explained the new inspector.

"Ah, well, it seems a very short name for so grand a gentleman," replied the duke. "Congratulations to you both. If there is anything the duchess and I can do to help with the wedding, we'd be honoured."

Esther cleared her throat and then glanced at her future husband. "Well, sir, we'd hoped to get married here at Branham. There's a lovely, little prayer chapel in the north wing that's just the right size for us."

Charles smiled. "Of course! I'm sure my wife would be delighted. When? Have you set a date?"

Baxter patted Esther's hand lovingly. "We thought May, sir. It's a busy time with the fête and all, but then it would be a very small wedding."

"Choose your date, and we'll make it so, Inspector Baxter. Now, my own bride awaits upstairs; though, she's probably fallen asleep. As the staff are on holiday tomorrow, we'll all sleep late. Goodnight."

The duke smiled as he climbed the grand staircase, towards the master apartment. He was still smiling when he entered the quiet parlour. Bella and Briar had decided to sleep with Adele again, and Samson returned to his mistress for the night. Dumpling snored beside the queen in a nearby apartment, leaving the master bedchamber a realm of peace and quiet.

Charles quickly changed into a night shirt and slipped into the warm bed. Beth lay on her left side. He pulled her close and placed his right arm round her waist. Shutting his eyes, Sinclair began to count his blessings. In only a few months' time, he'd regained his lost family, married a beautiful wife, and now had twin children on the way. No matter what the enemy night try; no matter the stratagem, no matter the plot; he would trust in the Lord to guide and protect them.

Georgianna, he thought happily as he drifted to sleep. *One day soon, I'll hold you in my arms again. And then, the world will be complete.*

CHAPTER SIXTY-TWO

Boxing Day, 9:11 am - Branham Hall

With the entire staff given the day off, breakfast that morning consisted of pastries, breads, sliced cold meat, and salted kippers. Nearly everyone slept late, except for Adele, who greeted each guest as he or she entered the dining hall, where Mrs. Stephens had laid out a self-serve buffet. Della giggled as the troupe of dogs wove in and out of the men's legs, as though performing some new trick. Sitting at the long table, she handed a bite of biscuit to her new puppy. The sleepy animal licked at the treat, trying now and then to take a small nibble with its razor sharp teeth.

"You mustn't feed her too many sweets," her brother warned as he joined her at the table. "She'll get fat."

"Cousin Charles eats sweets all the time, and he isn't fat."

Paul laughed, slicing through a juicy orange. "True, but Charles doesn't sleep all the time. When Napper is bigger, she'll need good food to build muscle and stamina. Have you gone to the stables yet?"

"No," she answered, taking a bite of ham. "Why? Isn't it too cold to ride?"

"Not at all. Horses don't mind cold weather. They do live in a barn, you know. Besides, the sun's already warming the air. It should be a fine day for riding."

"Does Beth have a horse my size?"

Charles had just filled his plate and took a seat opposite the youngster. "Horses? Are we discussing the sleigh ride?"

"Will there be a sleigh?" asked Della, excitedly. "We used to have one at Briarcliff, but one of the runners broke, and Mr. Gower never repaired it."

"I'm told the hall has three sleighs, and all will be put to use this afternoon. How's Holloway this morning?"

"Restive, so says Henry," replied the earl. "Our patient tossed and turned all night."

"Which means our doctor also had a poor night. And Cordelia?"

Paul smiled, his eyes lighting with joy. "Doing much better, though her bruises still hurt. She'll be down in about an hour. Mrs. Alcorn suggested a soak in Epsom salts to relieve the ache. Her mind is much clearer, now that she's no longer taking that dreadful elixir."

"And you? Are you happy with a wife, Brother mine?" asked Adele.

"Very happy, Sister mine. Now eat your breakfast. Good morning, Auntie Drina," he said as the disguised sovereign entered the dining hall. "How did you sleep?"

"Like a pampered puppy," she said with a wink at Della. "Is Napper the official name, then, or has it changed since last night?"

"Napper is the name," answered Adele brightly. "We're going to ride on a sleigh ride today, Aunt Drina. Won't that be fun?"

The queen sat while James Stuart filled two plates with a bit of everything. "Not too much of the fish, James. A second scone, though, I think. One with currents, if there are any left."

Drummond obeyed and joined the table. "Have we offered the blessing?" he asked his family.

Sinclair set down his fork. "Our casual setup has left us out of step. James, would you offer it?"

The Scotsman reached for the queen's hand, who then took Charles's. One by one, every person at the table held the hand of another. Edmund and Emily Reid, Paul and Adele Stuart, Cornelius Baxter and Esther Alcorn, Malcolm Risling, and Thomas Galton. Riga and the others still slept, having stayed up late reading. Just as James was about to begin, Duchess Elizabeth squeezed into the spot to her husband's left, near the head of the table.

"Forgive me, everyone, for being late. I stopped in to say hello to Seth."

To his surprise, Charles felt no jealousy at all, and he praised God for it. "We're about to pray, little one," he said.

She turned to look at him; as though she could read his thoughts. "You're a wonderful man. I'm so very glad I married you, Captain."

"So am I," he whispered.

"Let's seek the Lord's face," said Drummond with a grin, happy to see his family and friends gathered round. He spoke in a soft Scottish accent. "Lord of all, we come to you this morning as a family of miracles, for the blessings this Christmas surpassed all previous years, my Lord. I eat with my beloved granddaughter and long-lost nephew, who is father of my great-grandchildren, who'll arrive next June. Adele grows brighter and wiser each passing day, and Paul has taken a bride. It's my prayer that this new marriage will blossom like a rose, revealing ever changing colours and hidden depths as it matures. May Cordelia enjoy being a Stuart, and may you bless their union with many children.

"The future of our family sits here, my King. Children conceived and yet to be born. Twins who await their time upon life's stage. Be with them now, as you've been with their mother—my beautiful granddaughter—and may they honour and serve you all the days of their lives. Thank you for my sister Victoria, for our pretty Della, and for friends like the Reids and Henry MacAlpin; for Martin Kepelheim and Tommy Galton. For Risling, Ed MacPherson, and all the many agents who guard our steps. Thank you for Riga, Blinkmire, Anderson, and Stanley. And for the Patterson-Smythes. And thank you, my Lord, for this dear lady sitting beside me: our blessed Alexandrina. May she live many more years with as little discomfort as possible. And may she and I live to dance at many a wedding! Bless this food to our bodies so that we may face the day with purpose and strength. In Christ's name I ask it. Amen."

As he raised his head, the duke noticed his childhood friend dabbed her eyes. "Is everything ok, old girl?"

"Yes," answered Drina. "It's just I've not heard you pray in a very long time, James. It always touches my heart." She looked at Charles. "We are talking later today, I hope? Discussing that 'matter'?"

"Yes, of course, we are. We can meet after the sleigh rides, if you like."

"Oh, yes, for I must join in, you know. I've brought ample furs and warm clothes, but I imagine you'll have plenty of rugs in the sleighs. Beth, I'd like to visit the stables later this morning, if you don't mind, and pay my respects to Paladin. I hope to hire his services for three of my Arabian mares. Improve the stock, you might say."

Beth spread butter on a scone. "If you want to hire him, you'll have to ask Charles. He owns Paladin now."

Della looked up from her plate. "Really? Oh, I'd love to ride Paladin! May I?"

Charles answered. "Perhaps, but only with me. You know, there might be another horse you could ride, all on your own. Finish breakfast, then dress warmly, and we'll take a look."

"No skirts," Beth told the girl. "Remember, what I said last night. Skirts can be dangerous if a horse bolts. Wear those riding breeches Tory had made for you."

"I will. Does Henry also plan to ride?" she asked, putting her puppy into the basket near the fire.

"I don't know. Why?" asked the duchess.

"No reason. I just thought he might enjoy riding Paladin with me."

Sinclair watched his little cousin's face carefully. He'd noticed Della had made other interesting statements regarding the viscount of late and wondered what lay at the root of it all. "I'm not sure Paladin will allow it, but it's up to Henry. Now, let's all eat our breakfast. The villagers and farmers arrive at midday, which means we must all be ready to act as hosts."

"And I shall open the games," Adele declared. "Cousin Beth said I may."

"Along with your Cousin Charles," the duchess corrected. "Is there any more boiled ham?"

Charles gazed at his pregnant wife, who'd quickly cleaned her plate. "You're still hungry? Little one, if there's no ham on that table, I shall rummage through the larder myself, until I find some. You've no idea how pleased I am to see you eat!"

Beth laughed. "You say that now, but when I'm fat, you'll change your mind, Captain."

Emily Reid, a moderately plump woman of thirty-six whose figure had thickened after bearing two children, ate heartily as well. "I can't imagine you ever getting fat, Duchess. I used to be quite thin, but carrying our Harold changed all that. Our daughter came first, but the boy left me with an insatiable sweet tooth. I wonder if twins make a difference?"

"I'm sure they do," declared the queen. "Eat all you can, my dear," she told the duchess. "I think your Captain will love you no matter what."

12:45 pm – Branham Stables

Paladin greeted his new master with a nudge and a whinny. Charles offered the magnificent stallion half an apple, which the horse consumed in two bites. Adele stood nearby, and she stroked Paladin's nose. "He's so very beautiful. I used to have a pony at Briarcliff named Kipper, but he died of pneumonia last winter. Paul says I must wait to get another."

"Did I say that?" asked the earl as he drew near with Cordelia on his arm. "Strange. I don't remember it."

"Well, you practically said it," the girl replied. "I'd be very good to a pony, though, Paul. Really, I would!"

Charles took Della's hand. "Shall we take a short walk?"

"Where?"

"Not far. Just the next stable. Perhaps, Paul and Delia would like to come along."

"We'll stay here," the earl answered. "I want to show my wife the Friesian mare Beth bought last month."

The young duke escorted his cousin out of the heated stable and into a slightly smaller one next door. The mews of Branham included six stables, three carriage houses, and a dormitory for the grooms. Their boots made a crunching sound as they made their way through the snow drifts. A paddock separated each stable from its neighbour, and doors allowed certain animals to share outdoor freedom according to a set schedule. Presently, only a Halflinger ate from the hay-filled manger, nodding its flaxen-maned head as they passed.

The next stable felt warm as they entered, heated by two wood stoves. Charles led Della to the third stall on the right, where a small white horse had just been saddled. The name on the stall read 'Christmas Star', and Adele noticed the blanket was embroidered with a thistle, an oak, and an acorn.

"This is a sweet little horse," she said as they stopped. "Is she new?"

"She is," answered Charles. "Her name's Christmas, because she was born on Christmas Day, three years ago. Do you like her?"

"Very much," the girl answered as the pony nuzzled her gloved hand. "Is she fully grown?"

"Yes. She's a Welsh Pony, but the breed is actually a small horse. Did you notice the stitching on the blanket?"

"Do they mean something special?"

"They're symbols of the House of Stuart. Your house, Della. And if you examine the saddle, you'll see it's tooled with the owner's name."

"Who?"

"You."

This took a moment to sink in, but as it did, her expression changed from curiosity to unabashed delight. "Mine?" she exclaimed, bouncing up and down. "All mine? Really?"

"Happy Christmas, darling," he said, lifting her into his arms and giving her a fond kiss. "May this pony lead you into many wonderful adventures."

"Oh, Charles, you are the nicest cousin ever! Georgie will be very lucky when she's born, for you'll be her father! I miss mine, you know, but I like to think of you as one. Do you mind?"

He began to cry a little. "Not at all. That makes me very happy, Della. I've come to love you as if you were my own. Now," he said, placing her back on the ground. "This pony requires exercise. Mr. Clark's men have her all ready to travel. Would you like to ride beside me, whilst I'm on Paladin?"

"Oh, yes! But you mustn't go too quickly. I don't think her short legs will keep up with his. She's so very pretty, Charles. I think I'll call her Star. Is that all right?"

"It's perfect, Della. She's a lovely little star, just like you."

He kissed her again, and she wiped the tears from his cheeks. "Shall I help you up?" he asked.

"Perhaps, a bit of help."

He lifted her onto the pony, and placed her booted feet into the iron stirrups. "Comfortable?"

"I think so. Will you stay with me until Star becomes used to me?"

He took the reins from the groom, a boy named Afton.

"Say the word, and I'll walk you out."

"Ready," she said, once she'd settled.

Charles slowly led the horse and rider onto the snowy road, finding Paul and Delia waiting. Paladin had been saddled, and Clark held the tall stallion's reins.

"Do you need me to go along?" asked the earl, his arm through his new wife's.

"Not unless Delia wants to ride, too," Charles answered as he mounted the stallion. "We'll just ride a short ways along the main road. Where's Beth gone?"

"Walking with Drina, last we saw. Our special guest is reminiscing about long-ago Boxing Days. The villagers are already gathering near the maze, so don't ride too long. We'll start the sleigh rides soon."

Adele took the reins from the youth, who'd stayed close. "Thank you, Mr. Afton. I want to see how she moves, Cousin Charles. May we try several paces?"

"No galloping," warned her brother. "Keep to a cantor, Adele. You know how to control the gait. We'll meet you near the folly, all right?"

Charles turned Paladin northward, and Star walked alongside, the two animals taking their humans on a pleasant journey around the main gardens. As they rode, the duke conversed with his young cousin about life and Christmas.

"Do enjoy living at Briarcliff?"

"Not really," she said, surprising him. "It's awfully lonely sometimes, especially when my brother's away, which is most of the time. Paul travels a great deal. Is it true he may go to Egypt soon?"

"I'm not sure," replied Sinclair. "The prime minister had asked him to go, but now that he's married, I imagine all that will change."

"She's very pretty," Adele said. "But young. She's not much older than I am. Do you think I shall marry when I'm eighteen?"

He pulled Paladin a little closer, just in case Star made any unexpected movements. "I suppose you could. Wouldn't you prefer to go to college? I thought you were considering becoming a doctor."

She laughed. "Perhaps, I'll marry one, instead."

"Anyone I know?" he asked.

"I shan't say. When did you know you were in love with Cousin Beth?"

"Almost the moment I saw her in '84. She was sixteen years old and the most beautiful creature in all the world."

"Why didn't you marry her then?" she asked innocently as they passed to the left of the statuary park. "Was it because she was too young?"

"No, but because I was already married. My wife had left me for another man and lived in Ireland."

"Then, surely the law said you could divorce her," Della declared. "Aunt Maisie told me all about divorces. Her cousin just got one. Couldn't you have done that?"

"I suppose I could have, but it didn't seem right. Besides, Beth moved to France, and I had lots of police work to keep me busy. But I never forgot her, Della. Not for one day. Why do you ask?"

"No special reason," she replied. "But if I did meet someone interesting, do you think I must wait until I'm eighteen?"

"I suppose that's up to your brother. He's your guardian. You'd need his permission until your eighteenth birthday."

"Oh," she said as they neared a large group of children, playing in the snow. "I wonder, might someone else be named my guardian? Perhaps... You?"

He slowed Paladin, to allow the smaller horse to keep up. "Darling, I'd be happy to serve as your guardian, but isn't that up to Paul? Why is this on your mind?"

"No reason," she said as they neared a sleigh filled with four children and their parents. "But if Paul approved, would you be my guardian?"

He stopped, and Adele managed to pull up Star as well. "Della, I love you like a daughter already. If you ever need to talk, I'm here."

"I'll remember that," she told him. "But it's nothing really. I love you, Cousin Charles."

"And I love you, little one," he said.

The pet name caused her to cry. "You call Beth that."

"May I call you that as well?"

She reached for his hand. "Yes, please. Now, before I blubber like a child, I really should take Star back, I suppose. Might I trot just a bit first, though? Take her through the green?"

"It's really the 'white' today, isn't it? No galloping, Della. Remember what your brother said."

"Just a cantor," she said. "You can keep watch. Paladin can catch us up, if anything goes amiss. But she's a lovely little pony. Smooth and easy going. I love her, Cousin Charles. Really. May I go?"

"All right, but turn round before the woods. You don't know how she'll respond in there, and the paths aren't cleared."

"I promise!" she called, pressing her thighs against the horse's sides, causing it to lunge forward. He watched as they took the expanse easily, the horse's hooves kicking up the snow as Della passed by dozens of children building a snowman. Several gardeners, tasked to patrol the crowd and maintain order, waved as she cantered by them.

Charles saw Drummond and the queen sitting on a bench beneath a large marquee, erected just for the Boxing Day celebrations. Inside it, were tables of sandwiches, fruit, cookies, cakes, and steaming kettles of hot chocolate and sweet tea. He could also see the earl and his new wife walking towards the tent, arm in arm, and Elizabeth in a deep conversation with Henry MacAlpin. Salperton sat on a chestnut mare, bending down as he and the duchess spoke. Victoria and Dolly stood near the west entrance to the maze, waving to Adele and shouting something.

Charles paused his horse just before reaching the marquee, for he could see smoke rising up from the centre of the yew maze. Fearing a fire, he dismounted and handed the reins to a gardener, mentioning the smoke and ordering him to contact Powers immediately.

A part of the duke's brain recorded everyone's location as he neared the entrance. Tory and Dolly looking towards Henry's Woods, Beth and Henry by the folly, just at the wood's edge. Drummond pouring mugs of chocolate in the tent. Reid kissing his wife near the pond. Paul whispering into Cordelia's ear, and the girl laughing. Kepelheim with Riga, Stanley, and Blinkmire on the opposite side of the frozen pond, sharing a laugh.

And David Anderson on his own, not far from the row of yews that formed the maze's west entrance.

The smoke curled above the white-capped hedges, but no one else seemed to notice—except for Anderson. Charles could see him react, as though smelling the fire.

Then it all went wrong.

A horsefly, which had no business at all being alive in such weather, bit Christmas Star's rump, and the horse rose up on its hind legs, neighing loudly. Charles turned at the sound, for it cut through the cold air as though aimed at his ears. What he saw terrified him: Adele, barely hanging onto the horse as it dove into the dense foliage of Henry's Woods; Beth and Henry, reacting at once, and MacAlpin spurring his horse into the brush.

Paul was running. Drummond dropped his cocoa. Beth collapsed against the corner pillar of the folly.

Charles started to dash towards the rescue effort, but ran into a wall. Not a literal one, but a spiritual one.

"Come with me, or she dies," a voice said from the invisible barrier. "Into the maze."

"No!" he shouted, pushing at the wall.

"Then, I'll kill her now."

"What is it you want from me?"

"I want to talk," the barrier answered. "Come into the maze."

Charles watched the men and women—many of them villagers—rushing into the woods to help. Only Anderson saw the duke enter the treacherous maze. A chill of fear ran through him, and for a moment, it seemed history was about to repeat itself.

Go after him, a voice whispered into David Anderson's right ear. *He needs you.*

The former Rose House footman gulped, summoning up all his courage, and then David began to run.

CHAPTER SIXTY-THREE

Henry MacAlpin followed the Welsh pony's path for nearly ten minutes, but saw no sign of horse or rider. As he neared the enclosure of trees known as Faery's Copse, the track stopped, as though the pony had simply vanished. Henry saw no one anywhere in the area. He left his horse, leading the animal along the snowy path.

"Della!" he shouted, praying she was just ahead.

The packed snow grew lighter as he neared a rise in the ground, and he noticed hints of grass appearing within the mounding drifts. Just over the rise, the air warmed, and before him the woodland looked summery, with butterflies and bees attending to the many flowers. Turning to look behind, he could see nothing of winter, for all round had become impossibly verdant and luxuriant.

"Feelin' a bit muddled are we?" asked a woman's voice. "It can be quite confusin' round these parts, Henry MacAlpin."

Assuming he'd fallen asleep somewhere nearby, the viscount left his horse to graze and walked towards the plump woman. She wore a simple muslin dress with a checkered apron, which tied at the back of her ample waist. Her silver hair blew in the breeze, and he could see bee hives at the back of a simple cottage.

"You know me?" he asked.

"I've known you since you were a wee lad," she laughed. "Twas me sent you Droigheann, yer doggy. Aye, he was a right good companion for a boy. You're lookin' fer young Della, aren't ye, laddy?"

"Yes, I am. Has she come this way?"

"No, but she's all right. There's a girl waiting for you, though. She's just seen some right awful things, an' needs a bit o' tendin', ye know. Come in. I'll put the kettle on."

Inside the hedge maze, Charles felt strangely at home. Though he'd never in his life walked this maze before, he seemed to know every correct turn to reach the centre quickly. He even knew why. The Branham maze was identical to the one near his boyhood home of Rose House.

"This way," he heard a voice say. "Not far now. Come on. I'll not bite."

As he walked, he glanced down now and then, noticing footprints in the snow. They began as a large-footed man but transformed with each turn, finally becoming gigantic animal paws as he neared the centre. He instinctively reached into his coat for the weapon he kept there. Baxter's tale of Connor Stuart and a young Elizabeth finding a massive grey wolf at the maze's heart long ago passed through his thoughts. He wondered if he would come out alive.

As he neared the middle, he began to pray.

CHAPTER SIXTY-FOUR

"Come in," the woman told Henry, holding the blue wooden door open. "The girl's right inside."

The viscount removed his hat as he entered the cool interior of the cottage. A fire burnt in a creek stone heart, and Salperton instantly recognised the room as the one from the Stone Realms. "Forgive me, ma'am. Might your name be Hope?"

"Aye, sir, it is. Sit now. Take a load off. I'll fetch the lass."

He took the chair near the fire, noticing a pan of Bannock bread cooling on a stool. He could smell cinnamon and honey, and all round were hearts, hearts and more hearts. Entwined together as though forming a family.

"Here she is," Hope told him.

Henry stood again, turning round to find himself looking at the living image of the doll from the cavern. Instantly, he knew this was Elizabeth as a child.

"Hello, there," he said easily. "I'm Henry. You can call me Hal if you like."

"Are you here to take me home?" the girl asked.

"I am indeed. It seems I've been destined to do so for a long time. You're Elizabeth Stuart."

She nodded, moving close to the fire and sitting near the stone apron. "Yes."

"You're the Marchioness Anjou. Do you know there are lots of people looking for you just now?"

"Are there? I'm very sorry. I followed a woman into a tent near the maze, but then found myself in the woods, and it was snowing. How can that be? It's May, isn't it?"

He sat beside her. "Yes, so it is. I wonder, Beth, can you tell me what else happened to you?"

"That's what Miss Hope asked, too," she answered. "May I have some tea? I'm very cold."

Their hostess brought two cups of steaming tea, sweetened with honey, and left them on a table. "I'll be outside, if you need me, sir."

She then left the alienist alone with the child.

"You say you found snow?" he asked, handing her the smaller of the two cups.

Elizabeth took a sip and then held the drink in her lap. "Yes, and the faeries were making it," she said. "I think they were faeries. I once heard a story about them. My Cousin Paul told me. He's not here now. He had to leave."

"Yes, so I heard," Salperton answered, though he wasn't sure what she meant. "You like your cousin, don't you?"

"Paul's the most wonderful man in all the world. He's at Oxford, you know. Merton College. He's twenty years old, but he's going to marry me someday. If my mother leaves him alone, that is."

"What do you mean by that?"

"She kissed him. I saw it happen—not far from the maze. Paul didn't like it, though. Are you and I related?"

"Yes, actually. Your grandfather and I are second cousins, which makes me your cousin as well. Tell me about these faeries."

"They stood next to a great rock. One was very tall, the other short and round like a toad. The tall one was making something. He gave it to me, but I really don't like it. It's that awful dolly. Why would they have my dolly, Cousin Henry?"

"Hal," he reminded her. "You can call me Hal, if you like. My mother called me that."

"I like that. Hal. You're very nice."

"And so are you," he replied politely. "What dolly?"

"The one that looks like me. The faeries were making a new one, but it looks just like the old one. They made me take it, and they laughed about it. The wolf laughed, too."

MacAlpin's eyes narrowed with worry. "What wolf?"

"There was a third faery, who was really a wolf. He turned into a sort of man just as I discovered them. I was very cold and had no coat, because it's spring. The tall faery waved his hand, and the rock became a house, made from willow branches and stone. But the snow remained. Why would their house be surrounded by ice and snow?"

"It is a puzzle, isn't it? I've no idea, really. But this wolf laughed at you?"

"Not at me, really. I think he was laughing about something else. The doll's in the other room. The lady told me to take it with me, and that my father would need to see it. I'm afraid to go home, Hal. What if Father's angry with me? I heard him shouting at Mother earlier."

"I'm sure he'll be delighted to see you again. He's looking everywhere for you, Beth. Shall we get this dolly and find our way back?"

"Through the snow?" she asked hesitantly.

"If we must, but you may wear my coat."

He placed his riding jacket round her small shoulders and then lifted her into his arms. "We'll need to fetch that doll, too, won't we?"

They did so, and left the cottage. As he closed the door, Henry noticed the entwined hearts once more on the exterior: two large hearts surrounding seven smaller ones.

"I wonder if Charles knows there are seven, not just two," the viscount muttered.

"Seven what?" asked Elizabeth.

"Never mind. Let's get you home."

CHAPTER SIXTY-FIVE

"Welcome to your future," said the wolf as Charles entered the maze's centre. Amblers navigating the labyrinth for a whim often gasped when they reached the pinnacle of their journey, for the middle of the massive green puzzle held a tall fountain, surrounded by a miniature of the maze made from boxwood.

The wolf stood before the fountain.

"Have you figured it out yet?" it asked him.

"I think so. You're the demon that killed my father."

"Demon?" the wolf echoed in disgust. "What an ugly word! I'm hardly a demon, Charles. Surely, you know that. We've spoken of it often enough."

"When have we spoken?" he asked the creature.

"When you were a boy, we spoke of many things whilst in the Rose House maze. It's a twin of this one and they're connected—spiritually speaking, of course. One doorway leads to the other. You tripped through that doorway as a boy and ended up here, startling poor Connor Stuart. It was that accident that started him and your father thinking you might be the one, for only you are able to open the spiritual doors, you see. You used to visit me in one maze or the other, nearly every day; but only when your father wasn't around. Your mother thought me your imaginary friend of all things! But I was very real indeed. I used the mirror to speak to you as a baby. Your blood needed to awaken, you see, and I tuned it to our voices. Only that annoying footman believed your stories. David Anderson kept watch on you. That's why I had to scramble his mind, but Samael's fixed all that now. What a troublesome fellow he is."

"What's your name?" Charles asked, mentally whispering a prayer for courage and guidance.

"I've been called many things. Sariel, Suriel, Surufel, Striga. Babel mixed up all the languages, causing over a hundred variations. Humans call me vampire, werewolf, trickster, skin-changer—I've even been called Loki by some. Which makes Raziel 'Thor', I suppose."

"Why's that?"

"Because, as Loki did with his brother, I've tricked mine. I lured Raziel to France with a promise he could conquer the prince who rules there, but instead Raza's been taken prisoner and now awaits judgement in the Dragon Court. Trial by fire, you might say."

"What do you want?"

Saraqael's wolfish appearance transformed into his usual suit of flesh: tall, dark-haired, icy eyes.

"There now. Much more civilised, don't you think?"

"I asked, what do you want?"

"Nothing much. Merely to elevate you to a higher plane, Charles. Isn't it time your true abilities were allowed full rein? But let's spell that r-e-i-g-n, with a 'g', which also begins the word, 'god', doesn't it? All we want is for you to fulfil your purpose. Claim your birthright. Take the job, Charles. It isn't so hard."

"What job?"

"King of England, of course. Trust me, the people will rejoice when you're crowned. It was foretold long ago. He who was dead, returned at last. Arthur reborn."

"And if I don't?"

"Then we kill Della," Saraqael answered coldly. "I care nothing for the girl, but you love her, don't you? Just as if she were your very own daughter. I can gobble her up in three bites, if I want, and you cannot stop me. No one can. Or better yet, I could send my friend to do it. You've met him, too. A mirror stood betwixt you then, and you saw—how is it that meddling St. Paul describes it?—*through a glass darkly?* But now, you *can see him, face to face*, Charles. Would you like to see my friend face to face, in all his fiery glory?"

Charles shut his eyes, trying to remember Georgianna's message: *Tell Father not to fear the Dragon. Tell him Della will be all right.*

"Not particularly," he answered in as casual a voice as he could muster.

You're never alone, Charles, Romanov's voice whispered. *Never alone. We are ever at your side.*

"Do you really think you'll get way with any of this?" he asked the fallen elohim. "Are you so full of foolish pride that you think the One isn't watching?"

Charles heard the cry of an eagle, and he looked up, seeing a great bird circling high above.

"The One sees only what he wants to see," declared Saraqael. "If you think he's sending help, think again. Samael's in France, losing a battle against our battalions there. No one is coming to rescue you."

"I am never alone," Charles proclaimed. "*Yeah, though I walk through the valley of the shadow of death, I will fear no evil, for HE is with me.*"

Sara laughed. "Oh, really? He isn't coming. But we could stand beside you. We can raise you up to the highest throne in all history, and soon you'd wonder why you resisted us for so long. Your true father is beautiful beyond all imagination, and his voice shakes the earth! Allow me to introduce you to him, Charles. He is my friend and follower—the Nachash of the Stone Realms, the terror of humanity, the great and wondrous Stone Dragon!"

The fountain disappeared, replaced by a telescoping tunnel of darkness. Through its chaotic lens, Charles could see thousands of eyes, staring at him. Swirling winds tore through the opening, and he heard the creature's wings. Then the eyes merged into one pair of crimson orbs, growing larger and larger and larger.

The Dragon was flying straight towards him.

CHAPTER SIXTY-SIX

"Shall I take the doll to my father?" Elizabeth asked her rescuer.

"Yes, I think that must be how it ended up in the cavern," the viscount muttered to himself.

"What cavern?" she asked innocently.

"Never mind. But someone very much like you told me to make sure you take it."

"The wolf man put something in a bag and tied it to the dolly," she said as he handed her the toy. "He told the other faeries that it would allow them to watch me. What did they mean?"

"I can't say," Henry answered. "But don't worry about it. Let me teach you a psalm that will help if you're ever feeling afraid. Do you ever feel afraid, Beth?"

She gripped his hand as they made their way back into the woods. "Yes," she admitted, gulping. "When the Shadows call to me."

"Then say this. *The Lord is my Shepherd, I shall not want.*"

"*The Lord is my Shepherd, I shall not want,*" she said. "I think I've heard this before. Father sometimes reads it to me before I go to bed. What comes next?"

"*He maketh me to lie down in green pastures; he leadeth me beside the still waters.*"

She repeated the line, and they left the summery wood and passed through a transitional section that linked the past to the future. Snow covered all, as though the world were dark and without any sun to brighten it. A thick veil covered every tree and rock, making it difficult to see the path.

"Hold onto me," Henry told her as he lifted Beth into his arms. "Keep tight against me, Beth. I'll protect you."

"Thank you, Hal," she said, laying her head against his shoulder. "What comes next?"

"*He restoreth my soul*," the viscount quoted. "*He leadeth me in the paths of righteousness, for his name's sake*."

The future duchess whispered the words, her eyes shut against the heavy snow and freezing rain. "I'm so very cold," she whispered after saying the verse.

"You'll be warm soon, dear. I promise. Let's keep praying, all right? *Yea, though I walk through the valley of the shadow of death, I will fear no evil, for though art with me.* Can you say that for me?"

"Yes," she muttered, her teeth chattering. "*Yea, though I walk through the...*"

"*Valley of the shadow of death*," he prompted.

"I don't like that part. Is it true? Why would the Lord take me into shadow? Is this the valley of death, Hal?"

"No, darling. And God is here. Right now. He'll show us the way."

All had gone black as night, with not one star to guide them. Henry nearly stumbled several times in the high drifts, for he couldn't see his feet. "Hang on tightly," he told her. "*Yea, though I walk through the valley of the shadow of death, I will fear no evil; for thou art with me*."

"Does that mean God is here with us now?"

"Yes, he is, dear. He's here. Somewhere. We may not see him, but he's always beside us. He's always watching after you, Beth."

Henry whispered a silent prayer, straining to make out the road. *Please, God, show me the path to get her home.*

Then a pinpoint of light appeared a hundred feet ahead. A brilliant star that brightened as Henry walked towards it. The guiding light hovered overhead, shining a beam of hope upon his feet and several yards before him.

"Is that God?" the girl asked. "Is he the light?"

"He is, darling!" Henry assured her, his voice choked with relief and joy. "He promises to be a lamp unto our feet and a light unto our path. We must thank him, mustn't we?"

She nodded, her face numb with cold. "Thank you, Jesus," she whispered. "Thank you for sending Hal to help me get home."

CHAPTER SIXTY-SEVEN

The whirlwind nearly cut Charles in two, the pressure was so intense; but the duke stood his ground. "Lord in heaven, may your will be done," he said aloud. "You are my rock and my salvation. I ask you to protect Adele and keep Beth safe, should this be my last moment upon earth."

A fierce roar split the air, and the Dragon drew closer.

Hello, boy. I'm here. Join me and we will rule the world.

A sweeter voice whispered into Charles's right ear: *There shall no evil befall thee, neither any plague come nigh thy dwelling. For he shall give his angels charge over thee.*

The eagle overhead rose up, transforming into a mighty warrior, and then turned about, diving towards the hedge maze.

Saraqael looked up, his eyes round in surprise. "Shelumiel! Come take me, brother! I'll tear you to shreds!"

The fallen angel leapt into the air, a sword in his hand.

Join me, boy. We'll rule the world together and end the reign of men.

"I am a man," Charles dared say to the Dragon.

You are the new man. The perfected man. You are MINE.

The snout had nearly reached the portal's edge, but the claws emerged first, each talon six feet in length. And all were aimed at Sinclair's head.

Just then, a miracle occurred.

Charles could barely hear it over the whirlwind's churning screams, but a small army rushed towards him, led by David Anderson. Baxter with a pistol, Count Riga carrying a shotgun, Stephen Blinkmire armed with nothing but his determination, and former Detective Sergeant Elbert Stanley, brandishing a gardener's rake. The ragtag rescuers rushed towards the Dragon without blinking an eye.

Baxter pulled his master from the area, placing himself twixt the duke and the monster. The others attacked the maelstrom; shooting, raking, and shouting scripture at the Dragon. Blinkmire grasped one of the claws and twisted it in his large hands, breaking it off, and the Dragon howled in pain. Using its other foot, it swept three of the brave Castle Company away, but Blinkmire held his ground. Despite their bravery, it looked to Sinclair as though the battle would be lost, and he pushed against Baxter to reach his friends.

"No, sir! I cannot let you!" shouted Cornelius.

"It's going to kill them all!" Charles cried out, weeping.

Don't worry, Father. Don't fear the Dragon, he heard his daughter say.

"Help us, Lord," he prayed, his eyes lifted up to heaven. "Help us!"

Then, the world slowed down.

Every movement stopped, and the fracas became a tableau, as though time had taken a breath.

The angel overhead threw Saraqael to the ground, causing the whole area to quake. Only Charles perceived it, for only he could move.

He stood, passing by a frozen Baxter. Sara stood as well, glaring at Sinclair.

"This isn't over!" he screamed before vanishing.

Above his head, the great eagle now turned its eyes towards the Dragon, and it changed form once more, becoming a massive hand and arm, which took hold of the Dragon and hurled it back through the portal. The monstrous entity screamed as it swirled into the telescoping eddies, until Charles could see it no longer.

Then, the hand slammed the portal shut.

With a thunder clap, the deed was done, and the menacing monster vanquished.

For now.

"Who are you?" Charles asked the rescuer as the hand and arm became a man. He wore a gardener's uniform, all in white, and his hair shone with white light.

"My warriors are ever beside you, Charles. Never fear. I am your refuge and your fortress." The man spread his hands, and Charles could see the nail prints.

The human fell to his knees, kissing the Saviour's hands. "I have no right to your kindness or your love. I am nothing but a sinner, my Lord."

"You are my child, Charles Robert. Arise and be strong. You will become a mighty man in England, and all will seek your counsel. Follow me, and I shall lead you into paths that will shake the world."

The Lord then kissed Charles on the head and rose up into the air, vanishing from sight.

CHAPTER SIXTY-EIGHT

11:50 pm – 31st December, 1888

Charles Sinclair sat quietly before the drawing room fire, watching the gas flames, his thoughts slowing, his mind already anticipating a good night's rest.

"Sleepy?" his wife asked as she joined him on the sofa.

"Contemplative. I was just thinking about the year ahead. In a few minutes, it'll be 1889."

"Would you rather be downstairs with Grandfather and the others, toasting the new year?"

"Not in the least," he answered. "I prefer spending it with you alone. Did I make the right decision?"

"About what?" she asked, snuggling close.

"The queen's offer."

"I think it's a brilliant compromise, and allows our estates to remain in the family. Are you second-guessing yourself?"

"No, just thinking ahead, I suppose. Will Parliament accept it?"

"If the prime minister and Bertie agree, which they've already pledged to do. Charles, this is already done and signed. You've agreed to become a shadow sovereign. Just yesterday, you received your first red boxes, addressed to 'HRH, Prince Charles'. Honestly, Bertie doesn't want to be king. He looked quite relieved when the Archbishop placed those ceremonial robes on you."

"Yes, but shadow king. Is it a coward's way out?"

"It's God's plan to place you in a position of authority and influence. Darling, this year is going to bring all sorts of changes to our lives."

"Good ones as well as... What I mean is, there will be shadows now and then, Beth."

"But we'll face them together," she assured him. "We made it through Christmas. Della loves her new horse, by the way. She'll have to train it to be more reliable, but Clark can help with that. Paul's made a start on his new life, and Seth is on the mend. Are you sure you don't mind having him stay at Branham?"

"Not at all."

"You don't suspect him any longer?"

He held her close, enjoying her raspberry and vanilla fragrance. "He can't have murdered Collinwood, and Patterson's death bears hallmarks similar to those in Whitechapel. Seth's innocent of any crime. Given time, I may even grow to like the man."

"I never would have married him, Charles. Yes, I care deeply for Seth, but it's you I love. Only you. My heart is yours alone."

"It's a precious heart," he whispered. "But I shall have to leave it now and again to pursue evil. I'll do my best to be home with you each night, but it may require long hours. There's a great deal to do in the coming year. I need to unmask the demons behind the crimes in Whitechapel, Beth. And find out what really happened to Lionel Wentworth. We've murders to solve, both here and in London. Do you prefer I put away my detective hat for good and store it in a box?"

She kissed his cheek. "Not at all, Captain. I married a policeman, after all. I may even buy you a new detective hat, should you require it."

He laughed, kissing her forehead. "The Lord is very good to us, Beth. I bless his name for all the wonderful things he's brought me this year."

"And next year?" she asked happily as the clock chimed midnight.

"*This* year," he corrected, kissing her mouth. "This year, we shall conquer a thousand foes, solve a thousand crimes, build a teaching hospital in Whitechapel that will heal the sick and instruct those with desire but no money—and we'll greet our children. Roby and Georgianna. What a year this will be!"

"The year of promise," she whispered. "Four hundred years since the Branham duchy was founded, and we'll celebrate by bringing a new set of twins into the world. Happy New Year, Captain."

"Happy New Year, little one. May the Lord keep us safe and in his wonderful hands, each and every day."

EPILOGUE

1st January, 1889 - Goussainville, France

Seven-year-old Marie du Pont had never seen so many outsiders in one place at the same time. "Mama!" she cried in French. "Come! Hurry! Horses and horses with great waggons!"

Louisa du Pont was a weary widow with six children, who took in washing, repaired clothing, and cleaned houses to support her brood. Even with three means of income, the thirty-four-year-old had trouble making ends meet. She'd been scrubbing out copper pots near a kitchen window when her daughter called, and she peered through the leaded glass. Marie had an active imagination and was prone to exaggeration, but this time, the girl's report proved true. Someone was moving into St. Roseline Abbey.

Du Pont dried her hands, checked her hair in the mirror near the door, and dashed into the yard of her small cottage.

"See, Mama?" sang little Marie happily. "Waggons and waggons!"

"Yes, I see," Louisa said, looking down at her clothing and wondering if she should change. Word had come to the village of a wealthy Romanian who'd purchased the crumbling abbey with plans to convert it into a home, but such rumours arose from time to time; and yet here was evidence.

Emile Brelon, the village blacksmith, ran over, a heavy hammer in his right hand. "Is this the man?" he asked Louisa.

Soon, dozens of villagers had gathered in the gravel yard of the small cottage, which offered the closest view of the abbey and its activities.

"Are they real or ghosts?" asked Marie as she tugged at her mother's apron.

"They are real, *mon petit*," she answered. Little Marie often claimed to see invisible people and animals, and even played with phantom friends from time to time, especially at night.

Upon the great waggons, they could see many large boxes, barrels, and draped furnishings—and on the last two rested a pair of matched stone rectangles: obsidian sarcophagi. In all, sixteen heavily laden waggons passed through the abbey's iron gates, and lastly a magnificent carriage appeared upon the horizon. A team of four black mares, stepping in perfect harmony, pulled the black and gold brougham. As it neared the gates, Louisa could see a red and gold crest upon its door.

"What animal is that, Mama?" asked Marie. "One is a bird, but what is the other?"

The entire group began to cross themselves, and the blacksmith clenched his hammer as though holding a weapon.

"What is this devilment?" asked Gerard Montpelier. "A dragon? Does this invader bring so hated a symbol to our sacred place?"

Father Henri Gigot, the local priest, disagreed. "It is the crest of his family, I should think. He does not intend it as blasphemy. I've observed this symbol in many of these old houses. Romanians see it as a sign of righteousness and defence of the church. We must not judge too quickly."

To the surprise of all, the coach stopped, close to where they stood. A footman in black and gold livery with braided red trim opened the door. The footman and driver bowed as the mysterious occupant emerged.

Louisa had never before seen so beautiful a man in all her life. His movement was that of the most graceful dancer, and he seemed to float as he approached them. His tall, muscular frame was bedecked in satin and silk, all of it black; but as he walked, she perceived red lining to the knee length coat. His hair was long and wavy and as black as night.

Despite their reservations regarding the crest, everyone bowed or curtsied as the man approached. He walked directly to Louisa.

"Good day," he said in accented French. "I am Prince Aretstikapha. It is a difficult name for some, but you may call me Prince Araqiel, if you wish."

"Prince Araqiel?" repeated the lovestruck widow. "Yes, it is easier. Welcome to Goussainville."

Father Gigot stepped forward. As curate of the church, he assumed command. "We were not told of your arrival. Had we known, we would have greeted you with flowers and music, Your Highness."

Ignoring the priest, the prince's intensely blue eyes bored into Louisa's, and it felt as though he entered her thoughts. Louisa listened in enthralled wonder as he whispered of primordial days and ancient wars. A hand tugged at her apron; her daughter, calling to her.

The spell was broken.

"Forgive us, Your Highness," she muttered. "My daughter does not yet understand how to speak to strangers. We see so few here."

"So I know," the prince answered. "It is why I chose to buy this so beautiful abbey. The quiet pleases me. I wonder, is there someone here who represents the village? A leader?"

The priest replied with another bow. "If you please, sir, I am Father Gigot. May I help?"

"Ah, forgive my rudeness. You are the local priest, of course. You and I will have much in common, Father Gigot. *Latine loqui?*"

"*Sic ego Latine loquimur*," replied the priest eagerly. "Though not fluently, of course. I'm sure the old abbot and his monks spoke it daily, but now we use it only for mass and rituals. My conversational Latin suffers for lack of use."

"Then, we shall see if we might improve it!" Araqiel declared, instantly winning a friend. "Might I ask the whereabouts of Sir Richard's estate?"

"Would that be Sir Richard Patterson-Smythe?" enquired the priest. "He is away in England at present, but his manor house is nearby. Five miles to the north."

"He is in England? Ah, such a pity. I had looked forward to inviting him to my home this evening. You see, he and his investment bank aided me in the purchase of this property."

"There's also Lady Victoria," suggested the local butcher, a man named Laconnier. "But she also is away in England. However, my daughter Yvette works at her château and tells me the good lady plans to return here in a few weeks."

The beautiful man bowed slightly, causing the gleaming locks of waving hair to fall forward. He brushed them back as he spoke; a gesture that sent the pulses of all the women racing.

"Thank you for your help. You have made me feel most welcome."

He smiled, and it seemed to Louisa that his white teeth had a sharp look to them. Somehow, she found the unusual formation tantalising.

Araqiel snapped his fingers, and a man leapt down from the nearest waggon. He was modestly tall—six feet or so—and wore an English suit. He limped as he approached, and he held his side as though in pain.

"Yes, my lord Prince?"

"Wentworth, these are the good people of Goussainville, and this is their religious representative, Father Gigot. I want you to work with him to arrange for my builders." The prince's gaze fell upon the priest. "This is Lionel Wentworth, sir. He is my manservant, you might say. If you would join together to assemble workers for my estate, I should be most grateful. There are many dozens of positions to fill. Perhaps, you could commence these plans tomorrow morning at ten. Go to the gatehouse and speak with my legal agent. Wentworth will introduce you. His name is Albus Flint."

"Yes, of course, my lord. We'd be honoured. I'll speak to M'sieur Flint right away."

The enigmatic prince bowed one last time, and then returned to his coach, followed by the loping Mr. Wentworth.

Slowly, the gossiping gaggle of villagers divided into small groups to discuss the extraordinary luck which had come their way. Dozens of positions? Apply to an agent? Did it mean work and money for their families?

Louisa was the last to depart, and she took Marie's hand, wondering if the prince might need a seamstress or a cleaner. Or perhaps even better... A woman.

"Did you see the funny birds, Mama?" her daughter jabbered as they entered the cottage. "Flying all around him? Funny little birds."

Our story will continue this fall in:

REALMS OF THE DEAD

ABOUT THE AUTHOR

Science, writing, opera, and geopolitics are just a few of the many 'hats' worn by Sharon K. Gilbert. She has been married to SkyWatchTV host and fellow writer Derek P. Gilbert for nearly twenty years, and during that time, helped to raise a brilliant and beautiful stepdaughter, Nicole Gilbert.

The Gilberts have shared their talents and insights for over a decade with the pioneering Christian podcasts, *PID Radio, Gilbert House Fellowship,* and *View from the Bunker*. In addition to co-hosting SkyWatchTV's flagship interview program and *SciFriday* each week, Sharon also hosts *SkyWatch Women* and *SkyWatch Women One-on-One*. She and Derek speak several times each year at conferences, where they love to discuss news and prophecy with viewers, listeners, and readers.

Sharon's been following and studying Bible prophecy for over fifty years, and she often says that she's only scratched the surface. When not immersed in study, a writing project, or scouring the Internet for the latest science news, you can usually find her relaxing in the garden with their faithful hound, Sam T. Dachshund.

Learn more about Sharon and *The Redwing Saga* at her websites: www.sharonkgilbert.com and www.theredwingsaga.com

OTHER BOOKS BY SHARON K. GILBERT

Ebola and the Fourth Horseman of the Apocalypse (non-fiction)

Blood Lies: Book One of The Redwing Saga (fiction)

Blood Rites: Book Two of The Redwing Saga (fiction)

The Blood Is the Life: Book Three of The Redwing Saga (fiction)

Realms of Stone: Book Four of The Redwing Saga (fiction)

Winds of Evil (fiction)

Signs and Wonders (fiction)

The Armageddon Strain (fiction)

CONTRIBUTING AUTHOR

God's Ghostbusters (non-fiction)

Blood on the Altar (non-fiction)

Pandemonium's Engine (non-fiction)

I Predict (non-fiction)

When Once We Were a Nation (non-fiction)

The Milieu: Welcome to the Transhuman Resistance (non-fiction)

Made in the USA
Coppell, TX
13 February 2020